THE GIRL BEHIND THE IRON GATE

HANNAH STANDHAFT

Published by Prelude & Prose Publishing, LLC

ISBN: 979-8-9934694-1-6

Cover design by Hannah Standhaft
Interior design by the author
Printed in the United States of America

First Edition: January 2026

LANGUAGE INSPIRATION AND PRONUNCIATION

My mother was born in Germany, so I knew early on that I wanted to draw inspiration from the language. Many of the names and terms in the *Conspiracy of Shadows* series are influenced by Middle High German, the form of the language spoken during the High Middle Ages (roughly 1050 to 1350). You'll also find occasional nods to French and Latin, because I couldn't resist creating a little linguistic chaos.

As a result, not everything in this world follows the rules of any single language. Some pronunciations differ from modern German, and others bend entirely to the needs of rhythm, tone, or meaning.

You are absolutely encouraged to pronounce names and places however they make sense in your mind as you read. But if you're like me, and prefer to say things "correctly" (or at least as the author hears them in her head), you'll find a character pronunciation guide and glossary of terminology in the back for quick reference. These cover only the names and terms that appear in this volume, not the full scope of the world in *Conspiracy of Shadows*. There's more to come.

Welcome to the conspiracy, challengers. At your marks!

Happy reading!

TRIGGER WARNINGS

Your emotional safety matters to me. Before you begin this story, I want you to feel prepared for the journey ahead. *The Girl Behind the Iron Gate* contains dark and potentially distressing themes, including violence, blood, weapons, death, and on-page sexual content.

While this book explores difficult topics, it does so with care and intention. Please take what you need, skip what you must, and know that you are never alone in this experience. Your wellbeing always comes first.

For a full list of content notes, please visit my website at https://www.hannahstandhaft.com/cos.

With love,

Do you prefer men written by women to actual men?

You're so real for that.

Anyway, this is for you.

Also, for Annie. Because while this dream is thrilling and important, *you* are the dream that will last me my lifetime.

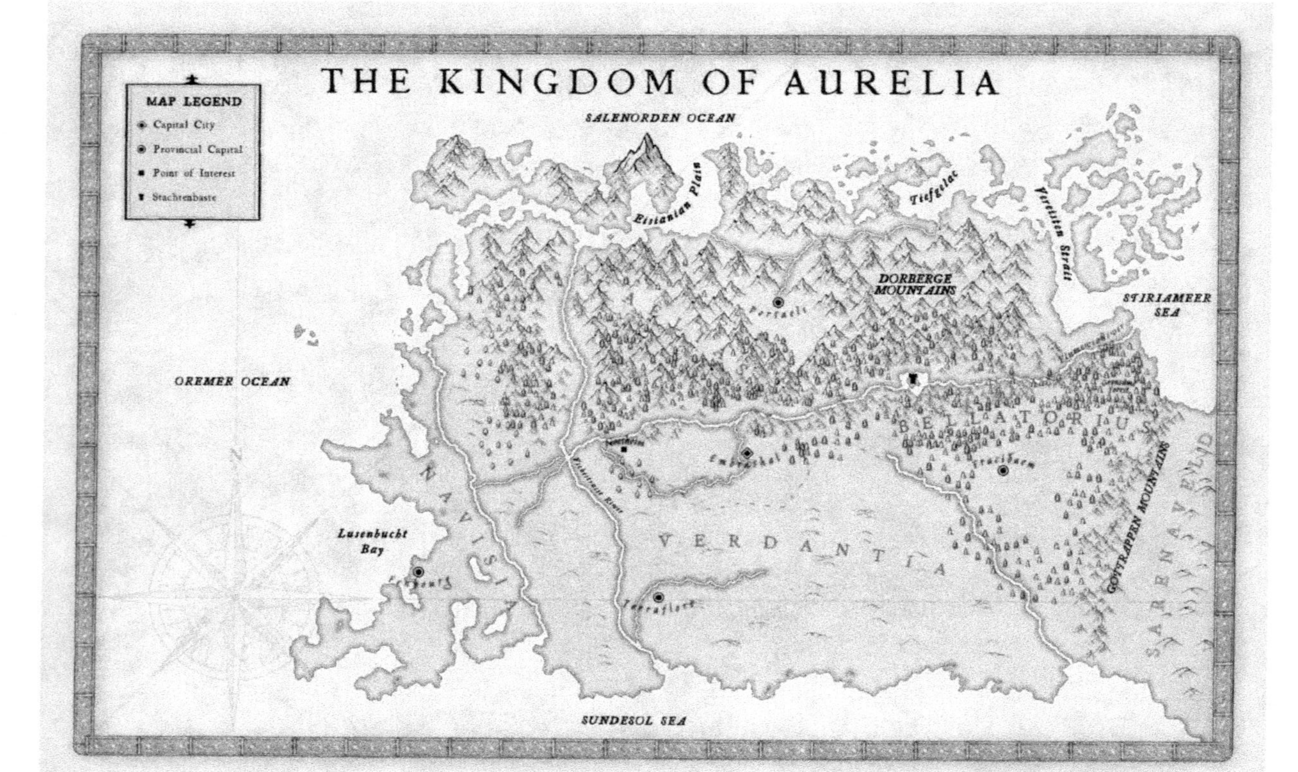

THE KINGDOM OF AURELIA
MAP LEGEND
Capital City
Provincial Capital
Point of Interest
Stachtenbaste
SALENORDEN OCEAN
OREMER OCEAN
Eisianian Plain
Tiefkelas
Vereisten Strait
DORBERGE MOUNTAINS
Portaele
STIRIAMEER SEA
BELLATORIUS
Noethein
Embrashal
Tracifarn
VERDANTIA
GOTTRAPPEN MOUNTAINS
SARENAVENLYD
NAVISI
Lusenbucht Bay
Terraflore
SUNDESOL SEA

CHAPTER ONE
Unqvenched

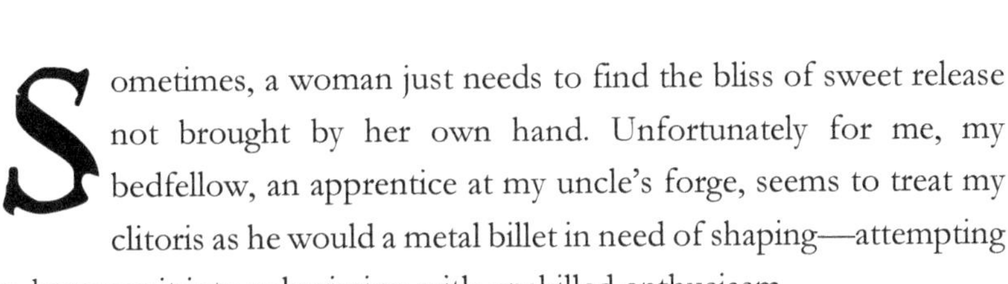

Sometimes, a woman just needs to find the bliss of sweet release not brought by her own hand. Unfortunately for me, my bedfellow, an apprentice at my uncle's forge, seems to treat my clitoris as he would a metal billet in need of shaping—attempting to hammer it into submission with unskilled enthusiasm.

I scrunch my eyes against the daylight peeking through the bed curtains. I try to focus on the man's lips on my neck and wiggle my hips, sliding them into a position that will afford Erwin more success, but he seems to take this as a sort of cat-and-mouse challenge and follows my body with his hands.

Sighing in frustration, I open my eyes and turn my head toward the bed curtains, trying to see through the narrow gap where I hadn't drawn them tightly enough the night before, without moving my head too much in case Erwin notices I'm not really paying attention to his ministrations anymore beyond the occasional wince.

I quickly abandon trying to fake my interest and sit up, pulling aside the emerald curtain, staring in dismay at the bright sun shining through the diamond windowpanes, shafts of dust-mote-laden light rollicking through the air from my sudden curtain disruption.

The distant sound of temple bells tells me it's eight in the morning.

"Blessed Sisters!" I gasp and push Erwin fully off me, scrambling out of my bed.

My legs apparently move at a faster pace in the morning than my brain, and I tumble gracelessly to the floor, sliding off the bed platform into a heap on the flagstones.

A blonde head pokes over the side of the bed. "You right, then, Greta?" Erwin asks me, and I stare up at him from my position on the floor before shoving my hair out of my eyes and standing in a huff.

"I'm fine," I say, wobbling and holding my head from the sudden rush of standing too quickly. "But I'm late for my duties, and you need to go. I stayed in bed far too long."

Erwin grins, resting his chin in his hands. "It's easy to lose track of time when pleasure finds you." He reaches out and pinches the generous curve of my left hip.

Pleasure must be blind, deaf, and stupid, because it hasn't found me with you yet, I think sourly.

I smack his hand away and shoo him out of the bed, pointing wordlessly to his discarded clothing strewn about my floor. When I invited Erwin to my room last night, I had such visions of lovely, diverting orgasms followed by whispered pillow talk and the comfort of strong arms embracing me in the afterglow.

Instead, I was left wide awake after five minutes of thrusting, my disappointed thoughts accompanied by the loud sound of Erwin's snoring. I must have finally drifted off at some point, despite the noise, only to be awoken this morning for "round two." The fog of sleep still hounds me, a tribute to my restless night.

I yank the bed linens and counterpane into place on my side and run around to the other side of the bed where Erwin is slowly gathering his clothing, unbothered by his nudity and my urgency. I fling open the bed curtains, fluff the pillows, and slap them into place a bit harder than necessary, glancing over my shoulder to see if Erwin has noticed.

Of course not. The man could write treatises on employing blissful ignorance.

I continue to glance at him periodically in the universal "I'm irritated with you" signal as I rush around my chamber, grabbing a linen shift from my wardrobe, followed by a serviceable dress I can move comfortably in throughout the day. As I pull the fabric over my head, I watch him finally begin to dress.

He has a sturdy, simple handsomeness to him, his wheaten hair shaggy and sleep mussed, brown eyes warm and languorous. What had first attracted me to him was the obvious strength in his shoulders and arms, owing to long hours at the forge. That and the way his eyes crinkle at the corners when he smiles, which he does nearly constantly.

Even now, he looks up at me and smiles, and I can't help but feel a flicker in my stomach. Of course the flicker is irritation, and it only grows with the evidence of his uncomplicated affability, wonderfully oblivious to the fact that I didn't enjoy myself or sleep well. Perhaps that isn't entirely fair of me to feel, since it's not as though I came right out and told him what to do to please me, and I didn't tell him that what he was doing wasn't working, but being tired doesn't improve my charitability.

I realize I never responded to his comment about pleasure, but it's been long enough now that it would be more awkward to say something than simply to leave it. He's still pulling on his boots while I've already put on more layers, including stockings and shoes, and made my way to the small table in my chamber that has my comb, hair ribbons, and hair pins. I told Clara, the maid who often helps me in the mornings, that she didn't need to assist me today, knowing I had invited Erwin to sneak in, and now I'm regretting it as I face the prospect of combing the snarls out of my hair, the result of forgetting to braid it before I drifted into dissatisfied slumber.

Sighing again, I pick up my comb and start dragging it through my hair, wincing whenever it meets a knot but resolutely pulling it through. The golden-brown waves are thick and normally not prone to tangles, but I didn't exactly go through my normal evening routine last night.

"You need to hurry, Erwin," I say impatiently. "I need to start with my duties, and no one can see you're here. My grandmother would have a fit. You'll have to go through the window."

That wasn't *exactly* true. My grandmother was as practical as she was proper, and while I don't think she'd be thrilled that I allowed a man into my bedchamber, I don't think it would be for the reasons most guardians would posit.

At nearly twenty-five, I was past the usual age for marrying, and I didn't exactly have many prospects considering how we de Veends keep to ourselves and the estate. And my grandmother has always said that "only men who've never earned a real woman place a high value on virtue." But I would be remiss if I didn't consider how it might affect my younger sister and *her* prospects if word were to get out that I'm cavorting with local tradesmen. Not to mention how she would react if she were to find out.

She would be mock scandalized and want all the details. As much as I love my little sister, I don't know how to discuss my sex life with her.

Erwin comes up behind me as I braid my hair and kisses the side of my neck. "Will I see you tonight?"

I turn and look at him guiltily, the confession on the tip of my tongue that I don't feel the chemistry for which I was hoping. But my tendency to please others wins out, and I give a noncommittal "maybe" before tying off my braid with a ribbon and pushing him toward my window.

"Do I really have to go out the window?" Erwin asks, looking at the drop from my second-story chamber.

"Yes," I say. "Now go."

Erwin presses, "Are you sure I can't just sneak through the door? I came in that way last night, and I was very quiet."

Erwin is as delicate as an ox, and his footfalls are twice as loud. I can't hold back the snort of laughter that escapes me.

Erwin, unwise to my humor at his expense, continues to look at me hopefully until I say, "No. Go!"

He leans over and kisses me firmly, my pulse fluttering slightly in response. If only his kissing ability translated to other physical talents. He grins at me, happily, of course, and in the next moment, disappears over the window ledge.

I watch as he dashes across the back gardens of the estate, and I turn toward the door, bracing my shoulders—prepared, if disheartened—to be facing the day unquenched and unrested.

I hurry from my chamber, darting through the kitchens to the small study in my grandmother's wing of rooms. I don't even pause to eat, shoving a dry scone in my mouth in passing, and chase it with lukewarm tea as I settle into the desk chair to balance the household accounts.

My grandmother insists I don't need to perform household duties such as monitoring the account books, taking inventory of household items and the kitchens, and supervising the staff. She's told me she can have one of the various staff members she's hired do so instead, but I've become accustomed to having a purpose here. The household is used to my methods, and it took me quite a while to figure out. Especially when it comes to the ledgers, since math isn't my strongest suit.

Admittedly, I now feel somewhat possessive of those tasks.

When the temple bells ring signaling midday, I close the ledgers and rise from the desk in the downstairs sitting room, tucking them into one of the drawers. I leave the sitting room, going in search of my younger sister, to see how she's getting on with her lessons.

Nearly a thousand years ago, the early inhabitants of Aurelia discovered they had been blessed by the gods with the gift of magic. Some received powers that enriched the world, such as healing, elemental control, telekinesis, and the creation of wealth. Others bore darker, more destructive abilities. They could manipulate minds, see the future, inflict harm with a mere thought, or even kill without a touch—though often at the cost of their sanity.

Aurelia's rulers, each gifted with the power to turn any material into gold, used their abilities to forge a flourishing kingdom that soon subsumed its neighbors in a growing empire. To govern these provinces and preserve loyalty, the King appointed magical representatives from each land.

These leaders formed the Aurenkammer—though, of course, anyone not completely high in the instep simply calls it the Gold

Council—a body that both advises the monarchy and serves as the voice of their provinces, wielding immense influence over Aurelia's wealth, resources, and military.

As power and privilege concentrated, the Gold Council decreed that those with magic could not marry those without it. The order was meant to preserve the rule of the Aurenclaste—the magical elite who dominate the aristocracy and hold all positions of power in the government. Meanwhile, the ungifted were consigned to labor, and those born with dark magic fared worse still, shunned or executed for the misfortune of their birth.

Therefore, Agnethe—a young woman of twenty years who is not in possession of magic—must present herself as a lady of refinement and secure an advantageous marriage, the surest path for one of her station to rise within Aurelia. The challenge, however, lies in winning the notice of one of the few young gentlemen of good standing—someone from a respectable family of the Lützenclaste, that small circle of society possessing rank but no magic.

Now Agnethe is receiving multiple lessons a week in languages, history, and music, as well as posture, etiquette, court manners, speech and demeanor, conduct, court fashions and dress, and expectations of a woman of Agnethe's status coming from a good-standing, wealthy, but non-magical family.

At first, Agnethe readily agreed to the lessons, both as something to fill her days, but also because she wants to experience all she can out of life, court, and Aurelia. But it's been more difficult to get her to focus lately. She's been frustrated with her routine since staying at our Uncle Eoforwine's home in Embrathal, our capital. In the weeks since returning from visiting for Lunoktium, the spring equinox festivities, she's been combative and sullen.

It's been like pulling teeth trying to get her to attend her lessons and not sass Madam Boeschg, her governess, to the point of having an attack of the vapors. The madam is very good at her job, but she seems prone to fits of nerves or offense in equal measure.

I hear conversation coming from the dining room and see Agnethe sitting in one of the chairs at the formal table. Madam Boeschg is standing beside Agnethe and gesturing to the place setting in front of her.

"This is your trencher, Miss de Veend, which is the anchor and base of your setting. It might be pewter or silver or sometimes ceramic." I wince in sympathy for Agnethe having to listen to the woman's unnaturally deep, but nasal voice for hours a day. "Then you have your knives for carving meat and, occasionally, one for dessert. A fork, for spearing fruit, sweets, or more delicate meats, and your spoon for soups, stews, sauces, and custards. Now, here's where it gets *quite* exciting, Miss de Veend—"

She and I have *very* different ideas about the definition of "exciting."

Agnethe spots me. "Greta!" She pushes her chair back and moves to stand until Madam Boeschg puts a firm hand on her shoulder and presses downward, keeping Agnethe in place.

"Miss de Veend, a lady does not stagger from her seat like a newborn foal. She rises silently and steadily, as if floating on a cloud. She glides her chair back smoothly and unhurriedly to greet her guests. Do you wish to attempt greeting your sister properly?" Madam Boeschg drones, raising an iron gray eyebrow at Agnethe.

I resist the urge to laugh as Agnethe's lips flatten into a mulish line. "No, Madam," she begins, but then turns toward me. "Only I can't see the point in all of this ceremony and etiquette. We never have *anyone* to dinner. We never host anything, and at the Lunoktium parties, no one was this stuffy and formal. Everyone was enjoying themselves and laughing and dancing."

"You can hardly compare a common *festival*," Madam Boeschg's prominent nose quivers in a disproportionate amount of shock as she continues, "with a formal dinner with your peers, the Aurenclaste, or at court."

I sigh and look at my sister. "She's right, Agnethe. It's not the same as court or more formal occasions."

Agnethe huffs, twisting an unfamiliar ring on her right middle finger, as she says, "Uncle Eoforwine had or was at parties nearly every night. I've *seen* court more recently than you have, and it's different."

I step forward and cup her hand in mine, looking at the ring. It's a signet ring. Old, the gold battered and worn and scuffed in a few places, with a red bezel and the shape of a raven's head engraved on it.

"Where did you get this?" I ask.

Agnethe snatches her hand back. "I found it in some old things, wandering the unused chambers," she explains.

"I've never seen anything like it in the house before," I reply.

"Then you haven't looked in the right places," Agnethe shrugs. "There are plenty of unexplored spaces."

I want to push her harder on the ring and remind her she can't just take things she finds for herself, but Madam Boeschg interjects. "Miss de Veend," she says to me, "we must continue our lessons if we're to complete them before the midday meal."

Agnethe looks mutinous, far more than appropriate for a young woman who is grown. I feel my irritation with her flare as I lean forward and say quietly, for only her ears, "I know you disagree with some of her teachings, but if you want to get married and move away from Noetheim, and it seems you do, you'll have to know how to be a proper lady."

Agnethe releases a long-suffering sigh but turns back to the place setting and begins to recite the items back to Madam Boeschg.

When in doubt, I think, *dangle a carrot.*

I nod in thanks to Madam Boeschg and leave the dining room, making my way down the gallery toward my grandmother's rooms. I trace my hand along the dark wood paneling that covers the bottom half of the walls, feeling my fingertips brush the grooves in the wainscoting, my eyes wandering to the de Veend family portraits spaced evenly along the hall.

I love Noetheim, the de Veend family estate situated on the fringes of Vallaurium. I love the mountains in the distance, the smell of the pine trees to the north, the just-blooming maple trees to the south, their small red flowers a colorful foil to their green leaves. I love the peace and quiet, my work in the home and at my uncle's forge. I can't understand why Agnethe would want to leave it, but as I've come to realize lately, Agnethe is very different from me and wants different things. More.

I don't begrudge her those desires, but I do feel trepidation at the thought of her going out into the world. Marrying. Leaving me.

The sound of a crash comes from the direction of my grandmother's drawing room, and I pick up my pace, hastening there to find her on the ground, her tea tray upended, delicate saucers and mugs shattered.

Naturally, my grandmother is stubbornly refusing the arm that Sunna, one of our maids, has offered to help her rise from her place on the ground.

"Grandmother!" I say, rushing to her side. She bats me away and crawls to her nearby chair, using it to brace her arms and pull herself up. She reaches for a linen napkin that managed to escape the fate of its sister, lying in a puddle of tea. She dabs at her dress until it's no longer dripping, then hands the cloth to Sunna.

"Sunna," I say, turning to the freckle-faced girl. "Can you fetch Madam de Veend another tray of tea?" Sunna nods and bobs her head before quickly exiting the drawing room.

I turn to my grandmother. "Honestly, Grandmother, what were you doing?"

My grandmother sits on her cushioned chair slowly and sighs, draping her hands on the padded arms.

"I was merely trying to set up our tea, *herzeline*, but the tray wasn't in its usual spot and my hands are troubling me today," she says, abashedly, holding them up for my observation. Her fingers have become increasingly swollen and gnarled over the last few years.

I smile at the endearment from my grandmother, who is not truly my grandmother. Agnethe and I were orphaned, our parents distant de Veend relatives who passed from fever when I was four years old and Agnethe was just an infant. We were taken in and adopted by Merel de Veend and her husband, Andebert Vergildetbach, and lived there very happily before they, too, perished from illness not long after.

My earliest memories are of my adoptive parents: Merel's fiery spirit, Andebert's gentle calm. When word of the *Fiebernacht* began to spread and one of the small number of household staff fell ill, they sent us away with our nurse to Noetheim, where Odina de Veend, Merel's mother and now my adoptive grandmother, resides.

We never saw our parents again.

Odina tried to be both mother and father to two young girls with nothing but a history of unintended abandonment, but as an older woman who had raised her children, she could only do so much.

So, it became me and Agnethe against the world. I was her older sister, her surrogate mother, her confidante, her best friend, and she was mine. For a long while, that was enough.

Now, it seems she's outgrown me. Part of me is happy for her to build her life, to grow. Part of me mourns the relationship I know will be forever altered once she goes.

I shake off my melancholy, a product of being overly tired, no doubt, and walk to my grandmother's chair. I gently lift her hands and inspect the joints.

"They do look a bit more swollen than usual. Maybe there's rain coming," I say, setting her hands back down on the arms of the chair. "I'll see if Gernot can gather comfrey for me to make a poultice. That should help ease the ache a bit," I add, making a mental note to speak with the steward this afternoon.

Grandmother smiles. "What would I do, *herzeline*, without you here to take care of me?"

I feel a rush of pride at my grandmother's words. I like being needed, useful.

Sunna enters the room with a new tea tray, setting it down on the side table, preparing my grandmother's special blend in two cups and bringing one to each of us. I sit in the chair opposite my grandmother.

"Where's Agnethe? She should drink some, too. It's good for your health," my grandmother urges, gesturing at me with swollen fingers to drink.

"She's in lessons, Grandmother. She can't join, but I'll make sure she drinks some later," I assure her.

My grandmother is very particular about her teas, and she insists that Agnethe and I have at least one cup of her unique blend daily. It's made from a certain kind of leaf from Caelias; and while I'm not sure if it truly benefits my health, it doesn't seem to harm me. So, I indulge my grandmother and drink the slightly sweet, slightly bitter brew.

"And how are lessons coming for Agnethe?" She asks, knowingly, looking at me with raised, silver eyebrows.

Time may have claimed my grandmother's hands as her sacrifice to its inevitable passage, but it hasn't dimmed her beauty. Though her once-dark hair has long since given way to a glossy, silvery white, her sparkling blue eyes are still clear, her delicate, patrician features still prominent in a face that bears few wrinkles save those around her mouth and eyes from smiling.

Although she rarely leaves the estate, she has her hair pinned to perfection in a sleek chignon every day, elegant jewelry often graces her ears and neck, and her gowns are rich in fabric and design.

Today is no exception. Her crimson gown is a stunning display of the iridescent wonder of silk, silver thread shot through the cuffs and collar that glitters in the light when she moves. Rubies decorate her neck and dangle from her ears.

"She's not enjoying them," I say, sighing. "She doesn't seem to see the importance as much as she once did. I tried to convince her that it's needed. I hope I got through to her today."

"Mm, perhaps a reminder is needed about the disadvantages of having no magic and her limited marriage options?" Grandmother asks. "After all, it's not as if Agnethe can become part of the Aurenclaste through marriage," she points out. Since Aurelian law prevents those with magic from marrying those without it, we both know Agnethe has a very shallow pool from which to draw.

"I'm not sure," I reply. "Just today I reminded her that if she wishes to go off and start her own life, she needs those lessons. It seemed to register with her, but I wish she understood how lucky she is to be part of our family and have the privileges she does."

"She's very lucky," Grandmother agrees, "that her enterprising de Veend ancestors sought to establish themselves as premier bladesmiths." She sniffs and sips her tea once more.

"Yes, I'm sure our ancestors had the social lives of young ladies in mind when they decided to smith weapons for the Aurengarte," I say dryly, referring to when our family supplied blades to the Aurelian military forces. "At any rate, if Agnethe continues to object to lessons, perhaps you could speak with her, Grandmother. She usually listens to you."

"I would be happy to, but maybe it's simply that the allure of escape and adventure has dimmed?" Grandmother poses.

I shake my head in the negative. "Definitely not. If anything, it's more acute than before. She seems…unsettled," I explain, trying to define the undercurrent of feeling I've sensed in Agnethe since she returned from Uncle Eoforwine's. "The lessons and a good marriage are the best way for Agnethe to achieve what she wants."

"She'll be grateful for them one day. You'll see," Grandmother says. Then she looks pointedly at my cup and adds, "Drink up; the tea is good for your lungs."

I roll my eyes. "My lungs are fine."

"Because of the tea," Grandmother insists.

I gulp the remainder of my tea and set my empty cup down. "Satisfied?"

"I'm always satisfied when I get my way," Grandmother says, the side of her mouth kicking up in a smirk. "Aren't you due at the forge today, *herzeline*? You know your uncle values punctuality," she adds, continuing to casually sip tea, utterly unbothered.

I look up at her. "What time is it?"

"The bells rang three several moments past," she informs me.

"What?" I say, frantically, rising to my feet. "I didn't even hear them!"

"Probably because you were too busy chiding your grandmother. Or perhaps you're losing your hearing. You should drink tea for that." She nods toward the teapot.

I don't answer, instead rushing out the door to the forge.

My uncle was *not* very happy that I was late for my duties at the forge. I normally arrive at two o'clock, and I was over an hour late, which means I didn't get nearly as far in my inventory cataloging as I could have if I'd been on time. I pacified him by promising to return to the forge tomorrow and arrive earlier than usual to make up for my lost time.

Once I arrive home, I trudge up the stairs, too tired even to eat, which is unusual for someone who loves food as much as I do. All I want to do is find my bed and forget last night and the mess that was today, but my day isn't over yet.

I make my way to Agnethe's chambers, the sound of plucking strings growing louder as I near the door. When I knock, the music stops and Agnethe's voice beckons me to enter.

I open the door and see Agnethe sitting in the chair by the fireplace in her room, holding her rotte, an oval type of psaltery, made from maple lacquered to a blinding sheen, with strings pulled taut across the body of the instrument. While it could be played with a bow, Agnethe often prefers to play with her fingers, the softness of the plucked notes appealing to her musical ear.

The rotte was the one lesson Agnethe didn't complain about getting. She'd taken to it naturally, already skilled at strumming and plucking tunes, insisting I sing along with her as she practices.

Tonight was no different.

"Sing while I play, *alouisse*, please? No one's voice is as beautiful," Agnethe begs, knowing I have a soft spot for her "little lark" nickname for me. Not that there's anything *little* about me, but the sentiment is appreciated, nonetheless.

I've been singing to and for Agnethe since we were small, and I enjoy sharing my voice with those I trust. I loathe being the center of attention and have never sung for anyone beyond family, but their pleasure in it brings me more than enough satisfaction. The thought of having to perform in front of a crowd is almost enough to give me hives.

"Just one," I acquiesce, and Agnethe's fingers begin strumming and plucking a familiar tune, her favorite. It's an old folk song about someone who promises to wait for their beloved in a golden meadow, even in death. It's beautiful, poignant, sad, and it twists a small part of my heart to sing it, though a part of me loves the pain, loves to feel the ache of the song's longing deep in my veins as I sing.

When the last notes fade from my voice and Agnethe's rotte, I smile at her, and she smiles back, softly, her beautiful face bathed in the glow of candlelight, making her gleam like a golden statue.

Despite being sisters, we share few similarities. Where Agnethe is petite and slender, I am tall—as tall as many men—and curvaceous no matter what restrictions I put on my food intake. So, I've given up trying to be slender and have accepted that I will always be full figured. Well…I've mostly accepted it.

Sometimes I feel longing for Agnethe's ethereal grace, wish we shared the same gold hair cascading in beautiful waves down her back and clear skin, fair but with a warm cast, glowing in any light as if she'd been blessed by the sun goddess, Soleinne, herself. In contrast, my moon-pale complexion looks as though I never see the light of day. Which is, unfortunately, mostly true, in part because the sun just turns me red, without any progression to brown before returning to the same milky hue it always is.

More than anything, I envy her self-assurance that upon entering a room, everyone's eyes will be focused on her.

Agnethe was born confident; and through her upbringing, with all those around her focused on ensuring she had a stable, loving childhood, that confidence was reinforced and solidified. Agnethe doesn't doubt herself, doesn't wonder if anyone disdains her. She travels through life assuming everyone will accept her as she is; and perhaps that confidence is influential, as they usually do.

Agnethe suddenly fills the silence and asks, "Do you ever tire of your life as it is?"

I sit back, surprised, and reply, "I am content here, with Grandmother, and you, and our uncles, and my work in the manor and forge."

"Do you ever want more?" Agnethe prods, clasping her fingers together after sitting her rotte on the chair beside her.

"More what?" I ask, puzzled.

Agnethe sighs, and her eyes grow fuzzy, unfocused, as if she's looking at something in the distance. "Just…more," she says, twisting the ring on her finger as she had done earlier.

I shift in my seat, more than a little uncomfortable with the direction of this questioning, as it's something I haven't quite settled within myself. But I'm not about to share my doubts and fears with my little sister when she's on the cusp of starting her own life and adventure. I don't need to dampen her excitement with my doom and gloom.

"I have all I need," I say firmly. "I'm needed, and that's good enough for me." My heart pinches as I utter it.

In a perfect world, I would have built my own life and family, as Agnethe will. Had my own home, a husband, perhaps children if the gods saw fit to bless me with them. But that wasn't how it ended up for me, and it's my duty to see Agnethe live to her fullest potential.

I stand, sighing, and walk over to her. I cup my hands around her cheeks and kiss the top of her golden head, then look into her clear blue eyes. "Don't you worry about me, *liebenette*," I tell her. "You are what matters most to me."

I say goodnight and make my way to my chamber, leaning against the door, closing my eyes and exhaling as fatigue settles into my bones now that I've finally stopped moving.

I'm not quite ready to find my bed, still having one unofficial task left for the evening. I go to the small desk in the corner of my room, where Clara has already thoughtfully lit a candle for me, and open the drawers, pulling out worn old journals, household account books, ledgers, and temple records.

Most of the documents are written in old Aurelian, which has fallen out of use in favor of the common tongue but is often the language in which older records are kept. I've always had a natural proclivity for languages. When my governess informed my grandmother of my ability to quickly absorb words, meanings, and pronunciations, she encouraged me to learn as many tongues as I could. And I have done so, becoming fluent in reading and speaking old Aurelian and able to decipher basic words and phrases in most of our other old languages—Caelish, Bellatorian, Verdantian, and Navisian.

I've even managed to sneak in some tomes written in the language of our fiercest rival nation, Sarenaveld. Not having anyone to learn it from in speaking form, I have no idea if I pronounce things correctly; but I can read some of it if I focus well enough.

I'm not sure if my knowledge of languages will be of benefit to me, but who knows? It might prove useful in the future, and I always want to be useful. After all, once Agnethe has started her own life, I'll need something to fill my days.

In the interest of usefulness, I dug through old chests in Noetheim's storeroom several months ago, unearthing family artifacts like journals, ledgers, household inventories, and censuses. Information that, while not its intention, told a story of the lives of those who were here before us. After that, I began the painstaking process of translating the old Aurelian into the common tongue in a journal of my own, often working into the night organizing the history I've uncovered. I intend to give the recordings of the de Veend family history to my grandmother for her seventy-fifth birthday in two months.

While I know my she'll love the gift, my desire to read through the family accounts is also somewhat selfishly motivated. I love learning about the history of my family and where I came from, as so much of my early existence is shrouded in mystery, lost to the recesses of fickle childhood memory. My grandmother doesn't know much about our lives before Andebert and Merel took us in, and I am unable to recall any concrete details.

I rub the back of my neck and roll my shoulders a few times before opening my recording journal and some of the old tomes lying on my desk. A puff of dust finds its way up my nose as I turn a page in one of the journals, and I can't hold back the loud sneeze that follows.

I shake my head and massage my nose, trying to clear out the residual ringing, and then resume bending over the journal, a particularly fascinating record from one of the previous mistresses of Noetheim, Sasse de Veend. From what I have been able to discover, she lived to be almost ninety-five years old, far surpassing the life of her husband and even all of her children. In fact, she died only about thirty years ago; and I am sad to have missed knowing her.

Her writing is poetic, beautiful, but often cryptic and difficult to discern meaning without heavy-handed and liberal interpretations. The page to which I turn tonight is no exception, the very first passage reading—

"Not all heirs wear crowns or rings,

Nor walk with steps alone.
Some bear the weight of shadowed things,
Their blood their legacy, their soul the throne."

I'm too tired to figure out the meaning behind the puzzling rhyme tonight but push on with my laborious translations. Who knows? Maybe one of these days I'll find something really important.

CHAPTER TWO
Smoke and Sparks

Three days later, I rush along my route toward the de Veend forge, late for only the second time in my years assisting Uncle Engilram, the oldest de Veend child of my grandmother and her long-departed husband and older brother to my adoptive mother, Merel.

Engilram is the second most serious of the de Veend brothers, eclipsed only by Burkhard, a Gleichvîger of the Heiligarte and head of the Order of the Blessed Sisters' building and land archives. Uncle Burkhard makes Uncle Engilram look like the life of any party.

But it's Uncle Engilram's disappointed frown I will have to face when I walk into the forge, and I dread the quiet censure I know is coming.

The forge is on the edge of the Noetheim grounds, bordering Uncle Engilram's lands, tucked into a rocky hillside with a slanted slate roof and stone-and-timber body. Thick stone walls keep the heat contained within, and smoke from a tall, soot-streaked chimney can be seen curling up to the sky most hours of the day. As much as I love Noetheim, I think

I love the forge more. There's something about it that makes you feel as if you're in a different world, with only the sights, sounds, and smells of smithing to fill your eyes, ears, and nose.

I can see Engilram's horse, Smit, in the small paddock beside the forge, peacefully pulling some of the new spring grasses from around the fence posts. Engilram could have assumed ownership of Noetheim upon his father's passing twenty years before, but he is a man used to routine and settled into his home in an opposite, albeit nearby direction from Noetheim in relation to the forge. He sees no reason to move his mother from her residence just to live in a house with more rooms than he could ever possibly use as a perpetual bachelor married to his profession.

As I run past the paddock toward the doors, I see two unfamiliar horses grazing behind Smit and feel apprehension rise in my throat, but I can't take time to pause and wonder who could be here aside from Uncle Engilram and the few hired workers he employs. None of the employees have horses of their own, instead walking from the village a brisk thirty minutes away or from Noetheim's servants' quarters, depending on where they live.

I burst through the door, not giving myself a moment to feel more anxious. Erwin grins vacantly at me from where he feeds logs to the hearth, while Tilo, the young assistant about Agnethe's age, pours water from the nearby river into the quenching trough. Lorenz, one of the other fully trained smiths, lays out his tools near one of the anvils.

I'm about to open my mouth to ask where my uncle is when I hear a roar followed by the sensation of strong forearms wrapping around my waist from behind me. I screech loudly as I'm lifted off my feet and push backward as hard as I can to get away from my assailant, when I hear laughter behind me. All the men in the forge are smiling good-naturedly at whomever is there.

I'm abruptly dropped back onto my feet, and I throw my hands out to balance myself before whirling around to see my Uncle Walter standing not two feet in front of me.

"Uncle Walter!" I exclaim in happy surprise, jumping into the tall man's embrace. "When did you get in? How long are you here for? Have you seen Grandmother and Agnethe?"

Walter throws back his head and laughs loudly. "Still full of questions, I see, *liebelín*, aren't we?" He tweaks me on the nose and calls me "little love" in old Aurelian, as he has since I was a child. There's something about being among older relatives that makes me feel as though I'm still seven years old, not twenty-four, and peppering him with question after question about his travel adventures.

I hang my cloak on a hook behind the door as I say, "It's been ages since I've seen you! You can't blame me for wondering all those things when I didn't even know you were coming home!"

"Well, I wanted to see my mother and nieces, of course! And I suppose my brother, even though he's really settled into his title as Duke Dour." Walter grins at me and nods toward Engilram's office.

I grin back, because I can't help it. Walter's humor is contagious, and his booming voice and zest for life made him the perpetual subject of my overactive imagination when I was younger. I used to dream that Uncle Walter and I would go on sea voyages together, exploring uncharted lands, finding hidden treasure, and battling pirates. His stories, that made it sound as though he did nothing *but* have those kinds of adventures, only fed my daydreams even more.

That is, until pragmatic Uncle Engilram told me that while Uncle Walter *does* fancy himself a world-explorer-treasure-hunter-pirate-killer who *occasionally* dabbles in archaeological research and diplomatic visits for Aurelia, it's really the reverse. I indulge my larger-than-life uncle in letting him paint it as he does because I love him; and, well, even if his real life is more boring than he portrays, it's still far more thrilling than my day-to-day routine.

"Ah, yes, well, while we wait for the duke to join us, tell me where you returned from?" My uncle always begins with plans and then you discover later that he ended up somewhere completely different.

Walter pulls a sooty stool toward him with his boot and drops onto it, either oblivious or uncaring as to how it might dirty his trousers. He tosses his head back, his long, black hair—now liberally streaked with silver—fluttering back from his shoulders as he spreads his arms wide, fingers splayed, and says, "Picture this: an unnamed, uncharted tropical island in the south Oremer Sea, brimming with untapped culture, a civilization of people untouched by modern conveniences, whose entire population has no magic."

My eyes go wide. "*No* magic? Like, none whatsoever?" I ask, as I pull down my dusty inventory logs so I can continue cataloging Uncle Engilram's supplies and tools.

"None," Walter confirms dramatically. "Their holy man, the only one who spoke the common tongue, seemed unimpressed by the fact that we do. Seemed to think it was the tool of evil."

I reply, "How do they live as a society then? How do they replenish resources or heal their people?" I start setting aside tools, as I tick them off in my log, making sure the inventory matches what's present.

I hear the sound of metal striking metal behind me, signaling that someone has begun working on a piece. I glance over my shoulder to see Lorenz calmly hammering a red-hot billet until the once-rectangular bar of steel is pitted and uneven. He'll alternate between heating and hammering until the blade shape and length begin to emerge, then refine it into the weapon it will eventually become.

The de Veends have owned and operated a forge for centuries, ever since a long-dead ancestor—a royal bladesmith of such skill that the Aurengarte commissioned his weapons—amassed enough wealth to establish the personal, family forge that carries on his legacy. My family doesn't speak of the reasons we no longer supply those blades to the military. In fact, Grandmother rarely speaks of Hrafn, her husband, and the last de Veend to arm the Aurengarte before his sudden death decades ago. Uncle Engilram deflects whenever I ask. What little I do know has come from Walter and Eoforwine, two of my more loquacious uncles, though even they offer only wary fragments—as if they, too, in this matter, believe some truths are best left unspoken.

The ledgers and journals over which I pore do hint at more, but their secrets remain locked away in cryptic household verse and buried between itemized figures, challenging me to decipher the past.

I watch for a few moments as Lorenz continues to hammer the metal into shape, slowly but surely forming the point of what looks like a dagger, based on length. In my years helping in the forge, I've never attempted to smith anything myself, knowing I lack the upper body strength and the motivation to shape metal into anything resembling a useful tool or weapon, but I still usually recognize the items the smiths make. Though the forge no longer supplies the Aurengarte, the de Veends still have an exemplary reputation for bladesmithing and blacksmithing, and many Aurenclaste nobles and wealthy Lützenclaste citizens still seek out my uncle for crafting blades or other metal materials. Thus I have been able to witness their craft firsthand many times over.

There is something poetic about shaping something as hard and unyielding as a block of steel into something as delicate and sleek as a blade. The crude shape of the billet giving way to the elegant curves of a sword or dagger or spear, the blunt corners honed into edges so sharp they can cut you just from looking at them. I've long loved watching the smiths at their craft—bringing the fire in the hearth to roaring life with a bellows, heating the steel until it's so hot it turns orange, then red, almost pulsing with life, laying the heated metal on the anvil and giving the hot steel purpose with nothing more than smoke, sparks, muscle, and determination.

I'm jolted from my observation when Walter's voice fills my ears. "They live off what their land gives them," he answers my question. "Natural rains help their crops grow, livestock is raised by breeding programs, and those who are sick or injured are healed best as commonfolk are in Aurelia. For those too far gone with illness, they pass on."

"How do they explain their rejection of the gods' magical gifts to them?" I ask.

"Simple. They don't believe in the same gods, *liebelín*," Walter replies.

Surprised, I query, "What do they believe, then?"

Walter says, "They believe in similar types of deities, those who oversee earth, weather, life, death, and more. But they call them by different names, pray to them in a different manner, and their civilization seems to operate under the belief that any power beyond what the body is normally capable of is unnatural."

A loud sizzling sound fills the forge, and I look over to see Lorenz plunge his basic dagger blade, quenching it, into the water trough to cool and harden the metal. At that moment, I notice Erwin none too subtly trying to catch my eye by winking. Mortified, I look at my Uncle Walter, who is watching the young man curiously.

Erwin must have decided that my turning my back on him was an invitation to come over, and he approaches us, saying his typical, "You right, then, Greta?"

How did I never notice before that he always says that?

I smile tightly. "Fine. Thanks, Erwin. Just talking with my uncle."

"Right, we met earlier this morning. Fascinating tales, those, Mr. de Veend," he says, nodding to Walter. "Love the ones about the naked savages."

I cough suddenly, shocked and embarrassed that Erwin would mention something so crass in front of me while my uncle is there. "Um, Erwin, perhaps now is not the best time to discuss the, er, *fashion choices* of foreign civilizations." I try to look at him in a manner that tells him to stop talking, but this appears to be lost on him.

"No, it was great fun! Walter, here, was telling us about the savages and how their tits were out plain as day, just for anyone to see." He holds his hands in front of his chest, cupping his fingers in the air as if cradling a pair of breasts, and the only thing keeping me from hitting him on the head with the hammer I'm clutching is the fact that there are witnesses.

Walter smothers a laugh with a cough of his own and says, "I do believe, Erwin, that I mentioned quite a bit about their culture as well. And they're not savages, truly, just different to Aurelians."

Erwin smiles moronically. "Well, I can't think of anyone here just walking around naked, can you?" He looks back and forth between us. My uncle is clearly trying to contain his laughter at this point.

"Erwin," I say through clenched teeth, "did you need something?"

"Ah, right!" He exclaims, as though he had already forgotten the reason he came over—other than my embarrassment, it seems. He glances at Walter quickly and leans toward me, saying in a stage whisper, "Well, I was wanting to know when I'd see you next, since you've not said."

I close my eyes, my hand tightening around the handle of the hammer once more. *Murder is illegal, murder is illegal, murder is illegal,* I tell myself repeatedly until I'm calm enough to reopen my eyes and look at the object of my ire.

"We'll see," I say with false cheer, only because I want to get rid of him, and I don't want to have this conversation right now.

"Right, right. Bless the Sisters for that then." He grins, continuing to stand there, looking between me and Walter, smiling affably.

The dimwit.

"Erwin, don't you have somewhere to be?" I ask, all pretense of cheer dropping from my voice.

"Right as a rivet! I'll speak to you later," he says to me with a wink and walks back to the hearth.

Uncle Walter turns to me, meeting my embarrassed expression, and asks, "Friend of yours?"

"Definitely not," I say, pressing my lips together, irritated at Erwin for being an imbecile and myself for not considering how awkward taking up with him would be for me since I help at the forge.

Walter chuckles softly and says, "Poor fool him then."

"Uncle, I—" I begin, trying to find a way to explain terrible sex with idiots to my uncle without *actually* explaining terrible sex with idiots to my uncle, but he interrupts by raising his hands.

"No need to explain, *liebelîn*, it's your business. I was just being a nosy old man," he says, pointing to his own nose, crooked from several ill-mended breaks over the years of adventuring. "I'd love to see you settled and happy with someone deserving of you. Not, mind you, that there is anyone who fits that description," he adds, raising his eyebrow at me.

I smile, shoulders dropping in relief that my lack of bedroom chemistry with Erwin can remain a private disappointment and not a public humiliation. "I'm happy, Uncle. I have Grandmother and Agnethe. What would I need a man for, anyway? They only bring trouble with very little adventure," I grumble.

"Speaking of adventure," Walter's eyes twinkle as he changes the subject. "Wait 'til you hear about the reason I'm back early! We were heading back to Navisia to replenish supplies before heading out west, but we got blown off course by a storm, ended up having to go east and north, ended up in the Stiriameer," he says excitedly.

The Stiriameer Sea was in the complete opposite and northerly direction to Navisia and required either going north above Caelias or east and around Sarenaveld, which poses its own dangers.

My eyebrows raise. "That's quite a detour."

My uncle nods. "Yeah, almost ended up in a skirmish with some Sarenaveldan privateers off their northern coast. Didn't even notice them until we were practically upon them! I thought we were going to have to go past the Gelinsels through the Vereisten Strait, but they never advanced, so we were able to curve west and head down the Flumevian River and cross over."

At the mention of Sarenaveldan privateers, my eyes almost fall out of my head. "What kept them from advancing?"

"Must've been able to tell we were a ship of seasoned travelers and would be able to fight them off!" Walter says, picking up a discarded dagger from the worktable and moving it like it's a sword.

"If you're going to fill the girl's head with tales, brother, at least try ones that wouldn't insult the intelligence of an ox," a smooth patrician voice says behind me.

Turning, I see my Uncle Eoforwine leaning against the door frame of the office, Uncle Engilram beside him. Eoforwine is holding a glass of wine in one hand and looking at the fingernails on his other one, as if meeting his brother's gaze after delivering such a set down would be uncouth.

Walter sputters as Engilram adds, his voice as steady and calm as ever, "Really, Walter, do you expect us to believe that tripe?"

"Uncle Eoforwine!" I say cheerfully, interrupting what was surely going to be a brotherly spat. "It's so wonderful to see you."

I go to him and hug him, which he obliges with only a slight sideways glance at my sooty dress, before he steps back, holding up one of my arms, since one is occupied by his wine. Where did he even get the wine?

"Let me look at you, darling. It's been an age since I've seen my eldest niece," he says, eyeing my plain day dress with its serviceable apron, my practical braid, my sturdy shoes. "We simply must get you to a better seamstress, *liebelîn*," he clucks at me. "This gown is doing *nothing* for your exquisite figure," he gestures to the unembellished, high-necked navy wool dress encasing the ample flesh of my breasts and hips.

All my uncles have some sort of profession that affords them the lifestyle of their choosing. Uncle Eoforwine, however, has always wanted the lifestyle of his choosing minus the profession. If being a professional courtier were a job, that's what Eoforwine's would be. He seems content to live on his inheritance in Embrathal and attend loads of court parties and balls and knows everyone who is anyone as well as many who are less than that but still entertaining, as he says. He also thinks fashion and socializing are the most important things in the world, after gossip and drinking wine.

It's somewhat surprising, then, that Eoforwine has made the day's journey to Noetheim from our capital to poke around in the forge, in which he has never shown a flicker of interest. A fact which couldn't be more obvious based on his silk, harlequin-patterned gold and black hose and his red velvet doublet topped with a dramatically draped cobalt-blue wool cape that falls past his waist. I'm never certain if Eoforwine's fashion choices are the rage in the capital, as I've not been since I was young, or if he's a bit eccentric, because I can't imagine a room filled with so many brightly colored peacocks if this is what they all choose to wear.

"My thanks, Uncle, but I'm not sure how much opportunity I would have to wear anything fine," I say, trying to avoid my flamboyant uncle's selecting my garments. My goal has always been to blend in, not stand out, and my clothing reflects that.

"Hmm, I'll have to speak to Mother about your making a visit, just as Agnethe did, yes? Perhaps for summer vröudenfeit season!" He says, excitedly, referring to the period during early summer in Embrathal when the court holds even more parties and festivals than the equinoxes to welcome in the warmer season.

I can't imagine something I'd rather do less. Except, perhaps, mathematical calculations or running. My "exquisite figure" is not built for speed. Far too much chafing happens.

I shrug and say, "Perhaps," with a noncommittal smile and quickly change the subject. "What brings you to the forge, Uncle?"

Eoforwine stares into his wine goblet briefly before answering. "I heard the de Veend name on a few curious tongues. No one important, though the Aurenclaste don't whisper for no reason. But when I saw my adventurous brother had returned, I realized it was merely curiosity and excitement about the fairy tales he's so eager to tell."

"They are *not* fairy tales," Walter huffs. "You wouldn't know an adventure if it bit you on your silk-covered arse—"

"If you're not going to leave then you need to start working, brothers," Engilram interjects calmly as he sits in front of the wheeled grindstone. He picks up a hammered dagger for the first stage of honing and sharpening.

Walter grumbles and says, "Any hammering that needs doing? I suddenly feel the need to hit something."

Eoforwine lazily raises a black brow at his older brother, runs a leisurely hand over his wavy black hair and neatly trimmed goatee, ever unruffled, as he says, "I will take any mention of getting dirty to be my indication to take my leave. I will go on to Noetheim to visit Mother, then journey back to Embrathal tomorrow. Brothers, will you join me later?"

Engilram answers without looking up from the grindstone. "Walter is lodging at Feuhūs for the duration of his visit," he says, indicating his own home.

Walter adds, "I had planned to visit Mother later this week."

Eoforwine sniffs. "I should think you would want to visit our Mother sooner, rather than later, as she's not getting any younger. Will you at least be home for her birthday?" He asks Walter.

Walter says, "That's months from now, yet, and I can't be certain which way the tide will turn. Spare me the silk-gloved slap, brother, I will do my duty to our mother in my own way."

Eoforwine huffs slightly and sets down his wine goblet. "Well, then I assume my brothers will at least see me off as I depart."

Engilram gives Walter a stern look. "Certainly, brother, we shall. Greta, join us."

Walter and Engilram follow Eoforwine, as he sweeps, nose in the air, out the front doors of the forge and makes his way toward the paddock. The additional horses there now connect in my head as belonging to Walter and Eoforwine.

Eoforwine turns to me. "Greta, *liebelîn*, I will see you for dinner then at the manor?" He doesn't wait for my answer, as he faces his brothers next and says, "Blessed Sisters be with you, brothers. I—"

Whatever he's about to say is cut off by the thundering sound of hooves hitting the ground at a fast pace.

"Sounds like an army," Walter jokes. But he's right; it's extremely loud. There must be many riders.

We move out to the side of the forge so the road that passes behind the hill is visible. Clouds of dry dirt are billowing as a group of riders barrels down the lane. The horses are large, like those built for combat. As they draw nearer, I can see that the figures on the horses are all wearing the same uniform—dark with gold and black heraldic surcoats. Some kind of soldiers?

"What is the Palastgarte doing here? Are they here for a commission?" Eoforwine asks Engilram, his smooth and practiced court cadence of speech dropping in favor of sharp concern.

The Palastgarte are the royal guard of Aurelia and have about as much reason to be here as our monarchs themselves.

Uncle Engilram's mouth presses into a thin line. "I'm not expecting them, so it could be for anything. They might not even be headed to the forge," he says.

As the soldiers near, their speed doesn't decrease, and before I know it, they are right by the forge. They continue, however, never glancing our way as we gawk at them. There are half a dozen riders, on my count, headed in the direction of Noetheim.

It could be nothing, I tell myself. Just a delivery. Just a visit. They might even pass Noetheim to go on to another location. But the fire burning in my chest tells me otherwise. Somehow, I know that none of those is the reason. I feel fear, as sharp and burning as any blade, coiling in my gut.

I take off in a run toward home.

CHAPTER THREE
Through History's Eyes

I run so fast that my breath is burning in my chest as I dart through the trees between the forge and Noetheim. What could the royal guard want here, if anything? I know they could continue past Noetheim, but given its isolation that seems unlikely.

Normally, when walking to and from the forge, I exit and enter through the front doors of the manor, cross the grounds and bridge, and take the main road, since the dirt has been worn down from riders and wagons to the point of hardness and is an even, easily traversable path. This time, however, I don't want the Palastgarte to see me if they are there, so I take a diagonal path through the woods, past the family crypt, and make my way to the edge of the tree growth.

Lucky for me, Noetheim is surrounded by a sizable moat, and the front entrance, which is the only visible entrance to the grounds, is on the opposite side of where I am.

Even luckier for me, Dunstan, our incredibly stubborn groundskeeper, is mostly deaf. He's also arguing with the Palastgarte soldiers, who are, in fact, outside of the entrance to the bridge.

"Move aside, man. We have business with the lady of Noetheim," the man at the front of the group of soldiers says.

"'Baby of Noetheim'?" Dunstan asks incredulously. "Lads, I think you are mistaken, there hasn't been a baby here in many decades."

"Not a baby, the *lady*," the head soldier clarifies.

"Well, now, I don't know what gravy has to do with anything, lad, but state yer business so's I can return to my tending."

A groan of frustration sounds. I thank the Sisters for our curmudgeonly old groundskeeper, who has given me enough of a distraction to get through the clearing and to the secret door that leads to the tunnel beneath the moat.

I heave open the heavy door—its hinges stiff from disuse—nearly flush with the earth at the moat's rear. It was built to allow residents of Noetheim to escape during more contentious war times throughout our history. While I'm grateful we've had no cause to use it, I'm equally grateful for its existence now. I take a deep breath and brace myself, uncertain what might crawl across my path, but I know I can't take the time to consider it or I'll never work up the nerve.

Without any further mulling, I descend the stone stairs into the depths below the moat.

The darkness spares me from seeing what else might lurk in the tunnel, but it also means I stumble, tripping on unseen stones. I press my hand to the wall to steady myself and encounter sticky wetness. Trying not to think too much about what *that* might be, I press on. The only sound that finds my ears is that of the gently moving moat some distance above me, a logical accompaniment to the stifling, loamy smell of damp earth permeating the stone walls.

I know I'm nearing the entrance to the house when I start to hear and smell things beyond the water. The tunnel supposedly empties into the storeroom beneath the kitchens, and I almost panic when I reach the door and it doesn't budge as I pull the handle. I dig my heels into the ground, spread my feet to shoulder width, and pull on the iron ring with all my might, sweat trickling along my hairline at the back of my neck from the effort.

Finally, the door groans and gives way, and I breathe a sigh of relief that I don't have to retrace my steps back through the tunnel, as I'm sure the Palastgarte will be on the grounds soon. My hope is that I have time to find Agnethe and my grandmother before then so I can get them out of here.

I race through the storeroom and up the steps to the kitchens, bursting through the door, ignoring the startled looks of the kitchen staff as I run past them, not pausing to explain. I stumble into the dining room where Agnethe is at lessons with Madam Boeschg again. Agnethe jumps up from her seat in fright, staring at me with saucer-wide eyes. Madam takes in my dirt-streaked gown, my right hand covered in tunnel muck, and her prominent nose quivers as she inhales deeply, no doubt preparing to deliver what will be a blistering admonishment of my comportment.

I speak before she can even open her mouth. "Agnethe, go upstairs and pack your things, just a small bag, we need to leave quickly."

"What? Why?" Agnethe asks, her eyes widening.

"What in the world is wrong, Miss de Veend?" Madam Boeschg sniffs.

"I don't have time to explain, you both need to go upstairs, and prepare to leave. If you hear any male voices or yelling, do *not* come downstairs. Find a place to hide and stay there," I instruct, hoping I'm overreacting, that the Palastgarte isn't here for anything serious and we'll all laugh about this afterward.

Agnethe crosses her arms. "Greta, I don't understand what's going on, but I'm not going anywhere until you tell me."

My heart is pounding with fear and exertion from rushing, and suddenly I'm so annoyed with her and so afraid that I can't hold back from yelling. "For fuck's sake, Agnethe, for once just do as I tell you!" I grab her arm and start ushering her out of the dining room toward the stairs.

Agnethe pulls her arm from me and stares at me as though I've grown three heads and committed the utmost betrayal. Thankfully, though, she runs upstairs. I sigh inwardly, knowing I'll have to give a serious apology to her later.

"Madam," I say firmly to the governess, more direct than I've ever been with her. "Please see that Agnethe does as I say. I would also like for you to prepare yourself to leave with us."

Surprisingly, she doesn't argue; she only nods once and follows my sister up the stairs.

Relieved that I've gotten that task started, I know the more difficult one is ahead with my grandmother, and I hurry down the hall toward her drawing room, throwing open one of the doors.

I find her sitting in one of her chairs, calmly sipping tea.

"Grandmother! We must leave. We must leave Noetheim," I say as I charge into the room, rushing to her chair and seizing the teacup from her, setting it down gently on the tray before grabbing her hands to pull her up from her seat.

"Greta, I'm not going anywhere," my grandmother says.

"You don't understand, Grandmother, there are—"

"I'm afraid, *herzeline*, it is you who does not understand, and much of that is my fault. Sit," she says, gesturing to the chair beside her.

"Grandmother, we don't have time for thi—"

"Margarethe Amelina de Veend, sit *down*," she says so forcefully that I immediately drop into the chair. I'm so surprised, I forget that my dress and hand are covered in mud until I touch the upholstered arm and leave a dark streak on the delicate fabric. I grimace apologetically at my grandmother.

She picks up her teacup, takes a sip, and looks at me before saying, "I haven't been entirely honest with you."

"About what?" I ask, eyes darting to the doorway, ears straining to hear if anyone is coming. Surely, Dunstan couldn't have distracted the Palastgarte for so long. It takes a few minutes to get from the bridge to Noetheim's entry doors, but not so long that they won't soon be upon us.

"About magic," she says calmly.

My gaze snaps to hers. "Magic? What magic?"

She replies, "My magic."

My heart rate increases, and the sound of rushing blood fills my ears. "But you don't have magic, Grandmother."

"I do," she says simply.

"Are you going to explain that loaded statement or just leave me to wonder about it as the Palastgarte descend on the house?" I demand, frustrated, hoping to shock her with this information.

Grandmother sighs. "I know they're coming, my dear."

My stomach drops. "You do?"

"I saw it," she says.

"You…saw it," I repeat, knowing what she's about to say but unable to voice it. Doing so would make it too real, and I'm not sure I'm ready for that.

"I have the gift of sight, Greta. I sometimes get visions of future events. As I've gotten older, they've gotten less frequent, less crisp. But the vision of the Palastgarte coming was, I'm afraid, as clear as any vision I had in my youth," she says, setting down her teacup, clasping her arthritic hands in her lap.

"Wh-why didn't you tell me?" I sputter, and I can't help but feel stung. Betrayed, even. I thought my grandmother trusted me.

"I've told precious few in my entire life, *herzeline*, and most are gone now. Having dark magic isn't something you share with just anyone," she explains. "You know the law."

"Who else knows?" I ask, somehow afraid of the answer; to know who my grandmother trusted with her deepest, darkest secret above me. I know this isn't completely fair. She's right that it's not a safe secret to share, even with those you trust. For one slip of the tongue, one secret spilled, can be your end.

"Hrafn knew," she says. "My parents. Merel. And Engilram was told when Hrafn died."

My mind is reeling. "But I don't understand, how does it work, how—"

My grandmother smiles. "Ah, always with so many questions, *herzeline*, but for once, I cannot indulge you by answering them all. There simply isn't time. The Palastgarte are, indeed, coming, as you said, and I saw it happen. It's important that you take Agnethe and hide. Go through the tunnel, as you came in. Head to the forge, or to Engilram's home, and don't emerge until you're certain they're gone. Then you must leave this place."

"But you're going to come with us," I protest.

"No, *herzeline*, I'm not," she says, sadly.

"But I—" my reply gets lost in the din coming from the front of the house. Shouts and male voices. Stomping. The whine of steel against steel.

"We have business with Odina de Veend," the Dunstan-arguing soldier's voice reaches me.

"You must hide, darling," my grandmother urges, getting up quickly and pulling me toward the portrait of Hrafn on the opposite side of the room. She runs a finger along the bottom edge of the portrait and I hear a latch release before the wall panel swings outward.

Before I can say anything, my grandmother pushes me behind the wall panel far more forcefully than I would've thought her capable. She closes the panel, and I'm sealed in the small chamber no bigger than a closet, the space still and dark save for a small shaft of light I assume is coming from the drawing room. Something which allows the person in the chamber to view the room undetected.

How typical and trite, I think.

I hear voices coming toward the room, growing louder, and just as my grandmother has settled herself in her chair again, the group of Palastgarte burst through the door in much the same manner as I had not many minutes ago.

Thanking the gods for the stereotypical hidden eye holes in the stereotypical room hidden behind a portrait, I lean forward so I can see into the drawing room.

The guard who had argued with Dunstan, clearly the leader, steps forward and addresses my grandmother. "Odina Roswita Foerstnerg de Veend?"

My grandmother nods regally. "I am she."

The Palastgarte soldier nods and turns to one of his comrades behind him, handing him the odd axe-and-spear combination weapon he was holding and the other soldier exchanging it for a rolled piece of parchment.

He clears his throat, unrolls the scroll, and reads, "By the Authority of the Crown and the Succession and Holdings Law, revision two-hundred forty-six, in the reign of his Royal Majesty, King Heinrich the fifth, under the purview of clause twenty-two, concerning dormant heirship and relief forfeiture, you are hereby summoned to present yourself before Crown-appointed assessors for inquiry regarding recent wardship declarations, alteration of estate documents, and custodial conduct concerning the inheritance of the Noetheim estate and lands.

"You are also hereby ordered to identify and present for interview any individuals named as wards within the aforementioned declarations, particularly where their station, age, or relation to the estate may influence future succession, custodial obligations, or relief outcomes.

"Said individuals shall be questioned for the purposes of establishing familiarity with estate matters, and awareness of custodial designation."

My heart is pounding so loudly I'm sure that everyone in the room can hear it, only no one turns in my direction at all. What were they even saying? Had my grandmother somehow named us as wards or heirs? Were they trying to determine succession of Noetheim? Clearly, that goes to my Uncle Engilram, so what were they doing here?

Grandmother says, "Goodness, gracious, what an awful lot of words to tell me that the Crown is inserting itself into family matters which do not concern them."

The Palastgarte soldier stiffens and says, "Madam de Veend, according to clause twelve of the Succession and Holdings Law, where an estate possesses a lawful heir of direct descent, yet said heir has not formally petitioned the crown for relief nor assumed legal stewardship of lands or revenues, the estate shall remain in custody under its current holder. However, this delay in succession may be interpreted as forfeiture of claim or evasion of relief tax obligation, especially if alternate custodians or wards are appointed in lieu of rightful heirs. In such cases, the Crown reserves the right to inspect the estate for mismanagement, undue influence, or dereliction of fiscal duty."

"Sir, might I have your address?" My grandmother asked, seemingly disregarding his entire mouthful of legal language.

His mouth thins into a straight line. "It's Captain Fiedlerg, Madam."

"Captain Fiedlerg," my grandmother begins, raising her teacup to her lips, not a tremor to be seen in her hands. "How did the Palastgarte come to be involved in matters of primogeniture, succession, and wardship?"

"The Palastgarte operates on behalf of the Crown and its representatives to execute lawful duties in the interest of the Crown as ordered," Captain Fiedlerg replies.

"And upon whose authority have you stormed into my home and demanded that I prove my wards are not swindling me and my eldest son out of his inheritance?" Grandmother asks coolly, setting down her teacup once more.

The captain flushes and says, "Lord Chancellor Rocheburn authorized and commanded the Palastgarte to proceed to the estate of Noetheim to execute the duties I have already outlined, Madam, including among others."

"What might those others be?" Grandmother inquires.

The captain unfurls the scroll once more and reads, "Inspecting the household function, the current holdings and revenues of the Noetheim estate, including tenant contracts, unpaid reliefs, and any transfer of stewardship not yet registered with the Royal Chancery."

My grandmother smiles and leans back in her seat, her arms draped casually on the cushions of the chair. "Ah, well, I can assure you, there have been no such unregistered transfers. As for the household holdings and revenues, you are welcome to inspect them. However, Noetheim has been in existence for hundreds of years, and being an old woman, I cannot ascertain exactly which order its records might be in, so you might be here for quite a time. Lastly, my wards are not present on the estate at this time, and as I will not be leaving my home, you will have to return with the Lord Chancellor if you wish to speak with them and me."

The captain looks at his fellow guards. "Madam, I must warn you that resistance or failure to comply with these orders may result in us forcibly escorting you to the Royal Chancery to be held for questioning pending resolution or royal directive," he says, clearly uncomfortably with the idea of manhandling an old woman.

As he should be, I think, fuming. I am three minutes from breaking free from my prison when my grandmother says something I don't think any of us would ever have guessed she would.

"On the contrary, Captain Fiedlerg. I am not resisting or failing to comply. It is only that I wish to save you a journey hefting the corpse of an old woman with you to Embrathal. You see, I've already ingested hemlock," she says, gesturing to her teacup. "So I shall shortly find myself unable to answer any more questions or respond to summons, as I will be quite dead."

My ragged breaths sputter to a stop in my lungs. Is it possible to still live when you can't breathe? I seem to be accomplishing that very feat now. My fingernails dig into the paneling of the wall in front of me so hard I can feel them snagging and tearing on the rough surface of the unfinished wood. I bite my lower lip to keep from screaming, wanting to call out, but my grandmother might be lying about the hemlock to get them to leave, so I can't reveal myself just yet.

The Palastgarte soldiers have all frozen with shock. Captain Fiedlerg squares his shoulders and asks, "You are quite certain you have ingested such a substance, Madam?"

My grandmother nods. "Indeed, I am."

The captain nods and says, "Very well," and turns to the comrade holding his strange weapon, who passes it back to him. He turns back to my grandmother and bows stiffly at the waist.

"Allow me to save you a torturous death then," he says and shoves the spear tip deep into my grandmother's stomach.

When the captain removes his spear from her torso, my grandmother immediately clutches her abdomen, blood pooling over her knobby fingers, but she doesn't utter a word, instead sinking deeply into her chair.

Blood thunders in my ears. I'm dizzy, on the edge of collapse. I don't know what to do. I am terrified, frozen, angry, heartbroken; how can someone be so many different things simultaneously without shattering into a million pieces?

The captain turns to his fellow soldiers before they quit the room and says, "Find the wards. His instructions were clear: bring them in at all costs."

CHAPTER FOUR
The Keeper's Legacy

I woke in a strange room, fabric surrounding my bed. I was terrified I had been made a prisoner somewhere, that I had been stolen from my parents by an evil ogre or wicked dark magic wielder like the ones in the stories Papa would tell me, and I'd have to wait for a brave prince to save me. I heard a door open nearby and shrank into the bed linens further, trying to hide from whomever had entered the room.

The bed fabric parted suddenly, and a familiar, friendly face smiled kindly at me.

"Ach, wee one, are ye still abed? The sun is high in the morning sky, and ye're wasting away the day," my nurse, Valda, said to me.

"Valda!" I exclaimed, jumping up on my knees in bed and flinging myself into her arms. "Where am I? Why does the bed have blankets on the sides? Don't people get cold with the blankets on the side of the bed and not on them?"

Valda threw up her hands in mock frustration. "Goodness me, Greta-girl, you'll make me daft with all these questions! All is well. Ye're at a fine lady's house in the north, y'are, and I'm to take you to meet her."

Nervous, I clutched the bedsheets. "Is she a princess? Do I have to curtsy? Because Mama hasn't taught me that yet," I said, worriedly.

Valda chuckled. "No, my sweetling, she's not a princess, but she is quite a fancy lady. Now, let's find somethin' for you to wear to meet her."

Valda dressed me in one of my nicer dresses, a navy wool that I liked because it hid grass and jam stains, and I stared around the lavish room as she combed my tangled hair and braided it, securing it at the end with a matching navy ribbon.

The floor was covered in large, square, gray stones. Stones that looked like I'd have to hop at least three big hops to cover the distance of just one. The walls were a lighter stone, stacked so high I had to tip my head back to look at the ceiling, and covered with fancy blankets that had people and horses and birds and flowers on them. The wall the bed was against was smoother, as if someone had smeared mud over the stones to cover them, and colored a deep red. The bed itself was a dark wood with ornate carvings on the headboard and footboard, ones that just begged me to trace them with my fingers.

"Valda, where is my sister?" I asked, suddenly remembering my baby sister, Agnethe. She was little, and she drooled a lot on herself and me, but Mama and Papa said I must look out for her since I'm her big sister. I was ashamed of myself that I had forgotten in my worry.

"Don't you fret none, Greta-girl. She's in fine fettle in another room in the nursery," Valda assured me, reaching down and taking my hand, leading me to the door of the bedroom. "We'll go visit her once we're done meeting the fancy lady, yes?"

I nodded, my tummy quivering with nerves, but I wanted to be brave like the heroes in Papa's stories.

I let Valda lead me down a large staircase, the stone steps so high I had to clutch the wall as I descended them, and I almost tripped and fell a few times. She then walked me down a long hallway that had lots of drawings of unhappy-looking people in funny clothes, the bottom halves covered in more of that dark wood, and this time I did trace my fingers along the ridges as I walked.

We stopped in front of a set of double wooden doors, and Valda knocked briskly and waited until a woman's voice called for us to enter. Valda turned the handle on the door and pushed it inward, revealing the fanciest sitting room I'd ever seen. There were cushioned chairs in brightly colored fabrics, multiple wooden tables with delicate legs, and a wall with a portrait of a man with hair as black as night and serious dark eyes that was so large I thought the painting must be taller than I was. A cheery fireplace already crackled with flames on the opposite wall.

In one of the brightly colored chairs sat the fanciest lady I had ever seen. Her dark hair, silvery at the temples, was swept away from her beautiful face in a low bun at the back of her neck. Her skin was a warm, glowing ivory, her figure slender and elegant. Her dress was long and a deep sapphire blue in a soft-looking fabric with a slight sheen and gold stitching on the hem, cuffs of her sleeves, and the collar. Sparkly gems winked at her ears and throat.

It was then that I noticed her eyes, though, and her eyes were my favorite part of her. A clear, bright blue, sparkling nearly as much as her jewels, and almost exactly like Mama's. In fact, I thought frowning, she quite looked like my mama, too, except she had fine lines around her eyes and mouth, as if she smiled a lot, which I liked. I'd hoped I'd get to see them crinkle.

My wishes were granted much sooner than I'd anticipated, and she smiled at me then and said, "Welcome to Noetheim, Greta."

"What's 'no-time'? I thought Valda said it's still morning," I said, confused.

The fancy lady leaned her head back and let out a sparkling laugh, and I decided that was my new favorite part of her. Oh, I'd give anything to hear her laugh again! It sounded like the most beautiful bells tinkling, more beautiful than temple chimes, and I loved temple chimes. It was almost as beautiful as Papa's singing, and that was the most beautiful sound I'd ever heard.

"Noetheim is the name of my home, dear, and it will also be your home now," she said, smiling.

"Are my mama and papa also going to live here?" I asked.

The fancy lady's smile got a little smaller. "I'm afraid not, dear. Your mama and papa got very sick, and they," she took in a deep breath and it shivered, like she was cold even though she was sitting by the fire. "They have passed away and gone on to Nachternel."

"Where's knock-or-nell? Can I go see them?" I asked.

"Nachternel is where the dead go when they've passed on from life, and I'm afraid it's not yet your time," the fancy lady says.

Dead. I knew that word. My stomach hurt and I suddenly wanted to sit down. Valda seemed to sense this, and she walked me over to the chair beside the fancy lady and helped me into it before leaving me in the room with her, promising to come back soon.

"Dead like my first mama and papa?" I asked, twisting my hands in my lap.

The fancy lady nodded. "Indeed."

I liked that she didn't tell me I would feel better soon. Grownups were always trying to tell me that things would be better soon, but I didn't want them to be better, I wanted my mama and papa.

"I'm sad, lady," I said, whispering, tears filling my eyes, to my horror. I didn't want to cry in front of the fancy lady in her fancy house and fancy room.

"It's quite all right to be sad, Greta. It is a sad thing to lose the ones we love. I am sad, too," she said, leaning close to me, as if telling me a secret.

I looked up at her, the tears spilling over from my eyes and onto my cheeks. "You are?"

The fancy lady nodded. "Oh, yes. You see, your second mama, Merel, is—or was, rather—my daughter. I'm her mama. And I'm going to miss her very much," she said, and she reached out to lay her hand on top of mine. Her sparkly eyes were shiny, like she wanted to cry too.

"What will I do without them, lady? And what about Agnethe?" I asked, sniffling. I had to make sure Agnethe was all right. She was my responsibility now.

The fancy lady leaned back and said, "Agnethe will also live here. And as for what we'll do, herzeline, *for now we will feel sad. And we might still feel sad tomorrow, and the next day, and even the next. Eventually, though, we will still feel sad, but we will also feel happy again. Does that sound all right to you?"*

I thought about it for a while and then nodded. "Yes. Only, what's hairts-a-lean-uh? Am I getting a haircut?"

She smiled at me, laughed softly, and said, "Herzeline means 'little heart' in the old language. I will teach it to you some day, if you'd like."

I nodded and said, "Yes, so I can understand old people when they talk."

She laughed one of her bell laughs again. "Oh, my, yes, we are quite difficult to understand sometimes, are we not? Would you like some tea?"

I nodded eagerly and watched as she poured steaming tea from a pretty, delicate pot into delicate teacups painted with flowers. Grownups all seemed to drink tea, and I had always wanted to try it. Since I was almost six and nearly a grownup, I decided it was time. She placed the teacup on a plate and set it on the small table beside my chair.

"Now, Greta," she said, "you must hold your teacup like you hold a secret. Keep it close, but not too tight, or it might spill out." She showed me how to hold the teacup in both of my small hands so the liquid didn't spill.

I took a sip of the drink and wrinkled my nose a bit at the bitterness. "This tastes a bit funny, lady. Why do grownups like it?"

She laughed. "I suppose it is an acquired taste, but like most things in life, it can be improved greatly by the addition of a bit of something sweet," and she pours a few spoonfuls of glittery, white sugar into my cup.

"And Greta," she added, and I looked up from my teacup into her sparkling eyes. "You must call me 'Müterine,' which means 'Grandmother.'"

I fumble with the inner latch of the compartment in the drawing room with clumsy, icy hands before I finally hook it with my index finger and lift the hidden door free.

"No, no, no, no, no," I say as I run to my grandmother's side, grabbing her hand.

"Don't fret so, *herzeline*," Grandmother says through pained breaths. "It is only a scratch," she jests.

My eyes burn, tears beginning to make their presence known, and I blink rapidly to clear them so I can see as I lift my grandmother's hands away from her stomach, blood still steadily pouring from the wound.

"We need to find a healer," I say frantically, looking around me for something to stanch the blood but finding nothing. I grab the skirt of my dress and press it into my grandmother's stomach. The viscous liquid bubbles beneath my fingers, saturating the fabric, the heat of it unexpected and disconcerting.

"It's too late. I took the hemlock," she says, reaching up to touch my cheek. "Help a poor old woman to lie down?" I nod, tears silently streaming down my cheeks as I gently lower her from the chair to the floor, cursing myself for not being strong enough to lift her with ease.

"I'm so sorry, *Müterine*," I whisper thickly, tears clogging my throat as I revert to my childhood nickname for her. I clutch one of her hands in my left, my right still determinedly pressing the skirt of my dress into her stomach, despite the blood that's now seeping onto the carpet beneath her body and my knees.

"My darling, sweet girl," she says, raising her hand once more to cup my face. My cheek registers the sticky warmth of her blood on her palm.

She continues, "There's no need to apologize. I knew this was coming. Have had time to prepare. I only wish…I only wish I could've prepared you more."

"Why didn't you?" I ask, her face blurring in front of my eyes as they fill with more tears. "We could have had more time together, I could've helped you get things ready, made things easier, prevented this from happening."

"Darling, you have given so much of yourself to me, and I eagerly took it, selfish woman that I am. But I must tell you…" she gasps.

"Don't speak more," I say. "Conserve your strength." A sob chokes the last word of my sentence. How I wish I were stronger than I am in this moment.

"No, I…I must tell you. Seek the sign…where shadow and feather meet. Let the keeper's legacy guide your way. Tell no one. Not even Agnethe." Her breathing becomes more labored, her chest rises and falls more slowly, the breaths fewer and farther between.

"What does it mean?" I ask. "I don't understand."

Grandmother says, "You will in time. When…you're ready."

Sobs wrack my body now as I say, "I'm not ready. *I'm not ready.* Please don't go. Stay with me. *Stay,*" I beg in earnest, coughing raggedly, my tears choking me.

"You are ready," she assures me. "And I am ready to go. To see…Hrafn. Merel. I am not afraid," she smiles at me, her thumb softly stroking my cheek before her hand falls away from my face as she weakens further.

I grab her hand as it falls and urgently press it back to my cheek, willing her to stay with me. "*I'm* afraid, *Müterine.* I'm afraid of it all, I need you."

"You've not needed me for…a long while," she says, smiling gently. "You must go…find your life outside Noetheim. Take Agnethe. Escape. Feel sad. Then feel happy again. I have always believed…that you were meant for more than this."

"I don't know if I do," I whisper, tears still falling steadily, the drops hitting her gown and staining the delicate lavender silk.

Grandmother looks at me with soft, distant eyes and says, "Then I shall believe in you…for us both."

Her eyes flutter shut, her lips part as if to say one more encouraging word, one more expression of love, but nothing comes. Just silence. A silence too full to bear.

Her breathing slows. Her hands slacken in mine. Her head rolls to the side. She is still.

And with that quiet departure, it feels as though I could die along with her from the pain of my heart cracking in my chest. It consumes me, burning behind my sternum, my stomach spasming painfully, the air leaving my lungs in a sudden, violent exhalation.

It's not long, however, before I'm reminded that I am still very much alive, and I am forced to acknowledge the searing pain from lack of air by finally taking in a deep, shuddering breath. Another cough rattles in my chest, wet and thick with grief and weeping. I squeeze my eyes tightly shut to the sight of her still form on the floor, all the while hot tears continue to leak from between my lashes. I feel the urge to scream, to rage at the gods and the world and everyone, building in my chest.

Overcome with a sudden rush of anger, my eyes snap open and I grab her upper arms and shake her. "No," I deny her death fiercely. "Wake up. *Wake up!* Come back, I…" my voice cracks, and I lean my head forward, body shaking with quiet, staccato sobs as I touch my forehead to her rapidly cooling shoulder. "I need you. I love you," I whisper.

But nothing changes, even with my pleading. She remains still, and I remain broken.

That's when a scream shatters the silence of my despair, raw, unconfined, echoing through the halls like a broken hymn.

My head snaps up and I gasp, "*Agnethe!*"

CHAPTER FIVE
The First Lie

I run out of the drawing room, my feet pounding on the stone floor as I tear down the gallery hall toward the staircase near the front of the manor. As I near the door to the entryway, I can see Agnethe struggling against the hold of the two Palastgarte soldiers holding her by each of her arms.

"We found the old one hiding in a closet in one of the chambers upstairs," one of the soldiers tells the captain, nodding toward Madam Boeschg, who is unrestrained but looks terrified. "And *this* one came running out, screaming at us like a demon and starts hitting Ecksteing on the head and shoulders with a rotte bow." He yanks on Agnethe's left arm harder than necessary, and she cries out in angry protest.

Fire races through my veins, and I come storming out of the hall. "Unhand her!" I bellow, the volume so unexpected that several soldiers start, turning toward me.

"And you are?" The captain asks slowly, taking in my bedraggled state, his gaze freezing when he sees the blood staining my dress.

Agnethe sees me then and screams, "Greta! Help, they're trying to take me and Madam Boeschg, and why are you covered in blood? Are you bleeding?" Her voice rises in pitch and volume with each question, and if I didn't have the angry rush of blood filling my ears, I'm certain I'd be wincing from pain in my eardrums.

"Margarethe de Veend," I say to the captain without ceremony.

The captain looks at his closest associates and nods once. "Seize her."

"No! Where are you taking her?" Agnethe screams.

The captain begins, "You're being taken in for interviewing by the Lord Chancellor under clause twenty—"

"It's a silly clerical error regarding Grandmother's will, Agnethe, nothing to concern yourself with. I hardly think this is cause for us to be treated like prisoners," I say to the captain, haughtily.

Just then, Engilram, Walter, and Eoforwine come crashing into the front hall, each carrying a weapon, no doubt grabbed from the forge before hastily leaving. "Greta, Agnethe," Engilram begins, looking around at the guards in the room. "What is the meaning of this?" He demands, drawing himself up to his full height and looking down his nose at the guards.

Captain Fiedlerg asks, "Is one of you gentlemen the heir to Noetheim?"

Engilram frowns and answers, "I suppose that would be me; however, my mother has been custodian of the estate since my father's passing. Let my nieces go, and we shall find her to clear up whatever misunderstanding this is regarding."

The captain's voice is tight as he says, "I'm afraid Madam de Veend has died."

All three men look shocked.

Walter charges forward as he roars, "What did you whoresons do to my mother? I swear I won't rest until each of you is separated from his head," and he brandishes his sword at them, lunging.

The soldiers holding Agnethe let go of her to block Walter from attacking the captain, and Engilram and Eoforwine are trying to yank Walter back by the fabric of his tunic. In the confusion, Agnethe rushes to my side, and I grab onto her, pulling her tight to me to reassure myself that she's whole and basically unharmed.

"Greta, what's happened? Is Grandmother really dead?" Agnethe asks, her eyes swimming with tears.

I swallow hard. "Yes, I—"

The sound of a man's harsh groan interrupts my explanation. Walter has been wrestled to the ground, his right eye rapidly swelling shut, blood gushing from his nose.

"Madam de Veend perished by her own hand; there was naught we could do to prevent it by the time we reached her. I merely hastened what would've been a long and unpleasant end from hemlock poisoning," the captain says blandly, as if he didn't just confess to stabbing an elderly woman.

On his odd-looking axe, I notice dark smears of blood. Bile rises in my throat, knowing to whom it belongs, how it got there.

Engilram looks to me and asks, "Is this true, Greta?"

I nod and reply, "Yes, Uncle. Grandmother told me the same herself when I found her." I don't want to alert the Palastgarte that I was present during their entire interaction. "She's…she's gone," I say, my voice cracking. I clench my teeth to keep my jaw from trembling.

While Engilram isn't nearly as hot-blooded as Walter, his anger is plain as day as he says, "I want someone to explain to me what is going on immediately before I bring the wrath of the law down on your miserable heads."

The captain clears his throat and pulls out his scroll. He reads the same notice he had given to my grandmother regarding the Succession and Holdings Law, the supposed investigation into a new will, the dormant heirship and relief taxes for Noetheim, and my grandmother's recent declaration of wards in that new will.

Eoforwine finally speaks. "I fail to see why the Crown is becoming involved in matters of inheritance," he echoes what my grandmother had also said to them.

Captain Fiedlerg says, "Sir, the Crown reserves the right to inspect the estate for mismanagement, undue influence, or dereliction of fiscal duty when an heir has failed to step forward to claim their birthright and updated documents of elderly persons have been filed with the chancery.”

Engilram says, “This is a mistake. I haven’t failed to claim my inheritance; I did not want to move my mother and nieces from their home when I already possessed one of my own. I shall write a letter to the Lord Chancellor and clear up this entire farce. You may leave my family’s home and rest assured I will address this matter promptly.”

My heart races at my uncle’s words. Could it really be that simple?

The captain smiles stiffly. “Unfortunately, sir, I am under orders to bring the new wards in for interviewing and, as your niece assaulted one of my officers—”

“That’s preposterous!” Uncle Eoforwine snaps.

“I wish I’d had a sword to treat you as you did my grandmother!” Agnethe yells angrily.

I clap my hand over her mouth. “Kindly shut up, Agnethe,” I say quietly.

“Miss de Veend, that is quite enough,” the captain censures sharply.

“I do not permit you to take my nieces from this estate; this is nothing short of abduction,” Engilram says, stepping in between the soldiers and me and Agnethe.

“Sir, if you do not step aside so that we might complete our orders, I will be forced to have you arrested,” the captain says. I decide then that I have never hated anyone as much as I hate this man.

I think of my grandmother’s body, life force soaked into the carpet of her drawing room, and I’m suddenly terrified for my uncles. “Uncle, it’s all right. We’ll go. We’ll speak to the assessors and assure them there is nothing untoward in Grandmother’s will. It’s all just a misunderstanding,” I say, speaking far more calmly than I feel inside.

Uncle Engilram’s brows draw together in concern. “Greta, I do not think—”

“No need to worry yourself, Uncle. We shall return soon,” I plead with him with my eyes to not protest further, my fear for him and my other uncles reaching a fever pitch.

Something in my face must convey enough of what I’m feeling so that he nods once and steps back. “Very well,” as he turns to the captain and says, “but make no mistake, I will be seeking counsel on this and if my nieces are not returned to Noetheim promptly, I will be coming to retrieve them."

It is the most I've heard Uncle Engilram speak in one sitting in years. My heart swells with love and gratitude for him, my somber but caring uncle who has tolerated my distracted management of his forge, giving me another place to find sanctuary instead of casting me aside.

"I will journey immediately to Embrathal and take up this matter with the chancery," Uncle Eoforwine says.

I nod my acknowledgement as I let the captain lead Agnethe and me out of the front doors of Noetheim. As we cross the threshold, I look over my shoulder at my three uncles, feeling sure that the next time I see them, it will be under far different circumstances. Whether they are happy or otherwise remains to be seen.

The Palastgarte soldiers escort us outside to their waiting horses, where Agnethe and I are each paired with a female soldier with whom to ride.

"Where are you taking us?" I ask the captain, stopping near the waiting horse. I'm not a particularly skilled horsewoman. I can stay on, but I have never been fond of it. With few sojourns away from Noetheim, I'm not accustomed to long rides. Agnethe is in the same boat as I am, and is currently eyeing her horse with wariness.

I want to know where we are going before I climb onto the smelly beast before me. The Palastgarte had told my grandmother that she would see "assessors," but then the captain had mentioned that "he" said we were to be brought in at all costs.

While I gave the outward appearance of being unconcerned and believe this all to be a misunderstanding, the specter of my grandmother's cryptic deathbed instructions hovers in the back of my mind. I can't help but wonder if this is all very much on purpose. To what end, I hope to discover soon.

The captain turns to me. "We travel to Embrathal, where you will interview with Lord Rocheburn per the law, to ascertain any influence or perfidy regarding Madam de Veend's recent adjustments to her will."

"But how will we be able to prove such a thing when my grandmother is dead?" I demand, my temper flaring at the captain's continued recitation of the same information.

"I'm afraid I've given you the information I know and am at liberty to share. We will change horses at the posting station after the river's cross, and you and your sister will ride by carriage from that point on," he tells me before walking over to his own horse. He swiftly mounts it, not sparing me another glance as he says to his soldiers, "Move out."

The soldier I'm to ride with wordlessly gestures to the horse beside us. I place my foot in its stirrup and grab hold of the saddle's pommel. My muscles burn as I struggle to lift the entire weight of my body using only my arms and the propulsion of my leg in the stirrup. I clamber onto the top of the horse, trying to swing my leg over to straddle it, restricted by the skirt of my dress. I hear a distinct rip as the fabric of the skirt tears to accommodate my seat on the animal.

As the soldier climbs up behind me, I turn my head and see Agnethe climb onto her horse with her riding partner. She manages to do so far more gracefully than I have. She looks to me after she's seated, her eyes glassy and mouth pinched with worry. Her hands grip the pommel so tightly that her knuckles turn white.

As we begin to make our way across the grounds and to the bridge, my teeth clack in my mouth with every cantering step. I grip onto my saddle's pommel and quickly realize that I would've benefited from asking for gloves so my hands aren't rubbed raw and a cloak so the breeze kicked up from riding doesn't chill me. Especially considering the bottom half of my dress is still soaked in blood and clinging wetly to my knees.

When we reach the end of the bridge, Dunstan is tending the roses that grow along the bank of the moat. He sees me and calls out, "Where are ye headed, girl? Did ye find the gravy?"

A perverse part of me has to hold back a laugh. After all the things that have happened today, I can't seem to muster a more appropriate reaction to Dunstan's question.

I reply, "To the capital, Dunstan, but we'll return soon!"

Dunstan says, "Well, now, Miss Greta, you may be cursed by the moon, but that's no reason to put you to the catapult."

We're riding too quickly for me to answer him. I suppose the sight of half a dozen horses heading in his direction without any sign of slowing prompts Dunstan to wisely step to the side of the gate so we can pass. As we turn after exiting the gate, I have one last look at Noetheim. We pick up speed and thunder past the grounds, headed north to the bridge that crosses the river.

Noetheim is in Vallaurium, Aurelia's central and capital province, but the small river snaking past it bisects the land. The majority of the province, including our capital Embrathal and the royal castle, is east of the river, and the remaining small portion is to the west.

The air has cooled considerably even during the relatively short distance to the northern crossing bridge. As we near in proximity to the Dorberge mountain range that dominates most of our northernmost province, Caelias, I regret my lack of cloak even more. Agnethe and her rider are behind me and mine. I try to look over my shoulder toward her, but it's difficult to focus on her expression when I'm bouncing up and down, and at a distance. I sigh and cross my arms, and the icy air and even icier reality sink deep into my bones.

Grandmother is dead. I'm alone again, except for Agnethe, who will eventually leave and strike out on her own, once this mess is sorted. My grandmother told me to find my life outside of Noetheim, but I don't even know what that is or would be. Had she seen something with her gift of sight? Oh, how I wish I could ask her so many more questions about my future, about Agnethe's.

I would give anything to return to the gallery, walk to her drawing room, and reluctantly drink her tea, but that will never happen again. My eyes burn as I recall her telling me she believed in me. If only I had half as much faith in myself as she seemed to. I feel proud and humbled that she trusted me so much to make more of myself than a glorified housekeeper for her and my uncle. But a part of me is also angry at her. She withheld so much from me, so much that might've helped me to find my way and cope a bit better. Now I feel as though I've been left holding the bill, so to speak, without having any knowledge of the order.

As far as deathbed confessions go, it was definitely lacking. I feel like my grandmother could have helped me out just a bit more, especially since it seemed so important to her.

Seek the sign where shadow and feather meet. Let the keeper's legacy guide your way. Tell no one. Not even Agnethe.

I look guiltily in Agnethe's direction, and she's watching me, her face a mask of concern. Perhaps she's worried for me, and knowing I'm holding some big, secret clue wouldn't help that. I attempt to decipher it mentally but come up short.

We cross the bridge and make it to the outpost, where the soldiers exchange their horses for freshly rested ones. Agnethe and I are stuffed unceremoniously into a small, uncomfortable carriage. But at least it's closed to the elements, since neither of us is dressed particularly warmly. Captain Fiedlerg says we will ride until sundown, when it's no longer safe for the horses to travel.

I lean back against the hard wooden seat, which has no cushioning or softness to recommend it, only scuffed boards coated in travel dust. I'm too tired to even care about a bit of dust, considering what other substances stain my dress—tunnel muck, dirt, mud from the road as we traveled to the outpost, and, of course, my grandmother's blood. The skirt fabric is now stiff and dry on the front from my knees down, stained dark brown where the blood has oxidized. I feel revulsion rise in my throat, and I look away from it abruptly, unable to stomach the evidence of my grandmother's loss of life stamped so clearly onto my clothing. I see Agnethe looking at it also, but she must be able to sense that my gaze is now on her because she looks up at my face.

I don't say anything to her, which is unusual and must make her nervous, because she clears her throat and says, "Are you going to say anything?"

Immediately, I feel the heat of irritation flare in my chest, prickling across my shoulders, down my arms, causing my fingers to twitch. Why is it always up to me to say something first? To bridge the gap of hurt feelings and to do the mending. Don't I deserve to have someone else do the work of that sometimes? I know that my grief is coloring my emotions, but I am aware of my control over my anger slipping as it pulses through my veins. I lean forward and wrap my fingers tightly around the edge of the wooden seat, as if I can somehow contain my ire and keep it from bubbling over.

"You didn't listen to me," I say tightly.

Agnethe looks surprised. "What? Listen to you about what?"

I reply, "You came out screaming and beating a soldier whose purpose was unknown to you. I told you to stay hidden."

"I'm not a child, Greta. I'm allowed to move about when I wish to," Agnethe challenges. She is right; she is allowed to do that.

"If you don't want me to treat you like a child, perhaps you should stop acting like one," I retort.

"What did you just say to me?" Agnethe's eyes narrow, and her fingers go to toy with her ring as she waits for an answer.

I respond, "You heard me. If you want people to treat you as an adult, you need to be one. Stop pouting, stop complaining about your duties, and Blessed Sisters, try to listen to me, damn it. If you had, we wouldn't be in this mess now."

Agnethe looks hurt and twists her ring. "I know things didn't go exactly as planned, but I can hardly be blamed for everything that—"

"I'm not blaming you for everything, Agnethe, I'm holding you accountable for your actions," I say, interrupting her. "Your actions that have directly influenced our current position, which is far more dangerous than I let on to our uncles."

"I did what I thought was right at the time!" Agnethe says, loudly. "It's not like I was privy to any of this danger you obviously know about. You never tell me anything. You're always trying to protect me from the world, to keep me from getting hurt, when it's *you* who is always doing the hurting!"

My head jerks back as if slapped. "I see. I didn't realize that seeing you get everything you want was hurtful."

Agnethe says, "I don't want you to get me everything I want, I want to do some of that on my own, to find my own life outside of this, of Noetheim."

Her words are so close to what my grandmother told me to do for myself that I am shocked into temporary silence.

"Maybe I have held you too tightly sometimes, but it's because I know how it feels to fall, and I don't want that for you," I say quietly. I look at my hands where they still grip the seat, the knuckles of my fingers white.

The carriage begins slowing down, and we're unable to say more to one another without fear of being overheard by the Palastgarte. Besides, the last thing I want them to know is that there is any tension between Agnethe and me. Who knows how they, or anyone, might exploit that if they were to find out?

When we stop, Agnethe and I sit in confused silence for several minutes until the sound of footsteps on the ground can be heard. The door to the carriage suddenly swings open, and one of the soldiers steps back from the door to the carriage and motions for us to climb out of it. The rapidly fading daylight turns the sky shades of pink and orange behind her shoulders.

As I awkwardly descend from the carriage, my legs and back stiff from the hard seat, I can see we've stopped in some kind of clearing, surrounded by forest on all sides. The breaths I exhale turn cloudy white as they meet the rapidly cooling air. The smell of the pine needles and wild heather around me and beneath my feet reaches my nose. So I don't give over to my exhaustion, fear, anguish, and the anger I was just feeling, I take a moment to inhale deeply.

"We camp here for the night so the horses don't turn a leg in the dark; we depart at first light," the soldier tells us, gesturing to where the Palastgarte soldiers are erecting small tents.

"We're to sleep…outside?" I ask tentatively, unsure if I interpreted her statement correctly.

The soldier's eyes glint in amusement. "Unless you're aware of a nearby castle we can prevail upon, I'm afraid the ground will be your bed tonight and the stars your blanket," she says.

I shudder, thinking of all the possible things that might sleep on the ground with us—bugs, snakes, and any manner of beasts that could try to rip out our throats. I have never been a particularly outdoorsy person, preferring the comforts of a home to being in the wilds of nature. Many flowers make me sneeze, grass gives me itchy spots, and I don't like being dirty or sweaty. I glance ruefully at my blood-encrusted dress and think that, perhaps, it can't get any worse at this point.

Agnethe and I don't speak to one another as we are directed by the soldiers to assist in setting up camp by clearing twigs and branches from the ground so the tents can lie flat, piling the same twigs and branches into heaps to use for the cooking fire, which will also serve as a way we can warm ourselves later. Several soldiers have split off to hunt for dinner and to water and feed the horses. I observe the clearing and wonder if there is any way Agnethe and I can escape from here but quickly disabuse myself of that idea. We have no idea where we are, it will soon be dark, we aren't near civilization, and we are not accustomed to weathering the outdoors for long stretches of time.

The hunters return with several rabbits and some wild vegetables, mostly mushrooms and onions, and set about making a stew in a battered pot set up over the fire. After dinner, the soldiers plan watch rotations to look out for wild animals that might be on the nocturnal prowl, as well as guard duty shifts to supervise Agnethe and me.

They shuffle us into a tent that, thankfully, we don't have to share with any of the soldiers. It's a small comfort, though, since we would easily be seen or heard were we to exit the tent or have anything but a whispered conversation.

With nothing else to do and almost no light from the fire, I lie down on the bedroll they've provided me. I still wear my dirty dress, but with nothing else to change into or sleep in, I have no choice but to remain in it. I pull the furs they gave us over my body, up to my eyes, to combat the worsening chill as night fully settles into the camp. I hear rustling from Agnethe's side of the tent and assume she's doing the same, but I can't see her given the low light and the fact that I've turned my back to her. We've had spats before, but this feels worse than any fight we've ever had. Maybe because I'm always extending an olive branch before things get to this point of mutual silent treatment. I simply don't have the energy for that now. I will have to make up with Agnethe in the morning, though. We're all one another has here, and we need to stick together.

The rustling noises grow closer until suddenly I feel Agnethe pressed up behind me. Her arm wraps over my waist, and I hear her voice say, "I'm sorry, *alouisse*. I don't want to fight with you."

Guilt and sadness make my resolve crack, and I turn to her, unable to see much but the shining of her eyes in the dark. "I'm sorry, too. I don't want to fight, either. I just…wish things were different."

"Did she suffer?" Agnethe asks quietly, and I know she means our grandmother.

"If she did, she did not say, and it wasn't for long. She…she had only good things to say as her last words," I tell her, thinking of what she said to me, expressing her faith in me, her belief that I was destined for bigger things.

"What did she say about me?" Agnethe asks, and the guilt tightens around my chest, making it hard to breathe.

How do I tell her that my grandmother's only words of her were to caution me against revealing that cryptic statement and to escape? I know that I cannot. Why make both of us live with the knowledge unnecessarily?

"She said she loves you very much and that we're to have grand adventures together," I wrap my arm around Agnethe's shoulders, and she snuggles up closer to me, just as she did when she was young, her head on my shoulder. I rest my cheek on the softness of her hair.

"What kinds of adventures should we have?" Agnethe asks mischievously, and I know this is for my benefit, to distract me.

I smile against her hair. "I would say this qualifies as quite the adventure so far, does it not?"

Agnethe giggles. "As does hitting a Palastgarte with my rotte bow."

I laugh then. "Honestly, Agnethe, you couldn't have found anything heavier?"

We whisper to each other of all the grand adventures we'll have—me and Agnethe against the world, once more—until the camp quiets and she drifts off to sleep, head still on my shoulder. I stay awake, staring into the dark, haunted by my grandmother's final words to me and the realization that I've just lied to my sister for the first time.

Not a harmless fib to shield her from sorrow, nor a softened truth to ease a child's worry. This was a choice. A deliberate withholding.

I've never kept secrets from Agnethe before, not like this. And even though my grandmother told me to tell no one, it still sits in my gut, heavy and sour, its sting sharper than any blade. As sleep comes to claim me and my eyes drift closed, I wonder how many more lies I'll have to tell my sister before all of this is over. And if she'll forgive me if I do.

CHAPTER SIX
The Duke's Hospitality

My arse has had just about enough of this carriage. The Palastgarte soldiers seem to have no regard for our comfort or the speed at which they take turns and maneuver the vehicle. I've been bouncing regularly against the hard seat and have also gracelessly slid from side to side, crashing into the walls when they've made sudden turns. Earlier, I tried looking out the lone window in the door by pushing the curtain aside, but found the motion of the rapidly moving scenery to be nauseating.

Agnethe isn't faring much better. Several hours into our journey the next day, we have figured out a sort of bracing system where I, with my longer legs, reach across to her seat and press my feet flat against the wall on either side of her body, providing her a cage. She holds onto my calves with her arms to help keep them steady when there are turns or hard bumps. Of course, the cage is only as useful as its construction, and with my legs trembling more the longer we are in this demon conveyance, the more often I lose my footing.

The carriage takes another sudden, sharp turn, and we are thrown to the side, Agnethe clunking her head on the inside handle of the door.

"Fuck the Sisters sideways!" Agnethe exclaims, holding the side of her head where it struck the handle.

"Agnethe!" I admonish, but it doesn't land very convincingly, considering I snort with laughter at the same time. "Wherever did you hear such a blasphemous phrase?"

Agnethe grins. "During Lunoktium, visiting Uncle Eoforwine. I heard one of the servants say it at a party, and I've been itching to use it. This seemed appropriate," she says, wincing as she rubs the tender spot on her head.

"Is there a bump?" I ask, wanting to reach out to feel myself, but forced to hold myself steady by placing my palms flat on the seat beside me.

"No, it just smarts," she answers. "I wonder how much longer it will be. Do you suppose the assessors will have a proper bed for us to sleep in?" She asks hopefully.

I bite my lip. "I don't think we're going to see assessors. The soldiers made it sound like we're going to see Lord Rocheburn himself."

She looks confused. "Who?"

I sigh, exasperated. "Honestly, do you *ever* pay attention in your lessons?"

She shrugs, unashamed. "When it was a topic I enjoyed, yes."

I roll my eyes and say, "The Duke of Rocheburn. As in, the lord chancellor of Aurelia? As in, member of the Aurenkammer?" I prompt, hoping for a glimmer of recognition. When there is none, I add, "The Gold Council."

Agnethe pales. "A member of the Gold Council is going to speak to us about Grandmother's will? Why?"

I try to explain to her what I overheard from the Palastgarte, about how Grandmother must've filed a new will and named us as her wards, which she hadn't previously done. And because Uncle Engilram hadn't claimed the lands or house by paying the relicf tax that's required in order to assume ownership of the estate, there are questions about whether Grandmother was influenced by someone to update her will. Which will cause issues for whomever would claim the estate upon her death.

She looks baffled and sputters, "But that's ridiculous! Uncle Engilram just didn't want to uproot Grandmother."

"Exactly his argument," I agree, pointing out that Engilram said that very thing to the captain. "But I guess this is part of the lord chancellor's duties, to ensure that everyone follows this Succession and Holdings Law."

She snorts and replies, "It sounds more like he wants to make sure that people pay the Crown taxes for land they already own."

I'm somewhat surprised by Agnethe's on-the-nose cynicism, which exactly mirrors my own private thoughts. For all her lack of interest in her lessons on our government, she seems to have stripped bare the flimsy facade of law to expose the heart of the matter.

The carriage jolts again, and I bounce high enough that my head hits the roof. I can't quite bring myself to blaspheme as Agnethe did, even with my skepticism regarding the gods and their influence and whether such phrases would earn me a sudden lightning bolt directly from Luftella's hand, sending me to Nachternel and the afterlife in a blaze of sparkling glory. I do manage to utter a respectable "Shit!" in response to my head connecting with the hard surface, though.

A few moments later, the carriage rumbles ominously, vibrating more than it has during our entire journey, before suddenly riding smoothly. Agnethe and I look at each other, cautiously optimistic.

"I wonder if we switched road surfaces?" I say, and we both dive for the curtain on the carriage door, pulling it aside.

Sure enough, the view out of the window is that of small, ramshackle buildings that, as we proceed, get taller and closer together. A look down a cross street in the distance gives me a view of the cobbled streets on which we are now rolling and people bustling to and fro in the busy walkways.

"I think this is the outskirts of Embrathal," Agnethe says, excitedly. She would recognize it better than I would, having been here recently. I haven't been to Embrathal since I was a small child. Not being interested in parties and festivals, as Agnethe is, I never attempted to visit it as an adult.

As we travel through the streets, the view of the city becomes more prosperous, the buildings larger and more ornate, the streets clean and well swept, the people milling about better outfitted in sophisticated clothing that would put even my grandmother's lavish wardrobe to shame.

The carriage slows its progress, most likely owing to the fact that there is more foot and carriage traffic in the city, and I'm able to stare in wonder at the storefronts boasting dressmaker forms draped in silks in every jewel color imaginable, bakeries with curls of yeast-scented steam wafting from the windows and pastries and tarts glistening with sugary glazes sitting in sparkling glass display cases.

As we cross what is clearly more of the central area of the city, filled with shops and restaurants with which to divert yourself, we begin to pass more residential areas—elegant row houses giving way to stately manor homes surrounded by stone walls and elaborate wrought-iron fences.

We pass an enormous structure with tall spires complete with gargoyles on the roofs, surrounded by extensive grounds and enclosed with ivy-strung fencing, and I gape at how beautiful the building is.

"Is that the castle, Aurumstein?" I ask Agnethe.

Agnethe's tinkling laugh sounds, and I look over at her to see her blue eyes dancing with amusement. "No, Aurumstein is much larger. That's Magnivine, the magic academy," she says.

Magnivine. I've heard of it, of course, because even those of us without magic have heard of the prestigious school to which the Aurenclaste send their children when their magic manifests. There, they learn how to hone and control their magical abilities, in addition to the schooling typical for the wealthy, privileged class who will one day rule our nation. As someone who loves learning, I had always harbored secret, childish fantasies of attending Magnivine. Not for the magic part—as I had long since resigned myself to the fact that I wouldn't suddenly be able to control storms, create fire, or move objects with my mind, but for the lessons, the books, and the education so far out of reach to so many of us.

The bitter taste of resentment floods the back of my mouth at the thought of just how different those with the privilege of magic are treated compared to those without. And I know that I've had a far more comfortable life than most of Aurelia's citizens, forced to toil away at humble professions or enlist in the military simply to survive.

"It's somewhat shocking, isn't it? How much so few have," Agnethe says quietly. I turn, surprised, to see her watching my face. She must be able to read my emotions better than I realize.

I nod and say, "Yes, I suppose I have never seen it so clearly."

"Part of me hates them, and the other part of me wants to be one of them," Agnethe admits. I admire how she can so succinctly sum up the whole of my feelings on the matter.

"Well," I say, injecting false cheer into my voice. "No sense dwelling on what cannot be."

Agnethe murmurs a noncommittal agreement and turns to stare at the window, stiffening suddenly. I turn my eyes in the same direction and see why her posture has changed. We've pulled up next to another fence, this one housing a large estate, and the carriage has slowed considerably. Indeed, my suspicions are confirmed when we turn sharply to the right and enter through a gate onto the house's grounds. The carriage pulls up into a curved pathway that runs along the front entrance of the house and stops immediately in front of the stairs that ascend to the entry door.

A well-dressed older gentleman steps down the stairs. Lord Rocheburn, perhaps? The carriage door opens, and the gentleman is holding the door open. He says, "Welcome to Felsegeist Haus, ladies. The duke eagerly awaits your arrival."

Of course not the duke, I think, mentally smacking my own forehead. A man *this* wealthy and influential would have many servants to manage every aspect of his house. The man identifies himself as the steward of the manor as he ushers us into the large, stone entryway. As we move down the main hall, we pass by several servants, all dressed impeccably and moving silently.

"No doubt you'll wish to freshen up," the steward—whose name I've already forgotten—sniffs at me as he looks at my horribly stained dress and continues, "before joining Lord Rocheburn for dinner. Madam Schmidt will show you to your room and assist with providing the necessary garments." He gestures to a stern-faced woman of indeterminate middle age whose hair is swept up in a cap.

"This way, ladies," says Madam Schmidt, whose goat-like voice makes me long for the comparatively dulcet tones of Madam Boeschg, something I never thought I'd do.

We follow the house madam to two sparse, but clean, guest rooms on the third level, which are situated side by side. We're provided with changes of clothing, worn and serviceable, no doubt belonging to some poor servant woman asked to surrender some of her meager belongings. I look at the undergarments and dress for a moment before glancing down at my bloodied clothing. I decide that, for once, I will allow myself someone's offering of help without guilt. I strip off my clothing and make my way to the tub in front of the fireplace.

I quickly bathe myself and put on the chemise and stockings, not wanting to be completely naked in case a servant or the duke himself decides to waltz in, and sit in front of the fireplace to allow my hair to dry. A small knock sounds on the door, and deciding a man wouldn't knock so delicately, I bid the person to enter. Agnethe slips in the door, already dressed in her borrowed dress, her hair damp as well, and comes to sit beside me in front of the fire, as we used to do together when we were younger.

"For such a large and empty house, you'd think we'd be given better chambers than these," she says, gesturing to the bare stone floors and walls and the wooden bed devoid of any ornate carvings.

"I don't think we're exactly guests of honor," I say wryly. "It's puzzling enough that Lord Rocheburn would give us this much."

I gesture for her to sit in front of me. Using the comb Madam Schmidt provided, I begin detangling her mostly dry golden waves. After I braid and secure her hair, we switch places, and Agnethe begins to comb my hair. The teeth of the comb scrape deliciously over my scalp, and a languorous feeling enters my limbs, owing to the fatigue and stress from travel and the trauma of the past two days' events.

I'm struggling to keep my eyes open when a more-forceful knock sounds on my door. The knocker does not wait, and a moment later Madam Schmidt enters my room.

"Ladies, his grace awaits you at dinner." She gestures to the door, indicating that we should make our way to the dining room to meet our fate.

We follow Madam Schmidt down the long hallway and multiple flights of stairs to the grand main level again. The walls on this level are a mix of the exterior stone and rich wooden paneling, not unlike Noetheim but on a much larger scale. I also can't help but observe that while Noetheim had the cheer of a house well loved and lived in, Felsegeist Haus, for all its rich appointments, seems cold and soulless.

We stop in front of a set of tall double doors, and Madam Schmidt waits for the footmen on either side of the doors to open them, revealing an enormous dining hall, complete with a fifteen-foot trestle table and chairs with narrow, elegantly turned legs and red velvet upholstery. She ushers us into the dining hall and to the right, heading toward the three chairs that have place settings in front of them.

At the head of the table is a pleasant-looking man who, upon standing, is about the same height as I am, which isn't short, for I'm tall for a woman, but isn't particularly imposing for a man. His average build does nothing to add to my impression or give him the appearance of physical power. His hair, which was obviously once brown, judging by some of the strands I pick out, is mostly an iron gray color, and his eyes are a flat green that manages to be both unremarkable and unnerving.

"Ah, the Misses de Veend join me at last," he booms jovially, his deep voice startling me, so incongruous with his nondescript appearance as it is.

Agnethe curtsies, staying blessedly silent, for once, and I follow her with a clumsy dip of my own, having not had to employ such a gesture in many years, maybe not even since my own comportment lessons.

"Please, have a seat." Lord Rocheburn uses a hand to indicate the chairs on his left side. I don't know why they've placed me and Agnethe side by side instead of across from one another, but I can't remember enough of my table lessons to recall if there is a reason, or if Lord

Rocheburn wants to only look in one direction when speaking.

We sit in our seats, pushed in by an attending footman, and I watch Lord Rocheburn's face as he looks at the open doors and then the footman who has just moved to stand next to the buffet laden with dishes.

"Arnold," he says to the footman, "would you mind seeing that the doors are—oh, never mind, I'll see to it." Lord Rocheburn stares at the dining hall doors, and they abruptly swing firmly shut. I gape at him in surprise.

Lord Rocheburn has magic. I mentally scold myself. *Of course he does, you fool, the man is on the Gold Council, and you can't be on the Gold Council without magic.* Telekinesis, if I'm not mistaken, since he was able to move the doors with a thought. Quite a powerful one, too, since he did so without any outward gesture of his hands or body. It makes me wonder what else he can do and move with his magic.

In the world of magic, telekinesis, while useful, isn't seen as a particularly powerful or influential magic. Magic also has limits, often proximity related, so Lord Rocheburn likely cannot move objects all the way across the world without seeing them, only those within a certain distance from his person. The Gold Council positions, while originally and officially "appointed" by the king, are usually inherited by means of primogeniture, like estate or land holdings. To elevate his family line to the Gold Council, though, the Rocheburn line of telekinetic powers must be more significant than those that are typical. Through range, size, precision, or other means, such as the ability to move objects silently and invisibly, as he did.

He smiles at me and Agnethe. "There now, we may enjoy our dinner without interruption, save for asking for more wine!" He says good-naturedly.

I wait for the footmen to serve us from the various platters and bowls, my mouth watering. I've barely eaten anything in the past two days, and now that I'm clean and warm, my stomach makes its presence known with a loud rumble. Lord Rocheburn throws his head back and laughs as my face reddens in embarrassment.

"Far be it from me to keep a lady from her dinner," he says and indicates we should eat. Agnethe and I don't need further encouragement, and we both begin attacking our plates as much as polite table manners will allow.

Several minutes later, the sharp edge of my hunger is blunted, and I take more leisurely bites of my roasted chicken and potatoes, dunking the potatoes into the accompanying gravy before popping them into my mouth and chewing contentedly.

"Now, ladies, I'm sure you are wondering why you're here for a visit, but first I must inquire as to why Madam de Veend did not accompany you as well? I was so looking forward to her sparkling, witty company." Lord Rocheburn looks between us expectantly.

I swallow my bite of potato hard and cough slightly when I choke around the too-large piece. Lord Rocheburn knew Grandmother? She never once mentioned having met him or interacted with him, and although my grandmother wasn't prone to fits of nostalgia, I'm certain it would have come up in the twenty years I lived with her. Nonetheless, if he knew her, perhaps I can appeal to him and make it plain we had no knowledge of this new will. After all, Lord Rocheburn can't have known that my grandmother would poison herself or that the guard would hasten her exit. The man is simply doing his duty to the Crown.

I clear my throat and say, "Forgive me, my lord, but Madam de Veend, our grandmother, has passed away suddenly."

He looks dismayed. "My word, how tragic for you both. She was your grandmother, you say? How could I not have known that one of the de Veend sons fathered daughters? Are any of them wed?"

"No, my lord," I reply. "Our grandmother was not our grandmother by blood. Rather, we were born to distant de Veend relatives of Hrafn, her husband, and when they perished from illness, Merel de Veend and her husband took us in as their adoptive daughters."

His eyebrows raise. "Merel de Veend, as in the wife of Andebert Vergildetbach, the abdicated prince and brother of our king?"

I shift uncomfortably at his intense scrutiny. "Yes, Lord and Lady Vergildetbach were our adoptive parents until they, too, passed away."

Lord Rocheburn looks sad. "Ah, yes, *Fiebernacht*, correct? I believe I'd heard something of it when it happened. The whole household was affected. Such a tragedy to outlive the young." He clucks sympathetically.

I nod. "Yes, my lord."

"And how did you come to live at Noetheim?" He asked.

I set down my fork and look into his eyes. "I don't much remember, to be honest. I recall very little of that time save for a few scattered memories. I was very young, and Agnethe was even younger."

Lord Rocheburn's jaw tightens slightly. I may not have noticed it except that I hope to play upon the man's sympathies, and that means being observant.

"Naturally, you were," he agrees, his voice considerably cooler than it had been only moments before. "But surely you have memories of them?"

"Yes, my lord, I do," I agree. "But Noetheim has long been our home. We are eager to return to it. When might that be?"

He picks up his wine. "That all depends, my dear."

I clench my teeth. "On what, exactly?"

He sets his glass down and stares at me, eyes boring into mine, as if searching my very soul, and asks. "Do you know why your grandmother had not previously recorded you and your sister as her wards?"

"No," I admit. It's a question I have myself, and one it seems I'm unlikely to have answered by the duke.

"I find it curious, I must admit," the duke says. "And what do you know of the twin flame and the guardian?"

My blood freezes in my veins. Could this "guardian" be the same as the "keepers of the legacy" that my grandmother referred to? What is the "twin flame"? How do I admit my ignorance without giving any hints as to possible connections? My hope is that if I can convince Lord Rocheburn that I don't know anything, he will let us go.

I swallow and say, "I don't know what that means."

He watches me for several minutes, then stares at Agnethe, who says, "I don't know," to him.

"I'm sorry to have turned dinner to such sordid dealings as these. It can't be helped, I'm afraid, particularly since your grandmother is not here to answer to this herself. Did she, too, contract fever?" He inquires.

I'm not exactly sure how to broach the topic of the truth with him, so I begin delicately. "My grandmother, unfortunately, believed that the Palastgarte gentlemen, who arrived heavily armed, were a threat to her, my sister, and me. She resorted to drastic measures to ensure our protection, and the captain…" my voice catches, and in my mind's eye, I see Captain Fiedlerg stabbing my grandmother all over again. My eyelids flutter shut for a moment as I'm overcome by the memory.

Lord Rocheburn's hand comes to rest on top of mine. "My dear?"

For some reason, I want to snatch my hand back. The duke's cold, smooth skin feels wrong and invasive, but I force myself to leave it as I open my eyes, nod, and say, "The captain stabbed her, my lord. With his weapon." I remove my hand from his and place it in my lap, no longer hungry, and stare down at my hands. I see Agnethe's hand sneak into my lap and wrap around my left, squeezing gently.

Encouraged, I look up to glance at the lord's face and am startled by the change in his demeanor. Gone is the affable lord welcoming two young ladies to a casual dinner. In his place is one whose face could have been etched from stone; it's so still and hard, and those previously flat green eyes are almost manic looking with fury.

"Arnold," he beckons the footman, his neutral voice belying the wrath in his gaze. "Please send for Captain Fiedlerg." Arnold hurries from the room, leaving the doors ajar in his haste, the sound of his running echoing through the dining hall.

"No need to fret, my dears," he nods to us. "This will be taken care of."

Although he's saying the right words, his eyes are telling a different, terrifying story, and I'm suddenly so afraid for me and my sister.

The still tension is dispelled when Captain Fiedlerg marches into the dining hall. He bows to Lord Rocheburn stiffly, nodding his greeting wordlessly.

"Ah, Captain Fiedlerg." Lord Rocheburn leans back into his chair, assuming a calm and unaffected demeanor. "How was your journey to Noetheim?"

The captain frowns. "The journey was uneventful. We traveled across the northern bridge and through Vallaurium to make it to Felsegeist Haus within the time frame you indicated."

Lord Rocheburn nods once in acknowledgment. "And at Noetheim itself, did anything untoward occur?"

The captain now shifts on his feet, looking nervous. Does he, too, see the way Lord Rocheburn's flat eyes occasionally flash with rage?

"Ah, my lord, we did encounter some…difficulty…with escorting Madam de Veend," he says, struggling to get the words out, his hand flexing anxiously on the hilt of the sword strapped to his waist.

"What sort of difficulty, Captain?" Lord Rocheburn asks.

"The lady seemed to know we were coming. She took hemlock, my lord. She refused to leave the estate. To save the woman a far more painful death and to avoid any questions regarding poisons, I dispatched her with my krahbek," Captain Fiedlerg finishes, speaking so rapidly I'm not sure Lord Rocheburn will understand him.

The duke is silent for several minutes, and I find myself jiggling my leg nervously under the table until Agnethe rests a stilling hand on it. She knows I do it when I get worried.

"Captain Fiedlerg, did you verify that Madam de Veend had ingested hemlock before 'dispatching her'?" The duke asks, the subtle curling of his lip the only sign of his distaste besides his eyes. He swirls his goblet of wine, sniffing before taking a generous sip.

"Ah, not as such, my lord," Captain Fiedlerg admits.

"And did you question her prior to your final decision?" Lord Rocheburn continues.

"No," says the captain.

"And you wanted to avoid questions regarding poisoning a member of the upper class by stabbing her instead?" The duke sets the wine goblet down and twirls the stem between his fingers, watching as the glass spins in place, the liquid sloshing restlessly against the sides.

Captain Fiedlerg seems to consider how to answer without further damning himself. "It seemed prudent at the time to avoid additional scrutiny."

Lord Rocheburn's voice increases in volume, the tone positively incensed. "Did you not think that would garner questions?"

"No, my lord. I mean, yes, my lord. That is, no, my lord." The captain stumbles, and despite everything, I feel some sympathy toward him in that moment, as his growing fear is palpable.

"And on top of that, you failed to gain any useful information from her?" Lord Rocheburn is now shouting at the captain, and he suddenly lets go of his wineglass, which hurtles toward the soldier. He barely dodges impact, and wine still ends up spilling down his pristine dress jacket before the glass shatters upon the floor. I can't help but notice that the jewel-red liquid resembles blood dripping down the captain's coat.

"Your instructions were to return the wards by any means necessary," the captain protests, his panic increasing.

"You made a permanent decision without the authority to do so. You leave me no choice but to make a permanent decision of my own," the duke says, sounding as though he regrets whatever act he refers to.

"My lord, no—" the captain begins frantically, but is unable to finish his sentence, for at that moment, his sword ejects from his scabbard and swiftly lodges itself through his neck, nearly severing his head.

Agnethe screams when the man collapses, blood spurting all over the floor of the dining hall, spilling down the captain's jacket in a gruesome imitation of the wine splashes. Spots dance in front of my eyes, and I feel as though I might faint. I take in deep gulps of air, pushing my back against the chair, trying to breathe through the panic I feel rising inside of me, threatening to suffocate me.

Lord Rocheburn just *killed* Captain Fiedlerg using only his magic, pulling the sword from the man's belt and shoving it through his neck. I know there are types of dark magic that give the wielder the power to end someone, but I hadn't ever considered that other forms of magic could be used for the same purpose, and that anyone would. I can't say that I feel much sympathy, in principle, for Captain Fiedlerg, given how he treated my grandmother. But I also feel a sense of *wrongness* at the idea of someone's life being taken as a form of punishment, and by having an individual mete out that justice without pause or consideration.

Lord Rocheburn takes a delicate bite of his chicken and looks at me calmly, as though there's not a dead man on the floor ten feet away from him, his blood filling the crevices between the stones. The urge to laugh hysterically at the entire situation is difficult to suppress.

"Now, ladies, I regret that you had to witness such brutality, but it couldn't be helped," he says around his bite of food. "And I really must insist you answer my questions."

I stare at him silently, not sure if I should speak.

"You and your sister resided with Andebert and Merel Vergildetbach until they perished?" He prods.

"Yes, my lord," I say quietly. I'm not certain what these questions have to do with my grandmother's will, but it seems best not to further agitate the duke.

He pulls a sheaf of parchment from within his coat and looks at it, asking, "And who is Valda Eks?"

Agnethe's hand has gripped mine again, and so tightly that the tips of my fingers are pulsing as if with their own heartbeat. My heart pounds in my ears. Why is the duke asking about Valda? My sweet, old nurse, Valda, brought Agnethe and me to Noetheim. Valda, who wiped tears, kissed injuries, and tucked us into bed. Valda, whose cataracts have made working impossible, so she now lives as a permanent fixture at Noetheim. Whatever reasons the duke has for asking, I know they can't be good or trustworthy.

I abandon any idea of trying to prevail upon this man's decency to simply let us go and settle for lying, instead, as I reply, "I don't know who that is."

Agnethe's fingernails dig into the side of my hand. She might not know why I'm lying, but she doesn't refute it.

His eyes return to my face from the parchment, watching me, as if waiting for me to crack. "I don't believe you," he says flatly.

"I don't know who it is," I insist, fear making my voice edge higher. "Or anything about any flames, my lord, or a guardian. I don't know." I hope my panic convinces him that I'm ignorant and scared and not that I'm hiding anything.

"Perhaps you simply need some time to gather your thoughts," the duke says. He gestures to someone across the room, and two soldiers in Palastgarte uniforms pull out Agnethe's and my chairs and grab us each by an arm. Agnethe cries out in pain or fear or both, which I'm not sure.

"Let go of her!" I demand, struggling against the tight grip of the soldier.

Lord Rocheburn says, "Return the younger one to her room. The older one can visit the *loubenstille*. It seems she needs some prompting."

The *loubenstille*. Old Aurelian for "the silent hallway." What could *that* mean?

Agnethe and I are both screaming as they drag us out of the room, Agnethe in the direction of the rooms we were in, and me farther down the main hall toward the back of the house. I'm struggling violently against the hold of the guard, who laughs cruelly at my attempts, as if he's enjoying the fact that I'm fighting.

I'm still yelling for Agnethe when the soldier stops abruptly and says, "Pretty thing like you should keep her mouth shut—while she still has lips to speak with." He traces a finger across them, and I feel like I'm going to vomit. The attention of this man seems even worse than that of Lord Rocheburn.

I clamp my lips together and pull my head back from his touch. He grins and then resumes dragging me down the hall. He steers me through a door that only has descending stairs, which are narrow and dark, damp seeping through the stones on the wall. The staircase seems older than the main part of the house, as if it were forgotten during whatever era an enterprising Rocheburn decided to update their manor.

When we reach the bottom of the stairs, we're in a narrow hallway with four solid wooden doors, two on each side. The soldier opens the first door on the right to reveal a dark, windowless room with a bedroll to one side and a bucket in the corner. The smell of mildew and damp is even stronger here, and I instinctively recoil from the tiny space.

The soldier, strengthened by his sadistic pleasure in my fear and discomfort, shoves me into the room, slamming the door shut before I can even turn to try and open it. I pound on the wood and scream Agnethe's name until my throat is burning and raw and my hands are riddled with splinters. But, true to its name, the hall remains silent.

I run my hands over as much of the surface of the door as I can reach. Without light, I'm only able to rely on what I can feel, and my search yields no results. There is no door handle on the inside of the door, which means whoever gets put in this room is not meant to come out.

CHAPTER SEVEN
To Bleed but Not Break

*V*alda woke me from sleeping. I had had a sore throat and cough the past few days and was finally feeling well enough to sleep deeply, so I was difficult to rouse.

"It's time to get up, Greta-girl," Valda said to me softly.

I sat up slowly and rubbed my eyes. I looked around my room and realized it was still nighttime. "Valda, it's not time to get up; it's still dark."

"Aye, it is dark, but time to go even so," Valda said, pulling back my bed linens.

I climbed out of my bed, whimpering because I was so tired. Valda clucked as she bundled me in warm clothing—a wool dress, sturdy boots, a cloak, and she tucked my hair into a close-fitting linen cap tied under my chin, followed by a fur-lined hood.

"Where are we going, Valda?" I asked, fingering the button on my cloak, watching as Valda bustled around my room, shoving clothing pieces into a canvas rucksack that had been oiled to protect it from water and the elements.

"We're goin' fer a visit to a fancy house, Greta-girl, so you'd best hurry and gather what you need to travel. Mind you, only things you truly need," Valda cautioned.

I nodded and ran back to my bed, burrowing between the linens, a crow of triumph echoing from my lips when I found what I was searching for. A doll, knitted with scraps of fabric and stuffed with wool, so she was soft to hug and hold.

"Come, Geraldine," I said to my doll, whispering to the brown felt that was her hair. "We're to go on an adventure to a castle."

I had no idea if we were actually going somewhere as fancy as a castle, but I figured it didn't hurt to make Geraldine feel better about it in case she was scared.

Valda saw me holding Geraldine and asked, "Do you truly need to bring yer doll, Greta-girl?"

"Yes," I said simply. "If she gets upset, she'll cry and be a dips-brush-chin to the household," I said loftily, repeating what my mama had said when she told me I needed to mind my noise and not wake Agnethe from her napping.

Valda's face softened. "All right, then, but just the one toy, you hear?"

I nodded quietly, not wanting to push my luck for more toys and lose Geraldine in the process. I followed Valda into the hall, where we were met by Agnethe's nursemaid, Trude, who was holding the squirming baby, also bundled in warm clothing. Trude had tears silently falling down her cheeks, and I wondered if her tummy hurt, because I always wanted to cry when my tummy hurt.

I wanted to ask Trude about her tummy and tell her to chew on ginger root like Valda gives to me for tummy aches, but she handed Agnethe to Valda and didn't follow us downstairs. Confused, I trailed after Valda into my parents' sitting room.

"Where's mama and papa, Valda? Don't they have to get ready for the fancy house, too?" I asked.

Valda looked sad as she said, "I'm sure they'll be along soon, wee one."

I climbed onto my mama's green chair and swung my legs back and forth, counting the flowers on the fabric of the seat with my fingers as I waited. It felt like I had been sitting there forever when the soft rustle of fabric met my ears, and my mama turned into the room, her beautiful face a mask of worry. My papa was not far behind her.

"Greta!" She exclaimed and ran to where I was sitting, throwing her arms around me, cupping my cheeks in her hands, tucking errant strands of my golden-brown hair up under my cap. "How is your throat?"

"It's better, mama," I said. "Only Geraldine is tired and wants to go back to bed." I held up my doll. I didn't want to admit that I was also tired, and Geraldine didn't argue.

Papa came over then, too, and knelt before me. "You'll have to tell Geraldine that once she gets to her destination, she's allowed to sleep as long as she likes." He hugged me close, humming, his golden voice settling over me. My papa's voice was one of my favorite things in the whole world.

My forehead wrinkled. "Papa, how come you and Mama aren't coming with us to the fancy house?"

My mama coughed then, or maybe she was choking, like she swallowed a sweet too fast without chewing. "Oh, Andebert," she said to my papa, "she's so young; is this the right thing? She's just a child, perhaps we expect too much of her—"

I felt mad then, a hot rush beneath my skin that made me itchy and made me want to kick my feet. "I am not too young, I'm not a baby like Agnethe, I'm almost six!" Even though I didn't know what my mama thought I was too young for, I just knew that she was worrying for no reason. I would be fine until they came to the fancy house.

"Greta can be a big, brave girl, can't you, now?" My papa smiled at me, his golden eyes crinkling at the corners.

I puffed out my chest, thrust my shoulders back, and nodded proudly. "Yes, Papa! I can take care of me and Geraldine just fine! Don't worry, Mama, I'm very brave!"

My mama did that funny cough again, and her shoulders shook. "Of course you can, love," she gave me a watery smile, her blue eyes shiny in the candlelight.

"You must also watch over your little sister, Greta. Take care of her. You're her big sister, and she needs your help." My Papa's eyes looked a little shiny, too, as he said that to me.

"Yes, Papa," I nodded, a bit nervous. Why did they seem so upset? The fancy house must be really special if they were so sad to miss it.

He smiled at me. "That's my big girl," he said, and my chest swelled with pride.

Papa stood then and went to Valda, taking Agnethe from her arms, holding her close to his chest, murmuring soft words to her as he bounced the fussy baby, gently swaying.

My eyes swung to Mama when she said, "Greta, be good for Valda, and remember that Mama and Papa love you and Agnethe so very much."

I suddenly felt very worried, but I couldn't explain why; something just felt different from how my mama normally bid me goodbye. I reached out to her then, wrapping my arms around her neck and burying my face in her glossy black hair.

"Love you too, Mama," I whispered.

I feel her warm breath on my ear as she murmurs, "Remember, vögelein, *you always have a choice. And for every sorrow, there is joy. For every night, a dawn. And with every end, a beginning."*

I wake with tears streaming down my face, the tracks chilling my skin in the cold air of the chamber. Though I can't be certain of the time of day with the lack of light, I think it's likely that it's very early morning. At least, my body is as stiff as if I were lying on the bedroll for hours, though that could just be from the chilly temperature.

The dream took me by surprise. My parents' faces were so vivid in it, and I could tell that it was the last time I had seen them. Was this something my brain had filled in from the trauma of what's happened, or was it a genuine recollection, unearthed from the depths of my childhood memory?

Vögelein, my dream mother had called me. Old Aurelian for "little bird." I hadn't remembered that, but the sound of it tickles my brain with familiarity, which makes it more likely that the dream was a memory and not something conjured by an imagination under duress.

I wish I could tell how long I had been asleep for. I had pounded on the door of the room until I was sure no one was returning, and my hands couldn't take the pain of the impact and the rough wood abrading my skin any longer. I had lain down on my bedroll and pulled out as many of the splinters from the sides of my hands as I could in the dark, wondering if the throbbing in them was from the abuse I'd dealt them or from slivers of wood still piercing the tender flesh. Without light, I couldn't be certain.

In a way, the splinters embedded in my hands are symbolic of my emotions now—not necessarily visible, but pressing close to the surface and painful with very little prodding. A hundred needle pricks of helplessness and grief beneath my skin, and the only way to conquer them is by feel. Dislodging them torturously, slowly, and one by one.

I do my best to stretch my arms and legs in the small space. The room seems to be just long enough for the bedroll, based on what I can feel and the brief impression I gleaned when the soldier had opened the door to it last night before shoving me in. I roll over to my hands and knees, tentatively placing my hands in front of me, in search of the bucket I had seen in the far corner that I'm sure is intended to serve as my toilet.

How the mighty have fallen, I think sarcastically. Only a few days ago, I was languishing in bed, and the worst part of my existence was that man's hunt for the female orgasm remains elusive. Now, I'm desperate to find the bucket in my windowless chamber so that I can empty my bladder, and I may meet a very ignominious end over information I don't even have.

I manage to find the bucket and relieve myself, almost upending it gracelessly when my foot catches the metal handle on it. The force of my tripping causes the handle to dislodge, a combination of rust and wood rot of the body easily separating it from its vessel. The ends are sharp; I can tell by testing the pad of my index finger against them. I clutch the handle to me as a pitiful weapon, and with little else to do, I return to my bedroll and attempt to find ways to occupy the minutes stretching out in front of me.

First, I sing to myself. Folk songs I sang to Agnethe when she was little, a verse my father would sing for me at bedtime, lyrics from the bawdy tunes that Erwin and Tilo sing at the forge. Then, I recite translations to myself.

Is this what going insane feels like? I wonder. Maybe I've been down here longer than I initially thought.

I hear booted footsteps echoing outside the chamber, growing louder until they abruptly stop in front of the door. The sound of a key scraping in a metal lock fills my ears before light, blessed and painful, fills the chamber.

"Good morning, pretty thing," greets the leering soldier who led me down here. I shrink backward into the corner, not caring that my dress and hair are pressed against the mildewy wall, so eager am I to get away from this man.

"Don't touch me," I warn. My hand, which I reach back to steady myself, brushes against something cold that moves across the floor with a quiet whine. *The bucket handle.*

"Now, now, pretty thing, what makes you believe that you have any say in what I do?" He grins at me, but rather than the cheerful curve of a friendly smile, it has the hard edge of something darker, crueler, and menacing.

My fingers tighten on the metal handle, fingernails scraping along the stone floor and gathering dirt and grime beneath them as they do. I will not let him know how much he terrifies me. Surely Lord Rocheburn finds me too useful to let this brute assault me, doesn't he?

The man put you in a dungeon, Greta; he's not exactly a candidate for host of the year.

The soldier moves into the room and hauls me up roughly by my left arm, forcing me to a standing position. Only an arm's length away from him as I am now, I can see the almost feral glint in his eye, smell the violent anticipation rolling off him like steam. He pulls me toward him steadily, despite my resistance, his strength overpowering mine. I've never felt so helplessly weak as I do in this moment. When my body is pressed against his, he leans his face into mine and runs his nose up the side of my cheek, inhaling deeply. Revulsion, oppressive and all consuming, fills my body, starting where his skin is touching mine and radiating outward.

He leans over and puts his mouth against my left ear, his hot breath moving the small hairs at my temple as he says, "Best behave now, pretty thing. Or shall I seek out your sister?" My blood goes cold as he continues, "She's quite the treat, isn't she? Golden. Young. Sweet. I'd have fun breaking in a girl like that."

"You will not touch her," I seethe. "Stay away from her." My heart is pounding, I want to vomit and faint at the same time, and adrenaline is surging through me along with a heavy dose of fear.

"Tell you what. Scream pretty for me when I fuck you, and I'll leave your sister alone." The guard leers, dragging his tongue along my earlobe and up the side of my face.

Anger, as white hot as flame, blazes within me, and I reply, "You first."

My right arm, still clutching the rusty bucket handle, stiffens and rises, plunging the sharp end of the handle into the soldier's shoulder beneath his collarbone. Blood, hot and forceful, sprays my face, neck, arm, and chest. The inhuman howl the soldier unleashes sends a chill down my spine. I try to pull away, and at first it seems he will hold me in place, but it quickly becomes apparent that I've managed to seriously injure him. He stumbles, sagging into me, knocking me sideways into the wall. Blood continues to pour from the wound in rhythmic pulses, but it's slowing. His entire chest and stomach are covered in it, and there's a large pool beneath our feet.

He loses consciousness, and the dead weight of his body knocks me over, jarring my backside, shoulders, and arms. Frantic, I muster all my strength and roll my whole body into his, which forces him off me. His arms splay beside him, his left leg is unnaturally bent beneath him from his collapse, his skin is pale, and the wound is slowing to a trickle; a swath of blood covers the floor, soaking my dress.

This has to be some kind of record for blood staining on dresses, I think.

I don't wait to see if he awakens. I step over his body and through the door. *I'm free!* I think. I just have to find Agnethe and get us out of here. I climb the staircase the guard had me descend before, hoping against hope that I won't meet anyone along the way who'll try to stop me. I reach the door at the top of the stairs and slam my shoulder into it as I lift the latch, eager to be free of the confining lower level. Spots are flashing in front of my eyes, and I know I'm at serious risk of fainting.

Agnethe, I tell myself, *you must get to Agnethe.*

As I stumble down the hallway toward the staircase we climbed when we first arrived, I'm aware that none of my motions have been stealthy, and I'm certain I'll be caught at any moment. I run to the staircase, taking a moment to pause and look at the daunting number of steps, and begin to climb, holding onto the banister for dear life.

When I reach the third level where Madam Schmidt had originally placed me and Agnethe, I run clumsily to the doors of our rooms and, without warning or ceremony, I burst into Agnethe's.

Agnethe sits in a chair by the fireplace, her mouth covered with a fabric gag and her hands bound to the chair. I run to her and start trying to work on her bindings.

"Agnethe," I huff, out of breath. "We have to get out of here."

I pull down her gag, and Agnethe screams. "Greta, watch out!"

I spin around and come face to face with Lord Rocheburn, who points his sword at me and says, "I've been waiting for you to join us, Miss de Veend. Where is your guard?"

"I stabbed him," I respond without emotion.

"Interesting," Lord Rocheburn replies, as if he's discussing the weather. "And is he dead?"

"I don't know."

"Well, that simply won't do at all, my dear. We were going to have a nice, calm chat, but I can see now that a conversation with you will require more…restraint." Lord Rocheburn goes to the door, still brandishing his sword, and yells for assistance. Several guards appear only moments later, and they grab me by both arms, leading me out of Agnethe's room.

"No!" Agnethe yells at the guards, struggling against her bindings. "Where are you taking her? Bring her back, please! Please! Greta!" She screams so loud her voice cracks on my name, and the sound similarly causes a crack across my heart; the evidence of my sister's suffering and fear is almost more than I can bear.

"Agnethe!" I scream over my shoulder. "Don't talk; don't tell them anything. I'll take care of this."

"Greta!" Agnethe screams, and it's muffled suddenly by the slamming of her door.

"Lock her in," Lord Rocheburn instructs the guard. "I need to be able to focus on my discussion with the elder Miss de Veend."

The guards drag me farther down the hallway behind Lord Rocheburn and up a second, smaller set of stairs, likely intended for servants. When we reach the next landing, it's clear that this level is not often used. There is a layer of dust along the floor where it meets the walls, on the edges of the paneling that covers the bottom half of them, and in the ridges of the wooden doors.

The duke strides purposefully down the hallway, stopping when he reaches a nondescript wooden door. He opens it and gestures for the guards to take me inside. The room is empty, save for a table with metal tools laid out upon it and a chair next to it. Ominous, dark stains cover the wooden floorboards.

Old blood, I realize. At least I hope it's old.

The guards dump me into the chair and begin restraining me, binding me to it. My arms are pulled behind me roughly and tied at the wrists. My ankles are affixed to the chair legs.

Unlike my sister, however, I am not gagged. I guess the duke really does want conversation.

"Leave us," Lord Rocheburn says sharply to the guards, and in only a minute's time, we are completely alone in the room, a fact which leaves me anxious and afraid.

"Why are you doing this?" I ask him softly, shaking my head in bewilderment.

"Oh," he tilts his head to the side as he observes me. "It's complicated."

"I'm a quick learner," I retort.

Lord Rocheburn smiles, but it doesn't reach his eyes. The skin at their corners remains smooth, and they have returned to their flat, emotionless green color. I shiver, unable to maintain eye contact with his dead-like stare.

A pounding on the door interrupts the unnerving observation. Lord Rocheburn opens the door, and a new guard stands before him.

"We found Bushe in the *loubenstille*. Dead. Stabbed in the chest, and he bled out quickly. Poor bastard didn't stand a chance with a wound like that." The guard shakes his head mournfully.

I find I cannot feel sorry that the guard is dead, but I do feel horrified at my numbness to it, as well as my ability to follow through with it. How quickly I've been reduced to being a monster in these circumstances.

The duke thanks him, and the guard leaves. "You were busy today. Killing a guard, breaking into your sister's room. But I've had enough of these games. Tell me how to get to the location, where they're hidden."

I shake my head, confused. "I don't know what you mean."

"The heirlooms!" Lord Rocheburn throws his hands up. "Where did Hrafn hide them?"

"I don't know," I shrug, telling the truth. I honestly am not sure what he's talking about. What kind of heirlooms—something unique to Hrafn or some other keepsakes? And am I supposed to know where they are? It seems like my grandmother may have left out a lot of information.

Seek the sign where shadow and feather meet. Let the keeper's legacy guide your way. Tell no one. Not even Agnethe.

But what does it mean? Is this what Lord Rocheburn is looking for? My instincts tell me not to barter with him.

Lord Rocheburn nods in acknowledgment of my confession. Then he turns suddenly, his arm sailing through the air, and I see it almost as if time has slowed, before it suddenly connects with my jaw. Sharp pain explodes through the side of my face as I realize Lord Rocheburn has backhanded me, splitting the corner of my lips.

"Don't. Lie. To me." Lord Rocheburn says as he adjusts the signet ring on the hand he slapped me with. I feel a warm trickle at the corner of my mouth that I'm sure is blood.

"I'm not lying. I don't know what the heirlooms are, or guardians, or anything."

Lord Rocheburn is suddenly in my face, spittle flying from his lips as he screams. "WHERE ARE THEY? TELL ME NOW!"

I look down at my blood-soaked dress, the result of protecting myself against a would-be rapist. I think of my other blood-soaked dress, of kneeling in my grandmother's life force as she died. I think of the blinding pain in my face as Lord Rocheburn hit me. My face is still throbbing as I look at him. And I'm angry. No, anger isn't enough to describe what I'm feeling.

It isn't anger. It is a storm turned inward. Lightning behind my ribs, thunder in my veins, and wind trying to claw its way out through my mouth.

I look at Lord Rocheburn, lick my bloodied lip, and I say, "No."

"What?" Lord Rocheburn looks flabbergasted.

"I said no," I repeat. "I'm not going to tell you anything."

"Is that so?" Lord Rocheburn asks slowly.

"It is," I confirm, voice rising in volume as I continue, "in fact, even if I knew where the heirlooms were, I wouldn't tell you. I'd rather die."

Lord Rocheburn stares intently at the chair I'm in, and it begins to rise off the ground, wobbling in midair, floating. I scream and grip the back of it as best as I can with my bindings in place.

He turns away from me, heading to the door, and the chair drops to the ground suddenly, the legs breaking. I crumple into a heap, tangled in the broken chair pieces and trying to right my balance with my hands tied behind my back. The door swings open; I assume the duke opened it magically, as he never once touched his hands to the handle. He yells for guards, and there is no more conversation between us as we wait.

Eventually, the sound of footsteps on the stairs reaches me, and two guards cross the threshold. They look at me, struggling to extricate myself from the broken chair, and then at Lord Rocheburn, who appears as though nothing unusual has happened or is happening.

"Prepare for a journey, lads, you have a prisoner to escort," he instructs the guards, who nod and quit the room.

"A prisoner?" I say incredulously. "I'm not going back to that room," I add, but my voice trembles, a jolt of fear revealing a crack in my feigned confidence.

"Oh, no, definitely not," Lord Rocheburn agrees, his voice returned to the jovial tone it had when we first arrived. "You are far beyond that."

"What are you going to do with me?" I ask, swallowing hard, finally freeing myself from the broken chair pieces and pulling myself to stand, tripping on the hem of my dress, which is beginning to dry and stiffen.

"Well, my dear, it occurs to me that if you'd rather die than share information with me, perhaps the very real threat of that will improve your disposition and change your mind." He takes several steps closer to me, flat eyes boring into mine.

I shake my head and say again quietly, "I don't understand."

The guards reappear in the doorway to the room, and they've brought an extra two with them. I guess my reputation as a guard killer precedes me.

One of them walks forward, manacles in his hand. My heart drops in my stomach, and the fear grows, prickling across the surface of my skin like nettles. I try to back away, but I have nowhere to go; the guards are blocking the only egress. Once he's close enough, the guard grabs my arm and removes my bindings. The relief that it provides is temporary, though, as he pulls my hands forward and clamps on the heavy manacles.

Lord Rocheburn steps forward and says, "Margarethe de Veend, you are hereby charged with murder. Regardless of intent or cause—I, Lord Chancellor Reinhardt Muller, the Duke of Rocheburn, acting under the Crown's authority and in accordance with the legistadt established by the Aurelian Gold Council, sentence you to twenty-five years of service in the Aurengarte military. Effective immediately, you are remanded into the custody of the Palastgarte."

I can't breathe, and I'm actually going to faint. This can't be real. I clench my jaw and pinch the thin skin of my hand. As well as I'm able to with the manacles on, that is. Definitely real.

"Do I not get to argue my case?" I protest, looking around desperately for a way to sneak out.

Lord Rocheburn scoffs and says, "The Gold Council, under permission of the Crown, holds the sovereign authority to judge and sentence any individual whose actions present sufficient cause and whose guilt is supported by compelling evidence. You need not waste breath asking for a trial, Miss de Veend. When the truth bleeds so plainly, judgment requires no theatre."

The guards usher me down the stairs, surrounding me without touching me. I am too numb with shock to protest, so I don't resist their escort. My manacles clink ominously as I descend the stairs, their echo deafening in the stillness.

As I climb down, I hear Agnethe call my name and footsteps thunder down the hall when we pass the third floor.

"Where are you taking her? Why is she in chains? Greta? Where are you going? Stop! Stop, please!" Two of the guards block Agnethe from reaching me, her arms outstretched past them, between their bodies. I reach through the guards to my side, and my fingers brush hers as I pass.

"Don't worry, Agnethe; it will be all right," I reassure her. "I'll return for you, and we'll go home."

When we reach the main level and the entryway, the guards pause to speak with the duke, confirming travel plans, but I'm unable to glean any more details about where they're taking me.

Lord Rocheburn saunters over to me and gets far too close. So close that the tips of his shoes touch mine, and the fabric of his tunic, stirring as he moves, brushes my dress.

He leans forward and speaks in a tone low enough to only reach my ears. "When you're done playing this martyr game, Miss de Veend, send word to Felsegeist. I think you'll find your new home will quickly jog your memory."

He straightens and steps back from me, smiling benevolently as if he just bid a granddaughter or niece goodbye rather than threatening my life for some cryptic nonsense I don't even understand.

"Gentlemen," he turns to the guards. "Take her to Stachtenbaste."

CHAPTER EIGHT
The Bridge to Destiny Ends at an Iron Gate

*S*tone surrounds me on all sides. *The ground beneath me is made of rocky dirt. My heart pounds inside my chest as I turn, looking for a way out. Seeing a shaft of light pouring in from a doorway behind me, I run to it, not eager to stay in a confined space any longer than necessary.*

I race through the door and into a crop of trees, the canopy of their limbs above providing shelter from the harshest rays of the sun, which dapple through the leaves, creating a kaleidoscope of spots on the root-veined ground.

This isn't familiar to me. I turn in a circle trying to figure out where I am. Behind me is the room I was in, which turns out to be a crumbling tower of lichen-covered stone. Its roof tiles are missing in places; the rotting wood door is ajar, fixed open by the choking vines digging into it and the surrounding bricks.

Above the door, the stone lintel is cracked and worn, but the lichen is embedded in the shape of the bird engraved in it. Goosebumps spread on my arms, and the hairs on the back of my neck stand.

Heart pounding, I step back toward the tower and enter through the door. I've not even gotten my bearings in the dim space when I feel another presence inside. Terror claws up my throat, making it hard to breathe, and my vision turns red—

I jolt awake from the abrupt stop of the carriage, which has been my home for the last six days, shaking my head to clear it of the haze left by my dream. Was what I had seen real? A vision, like those my grandmother had? The idea that I might possess dark magic fills me with paralyzing fear.

I scan my memory, hoping for clues. An unfamiliar tower, a raven engraving above the door. *Seek the sign where shadow and feather meet.* Could the sign my grandmother had been referring to be a literal sign?

"No," I tell myself aloud to bolster my belief. "It was just a dream borne of fatigue and stress."

Similar to my trip to Felsegeist Haus with Agnethe, the escort stops to refresh horses at multiple posting stations; unlike my previous trip, however, I never leave the carriage, except to relieve myself. I learned very quickly that if I waited for my bladder to alert me as to its need, I would be forced to endure until the next posting station.

When I frantically asked one of the guards to stop to allow me to go, he said, "You think we stop for piss breaks, princess? Either hold it in or learn to walk wet." And that was that.

I thought availing myself of the bucket in my cell was bad enough. The idea of sitting in a urine-stained dress for days was far worse. Meal times are just as grim. I'm given bread, dried peas or beans, dried fruit, and hard cheese on occasion. As someone who is accustomed to three filling meals a day, the barely edible rations are as pitiful as they are welcome in my hungry state. Though I vacillate between feeling starved and feeling as though I may vomit at any given moment, especially when I think of my sister.

Was Agnethe all right? Did Lord Rocheburn put her in the *loubenstille*? The thought of my bright, vivacious, golden sister in a tiny cell with no light is almost more than I can bear to think of. But at night is when my mind runs rampant, torturing me with visions of Agnethe screaming and shivering in the windowless room. The very idea makes me want to attempt to escape again, which I tried the first time we stopped to refresh the horses. I tried prevailing upon the guards who were stationed at the posting station, but I was met with jeering laughter and immediately returned to my escort. The next time, I alerted no one and took off from the privy, but I was about as stealthy as Erwin and was quickly apprehended.

Since my failed attempts, they send a female guard with me so as not to waste time chasing me if I bolt. They also stopped removing my shackles when I go, and now the act of relieving myself is not only humiliating, but logistically difficult. I have ended up with an arse full of leaves after hitting the ground more than once.

Sleep is difficult in the carriage, as the guards care even less for my comfort this go around than they did before, and I am frequently roused when I tumble across the carriage or when we stop suddenly. I am tired and bruised, and my spirit has been bludgeoned to a pulp. The farther I get from Agnethe, the more hopeless it seems that I'll be able to return to her.

I hear footsteps approaching the door of the carriage, and I wearily pull myself to an upright position so that I can climb down more easily with my shackled hands. My stomach growls, one of the hungry times crashing over me. *How quickly we are reduced to animalistic behavior when we are treated no better than they are*, I think to myself, suddenly having great sympathy for all manner of creatures so unfortunate as to find themselves slaves to the whims of humans.

The key jingles in the metal lock on the door, and it opens, the waning light of dusk casting an anemic glow into the body of the carriage. The sound of rushing water echoes somewhere in the distance.

My typical facilities escort is nowhere to be seen. Instead, it's one of the male guards, who merely grunts at me and moves aside in a nonverbal cue to step down from the carriage. Confused, I awkwardly climb down the steps outside the vehicle but catch my foot and gown on them and stumble. With my hands bound, I don't think to reach out and brace myself. I clumsily drop to the ground, earning myself a face full of dirt to the amusement of everyone in the posting station yard, judging by the uproarious laughter.

"Are you all right?" A male voice asks me.

I lift my head from the dirt to see expensive leather boots only a few inches from my head. I attempt to tilt my face backward to look up at the man, but get a painful twinge in my neck and have to avert my gaze.

"I'm perfect," I say sarcastically.

"Silly of me to ask when you've just fallen," the man says cheerfully, but then his voice softens. "I suppose I should have asked 'are you injured' instead, but if you had been seriously injured, you wouldn't have been able to answer me, so I suppose that answers—"

I groan at the man's nattering and lay my head back down in the dirt. No one seems eager to help me.

"Oh, Sisters! Here I am going on; let me help you," says the voice, and suddenly I'm hauled to my feet gently by large hands that roll me over onto my back before helping me into a sitting position and pulling me to a stand from behind.

I turn around to see a tall, heavyset, friendly looking young man with disheveled light brown hair and eyes the color of spring grass. He is smiling at me, though his smile falters when his eyes drop to my hands and he sees the shackles.

"Thank you, sir," I tell him, trying to muster some dignity. I toss my dirty hair back and raise my chin, my pride taking over when he looks at me in such a pitying way.

"You're welcome!" He says brightly. "Only call me Otto. Otto Weber. 'Sir' makes me sound dreadfully old, doesn't it? Like my father," he grins. He has the easy friendliness of Erwin with the lilt of Verdantia in his voice. "Are you on your way to Stachtenbaste, too, then?" He gestures to my manacles, seeming to have gotten over the initial shock of seeing them.

My choking fear is back, only this time it's for my life.

Stachtenbaste is shrouded in mystery for those not in the Aurengarte, its inner workings and practices known only to those who've endured them. Yet even from the distance of a safe and privileged home, its very name carries a menacing weight. In Aurelia, crimes are dealt with severely. If not condemned to Sühneferme—the labor camps of Caelias, where the unfit or infirm are worked to exhaustion under the watch of its wardens—those arrested are usually offered a simpler choice of punishment: death or conscription into the military. For most, the Aurengarte is the lesser of two evils, so they take their sentence and serve their time in the armed forces.

Those who are not guilty of crimes but are in need of a regular income may enlist at the age of eighteen and serve for a period of five years, after which they may return to civilian life or remain in the ranks of the military.

Either way, they are sent to Stachtenbaste for training in combat and the arts of war, since our endless conflict with Sarenaveld ensures a constant demand for more soldiers. I cannot decide if meeting my end by slow death at Sühneferme or in war after what is surely a brutal regimen at Stachtenbaste, is the preferable fate.

Since he is not in shackles and appears to have no escort, I would guess this man enlisted.

I nod at him. "It would seem so."

"Well, then, I'll be glad to have a friendly face during training!" He replies happily, looking as though he genuinely means it.

I stare at him, nonplussed as to how someone can be this unflappably cheerful even when facing training to potentially die in battle.

I glance around the posting station yard, noting that none of my escorts has come to take me away yet. I lean toward the man and try to convey my urgency.

"Otto, can you help me?" I ask.

Otto looks worried and says, "Surely, I will if I can."

"I've been taken and held against my will," I say in a low voice, leaning closer to him, the words tumbling out now that I have an audience. "I need to get out of here quickly; I don't belong here. I'm innocent," I plead quietly as I look up into his eyes, hoping my gaze is appropriately pathetic.

Otto looks conflicted, his mouth opening and closing, when a voice sneers from my left. "'Innocent,' eh? That's what all conscripts say. Watch yourself, lad; this one is no simpering miss," an older man leading a horse to the nearby stables says to me and then Otto.

Incensed, I say, "You don't know me! You have no idea what I've been through."

The man stops and looks at me. "Aye, but I know where you are."

"And just where might that be?" I ask hotly, mentally preparing a scathing retort to whatever he says.

The depths of Nachternel? No, not forceful enough.

I would guess the gates of Sühneferme based on the welcome, but it's not nearly cold enough. That's it, that's the one. Hopefully, the reference to the Caelish labor camp will be a blistering insult to this curmudgeon.

"Glancspitze Mountain at Stachtenbaste," the man says, looking at me like I'm a bumbling moron, then continues on his way to the stable.

Oh. Oh. *Oh, gods*! I'm already here! I'm too late!

I start breathing hard, in danger of hyperventilating, when Otto says tentatively, "Um, miss? Maybe you should sit down. You look like you're going to faint."

I'm tempted to do as he says and sit down right there in what must be the stable yard, since I now know it's not a posting station. Looking around, though, I can't be certain that my bottom won't meet a pile of horse dung, and so I settle for leaning against the side of my escort carriage as I take gasping breaths.

I'm about to snap at Otto that, of course, I feel faint. I'm about to enter a training camp for the army, for gods' sake.

Me, who doesn't have a toned muscle in her body and whose greatest feats of athleticism include twisting my ankle in dance lessons before the music had even started, and outrunning the geese that patrol the Noetheim moat like moneylenders in search of retribution, now expected to fend off armed opponents.

Me, who held a funeral when I was thirteen for the mouse that the house cat had killed, now expected to dispatch enemies without thought or remorse.

Me, whose only crime was defending myself when someone working for the man who had imprisoned me threatened to rape me and my sister, now forced to mingle with criminals of the worst variety.

Me, who desperately needs to save my sister from a monster, now trapped hundreds of miles away, where I might die before I get the chance to rescue her.

I open my mouth to speak when one of the guards finally approaches me from within the stables, carrying a sealed missive, presumably from Lord Rocheburn, based on the expensive-looking parchment and the wax seal.

He grabs me by the manacles and pulls me away from the stables toward a dense cluster of trees. I would try to resist, but my fear and exhaustion give me just enough energy to move my legs without being dragged and injured, and I follow along quietly, inwardly disgusted with myself for doing so.

We walk through the trees for several minutes. I hear footsteps shuffling in the leaves scattered on the ground and look behind me to see Otto following. He waves at me pleasantly, and I want to break the fingers on his hand. I turn back toward the guard pulling my chains, noting the thinning trees and the increased sound of rushing water.

We break through the tree cover, and I stop dead, the guard accommodating my need to stare, dumbfounded, at the sight before me.

A massive stone fortress rises on a rocky island in front of me, appearing completely surrounded by stone walls at least forty feet high. From my vantage point, with the walls blocking my view of the grounds and lower portion of the fortress, I'm only able to see the crenellated outer walls of somber gray ashlar that are filled with patrolling guards, and the inner fortress's tallest towers.

The sound of crunching leaves reaches me, and Otto walks up to stand beside me.

"Incredible," he breathes with awe in his voice. "I've read that the fortress itself is capable of housing thousands of soldiers, and the island is about two-and-a-half square miles."

A single stone bridge leads from the patch of ground on which we now stand, crossing the river, and ends on the rocky island with a massive metal portcullis inside an arched doorway. The Flumevian river, the source of the rushing-water sound, and the very body of water my uncle mentioned having recently traversed, courses briskly along, its frothy surf crashing upon the rocks gathered along the bases of the support posts holding up the bridge and against the side of the island.

The water moves too rapidly for me to be able to discern how deep it is, but given how high off the ground the bridge and the island are, were I to fall or willingly jump to escape, I might not survive the plunge. Not to mention the Flumevian river bisects the provinces of Bellatorius and Caelias, the latter being snow and ice bound nearly all year round, which means the water is probably dangerously cold.

My escorting guard seems to lose patience with my gawking and propels me toward the entrance to the bridge, which is eerily unmanned. I suppose when a place like Stachtenbaste is to the front of you and a stable yard teeming with soldiers behind you, there isn't much need to guard the bridge that connects the two.

As we step up to the edge of the bridge where the stone begins, the guard unlocks my shackles, and the sudden absence of weight feels both odd and wonderful. I use my hands to rub the raw spots on my wrists, which are abraded but, thankfully, bear no open cuts or scrapes.

The guard pushes me onto the bridge, and I stumble into its side wall, thankful for its height, or I may have tipped over the side.

Otto, who has since come up beside me, helps to steady my arm and frowns at the guard. "I hardly think that's necessary," he chastises.

The guard turns the full force of his scorn on Otto as he says, "You want me to be nice to the murderer? Gods know how you're going to survive the Aurengarte, boy, if you can't tell friend from foe and if you're not willing to do what's needed."

I flinch when he calls me a murderer, which I suppose is what I am. Even though Lord Rocheburn had charged me with the crime, I had yet to think of myself in such terms. Awful as they were, both Captain Fiedlerg and the other guard are dead because of me, indirectly and directly. Those are two souls in Nachternel for which I'll have to pay penance in life and the afterlife.

Otto says nothing and drops my arm abruptly, as if finding out I'm a murderer is more than even he can excuse.

The guard laughs harshly and turns back to me, stuffing the parchment missive into my hand. "Here is where we part, princess. You'll meet your fate at the end of the *Destinbrug* or a sword."

Destinbrug. The bridge to destiny. How fitting that fate has led me to a place with such a name. Perhaps this is something for which I was always destined. Did my grandmother see this? Maybe that's why she told me and Agnethe to run. If so, it seems even she who could see the future was unable to alter my path.

I turn and face the long bridge, glancing over my shoulder at the sneering guard who remains, presumably to keep me from running away before I can meet said destiny. I glance nervously at Otto, who smiles kindly at me.

"Shall we?" He asks gently.

"I suppose there is only one direction in which to go," I reply.

"Forward! Exactly!" Otto agrees happily.

"I meant because he's blocking me in," I say dryly.

Otto deflates slightly. "Oh, I see. Well, still! The time to cross the bridge to destiny is upon us. On the other side of the wall, we will discover what we are truly made of."

I look at Otto curiously, as we slowly trudge across the stones. "Do you really believe that?"

"Oh yes," he nods. "My father always says that 'we are seeds in the soil of circumstance. Some grow and twist in shadow; others rise in bloom.' Me, I think the only difference between those who flourish or flounder is determination. And I'm determined to make my father proud!"

I absorb that information. "Your father sounds wise," I say, noncommittally, wishing I could believe that the only thing necessary to success is determination. For if that were true, I wouldn't be here.

Otto smiles enthusiastically. "I think so! At least, he's not steered me wrong so far."

Except you're here at a facility to train for your death, I think bitterly. I would hope a father wouldn't steer his son to such a fate as this.

As we reach the halfway point of the bridge, a gust of salty wind lifts my hair from my neck, strands slithering across my face, temporarily blinding me. I pull them away from my eyes and glance behind me to see if the soldier is still there, and I wonder if I can make a break for it, but he remains. My shoulders slump as I turn back to face the fortress, picking up speed, eager to escape Otto and his ceaseless positivity. A woman can only take so much when all she wants to do is wallow in her own self-pitying misery.

The sun is beginning to descend, and I shiver in the increasing shadows cast by the towering stone walls, which engulf me and Otto as we get closer to the door. As we come up to the portcullis, I can appreciate how truly massive the gate is; just the spikes on the bottom segment of the grid are as tall as my legs.

Behind the portcullis is a scarred wooden door that stretches just as high, and it begins to move inward after only a moment of standing in front of the gate. Simultaneously, the portcullis begins to lift, the sound of metal chains clanging against each other filling my ears.

A guard appears when the wooden doors have opened enough, and he looks between me and Otto curiously before he says a curt "orders" to us both and holds out his hand. Momentarily confused, I look down and am reminded that I'm holding the parchment from the guards, which I hand to this new guard as he gestures for us to step past the portcullis and into the gatehouse.

Otto also hands him a paper from inside his coat, and we stand there silently while the guard releases the chain on the portcullis, which slams back into place, trapping me within the walls of the island. The guard beckons us to follow him as he moves toward a door inside the gatehouse.

I turn one last time to look over my shoulder toward the end of the *Destinbrug*, seeking out the escort guard, but he's gone, having completed his task of seeing me imprisoned.

The guard leads us into a small, low-ceilinged chamber where another soldier sits behind a battered wooden desk with a record log. This one is older, wearier looking, and doesn't even look up as he barks, "Names?"

"Otto Weber," Otto says happily, holding out his hand to the soldier. "I'm—"

The soldier doesn't look up. "Didn't ask. Don't care."

Otto flushes and drops his hand, which he shoves into the pocket of his trousers, as if that were always what he had been planning to do.

The soldier still hasn't glanced up, so I say, "Margarethe de Veend."

The soldier looks up sharply at me and asks, "Did you say de Veend?"

"Yes," I confirm, hoping this means he's somehow gotten word that this was all a big misunderstanding, Lord Rocheburn had a brain aneurysm and died or had a change of heart, and that I'm allowed to go home.

The soldier slowly looks me up and down, frowning deeply, as if something about my appearance displeases him greatly. I raise my chin silently in a show of pride, not willing to let this man know that I'm at all intimidated by him or my location. His mouth quirks up slightly on one side, like he recognizes the gesture for exactly what it is: an act. He doesn't say anything to me, though, only stares, before turning his gaze to the guard who ushered us in.

"She come with papers?" He asks gruffly.

The guard hands him my sealed missive, and the soldier takes it and writes my name and Otto's into the book. He calls out to someone, and another young guard comes rushing in from the back of the gatehouse.

"Take this up to the citadel; it's to go to his lordship's hands only," he instructs the guard, who nods and leaves as quickly as he arrived.

"His lordship?" Otto asks. "Is Lord Corvilian present at Stachtenbaste then? I didn't think he lived here."

Lord Corvilian. Another one of the Gold Council members. This one from Bellatorius. He also happens to be the general of the Aurengarte. I feel the sudden urge to lie down. The man's reputation is well known, and it's not favorable. Am I never to be able to escape the Gold Council?

"He doesn't," the seated soldier says, reading Otto's orders. "He visits periodically to meet with the colonel and other officers."

"Well, it's pleased I am to meet him in person, finally! I hear he's got quite a presence," Otto says sunnily, oblivious to my shallow breathing and the trickle of nervous sweat making its way down my temple.

"There's a reason they call him the lion of Fracidaem." The soldier looks up. "And it's not for his gentle purring." I shiver at the man's acknowledgment of Lord Corvilian's demeanor. Wonderful. Just wonderful. A man who's nicknamed after a lion is overseeing my imprisonment.

"Fenne, take her to see Lord Corvilian; the orders were clear," he says to the guard who walked us in. He looks at Otto and grimaces. "Best take the friendly one, too. He might want to acknowledge him."

The guard nods and gestures with his head for us to follow him. We exit the gatehouse room and make our way toward its rear, which is enclosed by a second wooden door and portcullis. When the second portcullis slams down behind me, I don't even register the loud crash, as I'm distracted by the vast grounds stretching out before me, bustling with soldiers in the rapidly diminishing daylight.

Otto nudges my arm and then spreads his own, grinning, as he says, "Welcome to Iron Gate!"

CHAPTER NINE
Into the Den of the Lion of Fracidaem

I want to shrink back against the portcullis at the sight of so many soldiers moving about. I feel no small amount of trepidation around them now, after my recent experiences. My pride, however, won't let me show my fear, even if my knees are knocking beneath my skirt; so rather than betray my anxiety, I simply don't move at all.

"'Iron Gate'?" I repeat back to Otto as a question, hoping to distract myself.

Otto nods, smiling. "I've heard that's what the Aurengarte call it because of the iron portcullis. I figured I'd better start using the terminology."

The guard escort, Fenne, wordlessly indicates we should follow him with a tilt of his head, and he walks in front of us, making his way along the hard-packed dirt path beneath our feet.

From my position, I can see that grass covers nearly the entire island, which I assume is to make training easier. The grounds are flat, which allows me to see almost to the other end of it despite the distance. The stone walls do, in fact, encase the entire island, leaving me with little doubt that escape will be extremely difficult.

I can feel the weight of hopeless depression settling on my shoulders the farther we move away from the gatehouse. A part of me naively hoped that I would be able to slip out of the grounds and make my way back to Agnethe, and then we could disappear to somewhere Lord Rocheburn wouldn't find us. I could tell them I need to speak to Lord Rocheburn, to make him think I've changed my mind and will spill all the de Veend secrets, even if I haven't the foggiest idea what they are. Just so I can get out of this place.

The sight of the sword penetrating Captain Fiedlerg's neck surges in my memory. *No,* I think to myself, *there has to be a way to get out of here that doesn't involve risking Lord Rocheburn's anger even more. I just haven't found it yet.*

Now that we're within the walls, I can appreciate just how massive the citadel actually is. Its height is aided by its perch on a raised outcropping, but the fortress itself has towers of varying heights and diameters that shoot high into the sky above us. The buildings have brightly colored terra cotta roofs, at odds with the bleak desolation I feel inside.

To my left is a stone wall, though what's behind it I can't be certain, for even though the walls are far shorter than those of the exterior, they're still taller than I am and obstructing my view of what's inside. Judging by the sound of metal screeching against metal, however, it's likely some kind of training area separate from the vast field that stretches in front of us.

To my right is a long wooden fence and pasture, with cows and sheep grazing placidly, their teeth ripping up the clover and grass from the earth. The pasture itself has several wooden buildings within it that I assume are various barns or animal-housing structures, indicated by their straw-thatched coverings.

We proceed along the path beside the livestock pasture toward the citadel, following silently behind Fenne. Otto is swiveling his head back and forth, eagerly trying to take in all the sights, sounds, and smells, whereas I alternate between staring at Fenne's back and covertly scanning the grounds for any sign of exit possibilities.

There are soldiers everywhere—not only walking the perimeter and inner walls, as I had seen before I even entered the grounds, but also on the grounds themselves, sparring, exercising in formations, and tending the livestock in their uniforms.

A group of three soldiers nearby stops to stare and watch Otto and me walk toward the citadel. The woman in the middle, strikingly pretty with black hair pulled back from her delicate features in a tight braid, curls her lip at me, as if she's spied something extremely distasteful.

The soldier on the right, an elegant woman with vivid red hair, snickers at the sight, turning her back to us and talking to her companions, as if deciding we are no longer worth her notice. Her companion on the left, a haughty-looking fellow with pale blonde hair, slowly moves his gaze up and down my figure, not bothering to hide his smirk of disdain after he does so. Otto sees them watching and waves at them, unconcerned with the fact that they seem to find something abhorrent about one or both of us. Despite the fact that we've never exchanged a single word, I feel embarrassed and look away abruptly, focusing on Fenne's back once more.

We curve around the path, finally making our way along the edge of the outcropping and toward a set of large stone stairs built into the edge of the rock that leads up to the surface on which the citadel is perched. We climb the stairs behind Fenne, and by the time we've reached the top, I'm out of breath and trying to take in more air through my mouth as surreptitiously as possible.

If I can't even climb the stairs without getting winded, how am I going to survive a single day's training here? I think bitterly, wondering if I should just hurl myself off the island and into the churning waters of the Flumevian now to save myself what is sure to be complete and total humiliation when others see how non-athletic I am, which will almost certainly be followed by catastrophic injury.

Once we're on top of the outcropping, we continue along the path toward the entrance to the citadel, which is flanked by two octagonal towers. Everything about this place is so vast and sprawling, it's almost difficult to comprehend. I thought Noetheim was a large estate, but the grounds of Stachtenbaste could fit at least twenty Noetheims within it, if not more.

At the thought of my home, a feeling of longing pierces my chest so sharply that I nearly grow winded again from the ache. It's surreal to think that only a little over a week ago, I was home and everything was normal. How could I have ever possibly thought my life there was dull or boring? I would take it any day of the week over my new reality.

We pass through the opening in the wall, and I try to observe the goings-on within it to begin planning my escape. Despite the later hour, there are still many people milling about the compound, some appearing to be on their way to or from one of the outbuildings inside the walls, some entering and exiting the largest building, and some marching toward the grounds from which we just entered.

Fenne leads us to the set of double doors in the left-side octagonal tower. Once inside, we're met by another stoic-expressioned soldier, this time a woman.

"Two latest intakes to see Lord Corvilian," Fenne says, gesturing to me and Otto with his thumb aimed in our direction. The other soldier nods, and Fenne turns to exit the building.

"Aren't you coming with us?" Otto asks, sounding a good deal more nervous than he had when we first entered the grounds.

Fenne clucks. "Miss me already, do you? Can't blame you," he says, and I have to duck my head to hide my smile. "But I'm due back at the gatehouse. Blaug here'll see you to Lord Corvilian's study."

Without any further explanation or ceremony, Fenne turns and departs for good, quickly disappearing down the stairs to the fortress outcropping. Otto and I turn to the woman called Blaug, and we look at her expectantly.

"Right," she says briskly. "Before I take you to Lord Corvilian, there are a few things you should know. Don't speak unless spoken to, don't give more detail than he asks for, and for the love of the gods, don't argue with him. If you do all that, you should be fine."

I'd heard the stories of Lord Corvilian, of course. A man doesn't assume the rank of the general of the entire military force without having a certain demeanor. He's also supposed to be particularly bad tempered. I'd hoped, though, that the rumors were somehow overblown and unfounded. That despite the guard at the gatehouse calling him a lion, despite the tales that the man acted with his temper first and asked questions later, he would turn out to be a fairly normal, if powerful, man.

After all, I was getting secondhand information about him from Uncle Eoforwine. Blaug's warnings seem to indicate that the rumors are indeed true and maybe even worse than I'd heard, seeing as how Eoforwine would've only encountered Lord Corvilian in formal court settings, not on or around the battlefield. So even with his impressive knowledge of all the important people in Aurelia, his picture of the man was likely not entirely accurate.

I swallow thickly, trying to quell the panic rising in my throat. Beside me, Otto shifts from foot to foot, but stays quiet in response to Blaug's warning. I've only known Otto for maybe two hours, and already that strikes me as unusual. I feel a sudden rush of sympathy for the man, who was so excited when he first entered, that I catch his eye and smile as encouragingly as I can muster in the moment. His shoulders sag, and he returns my smile gratefully, seeming to understand what I was trying to convey.

What will the military do to the spirit of a young man like Otto? Will it redirect the unbridled enthusiasm he has into his training, helping him focus his energies into usable combat methods? Or will it seek to break him until he has no joy left in him and is only another of these obedient bits of war fodder we've met so far, destined to be sacrificed on the altar of Aurelia's bid for conquest?

The idea of the latter makes me so unaccountably sad, and I'm so buried within my own head that I don't initially notice that Blaug and Otto have begun ascending the stone stairs to my left. I rush up the first few to catch up to them, thanking the gods that they hadn't gotten farther than they did.

As I'm huffing and puffing up *more stairs*, I say breathlessly to Otto, "Are you afraid?"

I hear a snort come from Blaug, but she doesn't stop moving and doesn't turn around.

Otto, who seems to be in about the same shape I am and just as breathless, replies, "Not afraid, no, but nervous, perhaps."

"Do you know anything else about Lord Corvilian besides the

common rumors?" I ask him.

Why couldn't there be a banister? Perhaps Blaug will let me stop and rest for a few minutes or hours until I've stopped wheezing.

Otto frowns. "I'm not sure I've heard any rumors of him. We don't have occasion to mingle with those who would have intimate knowledge of his character, so I only know what my father has told me."

My eyebrows raise. "And how does your father know of Lord Corvilian?" I can't imagine how some rural Verdantian farmer would be familiar with a member of the Gold Council.

"Well, he doesn't actually know *of* him, but rather—" Otto begins, but he's cut off abruptly when Blaug exits the stairs onto a landing and proceeds down a hallway that seems to stretch on forever, though she stops at the first door.

She knocks on the door, a pattern of five raps, three long and two short. A man's voice bids us enter, and my palms are suddenly so slick with sweat that I have to wipe them along the skirt of my dress, two identical tracks of moisture left behind on the gray fabric.

Blaug opens the door, and I'm granted a view of a richly appointed study, with multiple bookcases brimming with volumes and stained a deep brown, polished to gleaming in the light of the many beeswax candles lit in the room—an extravagance on their own, without the clearly expensive furniture. Even at Noetheim, we only used beeswax candles in certain rooms and burned tallow tapers in all the others. I am so accustomed to the pungent smell of the burning animal fat that the sweet and honeyed fragrance of the beeswax candles is almost shocking.

Heavy drapes of sumptuous, red velvet hang from multiple points in the room, indicating windows, but they're drawn shut, so I'm unable to view out of them. Central to the room is a large desk of dark walnut, intricate carvings decorating the sides, elegantly turned scroll legs sitting upon the ornate wool rug that covers the flagstone floor.

As Blaug is standing in the middle of the room in front of the desk, I'm unable to see past her to the study's occupant until she crosses her right arm over her chest, touches her fist to her shoulder, and bends at the waist, revealing the man seated behind the desk in a huge chair extravagantly upholstered in fabric dyed to match the drapes.

"You may rise," he says to Blaug, who stands stiffly and waits silently. "These are the new intakes?" The man asks, lifting his chin toward us as a form of pointing.

"Yes, Lord General," Blaug says deferentially, addressing Lord Corvilian by his official title as head of the Aurengarte.

"Well, don't just stand there. Come forward. I haven't all evening," Lord Corvilian says suddenly, his gravelly voice soft but no less commanding for it.

Otto and I step around Blaug, who retreats through the doorway and pulls it shut behind her.

Coward, I think, uncharitably.

At a closer proximity to his desk, and because his address to us gives me the excuse to do so, I can finally look upon Lord Corvilian. He is a massive wall of a man, close to fifty years old, with dark red hair that's begun fading to silver at his temples and along the part on his crown. The lower half of his face is covered in a neatly trimmed beard that blazes bright copper. Fitting, since the man can create and manipulate fire, if I recall.

Initially, the most I can say that is physically intimidating about the man is his size. But then I meet his eyes, and they are what truly give me pause. They are so dark that the pupil is nearly indistinguishable from the iris, and I once again am struck by the urge to shrink back. I thought Lord Rocheburn's gaze was unsettling, but his has nothing on that of Lord Corvilian.

I can understand why they call him the lion of Fracidaem now. It isn't just because of his fiery coloring. No, it's because when he turns that inky stare on you, you know you're in the sights of a predator.

I've taken Lord Corvilian's measure, and it seems he's done the same of me, as he finally speaks. "So you're the de Veend girl that's wrought so much havoc, are you?" He taps a missive with a broken wax seal on his desk, which I assume is the one from Lord Rocheburn regarding me.

His voice slides down my spine, hitting every notch and nerve on its way, leaving me feeling shaken. There is something incredibly unnerving about the way it rasps along my form, as though leaving cuts and scrapes in its wake. I'm still considering how to answer when Otto, ignoring

Blaug's advice to speak only when spoken to, steps forward.

"Otto Weber, my lord! I must say it's an honor, a great honor. My father speaks very highly of you," Otto thrusts his hand forward in an offer to shake, and I have to resist the urge to yank him back from Lord Corvilian, lest he decide to really live up to his leonine reputation and bite Otto's arm off or something.

Lord Corvilian glances at Otto before flicking his stare back to me and drawls, "Weber is your father? I confess I thought Fabian's older son was past eighteen years."

I have to keep myself from starting at Lord Corvilian's words. Weber is Otto's last name. Fabian Weber is Otto's father. Fabian Weber, as in Lord Valenhof, the Verdantian member of the Gold Council. So when Otto had begun to tell me that his father doesn't know *of* Lord Corvilian, it was because he actually knows him personally. Not only is Otto an enlistee, he's a Lützenclaste of the highest order at that.

When non-magical children are born to the Aurenclaste, they can take a position in their family's enterprise, should they have one; marry well, if they're so inclined; or they can enlist in the Aurengarte at the age of eighteen years. While they're not permitted to hold positions of power within the government, such restrictions do not exist within the military. In fact, most high-ranking Aurengarte officials are the non-magical children of the Aurenclaste, having been fast-tracked to officer positions following completion of their military training, rather than having to suffer through seeing combat like conscripts or lesser-advantaged enlistees.

Otto flushes at Lord Corvilian's words. "Ah, yes, well," he stutters and rubs the back of his reddened neck, "my father insisted I wait to enlist in case I was a late bloomer, but when I reached my twentieth year, he could no longer hope that I would develop magic."

I don't want to like Otto. He's the privileged son of a Gold Council member, and I am predisposed to hate all members of the Gold Council at present and, by extension, their families. But I find I cannot feel hatred toward him. He seems so genuine and completely without guile or artifice. Not dim, like Erwin, just…kind. My grandmother would often say how rare genuine kindness is, and so I feel protectiveness creeping up within me. I don't want Lord Corvilian to hurt him or to break him.

Lord Corvilian, however, seems mostly disinterested in Otto and ignores him in favor of saying to me, "I understand you've given our lord chancellor quite the difficult time."

I feel anger flare to life beneath the surface of my skin, threatening to boil up and over like a water-filled pot above a fire. I know I can't afford to incur the wrath of yet another powerful man, but I can't seem to stop myself from blurting, "I would like to know how my grandmother's dying was any trouble to the lord chancellor."

Otto makes a choking sound, which catches my attention, and I look over to see him widening his eyes and nearly imperceptibly shaking his head at me as if to say, "*Shut up, you clodpole, do you have a death wish?*"

"Well, it couldn't have been much trouble for *you*," Lord Corvilian says snidely, still disregarding Otto, "since you benefit from her demise. I certainly wouldn't put it past non-magical gutter trash to falsify their relative's will and try to steal funds from the Crown."

The man has forgotten that my grandmother and the de Veends are "non-magical gutter trash," at least as far as he knows. So, his outrage at their purported betrayal is disingenuous at best and rooted in prejudice, even worse. Particularly since his position on the Gold Council means he is to serve all residents of his province, not just those with magic.

I open my mouth to argue further, when Otto blithely interjects, "Isn't your son, Ranulf, also non-magical, my lord?"

It's my turn to give Otto the *"shut up, you clodpole"* look, as I can't imagine a man like Lord Corvilian, who clearly believes those with magic to be superior to those without, will take too kindly to being reminded if his progeny is anything less than perfect.

Lord Corvilian's face tightens, his skin flushing a shade alarmingly close to his hair, finally giving Otto the full force of his attention. "Are you jesting?"

Otto stammers, "N-no, I simply couldn't recall the details, but thought I'd heard that—"

"The son of a Gold Council member whose bloodline was sullied with foreign *gesindel*," Lord Corvilian grits out, "could not be more different from an orphan of unknown origins, even if the king's brother did raise her."

I clench my teeth in an effort to keep from shouting at the man, lest he decide to set me on fire. I'm already in enough trouble as it is.

"Of course, my lord," Otto laughs nervously. "H-how stupid I was to ask."

Lord Corvilian responds, "I'm sure this is not the last time someone will consider you a fool, nor the first time they're right."

"C-certainly, my lord," Otto agrees.

"I believe the rigid structure of the military will banish any undeserved ideas of entitlement from your mind, girl," Lord Corvilian says to me, seemingly in control of his temper once more, satisfied that he cowed Otto into fearful submission.

Oh, if only to have Lord Rocheburn's telekinesis at this moment. I could cheerfully hurl many items at the general's head without regret.

"You're dismissed." The lord discards the missive he was holding, picks up a quill, and turns to a different piece of parchment on his desk, having decided he's done interacting with us.

Otto and I awkwardly shuffle out of the door to where Blaug waits for us on the landing. She enters Lord Corvilian's study briefly, and I hear him tell her that he's returning to Fracidaem at first light.

She ushers us back down the stairs, then out of the octagonal tower. We're met with darkness, the sun having set during the time we were meeting with Lord Corvilian. We follow her obediently into an outbuilding in the inner bailey that has a sign tacked to the door that reads, "Administration and Records."

Blaug deposits a uniform of a plain white tunic, gray pants, undergarments, and sturdy boots into each of our waiting arms, as well as bathing supplies. She then escorts us out of the administration building and into the octagonal tower on the right side of the entrance.

We are met by another guard inside. All the guards certainly aren't dispelling the "glorified prison" feeling this place is giving me.

"Aalfs will escort you to your dormitory," Blaug says, though I'm surprised she doesn't just call it a cell. "Report to Administration tomorrow morning, after your breakfast, to receive your assignment."

Having no idea what she means, but too tired to ask, I nod silently in agreement.

I peer curiously through the set of double doors in front of us that appear to lead into some kind of hall with dozens of wooden tables, but Aalfs leads us to the circular stone stairs to my right. I haven't eaten since midday, but I don't even feel hungry. In fact, the lingering smell of roasted meat and vegetables makes me feel slightly nauseated, and I just want to find my bed. Perhaps when I wake, I'll discover this was all another dream, a nightmare conjured from the depths of my too-vivid imagination.

I look up, and the spiraling stairs in front of us seem to go on forever. I sigh, resigned to more wheezing as I follow Aalfs and Otto up. And up. And up.

"How many-how many levels do we have to climb?" Otto coughs as we pass yet another landing. By my count, we've just passed the third one, but I'm concentrating too hard on breathing to even ask how much farther we have to go.

Aalfs, who seems unbothered by the climb, replies, "Just the next level. We're reaching near capacity, so the remaining beds are on the top floor with some of the gold unit."

"What's the gold unit?" Otto asks, and I'm thankful he still has the breath to speak, because I was wondering the same thing.

"Cadets are broken into units that have color names—gold, green, red—you get the idea. The units are broken down into squads, then teams. You'll be assigned a team tomorrow." Of everyone here, Aalfs has definitely been the chattiest.

He continues, "Teams share dormitories, and gold is the unit with teams that have beds left in theirs. Probably means you'll be assigned to it, but don't quote me on that."

Otto nods. "Many thanks, Aalfs."

We reach the top floor, which is the fourth level above the main entrance level, so fifth overall. Whereas the main level had one large room off to the side, the path to our right appears to have a long hallway filled with doors and, to our left, a long, empty hallway.

Aalfs turns and proceeds down the empty hallway, which gives way to what I assume is the upper level of the other octagonal entry tower, and continues down the narrow hallway, passing by at least half a dozen doors. We encounter a bend in the hallway, which has another stairwell to our left.

Aalfs points at the door directly across the stairwell on our right and says, "That's the nearest bathing chamber. Take care you use it. No one likes sharing living quarters with people who stink." He moves to the first door on our left past the stairwell. "And this is your dormitory; the available beds are probably toward the back. You'll be able to tell because they'll have no linens covering them, which you can get in one of the cabinets in the chamber."

"Men and women share together?" I squeak from a combination of my recovering breath and shock.

"Isn't much room for modesty in war." Aalfs shrugs. "You get used to it."

I don't think I will ever get used to having to bathe in the same room as men, but I don't tell Aalfs this and merely thank him for his help.

Aalfs nods at me, a small ghost of a smile on his lips. "Lights out is at nine bells unless you've got night watch, and we wake at dawn to be in the training yard at sunrise."

And just like that, Aalfs is gone, disappearing back down the hallway, the echo of his footsteps the only indication he was ever here.

"Well, Greta, do you suppose we should find our beds? I'm so hungry, but I don't want to climb the stairs again, and it's nearly nine bells, so I'd just as soon sleep," Otto says, and I can see the weariness in the slackness of his facial features, the slope of his shoulders.

I nod and say, "Yes, I think I'm too tired to even chew."

We enter the room, which is surprisingly empty, but lit by a few evenly spaced candles, enough light to make our way to the handful of beds that appear unclaimed. I look around at the expansive space, marveling at just how many beds there are in it.

"How many people do you think sleep in here?" I ask Otto, as we each retrieve linens from a nearby cabinet and cover our respective beds. At Noetheim, my mattress was filled with down and wool, and it was one of the softest things I'd ever lain my body on. If it hadn't already been abundantly clear, the straw poking out of the corners of my new mattress informs me just how much my circumstances have changed.

"I'm not sure," Otto says, glancing around. "But looks like it could be dozens."

Once I've tucked the linens underneath the mattress, I set my uniform and boots on the floor next to my bed and lie down on it. Although these sleeping quarters are a far cry from what I'm used to, my eyelids grow heavy, and sleep claims me only moments later.

CHAPTER TEN
Putting One Foot in Front of the Other and Into Your Mouth

I'm in the tower again and searching for the exit. I follow the beam of light from the doorway behind me, running into the clearing in the forest.

I turn in a circle once more, trying to better absorb my surroundings. The tree leaves are a mix of yellow, orange, and red, as though fall has come to the forest. The curled remains of their fallen brethren crunch under the weight of my shoes as I move, the sound deafening in the otherwise quiet holt. I close my eyes, ceasing all movement, and I'm able to register the sound of the blood rushing in my ears.

No, not blood. Water.

My eyes fly open. Somewhere near here is moving water. A river? The ocean seems unlikely to be close given the dense woodland. It's too far, however, for me to determine from which direction the sound is coming. Something tells me that if I were to go searching for it, I'd merely get lost and not necessarily be met with success. And would knowing there's a river nearby tell me where I am? Not without any other landmarks.

That leaves me to reexamine the building to find out why I'm here. I turn to the crumbling tower, once again noting the missing roof tiles, the lichen coating the stones *and embedded in the surface's pockmarks. My eyes lift to the stone lintel above the wooden door, barely hanging on its hinges, rusted from disuse. At the bird engraved into it.*

I inch closer to the door, never taking my eyes from the stone. The engraving is beautifully detailed, the bird's wings raised above its body as if poised to take off in flight. Up close, I can see that the engraver carefully etched the texture of the wings, the full plumes at its throat, the fan of feathers at its tail.

Seek the sign where shadow and feather meet.

Before, I wasn't sure this was the "sign" my grandmother spoke of to me, where shadow and feather meet, but I feel almost certain of it now. I hadn't assumed the sign to which she referred was this literal. But what indicated shadow? The inside of the tower?

Although the rushing blood in my ears grows louder, I step toward the doorway and cross the threshold into the dimly lit interior of the tower.

I'm afraid, but I force myself to take deep breaths, to look around me, to see what I might have missed in my panic before.

Where the roof tiles are missing, soft light pours into the tower, illuminating the floor and walls where it hits. I can see that the walls are full of holes, but not those which look to be from wear. These look purposeful, as if they are part of the design. They're evenly spaced and stretch from about three feet from the floor nearly to the roofline. As I peer into one, I can see that there is a depression in the stone at each of the points that I thought were holes. A compartment, as if meant to store things, but it seems impractical for items.

Given the sign above the door, I can only assume that this tower is meant to house bird nests, like a dovecote or rookery.

I step back from the wall and scan the tower once more for indications that I'm correct. When my eyes catch on one of the spots on the floor that has light coming in from above, I see a dark shape that sets my heart pounding.

I slowly creep forward and bend down to pick up the dark object, which I lift toward the light to get a better look at. Pinched between my thumb and index finger is a single, black feather. In the light, the feather shifts from coal black to indigo to violet. It's so perfect I can't imagine how it's survived in the tower, since it seems as though it's been abandoned for some time.

My heart nearly seizes when I realize that this feather must be new. I sensed a presence here before. Was it a bird I had encountered? But the presence had felt so…aware. Like a human.

Then, the feather's spine, where I hold it, begins to change, lighten. As if it's being dipped in molten gold in front of me, despite it never moving from my hand. The gold bleeds upward until the entire feather is now gilded and gleaming in the beam of light from the roof. In awe, I reach up with my other hand to feel the edge. It's cool to the touch, like metal. A sharp stab of pain hits the pad of my index finger where I touched the feather, and I see a bead of blood welling from it, wobbling briefly on the tip before dropping to the dirt beneath me.

It's as if my blood hitting the ground changes everything, and I once again feel that presence inside the tower. Crimson floods my vision, casting everything in shades of red—

A cacophony of bodily noises is my version of morning bells, and my eyes open suddenly. I sit up from the same position in which I went to sleep, my body stiff from lack of movement, and blearily assess the dormitory in the light of dawn that filters in softly through the few narrow windows.

Men and women shuffle around the room in various states of undress, yawning, grunting, and some even flatulating as they fully wake. When a young man struts past my bed, completely nude, I decide I've had enough of the morning routine and flop back down onto my mattress.

I'll just wait until everyone else leaves, I tell myself.

Shaken and groggy, I review my dream in my head once more, and it feels so real that my heart pounds with residual fear. I cautiously lift my right hand in front of my face to examine my index finger and feel ridiculous when there are no marks on the pad.

Did I think I was going to find something? It was only a dream. I am in the middle of mentally chastising myself when a face surrounded by a halo of dark curls suddenly pops into view above me.

"Hi," says the woman who looks close to my age, as she cheerfully waves at me.

At least she's fully dressed.

"Hello," I respond cautiously, keeping my eyes on her face, taking in her warm, hazel eyes, upturned nose, and rosy cheeks liberally sprinkled with freckles.

"I'm Cadet Grieves," she says cheerfully. "But you can call me Lotti! I thought you might need help getting around since you're new, right?"

I reply, "I am new. I just arrived last night. I'd be grateful for the help. Have you seen Otto Weber?" I ask her, not willing to look for him myself, considering he might be naked somewhere nearby.

"I'm here, Greta!" Otto's sunny smile appears over my face on the side of my bed opposite Lotti's. Thankfully, he is also dressed. "Good morning! Did you sleep all right?"

"Well enough, I suppose," I grudgingly admit. "And you?"

"Oh, very well! But I confess I'm starved," he says, glancing at Lotti, finally, and when he meets her gaze, his face turns bright pink.

Lotti looks between me and Otto with silent question.

"Oh, um, Lotti, this is Otto; he also arrived last night," I introduce them to one another, thinking these are the oddest introductions I've ever made since I'm still lying down.

"Greetings," Lotti says, smiling, and holds out her hand, which Otto shakes. "I was just telling...Greta, is it?" I nod, and she continues, "I was just telling Greta that I will show her around to breakfast and Administration for assignment. You can come, too," she adds, and both she and Otto turn to look down at me expectantly.

"Is everyone gone?" I ask, noticing how much quieter it is. "There are no naked people in here, are there?"

Lotti leans her head back with a peal of laughter, her rosy cheeks becoming even rosier as she chuckles. "I promise you'll get used to that," she says to me. "But everyone else has gone, so you're safe."

I sit up quickly and ask, "Is there a place for me to bathe and get dressed?" I lean down and retrieve my assigned clothing items from where I left them on the floor beside my bed.

Lotti nods. "The bathing chamber has cabinets for your uniforms and a dressing area, but you'd best make it quick if you want to eat breakfast," she says, and my stomach growls loudly.

She points toward the hallway and begins walking in its direction, with me and Otto following closely behind her.

We reach the bathing chamber doors, and another cadet comes barreling out as I enter, somewhat surprised by the relative luxury I find behind the doors. The chamber is utilitarian, to be sure, built for maximum efficiency. However, several large tubs occupy the space, with metal piping leading to each of them, which I assume feeds water into the tubs.

Lotti has followed me in and gestures to the piping. "If you turn the knob, there, water fills the tub. It's not hot, but it's definitely easier than lugging buckets up five floors. People often share the tubs since everyone bathes rather quickly, but you've got them to yourself since they're all gone."

I nod silently and reach for the knob on the piping of the tub closest to me and watch in wonder as water begins filling it at a rapid pace.

"Where does the water come from?" I ask, not taking my eyes from the spout.

"There are several cisterns that supply the citadel," Lotti answers. "For us, there is one on the roof that uses collected rainwater, or it's filled occasionally by cadets to keep the supply high enough, and it flows through the piping. The valves block the flow when they're turned a certain way, so once you've got enough water, you can turn it in the opposite direction and it'll stop."

I shake my head. "That's incredible. I've not heard of such a thing before." I look up at her.

My family was not destitute and lived well by most standards, but we did not have this sort of modern water-piping system that the citadel has. I reach over and turn the knob to stop the flow of water when I'm satisfied with the level. Since Lotti is the only other person present, and a woman, I peel off my dress and climb in, screech when my skin touches the water, and nearly leap back out of the tub. Instead, I hover over the surface with only my legs submerged to mid-calf.

"It's f-freezing!" My teeth chatter as I remain hovering.

Lotti nods. "Well, the cistern isn't heated, as I said, and it's a pretty impressive system, but we're so close to Caelias, the water is usually fairly cold."

She hands me a washing cloth, and I dunk it in the water, quickly swiping it over my skin. I'm dreading what's next, but I know that I can't go another day without washing my head and hair, as there have been many days already since I've been afforded the ability to do so.

"I can help, if you'd like," Lotti says, kindly, reaching for a pitcher on a cabinet situated near the tub.

I nod and grit my teeth, lowering myself into the frigid water. My body must have adjusted somewhat, as it doesn't feel quite as cold as it did only a few moments before. I still try to arch my back away from the flow of water Lotti pours over my head, clenching my teeth together as it clings to my skin once it's fully saturated.

"You get used to the cold, I find it helps wake me in the mornings," Lotti says conversationally as she hands me a bar of soap to lather my hair with, which I do quickly since, even though I've gotten a little more used to it, it's still very cold, and my head being wet doesn't help. I'm also really hungry and want to eat breakfast.

"I certainly hope that becomes true for me, or I might decide that lugging the buckets of hot water is still superior to this system," I say, wryly.

Lotti laughs. "I couldn't believe it when I got here, either; water that appears at the turn of a knob! But it makes sense since there are so many of us and so many levels; it wouldn't be practical to haul water every day. And we all get sweaty and dirty, so not bathing isn't really a good option, though some still seem to resist," she says, rolling her eyes.

"How long have you been here?" I ask, briskly scrubbing my head and hair with the soap lather, using the excess on my hands to also soap my body.

"A few months," Lotti answers. "Not that long. We all seem to trickle in when we enlist or are conscripted, so we didn't all get here at the same time."

I still and ask, "Did you enlist, or were you conscripted?"

Lotti pours water over my head, and I flinch. "I enlisted when I turned eighteen. My ma and pa can't afford to feed all of us. Taxes keep going up, which means selling more crops to pay those, which means less for us to eat and sell to keep the funds for ourselves. The stipend I'll get as a soldier will help them stay fed," she says.

I absorb that information silently. I knew I was lucky as a de Veend, but I have to face that fact once again, in a harsher light than before, as I process what Lotti's told me of her family. Not once did I ever have to worry where my next meal would come from. Not once had I ever had to worry that we wouldn't have enough to pay our way in life. It's obvious that's not a situation that is true for everyone, and based on what little I do know of Aurelia beyond its favorably storied history tomes and my life at Noetheim, it seems most likely that Lotti's existence is one that is overwhelmingly common for most citizens. Without the monetary benefit that comes from receiving a soldier's stipend, we wouldn't have nearly the number of soldiers we do. Perhaps, I think, that's a system of purposeful design.

Lotti helps me get out of the tub, and I dry off my body and wring out my hair as best as I can, securing it in a damp braid that falls down my back. I reach for the clothes I was given, sighing inwardly as I pull the linen smallclothes over my legs and up to my waist and the band designed to secure my breasts before donning the scratchy wool pants, which stretch tightly across my hips and arse, the laces cutting into the curve of my stomach. The white linen tunic is cut slightly bigger, but still clings to my breasts and pulls snugly across my shoulders when I move my arms.

Lotti frowns and says, "We'll have to see if we can get you a slightly bigger uniform. That can't be very comfortable, how tight it is."

I step into the scuffed brown boots I've been given, tie my superfluous belt at my waist, and say, "Perhaps they hope to motivate me to eat less and lose some weight. I'm not exactly slender, which doesn't really fit the physique of a soldier."

Lotti doesn't argue with me, but says, "You have a lovely figure." She sighs, looking down at her own slender build. "I'd give nearly anything to have curves like yours."

My mouth kicks up on one side. "Until your pants don't fit."

She laughs. "Even then, it might be worth it."

We exit the bathing chamber and see Otto waiting for us, and he flushes again as he looks at my uniform-clad body, then at Lotti's face.

"Thank goodness," he says, "I cannot wait to eat!" Otto is also not thin but doesn't seem to mind this fact at all.

Lotti smiles and replies, "I don't think we were in there that long. Greta was admirably quick."

Otto agrees. "Oh, no, no; only a few minutes, but I just haven't eaten since yesterday."

"Well, let's change that!" Lotti makes her way down the hallway, across to the other tower, and then down the stairs. We follow, beginning our long descent to the main level of the citadel.

When we get to the main level, the scent of bread and sausage reaches my nose, and my stomach growls so intensely it's almost painful. I'm about to ask Lotti which way we go to eat when she leads us to the entry door.

"I think we should go to Administration first," she says, glancing at us both apologetically. "Breakfast will still be here in a few minutes, and it's best to get your assignments so you can head to training after you eat. The officers don't like it when you're late."

Nearly groaning out loud, I follow Lotti as she leads us to the Administration and Records building we visited last night. Inside, there are a few soldiers, including one seated at a desk, which is where Lotti leads us.

Lotti looks at the soldier and smiles. "These cadets arrived last night and need assignment."

The soldier glances at us before grabbing a ledger book. He clips out, "Names," which sounds an awful lot like how Otto and I were asked to give our information when we arrived at the gatehouse yesterday.

We each give them to the soldier, who looks through what turns out to be a sort of record book, not a ledger. He reviews a few pages before he begins writing in the book and says, without looking up, "Right, both of you report to Lieutenant Broadbente for training. You're in first company, gold unit, arrow squad."

Lotti squeals, "You're with me! I was hoping that would be the case since we've only got seventeen and squads normally have twenty."

The soldier looks up from his recording, unimpressed, and addresses

Lotti, "I trust you can show Cadets Weber and de Veend the ropes?"

She gives an eager nod. "Yes, sir!"

The soldier looks back down and utters a dispassionate, "Dismissed," as his way of getting rid of us.

Lotti bounces out of Administration, and we go back to the main building, heading to the double doors, into the enormous hall fitted with dozens of wooden tables filled with soldiers in various stages of finishing their breakfasts.

As we pass by table after table of soldiers, many of them glancing our way curiously, I catch sight of the tall figure of a man crossing the room. His reddish-brown hair brushes the collar of his tunic, which stretches tightly across his shoulders. Unlike my too-tight tunic, it's clear that his fits snugly because of the sculpted, lean muscles bunching in his shoulders and arms. His face is clean shaven, which allows me to appreciate the firmness of his jaw, the warm gold skin, and the slight cleft in his chin.

Different from some within the hall, whose inexperience is evident even to my untrained eye, this man is clearly an experienced soldier, the column of his spine straight, his shoulders thrown back in confidence, and his stride that of someone who is assured of his place and rank. He glances my way, eyes briefly meeting mine, a flicker of curiosity in their chocolatey depths. His head pivots toward a table where someone has beckoned him, and I mourn the ability to look upon his handsome face as he turns his back toward us and moves away.

I turn to Lotti to ask who he is, but instead crash into a wall.

Only, it turns out it's not a wall at all, but rather a man so huge and rippling with muscle he feels as immovable as one. I look up and up into the face of the handsomest man I've ever seen in my entire life.

He looks as though the gods had carved him specifically for battle. I have to tilt my head back considerably to look at his face, as he towers over a head above me. I'm not a petite woman, but at a height of at least six-and-a-half feet, he looms over me with the same dark presence as one of the citadel's towers—and is equally imposing.

His dark brown, nearly black hair falls in waves past his shoulders. The ends are damp, as if he recently bathed, and lie against the fabric of his forest green tunic. The angles of his face, sharp as a whetted blade, are softened only by a full lower lip that curves with a sensuality far more dangerous than brute force.

The close-cropped beard, identical in color to his hair, bracketing his mouth and covering the chiseled edge of his jaw, and the bronze skin across his high cheekbones, give him the look of a seasoned warrior well versed in life and combat. A man who has earned his way through conquest, not lineage.

His eyes, dark and fathomless, appear black as pitch at first, but are actually the color of rich earth, the pupil only slightly darker than the iris.

I stare at him in surprise, and I see a look of equal shock mirrored on his face, as though he, too, is unsure how to proceed given the intensity of each other's scrutiny.

Suddenly, his lips part, and I hold my breath, waiting to hear his first words to me.

He belches. Loudly.

A table of soldiers near us bursts out laughing, and the man grins in their direction, straight, white teeth flashing in stark contrast to his sun-browned skin. The spell is broken.

"Watch where you're going, cadet," he says, moving to push past me. It adds insult to injury that his voice is deep, smooth, and exactly the kind that, were it attached to someone altogether less rude, I would listen to endlessly.

I bristle, once again feeling the temper I didn't know I had in me flare to life. I am exhausted. I have no patience left in me to accommodate anyone. Agnethe could be clinging to life in the *loubenstille*, and this man just burped in my face and laughed at me.

Who the fuck does he think he is?

"*You* bumped into *me*," I say as I turn to face his retreating back. "And you should take care to mind your manners."

He freezes and slowly turns to face me. The tables around us have gone completely silent, as if everyone is both afraid and eager to hear what he says in response.

He stalks back toward me, not stopping until our bodies are nearly touching, the fabric of his tunic only a hair's breadth from mine. He leans his face to mine, the scent of peppermint filling my nose, and stares into my eyes for several tense seconds.

Then he bursts out laughing. The tables around us are only moments behind, joining him with obsequious guffaws. My eyes are in danger of rolling so far back into my head I might be able to see my own brain.

He suddenly whips out a dagger in front of my face, and my breath freezes in my lungs. Why did I have to go and open my big, fat mouth? Why, all of a sudden, did the calm I pride myself on so much abandon me to irritation's caprice?

He smirks at my obvious fear. Instead of slashing my throat, though, he taps the dagger lightly on my shoulder and says, "Get over yourself, *künnle*." He smirks. "Your shit stinks, too."

I jerk back at his crude sentiment, shocked that a man so beautiful could say something so disgusting. And to call me *künnle*, the old Aurelian term for "princess" derisively, as if I were the one who deserved the world's scorn for being prissy, not him for being crass.

He turns from me again and begins to walk away. I open my mouth to argue further, when Lotti appears at my elbow and begins pulling me toward the back of the hall, closer to the area where they're handing soldiers bowls with breakfast in them.

"Don't, Greta," she warns, continuing to pull me, a feat of strength which belies her small, slender stature.

As we draw up next to Otto, who has waited for us again, I pull my arm from her grasp.

"What's wrong with standing up for myself against that arsehole?" I ask.

Lotti and Otto both flinch, and Lotti looks around us, almost as if she wants to be sure no one overheard me call the man exactly what he is. "Careful," she warns, shaking her head to tell me to stop.

I frown. "I don't understand. I was just walking, and he crashes into me, burps in my face, and acts like *I'm* the problem because I'm uptight? I mean, who does he think he is?"

Otto's mouth is compressed into a tense line, and he looks at Lotti, who says, "That's Ranulf Kriegeur, Greta. He's a lieutenant colonel here…and also Lord Corvilian's son."

CHAPTER ELEVEN
A Prison by Another Name

O h. Oh. *Oh.*

Fuck.

I just told Lord Corvilian's son that he needs to mind his manners. Lord Corvilian, the general of the Aurengarte. A man who seems like he'd burn you alive just for looking at him the wrong way. His son looks equally as lethal, based on his size, and equally as insufferable.

One of the attendants behind the wooden counter hands me a bowl of breakfast. I wonder if I should eat it or just fling myself into the river now to save myself the trouble of attending training.

As we're walking with our bowls, a group of cadets approaches us, and I eye them warily.

A young man with blue eyes and chestnut hair looks at me and asks, "Did you really challenge Kriegeur to a duel for not saying please?"

"What?" I blurt, shocked.

"Rumor's going around that you told Kriegeur to meet you at dawn with a krahbek and a sense of decency," one of the others says eagerly to me.

Lotti scoffs. "How ridiculous! Do you honestly think she said that?"

A third says, "I heard she challenged him for the next *Nachtrif.*" Her companions look impressed.

I don't even want to know what the "night fight" is, nor do I know how I would challenge a lieutenant colonel of the Aurengarte for it. How in the realms had news traveled so fast of my interaction with him? If Lord Corvilian gets wind of this, I will definitely pay a price. The river-flinging option looks more and more appealing with every second.

I follow behind Lotti and Otto silently as they weave their way through the tables to one in a corner where several other people are already seated. I curl my shoulders inward and hope no one else approaches me to ask me some ridiculous question about what happened between me and the lieutenant colonel. By the time we reach the table, I do *not* feel like socializing, but it seems I have no choice if I don't want to be completely alone and vulnerable to more interrogation.

"Hi, team! This is Greta and Otto, they're in the arrow squad with us!" Lotti announces cheerfully as she sits down on one of the wooden benches at the table, Otto to her left, and me on her right.

I dig my spoon into the bowl of food, some kind of savory porridge with bits of sausage in it. It's not the most flavorful dish I've had, nor the most elaborate. But it's hot, and I'm so hungry that anything would taste good. In the short span of time I've been seated, I've already managed to shovel several spoonfuls into my mouth inelegantly, but judging by the habits of everyone around me, I don't think anyone's even noticed my lack of grace.

After several minutes of silent eating, a pretty, dark-haired woman with olive-beige skin says to me, "Is it true you told the lieutenant colonel to go fuck himself?"

Lotti chokes on the bite of food she had been chewing, and Otto pounds on her back as she coughs.

"By the green goddess! What are you talking about, Berte?" Lotti asks after she stops sputtering.

"Well, everyone saw her talking to Kriegeur," the young woman, Berte, explains. "And then a bunch of idiots ran around afterward, telling everyone what had happened. I told you she didn't say that," she scolds the ginger-haired young man sitting beside her.

He holds up his hands in mock defense. "I was only repeating what someone else told me."

"Gods help you if you believe everything you hear, Jarl," says the rough voice of the man seated two down from him.

I turn to put face to voice and meet striking, leaf-green eyes in a face that looks as irritable as his voice sounds. He looks to be in his thirties, so most likely a conscript and not an enlistee, with brown skin and black hair that falls to his shoulders. A thick beard covers the lower half of his face and provides an emphatic border for his intense frown.

Jarl turns to the man. "I didn't say I *believed* it, did I, Stigander? Only that I'd *heard* it," he clarifies.

"A technicality to cover the fact that you nearly tripped over yourself to come tell us about it," Stigander says dryly.

"So you're agreeing I'm technically correct?" Jarl raises a ginger brow.

Stigander grunts. "I suppose I am."

Jarl grins. "Well, since being technically correct is the best *kind* of correct, I think we can agree that—"

"Gods, save us," says Berte, who turns to me. "What *did* you say to him, anyway?"

I open my mouth to respond, when a thin, young man, almost feminine in his beauty, comes running up to the table. "Did you hear some cadet told Kriegeur that his prick is tinier than a flea's?"

Now it's Otto's turn to choke on his food. Stigander breaks into a broad grin, Lotti sets her spoon down and frowns, and Berte heaves a significant sigh.

Blessed Sisters, is this how quickly my reputation will devolve here? If this is what rumors at court are like, I can't imagine why they appeal to Uncle Eoforwine.

"Cyneric," Berte says, then points at me with her spoon. "Firstly, the cadet is right here. Secondly, she was just about to tell us what she *actually* said, because do you think anyone is such a shit for brains that they'd tell a man who looks like Kriegeur that he's got a small prick?"

Cyneric replies, "Well, I certainly wouldn't. Gods, that man is positively delicious, I don't care how big his prick is. Though I have it on good authority it's considerably bigger than a flea's," he adds saucily.

"On whose authority?" Lotti demands.

Cyneric shrugs and smiles cheekily. "A gentleman never reveals his sources," he says and turns to me with raised eyebrows, eagerly awaiting my recount.

I clear my throat. "Erm, well, it wasn't anything *that* dramatic. He told me to watch where I was going, and I told him to mind his manners." The entire table gasps, and I hurry to explain. "But I didn't know who he was when I said that. I just thought he was being an arse."

Cyneric wedges his way between Lotti and me, who yelps in protest when he shoves her. "Well, well, well, the kitten has claws. Darling, I cannot *believe* you said that to him. What did he say back?"

"He called me '*künnle*' and told me my shit stinks, too." I stab my porridge with my spoon, imagining it's the lieutenant colonel's face. When no one says anything, I look up at the table to see everyone but Otto looking at me blankly.

"What's a *künnle*?" Berte asks.

"Who's a *künnle*?" Jarl adds.

"It's old Aurelian," I prompt them, which receives more blank staring. "It means 'princess,'" I explain.

The entire table lets out a long "oh" of understanding.

"You didn't know that?" I asked, surprised.

A middle-aged woman with short dark hair and light brown skin across from me says, "What cause would commonfolk have to learn old Aurelian?"

She hadn't said it unkindly, more matter of factly, but I flush from embarrassment at my apparent ignorance and say nothing. Of course she's right. What time would the Arbenclaste—the laboring commonfolk class—have to waste on dead tongues and the privileged sarcasm of the upper classes? The chatter quickly turns to other topics that those at the table are more familiar with than I am.

Cyneric turns to me and asks, "So where did they find you, darling?"

The sun cascading in from the tall windows casts a warm glow upon his golden hair. I'm struck by how much it reminds me of Agnethe's. A wave of fear and aching sadness crashes over me, so pronounced that my throat closes as I stare at him.

Where was Agnethe now? Was she still with Lord Rocheburn? What had he done with her? Thank the gods I'd killed that awful guard who threatened me and her, but I'm sure that where he came from there are plenty more just like him. I drop my spoon into my bowl, my appetite completely gone.

"I'm from Vallaurium," I respond quietly when my long-instilled politeness kicks in. "How about you?"

"Caelias," he answers. "As are Berte and Brock." He gestures to a man seated at the opposite end of the table, his white-blonde hair covering his eyes.

I look around at the rest of the table expectantly, and Jarl says, "I'm from Vallaurium, also."

"Verdantia," Lotti begins, which makes sense since she mentioned the "green goddess," which usually refers to Erdia, the goddess of earth and soil. Verdantians hold her above the other gods besides the sister goddesses of life and death. She then individually gestures to the rest of the people at the table, starting with the middle-aged woman across from me. "And so is Lillen. Stigander is from Bellatorius. Dagmar is from Navisia."

I look around for Dagmar but don't see anyone else at the table. "Where is Dagmar?"

Lotti squirms a little. "She has mostly kept to herself since her group of conscripts was brought in a few weeks ago. She might already be at training or work duty."

Otto asks, conversationally, "And are you all conscripts?" I almost want to hit him with my bowl, because the last thing I want is for everyone to ask me questions about why I'm here. I don't need everyone thinking I'm a back-talking troublemaker *and* a bloodthirsty soldier murderer.

Berte answers, "Stigander and I are," gesturing to him, and he grunts in agreement without expanding further. "As are Brock and Lillen."

"Jarl and I actually chose to be here," Cyneric drawls, draping his arm around my shoulders. "And our teammates think we're quite mad for that choice."

I decide that I like Cyneric and his irreverent attitude.

"What about you?" Berte looks at me and Otto, and my shoulders stiffen.

Otto's cheeks grow pink, but he answers first. "I enlisted, also. I didn't really have a career path open to me otherwise."

The pity catches me off guard. I never imagined I'd feel sympathy for the non-magical children of those blessed with it, for those born to power but left untouched by it. And yet, how cruel it must be to grow up beneath the weight of a legacy you are not meant to carry. To find that it's slipped through your fingers, all the same.

"There's no shame in it," says Jarl. "My family has a bakery in Embrathal. But I wanted to travel and do something different instead of toiling away by an oven for the rest of my life. I can't explain it, but I feel like I'm supposed to do more."

Do you ever want more?

More what?

Just…more.

The conversation I had with Agnethe not so long ago is still vivid in my memory. I wonder if that restless ache for something greater is the mark of youth, all hunger and impatience, or if it's woven into the fabric of their being from the start. Perhaps some of us are born with that pull toward the promise of potential, never content with what is, always chasing what might be. I have never felt that need for adventure, being so focused on my duty and responsibility. While I would like to feel fulfilled, I'm not sure I long for the same excitement Agnethe seems to want. All I know is that I want her to have the chance to find out what kind of person she is, which she'll never get to do if I don't get myself out of here somehow.

I start to jiggle my leg anxiously, and my palms grow sweaty. I want to snap at Jarl and say that having the luxury of choice must be nice, but I refrain from doing so. My self-control seems to have returned following my interaction with the lieutenant colonel. Stigander, on the other hand, doesn't keep his disdain from showing.

"And is this what you imagined as being 'more'?" He gestures around the hall, to the windows, to the uniforms, to the simple food. "Training until you can barely move at the end of the day, work duty in the kitchens where you still stand by a hot oven until the smell of onions permeates your hair; in the laundry until the skin on your hands is raw and burning from lye; in the forge until your eyes burn from the heat of the flames; until your very soul aches, knowing that you will never, *never*, be treated the same as those *pompous*—"

"Stigander," Lotti hisses at him, and his mouth snaps shut.

Berte says softly, "Watch your surroundings, my friend. You never know who's listening." Her eyes scan the room as if looking for someone who might berate Stigander for his frustration. Or even worse.

I try to change the subject to avoid having to answer about my own reasons for being here and inquire about something that's been mentioned twice already. "Work duty? Is that what you do besides train?" I ask.

"Yes. Iron Gate is mostly run by the cadets and officers," Jarl supplies.

Berte adds, "There are a few servants and permanent residents, but we get assigned various duties around the citadel and grounds to keep it running."

I feel a thrill of apprehension. "What kind of duties?"

Lotti chirps, "All of them, like Stigander mentioned! The kitchens, the laundry, the infirmary."

Stigander then chimes in, having recovered, "The forge, the barns."

Cyneric adds, "Cleaning, organizing, all the grunt work. The only thing they don't use us for is the loading docks." He delicately spoons porridge into his mouth, his statement about the loading docks said so casually as to almost be neglected.

"Why don't they use us for the loading docks?" Otto asks, but he's ignored.

Lillen states, "Teams rotate each week, this week's kitchen duty, so helping with cooking, getting meals to tables, prep work, gardening, whatever the cook assigns us to."

"What about your free time?" I ask, hoping to find out when I'll have the opportunity to search for escape routes alone.

The entire table, except for Otto, starts laughing. He shrugs at me as if he, too, doesn't understand what's so funny.

"Free time?" Berte asks, incredulously. "Do you think we're here to enjoy ourselves?"

"Well, I—"

"This is a prison with a different name," Stigander states baldly and turns to Otto. "They don't use us at the loading docks because it's a possible escape route."

My heart leaps at his words. This is it. This is how I'll get out of here. I just need more information from Stigander about it.

"But even if you managed to get on a ship, there would be nowhere to hide, and as soon as you're discovered—and they *will* discover you— they'll kill you," he adds darkly.

My heart sinks, the brief swell of hope dashed as swiftly as it rose, wrecked against disappointment like a ship shattered on jagged shore.

"How do you know they'll kill you?" Otto inquires.

"Because I saw it happen," Stigander says, and offers no further explanation. The whole table goes quiet.

Otto clearly feels awkward and tries to cover that fact. "So, everyone just trains and does work then?"

"Pretty much." Berte shrugs.

Lotti adds, "We train in the mornings, then work duty at midday and lunch, then more training, then evening work duties, then lights out if duties take that long or more training if there's enough daylight."

Otto laughs nervously. "Oh, is that all? Then I guess we all get assigned our positions?"

Berte scoffs. "Our positions? You must be from an Aurenclaste family," her eyes narrow at him. Otto doesn't answer and looks petrified to confirm or deny.

Cyneric says, "Only Lützenclaste soldiers get assigned positions. Conscripts and Arbenclaste enlistees get sent to the front."

The front, meaning the border of Bellatorius and Sarenaveld and the location of most of the combat. And death. Panic rises within me, and I start jiggling my leg again.

"And the officers here were assigned?" Otto asks, clearly trying to figure out where his post would be.

Lotti answers, "Officers are required to do a three-year post at Iron Gate to help train cadets. They might get assigned immediately or later after serving somewhere else, with only a few exceptions."

"Who are the exceptions?" I ask. I have a feeling I know who at least one of those might be.

Jarl confirms my suspicions about the lieutenant colonel. "Kriegeur is one of them."

Otto's voice interrupts my thoughts. "Why is Lieutenant Colonel Kriegeur here permanently?"

Berte shrugs. "Not sure, he doesn't seem to do much apart from sleeping with female officers and cadets, drinking himself stupid, and the occasional weapons training."

I snort derisively. "Imagine being so bad at your job that your father is the only reason you still have one."

Jarl interjects, "Kriegeur's not a bad soldier. He's a very, very good one."

Cyneric turns to me. "He was the youngest cadet ever at Stachtenbaste. That man was made for war, sculpted to perfection," he sighs wistfully.

Lotti adds, "He was a hero at the Battle of Vitaheim, apparently, but was permanently injured and walks with a limp."

I frown, having been too struck by his appearance and boorish attitude to notice any unusual gait.

Stigander says, "He's *just* equal parts stupid and violent, so unless you want to fuck him, I suggest you avoid him."

Cyneric says, "*I* want to fuck him."

"We know," say Lillen, Lotti, Jarl, and Berte.

"Young Cyneric is destined for disappointment," Stigander explains. "He doesn't have the right equipment to appeal to the lieutenant colonel."

Cyneric wiggles his eyebrows. "Or so he thinks."

I feel a smile tugging at my lips at his saucy determination.

Otto asks, "So, avoid the lieutenant colonel; seems easy enough.

What about anyone else?"

Berte answers with a scowl, "Just Brat-ley and her crew of toads."

Everyone begins standing from the table and gathering their dishes, carrying them to the crates positioned every few feet along the walls and depositing them there for some kitchen servant or cadet to wash later. With my luck, I'd be meeting my bowl again very soon in the kitchens.

"Who?" I ask as we exit the hall and make our way to the training grounds as a group.

Lotti points to a group of three cadets speaking with someone wearing a different uniform. I recognize the cadets; they're the same ones who laughed at me and Otto when we arrived yesterday.

Gods, was it only yesterday? It feels like it's been far longer. Maybe because I've endured so much change over the last week and a half, my brain can't comprehend how fast the time is moving.

How a life can be altered entirely in just a moment.

Suddenly I can see my grandmother dying next to me, feel her blood seeping into my dress, hear her gasping her final breaths. I had known then that my life was forever changed but had no idea just how much.

I wonder if Uncle Eoforwine has had any luck appealing to the court or Lord Rocheburn on my behalf. Maybe there is still a glimmer of hope despite the obstacles that seem to continue dropping in front of me.

"That's Belinda Bradleye," Lotti says, pointing to the black-haired young woman. "The redhead is Mette Bosques, and the man is Hartwin Faerberg. They're all children of Aurenclaste parents and enjoy making everyone around them as miserable as they are. The officer is Lodema, Belinda's older sister."

Cyneric drawls, "Apparently it was a catastrophic disappointment to their parents that *both* of their children ended up having no magic."

"Lodema is a lieutenant on rotation at Stachtenbaste. She got assigned here immediately after finishing training," Lotti adds.

"Of course, that might be because a certain Gold Council member was hoping to marry his son off to her." Cyneric tilts his head conspiratorially. His penchant for gossip seems to be equal to Uncle Eoforwine's.

"And the lieutenant colonel doesn't want to marry her?" Otto asks.

Berte snorts. "I don't think Kriegeur is capable of devoting time to anything but weapons and his own reflection, much less marriage vows."

Lodema and Belinda Bradleye are both fair of skin and face, with inky black hair and tall, toned figures.

"They're both beautiful," I say plainly.

"Yeah, they know. Just ask them," Berte retorts.

"Well, my thanks for your advice. I'll just try to stay out of their way. How often do you get leave?" I crash into Jarl's back when they all stop and turn to look at me.

"'Leave'?" Berte repeats back to me.

"There's no going back home, darling." Cyneric wraps his arm around my shoulders again.

I feel the blood drain from my face. "What?"

Stigander adds, "Training is six months, and you don't ever get time off in the Aurengarte, not if you're a conscript. Appointment is until you complete your sentence."

Everything sounds far away as I recall Lord Rocheburn sentencing me to *twenty-five years*.

I'll be almost fifty years old by the time I am allowed to leave if I don't do something—either a false confession to Lord Rocheburn or an escape from Stachtenbaste. That is, if I don't die first.

An escape to *where*, though? This is the farthest I've ever been from home. I don't know anyone outside of Noetheim and my family. And, if I were to break out, they can't take me back safely; I wouldn't risk them that way. Desperation begins pounding in my body to the tempo of my thundering heart, taking root behind my temples and burrowing its way into my head, quickly becoming an intense headache.

"I have to get out," I say, rubbing my temples. "I have to get back to my sister."

Lotti, Cyneric, and Otto look at me with sympathy. The others don't say anything at all, but at least they don't mock me.

"I'll have to escape," I blurt out.

"I already told you: you can't escape," Stigander reminds me.

I begin, "But maybe there's a different route or a way we can sneak out the loading docks—"

"No," Stigander interjects. "You can't. The Schulz brothers are the other exceptions to the rotation rule for officers."

"Who are the Schulz brothers?" Otto asks.

"They're the only people on the island with magic," Lillen answers.

"They're the reason you'll get killed if you try to break out. It isn't just that it's an island with little to no civilization around," Berte explains.

Stigander finishes for her, "They're shields. They can project a barrier that alerts them when someone tries to go through it. So even if you tried, you won't make it," he adds flatly.

I feel like someone has punched me in the gut with that news. Even if I find some kind of escape route, I'm never going to be able to do it. They'll know as soon as I try.

"You're sure?" I look Stigander directly in the eye.

"Positive," he adds. "I had a plan to escape, but someone else beat me to it. He made it onto a supply ship, tried blending in with the cargo, but they caught him as soon as they hit the barrier. They dragged him to the training yard, and Colonel Richter executed him immediately. They made an example of him and told us about the shields then."

My mind starts spinning, wondering if there is some way I could charm one of the Schulz brothers into letting me escape from this place—

Berte must understand what I'm thinking, because she says, "Don't even think about it. Lieutenant Kriegeur sleeps with officers and cadets who are willing. I've not heard the same about the Schulz brothers. 'No' doesn't seem to be in their vocabulary. Steer clear of them."

I'm not sure if I should laugh or cry.

"Has anyone ever gotten out of here?" I ask.

Stigander says, "The only way out of Stachtenbaste is to finish training or to take a one-way journey to Nachternel."

In other words, the only people who get out of here before their training finishes are dead.

CHAPTER TWELVE
Pride and Potatoes are Both Easily Bruised

I follow behind my team, the apprehension inside me mounting with each footfall, until fear is screaming so loudly in my head I'm certain the others must hear it. I've only been awake for about an hour and a half, and though it's only my first morning, it feels far longer from an exhaustion standpoint.

Each step I take requires effort, like I'm walking through sap that's clinging to my feet, making my limbs feel clumsy and leaden. Lotti looks over her shoulder at me as we cross the field and hangs back from the group until I catch up.

"Are you all right?" She asks, then frowns and says, "How silly of me, of course you're not all right. But, well…are you?"

"No," I admit.

No, I'm not all right. Two weeks ago, I was organizing hammers and tongs in the forge and wondering how long the jam in the larder would last in the impending summer's heat.

Now my grandmother is dead, my sister is suffering, our home is in metaphorical shambles, and I'm here in this place that feels like the gods must have forgotten about. One moment, I'm hiding in the wall while soldiers destroy the only life I've ever known, and the next I'm being carted off like a prisoner of war.

I didn't even get to bury her. Or really say goodbye. I saw my sister restrained and screaming. I can't help but wonder what torture is next on my agenda.

None of it feels real. It's like I fell into some cautionary tale parents tell their children to keep them from misbehaving. And I'm supposed to learn how to train? To fight? To become one of them? As though I'm not still reeling from everything that's happened? As if the very thought of having to fight someone doesn't make me quake inside?

I feel like I'm just one more bad thing happening from completely shattering into a million pieces.

Lotti grabs my hand. "I know it sounds trite, but time really does make it better."

I look into her earnest brown eyes and smile slightly. "You're right…it does sound trite."

Lotti laughs and pulls me along with her, farther across the grass. The grounds have some gravel walkways on the fringes leading to and from the outcropping to a few areas of the fields, but mostly grass stretches in front of us. It's missing and muddy in places, a testament to the dozens of feet that have crossed those areas before us.

We pass by the area of the training yard I noted yesterday. The area that's walled off. I can see through the metal gate in one section that it does, indeed, appear to be a training yard since soldiers are sparring within it. My steps slow as I watch two of them circle each other, both holding two swords—one in each hand. It's almost elegant, like a dance, the way they spin and sway, their arms arcing as they bring them up to clash their blades against each other's. It's intimate, in a way, how their focus is solely on one another during their macabre waltz. Though I suppose killing someone is an intimate act.

The memory of blood, hot and metallic, spraying my face, returns unbidden, as I recall the last torturous minutes of that horrid guard's life at my hands. To kill someone strikes me as one of the most personal acts you can commit. Like lovemaking, it strips you bare, brings you closer than most ever dare to go. And once you've loved someone—or killed them—they never entirely leave you.

Just then, Lieutenant Colonel Kriegeur crosses in front of the gate from the other side, his gaze finding me. I startle, tripping slightly on my own feet, and he smirks before turning away, facing inward toward the smaller training yard.

Lotti catches the direction of my eyes and looks toward the training yard before turning back to me, her face grim. "That's the officers' training yard," she explains. "That's where the lieutenant colonel spends much of his time. I suggest avoiding it."

"Does he even *do* anything besides drinking and sleeping with women, like Berte said?" I ask, kicking a piece of gravel that has traveled from one of the paths.

"He gives weapons lessons to the cadets," Lotti replies. "He's skilled in most of them, although I've heard his specialty is the krahbek. We haven't learned that one yet."

I dispatched her with my krahbek.

I can still hear the dispassionate tone of Captain Fiedlerg's voice as he explained how he ended my grandmother to Lord Rocheburn. If I were to judge a man by his weapon of choice, then it seems the lieutenant colonel is as much a monster as the captain had been.

We curve along the field, and I see another bank of shorter stone walls, beyond which is a towering circular structure of stone.

"What's that?" I ask Lotti, pointing to it.

Lotti turns to where I've indicated. "Oh, that's the arena," she says.

"The arena?" I repeat. "What do they use it for?"

"Oh, many things," Lotti says a bit too casually. "Competitions and the like."

I can't help but feel that Lotti is avoiding fully answering me, but I don't have time to pry her for more information because we've reached a cluster of cadets standing in front of a tall, handsome man who looks to be about my age with brown skin and a somber expression. He is speaking, and his voice isn't loud and booming by any means, but it manages to carry nonetheless.

"Before we pair off, we'll begin with laps." The entire group groans, but takes off to the closest part of the gravel path and begins jogging away from us. The man turns toward what looks to be an equipment shed, with wooden weapons leaning against its stone walls, when he spots me and Lotti.

"Lieutenant," Lotti chirps. "This is Greta! I mean, Cadet…well, um." And she trails off, clearly realizing she never learned my last name.

"De Veend," I supply, and it's then I see the man from the dining hall with the reddish-brown hair stroll out of the equipment shed. I feel the flame of bashfulness crawl up my face, heating it as he looks upon me. I can't hold his stare for long before I must turn my eyes away.

"Yes, de Veend!" Lotti nods, as if she knew it all along. "She's new, arrived last night with Otto Weber."

The lieutenant nods and simply replies, "Laps," points to the gravel path, then gives us his back.

Lotti sighs and turns dejectedly toward the path, waiting for me to follow. When I line up with her, she takes off in a slow jog, and I begin to follow, looking back over my shoulder. I'm surprised to find the auburn-haired soldier is watching me still. I quickly swivel my head back toward Lotti and take off after her in earnest.

A few minutes later, my airways are blazing behind my sternum as I take unabashed, open-mouthed gulps of air, and sweat trails uncomfortably down my temples, the back of my neck, and pools beneath my eyes and above my upper lip. I swipe a hand across my face, trying to banish the moisture from it, but as soon as I wipe some away, there is instantly more to replace it.

Even though we aren't far from Caelias' icy peaks, and the air still carries a snowy bite, the sun's rays are steady and strong, and I am not built for this kind of activity. My breasts shake painfully with every jarring step I take, my inner thighs rub together to the point of burning, and my feet feel like they're pulsing inside my boots.

Lotti initially takes pity on me and stays with me, but she obviously wants to get the running over with, so I encourage her to go ahead of me. At least with no one around, I can struggle to breathe in peace and without embarrassment. Otto is the only one doing worse than I am, even though he began before I did. He trails behind me a good fifty feet, his face an alarming shade of red, and sweat pours down his face.

I finally wrap my way around the grounds near the gatehouse, and turn to make my way back to the upper training yard where my team has, no doubt, begun their next bit of training without me. I trudge my way past the officers' training yard. I don't even think what I'm doing can be called running. I lightly place my hand on the stone wall to steady myself.

As I pass by the gate, Lieutenant Colonel Kriegeur's face appears behind it, watching me with a stupid grin on his stupid face. I want to ask him if he has anything better to do, but I lack the air and hydration to even form the words. I lick my parched lips and continue past the gate, and he thankfully stays silent. But I can feel him watching me as acutely as if he were touching me.

I clench my jaw and push myself through the final burst of the lap, making my way to the back of the group standing in front of the stony-faced lieutenant. Many people are breaking off in pairs, and I gratefully take the waterskin Lotti holds out to me as the lieutenant pins me with his dark gaze.

"Cadet de Veend, Cadet Weber, how nice of you to join us. Did you enjoy your stroll?" As Otto draws up beside me, the sound of snickering reaches my ears, and if my cheeks weren't already pink from exertion, I'm sure everyone would be able to tell I'm blushing.

I haven't caught my breath enough to muster a response to the lieutenant, but he doesn't seem to require one. He gestures to a woman of about forty standing a few feet from him.

"Brevic," he directs, "pair with de Veend for sparring."

I thank the gods that I'm paired with a woman, but when she turns toward me and looks me in the eye, that relief immediately sputters and dies.

She's tall, even taller than I am. Where I'm curvaceous and prone to plumpness, however, she is thin and rangy. The lean muscle running along the curves of her biceps and forearms tells me her build does not mean she lacks strength. Her dark brown skin glows in the sunlight, stretched across prominent, elegant cheekbones, along the delicate slope of her nose, above the graceful arch of her black brows. She has full lips that she compresses into a line upon seeing me, and her eyes—a piercing, crystalline blue—narrow in disdain.

"Lieutenant Broadbente," she says to the young man for whom I now have a name. "Permission to spar with a different partner?"

I feel like I've been punched in the gut even though no one has yet laid a hand on me. There is something so humbling and humiliating about someone so quickly taking your measure and decisively determining you've come up short.

"Buck up, Brevic," Lieutenant Broadbente says, a ghost of a smile twitching his lips. "Just think of all you can teach Cadet de Veend."

Cadet Brevic rolls her eyes but doesn't argue. I notice that many other pairs of cadets have begun sparring. Unlike the weapons sparring I was prepared for, however, the only thing the cadets seem to be fighting with is their bodies. The foreboding that had left me when faced with the arduous task of continuing to breathe while running comes rushing back.

Brevic stalks away from me, makes her way to an empty span of grass, and waits for me, an expectant look on her face.

"What are you waiting for, de Veend?" Broadbente asks me, arching an eyebrow.

"What, erm," I cough delicately, "what am I meant to do?"

Lieutenant Broadbente stares at me for two, three, four, five seconds, before he says, "You spar, cadet. Hand-to-hand combat."

"But I don't know how to spar," I say, my voice making an alarmingly fast approach toward quavering.

Lieutenant Broadbente looks me in the eye as he states, "When fists fly at your face, you learn pretty quickly." He flicks his hand in Brevic's direction and then turns to Otto, indicating he will partner with him.

Irritated and afraid, I turn toward Brevic, dragging my feet as I make my way to the patch of grass where she stands.

When I reach her, I clear my throat and hold out my hand. "I'm Greta de Veend," I say, hoping to soften up my opponent with manners.

Her eyes snap to mine, surprised, but then she scowls. "We're wasting time."

I sigh and withdraw my hand. "Fine, I suppose we should get this over with."

She nods, draws back her right hand, and punches me in the face. Pain explodes in my cheek. I thought the slap from Lord Rocheburn was painful, but it turns out I had no idea what painful was, because he definitely hadn't hit me this hard.

Brevic reaches for my waist, and I step back instinctively, trying to escape her grasp. She growls in frustration and swipes at me, but I spin away again, squealing. I'm soon running circles around her.

I mean literally. I'm running around the group of cadets, much to Brevic's frustration. I know I'm not fast, but she seems unwilling to chase me, as if that's beneath her. Instead, she growls at me to stop running while trying to swipe at me. She tries to grab a handful of my tunic or the end of my braid to still me.

"De Veend," barks Lieutenant Broadbente. "Stop running and spar, for fuck's sake. Brevic, stop letting her lead you on a chase."

Despite her dark skin, the unmistakable flush of humiliation is visible on Brevic's face. As if she's decided there's no dignity in continuing to let me run around, she suddenly charges, yelling. I scream as she comes barreling toward me but am not prepared for her speed or the force of her ire as she rams headfirst into my stomach.

The air whooshes out of me, and I stumble back, only managing not to fall by grabbing onto her shoulders. I scramble as she wraps her arms around my waist, pinning me, and my feet dig uselessly at the ground as I attempt to twist and turn away from her.

It's then that I spot the auburn-haired man again, watching me. His handsome face is unreadable, so I'm unsure if he's looking upon me with judgment, pity, morbid curiosity, or indifference. Humiliated, I twist out of Brevic's grasp and turn to face her, determined to land a blow. I swing my right arm wildly and miss entirely, but Brevic doesn't.

I watch in horror as her larger hand grabs onto my fist and holds on tight, fingers digging into my skin. I try to pull my hand out of her grasp, movements increasingly jerky and desperate as I become aware that everyone has stopped sparring to watch us. I manage to raise my left arm to block her other hand from striking me, but I make the mistake of glancing at the auburn-haired man again when I see a flash of red in the corner of my eye. He is still watching me, as is everyone else within a thirty-yard radius.

The break in my attention costs me more ground with Brevic, and my arms, already trembling with effort, begin to shake more violently. My left arm droops, and the loss of rigidity enables Brevic to snake her fist beneath it and make a significant punch to my left side.

Howling in pain, my entire body loses its fight. My right fist slackens in her hand, and she lets go of it, so I cradle my left side with that hand. She bounces back on her heels, as if deciding where to strike next.

I shake my head, pleading and say, "No, no, please—"

Another blow to my face.

A jab to my left side again.

A solid fist to the center of my gut.

Then, she shoves into my torso with her shoulder, pushing me to the ground. The wind is knocked out of me, and I'm frozen. I'm only able to watch as she straddles my hips and draws back her fist for what will no doubt be a devastating blow.

A man's hand suddenly wraps around her wrist.

"You win, Brevic. No sense kicking a woman while she's down. That's the kind of low blow we expect from Sarenaveldans," a deep voice says calmly from above me.

Brevic stands, begrudgingly holding her hand out to help me up. I take it, too pained to disregard the assistance. She yanks me to my feet, none too gently. I hear her mutter "pathetic" under her breath before she turns away from me and heads toward the citadel building with the others, most of whom have already departed.

Confused, I look around for my savior and see the back of the auburn-haired man retreating toward the officers' training yard.

Lotti comes bounding over with Otto. "Greta! Greta, are you all right?"

Otto grimaces at my face. "That's *definitely* going to leave a mark."

I reach my fingers up to prod my cheek gingerly and am met by pain and the wetness of a trickle of blood from the corner of my mouth. I move my tongue around on the inside, and a metallic tang from the inside of my cheek greets my taste buds. When Brevic hit me, my teeth must've cut the flesh there, I realize.

"Where did everyone go?" I ask thickly. It feels like my mouth is full of cotton on the left side.

"Kitchen duty before the afternoon meal," Lotti answers, looping her arm through mine, and steers me toward the direction of the citadel. "Don't worry, we'll let you take an easy job today so you can rest before afternoon training."

I groan. "Oh, gods, I have to do *more* of this?"

"Probably just drills and running," Lotti says.

More running?

Otto laughs at my expression, which must convey my horror. "Maybe they'll go easy on you for a few days."

"Unlikely," Lotti says sympathetically. "We are training to be soldiers after all. But they also need us for work duty, so they can't destroy us too much, thankfully."

"Hmm, yes, I'm glad I was only destroyed a little just now," I quip.

Lotti grins. "I still can't believe Captain Everbrandt stepped in."

"Who?" Otto asks, but I can already guess.

"Is that the man with the reddish hair?" I query.

"Yes," Lotti nods. "He's the head of the Gold Unit. He's usually out here moving around and watching training, but I've never seen him step into a fight before."

"Gods, he must have thought I looked truly pitiful, then," I groan. *Pathetic.*

Lotti's eyes dance. "Your dismay wouldn't have to do with the fact that Captain Everbrandt is ridiculously handsome, would it?"

I flush but say haughtily, "Of course not. I just don't want my commanding officer to think I'm a lost cause."

Otto gently elbows me while smiling. "Such a dedicated cadet."

I scowl at Otto, but feel the corners of my mouth twitching not too long after. "Oh, come off it, then. How bad did it look?"

"The part where you got repeatedly punched in the face or the part where she knocked you over?" Otto asks.

Lotti adds, "Or the part where you got repeatedly punched in the ribs?"

"I'm sorry I asked," I say dryly.

"I'm sure she'll be gentler on you next time. Dagmar is probably just upset because she got to spar with Lieutenant Broadbente before you came along."

I stumble. "That's Dagmar? She's on our team?"

I knew she was in our unit since we were in the same training group, but I didn't realize it was even worse than that. Wonderful, now I have to find a way to work alongside the woman who just beat me up.

We make our way up the steps of the citadel, which my sore ribs are not happy about, through the entrance into the inner bailey, and toward one of the large outbuildings past the Administration and Records building. Smoke billows from multiple chimneys spaced along the terra cotta roof, and people bustle in and out of the doors, arms laden with items from what I assume are storehouses since they're smaller buildings directly across from the larger one.

We enter through the doors in the center of the building, and Lotti points out various areas of the kitchens. To our left and through a large opening is the bakehouse where they bake bread and other pastries like meat pies and the occasional dessert, although I can't imagine they care too much about giving us sweets. To our right is the smokehouse where meats are preserved. Unlike the bakehouse, there is no entrance to it from within the kitchens; it can only be accessed outside in order to keep the smoke in the smokehouse and out of the kitchens.

Lotti shows me the staircase in the rear of the kitchen that leads to an underground tunnel down to the larder beneath the dining hall in the main building. The smaller outbuildings directly across from the kitchens house the granary and pantry.

As she shows me around and allows me to catch my breath from climbing the stairs, a sour-faced woman with graying blonde hair bustles over to us.

"You," she says to Otto, "see to carting the lentils in with one of the other lads."

"Yes, madam," Otto says, cheerfully bouncing out of the kitchens.

"You," she says to Lotti, "go see Arna about the bread dough." She points toward the bakehouse.

"Yes, Irmela. Only, Greta got hurt in sparring, so she might need light duty," Lotti tells the woman before smiling sunnily at me and making her way toward the bakehouse.

Irmela turns to me and looks me up and down, her gaze remaining on my face for several seconds, presumably where a bruise is rapidly blooming across my cheek.

"Well, now, girl, what experience have you in a kitchen? You're looking like one of the posh ones." She curls her lip.

Okay, clearly not a fan of the Lützenclaste, I think.

I take a deep breath, wincing at the sharp stab that lances through my side with the motion. "I have experience managing the kitchens from my grandmother's estate. I assisted with planning menus, I oversaw the staff and dish presentation, managed orders and the budget, and kept the records."

The cook looks at me shrewdly, deciding where she can best use my skills, which are fairly impressive, if I do say so myself. Surely that experience warrants me a slightly better task than some of the most menial ones.

"Right," she nods. "Potatoes."

I gape at her. "What?"

"You've got no practical experience, girl, so we'll start you on the potatoes." She walks me over to a block of knives and hands me a battered paring blade, then directs me to a corner of the kitchen with a stool and a mound of potatoes at least two feet tall. Another girl dressed in servant's garb is seated on a stool, settling in to begin peeling.

I sputter. "But didn't you hear all I can do? I do have experience," I protest.

Irmela turns to me, eyebrows raised. "And just where do you think menu planning and presentation fit in here? We're cooking for soldiers, not royalty. Now be grateful you get to sit, girl, and start peeling."

I pick up a potato and begin awkwardly carving it. I know I'm taking off more skin than is necessary, but having never peeled a potato before, I can't seem to get a rhythm going. When I finally finish my first potato, I look up to compare it to the girl sitting across from me. An entire bowl full of peeled potatoes sits in front of her. I stare in shock at her pile. Surely, she must have some kind of potato-peeling magic to have accomplished that so fast. She doesn't even spare me a glance, and I watch, slack-jawed, as she smoothly peels a potato in a single, continuous, spiral motion.

Sighing, I pick up my second potato and set my knife to it.

That evening, after afternoon training, which was drills and running, just as Lotti said, and more potato peeling, my body is one walking bruise. My side aches, my face hurts, my fingers are stiff and cramped, and there is a slimy feeling on the skin of my hands even though I've washed them several times. As if the potato starch still clings to them.

As soon as I'm permitted to leave, I stagger up to my dormitory, which takes me far longer, with my sore ribs, than it did last night. I consider bathing before bed to help me relax, but the thought of the freezing-cold water makes me decide against it. I make my way to the back of the dormitory and my bed, wondering if this will ever get any easier. Everyone here seems to have taken to their work much better than I have—even Otto.

I collapse onto my bed, too tired initially to even undress. After several minutes, though, the weight of my boots on my feet, which are hanging off the edge of the bed, becomes too much, and I sit up to remove them, only to face the figure of Dagmar Brevic lowering herself into the bed next to mine.

She glances at me but says nothing, quickly covering herself with her blanket and turning her back to me. Sighing, I lie back down on my mattress, stare at the ceiling for several minutes, and anticipate my routine tomorrow with dread.

Sparring.

Drills.

Potato peeling.

Running.

As I drift off to sleep, I wonder if I can trade running for getting punched in the face again.

CHAPTER THIRTEEN
The Art of Surrender and Surprise

I am back in the aviary, watching the bead of blood well on my fingertip again before it falls to the ground. Instead of my vision flooding red, everything in the tower goes dark, as if someone has placed a blindfold over my eyes. Without my vision, my other senses heighten. I register the sound of my shoes rotating in the grit beneath my feet, the rush of the river through the trees, the delicate rustle of leaves kissing the ground as they fall, the feeling of stinging warmth on the end of my finger where the cut pulses with the beat of my heart.

In my ears, the rush of the river, of the blood pounding through my body, gives way to distant whispers, their vowels and consonants indistinct but distinguishable from the other sounds present. I turn toward where I think the door is, hoping the daylight will reappear and guide me out of this unnerving place, and see the faintest glow around what looks to be the shape of a door. But was the door even capable of shutting? I hadn't closed it when I entered the tower. I reach my hand out and creep slowly to the side until it brushes against one of the stone walls. My fingers dig into one of the indentations, meeting leaves and dirt and the stickiness of cobwebs. I begin to jerk my hand back, to avoid any spiders, when it brushes something cold as I retract it. I wrap my fingers around the object, which feels like metal, and transfer it to my *other hand before placing my palm back against the wall. With the stone anchoring me, I move toward that anemic light.*

As I near the door, I hear it.

The unexpected whoosh of air beside my ear.

My hair shifts, as if blown by some errant breeze, out of place in the stillness of the building. Adrenaline floods my system, and I hasten toward the door, frantically feeling along it for some kind of handle or lever. When I reach a metal ring, I pull hard, dislodging the wood from its frame, and dash outside.

The faint light I had seen was from the moon, obscured by clouds, but emitting enough of a glow to give distinction to the shapes of the forest around me. I feel another gust of air beside my ear, and terror grips me, forcing my limbs into action, and I begin to run from the aviary with no destination other than "away from here."

I trip on a tree root and fall, the metal object in my hand biting into my palm as I crash down onto my hands and knees. I look over my shoulder to determine how far behind me my assailant is, but I see no moving shapes, no indication that there is someone or something headed toward me. The only motion around me is the slight sway of the tree limbs and the gentle drift of the clouds above. Perhaps it really was just wind. After all, there are holes in the roof of the aviary, and there is a slight breeze outside.

I groan as I pull myself to my feet, fingers clasping the bit of metal, pulling it from the ground along with some stray leaves and dirt that becomes caked under my fingernails. I open my palm flat and turn so that what little light comes from above can shine on my hand. I pluck the leaves and twigs off and drop them back to the forest floor. My eyes have adjusted to the dark, and I can see and feel the object is a ring. I trace my fingertip along its edge, frowning when I encounter a flat side with ridges, as if something is carved into it.

Suddenly, the clouds part to reveal the moon, which glows an unnatural pink.

A blood moon.

Shivering, but not from cold, I look down at the ring in my hand. Now illuminated by the moon's eerie brilliance, I can see it's a signet ring. I grasp it between my fingers and turn the emblem to the light of the moon to better see the engraving.

Blood red enamel gleams brightly from the ring's bezel, and in the center, engraved with delicate precision, is a raven's head.

I jerk awake from my dream, the lack of light that comes in through the windows tells me it isn't quite time to rise. Still, I haven't become accustomed to bathing in front of my fellow cadets, so I grab my clothing and tiptoe out of the room to the bathing chamber, which is, thankfully, empty.

It's been a week since I arrived at Stachtenbaste, and I am a map of pain, each bruise a different symbol on its legend. The sickening mix of purple, green, and yellow coloring my face and side, where Dagmar struck her first blows, has been joined by newer, sharper coordinates on the topography of my body. A red ring around my wrist where she twisted my arm to hold me still, a monstrous contusion on the side of my knee created by her boot, innumerable nicks on my hands from the potato knife, a burn on my inner forearm where a blazing-hot pot sought to punish my clumsiness with its particular brand of retribution.

Then there are the bone-deep aches that seem to be a permanent fixture now, to the point where I'm not sure where one ends and the next begins. I only know that the very act of breathing is a daunting exercise by the end of each night.

And there is the psychological and emotional fallout from being here. Beyond the physical pain, which is significant but pales in comparison to the torture my mind brings me. Thoughts of Agnethe, starving, cold, afraid, and alone, fill my mind when I give myself even a moment to let it stray. The feeling of utter helplessness that assails me when I try to envision the landscape of my future. How I'll escape, how I'll get to my sister, how I'll survive.

Even in my sleep, I'm not free from the torment. While they don't occur every night, my dreams are frequent, repetitive, and disturbing. While I could explain them away as the product of an agitated and anxious mind, I worry that I'm somehow experiencing visions, like my grandmother did. Becoming something feared and forbidden, slowly driven mad by the inner workings of my own consciousness. Am I seeing reality in my dreams, a premonition of things to come, or am I experiencing the fevered works of a distressed mind?

In only a week, I have been whittled down to the barest existence—only eating, sleeping, and working, to where I hardly feel human. I wonder, though, if the dehumanization is purposeful. After all, a soldier who is wearied of body and spirit can hardly put up much of a fight beyond what it takes to simply survive. I haven't even tried to look for a means of escaping. Not only have I not had the time, but I can barely muster the energy to do the simplest tasks, let alone plan some daring exit.

I hear doors opening and closing in the halls and swiftly exit the bath, dressing quickly before towel drying and braiding my hair. Lotti had helped me get a bigger tunic and pants from Administration. Still, the sizes that fit my hips and breasts with enough room were made for much larger men, and caused me to trip, so I was left with having to wear items that were still snug, but simply less so than my initial uniform.

I gather my night clothes and quit the bathing chamber just as several cadets burst in, making for the garderobes and baths. Back in my dormitory, I fold my nightshirt and place it in the chest at the foot of my bed, then begin pulling the bed linens back up the mattress, tucking them under, and neatening it to kill time before Lotti and Otto find me to go to breakfast, as they have each morning.

As I pull my blanket tight over the side of the bed, smoothing it with my hand, Dagmar sits down on the edge of her bed, her hair damp from a bath, and pulls her boots on over stockinged feet. She doesn't say a word to me, doesn't even look at me, before she stands and leaves the room.

Despite my efforts to appeal to her with every nice gesture and polite manner, I've made no progress with her. I've tried to make conversation in the dormitories, taken on some of her kitchen duties, and the woman not only beats me up without remorse during training, but barely hides her derision as she does so. I'm not sure what I've done to earn her scorn, but it seems redemption with Dagmar is to be a hard-won, if not impossible, achievement.

Otto, Lotti, and Cyneric retrieve me to go down to the dining hall for breakfast. I say little, letting the sound of their lively chatter wash over me.

"But what would you even do with that amount of money?" Lotti asks Cyneric, laughing. I have no idea what they were discussing, having not been paying attention until now, but it sounds like it's been entertaining.

"What wouldn't I do, darling?" Cyneric asks, grinning.

"But what would you buy?" Lotti prods.

Cyneric looks thoughtful as he takes his bowl from the attendant in the dining hall, nodding his thanks. "A way out of Caelias for my family," he says seriously.

He'd told me how he planned to send his soldier's earnings to his family back home. They work in the mines, and his father is sick and needs medicine for a lung ailment.

Otto, Lotti, and I don't say anything to him about his somber admission, but Cyneric seems to snap himself out of his own dreary mood. He smirks. "And then, furs, jewels, men."

Otto laughs. "I don't think you can buy love, Cyneric, or every wealthy person in Aurelia would be much happier."

"I didn't say 'love,' I said *men*. There's a difference." Cyneric winks at him.

We sit down at a table, and Lotti looks at him, eyes twinkling. "What kind of jewels would you buy?"

"Emerald necklaces, ruby rings, diamond earbobs," he says, ticking off the imaginary items on his fingers.

At the mention of ruby rings, a shiver creeps down my spine as I'm reminded of my dream and the ring with the red enamel bezel and the raven carving. It looked just like the one Agnethe had at Noetheim; only it looked newer in my dream, less battered and worn. Did it mean anything? Or was my brain trying to fill in explanations for things where I had none?

Cyneric turns to me. "What would you do with endless wealth, darling?"

I smile at them. "Oh, I don't know," I shrug. "Buy lots of books."

"That's no fun," Otto says in an uncharacteristically grumpy voice.

I sigh. "Fine. I'd…I'd pay a bard to follow my enemies around and sing every failure of theirs in rhyme," I say dramatically.

Cyneric grins. "Now you're getting somewhere!"

Lotti looks at me doubtfully. "You have enemies? Somehow that seems unlikely."

I scoff, "Pfft, you don't know my whole life."

The others laugh at that, not knowing it's far from jesting to say there are those who are enemies to me.

After breakfast, we make our way to the training yard, and I shuffle along behind the others, my body already aching in anticipation of the pain it will endure at Dagmar's hand. The harsh realities of my routine at Stachtenbaste have forced me to confront just how privileged and sheltered my life was at Noetheim. Every day here is a relentless grind of exhaustion and, in my case, with anything training-related, failure.

We reach the training yard and pair off with our sparring partners, having been spared the torture of laps first. I look longingly at the equipment building, wondering what sort of wonderful weapons might be in there that I could use instead of my useless body. I am so busy picturing gleaming sword blades and piercing arrow shafts that I don't even see Dagmar's kick coming. All I can do is react as she lands a hit to my stomach, pushing me back onto my arse on the ground.

Lieutenant Broadbente comes over to us, frowning.

"De Veend, I'd expect you to have at least learned an ounce of technique after a week's worth of training."

I groan as I roll onto my hands and knees, slowly climbing to my feet.

When I say nothing in response, he adds, "Your reaction time is far too slow."

"Trust me, my myriad bruises and I are very aware of that fact, sir," I say as I make eye contact with him upon fully rising from the ground.

His mouth compresses into a line. "If you can't block or counter in time, you need to find a way to throw your opponent off balance. Especially as a means of regaining your footing after a blow."

"I suppose you could say sparring isn't my strongest suit, sir," I say wearily. The admission tastes of defeat on my tongue, heavier and more painful than the bruises on the rest of me.

What I lack in physical ability, I certainly make up for in pride.

Dagmar snorts inelegantly at my words, but thankfully stays silent otherwise.

"Speed of mind can make up for a lack in speed of frame. Try feinting and shifting. Make them commit to the wrong motion. Forget your fists for striking; you lack the strength in your arms. Use the weight of your shoulder or entire frame to knock her over. Sweep her feet out from under her or hook her shin. If she can't stand, she can't swing."

I frown at his advice. "You make it sound so simple."

"It is simple, de Veend," the lieutenant says, "you're not quick, so be clever. Fight like you're cheating. There are no rules in combat besides staying alive."

I consider his words and open my mouth to respond when a hair-raising scream echoes across the training yard from the direction of the gatehouse. Everyone freezes in motion as if uncertain what to do, looking at each other for indications of their subsequent actions.

Who was that? I think. Another scream rends the air, and this one a bit closer than the first.

Lieutenant Broadbente barks at us to stay where we are and runs toward the gatehouse, but none of us listens, and we jog after him.

A group of prisoners is escorted into the lower training yard. I'm puzzled that they all seem to be moving as cautiously and quietly as I did when I arrived, when I hear another scream. My gaze drags toward the officers' training yard, where a grim-looking Lieutenant Colonel Kriegeur is pulling a hysterical man through the gate by a chain draped between the shackles encircling his wrists.

I haven't seen the lieutenant colonel at all since that first morning after I arrived. It initially puzzled me, as I expected the man to be a giant thorn in my side after our initial interaction. Lotti had made offhand mention that he sometimes assists in bringing in the new waves of conscripts by traveling to Embrathal or Fracidaem to retrieve them; I guess this was one of those occasions.

The conscripts are disheveled and dirty; they look exhausted and as broken as I feel. However, the man the lieutenant colonel is dragging is frenzied in his resistance. The whites of his eyes are visible, even from a distance, as they roll back in fear—his head darts from side to side, looking for an escape.

"No, please, gods! No!" The man screams as the lieutenant colonel drags him toward the citadel. Despite Kriegeur's size, he's unable to make swift progress, as the man is resisting him with every ounce of strength he has.

Lieutenant Broadbente and Captain Everbrandt have reached him, and they both offer assistance. Lieutenant Broadbente grabs the man's left arm, Captain Everbrandt his right, while Kriegeur remains holding the man's shackles.

The man begins crying and pleading, snot running down his face and chin as his body shudders with sobs. "Please. No," he says, "I'm innocent! I don't want to go to war."

"It's that or the executioner," Lieutenant Kriegeur says bluntly, and I flinch reflexively at how cold he sounds. That is the voice of the warrior others have told me he is.

"You can't make me fight those savages!" The conscript shouts.

Kriegeur moves to pull the man's chain, but he screams in fear, head butting Kriegeur in the torso. Broadbente and Captain Everbrandt appear so shocked that their grip slackens, and the man breaks away, making a run for the livestock pasture.

With a thunderous expression, the lieutenant colonel gives chase, moving with a speed that belies a man of his size. It's not long before he has reached the hysterical conscript, and I wince sympathetically as he yanks the man back by his tunic, knowing whatever comes next isn't going to be pleasant for anyone witnessing.

Kriegeur grips the man by his throat, fingers digging in to the point of his knuckles going white, and he leans into the conscript's face and says something so quietly I can't hear it. Everyone around me looks just as puzzled. The conscript looks as though he can barely breathe but manages a slight nod and blink of his eyes, and Kriegeur releases his throat. I take a deep breath in sympathy, grateful for the air pushing its way into my lungs.

Colonel Romilde Richter, the managing officer of Stachtenbaste, appears on the path next to the livestock pasture, having come from the direction of the citadel. Captain Everbrandt and Lieutenant Broadbente have joined Kriegeur and Richter in conversation, and there are several minutes of tension while everyone stands and watches the interaction.

A tall woman of about thirty with short, curly black hair and brown skin has made her way up behind the colonel, and I hear Otto ask Lotti who she is, and Lotti tells him that her name is Major Berger. I refuse to move my eyes from the officers' conversation to engage with my fellow cadets in their whispered discussion.

Colonel Richter nods once and steps back, then gestures to the lieutenant colonel and points to the ground. Kriegeur looks pissed. I'm sure his pride is suffering from so many people witnessing the conscript get the better of him, albeit extremely temporarily. He pushes the sobbing man onto his knees on the ground. For his part, the man seems to have been subdued, no longer fighting, just blubbering to himself.

I watch in horror as Colonel Richter unsheathes the sword from the scabbard at her belt, and feel a scream building in my throat that lodges there as abruptly as the conscript's head separates from his body.

A few shouts and screams echo through the crowd of onlookers as the man's head rolls several feet, coming to a stop with his sightless eyes pointing to the sky. His headless body slumps to the ground, blood pouring from the neck onto the grass, creating a massive lake of crimson.

I sway on my feet and feel as though I'm about to faint. The blood steadily pulsing from the man's neck, owing to the still-pumping heart that hasn't yet registered its owner's demise, reminds me of watching my grandmother try to hold her own blood in as it left her abdomen.

I feel a hand reach out to steady me and look over gratefully to see Otto watching me with concern. He doesn't directly ask me, but I can tell by his expression that he wants to know if I'm all right. I stare into his green eyes for several seconds, forcing myself to breathe through my nose, until the wave of dizziness passes and I'm able to nod in confirmation.

I'm not all right, but I'm not in danger of losing consciousness.

Colonel Richter turns to the group of onlookers and says, "The conscript struck a commanding officer during his intake. He was restrained and warned. He was given a chance to stand down. He chose to disregard that." That wasn't what I recalled seeing. Yes, he head butted the lieutenant colonel and tried to run off, but there didn't appear to be much "chance giving" going on.

Colonel Richter continues, "There is no room for hysteria in battle. There is no excuse for cowardice. And there is no justification for violence against the command."

She nods at Kriegeur, who says nothing, before turning on her heel and marching toward the citadel, Major Berger behind her.

Lieutenant Broadbente walks past us and thunders, "Gold Unit, return to your training!"

We all scramble after him, rushing to return to the area of the training yard we had been sparring in. We all nervously group in front of him, waiting for his direction. Captain Everbrandt has followed behind, standing beside us to address him.

"What you just witnessed was entirely preventable. Discipline is what keeps you alive in combat. Lose that, and you lose your place, your rights, and your head." Captain Everbrandt looks across the Gold Unit cadets as he speaks.

Lieutenant Broadbente adds, "You are replaceable. Act accordingly." His eyes meet mine through the crowd, and I feel as though he's speaking directly to me. A frisson of unease dances down my spine.

Captain Everbrandt says, "Let's see if this lesson has spurred any improvement."

The lieutenant nods and says, "Brevic, de Veend. Spar."

Confused, I look around at our unit. No one else has begun sparring. Instead, they've moved to the side, creating a wide circle around me and Dagmar.

"De Veend, you are the weakest hand-to-hand fighter in the unit," Lieutenant Broadbente explains. "That weakness can cost your fellow soldiers their lives. You will spar with Brevic, and we will observe."

My stomach drops. No, he can't mean for me to fight in front of everyone, can he? To put my ineptitude on public display? When no one moves and the officers look at us expectantly, I can see that's precisely what he means.

I turn and face Dagmar with limbs as heavy as iron. Rather than being motivating, watching that man die has had the opposite effect. I just want to curl up in a ball and cry instead.

As if sensing how stricken I am, Dagmar sneers. "Well, de Veend, unless wars are fought with etiquette and tea parties, you're as good as dead."

The casual cruelty of her remark cuts me deeper than a blade would, and it drives home a brutal reality: I might actually end up on a battlefield. Lord Rocheburn's warning—that Stachtenbaste was meant to "jog my memory"—looms darker in my mind. Maybe if I can figure out a plausible lie, it would give Agnethe and me enough time to escape and get me out of this place.

Before I can spiral further, though, Dagmar kicks me in the gut again, knocking me flat on my back. I'm once again stunned, the wind knocked out of me, unable to move. Dagmar's face appears as she stands above me, leaning over so I can witness the full force of her contempt.

Something primal stirs within me upon seeing that derision. The events of the past several weeks run rapid fire through my head: the tragedy I was forced to witness, the fear I was forced to feel, the pain I am forced to endure. On top of all of that, this woman acts as though she is somehow superior to me. As if she holds a majority on misery.

A red haze washes over my vision, and without thinking and with more speed than I would've ever imagined myself capable, I sweep my leg out, catching both of Dagmar's with it. Completely off guard, Dagmar falls to the ground like a stone. I seize my opportunity and roll on top of her, pulling my arm back and striking her across the face.

I want to scream at the pain radiating from my hand. It was not elegant. It was not smooth. It was not skilled. But damn it, it felt good.

Dagmar grins at me, blood from a split lip smearing on her teeth. "Finally going to fight back, are we?"

I stare, puzzled at her remark, but the adrenaline coursing through my veins is invigorating.

Lieutenant Broadbente steps forward and looks at me. "Good. Catching your opponent off guard and off balance is the right choice."

Pride fills my being, and I feel my shoulders lift in response.

He continues, "Now, however, you must do it consistently, and finish the fight when it counts. If Brevic wanted to, she could have taken you out when you paused after you punched her."

And just like that, my pride is gone.

I roll off Dagmar and struggle to my feet, brushing the grass from my pants. Clenching my jaw, I look past the lieutenant and clash eyes with Captain Everbrandt, who watches me with an inscrutable expression. Irritated by his intense study, I notch my chin up slightly. His lips twitch in response, as if he's trying not to smile.

Surprise tingles in my stomach, and my cheeks flush, but I force myself to turn to Dagmar and assume my sparring stance, determination flooding my limbs.

I won't end up like that conscript. I will get out of here, and I will save my sister.

Gritting my teeth, I look Dagmar in the eye and yell, "Again!"

CHAPTER FOURTEEN
Nachtrif and Nightmares

I've never imagined I'd make a big mark on the world or even at Stachtenbaste. I've never been one to flaunt any talents or intellect. But I thought I'd at least leave some kind of imprint that signifies I was *here* after I'm gone. I didn't realize that mark would come so soon.

Of course, the imprint I'm currently leaving is one in the shape of my rear end in the grass of the training yard, Dagmar having flattened me *again*.

My success in sparring with her several days ago seems to have been a fleeting moment of brilliance. A spark of flame in kindling—impressive for an instant, but then gone just as quickly as it arrived, leaving only the smell of singed pride.

Otto leans over me from the left, his hefty frame blocking the sun's brightest rays. "Is she unconscious?"

Lotti's head appears next on my right. "She's blinking. I think that's a no then."

Cyneric's face emerges from above my head. "Perhaps she needs a moment to recover. Did she hit her head?"

Berte slides in next to Otto. "I don't think so; she just got knocked on her arse."

Jarl shoulders up beside Lotti, frowning. "Maybe she got stunned."

Otto looks me in the eye and begins speaking slowly and loudly, as if I'm too addlebrained to understand, "Greta? Are you all right? Do you need to go to the infirmary?"

"Do you need water?" Lotti asks, dangling a skin from her hand and speaking just as slowly.

I look at each of the five faces staring at me, irritated. "I'm fine. Berte's right. I just got knocked on my arse."

Jarl and Otto hold their hands out to me, and I take one from each of them, allowing them to pull me to standing, gritting my teeth as my sore muscles groan in protest. I place my palms on my backside and rub a few times, trying to soothe the ache there. It's a good thing I've so much padding there, or it might be far more bruised considering how frequently I fall on it during training.

I gratefully accept the waterskin from Lotti and take several deep gulps before handing it back to her. Cyneric, Jarl, and Berte have joined Stigander, Lillen, and Brock as they head toward the citadel for the afternoon meal, having finished morning training. Lotti and Otto remain behind, waiting for me.

After we eat, we'll head to the infirmary for this week's work-duty rotations. I've found I am far more comfortable in the den of the healers, working in the apothecary or with those who are injured or ill, than I was in the kitchen. Sorting bandages for wounds and herbs for medicines is certainly easier compared to the back-breaking drudgery of kitchen work.

I stretch my arms above my head and rotate my neck, trying to work out the kinks. I turn to Otto and Lotti to tell them I'm ready to head to the citadel when I hear steps behind us.

"Well, well, well, she's finally standing. I thought for sure they'd have to haul you to the citadel by your ankles, de Veend," Mette Bosques drawls at me as she, Belinda, and Hartwin slowly stroll by us.

Belinda smirks. "She should be used to lying flat on her back, don't you think?"

"She certainly looks like she spends a lot of time on it," Hartwin says, his pale eyes trailing slowly up and down my body, which leaves me feeling like I need a bath.

Lotti, Otto, and I all stiffen at their words. I open my mouth to respond, but someone beats me to it.

"If your sparring were half as sharp as your tongues, you might actually be dangerous," Dagmar says as she saunters out of the equipment shed.

All of us turn toward her in surprise. My jaw nearly hits the ground. Since I managed to knock her over, Dagmar's demeanor has continued to be reserved, but I have felt a shift in our interactions. She's stopped treating me as if I'm something beneath her shoe and more like someone she can at least tolerate. And I haven't even had to do any of her work duties.

Belinda looks incensed as she addresses Dagmar, "What did you say to me?"

Dagmar smirks. "You know exactly what I said. If you spent less time sneering at others and being a cunt, you might finally be able to hold your own in training."

Belinda's face is bright red. "Why, you—"

Captain Everbrandt is suddenly striding toward us, his expression one of impatience. "You'll miss your meal if you dawdle before your afternoon work duties and training."

He doesn't move; he simply watches us stonily until we all turn and hurry toward the citadel. Belinda tosses a look at us that promises retribution before stalking off. I keep my steps purposefully slow so that the trio of toads surges ahead rather than walks beside us.

"Thank you," I say to Dagmar, "for defending me."

She grunts and then picks up her pace, enlarging the distance between her and us.

I look over my shoulder as we walk toward the dining hall and see the solitary figure of Captain Everbrandt still where we left him, watching, a thoughtful look on his face. I suddenly want to know everything he's thinking, no matter how mundane.

Flushing, I turn my head back around, hoping Lotti and Otto haven't noticed, and smile at Lotti, who definitely *has* noticed me ogling the handsome captain. She says nothing, though, instead looping her arm through mine. Otto smiles at us both, and a pleasant warmth settles in my belly. I'm not sure what I expected to find beside misery when I came to Stachtenbaste, but allies would've been last on my list of possibilities.

Still sore from this morning's training, I walk stiffly through the door to the infirmary building following the afternoon meal. My first encounter with the infirmary was soon after I arrived, when I was issued my requisite pregnancy-prevention tonic. The visit would have been far more humiliating if the head matron, a practical, no-nonsense woman called Hildegarde, hadn't been so blasé about it.

The infirmary at Stachtenbaste is medically advanced, the healers and apothecary accustomed to treating gruesome wounds earned in training and of the Aurengarte officers during patrol duties, as well as any number of maladies and afflictions. Some of the conscripts arrive in rough shape from whatever holding jails they've come from and require treatment before they can begin training. There are lung and stomach ailments that come in waves through the compound, and then there are those who suffer from "wounds not of the training field," as Hildegarde told me when giving a tonic to one of the new conscripts who was feverish, shaking, and screaming at horrors only he could see.

Should they fall ill, the officers and wealthy visitors benefit from the ministrations of Zan Amalric, one of the magically blessed healers capable of stitching together wounds and remedying illness in the time it would take me to count to sixty. Everyone else sees the matrons for whatever ails them.

I pass through the rows of beds toward the matrons' station to check in. The air smells sharply of herbs and tinctures, their astringency only barely masking the odor of sweat-soaked bed linens.

"She lives to see another day," Hildegarde says wryly, without looking up from the log in which she's writing.

"Just barely," I quip, smiling slightly. Of the servants and permanent residents I've met at Stachtenbaste so far, Hildegarde is one of my favorites. She has a low tolerance for fools but enormous compassion for the sick and injured. At times she reminds me of my grandmother; at others, of Valda. I find myself wanting to be near her, if only to remind myself of the two older women I miss so much it hurts.

"It's bandages you'll be sorting and folding today," Hildegarde says, as if I've done anything else during my other shifts. With how many bandages I've ripped, sorted, and folded, I would think that Stachtenbaste was on the brink of being smothered by the mound of linen, but there seems to be a never-ending demand.

I head to the supply room where Lillen and Brock soon join me, and we sit in quiet while we complete the monotonous task of tearing old bed linens too worn to be used for their original purpose into long strips of bandage. Of the members of my team, I interact with them the least. Lillen, because she's older and seems mostly uninterested in me, and Brock, because he is painfully shy and barely speaks to anyone. But sitting in total silence while ripping strips of linen quickly gets boring, and to keep my mind distracted from my circumstances and worrying about Agnethe, I've tried to chat with them here and there.

I've learned that Brock was arrested after attempting to skip his duties in the Caelish mines for several days because of a lung complaint. He was offered either time in the work camps or training here as a conscript. The benefit of the work camps is that your sentence is reduced. The drawback is that there is even less freedom there than at Stachtenbaste and even worse conditions. Even now, Brock is thin and fragile, his skin even whiter than mine, but lacking my perpetual pink flush.

Lillen was a tenant farmer on a Verdantian Aurenclaste family's lands, barely making enough in crop sales to survive after giving her dues to the vassal. She attempted to withhold several pounds of potatoes to sell at the market and claimed a blight had taken them. When it was discovered that she had lied, she was arrested for stealing.

In both cases, their stories are those of hardship, of pain, and of sorrow. I feel great sympathy for them both. They were only trying to stay whole in a world determined to shatter them. It seems criminal to me that our rulers and leaders would, at best, turn a blind eye to the suffering and oppression of their citizens and, at worst, actively participate in their subjugation in favor of benefit to a select few.

I debate whether I should strike up more conversation to fill the silence and distract myself from my body's general misery, wishing for the hundredth time that I had Lotti, Otto, or Cyneric to talk to. Gods, even Dagmar and Stigander make more conversation than this.

The infirmary requires minimal assistance from cadets, though, since they don't trust us to be unsupervised with many of the supplies. Because of the nature of the work, they are usually adequately staffed with permanent residents and servants to perform actual healing duties, so our team is split across menial supply tasks here and with the fletcher making arrows for training and the Aurengarte guards on watch.

A loud bang comes from the front room, as if the door has been flung open and crashed against the wall with force. Brock, Lillen, and I startle at the noise and look at each other wordlessly when the sounds of several frantic voices and pained screams fill the space.

Hildegarde comes rushing into the room, looking uncharacteristically frazzled, and says, "Don't just sit there gawping, come help us!"

All three of us drop our linen strips and awkwardly pile into the main room, where Captain Everbrandt and an Aurengarte guard are holding down a soldier in a ripped and bloodied Aurengarte uniform in one of the beds. Blood pours from a wound on the soldier's left abdomen. For a moment, sounds are muffled, my vision blurs, and I'm back in my grandmother's sitting room. Watching her bleed out on the rug. It feels like a different lifetime to now.

"Cadet," Hildegarde barks at me, snapping me out of my daze. "Grab one of his legs. I need him still while I examine and treat the wound."

Brock and I each take one of the soldier's legs, pressing them into the mattress to still his thrashing. At the same time, Hildegarde orders Lillen to grab a knife, bandages, water, a strip of leather, and, from the apothecary, a sedative tonic and whiskey. While Lillen runs off to gather supplies, Hildegarde briskly cuts the soldier's tunic and trousers from his body and discards them. I can't even be embarrassed by the man's nudity; his injury is too ghastly, his suffering too pronounced.

"Tell me what happened," Hildegarde commands Captain Everbrandt as she probes the soldier's torso, much to his distress. If I weren't struggling to hold the soldier's leg down, I would raise my eyebrows at how she spoke to the officer.

He doesn't seem to think anything of it and replies, "Krahbek sparring with Rafe."

"Rafe?" Hildegarde asks.

"Lieutenant Colonel Kriegeur," he clarifies. I *do* raise my eyebrows this time at the informality with which Captain Everbrandt refers to the lieutenant colonel. Could they be friends? The idea makes me frown.

"So sparring with a man well known for his skill in the deadly arts with his weapon of choice. Not the wisest decision," Hildegarde quips.

"Yes, matron," Captain Everbrandt confirms. "He challenged the lieutenant colonel to a match, attempted to win by cheating, and caught himself on the spear tip of the krahbek the lieutenant colonel was wielding."

Hildegarde frowns. "He's lucky the lieutenant colonel wasn't actually attempting to inflict damage, or he'd be meeting Detlef in the crypt instead of me. I've seen more than my fair share of krahbek wounds, and they're never pretty."

I swallow hard.

Lillen returns with the items Hildegarde requested, and the matron proceeds to stick the strip of leather between the soldier's teeth, instructing him to bite down, and pours water over the wound in the man's side.

He groans, but his thrashing doesn't worsen; it's lessened, owing to the fatigue from his injury setting in and blood loss. However, his calm is short lived because Hildegarde pours the whiskey over the wound next. He screams so loud the hair raises on my arms, and I watch as Captain Everbrandt shoves the leather strip back into his mouth and tells him to keep biting down.

The captain's eyes meet mine then, and I wonder what thoughts are racing behind their chocolate depths. Is he upset? Anxious? Angry? He's difficult to read. My attention returns to the injured soldier, when Brock is suddenly thrown back by the kicking of the man's leg. Lillen dives in and pushes down. The sinew in her arms, honed by years of back-breaking labor, bulges as she does so.

"Why don't you give him the tonic?" Lillen asks Hildegarde.

"It's got henbane," Hildegarde says, as if that should mean something.

"So?" Lillen says.

Brock has regained his footing and moves beside Hildegarde, handing her the items she asks for in terse instructions.

"Henbane is finicky. Easy to give too much, and then you're in trouble."

"Why?" Brock asks as he hands Hildegarde a knife.

"Because it will kill them," she explains. "I only asked for it in case it's absolutely necessary. The tip of the spear broke off and is lodged in his wound. I'll have to dig it out."

I swallow hard, dread pooling in my gut. Hildegarde wastes no time in digging the blade into the man's side. I look up at the ceiling as I hold onto the man's leg, my arms growing tired from the effort of holding him down while he struggles against us, shouting.

Why didn't he faint? People in novels always faint when they feel extreme pain; shouldn't that be happening? In this moment, I am greatly disappointed in the accuracy of those novels.

Hildegarde makes a slight sound of triumph and holds up a bloodied shard of metal between her fingertips. "Right; time to cauterize," she says.

"What?" I whisper and see Brock's face blanch. I wouldn't have thought it possible for him to turn even whiter.

"Have to stop the bleeding," Hildegarde explains. This time, she does reach for the henbane tonic, but only drops one or two drops onto the man's tongue before resealing it and picking up a new knife.

She walks to the nearest hearth and sticks the blade into the open flame, waiting until the metal is nearly glowing. The soldier's thrashing has become more sluggish, whether from further blood loss or the addition of the henbane to his system, I'm not sure. I'm able to relax my hold on his leg slightly, my biceps twitching in response to the sudden lack of tension.

Hildegarde returns to the man's side and looks at me, Lillen, Captain Everbrandt, and the other Aurengarte soldier, saying, "Right. He moves too much, and I'll cut him more. Greta, Lillen, keep those legs still. Lie on them, if you must."

Lillen and I look at each other and shrug, then lie across the soldier's legs. Unfortunately, this puts me right in position of having a prime view of the wound. I watch in mounting horror, unable to tear my eyes away, as Hildegarde brings the heated blade to the soldier's side and presses the flat side of it to the open wound, and the smell of his burning flesh fills my nostrils.

A hair-raising, bloodcurdling scream rises from the man's throat before he finally, thankfully, succumbs to unconsciousness.

Everyone immediately releases their hold on him, and Lillen and I roll off his legs. I stand on shaky legs, unsure what to do, until Hildegarde instructs Captain Everbrandt and the other soldier to move the man to one of the beds in the corner, where he can rest more peacefully. Lillen follows behind them with additional supplies, and Brock is sent off to gather some of the linen strips we had made to cover the man's cauterized wound in case it opens or weeps.

I bend down to gather the man's clothing, which is covered in the discarded bandages Hildegarde used to absorb blood as she dug out the spear tip from his side. When I move a set of bloodied linen, the warmth I feel on my fingers fills me with revulsion, and the urge to lose my lunch is so strong I have to take several steadying, deep breaths through my nose to quell my nausea.

When I move the bandages, something glints among the fabric of the soldier's pants. I pick up a small gold coin with a symbol etched into it: a single, cresting wave with three teardrops falling from its highest point. I recognize it as the sigil of Aquaemus, the god of the sea.

This must be a gods' token. An item used to pay favor to one of the gods. I've read that Navisians toss coins with Aquaemus's sigil into the fountains that dot the province, to pay homage to the ocean god and receive the wish he is said to grant for such an offering.

I'm surprised that an Aurengarte soldier has a token made of gold that he hasn't yet offered to the god, considering its value. It must have some sentimental meaning to him, I realize. I drop the coin into my pocket to hold for him until he wakes. It must be important if he carried it all the way with him from Navisia.

"You did well," a deep voice says behind me.

I jump and spin around to face Captain Everbrandt, who has managed to sneak up on me while I was deep in thought.

"What do you mean?" I ask, puzzled.

He explains, "In assisting the matron. You did well. You didn't panic, and you held your own."

I feel a flush rise in my cheeks. "Oh, thank you. I didn't really think; I just reacted."

"And that tells me you have good instincts," he counters.

"Thank you, sir," I reply.

We stand there awkwardly for several seconds before he clears his throat, looks away, and says, "Yes, well, um…I just wanted to tell you that I was impressed."

With that, he turns on his heel and exits the infirmary, leaving me to stare after him in shocked silence.

A moon of the palest shade of pink hangs overhead.

I stand in the clearing, holding the signet ring, running my finger over its ridged surface. It has to mean something, this ring with the raven's head, the aviary. But what? I feel like I'm on the cusp of figuring that out, but can't make the last connection.

A breeze shuffles the leaves above me, and they flicker ominously in the moon's beams, their forms casting eerie shadows on the forest floor.

I feel the air move beside my ear again, and I scream, wondering what monster the night has sent to find me. When I turn in the direction of the air movement, however, there's nothing and no one there.

I spin in circles, looking for an answer, a sign, anything that tells me what's going on, why I'm here.

Seek the sign where shadow and feather meet.

I look back toward the aviary and square my shoulders, deciding it's where I need to go for answers. I slide the ring onto my finger for safekeeping and march resolutely toward the doorway.

When I cross the threshold, the whispers start.

They're less fuzzy this time, more discernible; snippets of consonants and vowels make their way to my ears.

"Who are you?" A whisper asks.

"I'm Greta," I say, shakily.

"Greta who?"

I turn in another circle, looking for the source of the voice. "Greta de Veend," I say, distractedly.

"Where are you?" The whisper-voice inquires.

I pause, frowning. "What do you mean, where am I? I'm here, in this stupid aviary. Where are you?" I'm not even pretending to be polite at this point.

Silence meets my question, and the whispers in the aviary abruptly stop. Unnerved, I dig my fingernails into my palms, feeling the edge of the signet ring cut into the skin of my fingers.

Suddenly, a scream erupts in the dark, coming from out in the forest, and I'd know that voice anywhere.

"Agnethe!" I gasp and dash from the aviary and into the woods.

Another scream rents the silence, and I try my best to follow its direction through the trees, barely breathing, barely seeing, barely thinking.

I follow a third scream through the trees and onto a narrow ledge of rock overlooking a churning, frothy river. Only, instead of glittering black with the shadows of night, it's scarlet and thick.

Blood, *I think*, the river is filled with blood.

Horrified, I turn to try to escape from this nightmare and hear another scream.

"Agnethe!" I yell in response. The screams are coming from across the river. She's on the opposite riverbank.

I must get to her. I pull off my boots, braid back my hair, and tuck the ring into one of the snug pockets of my pants.

I step to the edge of the rock ledge and watch for several seconds as the river flows, the speed and turmoil causing red froth to stir where it meets the rocky shore. I brace myself, not sure what to expect. Will it feel like blood? Will it taste like blood? But I shake it off, because all of that is irrelevant if it means getting to my sister.

"I'm coming, Agnethe," I whisper into the night, and dive into the crimson water.

I wake abruptly, sitting up in my bed, heart pounding.

In the quiet solitude of the sleeping dormitory, I hear the ominous clang of bells coming from the temple outbuilding. I see cadets rushing to dress—pulling on trousers, yanking boots over stockinged feet, securing tunics in place, tying back unruly hair.

I look around the room for Lotti and Otto but don't see them. I whip around in the other direction and meet Dagmar's icy blue gaze. She sits across from me calmly on her bed, as if waiting for me to ask what is happening.

I don't waste any time. "What in the world is happening, Dagmar?"

She looks at me grimly. "The *Nachtrif.*"

CHAPTER FIFTEEN
Wings on Stone and Broken Bones

I rush to dress, pulling on the uniform pants I had discarded before bed, my tunic, and boots. Dagmar is also dressing, though with less urgency than some of the other cadets.

"What's the *Nachtrif?*" I ask Dagmar, watching in confusion as cadets hurry around the dormitory before barreling out the door.

She looks at me and says, "You'll find out soon enough."

She stands, brushing invisible lint from the front of her pants, and then turns abruptly and heads to the exit. I watch her, afraid and exasperated, and only look around after she's disappeared entirely through the doorway.

Lotti rushes over to me. "Greta! We have to go," she says, breathlessly.

I will ask her what this is all about, but I don't have time before she grabs my arm and pulls me up from my bed, forcing me to follow along or fall over.

We thunder down the spiral stairs so quickly I'm dizzy by the time we finish our descent. We rush toward the front door and out of the building, falling in with the mass of other cadets and Aurengarte soldiers doing the same. I look around, confused as to why we're going outside and where we're headed.

"I don't understand, Lotti," I say, still allowing her to pull me along by my arm as we tramp down the stairs from the outcropping to the training yard. Everyone is moving on the gravel path that snakes alongside the northwest end of the outcropping, past the orchard and the kitchen gardens.

"It's the *Nachtrif*," Lotti says, not stopping her forward march, shoving her way through the throngs of cadets and soldiers.

"So I've heard! But what is it?" I yell to her so I can be heard over the din.

Lotti stops suddenly, and I go crashing into her back. The person behind me collides with my body, giving me a dirty look before continuing, and soon everyone parts around me and Lotti as we stand on the gravel path, rejoining once they've passed us.

"No one told you?" Lotti asks, her face a pale oval in the full moon's light.

"Told me *what?*" I throw up my hands in an "obviously not" shrug gesture.

"The *Nachtrif* happens every month on the full moon," Lotti begins, looking around nervously.

"Okay, and?" I question.

"It's a fight," she blurts.

Well, that explains the literal translation from old Aurelian for "night fight."

I frown. "Who's fighting?"

"Two cadets," Lotti says. "It's a sparring match between two cadets. Everyone else watches."

"That's awful," I say, still feeling as though she's holding something back. "But why are you so worried about it? Is it you?"

Lotti looks at her feet before looking me in the eye. "No, Greta, they usually pick two of the newest cadets."

I wrack my brain, thinking of the latest batch of cadets to arrive with the man Colonel Richter beheaded.

"But how are they going to fight?" I ask her. "The ones who lived are in isolation in the infirmary with a lung ailment." I know because I heard Hildegarde talking about it to one of the other matrons. One had already died, and the others were not well. "Do they make them fight anyway?"

"No," Lotti says quietly.

I think of those who arrived before this last batch. "But that would mean…" I look at Lotti; her facial expression confirms my train of thought.

Otto…and me.

Lotti looks stricken with fear. "I'm *so* sorry, Greta, I had no idea you didn't know!"

"They're going to make Otto and me fight?" I ask, my voice rising in pitch along with my apprehension.

Lotti nods. "Most likely."

"But how can they do this without the officers knowing?" I question, thinking of just how many people were exiting the citadel on our way here. Even now, people are still streaming past us.

"Greta, the officers run the *Nachtrif*," Lotti tells me.

I'm truly fucked.

I know Otto won't hurt me if he can help it, but he also must listen to orders, and he's bigger than I am, and while he's not any more coordinated, he has the advantage of far superior strength.

Lotti loops her arm through mine and gently pulls me along the gravel path. I stubbornly and stupidly want to dig in my heels and refuse to go, but I know that's not possible, so I don't put up a fight as she ushers me behind the thinning group of soldiers.

We shuffle along the path past the gardens to the stone wall that encases the upper training field with the arena Lotti had mentioned, but I hadn't questioned her on it again. If only I had thought to do so, I could've feigned illness or injury to get out of this.

As we enter through the gate to the arena grounds, I'm struck by how large the additional field is that surrounds it. It's difficult to appreciate from beyond the stone walls that enclose it. The amphitheater, a colossal round structure, climbs several stories above us, and torches line the outside to light the way to the multiple arched doorways spaced equidistantly along the perimeter. The crowd slows its progression as we near the doorways, and the congestion of the number of people causes delays in entering the arena.

Lieutenant Broadbente spots us from his vantage point near one of the doorways and comes trotting over, presumably to inform me of my gruesome fate. He looks unusually frazzled for a man whose demeanor is normally so calm. I've often wondered if he takes sedative tonics.

"Grieves," he nods to Lotti before turning to me. "De Veend, wait for my signal, you may not have to fight. Aric is trying to convince Rafe to choose someone else."

"Aric?" I ask, perplexed.

Lieutenant Broadbente shakes his head, as if chastising himself. "Captain Everbrandt."

Aric, I think to myself. The name suits him.

"Why do you think the captain will be able to convince him?" I ask as we shuffle through the doorway to the arena.

"Because they're cousins," the lieutenant answers plainly.

My eyes snap up to meet his. "*What?*"

He nods. "The captain's mother was Lord Corvilian's sister."

"Was?" Lotti asks.

Broadbente looks uncomfortable, as if he realizes he's been airing his superior officer's sordid family history. "She's dead." He doesn't offer any more explanation.

"Thank you for trying to help me," I tell him, unsure what else to say.

He nods. "Don't thank me yet. You'll know soon enough if we're successful."

He nods at us both and heads into the arena, disappearing into the crowd of people making their way to the stands. As the horde of people thins, I'm able to see row upon row of stone seats towering above us, pitched at an angle so the rows farther back can still view whatever destruction is occurring in the center ring. Cadets and Aurengarte alike press in on the rows closest to the ring, shoulder to shoulder, their voices chanting, braying laughs echoing, the light from the torch brackets driven into the stone glinting off their sharp eyes and even sharper smiles. They are hungry for blood, not just out of sheer cruelty, but relief that they aren't the ones being thrown into the fight.

When we climb to our seats, we find Otto waiting. He's just as nervous as I am. I look down into the center ring, and my eyes immediately find the tall figure of Captain Everbrandt, who is standing on a raised stone dais at one end of the ring in Kriegeur's imposing shadow. The lieutenant colonel is currently listening to the captain speak, his massive arms crossed over his massive chest, a scowl fixed on his face like a petulant child.

"Maybe you'll be able to get out of it," Lotti says hopefully.

I don't want to pin all my wishes on the lieutenant and captain—Aric—being able to convince the brutish lieutenant colonel not to subject me to the fight, especially since I very recently insulted him publicly. I turn to look longingly at the doorway through which we just entered, wondering if I can make a break for it. Beyond it, the tallest towers of the citadel are just visible over the edge of the arena walls, rising high and silent, mute witnesses to the ritual violence that's to occur this night.

Despite its size, the crowd falls eerily silent as Kriegeur claps Aric on the shoulder and steps forward to address the audience. It's then that I notice the limp Lotti mentioned on my first day. Each step taken with his left leg is quicker than his right, telling me he favors it and places more weight on his right side. I would feel sympathy if the man weren't about to order my beating.

"Welcome to the *Nachtrif!*" He says as he throws his arms out dramatically, grinning when the crowd cheers wildly. He waits for several seconds, while the noise dies down, before continuing, "For those unfamiliar with our tradition, tonight is not about drills or rules. Tonight is about proving you can hold your own in battle. Tonight, you prove you belong." He's turned his head to our section of the stands, and, even though he's far away, I swear he's looking directly at me as he speaks.

Fear spikes my blood pressure to an alarming pace.

He turns away from my section and addresses another, but his commanding voice booms across the space, even so. "Two cadets," he says, holding up two fingers, "enter the ring. The rest of us get to watch what happens when the illusions of safety, sympathy, and camaraderie are stripped away."

A snort sounds behind us, and I turn to see Stigander, Berte, Cyneric, and Jarl seated there.

"There's safety here?" Berte asks sarcastically.

"Don't forget the sympathy," Stigander reminds her.

"It's almost beautiful in its simplicity," continues the lieutenant colonel. "Some think this a punishment. Others, a lesson. I prefer to think of it as entertainment." He grins again as the crowd cheers, and I wish I could challenge *him* to a fight just to wipe that stupid smile off his face.

"At least we're entertaining," Cyneric says behind me.

"Entertainment, yes," Kriegeur continues and turns toward our section again. I freeze.

He continues, "But with purpose. The enemy won't wait for you to catch your breath on the battlefield. Your commanding officer won't hold your hand as you ease gently into combat. Training makes you a soldier. Conflict. Struggle. *Pain.* That's what makes you a fighter. That's how soldiers become warriors."

The crowd cheers, and my team remains silent in the aftermath of his words. I can't disagree with his sentiment, but I fail to see why the *Nachtrif* is necessary, considering war will make us "fighters" soon enough.

"Normally," he proceeds, "we ask the two newest cadets to join us and prove their mettle in the arena. By request of our most esteemed Captain Everbrandt, and after some consideration, tonight's match will feature a bit of a change."

The crowd collectively sits on the edges of their seats, waiting to hear what the change might be. My fingers are digging into the palms of my hands so hard I'm certain I'll draw blood at any moment. Kriegeur turns to our section of the stands again, and this time I'm positive he's staring directly at me.

"Cadet de Veend will not be facing Cadet Weber," he announces, and the crowd starts booing. I almost sag in relief. Thank the gods the captain convinced him not to make me fight. Kriegeur waits patiently to continue speaking until the noise dies down. Even I'm curious about the change now that the threat of the fight is gone.

"As I said, Cadet de Veend will not be facing Cadet Weber. She will face Cadet Bradleye."

The crowd roars with excitement, and I feel like I'm observing it all from above. My brain has separated from my body in an act of self-preservation. I see Belinda's dark head emerge from the stands across from ours, and she makes her way down the stairs to the center of the arena. I stand slowly and make eye contact with each member of my team.

Lotti and Otto are holding hands and looking worried.

Cyneric reaches out and pats my hand in sympathy.

Jarl nods his carroty head at me encouragingly.

Berte lifts her chin at me as if to tell me not to let them see me afraid.

Stigander is the first one to speak, "Make her work for it."

I swallow hard and nod in silent thanks to each of them before I sidle past Lotti and onto the stairs nearest us and begin descending them toward the arena. As I pass, there are jeers and catcalls, whistles, and a few shouts of encouragement. I'm about to break through the stands to climb into the arena when I feel a hand slap my arse hard.

Incensed, I turn toward the offending soldier, a stocky man with short blonde hair and a leering grin.

"What?" He asks innocently. "Just trying to show my support."

A boot hits his torso in the vulnerable, fleshy part of his side, and he's knocked to the ground. Startled, I look to the row above him and directly into Dagmar's icy blue eyes.

"What?" She questions, sounding just as innocent as the soldier. "My foot slipped."

No one argues with her recount of events. *I bet Dagmar wouldn't be afraid if she had to do this*, I think bitterly.

The closer I get to the ring, the shakier my knees become, and by the time my boots hit the dirt floor, I am barely holding myself up. Despite Dagmar's taunts to Belinda that she isn't a good fighter, her frame is tall and lean, and her toned muscles indicate a body well-versed in athletic pursuits. I've been here for a few weeks and have yet to notice any change in my own fleshy figure. I even still get winded on the stairs to the dormitory.

I move slowly toward the platform where Kriegeur is standing with Belinda. Something dark flutters in the periphery of my vision, and I turn my eyes to see an enormous black bird land on one of the pillars on the upper stands of the arena.

A raven.

It's black as coal and unnaturally still, almost like it's observing the ring from its perch. The flickering torchlight casts amber shadows that dance over the arena floor and the stands. Where the raven sits, however, seems shrouded in shadow save for the faint glow of the moon that casts an iridescent shimmer on its feathers.

Like when I sat in the stands and watched Kriegeur speak, I can't see its eyes, but I swear it's staring directly at me. My scalp tingles faintly, whether from awareness or foreboding, I can't be sure.

What is a raven doing this close to people? I don't know much about them, but they were a particular favorite of my grandfather, Hrafn, and there were several books on ravens at Noetheim. I seem to recall reading that they're fairly solitary. This one, however, appears wholly unbothered by the roar of the crowd, a silent but willing spectator of the carnage that's about to unfold.

I climb the steps on the platform and stop when I'm a few feet away from the lieutenant colonel and Belinda. They're both smiling at me, the lieutenant colonel with excitement, Belinda with derision.

"How kind of you to join us before we expire, cadet," Kriegeur says, and I feel my eyebrows draw inward in a scowl.

Doesn't he have the decency to at least *pretend* he's not looking forward to seeing me get my arse whooped? I send a silent prayer to the Sisters that I pass out quickly and don't have to endure for long.

"I don't think someone of her size is capable of moving any quicker," Belinda says snidely.

A throat clears behind Kriegeur, and the three of us turn to see Captain Everbrandt standing there, eyebrow raised at Belinda. She has the intelligence to flush and look embarrassed, but doesn't apologize to me. The captain then turns his gaze on his cousin, who seems completely unfazed by his irritation.

"Is there an issue, cousin?" Kriegeur asks him blithely.

"A moment with my unit member, *cousin?*" The captain asks.

Kriegeur raises a dark eyebrow right back at Captain Everbrandt. "That is not customary, but I see no harm. Thirty seconds," he warns, and the captain grabs my arm and pulls me to the side of the platform.

"I couldn't get you out of this; I'm sorry. Rafe's creativity seems to only extend to this form of cruel punishment," the captain explains to me.

"You didn't have to do that, especially since it seems as though many go through this. It's hardly singling me out or even a punishment," I tell him.

He frowns. "You misunderstand. He is punishing *me* for asking."

"Then why ask?" I question him.

The captain opens his mouth to respond when the lieutenant colonel's voice barks out, "Fifteen seconds!"

"Remember what Eduart—Lieutenant Broadbente—told you. Take her by surprise. Be clever," he instructs me. He looks like he'll say more, but then Kriegeur walks over.

"Time's up on the conference, cousin." He jerks his head toward the area of the stands where officers are sitting, watching, as if telling him to go up there.

The captain hesitates for several seconds, and Kriegeur says curtly, "Dismissed."

The tone of his voice, deep and intimidating, raises the hairs on my forearms and seems to snap the captain out of his internal battle. He nods at me and quits the platform, going up to where the other officers are seated.

Kriegeur ushers us down the platform stairs and to the middle of the ring.

"Right then," Kriegeur turns to me and Belinda. "Rule number one, cadets: there are no rules. Rule number two: no killing blows."

Belinda frowns. "But you just said there aren't any rules—"

Kriegeur has turned away from us already to address the crowd, apparently too stupid to notice his mistake. If I weren't so terrified, it would be laughable.

"Officers, members of the Aurengarte, cadets," he booms. "Proelian is surely looking down on us with favor," he adds, referring to the god of war. "Cadets, prepare to fight."

I step back from Belinda nervously and watch as she effortlessly assumes a sparring stance. I try to mirror her and am sure I look nowhere near as practiced.

Kriegeur climbs back up onto the platform and waits for the crowd to quiet before yelling, "*NACHTRIF, HEB AN!*"

Nachtrif, begin.

My heart pounds so loudly that the noise of the crowd sounds far away. I'm not ready. But I've been struck before, haven't I? I've been bruised and I've bled and I've survived. I can survive this, too.

Suddenly, she charges at me and her fist plows into my gut. My breath whooshes from between my lips as I stagger backward from the force of the strike. Immediately following, I realize two things. One, I was right that Belinda is a far better athlete. And two, unbelievably, it seems Dagmar has been going easy on me the whole time.

I try to recall the advice of Lieutenant Broadbente and Captain Everbrandt and think cleverly. When Belinda moves toward me again, I crouch low and sweep my leg out, trying to catch her off balance. My foot connects with her leg, and she stumbles but doesn't lose her balance.

She swings her fist at me, and I barely have time to bring my arms up to protect my face from the blow. The crack against my forearm sends pain shooting up to my shoulder. The crowd cheers. Not my name or even Belinda's. Just the indiscernible chorus of fevered bloodlust. We could be anyone, and they would yell all the same.

I stagger back, my booted feet kicking up dust clouds from the dirt floor. With one arm blocking her, my side is vulnerable, and I realize my mistake of leaving it open too late. Her other fist slams into my ribs, in a similar area to where Dagmar first hit me. It's not a punch, but a battering ram, fueled by Belinda's superior strength and her anger at my audacity in trying to fight back. For a moment, I can't breathe. My body folds, my ribs screaming in protest, but I don't fall. Not yet. While hunched over and appearing completely incapacitated, I bring my own arms up, wrap them around her torso and land a quick jab to her kidney.

With a howl of pain-fueled rage, Belinda spins around until she's behind me and kicks the back of my knee, forcing it into a bent position, which makes me drop like a stone to the ground. On one knee, I start to push off the dirt to resume standing when she kicks me in the side. The pain is blinding and sharp in my lower back just beneath my ribs. It jolts up my spine and through to my stomach. Nausea, instant and violent, rises in my throat, and I bend my head and heave the contents of my stomach onto the dirt, saliva and snot dripping from my mouth and nose.

I see her boots appear to my right as she circles around to my front, and I know I can't afford to let her get in another hit. Without thinking, I punch the side of her knee as hard as I can, and she falls onto it, crying out in surprise. The crowd's cheering has reached a fever pitch, beyond excited by Belinda's bloodthirstiness and my feeble attempts to fight back.

I force myself to my feet, to step back so I'm out of her reach. I could try to land another blow, but it would put me within striking distance of her, and I decide I need a moment to think more than I need to hit her again. Belinda stands also, and her face is a mask of unmitigated rage.

"You filthy piece of *gesindel*," she spits at me. "I will destroy your fat arse for this."

I could make a retort, but I want to conserve my energy, so I wearily bring my hands up in an attempt to shield my face as she advances. Before, the sudden white-hot flame of anger fueled my bursts of athletic brilliance; now I seem unable to muster even the slightest spark. My brain feels sluggish, and my limbs feel like I'm treading through water.

She swings, and I duck once more and desperately attempt to sweep at her legs again. But it seems she's learned from her previous mistakes. Instead of allowing my leg to impact hers, Belinda steps back out of reach, avoiding toppling over. I reach my arm back and swing my fist, but she's ready and blocks it.

She hits my side again, and when my breath leaves my body, she swiftly pulls back and punches my jaw. My head snaps back, and I feel the echo of her blow in the throbbing pulse of blood that rushes to my face where she struck.

Dazed, I fall to the ground and shake my head to clear it, which barely helps.

"Stand up, *schnecke*," she sneers.

"Better a…snail…than a snake," I gasp.

Face contorted with fury, Belinda's arm draws back and thrusts forward. I almost see it coming toward me at reduced speed, everything in the world slowing to the movement of her fist toward me. But despite seeing its advancement, I'm unable to stop its progression.

Pain blooms white-hot behind my eye.

The world tilts.

I register someone calling my name from far away.

And then, nothing.

CHAPTER SIXTEEN
Bedside Manners

I'm running through the woods beneath the blood moon. This time, Agnethe's screams beckon me from the opposite direction of the river, as sharp and piercing as an arrow, and I frantically search the shadows for any sign of her.

My breath frosts in front of my face, a contrast to the burn in my lungs with every aspiration. I crash through the trees, my hair and clothing snagging on low-hanging leaves. The whip-like branches strike my face, leaving stinging paths across my cheeks and neck.

I stumble out of the forest cover into a clearing bathed in the glow of the moon. In the center of the clearing is a glittering pond, its surface reflecting the glowing pink orb in the sky. I hasten to the water's edge, desperate for a drink, and I fall to my knees, cupping my hands and drawing water to my lips. It's icy and refreshing and soothes the fire blazing in my throat from running.

The next time I dip my hands in for more water, I feel a distinct sting on my hand. Pulling it from the pond, I stare at it, fully visible in the bright light of the moon. There are multiple cuts on my hand—on both of them, actually—just deep enough to bleed. On my ring finger sits the signet ring, and I stare at it, wondering what it all means.

I rub my finger over the engraving and feel a stirring at my back, see a shadow flutter in the reflection of the pool of water. Gasping, I look behind me and stumble back, one of my hands dunking into the frigid water as I edge closer to it.

There's no one there.

After several minutes of waiting where no one appears, I turn back toward the pool, wash the mud from my hand, and see the flutter again. I feel the stirring on my back once more and realize there is something behind me. Cautiously, I lean forward to get a better look and gasp in horror at what I see.

Wings. I have wings.

My eyelids open and immediately flutter closed, still overcome by exhaustion. But I want to know what happened and where I am, so I force myself to pry them back apart.

Above me is not the tall ceiling of the dormitory to which I've become accustomed, but rough-hewn wood beams and plaster at a far closer distance. I can hear a fire crackling nearby and the low hum of voices and smell the astringent odor of vinegar. As my eyes become more focused, I turn my head to the side and see the long row of beds to my right and across from me.

I'm in a bed in the corner of the infirmary.

A fact which I'm sure Hildegarde is thrilled about. Blankets are pulled up to my underarms and tucked around my torso, almost suffocating in their snugness. A few candles gutter around the room in addition to the fire in the hearth, but it's mostly dim. The faint light coming through the windows is from the soft beams of the moon, not the bright rays of the sun, so I know it's night.

At the sight of those beams glowing softly on the interior of the infirmary, I recall my dream. I had wings. Black, iridescent wings. Like those of a raven. At that, I'm reminded of the odd appearance of the raven at the *Nachtrif,* how it seemed to be watching the proceedings, studying them, perhaps even looking for someone.

Now I understand why they're often thought of as bad omens, I think with a wince.

All of that seems ridiculous, though, now that my mind is fully awake. The obvious explanation is that the raven was a coincidence, drawn by noise, blood, or some other innocuous reason, and my dream was spurred by seeing it, followed by being hit in the head. Although a part of me still fears that something is happening to me with my dreams, that I'm beginning to have visions like my grandmother, I try my best to push those thoughts from my mind and focus on my immediate problems.

I shift slightly and let out a groan of pain. My body is one giant ache. I can feel the bruises on my ribs with every breath, the pulsing around my eye that tells me, without the aid of a mirror, that I have a pretty nasty mark there.

Memories of the fight come back to me in bits and pieces. The jeering yells of the crowd, the force of Belinda's first blow, the burn of acid as I vomited into the dirt, my leg sweeping hers. And finally, her fist flying toward my face.

I open my mouth and shift my jaw, trying to work out some of its stiffness from where I was struck. Gods, even my teeth hurt. With a groan, I place my palms flat on the mattress on either side of my hips and start to awkwardly push myself into a seated position.

"You're awake," a voice says, and I jump, turning toward the direction of the sound.

If I weren't already lying down, I probably would've fallen over at the sight of the captain—Aric—sitting in a chair beside my bed. As it is, my hands still slip on the mattress, and I slam back down onto my back with a loud "oof."

I don't even know why he's here. My frown deepens, and my eyes narrow. Wait, why is he here? Why would the captain of an entire unit sit by the bedside of a lowly cadet who got knocked out in a fight? It seems beneath him.

"Why are you here?" I ask, my voice cracking from dryness. "And what time is it?"

He silently hands me a glass of water, which I gulp greedily, and says, "It's two in the morning. The *Nachtrif* ended a few hours ago," he explains, and I feel the heat of embarrassment about just *why* the *Nachtrif* ended. "And checking on cadets in my unit who are injured under my watch is my responsibility."

I gape at him for several seconds before replying, "Seriously?" Because I can't believe he thinks I'd take such a statement at face value. The man has barely interacted with me since I've arrived, but I'd like to believe that he has at least been able to determine that I'm not a fool.

"I wasn't able to get you out of the *Nachtrif*. I am as responsible for your injuries as Belinda," he says solemnly, and I turn to look at the ceiling while I gather my thoughts.

I'm surprised at how disappointed I feel at his explanation, even knowing I shouldn't be. The logical part of me knows this is ridiculous. The fanciful part of me hopes he is as intrigued by me as I am by him and that he wanted to chivalrously save me in a moment of uncontrolled, romantic worry for my safety.

I turn my head back toward him and stare unabashedly at his face, since he's given me such a plausible reason to stare. The firelight dances across his auburn hair, lighting it ablaze as if the flames burn within its waves. It flickers playfully on the angles of his cheekbones and across the lower plane of his jaw, where the beginnings of stubble, glinting more copper than brown, have appeared.

He's so handsome it's almost enough to rob me of breath, and my ribs are already doing a fine job of that. As soon as I have that thought, though, I scowl, angry with myself. It's bad enough that between training and work duties, I haven't been able to look for escape routes, but to allow myself to get further distracted by a handsome face makes me feel silly and shallow.

Maybe I am a fool. Only someone foolish would be upset that her superior officer didn't participate in some kind of emotional entanglement with her while she's desperately trying to survive so she can save her sister.

Shame fills me as I realize that, in my disappointment, I wasn't thinking of Agnethe. I was only thinking of myself. She is the priority. I need to find a way to reach her soon. Not lose focus lusting after handsome, enigmatic, emotionally distant captains.

I look down at my hands and twist my fingers together to try to stem the tide of emotion rising inside me. I feel brittle, like the slightest shift, be it kindness, pity, arrogance, anything, could fracture my composure and unleash everything I've been holding back: the fear, the helplessness, the grief.

In a place where I control so little, I want to keep hold of whatever pieces I still can.

And for Agnethe, I will outlast Stachtenbaste and claw my way back to her.

"I can help you," he says.

I'm so surprised, I look up at him sharply. "What?"

"With sparring. I can give you lessons. They'd have to be early—before breakfast," he explains.

I shake my head. "Why would you do that?"

He leans back in his chair and looks at me critically. "Your current weaknesses slow down the unit. Efficiency is critical, both in combat and as part of training later, where units have to compete against one another. Victors earn better positions after Stachtenbaste. Losers are forgotten."

My face flushes in embarrassment, and my knee-jerk reaction is irritation. Who in the realms does he think he is to judge me for my shortcomings in battle? I never wanted to be a soldier; I never wanted any of this. I'd like to see him do better in my shoes.

"I'm a conscript, Captain. Better stations hardly matter, as they are unlikely to happen for me," I point out bitterly.

Aric says quietly, "I was a conscript, too."

My eyes lock on his, trying to ferret out any untruths in their chocolatey depths. "You were?"

He nods. "As was my cousin."

Too shocked to hold my tongue, I ask, "For what crimes?" Could it be that Aric understands the desperation of self-defense? Of survival?

He answers, "Circumstance of birth."

An involuntary enlistee versus a conscript, then. I can't help but imagine his experience would have been *very* different from mine.

He continues, "And while you might think being the nephew and son of the general of the Aurengarte afforded us some kind of physical or strategic advantage when coming here—"

That's exactly what I think.

"—it did not."

Oh.

"Neither one of us was prepared for it," he adds. "And I'd argue that we managed to get decent positions despite that."

I digest his words, my eyes never straying from his. "How did you do it?" I whisper.

"I can't speak for my cousin, but for me, it was training. Discipline. Relentless pursuit of perfection," he states. "If you work hard, your efforts will be rewarded."

I stare at him, unsure how to respond to a level of optimism and trust I don't share given my interactions with not one, but two of the most powerful people in Aurelia. Interactions that proved to me character, honesty, faith, and trust are not always enough.

I decide to tell him how I feel when the sound of off-key singing reaches my ears.

"There was a maid in Embrathal,
Whose tits were round as she was tall.
And e'ery night, before she sleeps,
She spread her thighs, and there did weep."

My face turns bright red, and I avoid Aric's gaze, hoping we can just ignore the singer until he goes elsewhere. To my dismay, though, the voice continues to grow closer to where we are, drifting through the drafty infirmary windows. I reach for a glass of water on the table beside my bed to keep my hands and mouth busy.

"There dwelt a lad on Fenbourg's coast,
Whose hose concealed a mighty post.
And when he stepped on shore at last,
He sought a lass to scale his mast."

I let out a noise somewhere between a sputter and a cough, spraying water indelicately. I can't resist glancing at Aric, and instead of looking amused, as I feel inside, he seems irritated. His uptight frustration makes the song all the more funny, and my lips twitch uncontrollably as I try to hold in my laughter.

> *"So maid and lad by chance did meet,*
> *He asked to glimpse her weighty teats."*

I choke on my water, and a little bit dribbles down my chin.

The door to the infirmary crashes open, letting in a gust of chilly night air. Rafe Kriegeur waltzes inside the infirmary, clutching a nearly empty bottle of amber-colored spirits in one hand and a dagger in the other. He spreads his arms wide as he continues to sing, his voice cresting inconsistently on notes I'm quite certain only he has heard of and that don't truly exist within the bounds of music.

> *"She then agreed, and to his shock,*
> *She wrapped her lips around his—"*

Kriegeur takes a deep breath as if to continue his song, but Aric snaps at him. "Rafe. What are you doing here?"

Kriegeur turns to us, and his eyes brighten, as if we were exactly who he was looking for. He stumbles over, reeking of alcohol and poor decisions. His dark hair looks slightly disheveled, and his black eyes glitter in the candlelight, which burnishes his skin to a lustrous glow.

"Congratulations, *künnle*," he slurs. "That was great fun!"

"Rafe, you're drunk," Aric accuses.

And the sky is blue, I think to myself sarcastically.

Rafe looks deeply offended by his cousin's words. He clutches his bottle to his chest, sniffs, and says, "I am not."

He then begins to walk forward, trips over his own feet, and catches himself on the edge of the bed, nearly toppling to the ground in a muscled heap. He sets his bottle down on the table beside my bed as he rights himself, pulling his twisted tunic back into place, and grins at me while swaying slightly.

He leans over to me, his hand pressing into the mattress beside my body, and the scent of mint reaches my nose as he gets closer. "I might be just slightly tipsy," he says in a conspiratorial whisper, holding his thumb and forefinger in a pinching motion while gripping his dagger with the other fingers. I eye the weapon in his hand warily, wondering how wise it is for a drunk person to be brandishing a blade with so little concern for his surroundings.

Aric rolls his eyes at his cousin, clearly annoyed, but also does not tell him to leave. Instead, he asks, "What are you doing here, Rafe?"

The lieutenant colonel stands quickly, which causes him to bob. "I had to come—" A hiccup sounds. "Check on the patient. Fell harder than a sack full of stones, that one. It didn't even look like Bradleye hit her that hard from my viewpoint. Though to hear her tell it, it was the blow of the century."

I feel a blush heat my face again, humiliated by the lieutenant colonel's casual admission that I am a woefully deficient fighter. I can't even take a punch well, let alone throw one. I feel as pathetic as Dagmar accused me of being during my first training session.

"Yes, well, it wouldn't have happened if you'd just had two other cadets fight," Aric says tightly. I look at him, wide eyed, that he'd challenge a man like Kriegeur. They might be cousins, but Kriegeur is his superior and has a reputation for being unpredictable. I definitely don't want him sticking his neck out for me.

Kriegeur turns to his cousin, eyebrow raised, suddenly more eagle eyed than he previously appeared. "Why do you even care? You've never objected to the *Nachtrif* before, nor asked me to change the fighters. Can't recall ever seeing you at a cadet's bedside either," he drawls.

I make a mental note that even when drunk, the lieutenant colonel was not to be fucked with. He is more observant than I would have given him credit for. It seems my team was right in telling me he was actually a good soldier.

It's the captain's turn to flush, and I watch him, puzzled, as he says, "It's clear that de Veend isn't accustomed to fighting. I thought it wise to postpone her *Nachtrif* participation."

Was anyone here really prepared for fighting besides a select few? Certainly none of the conscripted cadets had asked to be here; nor had they been "accustomed to fighting" prior to their arrival, except maybe in the most desperate and dire of circumstances. This seems like a poor excuse for singling me out as someone being coddled by the officers.

It seems the lieutenant colonel and I share a similar line of thinking. "You put a target on her back as big as a war banner. You really think the general won't hear about that?" I hadn't even thought of that, and feel my face pale. The last thing I want is for Lord Corvilian to take additional notice of me, because I want to get out of here. However, I do find it odd that Kriegeur refers to his own father as "the general."

The captain opens his mouth, clearly to argue based on the mulish expression on his face, when he stops because his cousin is busy chugging the remains of his bottle of liquor, tilting his head back, the strong column of his throat pulling with each gulp of liquid until he's bled it dry. Belching loudly, Kriegeur sets the bottle down on the table next to my bed and wipes his sleeve across his mouth. I want to be disgusted, but something about this whole conversation just makes me want to laugh instead, and I feel my lips twitching dangerously, and a small cough breaks through them before I can hold it back.

Kriegeur grins at me, his eyes looking glassier than they had moments before. He sits down on the edge of my bed, pinning me under the blanket, and his bulk is such that I roll slightly toward him from the dip in the mattress and uneven weight distribution.

"Now, *künnle*, did we learn anything valuable about fighting tonight?" He asks primly, twirling his dagger on its point against the pad of his index finger, a smirk kicking up the corner of his mouth.

I open my mouth to answer, but Aric reaches over the bed and swipes the dagger from Kriegeur's hands. "You shouldn't be waving a blade around when you're inebriated," he says stiffly.

The look on the lieutenant colonel's face makes me shrink back into my mattress. All the good humor is displaced by thunderous anger. He stands, and for a moment I think he will strike the captain. Instead, he simply swipes the dagger back from his cousin.

He says in a low voice that's utterly devoid of humor or warmth, "No one touches Rosamunde." He tucks his hand behind him, and the blade disappears. I surmise that he shoved it into some sheath on his person.

Aric stands to face his cousin across my bed. He's not as tall as

Kriegeur, nor as bulky, but he looks just as angry. My eyes dart between the two men, casting furious shadows over me. A tension that seems far deeper than is warranted for the situation simmers between them. It's like I'm not even there. Nor do they even really need me in order to be angry at each other.

Desperate to diffuse the situation and irritated that they haven't left me alone to sleep, I ask, "Your dagger has a name?"

The spell between them breaks. Aric steps back from the bed, and Kriegeur turns his black gaze on me. His face loses some of its rigidity as he looks at me and says, "Yes. It means 'protection.'"

I laugh nervously and say, "Do you even need a dagger to save you?"

Kriegeur looks at me intently and says, "Everyone needs saving from something."

I can't look away from him after he says it. While it's true, I can't help but wonder what this formidable man could possibly need protection from. Part of me is morbidly curious to know what it is. Still, the larger part of me thinks that whatever Kriegeur is afraid of must be truly terrifying, considering his reputation.

Aric clears his throat, and I jump at the sound, looking over at him. I take in his clenched jaw, his eyes pinched with irritation. He says to Kriegeur, "Are we done here?"

I almost want to hiss at him to shut up and stop angering the volatile, "tipsy" lieutenant colonel, but I keep my mouth shut. Kriegeur turns toward his cousin, looks at him slowly from head to toe and turns back to me without ever saying a word to him. I want to wince at the slight but keep my face as blank as I can.

A silly smirk breaks over Kriegeur's face. "Well, *künnle*," he says, "I have a feeling the Freiheit will be far more interesting with you around. I look forward to it. Now," he stands and swipes his empty bottle from my bedside table, "I'm off to the gatehouse."

Aric frowns. "Why the gatehouse?"

"Meeting the Schulz brothers," he explains, wobbling toward the door. "Going to see if we can find any lingering patches of snow, piss our names into them. Care for a signature?" He turns back toward us, his face an expression of inquisitive expectation.

My eyes widen, and I press my lips together to keep from laughing hysterically. Aric—the captain, I should stop thinking of him so casually—looks somewhere between disgusted and exasperated.

Kriegeur moves his index finger back and forth between us, waiting for us to answer. "Yes. No? Any takers?"

The captain begins, "Rafe, I don't think—"

"I'm not hearing many ayes, so I have to assume they're nays." He looks disappointed. I feel a laugh bubbling dangerously close to the surface.

The captain looks at me and then back to his cousin. He must decide that arguing with him further isn't worth it, because his shoulders drop, and he only says, "No, thank you." And for some reason, the fact that he thanks him strikes me as even funnier. I let out a wheeze and am trying so hard to hold back the laughter and avoid angering Kriegeur that I start coughing.

The captain comes over and hands me another glass of water. The lieutenant colonel looks at me curiously, then shrugs and says, "Suit yourself," and sways out of the infirmary, resuming his bawdy song when the door shuts behind him.

I feel physically and emotionally wrung out by that interaction. I don't know what kind of relationship the cousins have, but it seems it's not one of familial love based on what I've seen pass between them. Casual indifference at the best of times. Blatant disdain at others.

"Is he always like that?" I ask the captain after I've finished drinking my water, and he returns to sitting in the chair beside my bed.

"Rafe? Yes. There was a time when I'd thought that—" he begins, but then seems to stop himself from explaining further. My curiosity is piqued, but I decide now isn't the time to press it.

Instead I switch topics, frowning as I remember something Kriegeur had said. "What's the Freiheit?"

Aric looks at me sharply. "What?"

"The lieutenant colonel said that the Freiheit will be more interesting with me around. What is it?" I ask again, watching his face closely.

A shadow crosses the captain's face at my question. "It's nothing you need to concern yourself with."

"It seems as though I do, since the lieutenant colonel seems to think I'll be involved in it," I point out.

His jaw tightens, and he looks away, as if trying to decide how much he wants to share with me about this Freiheit thing. "You'll find out soon enough, I'm sure."

"I'd rather find out now," I press.

He stands suddenly, tension vibrating through his frame. "Don't presume to give me orders, cadet."

I bristle at his words, but they also act like a dousing of ice-cold water over my head, bringing me back to the reality of my situation. I don't know him. I shouldn't feel comfortable around him. He might be handsome, and he might have treated me with some kindness, but his motives as to why are unclear, and I won't even be here long enough to discover them, if I have my way.

"My apologies," I say, looking down at my hands, which are clutched in my lap again.

He sighs, and I look back up at him. "No need. I spoke too harshly. Rafe just has that effect on me. You should rest tonight. Meet me at the officers' training yard tomorrow morning at dawn."

He, too, quits the infirmary, leaving me alone to replay the entire puzzling interaction. As I lay back against the pillow, my eyelids become heavy once more. The exhaustion from the fight, the tension of the conversation with Aric and Kriegeur, and the weight of my entire situation seem to press heavily upon me, making me feel so soul weary I wish I could sleep for an entire week.

As I begin to drift off, my mind wanders to the Freiheit thing that Kriegeur mentioned. Based on Aric's reaction, whatever it is, it's nothing good.

CHAPTER SEVENTEEN
A Fool's Hope

I arrive at the officers' training yard three days later. Hildegarde didn't release me from the infirmary until yesterday, telling me that I had a concussion and if I didn't rest, I would make it worse. I had received a missive from Captain Everbrandt the morning after the *Nachtrif.*

"Meet me at the officers' training yard at dawn the morning after you're released. Yours, A.E."

I thought of the words for the entirety of my remaining stay in the infirmary, even though I had burned the missive out of an abundance of caution, breaking it down multiple ways in my head to decide what it all meant. Lotti and Otto visited me when they were able, and though I told them about the tense meeting between the captain and the lieutenant colonel at my bedside, something keeps me from confessing the captain's promise.

I'm not sure if private training is allowed, but I'm not about to try to find out and ruin any chance at improvement I might have. At least that's what I've tried to tell myself is the reason for keeping it a secret. It seems my stupid, irrational heart cannot heed my head's warnings about getting distracted by a handsome face, and that part of me wants to see what happens.

Despite Otto's comprehensive knowledge of Stachtenbaste and its doings, he is unaware of the Freiheit and what it is, as is Lotti. I haven't asked anyone else on our team, not wanting to tell the others about my interactions with the two officers. So I've resolved myself to re-asking Aric—the captain—what do I even call him? He signed the missive "A.E." Does that mean I should address him by his first name? Oh gods, I'm in so much trouble.

When I stop in front of the gate, I look around and over my shoulder toward the citadel to see if anyone is watching me. Do I just walk in? I press the lever on the gate, and even though he told me to meet him here, I'm still surprised when it depresses and the gate swings inward, unlocked. Stepping through the opening, I close it behind me, jumping when the loud clang of metal against metal sounds across the otherwise silent training yard.

The sun hasn't yet broken the horizon. Though the early dawn light illuminates the grounds, the captain has still lit several torches that line the yard's perimeter to increase visibility. He is standing in the middle of the training yard, holding a sword and making motions against an invisible opponent. His auburn hair is pulled away from his face, and the sleeves of his tunic are rolled up to expose golden forearms sprinkled with glinting coppery hairs. A focused expression is visible on the side of his face turned toward me, and a vee of sweat soaks the back of his tunic where it clings to the muscles there. My mouth goes dry at the sight of him, and I watch in silence as he moves lithely toward his imaginary rival, thrusting, lunging, rolling, all while still holding the sword.

Eventually he turns and notices I'm there, and my pulse starts pounding in my veins, especially as his eyes slowly trail from where the bruises are still healing on my face and down my figure, hastily dressed in my tighter uniform, which strains across my hips and breasts. I curse myself for not being more careful and grabbing the one that fits me better, but I was eager and rushed.

"Good morning," he says.

This is the first time I've seen him since that night in the infirmary, and despite my earlier excitement, I now feel nervous, for many reasons.

This man holds the ability to improve or worsen my existence at Stachtenbaste, and I'd have little recourse if he decided the latter was to be my fate. I don't get that impression from him, but I haven't known him long enough to be certain, and haven't known enough of soldiers, in general, to trust them wholly. Then, there's the fact that he is able to help me with the skills I'm expected to learn while here, which might better prepare me to survive training, to escape, and to then disappear with Agnethe. In short, I need all the help I can get, and I mean to take it if he is willing to offer it.

Then, of course, there is the undeniable fact that looking at him makes my heart race, my stomach flutter, and my breathing erratic. While I know it would be beyond stupid to become entangled with him, and I don't even know that he wants to with me, part of me is sorely tempted to seize what little enjoyment I can find here. It's not as if I would expect it to go anywhere. After all, he's an officer in the very institution that I want to escape, and one that falls under the purview of the Gold Council, a body whose methods I've come to view as not entirely honorable or without bias.

Suffice to say, it's complicated.

The space is larger than I had imagined, not having been able to view much of it through the narrow gate, and it takes me a minute or two to reach him in the center. The officers' training yard is, of course, much nicer than those allocated to the cadets. I'm sure this is partly because of their rank and partly because not nearly as many people use it. But the grass beneath my feet is plush and vibrantly green, not having given way to mud in so many places like in our training yard. The gravel path circling it is well-kept, without many stray stones littering the grass. I can attest to just how often the gravel shifts, having found it with my hands and knees many times after falling during training. Against the back wall, which is one of the outer walls of the island, there rests an equipment shed not dissimilar to those positioned around the cadet training yard. The door is hanging open, and unlike our own shed, which is full of wooden practice weapons, this one's interior gleams with the shine of metal.

"Good morning," I respond as I come to a stop in front of him.

Up close, his eyes scan my face again, lingering on my hideously bruised eye. I would've felt more embarrassed about how awful it looks if I didn't see his jaw tighten in anger, obviously upset by the injury rather than horrified by my appearance.

A few moments pass as we stare at one another, and I wonder if he will bring up what happened with the lieutenant colonel in the infirmary.

"Well, then, shall we begin?" He asks, and though I feel a slight twinge of disappointment that he doesn't say more, I nod my assent, deciding it's best if we keep it professional.

"First, your stance," he says. "Show it to me."

I hesitate, feeling foolish. What if he sees how I stand and decides that I'm not worth the trouble to train? *The man saw you get knocked unconscious and is still here. Relax*, my brain tells me sarcastically. Sighing, I get into the stance I typically assume for hand-to-hand combat. He circles me, looking at my position.

"Right," he says when facing me again. "For maximum balance, you need to stand with your feet at the same width as your shoulders, with your dominant foot slightly back. Keep your knees bent so they don't lock and you don't fall over."

I listen to what he says and adjust my stance accordingly. He circles me again, and this time I feel his boot nudge my calves apart a little more, and he guides my right leg back slightly using the palm of his hand on my thigh, which makes my cheeks flame red.

When he's facing me head on again, he says, "Keep your hands around the height of your collarbone. This will help you guard your face and torso."

I follow his instructions, but he grabs my wrists gently and pulls them up slightly higher, adjusting the tilt of my shoulders. When he's satisfied with my stance, he nods and tells me to relax out of the stance.

"Now, repeat what you just learned," he instructs, and my eyes widen, not anticipating that I'd have to remember everything he just taught me.

We go back and forth like that, and each time he has me repeat it, I improve a bit more. On my fifth attempt, he declares that I've gotten it "close enough" and moves on to the next item of business: break falling.

"You're going to fall," he says bluntly. "So it's important to learn how to do it safely and return to your fighting stance."

Having just managed a "close enough" on my fighting stance, I fail to see how I'll ever be able to fall—and fall in the right way—and smoothly return to that stance. I say nothing, though, not wanting to betray how much I fear my own clumsiness, and watch as he demonstrates.

He tucks his chin, hits the ground with his forearms flat to absorb the shock, and rolls back gracefully to his feet.

"Is that all?" I say sarcastically, and he cracks a smile that makes my breath stop momentarily. I'm not sure how I'm supposed to do anything after seeing that.

He encourages, "You'll never know how well you'll do if you don't try."

I reply, "I'll also never have to face how bad I am if I don't."

"You'll also get injured," he shrugs, as if indicating it's up to me.

Gritting my teeth, I try falling in the way he taught me. On my first time down, I instinctively reach out my hands to catch myself, painfully slamming my weight down onto my wrists and palms.

He tells me, "That's a good way to break your wrists if you fall hard."

"But what if I fall in a way that doesn't allow me to land on my forearms?" I ask, pointing out that it might not always happen in a "good" way.

"You have to keep your momentum going in order to minimize the impact. So, if you feel yourself starting to fall, try to roll into it. If the ground breaks your fall rather than your body, you're going to get hurt worse than if you turn into it. Above all, make sure you protect your head." He raises his arms around his face to show me how to cage my head if I fall forward.

"So," I begin, "fall on my forearms, but roll into the fall, and don't forget to bring up my forearms to cover my head." He frowns, as if realizing upon my repetition of them that the instructions are less than clear.

I smile at him then and shrug. "I'm sure I'll get it eventually."

I practice falling, then I ask him to give me a nudge so I can drop more realistically. He walks behind me and pushes at my shoulders. His nudge is probably gentle to him, but it feels quite hard, and I stumble forward, awkwardly rolling onto my side and then flopping onto my back.

"That's one way of doing it," he says, smothering a laugh.

I glare at him but get back to my feet. Finally, after several attempts, I manage to roll into the impact and can tell right away that it's much easier on my body. The fall doesn't jar my hip and shoulder quite as hard, and the momentum of the roll itself effectively moves me away from him, so if he were my opponent, I would escape any kicks he might try to deal me.

"Good," he says, "do it again."

Groaning, I climb to my feet, my movements gradually becoming sluggish. I dread doing more of this not too long from now when I go to my regular training after breakfast. I decide there's no better time to ask him my question than now, both because I need to just seize the moment and because it'll give me precious extra minutes to recover.

"What is the Freiheit?" I ask, and have to hide my amusement at how shocked he looks.

"Why do you want to know?" He asks.

Because I haven't stopped thinking about it since the lieutenant colonel mentioned it as if it were something I should be preparing for, and if there is some other torture in my near future, I want to know about it.

"I just do. I'm curious."

He hesitates for several seconds before saying, "It's a tournament. Fall again."

"What kind of tournament?" I ask as I climb to my feet after another decent break fall.

He sighs and pinches the bridge of his nose between his thumb and forefinger. "Since you're obviously not going to let this go." He looks at me hopefully from behind his hand. I cross my arms over my chest, and he sighs again before continuing, "Conscripts here get the chance to enter and win their freedom from their sentence."

I'm glad I know how to fall properly because I'm about to collapse from shock.

"They...*what?*" I shake my head in disbelief.

He drops his arms and repeats, "Conscripts can enter the competition to win their freedom from the Aurengarte and combat, as well as a lifelong stipend."

"How did I not know about this?" I ask, breathlessly. "No one has mentioned it."

"There isn't much reason to bring it up outside of when it's happening, and that's only once a year. And I don't like to encourage people to enter," he explains.

I gasp. "Why not? People have a chance to escape their conscription sentences, and you just...don't tell them?" I ask, incensed.

"It's not that simple," he argues. "Only *one* person can win out of all who choose to enter."

"But it's a chance," I argue right back.

"A slim chance," he retorts. "The Freiheit Tournament is dangerous."

"Don't you think that the conscripts should be able to decide whether or not they take on that risk?" I demand.

He begins, "Of course I do, but—"

I interrupt him, "But what? What you could *possibly* argue against free will that—"

"People die in the tournament, Greta," he says softly. It's the first time he's ever called me by my first name. I didn't even realize he knew it. The change in how he addresses me makes me freeze in place more than the threat of death. I'm already under threat of death, after all.

I want to argue more, but I'm not sure what to say. I practice falling a few more times, and then he tells me we should try a push-pull grapple. He tells me that a slight shift in balance can throw my opponent off and force them to focus on adjusting their own bodies rather than attacking mine.

"Here. Try and push me," he directs, indicating I should move toward him. I charge toward him clumsily and reach out to push him, which he lets me do, but he grabs my arms and twists his body, which redirects my force. Next, we reverse our positions, with him pushing me. I try to mimic the movement, but I'm not as smooth as he is, nor as big. I stumble forward, and he reaches out to steady me by my arms, his fingers closing around my biceps.

When the world stops spinning, I register how close we are to one another. Close enough that when I take a deep breath, my breasts brush his chest. Following my inhalation, his fingers flex on my upper arms where he's holding me. He's taller than I am by several inches, but I'm tall enough that when I tilt my head back to look up at his face, our mouths are only inches apart, our breath mingling between us. His eyes lower to my mouth for a moment, then back up to meet mine. His pupils are dilated, and I wonder if he's thinking of kissing me like I am him.

Nearby, a sheep bleats loudly in the livestock pasture. Startled by the noise, I step back from him quickly. Too quickly. I stumble again but am able to catch myself.

He clears his throat. "Moving on. Next, we should try deflecting and escaping a grab."

He certainly seems to be an expert in deflecting, I think. I guess we're abandoning grappling today.

He says, "To escape a grab, you have to rotate and step into it to trap your opponent's arm."

Without warning, he reaches out his hand and clamps it around my wrist. Not tight, but firm, controlled. My body goes taut.

"This is how most of them will grab you," he says, "Quick, with their dominant hand, trying to drag you off balance. If you panic or pull back, that's when you lose."

I try to yank free anyway. It doesn't work. His grip doesn't even shift. He steps behind me, not touching me, but close enough that I can feel the heat rolling off his body.

"Don't pull back. Step in," he instructs.

My voice barely emerges as a whisper. "Toward you?"

"Yes," he agrees. "Surprise them by closing the distance instead of trying to increase it."

I shift my weight and step in sharply, aligning my body sideways to his, my shoulder brushing his chest. My heart starts pounding, but I can't make eye contact with him again.

"Now," Aric continues, his voice softer, "turn your wrist upward like you're about to elbow someone behind you. High. Good. See the line of my elbow? That's where the leverage is."

I nod, biting the inside of my cheek to focus. My free hand finds the bend of his arm, fingers pressing just above his elbow. I can feel the taut muscle shift beneath my touch, but he doesn't flinch.

"Control the elbow," he murmurs, "and the rest follows."

I rotate my body, drawing my arm across my own chest like opening a gate. My wrist twists as I turn, and his fingers slip, breaking the hold. I stumble back, hand still raised, surprised it worked, and on my first try. He watches me, expression unreadable.

"Well done," he nods.

"What do you have to do to win the Freiheit?" I blurt.

His expression shutters. "You have to beat everyone else."

I ask, "And how many is 'everyone else'?"

"Dozens, at least. Often well over a hundred. Sometimes far more," he answers.

"What does beating them involve?" I inquire.

"I'm not going to give you more information on it, Greta," he says. "It changes every year anyway; I couldn't tell you everything even if I wanted to."

"So you'll just refuse to help me?" I demand.

"What do you think I'm doing now?" He asks angrily. "Do you think I'm here because I do this for all cadets? Because I love giving up an extra hour of sleep?"

"I didn't ask you to help me train," I say hotly.

"No, only to tell you how to die," he says bitterly.

Furious, I shake my head. "Never mind." I step around him and move to walk toward the gate.

His hand shoots out and grabs my wrist. "Greta, wait—"

Instinctively, I react exactly how he taught me, stepping into his hold, rotating my hand, pressing on his elbow, and breaking free. We both stare at each other in shock.

He steps toward me. "Greta—" and something in his face makes me step back, my mind going back to several weeks ago, in a closed room, with a guard who didn't understand boundaries or the word "no." To a lord who wanted something and wouldn't listen when I told him I didn't know.

He stops moving when he sees my face and drops his outstretched arm.

"That was good," he says. "It's almost like you were afraid of me, though."

I scoff, lying, "I wasn't."

His eyes narrow on mine. "Weren't you?"

I don't answer him, and the silence stretches between us.

"Why are you here, Greta?" He asks.

I frown, confused. "What do you mean? To train. You said you'd help me."

He shakes his head. "Not here this morning. Here at Stachtenbaste. How did you come to be here?"

I freeze, fear making it feel as though my throat is closing. I'm not ready to trust him, not with Lord Corvilian's blood running through his veins. Maybe that's not fair of me, but the fact of the matter is that I don't know him well enough to know if I can share my secrets with him. Share my fears. My pain. No matter what my fluttering pulse and raging hormones try to tell me, he is still mostly a stranger to me.

A dark shape flutters behind his shoulder before I can even think of a plausible lie. I look past him to see a raven—enormous, dark as coal, and uncannily still—perched on the edge of one of the stone walls. Watching, as if waiting for something to happen.

My stomach dips. Crawling awareness slides over my skin as I return the raven's gaze. I blink and sway unsteadily.

"Greta?" Aric asks, his voice sounding concerned.

A wave of dizziness crashes over me suddenly. My knees begin to buckle, and I sag. Aric reaches out, catching my elbow gently before I can collapse onto the grass. I feel like I'm going to vomit. Gods, I hope I don't vomit in front of him. He gently guides me to sit on the ground and presses my head between my knees.

"Take slow, deep breaths," he encourages gently, his large, warm hand a comforting weight on my upper back.

I heed his advice and shakily inhale and exhale several times. The nausea and intense dizziness fade, but I'm still shaken as I pull my head up from between my knees to look at him gratefully.

"Thank you," I tell him.

"You need food," he states. "You're running on adrenaline and nothing else."

Food is the last thing on my mind, for once, but I don't refute his statement and allow him to help me to my feet.

"I'm all right," I tell him as he holds my shoulders and looks into my eyes, like he's trying to decide if I'll be able to walk of my own volition.

"You're not," he counters, "but you'll be better once you've eaten. But please, Greta, just forget about the Freiheit. It's a fool's hope. You're better off improving your skills and getting a decent position after you finish your training."

I don't have the energy, nor do I feel steady enough to argue with him, so I nod, knowing that I'm not going to forget about it but am simply choosing to drop the topic with him for the time being. He looks relieved at my gesture, and I know he believes he's convinced me to reconsider my curiosity regarding the tournament.

I sigh and let him lead me from the officers' training yard toward the citadel as the sun fully breaks over the horizon, illuminating a new day. As we step into the orange-pink rays that spill over the grounds, I look back over my shoulder toward the training yard wall.

The raven is still there.

It's shifted its position. Where it had been facing inward toward the officers' training yard, it's now facing our direction as we walk away. A frisson of awareness and apprehension shivers down my spine. In its gaze, I feel the unsettling, quiet promise that, though my life is already far from ordinary or peaceful, the worst of it still lies ahead.

CHAPTER EIGHTEEN
Breakfast of Champions and Future Casualties

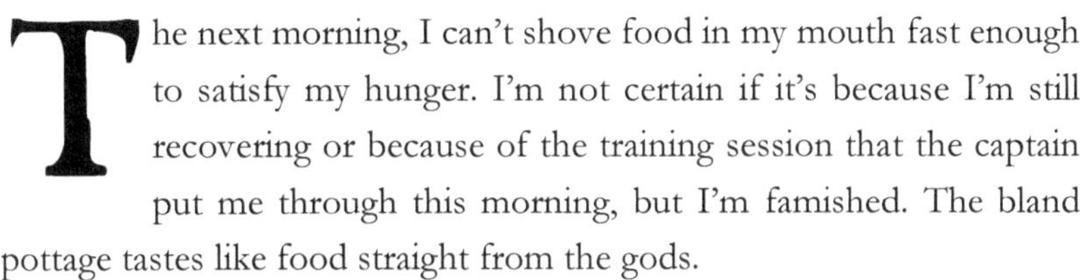

The next morning, I can't shove food in my mouth fast enough to satisfy my hunger. I'm not certain if it's because I'm still recovering or because of the training session that the captain put me through this morning, but I'm famished. The bland pottage tastes like food straight from the gods.

Around me, the team is chattering. Berte, Jarl, and Cyneric are bickering like always. Stigander listens with a sour expression and occasionally interjects with a wry observation. Otto and Lotti discuss the best time of year to plant turnips with Lillen. I look over at Brock, who is seated across from me, silently pushing his pottage around in his bowl.

"Are you all right, Brock?" I ask around a mouthful of food.

He looks up at me, startled. "Fine," he says, "just thinking."

Brock seems to think a lot with how quiet he always is. Not that I mind that he's quiet, really, but I do wonder how he fares mentally.

"Is your food all right?" I ask, pointing to his bowl with my spoon.

"It seems fine," he says.

I smile. "Unless you count the taste."

His lips curve in a small, reserved smile. "Still better than the mines. Most days, we just got dust in our teeth and called it dinner."

I frown at him. "Do you ever miss it? Home, that is."

He takes so long to answer, I think he isn't going to, but finally he says, "I miss the sound of silence. Have you ever been outside when it's just begun to snow?"

I consider his question but have to shake my head. "It didn't really snow that much at home, just dustings in the winter months. Nothing like what I'm sure you're used to seeing."

"I used to love to go outside when it was snowing, especially at night. When there was a bit already on the ground, and more still falling. I'd stand out in the cold, and my breath would cloud the air, and I'd just listen to the sound of the snowflakes touching the ground." He skims his hand lightly across the table as if he can picture it in his mind's eye.

"You could hear it?" I ask, surprised.

He shakes his head. "Not the snow itself, although when it would get really heavy, it would sometimes sound like it was creaking when you walked through it. But no, it was more…the absence of sound. The snow cover muffled everything. And it sparkles in the moonlight. There's something magical about the sound of that silence, about the glittering white. Like Lunoch had laid a blanket of diamonds across the ground for us to sleep upon."

To listen to him describe it made me believe in its magic. "You didn't find it too cold?"

"After a time, yes," he says, "and the cold would sometimes make my chest hurt. But I couldn't resist that quiet. It's never that quiet here," he laments.

"Do you ever think about what you'd be doing…you know, if you weren't here?" I ask him, and for some reason, I know Brock has. I see myself in the frequent, faraway look in his eyes, as if his mind is often on what might have been.

"I'd likely still be working the mines, which wasn't good for me," he says. "But I wish I could see it again…the night snowfall."

"You still can," I say, "after all this."

He smiles faintly at me. "If there is an after."

I know then that Brock has had the same thought I have about whether or not we'll survive combat. I often wonder if I'll even survive Stachtenbaste.

"Greta, darling, we simply must know yours." Cyneric's voice breaks through my melancholy thoughts.

I look up and see most of my team staring at me and Brock. "Know my what?"

"Your legend name," Jarl says. "What they'd call you after seeing you in battle or because of your reputation there. Like how they call Lord Corvilian 'the lion of Fracidaem.'"

Berte interjects, "I'd like to be known as Berte the Blade. Not for my sword skills but my sharp wit," she grins.

Cyneric places a hand to his chest. "And I will be Cyneric the Sinful, for obvious reasons," he says as he wiggles his eyebrows.

"I, of course, am Master of the Flame," Jarl says, winking at me.

Berte objects. "Because of your ruddy ginger hair?"

"No, because I set the ladies' drawers aflame with desire," he says saucily, and Lotti and I start laughing while Berte scoffs.

"Whisperknife," Lotti says. "You'll never see me coming."

"No, we'll just hear you yapping instead," Jarl quips and earns himself a wallop on the head from Lotti. "Ow!"

Stigander says, "Stigander the Stoic."

Berte snorts. "More like Stigander the Surly."

Stigander glares at her.

I look at Otto, Lillen, and Brock. "What about all of you?"

Lillen shakes her head. "Oh no, you're not dragging me into these children's games."

Jarl says grandly, "You shall be known as The Wet Blanket," which earns him a second wallop on the head, this time from Lillen. "Ow, fuck!"

Everyone laughs and calls out various ideas for Lillen, Otto, and Brock, and soon we're all shouting over one another to get our ideas heard. We've become so loud that we're garnering looks from some of the nearby tables.

"What about *you*, darling?" Cyneric turns toward me expectantly, and everyone else follows suit.

"She Who Broke Belinda," Jarl suggests, grinning when I send a withering glance his way.

"The Concussed Clod," Berte cracks, and I groan.

"I'm never going to live that down, am I?" I ask them.

Just then, Dagmar approaches the table and sits next to me.

"Well, if it isn't Dagger-mar!" Jarl booms.

Dagmar's head turns slowly in his direction, and her eyes narrow slightly. "What the fuck did you call me?"

Jarl swallows. "Shall I wallop my own head to save time?"

Lotti asks, "Did you come here from the training yard, Dagmar?"

"Had no choice," Dagmar grunts. "Was told Richter is making some kind of announcement."

I suddenly feel my stomach drop and wish I hadn't eaten so much. I have a feeling I know what the announcement is about, but I can't find the words to tell my teammates. Before I can even consider how to do so, Colonel Richter walks into the dining hall, followed by the other officers: Lieutenant Colonel Kriegeur, Major Berger, the Schulz brothers, and others whom I recognize as leaders in different units but whose names I haven't learned. Finally, Lieutenant Broadbente strides in, followed by Aric, who is the last to enter.

Colonel Richter leads them in a queue past the first bank of tables, including ours. The lieutenant colonel winks at me as he strolls by unhurried. I feel my face flush when my entire team turns to stare at me. When Lieutenant Broadbente and Aric walk by us, Aric looks directly at me and nods a greeting. I feel my face flush anew as I simultaneously want to melt into a puddle at the small acknowledgment and let the ground swallow me whole. My team is staring at me again.

"Maybe your name should be The Heartbreaker," Cyneric whispers so only we can hear. "Mine is positively broken that the lieutenant colonel winked at you."

There are a few soft snickers, but they quickly die down when Colonel Richter reaches the middle of the room and turns to face the cadets, the officers fanning out behind her.

She's not a woman who commands a room like some of her broad-shouldered male officers. She's of middling height, middling age, middling tan skin. Her short hair is a graying medium brown, and her eyes are an unremarkable shade of brown that I can only describe as "mud."

Yet, there is something in the way she moves. It's deliberate, economical, like she's calculated every step at least ten times before taking it. Her uniform is crisp without being so new as to look unused. Her boots bear the scuff marks of those that have been well used. The lines in her face have been carved by wind, by sun, by whatever battles she's seen before many of us had even taken our first steps.

She doesn't command the room. No. She owns it.

She looks across the expanse of cadets, as the silence tightens around the room like a noose.

"My fellow officers, soldiers, and cadets. By the will of the Gold Council under Lord Corvilian's exemplary leadership, I'm officially opening registration for the Freiheit Tournament," she declares.

The room begins whispering frantically at her announcement, including my own table.

"What's the Freiheit Tournament?" Berte asks, and it takes everything in me not to meet the gazes of Lotti and Otto, who are the only people I've told about it and who I know will be staring at me and will give everything away.

"Never heard of it," Stigander shrugs. "Must be some Aurenclaste horseshit. See which one of them can win against the other for the opportunity for more privilege."

"The Freiheit Tournament," Colonel Richter's voice cuts through the din, "is an annual tradition at Stachtenbaste. A chance for conscripted cadets to fight and compete for the ultimate reward: freedom from their sentence."

Unlike before, the room is stunned into silence.

She continues, "For those of you conscripted into the military, the Freiheit offers a singular opportunity. Victory means a full pardon and exemption from conscription, as well as a lifetime annual stipend drawn from the Aurengarte's coffers."

"What did she say?" Berte whispers, her face pale.

Stigander shakes his head. "I don't believe it. What's the catch?"

"This tournament is not for the fickle. It is not for the weak. It will test your mettle and whittle away the unworthy until only one remains. All but one who enters will fail," she pauses and scans the mass of cadets again. "And many will die."

At that, I can't help but look over to where Aric stands and see that he is staring directly at me. He shakes his head almost imperceptibly as if he knows I've still been considering the tournament. I swallow and turn my eyes back to the colonel.

"There will be eight trials. One each week for eight weeks. Each trial pays tribute, whether in structure or in spirit, to one of Aurelia's gods. The challenges differ each year. No one can prepare in advance beyond doing their best in the training they've already been given. Between each trial, you will continue your training and work duties as usual."

I look at each conscript at my table: Berte, Stigander, Lillen, Brock, Dagmar. They're all listening, their attention unceasing, because unlike me, they've never heard about the Freiheit and didn't know what's at stake if you enter. I didn't know the format, but I at least knew of its existence.

"If you fail a trial and live, you are eliminated immediately. You may also choose to withdraw at any point in the tournament. But make no mistake—failure or withdrawal comes at a cost."

I turn my head sharply to the colonel, knowing I need to hear if she explains the cost to us. I'm not disappointed.

"Failure will add five years to your conscription sentence." A low murmur ripples through the hall. "Withdrawal will add ten years."

My stomach plummets to the ground. That would've been helpful for Aric to tell me before I got my hopes up about the tournament. I turn to glare at him, but he's not returning my gaze. Instead, he's looking at the colonel as if she's giving the most fascinating speech he's never heard before. A few officers down from him, the lieutenant colonel is spinning his dagger—Rosamunde—by its hilt, the point digging into the pad of his finger. I feel my lip curl at the sight. Of course, the man is distracting himself while the colonel speaks. He couldn't give a fuck about the conscripts here. I don't care what Aric says, even if Kriegeur was a conscript, his father is still a member of the Gold Council, and his existence here was automatically bound to be better than that of the rest of us.

Colonel Richter addresses the room once more. "If you are not discouraged from entering, or if I've failed to impress upon you the importance of your certainty in doing so, I will share with you that one trial remains the same each year. The final trial is a duel to the death between the last two remaining challengers. No exceptions."

The room goes abruptly silent.

"Should you wish to enter, you will begin in two weeks. You must lodge your name with the tournament registrar no later than nightfall tomorrow. There will be no second call, and you will be at the point of no return once you have registered. Once entered, you will fail, you will die, or if the gods will it, you will be free."

After the final portion of Colonel Richter's announcement, she sharply turned on her heel and marched from the room, her officers in tow behind her. The room erupted with chatter, many of the cadets speaking excitedly about the potential for freedom.

I immediately felt a heaviness suffuse my limbs, which stays with me as I move throughout the day. Besides the excitement of the other cadets, both enlisted and conscripted, the day continues as if nothing has happened.

Around me, life at Stachtenbaste continues to carry on with its usual practiced efficiency, but I feel the quiet, crushing gravity of the choice I must make. What will likely be the most difficult decision of my life.

It might even be one of the *last* decisions of my life if I choose to enter.

There are two paths before me: I can risk death or even harsher conscription in the tournament or remain in a place that has sought to rob me of what little remains of my existence. For without grandmother, without Agnethe, what do I have left?

And if I compete, do I have the strength to survive what so few have before me?

So many snippets of my life flash in my mind's eye: the brown felt of my doll Geraldine's hair. My father's eyes closing as he held Agnethe to his chest, and my mother's murmured encouragement to me on the last night I saw them. My small hands holding a teacup like a secret the first time I met my grandmother. My uncle Engilram's look of intense concentration as he honed and sharpened a dagger against his grindstone. My grandmother's blood welling up through the fabric of my dress, and the sluggish rise and fall of her chest as she took her last breath. I can smell Agnethe's fear as I burst into her room at Lord Rocheburn's residence to find her tied to the chair, can hear the sound of her screaming my name as I was hauled away.

So many have paid a price for my life. Do I not owe it to them to at least try to regain it? It's not just me that I'd be fighting for if I enter the tournament. I'd be fighting for Agnethe, my uncles, and my grandmother's legacy. For a chance to reclaim the existence and potential stolen from all of us when Lord Rocheburn decided that whatever he sought was more important than our lives.

During evening training, I force my aching body to continue moving through the sword drills we're starting to learn, although I'm barely able to keep up. Holding a wooden practice sword, I practice basic diagonal cuts, horizontal slashes, and thrusts while moving through different guard positions.

Ox guard, drawing my wooden blade up and to the outside, just beside my head at temple height, pointing at a slight downward diagonal, toward my imaginary opponent. Plow guard, my sword is aimed at my imaginary opponent's chest this time, the hilt touching the front of my hip. Fool's guard is the one I find easiest. Probably because the point of my sword is lowered and touching the ground. It seems the fool's guard is most fitting, because I feel foolish, and it seems to leave me the most vulnerable to attacks.

In all of my cuts, my movements lack fluidity. My transitions are slower than the other members of my team, and even though we're using practice wooden swords that are ostensibly lighter than real blades, mine still drags behind each movement. My arms burn with every reset Lieutenant Broadbente demands of us. The blade feels like a dead weight in my grip, like it knows I don't belong here.

In footwork, we practice advancing and retreating in measured steps from starting position, with one foot forward and the other pivoted and pointing out at a forty-five-degree angle. It feels unnatural to my foot and ankle, and even though the lieutenant says it's supposed to help us maintain balance, I feel even more wobbly than ever. Passing, gathering, and lunging present different but equal challenges to my coordination. I overcommit or, worse, hesitate. My back foot slides on the mud. My breath comes too fast, but I don't want to slow down when I know others are watching. I feel like a puppet with tangled strings—off balance and off rhythm, with my arms and legs not quite where they should be.

When I have to work with Dagmar on parrying and counterattacking, I parry too hard, and the lieutenant barks at me that they're not angled. I get knocked by the force of Dagmar's blows. My counterattacks are late. When the wood cracks against wood, I flinch nearly every time. My blade sings, but it's an off-key, jarring melody with no rhythm. I think Dagmar might even be beginning to pity me, which says a lot about how terrible I am at this.

With every missed parry, every wrong step, my mind whispers that if I enter the Freiheit, I'll die.

For a moment, I allow myself to fantasize about what it would be like to escape without more injury, more blood drawn. I imagine what it would be like to have someone save me, for once, allowing someone to come to *my* rescue, *my* aid, instead of always the reverse.

But no one is coming. Not unless I lie to Lord Corvilian, to Lord Rocheburn, and pretend I know something I don't. Tempting fate by seeing if I can lie just well enough to get out of Stachtenbaste and run away with Agnethe seems too reckless. Who knows if I'd even have the opportunity to make a run for it, and I won't take that risk with Agnethe.

Unbidden, the memory of the conscript brought in weeks ago resurfaces. The man who was dragged into the training yard, screaming. The whites of his eyes as they rolled back in fear. The sickening thud of his headless body hitting the ground. The sight of his head rolling several feet, coming to a stop with his eyes staring at the sky.

Stigander called Stachtenbaste a prison by another name. Whether I make it through training and am sent to the front or enter the Freiheit, I risk my life. One of those choices would see me toil for decades before even having the possibility of freedom. While entering the tournament poses a higher immediate risk, at least my suffering would be shorter lived.

I plod my way through the remainder of training and wearily stow my practice sword in the equipment shed with the others. I break away from my teammates as we walk to the citadel, allowing them to proceed ahead of me so I can be alone with my thoughts and my decision.

I climb the steps to the citadel's outcropping and slowly reach the inner bailey where the outbuildings sit. As the sun descends behind the stone walls, I enter the Administration and Records building, which is surprisingly empty. Maybe, unlike me, others had a much easier time making their decision about whether or not to enter the tournament.

The tournament registrar turns the entry log toward me, and I see dozens of names scrawled on the lines of the page. Before I can question myself any further, I hastily print and sign my name, formally entering the Freiheit Tournament. As the ink rapidly dries on the parchment, so, too, my fate is sealed.

There's no turning back now.

I step into the dark, silent air of the evening. My surroundings haven't changed, but I have. I don't feel victorious in my choice, not even resolute in it. But I do feel decided. The woman who has hemmed, hawed, and hesitated all day is gone.

The one who remains must now survive or die trying.

CHAPTER NINETEEN
Careless and Careful Whispers

The air is thick with smoke and the smell of iron. Everything is cast in the orange glow of an open flame, whether the bricks blackened from countless years of fire, the iron tools hanging from walls sticky with soot, or the aging wooden beams in the ceiling above me. I'm in a forge, but it's not a place I know. I have never seen it, of that I'm certain, but it feels familiar all the same.

In front of me, a blade lies across the anvil, its form broad, curved, and unfinished. Something about it calls to me, and I find myself walking toward it. When I reach the anvil, I stretch my hand out to run along the metal, and though its edge has yet to meet a grindstone, it cuts me all the same. Pain flashes sharp and sudden, and I jerk my hand back as a thin line of blood appears across my palm, the cut forming a macabre smile that grins up at me. Though it's a small cut, the blood wells quickly and drips down my hand, following the path of my fingers to their edge until it falls onto the blade.

The moment it lands on the metal's surface, the blade begins to glow. Spreading from the point of contact, a strange pattern illuminates along the metal, a central path with many veins branching from it. My pulse roars in my ears.

Suddenly, fire erupts from the hearth, a gout of flame that sears the air, and I *can taste it on my tongue, hot and dry. Then, spreading over the surface of the ground toward the hearth is ice, white and brittle, creaking beneath my feet, and rising around me in jagged points. Wind gusts past my face, whipping strands of my hair across it. I reach a hand up to brush it away when sand blows into it, stinging my cheeks, and I'm grateful for the protection my hair affords as it covers my eyes. The scent of the ocean's brine invades my nose, and I reel back from the shock to my senses.*

My throat feels as dry as a desert and twice as hot, and I turn from the anvil, looking for a source of water to moisten it. I spy the quenching trough and stumble toward it, blinded and choking on heat and salt and smoke, my skin simultaneously on fire and freezing.

When I reach the trough, I crash into it, nearly falling to the stone floor on my knees from the impact, but manage to brace myself with my hands on its side, the impact sending a shooting pain through my wounded palm. Bending over the trough where the water's surface is eerily still, I reach a cupped hand down to scoop some of the precious liquid into my mouth. My face stares back at me—eyes and hair wide and wild, cheeks flushed and slick with sweat.

Rising behind me, black as the sooty walls and gleaming faintly with hints of violet and indigo, are massive black wings. I blink, but they remain poised on my back.

Panicking, I surge to my feet, whirling in place, looking for an exit. Seeing a door off to the side, I make a break for it, nearly sobbing with fear as I frantically pull on the metal door handle. Thankfully, it doesn't protest as I yank it open so forcefully that it slams against the wall. I run outside into the darkness of night, the only light illuminating my surroundings from the moon above me, though it's covered by clouds. I lift my eyes just as the clouds break, the night sky revealing its master.

A blood moon.

Unnerved, I look around for an escape route and see a shadowy figure standing several yards away.

"Who are you?" I ask them.

"I am the keeper of what was buried by blood and time. A legacy forgotten but not dead."

My blood freezes in my veins. I slowly creep forward in the direction of the voice, though every instinct in me is screaming to run in the opposite direction. The shadow hasn't moved but becomes no clearer the closer I get. I stop several feet before it and wait several moments before speaking.

"You…you're the keeper of a legacy?" I ask.

No answer. I inch forward.

The shadow shifts. Twin spots of red appear in the dark—deep, crimson red, the same color as the blood I spilled from my hand in the forge. They don't glitter like gemstones nor glow like lights; rather, they reflect my own face back at me, like an unnerving pair of mirrors. I stare at my reflection in them and feel something stir within me. Something ancient, knowing, powerful. Alive.

I repeat, "You're the keeper of a legacy?"

The voice doesn't answer, but the red spots disappear and reappear shortly after, almost like they're blinking at me. That's when it dawns on me.

Eyes. I'm staring into someone's eyes.

I open my mouth and scream.

I jolt awake suddenly but silently, sitting upright. The dormitory is still dark; the earliest light of dawn has not yet broken the night sky. My heart is pounding, and I can feel sweat along my hairline at the back of my neck where my braid lies heavily against it.

I lift my braid off my neck, flipping it forward on my head, and turn my pillow over before flopping back down onto my bed with a sigh. Trying to cool off, calm my still-racing heart, and banish the edginess I feel following my dream, I kick off the blanket. The sweat drying on my skin in the cool room, however, means I quickly feel chilly and have to pull it back up over my body.

I cross my ankles under the blanket. Then I uncross them.

I lift my head and slide my forearm beneath it. My neck starts to hurt, so I remove it.

I count the breaths of those sleeping around me.

I sing songs in my head, tapping my fingers against my leg, silently counting out the syllables.

I mentally recite the hymn of the First Blood about how the sister goddesses, Levitia and Mortuua, created the world.

Next, the Covenant of Balance.

I count the number of days I've been at Stachtenbaste—twenty-nine. I can scarcely believe it's been as long as it has and yet not very long at all.

Tomorrow, the Freiheit Tournament begins.

With that realization, my heart not only refuses to slow down, but it actually begins to pound faster. I feel the tingling thrill of foreboding travel the surface of my skin, and I know I'll never be able to fall back asleep. I throw my blanket back, grab my uniform and boots, and head to the bathing chamber, hoping the frigid water will clear my head or at least prove enough distraction to forget my fear and anxiety temporarily.

After I bathe, I braid my hair and head down the stairs and outside toward the officers' training yard where I'm to meet Aric for more practice. The compound is even quieter than when I meet him at dawn, eerily still. Though construction for the Freiheit has been going nearly nonstop since Colonel Richter announced it two weeks ago, even those workers are still abed at this hour. They've been working long into the evenings constructing gods know what kind of torture for the challengers, their craft hidden behind wooden planks affixed over the gates to the walled-off portion of the grounds with the arena in it.

The breeze coming off the Dorberge mountains tugs at my hair, blowing golden brown tendrils across my cheeks. The river beyond the walls courses briskly along, only halting its progress when it meets the island's rocks. If I weren't contemplating my very likely demise tomorrow, I'd almost find it peaceful.

Having made my way at a leisurely pace, I finally approach the gates to the officers' training yard. Aric hasn't yet arrived, even though dawn's faintest blushing beams have begun to shyly make their presence known behind the mountains. I lean against the wall of the training yard, humming to myself quietly, when a soft whoosh cuts through the stillness, followed by a snap, almost like that of linens blowing on a line. A shadow falls over me, and I turn to look at the wall behind me and make several hasty steps backward when I see a large raven sitting on its edge, only a few feet away.

We stare at one another for several long moments. Unable to resist, I quip, "We simply must stop meeting like this; it's highly inappropriate when we haven't been properly introduced."

The raven watches me silently, still save for its wings rustling in the breeze, and I feel tingling awareness spread across my scalp as it does.

I step closer to it. "You *are* the same raven I've been seeing, aren't you?"

It cocks its head to the side, and I swear it's almost as if it's listening to me.

I stop two feet from it. "Can you understand me?" I whisper.

Its head tilts in the other direction, and the dawn light has broken enough over the horizon to illuminate its face to where I'm able to distinguish its features. Shaggy feathers erupt from its throat and sit against its chest, like a lacy cravat made of iridescent black. Its large, stout beak is not a graceful dagger's blade like that of a crow, but rather like the stout, punishing blade of a butcher knife. Small feathers like the bristles of a brush decorate the top of it. And above its beak, its bright, curious eyes watch me.

Eyes a disconcerting shade of crimson.

I'm frozen, staring into the raven's blood-red eyes, so like those from my dream. I blink several times to be sure that what I see is not a product of a sleep-deprived brain, but real. Each time I open my eyes, though, the raven's remain the same. That isn't normal, for a raven to have red eyes, is it?

I back up a few steps again, and it's then that I hear the sound of boots on gravel. I turn and see Aric walking toward me, all calm, commanding presence and careful expression. We haven't spoken about the Freiheit Tournament since the day Colonel Richter announced it. But as the list of entrants was publicly posted following the close of registration, he'd be a fool not to know I signed up. I know he's angry, I can feel it in the pregnant silences that surround our practice sessions, but he hasn't mentioned it, hasn't indicated anything about it. The fact that he won't acknowledge it or ask me how I'm feeling about it hurts somehow. As if his anger is more important than my reasons for doing this. I'm not so foolish as to believe that we have the closeness I've developed with Lotti and Otto and Cyneric, but I thought that this time alone at least proved that we are more than mere acquaintances. Friends, even. And the attraction I thought I felt simmering close to the surface during our first session has been notably absent in every subsequent interaction, making me wonder if I imagined it.

As Aric approaches the gate, he produces a key and wordlessly unlocks it. It's bright enough outside that we don't need the torches, so he gestures that I should enter the training yard in front of him.

I hesitate, asking, "Did you see the…raven?" My voice trails off as I turn toward where the raven was perched, only to see that it has since gone.

"I didn't see it. Why?" He questions and again indicates that I should pass through the gate before him.

Flushing, I reply, "No reason," and hurry into the training yard.

Except for his terse instructions, we don't converse, as has been the case for the past two weeks. I execute my sparring drills followed by some of the sword-fighting guard positions. For his part, Aric corrects my stances without touch and without warmth. I feel the tension between us drawing tight like a bow string, and the awkwardness shifts into anger the longer this continues.

The tournament is *tomorrow*, and he can barely be bothered to speak to me. I would almost tell him not to bother with practice, but the truth is I sorely need it. My form is slightly cleaner, my reaction marginally sharper, but my core remains weak, my arm strength unpredictable, and while I've improved, my "improved" is still a far cry from "good" or even "decent." I'm trying, but it's not enough. I can tell Aric feels the same.

When I raise my hands and practice sword to the ox guard position, he finally speaks beyond the bare minimum.

"I want you to drop out of the tournament," he says.

"What?" I'm so startled I drop my arms, and my practice sword falls with a heavy thud to the ground, hitting my toes. "Shit!"

I step back and hop on my uninjured foot.

He repeats, staring directly into my eyes. "I want you to drop out."

Feeling nervous, I look away and bend down to pick up my practice sword. "You know I can't do that."

He snatches the blade from my hand. "Can't? Or won't?"

My temper flares. "Can't, Aric." If he is surprised that I've called him by his first name, he doesn't show it.

"I disagree," he says stubbornly.

I snap, "Withdrawing means ten more years. It means giving up on my—on what I need to do." I almost let slip about Agnethe, but I stop myself at the last minute.

"It means you'll live," he says, heatedly.

"For now," I counter, my voice sharp.

Aric huffs in exasperation. "I think you're being a bit dramatic, don't you?"

"No, I don't," I say. He opens his mouth to argue, and I cut him off, "Look at me, Aric. I can barely hold my godsdamned *practice* sword up for more than a minute or two. I trip over my own feet. I'm not strong enough or fast enough. If I see combat, I'll die."

Being forced to say it aloud makes me realize how much I believe it to be true. If I can't make it out of here, I'm as good as dead. Panic and despair crest within me.

"Not if you just keep trying—"

"*This is me trying!*" I yell at him and surge forward until I'm close enough to poke him in the chest. "I don't even know why it makes a difference to you. I'm another conscript! A criminal in the eyes of the Aurenclaste, and I'm a terrible fucking soldier to boot."

He grabs my hand and pulls it away from his chest, and for a moment, I think he's going to push me away and storm off. Instead, he pulls me closer, trapping my hand against his chest between our bodies. I stare at my hand, which presses flat against his chest. My brain refuses to comprehend what's happening but registers the steady thump of his heart beneath my palm. I slowly turn my head up to meet his gaze. This close, I can see flecks of gold in his chocolatey eyes, can see the way his lips part subtly as he stares at me, feel the way his heartbeat increases.

He bends his face toward mine, pausing when his lips are only a hairsbreadth from mine. "You really don't know why?"

My fingers tighten reflexively, bunching the fabric of his tunic in my hand. He releases my wrist and slides his hand up my forearm, my upper arm, until his warm, callused palm slips up the side of my neck to cup the nape with his fingers. My heart feels like it's going to leap out of my chest, and I'm certain he can feel the way my pulse is galloping in the side of my neck.

I swallow hard. "No," I whisper a moment before his lips touch mine.

He kisses me like he intends to show me why, not with words, but with heat and intent and quiet desperation. It's not clumsy or forced, not rushed. His other hand finds my waist, steadying me as if he thinks I might fall at any moment, and the world narrows to the places our bodies touch—at my neck, at my waist, at our mouths. My lips part involuntarily beneath his, and his tongue sweeps past them, claiming me. A sweet ache blossoms low in my stomach, twirling like a wisp of smoke, and I lean into him, chasing the ache.

His hand twitches at my waist, almost like he wants to move it farther but is restraining himself. I'm about to tell him to stop holding back when the sounds of boots on gravel and cheerful whistling approach the training yard. He must hear it also, because he suddenly, abruptly pulls away from me, dropping his hands from my body and putting a distance of several feet between us. His lips are reddened, his face is flushed high on his cheekbones, and he's breathing heavily.

Lieutenant Colonel Kriegeur opens the gate and strolls in, looking surprised to see us, the whistle dying on his lips when he does.

"Well, well, well," he drawls, "getting in some extra sparring practice, *künnle*?" He asks, and the way he says "sparring" as he arches a dark brow leads me to believe he knows exactly what was happening.

I look between Kriegeur and Aric, at a loss for words, unsure how to address Aric without tipping off Kriegeur, and Kriegeur without calling him an arsehole. My mouth opens and closes several times, but no sound comes out.

"We were just finishing up lessons here," Aric says to Kriegeur. "We'll be off shortly and out of your way."

"Not at all, cousin," Kriegeur says. "On the contrary, if you believe *künnle* is in need of lessons, I'd be happy to show her my techniques." He winks at me, and my face feels hot.

I say, "No need. I must be off for work duties. Captain, Lieutenant Colonel." I bow stiffly to each of them and, before either one can say anything further, rush out of the training yard.

CHAPTER TWENTY
The Gods' Assault with a Deadly Obstacle Course

The following afternoon, I stand shoulder to shoulder with over a hundred conscripts in the vast field surrounding the arena, tension buzzing in my limbs. The wooden stands erected on either side of the field groan under the weight of observing cadets, Aurengarte soldiers, and visiting Aurenclaste members. Their enthusiastic chatter, cheering, and jeering add to the din, competing for dominance with the pounding in my ears.

As more conscripts and crowd members filter in through the gates to what is now called "Freiheit Field," I scan the long stretch of land between the stands. Sprawled across its length is an obstacle course, its details unclear but menacing, nonetheless. A wall here, a platform there, an odd bridge-looking span, and somehow, most ominous of all, a stretch of open field in the middle. Gods only know what they have in store for us there.

When I look around at my fellow entrants, I catch sight of Stigander, Brock, Lillen, Berte, and Dagmar in the mass of bodies. All of them, like me, have signed up to gamble their lives for a chance at freedom. A flicker of movement flashes in the corner of my eye, and I look up into the stands to see Lotti and Otto grinning and offering waves and thumbs up. Gratitude floods my being as I look upon their encouraging faces. I don't know if they believe I can win, but they're here with me regardless.

On a covered platform separate from the regular stands are considerably nicer seats, upon which many of the officers are seated, including Lord Corvilian himself. He must have arrived expressly for the trials. Beside him is an extremely young, timid-looking woman with light brown hair and pale skin who is so draped in finery it's a miracle she doesn't collapse under its weight. His wife, perhaps? She looks too young to be Kriegeur's mother, so she must be a second wife if so. On her other side is a wizened old man in ceremonial temple robes, clearly a high-ranking member of the Order of the Blessed Sisters, like my Uncle Burkhard. Perhaps he's here to add spiritual gravitas to the ensuing massacre. Or to provide blessings to the dead. I grimace at the thought.

To Lord Corvilian's other side sits Lieutenant Colonel Kriegeur, who looks as if he'd rather be anywhere but his present location, one of his legs draped indolently over the arm of his chair. He is currently throwing his dagger end over end into the air and catching it between his fingers. Part of me hopes he pokes himself and looks like a moron.

Well…like even *more* of a moron. A more-on.

Seated in a row of chairs behind Lord Corvilian, his assumed wife, Kriegeur, the colonel, Major Berger, are the other officers—some of whom I don't recognize—including Aric. I stare at him for longer than I should, desperately hoping he'll search the crowd for me and I'll be able to convey what I'm feeling through my face. But he doesn't glance my way; he's in focused conversation with Lieutenant Broadbente and never once looks up the entire time I watch him.

When I ran from the training yard yesterday, I skipped breakfast, preferring to hide in the dormitory until Lotti found me and dragged me to training. Aric didn't attend, which was both relieving and disappointing. Part of me is angry with myself. I should have shoved him away instead of merely accepting his kiss. A kiss, after all, changes nothing—least of all my chances of survival here. No amount of kisses and coddling can armor me against the Freiheit, Lord Rocheburn, combat, death. I am also angry *with him*. Why now? Why right when I was on the precipice of something so dangerous, after weeks of brooding silence and barked commands? Was it pity or strategy, passion or control?

The other part of me…well, that part of me can still feel the press of his mouth on mine, the gentleness of his hand at my waist, the thud of his heart pounding beneath my palm. As I watch the sun glint on his chestnut hair, its rays casting a glow upon his golden skin, I find myself thinking of possibilities and filled with the fervent hope that he's not too upset to approach me after the trial so we can talk about what it all meant.

Assuming I make it out alive, of course.

Frustrated at my own line of thinking, I look down at the grass beneath my feet. One kiss and all thought of my true purpose, my duty, flees my silly head. I close my eyes, and Agnethe's face appears behind my eyelids. How can I indulge in stolen warmth, in such frivolous daydreams, when she may be suffering? Desire is not a luxury my sister can contemplate right now, so I should be sharpening my focus and my footing, not losing it over a man who won't even look me in the eye right now. Perhaps it truly meant nothing to him. But it meant something to me. And while part of me aches to feel it again, the other part knows it's a foolish fantasy. Longing dulls instincts, fractures focus. And I need all the focus and instinct I can get right now.

Clenching my fists, I shift my feet to shoulder width apart to steady my swaying form and center myself. I take several deep, stabilizing breaths. I think of Agnethe in the *loubenstille*, her blood on stone, her screams in that small, windowless chamber, and ice spreads through my veins along with even icier resolve.

Colonel Richter stands from her chair and steps forward to the edge of the platform, and just as quickly as my resolve filled me, it flees, and my mouth goes dry. She nods at a young woman standing in front of the platform who returns it, and as the colonel opens her mouth and begins speaking, the woman flicks her wrist, and a gentle breeze whistles along the colonel's form, ruffling her hair. Her voice is suddenly amplified across the entire field.

"A wind wielder," someone near me says in hushed awe. "She must be projecting the colonel's voice."

I had *heard* of many of the types of major magic, including the ability to manipulate, or even create, certain types of weather elements, but with a—mostly—non-magical family, and no cause to see wielders in the quiet countryside of Noetheim, I'd never seen a gift like this up close. I certainly hadn't considered some of its uses beyond various wielders' straightforward capabilities.

"Lord Corvilian, distinguished members of the Aurenclaste, officers and soldiers of the Aurengarte, and cadets of Stachtenbaste, welcome to the Freiheit Tournament!" She opens her arms wide, and the entire crowd cheers. A few conscripts around me give half-hearted applause, but most stay silent, and I suspect they're all just as nervous as I am.

"You have gathered to witness not only the beginning of the tournament, one of Stachtenbaste's sacred traditions, but the pursuit of divine judgment.

"Before you stand those who have chosen to compete—men and women conscripted into service, now bound by the rules of the tournament. For the next eight weeks, they are no longer cadets; they are *challengers*. United not by bloodline, origin, credo, or conviction; rather, by a single hope: to win.

"One victor shall earn the dismissal of all charges levied against them, release from conscription, and a lifetime stipend drawn from the Aurengarte's coffers. This is the promise of the Freiheit Tournament, the results of which are earned through sacrifice and tempered by the divine."

She pauses, scanning the crowd, who is hanging on her every last word.

"Each week," she continues, "the challengers will face one trial. Eight trials in total, each a tribute to one of Aurelia's gods or goddesses. These trials will test more than strength. They test resilience, resolve, intelligence; indeed, they test your very soul. No advantages are given to those born of a certain region, rank, or background. Only those who choose to fight, to endure, will triumph and continue. This tradition is echoed in our first breath as a people, and we are told as much in scripture. To reflect on those beginnings, we are joined by Pfaetr Joham,

Hochvîger of the Order of the Blessed Sisters, who will sing the hymn of The First Blood."

She steps back, but remains standing, as the old man seated next to Lady Corvilian slowly rises to his feet and shuffles forward. He looks as though a stiff breeze might blow him away, and I hope the wind wielder considers that before amplifying his voice and aims her magic very carefully.

Without pretense or preamble, Pfaetr Joham begins to sing the hymn, which is really more of a chant, the old Aurelian lyrics telling the story of how mortals came to be:

"From silence came the Sisters, eternal and entwined.
Levitia opened her palm and let her blood fall to the soil.
Mortuua knelt and shaped it—flesh and flame, root and river.
From blood came bone, from bone came breath, and from breath, will.
Thus, were mortals made: to live, to die, to choose."

Pfaetr Joham opens his eyes and addresses the crowd. "The teachings of the twin goddesses are ever essential as you challengers stand at the threshold of these ordeals. Levitia, goddess of life, protection, and rebirth, grants us the gift of first breath—the beginning of every life's journey. Her sister, Mortuua, goddess of death, endings, sacrifice, and the passage of time, takes us into her care following our last breath—the grace of an ending well met.

"Together, they are not opposites, but reflections—each giving shape to the other. This is the balance the Blessed Sisters give us. This is the rhythm that governs all things. And from that balance, comes the gift that defines all mortals: choice. The Sisters did not shape mortals and bestow balance only to govern our every step.

"It may feel as though your path became fixed the moment you put name to Freiheit ledger. But make no mistake, even now there is choice. In every moment of fear, every blow, every step forward, choice remains. Each of you has already chosen to be here, but that was only the first. The true measure of your will is not in entering the trials, but in how you choose to face them.

"When you do, remember that in all trials and tribulations, there exists a counterpart from which you can draw reassurance. For every sorrow, there is joy. For every night, there is dawn. And with every end, there is a new beginning."

My breath seizes in my lungs at his words. Had I not recently dreamed of the last night I had seen my parents, and my mother's last words to me, I likely would have never taken note. Though his words are not familiar scripture, they are also in keeping with the typical teachings of our gods. Was it merely coincidence then, that he recited the words from my dream nearly verbatim? Had my mother been quoting some little-known scripture to me? Or was the likelihood that I had somehow inherited my grandmother's sight higher than I had initially assumed? The thought sends a chill down to the very marrow of my bones.

Pfaetr Joham returns to his chair, and Colonel Richter steps forward once more. "Thank you, Pfaetr, for your guidance. Challengers, the Freiheit exists so that your choice might mean something. You chose to enter this tournament, and that choice will yield your future, for good or ill. Choice, however, comes with consequence. If you fail or withdraw, this will result in additional time added to your conscription sentence. To progress to the next trial, you must complete the current trial in accordance with its rules. Between trials, you will resume your assigned duties and training unless you are deemed unfit by our healers. Most trials are public, so your victories—and your failures—will have witnesses."

I swallow hard. I struggle enough with being the center of attention when I'm *good* at something, let alone when I'm bad at it. My humiliation at the *Nachtrif* still stings more than I'd like to admit.

"The good news, however, is that your triumphs in each trial will not come without reward. The winner or winners of a given trial will earn a crucial advantage in the next, except for trials four and eight, where all must stand equally before the gods. At the halfway point, following the fourth trial, select members of the Aurengarte will choose a challenger to mentor through the final four trials. Those selected by a mentor should consider this a privilege."

She goes on to list the mentors who will observe our first four trials before making their selections, which includes officers like Major Berger, Lieutenant Broadbente, and Aric. I look toward where Aric is seated again, hoping to catch his gaze. However, he still has not looked in my direction, whether purposefully or simply because he hasn't spotted me, I'm not entirely sure, but my pride sincerely hopes it's the latter.

"Today's trial will admit sixty to the second trial." A shocked murmur ripples across the entire crowd. Considering how many of us there are, that means a large portion of us will not progress. "The first sixty challengers to cross the finish line will advance. The rest, whether through failure or death, will not proceed."

She allows us to digest this information, and I look at my teammates in the crowd to gauge their reactions to this news. Berte and Brock look worried. Lillen looks unbothered. Stigander looks as surly as ever. Dagmar's expression is completely neutral, as if she sees even betraying her feelings about the rules as giving some kind of advantage to her fellow competitors.

"Challengers, this tournament will not just expose the most capable, the bravest, the most cunning. It will also force you to confront your weaknesses, your vulnerabilities, and your fears. Those who are too weak may falter, but the worthy—the truly worthy—let the trials temper them into something greater. The trials will burn, but not all fire is destructive. Some fire purifies. When all is done, let what remains of you be forged in valor and cast in strength."

Forged in valor. Cast in strength. The last lines of the oath of the Aurengarte.

As the crowd cheers, Colonel Richter returns to her seat, and Major Berger steps forward, white teeth flashing against dark skin as she grins at the challengers and onlookers alike. Where Colonel Richter is quiet strength and commanding stoicism, Major Berger is captivating flair and dramatic sensationalism.

"Challengers," she booms. "Allow me to introduce you to your first trial: The Gods' Assault."

"The Gods' Assault is a five-part obstacle course that challengers must complete in order to progress to the next trial. And, as Colonel Richter stated, you must be one of the first sixty to do so for that to happen. Further, each obstacle of the course must be completed before moving to the next one, and you must complete them within the stipulated rules—first, Erdia's Mountain. For the obstacle honoring our goddess of the earth and the mountains she's created, you'll encounter a vertical climb followed by a drop by rope or jumping. However, since the drop is forty-five feet off the ground and has a fifty-percent fatality rate and a one-hundred-percent chance of injury, I don't recommend taking a leap of faith." She grins at her own pun.

I happen to see Kriegeur grinning at her. *I wonder if they're friends*, I think wryly. They seem to share a similar sense of humor at least.

"There is no time limit for Erdia's Mountain, but the fastest challengers will proceed the quickest to the next obstacle, so time is of the essence. Next, Luftella's Breeze. You will pay tribute to the goddess of the skies by demonstrating the power of the wind she grants us. With a bow and arrow, you must strike a series of targets at increasing distances. Targets are placed at thirty, forty, fifty, and seventy yards. You will be allowed a maximum of five shooting attempts for the four targets and a maximum shooting time of six minutes, or you will fail the trial."

My stomach drops. Shooting *arrows*? I took basic ladies' archery lessons when I was younger than Agnethe is now, but that was almost six years ago, I was abysmal at it, and we haven't even begun to train with the longbow since I've been at Stachtenbaste. I'm doomed.

"Feuerignis's Flame. The god of fire's challenge will see you cross a field while facing various fire-laden tasks—avoiding flame-tipped arrows, traversing fire-hot rotating barrels, and capped off by leaping over a three-foot-high flame. There is no time limit for this step."

Oh, lovely. A wall of flame over half my height. No trouble. My palms are already sweating. My gaze darts to my fellow challengers from my team, and they look concerned also. At least I'm not alone in that.

"For Aquaemus's Sea, you will honor the god of the oceans and waters by crossing a bridge measuring thirty-five yards and suspended over water. Sounds simple, yes?" She scans the group of challengers, nodding. "By the way, the bridge is only a foot wide. Also, I feel I should mention that if a challenger falls off, they will not be permitted to climb back on and must swim the remainder of the way across."

"Blessed Sisters," someone beside me murmurs, horrified. It dawns on me then that some of the challengers might not know how to swim and will dread this step.

"Finally, if all of that weren't exciting enough," Major Berger paces the platform before us. "You'll end with a tribute to the goddess of healing, Heilane. However, I'll wait for you to make it to that point to find out just what's in store as our little welcome surprise." She winks at the challengers.

I feel a hysterical laugh bubble up inside me, desperate to escape.

Out of the corner of my eye, a black shape descends near the first obstacle. I almost know what I'll see but do not quite believe it. I watch as a raven perches on top of the wall of Erdia's Mountain. Though I can't see its eyes from this distance, there can be no doubt in my mind now that it's the same bird I've been seeing. Has it identified me as a friend and decided to follow me? Maybe, given its unnerving red eyes, it's decided my generous proportions are worthy of a snack. It seems entirely plausible that some kind of creepy, red-eyed demon bird would also be one willing to ingest humans.

I hear whispers nearby, but none of the challengers I can see are speaking, so it has to be the onlooker crowd murmuring, which makes my brow furrow in concern. What did I miss in Major Berger's instructions while distracted by the raven? I don't get a chance to figure it out, because the challengers are beginning to line up along the starting line. Swallowing hard, I step forward and risk one last glance toward Aric. He's watching me grimly, his mouth compressed into a line. As I turn my gaze from him, trying to quell the fear and disappointment that threatens to erupt from me at the lack of nonverbal encouragement, my eyes stall on Kriegeur.

To my surprise, he's watching me, too. When he meets my stare, he wiggles his fingers at me in a playful wave. I stiffen in shock, unable to resist looking at Aric once more, who is watching his cousin with an irritated expression. Frustrated with myself for rechecking his reaction, I turn back to the starting line. Only I would be worrying about what Aric thinks right before I die.

As I draw up to the starting line, I make eye contact with Stigander, then Berte, then Brock and Lillen, all of whom give me small smiles. Next, I find Dagmar, who only gives me a stiff nod, but from Dagmar, that's practically a confession of love.

The starting horn sounds, and the mass of challengers moves frantically toward the first obstacle. At the base, I stare up at the daunting, forty-plus-foot wall in front of me. The bottom half is composed of rocks stacked on top of one another, some with small notches for hands and feet to find, some protruding slightly for the same purpose, and some are sheared flat, making me wonder how we're meant to ascend, especially as most of those appear to be closer to the top of the rock portion. Following the rocks is a section of rope netting laid out in a grid that flexes with the slightest movement, from wind or challenger alike. At the top of the rope net is a long wooden bar from which multiple lengths of rope are knotted and disappear over the side. I can only assume this is the vertical drop by rope or jump that Major Berger mentioned with such cheek.

I stare at the obstacle before me, trying to stay calm by reminding myself not to rush, because there's no time limit. However, I also know it's necessary when I'm going up against challengers who are far more physically capable. In fact, many challengers are already passing me.

I scan the top wooden bar of the wall, looking for my raven stalker, but it seems to have abandoned me to the mercy of the wall obstacle. How far have I fallen into fear that even the continued, eerie presence of the dark bird would be a comfort to me? Shaking my head and gritting my teeth, I tell myself this is for Agnethe and that I've stalled long enough. I reach forward and dig my fingers into the rocks in front of me, looking for a foothold to boost myself up.

At first, the climb isn't so bad. I'm able to find some foot and hand rests and pull myself up with a modicum of speed. I'm thankful for the help my height provides in elongating my reach, thus shortening my ascent, and even more grateful that I'm not the last person to climb the obstacle, some still stuck on lower portions of the rock wall, some paralyzed with fear of heights before even beginning, and some have fallen to the ground, their hands or feet having slipped. I wedge my boot into another gap between stones and reach as high as I can, pulling myself up another few inches.

The foot and hand holds are getting fewer and farther between, and I've reached the flatter portion of the rocks I spotted from the ground. I wince as I dig my hand into a hold and feel a fingernail tear against the roughness of the rock. The holds are also becoming smaller. Having hoisted myself using ever-decreasing allowances of space, my arms are burning by the time I reach the end of the rock portion, and I fear for my stamina for the remainder of this obstacle, let alone the whole course. If I hadn't been practicing with Aric, I don't think I would've done half as well as I have on this part. If I don't plummet to my death, flunk out of hitting archery targets, get burned alive, drown, or expire from whatever Heilane-inspired torture awaits us at the end, I'll have to thank him.

I stretch an arm up from the rock and grab onto the first rope rungs of the next section of the wall. As I pull myself up to stand on the rungs fully, I suddenly feel a weight on my shoulder.

A hand.

In horror, I watch as the hand, belonging to a man I don't recognize, presses down hard on my shoulder before digging into it and pulling.

"Get out of my fucking way if you're going to be slow about it," he yells sharply.

His hand shoves hard into my shoulder, yanking me sideways. I can't resist crying out as I'm flung into the rope grid, my arms tangling instinctively to keep me from falling. One of my forearms hooks through a square, the rope biting into the tender skin under my arm.

My whole body whips backward. Suddenly, I'm facing the wrong way, the starting line below me. My arms start tangling in the rope grid; the fact that they're caught is the only thing that keeps me from immediately plummeting to the ground. As it is, I have to grab on with my right arm, hooking my forearm through another square of the grid, letting the rope dig into my underarm so I don't continue to slip. My swing outward means I've been thrust against the rope rungs back first and am facing the starting line once more.

My feet dangle for several seconds, frantically searching for purchase, and I nearly sob with relief when I feel one hook inside of one of the rope grids. I look down and see my ankle is tangled in it, and then I look down even farther to the ground. All the way down. I'm suspended at least twenty-five feet in the air with nothing but a bit of rope to keep me up here. I rock once. Twice. On the third swing, I twist hard, flipping myself back over with more grace than I knew I had.

I brace myself on the rope for a moment, trying to allow time for my racing heart to slow down. Instead of feeling calmer, however, anger surges through me, hot and prickling across my scalp and through my limbs. Ignoring the scrapes on my hands, I begin to climb, no longer hesitating or looking down. With anger fueling me, I make it to the top relatively quickly.

I throw my stomach over the wooden beam and nearly scream when I look down. I'm not normally afraid of heights, but the drop is farther than I thought it would be. Then I make the mistake of looking at the course facing me ahead.

The rotating barrels, the surging flames, the bridge so impossibly long I can't even see the finish line. The rage that had spurred me on and energized me only moments before is rapidly depleting in the wake of the dread I feel upon seeing what I have left to overcome.

I shakily straddle the wooden bar, then slowly swing my other leg over it until I'm draped over it, stomach down, my hands still gripping the rope net. Going purely based on feel—because I refuse to turn my head and chance looking down—I reach one hand out and pull a dangling strand toward me until it enters my field of vision. I hook one leg around rope thicker than my wrist and grip it so tightly with my fingers that my knuckles turn white. Then I wrap my other leg around it, but still hang over the bar. My remaining hand refuses to relinquish its hold on the rope net on the other side. I nearly vomit when I consider what I need to do next, but challengers are passing me, and fast. I need to get moving.

My other hand is still clutching the net.

I can't hold both. I have to let go.

I suck in a breath, shut my eyes, and release.

CHAPTER TWENTY-ONE
Blood is Thicker than Slaughter

Fire sears along my palms as I slide down the rope, and the scream that tears from my throat tells me I'm closer to beast at this moment than human. Fear has me keeping a death-grip hold on the rope, though, so the torture continues bit by bit as I descend at what feels like an agonizingly slow rate. Once I'm close enough to the ground to where I think I can jump, I let go of the rope.

An "oof" slips out from my lips as I hit the ground, which turns out to be farther from me than I had calculated. My boots make contact with the dirt beneath me briefly before I crumple into a heap, my raw palms burning in protest when they slap against the hard-packed earth. I know if I don't stand up quickly, I'll never be able to keep going, and I still have four more obstacles to get through before I reach the end.

I am conscious of the people running past me and that I need to make up ground, as well as the groaning bodies of fellow challengers strewn around me on the ground. As I haul myself to my feet, I catch sight of the too-still form of someone nearby. His head bends at an unnatural angle, and when I slog past him wearily, I can see his face is locked in a rictus of terror. Fear prickles, sharp and stinging, across the surface of my skin, and I desperately wish I could take a few minutes to gather my thoughts, drink some water, prepare myself for what I saw was coming next when I was on top of the wall, but I know time isn't a luxury I possess. So, I swallow that fear and revulsion and push myself into a half-hearted run toward the next challenge in the course.

Perhaps those laps around the training yard helped me a bit, after all, I think. Though I'd die before admitting it to Lieutenant Broadbente.

Luftella's Breeze demands precise shooting with a longbow and arrows at successively farther targets. Unfortunately, I don't think my previous comportment lessons will help me in this. This is a distance for which I've never trained. This is pressure that crushes the air from my lungs. A failure here ends my future, my life, Agnethe's life, not my social standing.

And precision? I scoff inwardly. My instructor told my grandmother that I was "too spirited" for archery. In other words, too impatient, but phrased in a way that was palatable to my grandmother, who was paying for their services. There is no tolerance here, no polite smattering of applause from the household staff. No shaded gallery. Just sand trickling through the slim neck of the hourglass I'm to turn over when I begin, and a line of imposing officers watching with stony expressions, waiting to judge whether I can proceed or if this is where my tournament journey ends. Whether I'm allowed to keep fighting for my life or whether I'm a lost cause. All of my hopes pin to the point of an arrow.

I step up to the closest station, and the officer nearby nods at the hourglass, which I turn over, panic rising with every grain that falls to the bottom. I reach for the bow leaned against the block, holding my hourglass, and I immediately know this will be harder than I had anticipated. My fingers are raw, stiff. The burns from the rope make my hands feel like they've been dipped in lye the moment I close my grip, and I swear I can feel my heart beating in the pads of my fingers.

So much for grace and posture, as I was taught in my lessons, my instructor neglected to teach me how to fire arrows with blood on my hands. I clumsily position the bow and nock an arrow, thankful that I at least had a jumping-off point from my lessons, or I'd be doomed already.

I take a deep breath in and exhale, staring down the shaft of the arrow at my closest target of thirty yards and release the arrow.

…and miss. Badly.

"Shit!" I hiss, flicking my fingers back and forth to soothe the additional pain brought on from the tension of the pull and release of the bow string on the flayed skin of my hands.

Now, I'm fucked. I had five attempts and four targets. Which means I cannot miss any of my remaining shots. Feeling my heart pounding, I nock my second arrow and am about to release it when I see the raven sitting on the farthest target. I watch it for a few seconds, and though it's far away, I can swear it's watching me back. Somehow, the fact that it's here makes me feel calmer. Though the anxiety still prickles across my skin, I manage to position my bow more smoothly than the first time, take a deep breath, and release.

It hits the target!

I almost whoop in triumph, but I'm so shocked and worried I'll somehow curse myself by celebrating prematurely, that I simply reach for my next arrow. Thankfully, I manage to dispatch the next two targets in much the same manner as I did with the first. My last target, however, is nothing short of daunting. Seventy yards away. I can make out the general shape of the target, the raven sitting atop it, but nothing else on it. I look at my hourglass, and my throat seizes when I see how little sand I have left. My patient and careful shooting has been all well and good for accuracy, but it won't help me if I run out of time.

I reach for the last arrow, fumbling with it several times before nocking it properly. I start to let my fingers slip away from the end when a gust of wind ruffles my hair, and I freeze, waiting for it to pass. I watch as several other challengers' arrows go astray, their cries of dismay both genuine and heartbreaking.

Haste starves the seed; patience gives it bloom.

I'm not sure where I've heard the adage before, but taking one last look at the depleting sand in my hourglass, I acknowledge that I can't rush or I'll miss. I pull back the bowstring once more, stare down the arrow's shaft, eye my target, and count to one…two…three…and let go.

It hits!

This time, I don't stop from letting out a triumphant shout, and the officer nearby almost looks like he wants to smile before he nods, letting me continue on.

"Thank you!" I yell over my shoulder as I brush past him and out of the archery yard, veering to my right toward the next obstacle step. Adrenaline and exultation fuel me as I plow my way to the beginning of Feuerignis's Flame. I see the raven elegantly sweeping the sky above me, and I wave my arms at it and cheer, not caring who watches, so heady is my relief.

When a scream pierces my ears, I look down just in time to see a woman tumble past me. She is frantically trying to beat out the fire from the flaming arrow protruding from her arm that's igniting her hair, and my relief immediately turns to lead in my stomach.

In front of me are challengers dashing across the field, trying to avoid flame-tipped arrows being shot from each side by archers with far greater skill than I possess. Beyond that, they balance across rotating barrels that set their boots to smoking when they make contact with the hot metal. Finally, at the end, I watch several challengers brace themselves as they prepare to leap over the wall of flames. I can't even begin to let myself consider what the writhing lumps on the ground near the flames even mean, the horror that has spurred the anguished cries of pain.

I decide the only way I will get through this is to focus on each step individually. If I allow myself to consider what I must face after each hurdle, I will be immobilized by fear. First step: flaming arrows across a field that looks to be several hundred yards. Since there is no time limit for this obstacle, and I can see many of the other challengers have been incapacitated, I take the time to watch the path of the flaming arrows, to discern the position of the archers, to try and determine their pattern.

It becomes apparent very quickly that there is no pattern. Rather, the archers watch the challengers, and they aim for them. *They are hunting them.*

There is no penalty for getting hit by an arrow, only for not finishing the portion of the course, so I know I have to run through, try to dodge as many as I can, and suffer through it if I'm hit. I feel that same prickling fear tingling across my scalp, and I have to resist the urge to score my nails across it in agitation. Now is not a time to lose my head.

There will obviously be ample time and opportunity for that within the trials.

I shake out my hands and feet and crouch, preparing to run as best as I can. When I notice a cluster of challengers break over the starting line of the obstacle, I take off after them without further thought, hoping I can avoid some of the arrows if I stay in a clump.

"Fuck!" I screech when an arrow narrowly misses my foot as I dash through.

The ground is dry, and the dirt kicked up by so many challengers' feet helps to obscure us from the view of the archers a bit more. A prickle of awareness tingles across the back of my neck, and I turn just in time to see an archer aiming right at me. When he releases the arrow, I fall to the ground, rolling and managing to tumble into a kneeling position before hauling myself back to my feet, having been separated from my cluster a bit. Impressed by my own burst of physical capability, I shake my head, but that feeling is short lived.

Suddenly, a barrel crashes into my calves and sends me sprawling. Only it's not a barrel, it's a person, and he's shrieking, clutching the flaming arrow jutting from his eye socket and melting the flesh of his eye down the side of his cheek. I frantically pull at my legs to dislodge them from beneath his writhing form, knowing the longer I lie here, the more likely I am to get hit. The only thing protecting me is my proximity to the ground and the dirt clouds stirred up by the man's rolling. Gagging at the sight of the gruesome injury, and angry at him for slowing me down, Lord Rocheburn for putting me here, and the world, in general, I shove him off my legs with rage-fueled strength and stumble to my feet once more.

When I emerge from the cloud of dirt, coughing, I realize I've managed to cross the field without getting hit. Trying to escape what I just saw, I set off in a run to the rotating barrels. I surge up the platform, not even taking time to consider how I should cross them. Adrenaline and fury and shock are suffusing my limbs with energy and leaving little left for my mind to think strategically. I take off across the barrels, my boots hissing as the soles make contact with the metal, leaving bits of them behind here and there, a monument to my passage across them. It's over before I even know what's happened, and I find myself drawing up short, heels digging into the dirt, as I suddenly stop in front of the wall of flame before me.

My lungs burn as surely as if they've been pierced with arrows, my hands sting and throb as if I've lost bits of them to the molten barrels, and my heart slams against my ribs, pounding them into blades like a smith's hammer. Blades that dig into my sides with every breath, only these are forged not of iron, but fear and desperation.

Beside me on the ground are the bodies of many of my fellow challengers, all with burns varying from awful to catastrophic. The woman closest to me has most of her clothing missing, but modesty is likely the least of her concerns given the bubbling flesh covering her body. She's hardly moving, and I creep forward to where she is and kneel beside her. Her eyes are barely open, but upon seeing me, they light up, their hazel depths glazed with pain and delirium.

"Minna? Is that you?" She asks me, her breath wheezing between her trembling lips.

"Actually, I'm—" I begin to dissuade her of the notion that I am whoever she thinks I am.

"It *is* you!" A smile stretches her parched lips. I wish I had water to offer to her. I realize quickly that she's dying, that her injuries are too severe for her to overcome, and that it doesn't matter who she thinks I am if it brings her peace in her last moments.

"Um, yes, it's me. Don't tire yourself, though; just rest." I smooth back her singed dark hair, trying not to touch any of the areas of burned skin.

"I was—was trying to get home to you," she gasps, her chest rattling, and I think my heart breaks then and there.

Every one of us here is just trying to get home to someone or something better than where we are. I want to give her some final words of comfort to send her to Nachternel, but she's already stopped breathing. I am too late.

Grief for this unnamed woman threatens to consume me, and I know I've let precious moments slip by, but if I were in her shoes, I would've wanted someone to stop for me. She deserved that much. This woman's fate could very well be my own in just a matter of minutes.

I stand and stare at the flames, at countless others attempting them, failing, or making it through, but not without injury. I'm suddenly so afraid, I don't want to continue. Is this worth dying for? Perhaps there is another way to get to Agnethe.

Only those who fly into the fire learn the strength of their wings.

I say a prayer of thanks to Gehrvania, the goddess of wisdom, for these bits of poetry that have found me today and have urged me on. I feel my resolve strengthen, that energy prickling in my limbs once more, across my shoulders, my neck, my scalp, until it feels like a suit of armor against whatever pain the flames may bring. Taking a deep breath, I back up as far as I can, getting as close to the molten barrels behind me as I dare, and then sprint forward, leaping when I'm nearly upon the fire, extending one leg in front of me.

I feel a sharp twinge in my extended leg before I hit the ground hard on my feet, collapsing and rolling when I spy the flames licking up my right pant leg. I don't look beneath the smoking fabric, too afraid to see what might lurk on my flesh beneath it, that it might keep me from moving forward, and instead stagger to my feet once more, winded and exhausted.

I look behind me at the towering wall of fire, not sure how I made it over with such minimal injury, and think of the dead woman behind it, and say a last prayer for her peace before turning toward my next obstacle. I haul myself up the wooden platform toward one of the bridges stretching across the pool in front of me. It's not long, as Major Berger had acknowledged, but the bridge is so narrow—only a foot wide—I fail to see how we will stay on it, exhausted as we are. In fact, I don't see many crossing the bridges stretching across the water, mostly challengers who have fallen into it and must swim, as the rules stipulate. There are multiple challengers per bridge, seemingly having decided it makes more sense to try to plow through than politely wait until the bridge is clear. I also see many of the challengers floundering in the water, despite it being no more than about neck high on me. It seems my suspicion about their lack of previous swimming lessons is being proven right.

Knowing it's now or never, I step across the platform toward the closest bridge. A shadow ripples across the water not far from me, and I look up to see my feathered friend flying above me. Bolstered once more, by its presence, I start to make the trek across the bridge, windmilling my arms several times to stay atop the surface that's already slick with water from challengers crossing before me.

I'm about halfway when I hear a male voice bellow, "Out of my way!" And I'm suddenly falling, flung into the water.

I break back through the surface, sputtering and spewing water, hair plastered to my head, and look up to see the same man who pulled me against the rope wall running across the bridge where I had just been. I wonder how he got behind me, but then I notice the multiple burns on his legs and arms, and realize they must've slowed him down considerably.

The heat of impotent outrage washes over me as I realize this man has attempted to sabotage me not once, but twice, and for no good reason. And I'm not in a position right now to fight back, to challenge him. Letting the anger propel me, I start to swim the rest of the way across the pond. I once again say a prayer of thanks to the gods for my experience, slim as it may be, and home at Noetheim, having fallen into the moat there several times and being forced to learn to swim out of it. I'm not the fastest swimmer, but I'm steady and don't falter as I make my way toward the opposite shore.

I hear a strange caw and look up in shock to see the raven suddenly dive down into the path of the man who pushed me, startling him to the point that he falls into the water on the other side of the bridge, apart from me. Unable to help the grin that breaks over my face, I push toward the pond's edge, dragging myself onto the grass by my forearms, trying to avoid direct pressure on my burned hands. They had a respite in the cool water, but now that they've broken the surface again, the fire has returned to them and my calf.

I look back behind me to the pond and see the man, an obviously inferior swimmer, struggling to make his way across. Feeling heartened, I look for my raven friend and see it following above me once more as I round a bend of trees to the final obstacle.

I'm exhausted, and the adrenaline is quickly vacating my body, leaving me dangerously weak. But I just have this bit left, and then I can allow myself to collapse. With that encouragement, I push forward. Around the bend, I can see the stone of the erected exit gate, with no indication of the obstacle except for some raised bumps at erratic positions—hurdles maybe—preceding it. This one was the "surprise" Major Berger had so gleefully announced, dedicated to Heilane, the goddess of healing. When I get closer to the exit gate, however, I can see the lumps on the ground aren't hurdles or some other kind of physical obstacle I have to climb over.

They're bodies.

Very still bodies.

My steps slow, the trepidation as to what atrocity awaits me leaving me feeling like I'm trying to wade through deep water. I make my way to one of the closest bodies, dread creating a pit in my stomach at the prospect of comforting yet another dying person into their afterlife.

When I reach the man's body, I see a shock of white-blonde hair, but he is lying prone, his face pressed to the ground, so I can't discern what happened to him or who he is. Reaching his shoulder, and ignoring the sensation of skin ripping on my hands, I use what remains of my strength to shove and roll him onto his back, looking for signs of his lethal injury.

When he lands on his back, I get a good look at his face, and while I can't see any injury, unlike the woman at the flame wall, I immediately know who this person is.

Lying dead on the ground before me is Brock.

I stumble back, startled, and fall on my arse hard, my injured palms slamming into the ground, but I barely register the pain.

Brock, who didn't say if he missed home, but said he missed the sound of snow.

Brock, who wondered if there would be an "after" Stachtenbaste for him.

A sob chokes me, and I suddenly feel sick, and though I managed to hold back my retching when I saw that man's eye destroyed by the flaming arrow, I can't contain it now. Bile—sour, sooty—rushes up my throat, fills my nose and mouth, and I turn onto my hands and knees, heaving into the dirt beside Brock's body.

When my stomach is done rebelling, I stand on shaky legs and look around me. I haven't seen any other challengers come around the bend, but I see officers up ahead, see the crowd in the stands in the distance, having looped around the entire obstacle course nearly back to where we started. I can even spot the platform with the leaders from my vantage point.

"Help!" I scream, my voice raw and lacking volume. "Help me!"

I grab Brock's hand and try to start pulling him toward the exit gate. He needs assistance—a healer, a pfaetr, *something*. I make it a few steps before I acknowledge he's too heavy for me to pull him the distance I have left to go, while also trying to complete the trial, which I don't even know how to do yet. Is this part of the challenge? This suffering?

Sobbing, I drop Brock's hand in the dirt and kneel before him. "I'm sorry, Brock. You'll see the snow in Nachternel."

I reach up and close his unseeing pale eyes, running my hands over his face, his shoulders, looking for any clues that he can give me as to how he died, but find none. Tears still pouring down my face, I move to the next body, and the next, and find the same, strange, absence of mortal wounds—though plenty of other kinds—to inform me about their demise.

I look up at the officers, the stands, the platform in the distance, and I know I haven't yet finished, that I'm overlooking something, but what?

Just then, the man who knocked me into the rope net, who pushed me from the bridge, who attempted to sacrifice me at the altar of his own success, appears around the bend of trees. He's limping toward me, water dripping from his form, breathing ragged, clearly exhausted.

He spots me kneeling by a body and sneers, slowing down to say, "You still here? So you're not just fat and slow, you're dumb as a fuckin' rock, too."

My spine stiffens at his words, surprised at his vitriol toward me. What did I do to him to earn this hostility? I shake my head in resignation, knowing I'm not likely to find out that information, as he seems inclined to think the worst of me and to view me as someone expendable. For a moment, I think he will come after me, take me out and eliminate me as a challenger, but he continues his run toward the exit gate.

Realizing he has no idea there is something dangerous about it, I call out to him. "Wait!" I can't let him die just because he's an arsehole.

He looks over his shoulder at me and smirks. "Sorry, girlie, best get a move on, I'm not waiting for—"

His feet cross through the gate, and he's suddenly blown back from it, landing on the ground with a thud dozens of feet away, unmoving. I race over to him and press my fingers to his neck and find no pulse. He's dead.

I feel pity for him in an abstract sense, but can't focus on it while also trying to keep myself alive. I approach the exit gate with hesitation, warily eyeing the officers standing a dozen feet beyond it. The man was killed when he crossed through the gate. The officers aren't injured. What are we meant to do to cross over safely? There's clearly a step that precedes crossing over.

What would a goddess of healing want in tribute in exchange for safe passage?

I stand there for several seconds, unsure how to proceed. A shadow on the ground alerts me to my raven friend flying above me. I look up at its form, soaring lazily through the sky, its inky wings turning purple and indigo in the tilting rays of the afternoon sun.

Not all crossings are meant for clean hands.

I frown, my brows drawing together. *What?*

I look down at my hands, burned, torn, bleeding, and covered in dirt, and watch as a drop of blood wells from one of the cuts along my finger.

"Not all crossings are meant for clean hands," I say, and the drop of blood beads and falls from my fingertip to the dirt.

Suddenly, I'm transported to my dream where a gleaming feather caused my blood to spill. An inky feather turned indigo and violet, then gold. In my dream, my blood hitting the dirt changed the outcome. I woke up.

What would a goddess of healing want in tribute?

Blood. She would want blood.

My way out of this is to offer Heilane blood. And the only place I can think to put it to allow my safe crossing is on the gate itself. I shake my hand rapidly, trying to increase blood flow to my already bleeding fingers.

"I hope Heilane isn't some kind of bloodthirsty healer, because this is about as good as it gets," I mutter as I squeeze my fingers, encouraging several beads of blood to appear and roll into my palm, flinching at the stinging pain it causes.

I approach one of the pillars of the exit gate and take a bracing breath. I shoot my raven companion a quick glance before reaching my palm out and smearing it across the stone, watching as my blood glistens across the rock. At first, I think nothing is going to happen, but then my blood suddenly absorbs into the pillar and vanishes, as if it had never been there.

Though I'm unsure how to react to that glimpse of magic, I also decide it's something I can puzzle over later. Without further hesitation, I cross the exit gate. The crowd beyond roars, but it sounds muffled to my ears.

My relief when I reach the officers standing nearby is so intense that I feel lightheaded. I hear someone call my name, and then I know nothing else.

CHAPTER TWENTY-TWO
Krahbek and Call

I'm flying. The shadow cast by my wings ripples below, a dark specter cast on the glittering white snow blanketing the ground beneath me. On either side, I can see the glisten of indigo and violet against inky black, slicing through the air, each undulation spilling across the sky like a well of ink overturned on parchment.

I spiral higher, gliding over the fluffy tops of evergreen trees crisp with anticipation of autumn's chill, their boughs enshrouding the woodlands below them like a fragrant, green petticoat.

The trees break and give way to a coursing river bracketed by the creamy-white tufts of delicate lace atop tall, slender arms from the meadowsweet plants that line the banks. On this misty morning, dew clings to their petals and dusky green leaves, and their scent—a soft and heady blend of honey and almond—is a lingering homage to the rapidly fading summer.

Small streams branch from the river like so many veins, smaller forests knotting the landscape like fists. I soar over cobbled rooftops tiled with chipped slate, their chimneys already bellowing gusts of smoke from within. A fortress's angled spires climb into the sky, chasing my ascent, their imposing vigilance reinforced by the thick, stone *walls surrounding the extensive grounds. From above, it seems peaceful.*

That peace, it so happens, belies a darker truth. As the sun rises over the stone walls, I see people rapidly filing into an area of the grounds fitted with rows and rows of wooden seats, positioned next to man-erected structures that speak of forthcoming torment: narrow bridges, rope mountains, a wall of flames. All of them tinged with an increasing sense of malevolent foreboding.

I dive down over the field to gain a closer look, propelled by the feeling that I need to bear witness to the events that are about to unfold. Some niggling instinct tells me I'm needed there. When I near the field, I see myself poised at the starting line of The Gods' Assault obstacle course.

I frown. That doesn't make sense.

I'm both in the obstacle course and watching myself endure it. I watch as stone scrapes beneath my knees, as I strain up the rock wall base. My hands begin to bleed as my fingers wrap around a rope and slide down, down. Pain causes me to let go, as I feel the sting in my hands, the pull of a rope in my shoulders, a burst of pain as something hot brushes my calf.

Then I'm fumbling with arrows, my jaw clenched, sweat slicking my palms, my brow. My hands won't close properly. The fingers refuse to bend. I am her, and she is fire. The arrow looses and sings.

The challengers stumble across molten barrels. One falls; another screams as they burn. The sound is high and bright and painfully short. I fly closer—no, I fall, and I'm in my body once more. Running. Leaping from barrel to barrel. Heat gripping my feet, my boots leaving pieces of themselves behind.

Then the wall of flame. Alive and licking at me like fingers hungry for my flesh. I watch myself back away from it, my face open and afraid but also determined. I can't feel the heat of the fire because I'm no longer right in front of it. Suddenly I am, though, and I'm in my body again; my feet are leaving the ground, and the world slows as I soar over the flames.

There's a splash when I hit the ground, and water briefly closes over my head. I break through its surface and begin swimming, but my arms are heavy. The water is as hot as blood and smells like iron. Hands are grabbing at me, dragging me down, and I see faces beneath the surface: Stigander and Lillen, silent and pale; Brock, eyes wide and damning; Berte, weeds wrapped around her neck; and Dagmar reaching out to me with fingers melted from the flames. Her eyes have oozed from their sockets.

Then I'm beside Brock as he lies still on the ground. He's dead, and I scream over and over, and then I'm watching myself as I scream and sob over him, as I puzzle over the exit gate, and I know I have to help myself break through.

Not all crossings are meant for clean hands.

The world goes indigo, then violet, then gold, and, finally, black.

I start awake, sitting up in bed, breathless and disoriented. While I wait for my heart rate to calm, I try to blearily assess my surroundings through stinging, crusted eyes. I attempt to clear them using my fingers, but when I raise them to my face, I find them encased in thick linen bandages, making them about as dexterous as if I had five sausages strapped to each of my hands.

I manage to rub the heels of my palms against my eyes a little and reduce the gritty sensation enough to look around me and determine I'm in the infirmary once more. It seems I'm destined to end up here after anything more physically taxing than minor exercise.

Determined to ignore the disturbing recollection I was just forced to relive in my dream, I set my sights on figuring out how to get out of bed with my hands wrapped in bandages.

After several minutes and much profanity, I'm able to grasp the bed linens between my bandaged palms and slowly peel them back from my legs so that I can swing out of the bed and go in search of someone, to find out what happened after I lost consciousness at the end of the first trial.

The sound of glass shattering sounds from inside the storage closet. "Did you break *another vial?*" I hear Lotti's incredulous voice ask.

"Lotti?" I call out, pulling myself to standing. I'm only in a nightshift, but this side of the infirmary appears empty.

A gasp, followed by more shattering glass, precedes Lotti's cloud of dark curls popping out from inside the storage closet. When she sees me sitting up, she exclaims, "Greta!"

She comes running over to me immediately and wraps her arms around me in a fierce hug. Otto, who was close on her heels, is quick to follow suit.

"I'm so relieved to see you awake!" Lotti gushes.

Otto nods. "It seems like you've been asleep forever," he says, dropping the glass vial he held.

"Seriously?" Lotti fumes, turning toward him. "Why did you even bring a vial out here? Hildegarde is going to *murder you*."

Otto shrugs. "I don't know. You just started running, so I followed you."

"Well, hurry up and sweep it, we've got to make it to breakfast, and it looks like Greta can join us!" She flings a uniform on my lap and moves to run off to some other part of the infirmary.

"Er, Lotti?" I prompt her.

She looks at me in question, and I hold up my bandaged hands in response. "Oh! Let me get Hildegarde; those can probably come off."

"No need, girl. I'm right here," Hildegarde mutters crabbily, no doubt having spotted Otto trying, none too subtly, to clean up the glass from the ground and becoming irritable over it.

She wordlessly gestures for me to hold out my hands, and she begins unwrapping my bandages. When Lotti spies what Hildegarde is doing, she steps back several feet. Hildegarde rolls her eyes.

"Never seen anyone less suited to healing than the two of you," she says to Otto and Lotti. "Why'd you volunteer for work duties here if you can't stand the sight of blood, girl?" She asks Lotti.

It's clearly a rhetorical question, because when Lotti opens her mouth to respond, Hildegarde continues her tirade by turning her frustrations on Otto. "And you. Clumsier than an ox with an earache. Put down that vial!" She scowls at him, and he sets down the vial he had picked up from gods knows where. It subsequently rolls off the side table and falls to the ground with a musical tinkling of shattered glass. Otto winces at the sound.

"Apologies, Matron," Lotti says sheepishly. "We wanted to help keep watch over Greta." She eyes my hands warily, her face looking slightly green.

"Oh, come off it, her hands are perfectly fine. Her skin is as fresh as a newborn babe's but completely healed," Hildegarde says as she removes the last of my bandages. "No blood whatsoever."

I marvel at the sight of my hands, which are indeed pink with newly formed skin but otherwise unremarkable. "How? How long have I been asleep? Oh, no…I failed the trial, didn't I?" I look at Lotti and Otto in dismay, knowing they'll set their calves' eyes on me and break the news as gently as possible that I'm here for even longer than I originally thought I would be.

"No, Greta, you made it!" Lotti says cheerfully, her color rapidly returning now that she knows she won't have to see my blood. "You just passed out afterward."

I frown. "But how long have I been asleep for that my hands are so well healed?"

"Three days," Otto says.

"But that's not enough time for that," I object. Could I have slept through the next trial?

Hildegarde answers, "*Wundsmeiten.* Special salve imbued with magic. Expensive, so they don't usually waste it on cadets, especially not ones who are foolish enough to enter the Freiheit," she looks at me with a raised brow.

Puzzled, I ask, "Then why did they give it to me?"

Hildegarde smiles slyly. "Well…you can thank a certain handsome officer for that bit of special treatment."

A handsome officer? *Aric.* Aric arranged for me to get special, magical medicine to promote my healing? After our argument and kiss, where I ran off, I confess I wouldn't have thought he would go out of his way to help me continue in the Freiheit, but it seems I was wrong. I stare at my palms in flushed astonishment, pleased beyond measure that he sought to help ease my discomfort.

Lotti and Otto watch me curiously, but say nothing. I still haven't told them what happened with Aric before the Freiheit, and with Hildegarde listening nearby, this isn't the time for it. With my hands freed, I rush to one of the bathing chambers off the infirmary and splash myself with cold water before dressing in the uniform Lotti brought me. If I've been asleep for three days, that means there are only four days left until the next trial, and I've lost time I could be finding out information about the next trial, not to mention several days of training.

I thank Hildegarde as we exit the infirmary and head toward the dining hall. She only grunts in response, and I get the feeling she's just relieved to have some peace and quiet after being subjected to Otto and Lotti's assistance. I follow my friends from the infirmary building across the inner bailey, my shortness of breath informing me that my time recuperating did nothing to help my stamina.

"How are the others?" I ask, swallowing hard when I think of Brock. Lotti and Otto spare me sympathetic glances, although neither one of them addresses what they surely know is on my mind.

Lotti instead opts for her usual optimism and says, "Berte, Stigander, and Dagmar also advanced. Lillen is alive, but she was disqualified in the archery portion."

I nod as I follow them through the dining hall doors. We make our way to the line for food, retrieve our bowls, and head to our usual table, where I can see most of our team is sitting, including, to my surprise, Dagmar. She spies me first out of the whole group. I can't be certain, but I swear her shoulders relax just a little at the sight of me, almost as if she's relieved I'm alive and awake. She settles on a terse nod rather than warm words of welcome when we approach, though.

"The invalid returns," Cyneric smiles and slides down the bench so I can climb in beside him. "How are you faring, darling?"

"Well rested." I smile back.

He laughs. "I'd imagine so. Gods know you earned it after such a dramatic finish to the trial."

The whole table sobers, and I know they're thinking of Brock also. "Poor bastard," Stigander mutters, breaking the silence.

"Did he say anything to you before he…well?" Berte asks me.

I shake my head. "He was already gone when I got to him. I only wish I could've stopped it from happening."

"It's better it was fast. Some of those burn injuries that went through were horrific," Lillen shudders.

"How are you doing, Lillen?" I ask, hoping she's grappling all right with her loss and increased sentence.

She smiles ruefully. "Oh, fine. It was a long shot for me. Quite literally, I had no hope of making that last one."

Dagmar says, "Many of us barely made that obstacle. You seemed like you got through the arrows all right." She turns her piercing azure gaze on me, as if she knows it makes no sense.

I shrug, unable to explain it. I also want to keep that knowledge to myself for reasons I can't be sure. "I had archery lessons when I was younger."

"Must've been some instructor," Stigander says curtly.

Jarl gushes, "I, for one, can't believe how well you leapt over the flame wall. I mean, I don't think I've seen you jump that high…well, ever."

A few people at the table laugh, including me. "There's something to be said for the motivational properties of fear." Jarl grins at me, and I turn to Stigander, Dagmar, and Berte. "How did you figure out the blood offering on the last obstacle?"

"Dagmar and I got there at about the same time. Saw another challenger smearing his blood on the gate and walk through, followed by a couple others who didn't and got blown back. Helped us to figure out what to do pretty quickly. Plus, the inscription made it clearer," Stigander explains, shoveling the remaining few bites of his food into his mouth.

I frown. "Inscription?"

Berte raises her eyebrows. "Yes, I was behind you and saw what you did with your blood but also spotted the inscription on the stone of the gate; didn't you?"

I shake my head. "No, I never saw it."

"How'd you figure it out then?" Berte asks.

"Instinct, I guess." But the explanation sounds hollow even to me, and I'm the one who lived it.

"Good instincts," Dagmar says, watching me quietly.

After finishing our meal, we make our way toward the training yard, and I ask what I've missed while asleep.

"We've begun training with krahbeks!" Otto says.

The name sends a chill down my spine, having been introduced to that particular weapon when my grandmother died and again when Colonel Richter executed the conscript.

"They're a kind of poleaxe," Jarl explains enthusiastically. "They have an axe, a spear point, and a hooked beak opposite the axe blade. They're great for keeping your opponents at a distance while giving you a long reach, and they can pierce armor pretty effectively. You can also pull a horseman off of their mount with it."

"It packs considerably more force than a sword," Stigander agrees, "but isn't as straightforward to learn."

We arrive at the upper training yard and immediately queue up at the equipment shed so that we can each retrieve a wooden practice krahbek for training.

"Yes, even Captain Everbrandt and Lieutenant Broadbente aren't as adept with it, so they had to bring in an expert to help train us," Lotti adds.

"Who is it?" I ask, as my hand wraps around the pole of one of the practice weapons.

A deep voice shivers up the back of my neck. "Sleep well, *künnle?*"

Startled, I whirl around to face Rafe Kriegeur's handsome, arrogant face, nearly hitting him with my practice krahbek in the process. I feel my expression turn sour the longer I stare at him.

"You're the krahbek expert?" I ask.

"Hmm, it would seem so. Did you dream of me these past few days?" He raises an eyebrow at me.

"Well," I muse as I tap my index finger to my chin, "I suppose nightmares are a *kind* of dream."

Berte and Lotti, who are standing nearby, choke back laughter. Otto looks dismayed, as if he's worried I'll get in trouble with the lieutenant colonel for my retorts.

For his part, Kriegeur seems to blithely ignore it and leans in, lowering his voice to a pitch suited only for the bedroom. "The only nightmare to be found in a bed is waking up to an empty one."

My face flushes at the blatant flirtation. I know he's only doing it to get a rise out of me, but it doesn't stop me from taking the bait. "An occurrence with which you must be *very* familiar."

Several of my teammates gasp at the blatant hit to his prowess. Something I'm sure the man isn't likely to take well. He surprises me, though, by throwing his head back and laughing. His laugh continues for several seconds, as if I've made the funniest jest he's heard in years.

"That's a very kind offer, *künnle*, but I'm not interested in fucking cadets." He places a heavy hand on my shoulder and looks at me consolingly.

I sputter. "But I—you—I wasn't—" and I'm unable to form a coherent sentence, so great is my irritation with this lummox, but my breath and fight abruptly leave me when I see Aric heading toward our group.

Suddenly, I remember that the last time I had seen him, we were alone—Kriegeur doesn't count, and he had kissed me. And despite everything I went through in the first trial, I'm no closer to knowing what to do around him now. It seems I will have to figure that out fairly quickly, though, because he heads toward me.

He stops a few feet away and nods at me. "Cadet de Veend." All proper soldier and captain. "I'm glad to see you looking recovered."

Resisting the urge to fidget, I reply just as stiffly, "My thanks, Captain Everbrandt."

"Brr!" Kriegeur says theatrically, appearing behind my shoulder and rubbing his hands up and down his biceps as if he's freezing. "You know, *künnle*, your people skills might be even worse than your combat skills. I'd happily offer my...services...should you desire." He wiggles his eyebrows at me with clear lascivious intent, and it's so ridiculous I'm torn between laughing and feeling mortified.

My cheeks turn pink when I notice Aric quietly watching my interaction with his cousin, though, which quickly kills any urge to giggle.

"Rafe," Aric says to him, and Kriegeur stands up straighter, suitably admonished, "you can begin the training."

Using his dagger to point, Rafe begins to pair the cadets off. Unlike Lieutenant Broadbente and Aric, he doesn't pair us with our typical sparring partners, seeming to want to mix it up at random. At least, that's according to Cyneric, who joins me at my practice dummy. I watch him take a few swings with the weapon, trying not to look at Aric too often to surreptitiously determine if he's watching me.

Picking up my practice krahbek, I'm surprised by the ease with which the motions come to me as I take some practice swings at the dummy. It's even easier when I imagine it's Kriegeur's face on it. The back of my neck prickles, and I turn after a missed swing sends me off balance, expecting to see Aric. Kriegeur faces me instead.

"Full marks for enthusiasm, *künnle*," he says, "but you stand as if you're afraid of the dummy and your weapon."

"I do not!" I protest hotly.

He rolls his eyes and walks toward me, unaware of Cyneric's swooning expression. "The krahbek's not a rapier, or even similar to a longsword. It's leverage and torque. Widen your stance. One foot slightly back, dominant side. Now swing."

I do as he says and frown in surprise when I don't wobble at all upon swinging. Kriegeur nods without any of his usual arrogance. "This gives you more control by improving your balance. Now, on being afraid, you don't always need the full reach. Choke up on the polearm when you want speed. Slide back for reach. And don't hold it like a sword. You're not fencing nobles in a practice ring, you're breaking through armor."

I test his guidance with several swings on the dummy, noticing how following his advice does precisely what he said it would do. When I choke up on the grip, I feel the blade slicing through the air much more quickly, almost with less resistance, and my strikes are that much faster to the dummy's head and body. When I slide back, it allows me to step farther from the dummy, the practice krahbek arcing gracefully through the air toward my target.

Kriegeur nods. "Better. Try not to muscle it through the air, though. Let it swing; guide it. Its own momentum will help propel the weapon for you. And practice lunges any chance you get. Holding something twice this weight. Do that until your legs feel like they'll give out. Then keep doing it."

I absorb his instruction and stare at him, unsure when the arrogance will come roaring back. I wonder if he's right about the lunges and momentum. Shockingly, Kriegeur isn't actually a bad teacher. I can't believe he's actually helping me so much.

"Now, *künnle*, keep going and learn fast. You can't depend on all your Freiheit competition taking themselves out like in the first trial." I scowl at his broad back as he strolls away.

And just as quickly as I thought better of him, he's awful again.

Cyneric rushes over to me, giddy. "Darling, I just cannot *believe* he spent so much time with you. What's your secret? Tell me everything."

"Oh, just unmitigated disdain," I say, glowering in Kriegeur's direction again.

"You really don't think he's handsome?" Cyneric asks, shocked.

"Of course he's handsome. The man's so beautiful it hurts your eyes," I acknowledge, and Cyneric nods his eager agreement. "He's also an idiot and an arsehole."

Cyneric grins. "Doesn't it make you want to tame him, though?"

I smile. "Completely changing your personality seems like an inauspicious way to begin a relationship, doesn't it?"

"Now, darling," Cyneric chastises, "when did you *ever* hear me use something as egregious as the R-word?"

We continue chatting and laughing and taking more practice swings at our dummy. I use the advice Kriegeur gave me because, arsehole or not, he is an expert at this weapon according to Lieutenant Broadbente and Aric, who are *not* idiots, and his advice actually seems to be helping me. By the time we put away our practice weapons, the sun hangs high in the sky, and I anticipate my lunch with glee.

I prepare to leave the training yard with Cyneric and catch up with Lotti, Otto, and the others, when a voice calls my name. I look back over my shoulder and see Aric walking toward us. My heart leaps into my throat. Sensing my nerves and need for privacy, Cyneric whispers a "good luck, darling" to me before hurrying off after our team, who are already walking back to the citadel.

Aric approaches me, his pace slowing as he nears, finally stopping a few feet in front of me. I find myself disappointed that he doesn't try to creep closer, even though I know other officers and cadets surround us, and that's probably not very fair of me to want.

"Yes?" I ask him, trying to sound casual, but wanting to cringe when I hear how breathless and eager I sound.

"I wanted to let you know I'll be in the officer's training yard before breakfast if you still want to train in the morning," he says, "Assuming you would like to continue."

My heart drops. Training. That's all he wanted to discuss with me. Not the kiss. Not the fact that he wants to kiss me more and maybe escape Stachtenbaste and find Agnethe and live happily ever after in a castle surrounded by baby animals.

I swallow my disappointment and nod. "My thanks." I start to turn away, and he grabs my arm.

"Greta, I—" he drops my arm when I turn back toward him. "I wanted to talk to you about what happened before the first trial. Between us."

My heart starts pounding in my chest. "What about it?"

He rubs the back of his neck, looking uncomfortable. "It's just that, um…the kiss was a mistake. I was concerned for you, as I would be for any cadet in my unit in your position and not thinking rationally, and I shouldn't have let my emotions get carried away. I hope we can maintain a professional cadet-and-superior relationship from now on."

My head rears back like I've been slapped. "'Professional?'"

He nods, avoiding my gaze. "Yes, I really think—"

"If anyone was lacking professionalism, it was *you*. You should've just kept your distance if that's how you really feel."

He steps forward. "Greta, it's—"

And much like I did the last time we spoke, I turn on my heel and run.

CHAPTER TWENTY-THREE
In Hot Water

I trudge wearily on my own up the many flights of stairs to my dormitory that evening, having told my team to go ahead without me, and helping Hildegarde finish neatening the infirmary in silence. She seemed to appreciate my ability to work without chattering or breaking things, and I needed the time to think, so it was a mutually beneficial interaction. My body protests every motion I've put it through since waking up. Every lift of my leg to another stair requires significant effort, thigh muscles burning, abdominals straining. I seem to have hit my physical limit.

My mind, however, is another story. I can't stop it from replaying what happened with Aric. As I swept flagstone floors, I thought about the day he kissed me. As I folded bed linens, I recalled the sensation of his hand grabbing my arm today. As I prepped the hearth and sorted tinctures in the apothecary, I broke down every word, every gesture and mannerism, each tic, trying to determine where, exactly, I could have gone so far in misinterpreting what had happened between us as to be stupid enough to think there would be more. That perhaps, Aric, too, was excited at the prospect of a small scrap of joy to be found in this misery. After all, happily-ever-after castle fantasies aside, it's not like I had any expectations. I didn't even know what to think of it all. But he closed the door on any possibility today. I sigh heavily. I suppose it's for the best. Anything that takes my focus off my ultimate goal of getting back to Agnethe is a distraction I should avoid, even if it's a welcome one.

It's just about nine bells, which means lights out is approaching, but I know I won't be able to find sleep immediately, if at all. Beyond the upsetting conversation with Aric, the second trial is still coming up in only a little over three days, which I have yet to contemplate.

I decide that I can afford a bit of rebellion and duck into the bathing chamber rather than the dormitory door, finding it empty, as everyone else has already made their way to their beds. I fill one of the tubs with water and quickly climb in, hoping the cold temperature will send my brain into temporary paralysis and keep me from thinking.

Unfortunately, instead, it seems to have created an arrow focus on anticipating the upcoming trial. Each pass of my soapy fingers across my scalp, washing away the dirt of the day's training from my head and hair, stimulates another thought.

They've said the trials are different every year, so no one can really prepare, but Colonel Richter also said the trials are meant to test you. I would imagine that can't just be physical, can it? I don't know if my body will survive another obstacle course like the one I just went through so soon.

Perhaps puzzles or riddles while someone's chasing us?

Oh, gods, what if it's climbing again? Maybe they'll just throw us in a pit and see who emerges first.

If Agnethe were here, I know she'd have all sorts of outlandish suggestions for them, to take my mind off the seriousness of what I'm facing. I can hear her voice now, suggesting a trial by pastry—fail to make a perfect tart and you're eliminated. Burned crust, burned challenger.

Or trial with a weapon we've never trained with and are expected to fight with. While blindfolded. Or with our non-dominant hands. Or no hands at all.

Bite your way out of the trial, challengers.

I smile at the thought as I climb out of the tub, but with it comes a fierce pang of longing and grief. Agnethe would hate that I'm here, would hate knowing what I'm going through, but she would make it more tolerable all the same. Just her and me against it all.

I pull on smallclothes and a nightshift from my designated cabinet and sit on one of the benches in the chamber, waiting for my thick hair to dry a bit before braiding it, so I don't have to sleep on a sopping-wet lump. My eyes are fluttering closed slightly but fly open when a knock sounds on the door to the room. Confused, I pad over to it, wondering why any cadets have bothered to knock when we're free to come and go from the bathing chamber.

I slowly pry open the door a crack and peer through it. I'm so shocked to see Aric standing there that I let go of the handle, the door slowly, creakingly, drifting open further.

"I—what are you doing here?" I take in his appearance, which is uncommonly disheveled. His hair looks as though he's run his fingers through it repeatedly, his clothes windblown as though he had been walking outside.

"I saw you go in, and I need to speak with you," he tells me.

"Aric, I've been in here for at least thirty minutes, and you've just been waiting out here?" I ask, flabbergasted.

"As I said, I needed to speak with you," he repeats.

"All right," I reply, warily.

"Is anyone else in there?" He says, gesturing to the inside of the bathing chamber.

I look over my shoulder before I meet his eyes once more. "No, only me."

He nods. "Good."

He advances, and I back into the bathing chamber. He shuts the door behind him and waits a breath before turning back to me. With maddening slowness, he lifts his hand, brushing his knuckles along the side of my face, down my neck, skimming his thumb along my collarbone. I don't pull away, I don't flinch, but I feel frozen, unsure how to proceed, and scared he'll stop if I move.

"You're shaking," he murmurs, his voice calm.

I swallow and let my eyelids flutter closed as his hand smooths over the curve of my shoulder. "It's hard not to," I whisper in return.

My eyes fly back open when his thumb brushes the corner of my mouth, and that's all the warning I receive. When he bends to kiss me, it isn't rushed, but intentional. He claims my lips as though he's been planning this, thinking of it for far too long, mapping out every breath and angle. He tastes like vanilla and smells like crisp night air.

When my lips open against his, he moves with precision, sweeping his tongue beyond their bounds to slide against mine with delicious languor. This isn't like Erwin's fumbling ministrations. This is unhurried and purposeful, just like the man holding me.

Aric presses me against the nearest wall, his hands sliding down to my waist and underneath the edge of my tunic. I gasp against his mouth when one of them finds my breasts, tweaking my nipples. I respond by hesitantly running my hands over his shoulders, his biceps, down his back. His hands tighten on me when my nails skim the rigid columns of muscle bracketing his spine, a pleased shudder reverberating through him. One of his hands drifts downward toward the waist of my smallclothes, and he hooks his finger inside it, running it along the hem.

"Tell me to stop," he murmurs against my mouth, and my stomach leaps at the sound of barely leashed control in his voice.

"Don't stop," I plead breathlessly.

His fingers dip beneath the edge of my smallclothes, seeking the wet heat between my legs. He groans against my mouth when he runs a finger up the seam, dipping inside and discovering just how much I want this, how much I want him.

He slides a finger fully inside of me, moving gently but firmly, his thumb teasing my clitoris with every thrust of his hand, and I lean my head back against the wall, letting out a moan, because it feels *that* fucking good.

Wanting to give him the same enjoyment, I reach my hands down to the drawstring of his trousers and pull at the cord, sliding fingers inside and wrapping them around the hot length of his shaft. Hissing, he inserts a second finger inside of me, which causes my hand to reflexively squeeze around his cock, and his answering groan makes my core tighten further around his fingers.

I ease him out of his trousers, moving my hand along his length in time with the thrusts of his fingers, mimicking the pace and motions we would be making if he were actually inside of me. His other hand, still on my breast, brushes my nipple insistently, and I feel the telltale tightening in my lower belly, the increase in my heart rate, the panting of my breath, all of which tell me my climax is fast approaching.

"Aric," I breathe, as a warning, and my hand on his cock becomes more insistent, more frantic. I want him to join me in it.

"Greta," he replies, "let go."

"But are you—" I begin.

"Gods, yes," he groans, and I smile.

"I'm so close," I tell him, to which he responds by swirling his thumb around my clit at the same time that he pinches my nipple, which sends me over the edge.

My hips jerk in time with the spasming of my lower belly, punctuated by the breathy moans coming from my mouth. With a thrust against my hand, Aric buries his face in my neck, and I feel his cock jerking, followed by hot moisture on my hand as he shudders with his own release.

We slowly disengage, my body still humming with pleasure. He finds a toweling linen in one of the supply cabinets and cleans himself off, then reaches for my hand, gently wiping the evidence of his pleasure from my skin. I feel overcome with shyness at the attention but steal a glance at him. He's not looking at my face; instead, he focuses on his task. He tucks himself back into his trousers, laces them together and discards the toweling linen down the laundry chute before finally meeting my gaze.

"That was…" I began hesitantly, trying to find the words to tell him what that felt like, what it meant to me to have my pleasure taken care of.

He releases a sigh, runs his fingers through his hair, and finishes for me, "Likely a very, very bad idea."

A chill washes over me, banishing most of the afterglow I had been basking in. "What?"

"I still meant what I said earlier, Greta. It's not a very good idea to get involved. I'm your superior, you're in the Freiheit. This isn't something I've done before." He paces back and forth across the length of the chamber.

I throw up my hands. "Then why did you? I wasn't seeking you out; I was respecting your call."

He stops and walks over to me, cupping my cheeks in both hands. "I just can't…I can't seem to stay away. From the moment I saw you, there was something about you—" he breaks off without saying more.

But I'm hurt. And confused. It shouldn't matter this much; I know it shouldn't. Whether he wants me in the moment or forever. I shouldn't want it. Shouldn't want his attention, his admiration, his hands, his pleasure, as much as I do. But I do want him, and I want to be wanted by him.

He kisses me like he's been planning it for ages, but then turns away like he's afraid of getting in too deep. He guards his thoughts, his motivations, and doesn't share what it really is that causes him to continue finding me. Some inexplicable physical attraction? Or more?

And, fool me, my instinct is to bend, accommodate, soothe, to understand, to tell him it doesn't bother me. To be suitable for the moment, to provide what he needs with little thought for what I want and need. Pretending I am content with being enough for holding, but not holding on to.

Now, though, there is so much at stake for me. My sister. My *life*. The fear and anxiety I feel whenever I consider the tasks laid ahead of me. Not just the trials but what comes after, if there even *is* an after.

So even though my inclination is to do whatever it takes to hold on, to keep those good feelings and ignore the realities behind them, I say, "If you're uncertain, perhaps it's best that you do stay away."

I immediately want to seize the words back, not to have uttered them. Especially when I see the surprise and hurt on his face as he steps back from me, his hands falling from my cheeks.

He looks as though he's going to say something, and his hands flex as though he wants to reach for me again. Instead, he nods stiffly and exits the bathing chamber, the only evidence he has been here in the fading rhythm of his steps.

CHAPTER TWENTY-FOUR
Efanwohl's Key

I'm at Freiheit Field in the center of the dirt-filled arena with my fellow remaining challengers, now only sixty. Tension is high, many of us are still riding the edge of pain, all of us pride, some of us anticipation.

On the leadership platform sits Lord Corvilian, Colonel Richter, Major Berger, Kriegeur, and the other officers, absent Lady Corvilian and Pfaetr Joham. I'm unsure if the pfaetr is missing because the Hochvîger only blesses the tournament at the beginning or because that stiff breeze took him out after all. Without him, the occasion lacks ceremony and grandeur, replaced by disquiet and barbarism. We are lambs at the slaughter, waiting for our time to step up to the chopping block.

I chance a look at Aric, expecting to see him pointedly not looking at me. Given our last interaction in the bathing chamber three-and-a-half days ago, I expect he will avoid any contact whatsoever. To my surprise, though, he is staring directly at me. I haven't spoken to him since then or even seen him. He seems to have avoided regular training sessions, leaving them to Lieutenant Broadbente and Kriegeur to manage our continued skills lessons with the krahbek. I haven't dared to venture out at dawn to see if he waits for me. I want to lie to myself and say it's because I stand by what I said, and if he's really uncertain of what path he wants to go down, he is better off avoiding me. In truth, I'm afraid that if I go out there and he's not waiting, I will feel crushed.

As it is, I've had to talk myself through every action I've taken since that night. Work duties in the infirmary with Hildegarde, practicing krahbek motions on the dummies, and even basics like bathing and chewing. It's as if this additional disappointment was one too many for my spirit to bear, and I'm barely keeping my head above water. It takes all my effort just to ensure I don't drown.

A glint of metal flying through the air catches my eye, and my gaze jumps from Aric's intense scrutiny to where Kriegeur tosses that dagger of his in the air and catches it again. I roll my eyes. It's a wonder the man has any appendages left with how careless he is with that thing. Like he senses me watching, Kriegeur turns his black gaze on me, catching his dagger by the hilt without ever breaking it, in an irritatingly impressive fashion. The man may be as dense as a log, but he's certainly gifted athletically. He wiggles his fingers at me again in a ridiculously delicate manner.

As is often the case with him, I find myself wanting to laugh. He's so huge that the very motion of his finger waving is incongruous with his person. Yet, he seems to suffer no self-consciousness for having made himself look foolish, which means he's extremely confident or even dumber than I initially thought. Perhaps both.

Colonel Richter stands and makes her way to the platform's edge, and I turn my eyes in her direction, suddenly overcome with nausea at what is facing me today.

"Challengers," she begins, her voice again amplified by the wind wielder. "You've proven you can run, climb, burn, bleed, and crawl your way through obstacles. Those were the demands of the first trial. Cresting the mountain, withstanding the flame, passing an ocean, enduring the pain of sacrifice. Your ability to push through pain, to endure, is not enough. Today, you must display rarer skills."

"Blessed Sisters," someone mutters, "how much rarer than jumping over fire can you get?"

Despite the fear, my lips twitch in response, because I wonder the same thing.

"Strength alone will fade. Muscles grow fatigued. Bones can be broken. Blood spilled. The foremost defensive and offensive tool a soldier has at their disposal is not their body, but their mind. A sharp mind is faster and deadlier than any weapon man can forge.

"In war, many things kill: blades, fire, hunger, hesitation, carelessness. Your survival depends on how quickly you move, yes, but even more on how quickly you *think*. On how well you're able to measure your opponent at a moment's notice, and even that is not always enough.

"A true soldier is never alone. In battle, you live or die by your fellow soldiers at your side. Trust is not optional; it is necessary. You must be more than the tip of the spear. You must be the hand that directs the strike, the eye that spots the vulnerability, the voice that leads the charge, and the shield that blocks the blow. There are no obstacles today except those you make for yourselves. No ropes, or flames, or arrows. Only choices. And your ultimate choice in this trial is whether to rise to the challenge or drag others down with you."

The crowd murmurs in confusion and suspense. Can it be that we won't face a physical challenge today? If so, I might have a fighting chance after all.

"Remember, challengers: a sharpened blade cuts deep, but a sharpened mind can end wars before they begin."

The crowd's murmurings grow in volume as the colonel yields the platform to Major Berger once more.

"Challengers, are you ready to turn the key on this challenge?" Major Berger asks slyly, her mouth tipped up in a smirk.

I look around me, confused, wondering if there was some clue I missed.

"Today's challenge is called Efanwohl's Key, honoring our god of wealth and prosperity!" She grins when the crowd gives a collective noise of understanding.

"Ha!" Kriegeur slaps his knee from his chair, reaffirming my belief that these two odd birds must be friends.

The thought of birds makes me wonder if I'll see my raven friend again today. It hasn't appeared since the last trial, although I've admittedly been distracted and not as aware of my surroundings.

"Efanwohl's Key involves a multi-step scavenger hunt," Major Berger continues, "Where you will follow a series of clues to reach your final goal of obtaining one of fifteen golden keys, like his fabled golden key of wealth, which will signify that you've completed the trial. Sounds simple, right?" She asks, mirroring the question she asked during her explanation at the last trial, so I know it will be anything *but* simple.

"There are sixty of you. There are fifteen keys. Challengers must be one of the first forty-five to complete the trial. This means you will work in teams." The crowd gasps. We all look from side to side, assessing each other and wondering who our best options are.

"Teams will be chosen at random," Major Berger motions with her hands for the crowd to stop chattering, and many look frustrated at this turn of events. Not only is our outcome not fully within our control, but we don't even get to choose the team we face the trial with. "In battle, you do not get to choose your comrades. You only have dominion over your own actions, so you must do what you can with the tools—that includes people—at your disposal," she chastises.

There are sounds of displeasure coming from the group of challengers when a voice, gravelly, soft, but penetrating, says, "I was under the impression that entry into the Freiheit Tournament is completely voluntary, is it not?"

Major Berger steps back to address Lord Corvilian, who has spoken from his chair, not even needing to rise for complete silence to descend upon the crowd, including the onlookers.

"It is, Lord General," Major Berger nods amiably.

"Well, then I will simply suggest that anyone who protests the design of the tournament challenges be voluntarily eliminated from competition," he says with a casualness that belies the venom in his black gaze.

His words of warning are enough to keep the crowd quiet as Major Berger says, "Just so, Lord General. Do we have anyone who wishes to withdraw? Keeping in mind the penalty for doing so?"

She waits thirty seconds before grinning and adding, "I didn't think so. Now! All clues must be completed in order. Before you get any sneaky ideas," she wags her finger at the crowd like they're so many naughty school children. "None of the team's clues are in the same order except for the very last one, so don't think to copy each other. Each clue will lead you to the location of your next clue, and that clue will lead you to the location of the next clue, and so on. Your last clue will lead you to the location of the key. Teams must remain together except on the last clue, and in order to complete the trial, you must finish together. The winner of the first trial and their team will get to skip one of the clues and proceed directly to the next one."

An appreciative murmur sounds from the crowd. I'll have to do a better job of trying to win where I can; who knows where the advantages might come in handy?

"Stand by and wait for your team assignments," Major Berger directs and heads to the registrar seated on the platform.

I feel the first blooms of hope burgeoning within me. A mental challenge! Something at which I have a higher chance of success than anything physical. I can only pray to the gods that my teammates are not entirely useless and, even better, that they bring their own acuity to the challenge.

"Brevic, de Veend, Wazo! Your team," Major Berger calls, pointing to a position near the platform.

I make my way over, nodding at Dagmar. "Looks like we're on the same team yet again," I say, trying to sound positive, even though I feel intimidated by her icy stare.

"So it would seem," she agrees, not even pretending to be enthusiastic.

I grind my teeth and turn to the man standing beside her with a heavy brow and sloped shoulders. "And your name?"

"Wazo." He nods.

"And your first name?" I prod.

"Wazo," he says again.

Dagmar turns slowly toward him. "Your name is Wazo Wazo?"

He shakes his head, jowls trembling. "Just Wazo, friend."

Dagmar scowls. "I'm not your friend."

I smile sunnily at Wazo. "Where are you from, Wazo?" He might be some secret intellectual weapon, and Dagmar has already written him off like she did with me, but I won't do that.

"Verdantia, friend."

Dagmar growls. "You fucking—"

"Now, now, Dagmar," I say in a sickeningly sweet tone. "I'm perfectly happy to be good friends with Wazo. After all, we are on the same team. Shouldn't teammates support each other?"

I stare directly into her icy blue eyes, my previous nerves banished in the face of her irritation. I know she can't hurt me during the challenge; she needs me to complete it. Therefore, I'm free to bait her as often as I like. The thought makes me practically salivate with *Schadenfreude*.

Dagmar's jaw clenches, but she says nothing else as Major Berger walks around, handing the twenty assembled teams a small, sealed bit of parchment.

"Challengers! At your marks!" Major Berger calls, and the groups all gather in the starting circle indicated by the supervising soldiers on the fringes of the arena.

When the starting horn sounds, Dagmar pushes us off to the side and tears open the parchment, clearly deciding she's taking charge.

"In the shadows where vigilance reigns,
Amidst quiet visions of past campaigns.
Seek the place where strength takes respite,
Amongst its brothers fresh from the fight.
Look where silence meets echoes of steel,
And there your next clue will soon be revealed."

Wazo groans. "I've never been good at poetry."

Dagmar rolls her eyes at him. "It's the training yard."

I frown. "What makes you think that?"

Dagmar points at the parchment. "'Echoes of steel,' meaning weapons? Either that or the infirmary, 'where strength takes respite.'" She raises her palms at me like I'm as dense as Wazo. "We're wasting time!" She says and takes off.

Wazo follows her dutifully as she races from the arena and across Freiheit Field. I try to keep up, but I'm not as fast, and I'm also attempting to remember the clue as I go.

When we reach the upper training yard, Dagmar yanks open the first equipment shed door. Wazo has begun wandering nearby, picking up rocks, looking beneath them, and staring at the ground.

Dagmar watches him for several seconds before saying, "You're a fucking moron." She turns to me. "You going to help search or not?"

I sigh and follow her into the hot and dusty equipment shed. We dig through several piles of wooden practice weapons before Dagmar exhales in frustration once more. "Let's move to the infirmary."

"We only checked one shed, and you were so sure, shouldn't we— agh!" I start and immediately have to take off after her as she runs from the equipment shed toward the citadel.

"This is going just swimmingly, Greta. You sure are asserting yourself. So much for baiting her and showing her you're not a pushover." My words, mumbled to myself under my breath, become increasingly breathless as I struggle to maintain even my current distance behind her. She's already reached the gravel path that heads toward the outcropping.

"I agree, we should push her over," Wazo nods.

I find myself rolling my eyes at him. "Not what I said, Wazo."

Several minutes later, we approach the bottom of the stone stairs to the outcropping, and I'm surprised to see Dagmar has waited for us, which I express to her.

"Have to, don't I? Those are the rules," she grunts. "Now hurry."

Wazo groans beside me as Dagmar nimbly bounds up the stairs. How did this man make it through the first trial? There must be something to be said for sheer, dumb luck.

Emphasis on dumb.

I follow Dagmar to the inner bailey and to the left toward the infirmary building, not eager to revisit where I had been sleeping for several days and then performing work duties. Still, I don't even have breath left to protest.

She slams open the door, smacking it against the wall with force, which is met by the sound of outraged disapproval from one of the matrons who comes running from their study at the sudden ruckus.

"Excuse me," she sputters, "we have patients resting!"

Dagmar looks around at the unoccupied beds. "Where? Or did we just interrupt nap time?" She asks, raising an elegant brow at the mousy woman.

I flinch, expecting the matron to haul off and wallop her. Still, I guess Dagmar intimidates everyone, because the matron swings her head back and forth in a comically exaggerated motion before flushing. "Well, we *could at any moment*, so keep the noise down."

"Noted. Do you know where the clue is?" Dagmar asks her.

The matron's rotund body vibrates with ire. "Even if I did, we're not allowed to assist challengers, so *no*."

Dagmar shrugs and starts diving under beds, lifting bed linens and pillows, searching for a piece of parchment.

My skin prickles like it did during the first trial, traveling up my arms and over my scalp, and in my head, I hear, "*When warriors dream, their battles might well follow them into folded linen.*"

I frown. Like in the first trial, veiled words of wisdom materialize in my mind. Only this time, it feels like the voice was not my own. I look over my shoulder nervously, but see only Wazo looking at us absently from the corner of the infirmary where he stands—holding a glass vial.

He drops the vial on the ground.

"Now, watch the mess!" The matron yells at him.

Running my nails over my scalp, I turn to Dagmar. "Can I see the clue?"

She sighs and hands me the parchment, and I read through it several times before I look at her.

"Shadows…quiet…silence. So somewhere peaceful?" I muse aloud.

"Yes, so the infirmary, then." Dagmar nods impatiently, gesturing to the room around her.

I shake my head no. "I don't think that's what it means. 'Quiet visions of past campaigns' suggests memories, and 'seek the place where strength takes its respite' suggests sleep. Especially when you combine it with 'amongst brothers.'"

Dagmar rotates her wrist as though urging me to explain myself. "So?"

"I don't think it's referring to a place where strength is honored or recovers from wounds; it's where strength actually *rests*. As in bed. Sleeping quarters," I clarify when she continues to stare at me.

She frowns, considering my words. "How do you figure?"

I feel the weight of her skepticism and shrug. "A hunch," I say nonchalantly.

She snorts. "Does your 'hunch' tell you which bed? There have to be thousands in the citadel."

I look at the clue again. "If we assume it means memories, then we should assume that it means whoever is dreaming is already a soldier. So, perhaps the Aurengarte quarters?"

In the corner, Wazo drops another vial.

The matron comes bellowing at him, "Get out of my infirmary, you great lummox!"

Dagmar grins. "I guess now is as good a time as any to try a different location."

I smile back, run over to Wazo, grab his hand, and pull him from the infirmary toward the main citadel building. We race up the stairs to the second floor, where the chambers of the Aurengarte soldiers are. These are the bedrooms of the soldiers who help monitor the tournament, man the gatehouse and Administration buildings, patrol the battlements, and keep cadets in line, like Blaug or Fenne.

During the day, the quarters are unoccupied, so we take a right and start opening doors down the hall. Unlike the cadet dormitories, which hold dozens of beds, the Aurengarte soldiers are afforded slightly more space, with only a half dozen or so soldiers per room. Even so, after a few rooms, it becomes evident that this is a daunting task, and not one we'll accomplish quickly.

"This is useless, there are too many rooms for us to search," Dagmar says. "We must be missing something."

I pull the crumpled parchment from my pocket and stare again at the words.

"In the shadows…" I muse. "Where does the night guard sleep?"

"What?" Dagmar asks, surprised.

"The night guard. When I first arrived here, the soldier told me that lights out was at nine bells 'unless you've got night watch,'" I tell her.

"Fuck if I know. They didn't give me such a thorough tour," she says dryly. "Who told you that?"

And now it's my turn to race from the room, back downstairs to the front right hall, to the guard station near the entry door, where I spot a familiar face.

"Aalfs!" I exclaim, my excitement adding to my breathlessness as much as the running.

He stares at me blankly. "Yes?"

"It's me, Greta. I mean de Veend. I mean, you helped Otto and me on our first night. Otto Weber." Verbal diarrhea has struck me in my eagerness.

"He doesn't need your life story," Dagmar says curtly.

"You showed me and another cadet to our dormitories on our first night," I say more calmly.

He smiles in recognition. "Oh, right!"

I nod. "You mentioned then that lights out is at nine bells unless you've got night watch."

"That's true," he nods.

"Where does the night watch sleep? Is it somewhere different from regular quarters?" I ask, tension climbing my shoulders as I pin my hopes on Aalfs' next words.

Understanding dawns on his face. "Oh, yes, second level, east tower, away from the stairs, there's a block of—" but I'm already running back up the stairs, Dagmar fast on my heels, Wazo wheezing behind us.

Dagmar and I tear down the hallway, cross the octagonal towers, past the leaders' studies and Aurengarte chambers. I would've run past it if Dagmar had not called out.

"These rooms aren't near stairs, and they're in a tower. Are we east?" Dagmar asks, breathing hard in front of a set of wooden doors.

"Never have I instinctively known what direction I'm moving in without the benefit of a compass," I quip.

Dagmar rolls her eyes.

"But there aren't stairs; we might as well try," I acknowledge. "But won't they be sleep—" I begin, but Dagmar flings open the door.

Angry shouts greet her entry as she dives into the room. Without thinking further, I run in after her, trying in vain to see through the dark, aided only by the sliver of daylight peeking from beyond the heavy drapes at the windows. I see a shadow moving swiftly through the room and hear several outraged cries. I can only assume Dagmar is pushing people from their beds in her haste to find the next clue.

I turn toward one of the beds and tiptoe over gingerly. "Sorry," I whisper delicately through my teeth before shoving my hand under what I sincerely hope is the pillow.

"Tempest's tits!" The guard occupying the bed exclaims—clearly Caelish based on that expletive.

I'm about to pull my hand back when my fingers brush against something stiff that crinkles. "Dagmar! I've got it!" I exclaim.

Her answering whoop sounds from across the chamber, and she crashes back through. I yank my hand with the parchment from under the soldier's pillow and stumble back when he tries to swing at me.

"Sorry, sorry, sorry!" I repeat rapidly.

"Blame the tournament designers," Dagmar says cheerfully before she pulls me out of the room and into the hallway. She slams the door behind her, and to avoid any angry soldiers who decide to chase after us, we dart back down the hall toward the front of the building. When we reach the entryway, we stop to catch our breath.

Dagmar says, laughing, "I wish I could've seen their faces."

Tears are streaming from my eyes. "Just think…we're only the first team to break in there."

We can't hold the full-throated laughter then, and my stomach aches when I finally stop. Wazo looks at both of us, puzzled.

"Did I miss a jest, friend?" He asks me.

I shake my head, a residual laugh still on my lips. I look at the parchment and then hold it out to Dagmar. "I suppose you'll want the next clue."

She looks at the clue, then at me, and says, "No. What does it say, and what do you think?"

"Where sun sets low and horizon meets sky,
And sentinels watch as time passes by.
Where tempests boast with showers and breeze,
And perspective reveals fiercest foe in the trees.
'Neath where the view meets the sun's brightest rays,
The next clue in your quest is hidden away."

I read our next clue aloud to Dagmar and Wazo, breaking down each line in the verse in my head in an attempt to understand it.

Wazo gasps, "The gardens!"

Dagmar stares at him. "Where the fuck did you get 'gardens' from in that clue?"

"Trees," Wazo says simply.

Dagmar leans toward him, brandishing her fist. "If you don't shut up, I'll kill you and bury you in the garden."

Wazo shrugs, unaffected by her threat.

She turns to me and says, "First line seems like it means the west."

I nod in agreement. "Sentinels are guards, so perhaps something about where they keep watch?"

Dagmar thinks in silence for several seconds. "A guard would see someone in the trees if they were standing watch outside."

I frown, considering her words. "And you'd feel the wind of storms, as the third line mentions. Which direction is the tree cover in?"

"Most of it has to be to the south, doesn't it? Caelias is to the north, and those mountains aren't as dense with trees. They're snowier," she states.

"So a location where guards stand watch, the sun sets, and from where you can see enemies in the trees from your position." I tick off what we've deduced on my fingers.

Dagmar says, "It has to be a position along the outer wall. Maybe a tower on the southwest corner of the island," she suggests.

I nod again. "We might as well try it, but how do we know which way is southwest?"

Dagmar shakes her head. "All these good instincts and hunches you seem to have, and yet the gods didn't see fit to bless that brain of yours with a sense of direction, did they?"

I frown. "Well, how do *you* know?"

She rolls her eyes. "Sun rises in the east and sets in the west. Midday, it's due south. It's midday now. All you have to do is face toward the sun and turn right."

"Oh, is that all?" I ask, putting my hands on my hips. "How do you know that facing toward the sun isn't a matter of perspective, and the direction could be mistaken?"

"It's a giant ball of fire in the sky, can you really miss it?" Dagmar asks sarcastically.

I huff but don't answer her since I don't have a witty rejoinder.

She smirks. "That's what I thought. Let's move!"

CHAPTER TWENTY-FIVE
Under Lock and Key-per

We exit the building into the midday sun, which is high and bright above us. We will have to make up time with some of these other clues if we want to finish and remain in the tournament. Dagmar leads the way down the steps from the outcropping to the training yard, making a sharp left toward the livestock pasture.

I eye the animals warily through the fence as we approach one of the gates. I haven't had much experience with farm animals, besides the geese that lived in the moat at Noetheim and the goat that bit me when I was young, neither of which were exactly positive. Even now, the memory of the goat's yellow eyes and oddly shaped pupils before it clamped down on my arm makes my stomach twist. Sure, the cows and sheep gnawing on grass look placid enough, but who knows when they might decide to strike?

Dagmar starts opening the gate to the main pasture, and I look around nervously, rubbing the place on my forearm that still bears the scar from the goat's teeth. "Are you sure you should be doing that? I mean, what if we get in trouble?"

She looks at me, confused. "We have work duties in the pasture. What are they going to care if we walk through it?"

"Maybe they don't want us traipsing through the grass; don't the animals need to eat it?" I ask, my voice rising in pitch when one of the cows starts plodding over curiously.

Dagmar grins. "I'll let you in on a little secret, de Veend: grass is a plant, and plants grow back."

Wazo nods enthusiastically and leans toward me. "She's right, y'know."

"See, even Waldo agrees," Dagmar says.

"Wazo," he corrects.

"Gesundheit," she replies.

Wazo scratches his nose, like he can't remember if he sneezed or not. Dagmar rolls her eyes at him and turns toward me, gesturing at the gate. "Come on, de Veend, we've got a clue to find."

With a high-pitched whine, I creep into the livestock pasture, trying not to scream when the cow gets closer to me. It's *huge*, and it *stinks*. Like a mix of manure, hay, and wet fur. There's grass clinging to its moist snout, which is ominously close to my arm, but I don't want Dagmar to think I'm spoiled or ridiculous. So, I force myself to stand still, suppressing a shudder when I feel the slimy, wet nose brush the fabric of my tunic, snagging it and leaving a smear.

Dagmar looks at the streak of cow mucus on my sleeve and then at me, and I have to close my eyes and breathe through my mouth. When I reopen them, she's grinning at me. "Just like a big dog, right?"

She starts moving away from the cow and toward the back corner of the pasture, aiming for the far corner of the island's curtain wall, where a tower sits at the edge of the pasture.

"Not quite," I grind my teeth.

When we near the edge of the pasture, I can see we've circled back around to the side of the outcropping that the citadel sits upon, but there wasn't any way for us to access this part of the island from it. To our left is the jagged edge of rocks propping up the citadel, and to our right is a looming, forty-foot-high section of the curtain wall surrounding the island's perimeter. There's a small door at the base of the enormous tower sitting at the corner of the pasture, and I hope to gods that it opens for us, that we aren't forced to go back through the pasture and find a different path, and that we're on the right track with this clue.

Dagmar pushes open the door, which gives way with no resistance save for that of wood swollen from moist air, being so close to the river. I see a small chamber off to the side when we enter the tower. Dagmar tests the door but immediately shuts it.

"Privy," she says, without further explanation.

One would hope the clue would not be stored there.

I eye the spiral stairs with dread but sigh and follow Dagmar as she begins to climb them, Wazo uncomfortably close on my heels. We climb in silence, reaching the top without conversing. Dagmar seems focused on getting there as quickly as possible. I focus on breathing. Wazo…well, I'm not sure Wazo can focus on anything.

When we reach the top landing, I stop at the sight before me, which causes Wazo to crash into my back.

"Oof," I say, pitching forward, throwing my hands out in front of me to maintain my balance.

"Sorry, friend," he says, stepping back.

I stare, puzzled, at the blank wall in front of me. "How do we get outside? Do you think the clue's in here?" I ask Dagmar, turning toward where she's disappeared around the curve of the stair wall.

She's waiting by a ladder. "This is how."

I look above the ladder and see a wooden door that must open to the outside. "A trapdoor?" I ask, incredulously.

Dagmar nods. "It's not like they're going to build regular doors for a guard tower. That's just inviting people in."

"Well, if you ask me, anyone who tries to break *into* Stachtenbaste kind of deserves what they get," I quip. "You go first."

She climbs the fifteen-foot ladder and reaches for the handle on the door, turning and pushing, which lets in a bright shaft of light. I feel excitement that our instincts were right and rush over to clamber up behind her.

When I break through the door, I'm greeted by Dagmar and a guard whose boring but peaceful day has likely already been interrupted by at least one other team. He looks none too thrilled to see more people joining him.

I haul myself out of the doorway so Wazo can join us and take in the area around us. It's hard to appreciate just how massive each tower is from the ground, but it's at least sixty feet in diameter, with crenellations whose merlons stretch at least a foot above my head. I walk forward to one of the embrasures and stare through the gap, and my breath completely leaves my body.

The view stretches wide and wild in front of me, a painted tapestry of blues and greens come to life. Below, the Flumevian river churns and rushes in silver ribbons, threading its way around the island's rocky base. Even at this height, the current's restless rush reaches my ears. Beyond the riverbank, the land rises in evergreen-cloaked mountains; the towering conifers holding vigil as surely as the guards do along the wall here. Their needles sway faintly in the breeze kicked up by the river's current, the vibrant emerald unmoved by the season. Still, I am sure I see a few burnished tufts of early gold and rust and orange peeking out where the pines yield their ground to the occasional maple.

Overhead, wispy cirrus clouds vein the startling blue sky, which stretches as far as my eyes can see. I place my hands on the sun-warmed stone in front of me, bracing myself so I can lean out and appreciate the spray of salt as it hits my cheek, the smell of pine and fast-approaching autumn, the feeling of flying that being up this high gives me.

"De Veend," Dagmar says, "let's look at the clue again."

Spell broken, I retrieve the parchment from my pocket. "'Neath where the view meets the sun's brightest rays." I turn to the guard. "Is the sun ever really bright when you're up here?"

He looks surprised that I'm speaking to him, but he answers, "Yes, but not usually until afternoon when it gets closer to sunset. I have to avoid sitting in the other corner, else the sun hits me right in the face."

I look around at the cobbles of the tower, up at the sky, then back at the stones beneath my feet.

"What are you doing?" Dagmar asks.

"Looking for a spot where the sun would hit," I explain.

Understanding dawns on Dagmar's face, and she tests stones on the ground. "This patch looks lighter," she says.

I ask the guard. "Is this where you avoid standing?"

He nods. "About there, yes."

Dagmar uses her booted toe to nudge stones, and her eyes snap to mine when one wiggles. She dives down and pries the cobble from its place, revealing multiple parchment missives, sealed for ours and other teams to find.

"We should take them all," Dagmar says to me.

"What?" I ask, surprised.

"If they don't have the clue, they can't go to the next step," She explains as if I'm as slow as Wazo.

"But they'll know someone cheated," I protest.

"There wasn't a rule against cheating," Dagmar points out.

I frown. "I don't feel good about that."

"Don't you want to win?" Dagmar asks.

I begin, "Of course, but it hardly seems honorable to—"

"Only two kinds of people cling to honor: the naïve and the dead," she says sharply.

Stung, I want to refute what she says, but the trapdoor flings open again. The guard groans in frustration. Three more challengers climb out and see Dagmar with the clues. It's too late now to steal them without being discovered. She grabs one, looks at me with irritation, and swiftly descends through the trapdoor.

Wazo and I follow her down the ladder, the staircase, and out into the livestock pasture, where we open the clue and read it, our previous sense of camaraderie diminished.

> *"In a chamber of steel with sword's sharpest edge,*
> *Where knights last prepare to make good their pledge.*
> *Hidden 'twixt spaulders and poleyns of gold,*
> *Shielded by limbs and fletching of old.*
> *Where blades' appetites are whetted anew,*
> *Upon dagger's point you will find your next clue."*

"What's a spaulder?" Wazo asks.

"I thought I told you to stuff it," Dagmar snaps.

"I don't know what it is," I say, shaking my head.

"It's parts of a suit of armor; so are poleyns," Dagmar says matter of factly.

"How do you know that?" I ask her.

"Surprised I have knowledge you don't?" Dagmar inquires sarcastically.

I merely raise an eyebrow at her and wait.

"Used to steal pieces of the Aurengarte armor since it has gold in it. Melted down, all looks the same, fetches a decent price, too." She shrugs.

I look at the clue again. "'Steel,' 'sword,' 'blades,' and 'dagger.' These are all weapons or have to do with weapons."

"The equipment shed!" Wazo says excitedly.

Dagmar whacks him on the back of the head with the clue parchment and says to me, "The armory."

"Agreed," I reply.

We trace our way back through the pasture, and although we're slowed down when Wazo steps in a cow pie, we make decent time and soon enough are nearing the gate. Dagmar is opening the gate when I feel a tug on my tunic sleeve. To my horror, when I look down, a brown goat has taken hold of the cuff of the sleeve.

Frantic, I start trying to pull my sleeve from its jaws.

"Come on, de Veend. This is no time to play with the animals," Dagmar says cheerfully.

"Let go, you shit-smelling, ugly bastard—just let go!" I yell at it, pulling harder. I hear the fabric begin to rip and try to pull harder, but the goat resists, bleating in its throat at me. Its eyes lock on mine— yellow, glowing. Unnatural. It tugs harder, as though determined to drag me down and trample me.

"Just kick it away or something; we're wasting time," Dagmar says impatiently.

"I'm not going to kick an animal, no matter how. Fucking. Much. I want to," I huff, continuing to pull, blinking against the fear sweat that breaks out on my brow.

I see more goats approaching curiously, more unnatural eyes catch mine, and I feel panic rising in my throat. This wasn't supposed to be a physical trial! I open my mouth to yell for help, and instead, a bloodcurdling scream erupts from within me. The goat holding my sleeve is so startled it drops the fabric, screams back at me just as loud, and promptly falls over dead.

"Oh, my gods! She's got dark magic! She's a goat killer!" Wazo exclaims, rushing over to me.

Horrified, I say, "No, I don't really, I just—"

The goat rolls over and stands up, running away from me when fully on its feet. The others that had been approaching have also scattered.

"What in the gods' name was that?" I ask Dagmar as I dart through the gate.

She can barely speak for laughing. "Fainting goats."

We rush toward the outcropping, and my humiliation from the goat altercation is such that I run faster than I ever have before to escape the scene of the crime.

We scale the stairs to the outcropping and enter the inner bailey of the citadel, making our way to the large building in the center, and the only one with guards: the armory. Dagmar holds up our clue when we reach the doors, and the guards stand aside, letting us enter.

We're the only team in the space, which is enormous and filled with rows upon rows of armor and weapons.

"There are the spaulders and poleyns." Dagmar points to rows of shoulder and knee covers.

We keep pushing through, passing rows of more pieces of armor, past old bows and arrows, identified by their limbs and fletching. I wheeze, "What does…the last part of the clue say again?"

Dagmar slows. "'Where blades' appetites are whetted anew, upon dagger's point you will find your next clue.'"

"Do you think there's a place they would sharpen the blades in here?" I ask her.

"Split up, and look around," she orders, and dashes off between rows of swords.

I point Wazo down what I hope is a row where he can't damage much and turn to squeeze through another aisle of longbows. When I turn the corner, I see dozens and dozens of gleaming krahbeks. It's so faint at first, I think there must be a draft coming through one of the windows near the top of the room, but none appear open. The air here is thick with oil and iron and heat from being enclosed. Still, I feel I can hear something, like someone is standing behind one of the weapon racks. Another challenger sent to torment or deter us?

My boots scuff against the flagstone as I pass a rack of battered shields and more bent arrow shafts. That's when the whispers grow louder. Still indistinct and more sensation than sound, but they're getting closer, like they're circling. Murmurings and thoughts not entirely my own curled around the edges of my hearing.

I reach the side wall and see a series of doors. Their contents are a mystery to me, but I head for the first, trying to open each, the whispering sensation getting louder as I move down the row, like blood rushing in my ears, but punctuated by staccato clicks of teeth and tongue.

When I reach the next door, the whispering has become almost overwhelming. I push on the handle and the door swings open, revealing what looks like a repair shop, with a small hearth and forge tools, an anvil, and a grindstone.

Sealed clues on the workbench are fixed to the scarred wooden surface with daggers. As I approach the daggers, one in particular stands out. The metal of the blade is darker, and there is a faint pattern within it, an almost ripple effect, like it's alive. When I'm so close that my stomach is bumping the workbench, I can see the ripples are actually a very fine veining traveling through the steel. When I reach my hand toward it, the whispers surge, like wind rustling through leaves but too fast to follow.

That strange prickling sensation creeps up my limbs, over my shoulders, up the back of my neck, over my scalp. I turn sharply, looking around me.

"Hello?" I decide it's best to address whoever is there head on.

The whispers stop.

Only the rasp of my own rapid breathing sounds in the space.

I yank the dagger from the work table's surface, dislodging the sealed clue, surprised when the hilt feels warm in my hand. Unnerved, I drop the dagger and quickly exit the room.

I find Dagmar and Wazo. "Let's read the clue outside; it's too warm here," I say.

Dagmar eyes me thoughtfully. "Everything all right?"

I laugh nervously. "Of course, just overheated. Maybe a little hungry."

Wazo nods dolefully. "Me too, friend."

"Wazo—" Dagmar begins in a menacing tone.

I break off from them and head outside, not waiting to hear whatever threat she's dealt the hapless man this time. When they meet me, I break open the seal of the clue, hoping Dagmar doesn't notice my fingers trembling around the parchment as I read.

"Inside draughty chambers where failing men go,
Where blended balm, mortar, and pestle call home.
Behind fragile panes that sleep remedies,
Above mended extracts and brisk recipes.
Where herb, oil, and bloom all combine,
With seeds of euphoria, your clue you will find."

"This has to be the infirmary," I say. "All the clues are medicinal—draught, balm, mortar, pestle, remedies. Seeds of euphoria are probably some kind of drug. Maybe the apothecary, specifically."

We rush to the infirmary building, and I'm relieved we didn't have far to go this time. The matron we had burst in upon earlier is nowhere to be seen, but Hildegarde is bustling around the beds.

"Hildegarde, can we look in the apothecary?" I ask, holding up the clue.

She cocks her head toward its direction. "Go on, then."

We rush toward the end of the infirmary, which is attached to the apothecary by a shared wall. Despite having been in the infirmary multiple times as a patient and for work duties, I've never entered the apothecary. It feels like a separate world sealed in glass and dust and old, dried things. Shelves line the roughened stone walls, some sagging under the weight of timeworn jars and stoppered vials, each one labeled in fading, curling script.

Bundles of herbs, crumbling and fragrant, hang upside down from overhead beams, tied with fraying twine. The scent in the room is thick and heady, a battle between crushed mint and eucalyptus and vinegar and lavender, with something bitter lurking beneath it all.

On the far edge of the room, mortars and pestles rest in neat rows on a work table that holds thick journals open to ink-splattered recipes and charts, their edges warped with age or moisture from spilled remedies. Above the work table, hanging on the wall, is a series of massive wooden cabinets with foggy glass panes guarding rows of tinctures and tonics, their contents steeped in liquids of garnet, moss, and viridian.

"The clue says, 'above mended extracts and brisk recipes.'" Dagmar points out.

I look at the cabinets on the wall and nod. "I suspect it'll be in something in the cabinets."

I hand her the parchment, pull a wooden stool over to the workbench, and climb up on it, opening the first set of cabinet doors to better see behind the dingy glass. I start pushing bottles aside, trying to find any that looks like it contains paper.

"What was the name of the medicine?" I ask Dagmar.

She looks at the parchment. "Seeds of euphoria."

I scoot over to the next cabinet and open its doors, hoping it'll share its secrets with me.

"These look to be more ingredients than actual medicines," I mutter. "The way it's phrased makes it sound like something that is already created or that occurs naturally."

I move to the next cabinet and open its doors, and my reward is the set of vials that holds tiny black seeds and pieces of parchment on the top shelf. The labels on the outsides of the vials have become brittle and stained with time.

"'*Samenivresse,*'" I read aloud.

"What'd she say?" Wazo asks, puzzled.

"It's old Aurelian. It means 'seeds of intoxication,'" I explain.

"Sounds euphoric to me," Dagmar quips.

I open one of the vials and gently pull out the parchment, tossing it to Dagmar before recorking it and climbing back to the floor. She breaks the seal and reads the next clue aloud:

> *"It's here where caprice of fate does confine,*
> *Where souls who have wandered must bide their time.*
> *Amid the stones where hope often wanes,*
> *The pathway to freedom hidden in chains.*
> *Behind rails of iron where none wishes to be,*
> *Your finish awaits 'neath lock and key."*

Dagmar looks at me blankly and says, "It's the gaol."

"Are you sure?" I ask her.

"If you'd ever been to one, you'd know straight away, too."

I could tell her about the small, dark room at Lord Rocheburn's. Let her know that I had, in fact, been imprisoned. Just as I haven't, Dagmar has never mentioned how she came to be at Stachtenbaste. I'm not going to ask her. But that one sentence, her confident assertion, tells me all I need to know. That I have no basis for comparison to what she's seen, where she's been.

As we head back to the infirmary, I ask, "I don't even know where the gaol is; how will we get to it?"

Dagmar shakes her head. "I'm not sure, I'd imagine somewhere underneath the citadel. We'll have to go out and—"

"No need," says Hildegarde. "You can get there through the storeroom.

We all look at her in surprise. Dagmar repeats, "The storeroom?"

Hildegarde nods. "There's a storeroom for the infirmary beneath the main building. Stairs are in the back; they lead down to the undercroft. There's an access door from the citadel's outer wall, but it's fastest to cut through there."

"How have I not heard it was there until now?" I ask, bewildered.

Hildegarde frowns. "Generally, if you get put in the gaol at Iron Gate, you don't return."

A shudder runs through me. I can imagine that what she says is precisely true. Stachtenbaste is already as akin to a prison as I can imagine. So if you're in the prison's prison, it's not a good sign. I can suddenly see the glint of the blade slicing through the conscript's neck in the training yard. For a moment, I'm frozen. Then I feel a gentle hand tug my wrist.

I look down to see Wazo pulling at my arm. "She's already left, friend."

I thank Hildegarde when she points toward the matrons' study and tells us the stairs are at the back. She nods once and returns to folding the bed linens she was working on, dismissing us as quickly as she helped. The door to the stairs is already open, and Wazo and I duck through into the dim light without pause.

The stairwell is lit by a few dim torches clinging to the walls, but the smell of damp reaches my nose and tells me to watch for any slippery spots so my feet don't find them. When we reach the bottom of the stairs, we're in a large store room, almost as large as the armory. Only, instead of shelves brimming with implements of destruction, these are lined with tools for healing: bandages, bed linens, and medicines.

We hear a shout at the end of the room and rush toward it, finding Dagmar waiting at a set of pockmarked wooden doors. If it weren't so dim in here that I doubt myself, I could swear she looks a little green around the edges. It's almost as though she's afraid, but I don't point that out and simply allow her to open the doors, which reveal a room with a guard station and a wooden door with a small iron grate near the top of it.

A soldier exits the guard station. "Clue?"

Dagmar holds up the parchment. The guard nods, produces a large metal key from a ring at his waist, and opens the wooden door, revealing a long hallway bracketed on either side by cells walled with iron bars. In the largest cell chamber, several other challengers are waiting, including Stigander. When the guard opens the door to the cell, we rush in to see him.

"Are you all right?" I ask Stigander.

He nods. "Yes, but—"

"Which two will be staying?" The guard interrupts, addressing me, Dagmar, and Wazo.

Dagmar frowns and visibly pales. "What?"

I take the clue from her shaking hand. "“The pathway to freedom is hidden in chains. Behind rails of iron where none wish to be, your finish awaits 'neath lock and key.'"

Stigander looks grim, and Dagmar says, "So? That's the goal. We're here."

"It says, 'the pathway to freedom' and mentions our finish, but it doesn't say the clue is here. All the other clues mentioned the next clue," I point out. "So that must mean—"

"There's another clue," Dagmar says quietly.

I nod stiffly. "Or another step. Remember, Major Berger said we had to stick together until the last clue. I think two of us have to wait down here while the third goes and finds the key. Breaking the two team members out of the gaol must be the last part of the trial."

Dagmar looks at Stigander for confirmation, and he shrugs. "That's what my team also assumed, but the one we sent out has been gone a while. Seemed like a right fuckwit," He says.

"Why didn't you go?" I ask.

"Can't read," he says.

I stare at him, his words striking horror into my heart. What if a team were made entirely of challengers who couldn't read? They'd be eliminated.

"Challengers, who stays?" The guard asks, sounding impatient.

I look at Dagmar. "I know you don't want to stay in here, but do you trust me to find the key and come back for you as soon as I can?"

She watches me for several moments and nods. "Yes, because you have to get me if we're going to pass the trial."

I laugh quietly. "Thank you for trusting me."

Dagmar levels me with a hard stare. "Trust is a luxury I can ill afford. Don't make me regret it, de Veend."

I nod and turn to the guard. "I'll go."

He reaches into his belt, then places the last clue in my waiting palm.

CHAPTER TWENTY-SIX
A Dull Blade Still Cuts

Where matters of metal and might first arise,
A kingdom's conquests are drawn and devised.
Amidst ink and parchment, where victory begins,
You'll find there, at last, the key to your win.
When granted the key, their tethers will rend,
Then seek the prelude to reach trial's end.

Standing outside my teammates' cell, I read the clue three times. Turning to the guard, who is shifting from foot to foot impatiently, I say, "Is there a library here?"

He looks at me as though I've grown three heads. "Of course, there's no library here. Does this really seem like a place with a library?"

"What's the clue say?" Dagmar asks, approaching us and looking over my shoulder through the bars of the cell.

Stigander wanders over, Wazo close behind him. "Anything straightforward?"

"Don't you already know?" Dagmar asks him, eyes narrowing.

"Our team member didn't stay down here like de Veend, so no. Probably should have. That fuckwit."

Surprised, I say, "You want to help us?"

He shrugs.

"But don't you want to win?" I blurt.

His eyes narrow. "Victory is survival disguised as honor. I'd rather lose with my soul intact than win with blood on my hands."

I'm so surprised, I don't know what to say.

"Are we going to die, friend?" Wazo asks, sounding afraid.

This time, I roll my eyes. "No, Wazo."

"But he said somethin' about blood," he whines.

"It's an expression," Stigander says, then looks at me with a "where did you find this idiot" expression.

"Thanks for your help," I acknowledge Stigander's offer.

He nods. "Seems like the first three lines are what you need to get there."

"If there's no library," I say, "where else would they have ink and parchment or documents for strategy?"

"What kind of strategic documents?" Stigander muses.

"Ledgers?" I suggest. "Or maybe journals? Letters?"

"Maps?" Dagmar throws out.

"There are maps in Lord Corvilian's office," Wazo says.

All three of us turn slowly to face Wazo, who is turning in a circle, trying to figure out how to get the twist out of his belt. Dagmar slaps her hand on his shoulder, stopping him in his tracks.

"How do you know that?" I ask him.

"Saw 'em. Had cleaning rotation of the leaders' studies. Lots of papers." He nervously twists his tunic sleeve in his hand, likely unaccustomed to such rapt attention.

"And you're sure they were strategic?" I ask.

He shakes his head. "Can't read, can I? But they had ink on 'em. Writing, I s'ppose. And I know what maps look like."

I look down at the clue again. "'A kingdom's conquests are drawn and devised.' I think he's right," I say to Dagmar and Stigander.

Dagmar is staring at Wazo. "I can't believe your idiot brain figured it out."

Wazo smiles. "A dull blade can still cut now and then."

I grin, and Dagmar and Stigander both surprise me by smiling also. Without another word, I head out of the gaol hallway, past the guard station, and into the still infirmary storeroom.

As I cross the threshold into the linen-and-lavender hush of the storeroom, the door clicks shut behind me with an echo far louder than I anticipated. I didn't get more than a cursory glance here before when we were rushing toward the gaol, sure of our final destination. When I walk back through this time, briskly but not at such a mad dash, I can absorb the scent of dried herbs and old tallow filling the cool, damp, still air of the undercroft; the dust motes fluttering through the air illuminated by the stairwell torchlight.

I feel it when I'm nearly at the stairs that go to the infirmary.

A feathering along the edge of my thoughts. A quiet too deliberate to be merely contented silence. The sensation, like before, is faint at first—like someone murmuring from behind a closed window, their voice muffled from the glass. I'm alone, yet something deep in my marrow knows I'm being watched.

I lift my foot to the bottom stair, and the whispers begin. Not discernible sound initially. More like…a texture. The edges of my consciousness, frayed like a carpet, skimmed through by claws that then bump along my spine, hitting every knob and ridge with prickling precision. The murmurs scrape against the inner shell of my skull, impossible to locate.

Behind me? I turn my neck rapidly to look. No.

Above me? I pivot my gaze to the rafters and stone above me. No.

Within. The way a dream or memory sometimes lives inside you even after you wake.

I press onto the first stair, and the higher I climb, the louder the whispers become.

The whispers don't sound angry. They aren't even distinct. But while they lack intent or shape, I feel certain they are trying to reach me. I reach the landing in front of the door to the infirmary and brace my hand on the wall beside the door, trying to steady myself.

"The memory waits," a whisper sounds.

The words settle between my ears. With it comes the screech of steel, the distant clang of hammer on anvil, and a low, rhythmic sound beneath it. Like a heartbeat.

"The guardians remember," it intones ominously.

I nearly scream, pressing my hand to my chest, trying to drown out the whispers with the sound of my own breathing. In. Out. The moment stretches, and I fear any moment my mind will shatter into a thousand shards of glass across the stairs.

I crash through the door, whispers nipping at my heels. Not with fury, but knowing. When I burst into the nurse's study, Hildegarde looks up at me sharply from the chair in which she's seated.

She spots the parchment in my hand. "Found your clue, did you?"

The weight of her no-nonsense, unbothered gaze grounds me.

The whispers stop. My fear, and the unease, lingers.

Relieved, I nod. "Yes." My voice sounds breathless to my own ears.

She frowns. "Are you well?"

I'm not about to tell the matron that I think I might be hearing voices, possibly going insane, and in possession of the same prophecy magic my grandmother possessed. The same *illegal* magic.

"Fine!" I reply with forced cheer. "Just winded. It's been a long day."

"Best be on, then. Faster you do, sooner you'll be finished." She looks down at the book in her lap, finished with our conversation.

I dash out of the infirmary and into the bustling inner bailey, passing several teams of challengers as I go, wondering how far along they are in their quest. One is heading toward the infirmary as I depart on the path away from it and toward the main building. But rather than enter the right-side tower that leads to the dining hall, I enter the left-side tower. The very same one Otto and I entered our first night here. When we met Lord Corvilian. It seems I'm to do so again.

As I cross through the door and pass the guard station on that side, I wave my parchment at the bored-looking soldier, who simply nods at me without even rising from his seat. I immediately head for the stairs and begin climbing.

Again, the moment my boots strike the first step, it begins—that slow, insidious murmur at the base of my skull. Like something waking, that at first is no more than a suggestion, but with each step it grows teeth.

Just a chorus of fragmented words that curl beneath my skin. My fingers twitch, and the parchment of my clue crinkles in my grip.

"*Remember*," the whisper beckons.

My heart kicks against my ribs, trying to break free. A spike of pain pierces my temple, behind my eyes, so fast and sharp I nearly cry out. I stumble, bracing my hand on the wall near me, again, for balance. The stair bows beneath me. No, not the stair. I'm just dizzy.

Through the whispering, a single voice emerges. Louder, distinct. Deep. Ancient. Commanding.

"*Find me*," it says.

I pause, the words spilling down my spine like frigid water. My vision wavers, then sharpens. Every stone in front of me, every groove and pock in the mortar, the hair on my forearm leaning against the wall, all suddenly too vivid. My fingers touching the wall are both icy and burning up.

What's happening to me? I wonder desperately.

Just then, a whistle pierces the noise, sharp and casual. It's as if the sound cuts the noise in my head cleanly in two just as Rafe Kriegeur saunters into my sight, leisurely descending the steps above me.

"Head paining you, *künnle*?" He asks, nodding to the hand pressed against my temple.

"Even more now that you're here," I say tartly, dropping my hand abruptly in hopes he doesn't question me about it further.

He nods sympathetically. "It's painful sometimes to be faced with such a shining presence." He lowers himself to the same stair and leans against the wall opposite me, grinning.

I clench my teeth. "Do you ever tire of talking about how great you are?"

He looks thoughtful, pulling his dagger out from behind his waist, twirling the point against the pad of his finger as he often does.

"Hmm…no."

I roll my eyes.

"You know, *künnle*, you really ought to be more respectful toward me as your superior officer." He wags the dagger at me in a playfully chastising manner. "That smart mouth of yours could get you in trouble around others with thinner skin than I have."

"I'll be respectful when you've earned it. Until then, you'll just have to deal with my 'smart mouth,'" I retort.

His eyes briefly dart to my lips. I almost think I imagine it; except after a few seconds, he clears his throat. "What are you doing in the leaders' wing if you're not looking to use your mouth for more…pleasurable pursuits?" His black eyes meet mine with challenge.

I flush, thinking about my "pleasurable pursuits" with Aric, an officer. Not that that was in the leaders' wing, but still. Kriegeur stares at me, almost as if he knows, his dark brows slowly climbing up his forehead.

"I'm in the middle of a trial, remember? I have to get to Lord Corvilian's office." I wave my clue at him.

His shoulders stiffen the tiniest amount. I would've missed it if I hadn't been watching him, because he quickly relaxes them and pulls away from the stone wall.

"Do give my father my regards, will you? I hope your task isn't to dislodge the stick up his arse. I fear that's permanent," he says, as if imparting disappointing news.

I can't help it, the laugh bursts from me unbidden. "No," I reply, lips continuing to twitch in amusement.

The ghost of an almost sweet smile chases Kriegeur's mouth before he inclines his head toward the stairs. "Go."

I pass him, shaking my own head in puzzlement as I climb the stairs. What an odd conversation. Of course, Kriegeur is kind of an odd fellow. Although I'm itching to look behind me to see if he's still there, my pride refuses to give him the satisfaction of letting him know I'm curious.

As I exit the stairwell onto the floor of the leaders' wing, I almost walk directly into Major Berger, who is heading toward the stairs herself.

"Challenger?" She asks, as if she doesn't know where I'm heading.

"Lord Corvilian's study," I say, waving my clue again.

She nods and starts to go around me, but stops, turns back, and again says, "Challenger?"

I face her fully. "Yes?"

She replies, "Be on your guard. Lord Corvilian isn't a regular soldier. He will end someone without regret. Don't hand him the noose."

I nod nervously, whirling and darting toward the door I remember as the lord's study. I knock on the door and hear his voice bid me to come in. Turning the handle, I once again enter the den of the lion of Fracidaem.

I cross the threshold into Lord Corvilian's study and immediately catch sight of the man's unnerving dark gaze. While he and Kriegeur share the same eye color, Kriegeur's are merry, often dancing. Lord Corvilian's still remind me of a predator. I quickly pick a spot on the wall behind him to look at instead of directly at him, unnerved by his calculating scrutiny, especially on the heels of the whispers in my head, which have left me feeling scraped raw.

"Cadet de Veend," he says, by way of greeting.

Surprised he remembers my name, I stutter, "I, um, am here to collect the key for my team for the end of the challenge."

He makes no move to reach for any kind of drawer or box that might contain the key I need, instead leaning back against the red tufts of his chair. "I confess I'm surprised to see you've figured it out. Your family doesn't seem as much inclined to…intellectual pursuits."

I stiffen, eyes briefly flashing to his. "My family? My uncles are very accomplished. Engilram runs the forge, Walter is a diplomat, Burkhard serves the Order." Although I'm sure he already knows this, my mouth won't stop moving. I look at the wall beside his face again.

"And the courtier and the actor?" He asks sardonically, referring to Eoforwine and Herman, my youngest uncle.

I flush. "Uncle Eoforwine and Uncle Herman are more creative."

"They're frivolous," he retorts.

"They're spirited. And still of good family," I argue, becoming more heated.

"Ah, and yet," he drawls, "here you are, conscripted like any *trübvolk* girl."

My shoulders stiffen. *Trübvolk* is old Aurelian for "lackluster," and something only the Aurenclaste wield against the non-magical classes, as though insult can cement social hierarchy. It's intended to humiliate, to keep the commonfolk's necks under the heel of the Aurenclaste's boot. The use of it prickles beneath my skin, but I refuse to give him the satisfaction of an irate response.

He adds, "Lord Rocheburn has asked after your well-being."

I feel my blood freeze in my veins, but I try to sound casual as I glance at his face and ask, "Has he? Have you seen him?"

"I have," he confirms.

I swallow hard, then look at the floor. "And…Agnethe? I mean, my sister? Have you seen her?"

He asks, "You mean Lord Rocheburn's ward? I met her briefly, but she seems to keep mostly to herself."

My heart squeezes, and I whisper, "When did you see her?"

He cocks his head. "It was several weeks ago. Polite girl, if a bit wan." He taps his fingers on the blotter on his desk, and my eyes follow their rhythm.

"She's not with my uncles?" I ask, knowing Lord Rocheburn would have tried all he could to keep her to force me to comply, but hoping Eoforwine would be successful even so.

His fingers still. "You don't think your sister is better off with a member of the Gold Council? With every privilege possible available to her?" I can feel him staring at me.

I dart a glance at him, frowning. "She should be with her family."

He gives a lazy shrug. "I admit I didn't follow why Lord Rocheburn initially took such an interest in the two of you. Though after learning about your history, I understand a bit more. I must say, it's unusual that your grandmother didn't bother to register children of Andebert Vergildetbach, even if his wife was a Lützenclaste whore. He's fortunate the king only made him abdicate for that offense."

I almost yell at him. Almost tell him exactly what I think of his mean-spirited, prejudicial words, but when I look at him, I see the smirk on his face, and I know that's exactly what he wants. Major Berger's words echo in my head. I won't give him the satisfaction of being able to punish me.

I close my eyes briefly and take a shuddering breath to calm myself before staring slightly above his head and replying, "Agnethe and I are children of a cousin of Merel's. She and Andebert were kind enough to take us in when our parents perished when Agnethe was only a few weeks old."

"Of course," he says, "my mistake." He doesn't seem like he believes it.

He stands, reaching into a drawer in his desk, and pulls out a heavy gold key. He walks around his desk and stops just in front of me, my eyes level with his chin. The man is almost as tall as his son.

He says, "As I can deduce you've completed the previous clues of the trial successfully, since you are now here in my study, you may go rescue your teammates."

"Thank you," I say, deciding manners are called for since he's standing so close.

He holds up the key with one hand and gestures with the fingers of his other, as if he wants me to take it from him. I reach out and wrap my fingers around the key. I try to pull it from his grasp, but he holds tight for several seconds. I look at his face now, nervous and frustrated.

"I'll be following your progress in the tournament closely, Cadet de Veend," he says.

I'm certain his not doing me the courtesy of addressing me as a "challenger" is a purposeful slight, just as I'm certain that his keeping tabs on me is *not* a good thing for me.

"I'll be sure to pass along your well wishes to Lord Rocheburn and his ward. Don't fret, he has a way of shaping the malleable." The smile that curves his lips is full of malice. "Run along now. And do try not to fail too spectacularly. You wouldn't want to humiliate that 'good family' of yours more than I'm sure your being here already has."

The shame that crashes through me is acute, and I reflexively pull on the key again to escape this conversation as quickly as possible; this time, he relinquishes it to my grasp. I turn wordlessly to exit the study, but as

I go, I feel cold rage replacing the shame.

How dare he deliberately play upon my sympathies, my ties to my family, my station, my sister, *everything*?

That impractical, ill-advised temper that I've so recently found flares within me, and I can't resist twisting back to face him.

Finally, I look directly into his glittering black eyes without hesitation as I say, "I wouldn't underestimate my sister, my lord. Or me."

CHAPTER TWENTY-SEVEN
Method or Madness?

I race back down the stairs to the entry hallway, trying to outrun what I just said to Lord Corvilian lest he decide to turn my back into the perfect flaming arrow's target. I also hope to outpace the return of any whispering that might try to chase me as I hurry along alone, which is when it seems to find me.

As I barrel down the stairs, I shove the key and the extremely crumpled clue parchment into my pocket, flying past the guard station and out the door, back into the inner bailey.

I have no idea how far along the other teams are, but now is not the time to waste on leisurely returning to my teammates. I run along the gravel path toward the infirmary, certain Hildegarde will let me approach the gaol that way again, since I'm not sure how else to access it. Gravel kicks up beneath my feet, stinging against my calves through my uniform trousers, but I barely notice.

I throw open the infirmary door and rush back toward the matrons' study. I hear voices inside it and wonder if Hildegarde was generous enough to anyone else to allow them to access the gaol through those stairs. Although, I think, frowning, they had said none of our earlier clues would be in the same order. The only one shared is the last, so none else would have gone to the gaol from the infirmary.

I'm not sure what instinct tells me to do so, but I slow my steps, quieting my boots' footfalls on the wooden planks of the floor. I don't want to interrupt a serious conversation about a patient, but I don't know why I feel as though that's not what this is.

I find I'm right when I approach the door, which is slightly ajar, and see Kriegeur talking to Hildegarde.

"I need more of it," he insists.

"It'll have to wait," Hildegarde says. "With the Freiheit, shipments are slower, inspection is higher. The visiting Aurenclaste means we have greater demand for medicines and treatments. And covers," she adds tartly.

Kriegeur makes a scoffing noise. "Can't imagine the Aurenclaste wanting to *decrease* their own potency, can you?"

"Even so," Hildegarde says, "doesn't seem like you can afford to have anyone looking too closely at what you're doing, my boy. Not when you cut it so close last time."

"You sound just like Conrad. *Now* is the time. Maybe scrutiny is higher, but so is distraction. You've seen the parade of broken limbs, burned skin. No one's going to question a few more exits."

I'm surprised at how…sharp…Kriegeur's voice sounds. I've never heard him speak to someone the way he's doing so to Hildegarde. He's clearly comfortable with her, but in command, and altogether more astute than I ever would have expected from him.

I watch as Hildegarde presses a paper envelope into his large, waiting palm. "This is what I have. I'll send a note when I get more. I can't completely deplete the supply, or the others will notice and become suspicious."

"Be creative," he urges. "You always have been when it matters."

"Patience, Rafe. No one rushes to bury the dead."

Bury the dead? I mouth to myself.

She called him *Rafe.* The familiarity is shocking. Weeks ago, when Kriegeur injured that soldier during practice, Hildegarde seemed not to know what Kriegeur's nickname was. Was that a performance? Has she known him all along?

And the envelope. *Why is she helping the son of the Aurengarte general obtain what I deduce is some kind of drug? Is he addicted to something? Something that the Aurenclaste would want to know about?*

"I want notice the moment you can find more," he says. "If you can't…I'll find another way."

The door opens fully then, causing a gust of air to stir my face. Kriegeur is there, but looking over his shoulder at Hildegarde. Quickly, pretending as though I just arrived, I raise my hand in a knocking motion.

"Oh, apologies," I say cheerfully.

Kriegeur's head snaps toward me sharply. His dark, earth-rich eyes meet mine in shock, which is quickly replaced with his standard twinkle.

"*Künnle,*" he says lazily, leaning against the doorjamb. "You simply have to stop pursuing me so obviously. What will the others think?"

I roll my eyes. "What others?"

"The other cadets, of course," he clarifies. "You don't want to give them the impression that I'm at all…favoring you…do you?" His eyes travel down the length of my body, and I feel myself flush.

I'm not stupid. I know he's trying to discern how much I heard and to hide how much he cares about the topic. Still, though, he has the ability to get under my skin, even when I know that's precisely what he's trying to do.

"I was *trying* to get back to my team. I was hoping Hildegarde would let me go through the storeroom again," I lean around him, finding Hildegarde's concerned gaze.

She immediately looks relieved, not nearly as good at hiding her reactions as Kriegeur apparently is, and nods.

I duck into the study underneath the arm that he's draped across the doorway. "Thank you, Hildegarde, I'll go get them, and then we'll be on our way."

She doesn't say anything, simply nods again, her hands tightly gripping the fabric of her skirt. I don't want to give away that I overheard anything, so I smile blithely at her before yanking open the door to the stairwell, not sparing Kriegeur and his stupid face another glance.

I don't care what drugs he's addicted to. I'm not at all curious. Of course, that's a lie, but I'm also a little busy at the moment. I force myself to focus on my task, bolting down the stairs and careening through the storeroom. I'm rushing to my team, but also still trying to outrun any whispers and now my own curiosity about Kriegeur. I pull open the door to the hallway near the gaol, and dart past the guard station, not bothering to stop and acknowledge him. I have the key, so I no longer need him.

When I approach the cell my team members are in, I see some new faces waiting, as well as some missing.

"Did Stigander's team member come get him, then?" I ask Dagmar, who has rushed to the door with Wazo fast on her heels.

"Just a few moments ago. Seems like there are still plenty who haven't figured it out," she says nervously, looking over her shoulder at the numbers still waiting. We can't be sure, though, how many were here before us.

I fit the gold key into the lock on the door, and it unlocks with a loud *clang*. Dagmar and Wazo bustle out of the door, which I shut behind them, sealing the other challengers back into the cell.

"What's next?" Dagmar asks. "Read the end of the clue again."

I pull out the parchment, which has seen better days, and read the clue once more.

"Where matters of metal and might first arise,
A kingdom's conquests are drawn and devised.
Amidst ink and parchment where victory begins,
You'll find there, at last, the key to your win.
When granted the key, their tethers will rend,
Then seek the prelude to reach trial's end."

"'Seek the prelude,'" Dagmar frowns, thinking over the last line.

"Well," I begin. "In music, a prelude is an introductory piece to a larger movement. At the beginning."

Dagmar says, "So we have to go back where we started."

I nod. "I think so."

"Makes sense," she agrees. "Move out!"

We head down the hall to the guard station, and when we reach it, I call out, "Which is the regular way out? Not through the storeroom?" I ask him, not eager to face Hildegarde or potentially run into Kriegeur again and have to fake my knowledge or hide it from Dagmar.

He points over his shoulder at a door in the back of the guard station, not rising from his chair. "Through there."

Dagmar reaches the door first, opening it with force, and we're greeted by a large stairwell that simply leads upward. At the top of the staircase, another door leads us out the side of the outcropping, between it and the orchard and vegetable gardens. Above us, on the ledge of the outcropping from where we've emerged, are the crumbling ruins of a small, stone building sitting beside the wall of the citadel.

"What is it?" I ask.

"The old chapel," Dagmar answers. "Heard the grounds warden mention it but hadn't seen it yet. They left it here even after they built the new one in the inner bailey."

She takes off, obviously not interested in examining the old chapel or its existence any longer, and I'm forced to follow so we can stick together. As we race across the training yard and approach Freiheit Field, I can hear the hum of the crowd, which rises to a roar when we break through the arena's gates and enter the middle. Dagmar waits for Wazo and me to catch up to her, and then we make our way to the center of the arena. I chance a look at the platform, searching to see if Kriegeur is present, but he's nowhere to be found. My gaze flits to Aric, whose tense face relaxes upon seeing me enter the starting circle, where several other teams are already waiting. We hand our key and parchment clue to Major Berger.

"The eighth team has arrived!" She announces to the crowd, who cheer.

Eighth! We made it! I can't help it. I am so excited, I fling my arms around Dagmar in a hug, jumping up and down. She stiffens for a moment but then allows the embrace, although she doesn't return it.

"Not so bad, de Veend," she says. "Though I had begun to worry when it seemed like you took forever with Lord Corvilian. He give you any trouble?"

If I didn't know better, I'd think she seems almost concerned for me, her question going beyond simple curiosity, but that can't be it.

I shrug. "No more than a pompous arse like that usually would."

She grins at me.

"Well met, friends," Wazo says, smiling.

"Wazo, don't take this personally, but I hope we never speak again," Dagmar says.

Just like that, she wanders over to Stigander and Berte, who are in clusters with their teams, and the spell of our forced fellowship lifts. Wazo also drifts off to another group, perhaps to join some other dim-witted, absent-minded friends. Sighing, I shake my head and give myself a moment just to enjoy the fact that I have made it to the next trial—and without any injuries like last time.

A flutter in my peripheral vision has me looking up into the stands of the arena to see my raven friend perched on one of the empty benches. I feel pleasant surprise at the sight of it, but then a subtle, prickling sensation creeps over my shoulders.

"Greta," a voice says to my right.

I turn abruptly, looking into Aric's chocolatey eyes with surprise, all intelligent thought leaving my head.

"Yes?" I ask, hating how eager I sound that he's approached me. I want to maintain a facade of cool indifference, but instead I'm nothing but warm interest.

"I need to speak with you," he says.

"About what?" I ask innocently.

"Just say you'll meet me later. In the south officers' bathing chamber. Third level." His face is pleading.

My mind goes blank when he says "south."

"Uh, which chamber is that?"

He smiles. "Over the dining hall, nearest the stairs."

I nod. "I'll think about it."

"I'll be there," he says firmly. "Come after lights out."

I creep down the stairs to the third level an hour after lights out, knees knocking, my arms flailing when the toe of my boot finds a rough edge of stone and I nearly fall. I've never been a rule breaker, but it seems that the last few months have not only completely interrupted my life, but also my habits, as I'm turning into someone I would've never thought myself capable of being.

That someone is easily irritable. Reckless. But determined. Maybe even a bit brave.

When I reach the third level, I go to the closest door, praying to all the gods that it's the right one. I'm still not great with directions. I push it open very slightly and breathe a sigh of relief when the better-lit plastered walls of a bathing chamber come into view.

The cadet bathing chambers already seemed lavish to me compared to what even many wealthy Aurelian households would have, especially given the running water. However, they pale in comparison to those the officers are afforded.

The air shimmers faintly with residual heat from a fire banked but slowly diminishing in a large stone hearth on the far side of the room, its remaining embers glowing low in its marble depths. A series of copper tubs, each deep and wide enough to stretch out in, are spaced evenly along the tiled central aisle. While their edges are worn smooth from years of officers slipping in and out of their confines, they are polished to gleaming, their surfaces adding to the soft, warm glow of the room.

Near each tub stands a low table bearing folded linen cloths, brushes, and vials of soaps and salves. Along the plaster walls are richly embroidered tapestries depicting various brave, Aurengarte-fought battles, well positioned to banish any autumn and winter chill from the room during the colder months. The rug beneath my boots is thick and luxurious, muffling every footfall, a deep burgundy woven with moss greens and golds in intricate curling patterns.

In a discreet alcove to one side of the chamber are several garderobe closets with wooden doors and brass latches. In the opposite corner, near tables with washing bowls atop them, and close to their storage cabinets and dressing area, are upholstered chairs and a settee covered in wine-colored velvet, carved vines twirling around elegant mahogany limbs lacquered to a glossy finish. This is a place not just for bathing, but for respite and retreat, for officers to shed the grit of the day's efforts and emerge refreshed and reborn.

Suddenly, a hand closes around my wrist, and I gasp, ripping it from Aric's grasp in surprise.

"I didn't mean to startle you," he says apologetically.

"I was admiring the room," I tell him. "It's certainly a step up from the cadet bathing chamber."

He smiles. "I suppose they don't want us to complain too much since we have to be here for several years."

I nod. "I suppose. What did you want to speak with me about?" I ask him, cutting to the chase.

"How was the trial?" He asks, eyes scanning my face, as if searching for any sign of illness or injury.

"You could've asked me that earlier without requesting I break the rules to do so," I reply bluntly, irritated he dragged me from my bed just for trivial conversation.

I shouldn't have come.

"I'm just trying to talk to you, Greta. You shut me out," he protests.

"Can you blame me?" I ask him. "You haven't sought me out, either."

"I did today," he says.

"To ask me about the weather? The trials?" I press, my frustration growing. Surely he can't be this obtuse.

"To ask you—" he runs his fingers through his hair and then expels a heavy breath. "I don't know. To see you, I guess, really."

My heart kicks up in my chest, and my stomach drops.

"Why?" I whisper.

"This isn't…this isn't going at all how I'd imagined," he confesses. "I thought we could be civil. Friends."

My heart sinks. "You want to be friends."

"What I want doesn't factor into this," Aric says, pacing away from me.

"Aric," I say sharply, and he looks up at me. "What. Do. You. Want?"

He stares at me from his position across the room for several moments. His eyes move to my mouth, down my body, all the way to my toes, before traveling back up to my face.

"What do you want?" He asks me, seeming hesitant to voice his true feelings.

I walk toward him slowly. "I think I asked first."

"Greta," he murmurs as I stop a few inches before him. He swallows. "I think this was a foolish idea."

"Very foolish," I agree.

He frowns. "You agree with me?"

"If you only want to be friends, Aric, then it's foolish for me to be here." I nod. Trying my best at seduction, I look up at him through my lashes and lower my voice, "So what do you want?"

He reaches for me, his lips pressing against mine, fingers digging into the indentation at my waist. My hands slide up his forearms, over his biceps, to settle on his shoulders as he deepens the kiss, his fingers grasping the hem of my tunic and pulling upward.

I lift my arms, allowing him to remove the tunic from over my head. I reach for his, but he brushes my hands away and removes it, revealing sun-warmed skin burnished to a golden glow in the low firelight. A smattering of auburn hair dusts his chest and trails down the tight muscles of his abdomen, disappearing into the waistband of his trousers. I swallow nervously, hands trembling as I press them to his chest, and he lowers his mouth to mine again.

I feel his fingers brush the skin of my back, sending shivers down my spine as they gently dislodge the banding securing my breasts, their heavy weight spilling from the fabric falling to the ground. I sigh a breath of contented relief when the air brushes my skin, nipples tightening in response to the stimulation. Aric looks down at my bare breasts, and I nod at his questioning glance, which asks for my permission. His hands drift around the front of my abdomen, sliding up to cup them, thumbs brushing the taut peaks with aching tenderness.

"You're so beautiful," he says thickly, running his lips along my cheekbone, then down the side of my neck.

His mouth continues to trail down across my collarbone and the smooth expanse of skin along my chest. He reaches the peak of my left breast and closes his lips around it, pulling it into his mouth, sucking firmly.

Gasping, I lean my head back, running my fingers through his hair, digging my nails into his scalp, which is met with a groan from him. More urgently, he reaches for the waist of my uniform trousers, and I kick off my boots as he pulls the trousers and smallclothes over my hips to pool at our feet.

He urges me over to the settee, seating me on the edge as he removes his own boots and trousers before standing tall and bare before me. I've never seen anyone as handsome as he is naked before. His body is sculpted lean muscle, all angles and dips and strength, dusted with that coppery hair across his legs, forearms, chest, and drifting from his stomach to where I can see his cock jutting out eagerly from him.

I reach out, wrapping my hand around his shaft, feeling a tightening in my lower belly at the groan he emits, his own head tilting back now, his hands finding their way into my hair.

"Greta," he murmurs my name as he reaches down and brushes my nipples again, which causes my hand to reflexively tighten around his cock.

He pushes me onto my back on the settee, and I'm suddenly glad that I had to suffer the embarrassment of my mandatory contraceptive tonic visit when I first arrived. It was worth the discomfort to now not worry about any potential consequences of this interlude. More people must find time to do this than I initially thought.

He covers my body with his, which presses my arse into the velvet of the settee, his lips finding mine again, pushing my thighs open to cradle his hips with mine. The heat of his shaft brushes against the wetness between my legs, and we both hiss in pleasure when it rubs against my clit, eased by the slick moisture already gathered there.

He reaches a hand in between us and traces circles around my clit with his thumb, which makes my whole body tighten like a bow string, eager for a repeat of the release I found with him days ago. He trails a fingertip down to my entrance, circling it teasingly before sliding one fully inside of me.

He groans against my mouth and shudders. "You're so wet."

I can't speak, nodding frantically against his mouth, not wanting to break the spell he's casting over my body with his. I can feel release fast approaching, and I chase it, the stress and tension of the day leaving me little patience for gentle caresses and measured lovemaking. I just want to feel something, *anything*, good.

I shatter around him, and through the clench of my inner muscles, feel the press of his cock at my entrance behind his fingers, stretching me open to accommodate him as he slides in until his hips are touching mine. Despite the orgasm that just crashed through me, my body responds to the firm, steady thrusts of his hips, the push and pull of his body within mine, the drag of every ridge of his cock along the inner walls of my core.

He increases his pace, and I meet each forward thrust with an upward one of my own, wanting the violence, the ferocity, to hear the sound of skin slapping against skin as he takes me. I can tell he wants to slow down, to take his time, but I want more, now. I bend my knees and wrap my legs around his waist, pulling him deeper into me, the act of which results in a shaky moan from him.

I reach my arms above me, bracing them on the settee, as he thrusts into me harder and faster, my breasts bouncing with each inward motion, drawing his eye. I can see the feral gleam in his gaze as he watches my body move beneath his, and I pull his head to my breast, encouraging him to suck on my nipples once more. He obliges, and as soon as his lips close around one of their peaks, I dissolve around him in a second release, my body clutching his in desperate, eager spasms.

He gives a few more thrusts and then buries his face in my neck, his deep, satisfied groan followed by a hot gush telling me he found his own pleasure.

We lie like that for several minutes, our breath calming in the stillness of the room. I let my legs fall away from his hips, and he slowly dislodges from me. He reaches for a toweling linen and wipes himself off, then helps me to clean myself, which brings a flush to my cheeks, before he lies beside me on the settee, stretching an arm beneath my head.

Soon, I feel my eyelids start to grow heavy, and I know I'm in danger of falling asleep, but I don't want to lose the glow of this moment, the good feeling. Smiling, I look up at Aric's face, and feel dread in my gut when I see his somber expression. He is looking at the ceiling, as if deep in thought, and the thoughts can't possibly be good.

"Is everything all right?" I whisper, tracing the frown lines in his forehead.

He looks at me, brow smoothing, and says, "Yes, but you should probably get back to your sleeping quarters so as not to arouse any suspicions."

I feel he's not being entirely truthful with me and that he's having doubts or worries again. Perhaps he doesn't want to voice them for fear of upsetting me once more, which is a valid concern given that I already feel upset and he hasn't even let me down yet. The warm afterglow I had been basking in has already left me, and all I have remaining is chilly regard, perhaps mixed with regret.

We quickly dress, and he walks me to the stairwell. He kisses me goodnight but then disappears quickly down the hall and around the corner. It makes me wonder if I've misread everything and all he wants is something physical. I suppose that wouldn't be the worst outcome considering everything I have to face here, both in the trials and after with Agnethe, but I can't help my traitorous heart from wishing I had more.

Trying desperately not to cry, I climb back up the stairs to my dormitory and fall into my bed, my shattered hope my only companion as my eyes drift closed.

I'm in a temple I don't recognize—one whose walls are slick with age and forgotten history. Mournful cawing fills the air, along with the sound of wings beating

against the thick silence.

Shadows stir around me, suffocating and menacing, their presence pressing in from every angle, making me feel as though I'm choking. In the shifting darkness, a figure emerges.

A man.

A man with hair as black as pitch, skin as pale as the moon, and dark, fathomless eyes.

Before I can even address him, he changes in front of my eyes, his nose growing, elongating; his figure hunching; his arms stretching out on either side of him. Skin, clothing, and hair are replaced by feathers as dark as night, iridescent with indigo and violet.

A raven.

A raven with unsettling crimson eyes.

The raven's gaze locks with mine. Its beak opens, and a deep, resonant voice pierces the air from within its breast.

"The guardians' memory pulses through your veins. You bear the blood of night within you. Awaken."

My eyes fly open, and I'm awake.

Awake and standing barefoot in the grass in front of the old chapel. *How did I even get here?* Panicked, I turn, looking for the path to get off this side of the outcropping and back to my room. I'm so unnerved by the fact that I managed to climb through the weeds and overgrowth blocking the way to the front of the citadel *while sleeping* that I don't initially notice the dark shape sitting nearby.

Clouds part in the sky above me, allowing the moon's bright glow to break through, illuminating the space before me as I turn toward the ruins once more. The raven is seated on a cluster of crumbling stones in front of me. I can see how large it is when it's this close. Far larger than a common raven.

Its eyes are a disturbing shade of crimson that study me solemnly.

I break the silence, not even caring that I've reached the point of insanity where I'm earnestly speaking to a bird. "What's happening to me? Am I going mad?"

I shake my head, bringing my trembling hands into my hair, and sink into the damp grass on my knees. The raven watches me for several minutes more without moving. Suddenly, I feel that sharp pinch in my temple again, and a prickling sensation ripples across my scalp, making the hairs on the back of my neck stand on end.

In the quiet of my mind, a voice speaks. One as ancient as the stones upon which the raven now perches, worn smooth by centuries of wind and legend, echoing with truths long since buried.

"Madness is forgetting who you are. You, Margarethe de Veend, are just beginning to find out."

CHAPTER TWENTY-EIGHT
The King Without a Throne

My legs are stiff as I rise, the damp grass clinging to me like fingers refusing to let go. Every rustle of the breeze sets me on edge. I scan the tree line of the nearby orchard, even the low bushes and weeds, anywhere a voice might have hidden itself. But there's nothing. Just the raven, black as ink, perched motionless like a statue carved from night.

I take a hesitant step forward. Then stop.

This is ridiculous. This is *insane*. Birds don't talk. Not even in nightmares. And if they do, they don't sound like they know what I'm thinking.

The raven tilts its head, and the prickling returns to my scalp. The voice doesn't echo in my ears; it rather feels like it coils *behind* them, somewhere deep inside my mind. A soundless thing that also rolls like thunder through the clouds of my consciousness.

"Any more insane than conjuring fire from thin air, or the weather, or moving objects with your mind?"

The voice snaps across my thoughts like lightning cracking through those clouds. I stumble, my heel catching on a loose stone, and fall to my arse hard on the ground, air knocked from my lungs in a gasp. As I stare, bewildered, at the raven, I can feel the dew clinging to the blades of grass quickly soaking into the fabric of my night clothes.

"How-how did you know what I was thinking?" I ask the raven.

The voice replies, "When the bond stirs, thought becomes a thread between us."

"So…you're speaking to me? Into my mind?" I ask it.

It raises its wings slightly, almost like a bird equivalent of a human throwing up their hands in frustration, and its head bobs up and down, as if nodding to me.

"I don't understand," I whisper. "This is magic, and I…I don't have magic. And I've never *heard* of magic like this."

"Your blood sang to me. Not with one voice, but two. Feather and fortune. Gleam and shadow," the raven intones.

"How did my blood sing to you? How did you find me?" My fingers dig into the wet grass, looking for something to ground me, to keep me from keeling over in shock.

"The sum of such knowledge is not gathered in a single night, nor even in a lifetime. Each truth is a feather in the wing—only when enough are borne, can you take flight."

Great. Metaphors. Super clear.

The raven does the wing-raising thing again, like it knows *exactly* what I was just thinking and is irritated by it.

"I still don't understand," I tell it.

"Understanding comes with time. Suffice it to say, your life is not what it once seemed to you."

"Is this what my dreams were about? And caused by?"

I want to believe this is another dream, that I'm hallucinating. That I've finally cracked under the pressure of everything. Grandmother's death, Lord Rocheburn, separation from Agnethe, Stachtenbaste, the trials, fear, grief, pain, and all in between. Something else inside me, though—some fragile, buried shard of emotion—hopes it's true. Hopes it means I don't have some terrible, secret prophecy magic like my grandmother. Of course, it would mean I have some other, terrible, secret bird-talking magic, but at least that's not documented as illegal, as far as I know.

"The blood of ravens stirs differently within each guardian's veins. Some guide the darkness, some change form, some recall that which no other can, some view the world through their bond's eyes, and you…" It cocks its head at me. *"Well, you are something I've never seen before. You walk with two ghosts at your heels: one with wings, one with burnished brow."*

"So, you're telling me that not only am I magical, but it's a magic I've never heard of and even *you* aren't familiar with in all your birdy wisdom?" Now it's my turn to throw up my hands in exasperation. I bet if I had wings, it would look much more impressive.

The raven's feathers bristle. *"I am not a 'birdy.' Once, I soared with sovereign's pinions. It is thanks to man's delusions of grandeur that I linger in the realm of forgotten memory."*

I realize I've insulted him. Somehow. This poetic, also somewhat snobby, raven?

"Apologies, um, your highness. That's what you meant, right, that you were king of the ravens?" I ask hesitantly.

The raven's feathers smooth. *"Not all ravens, for there are many kinds. But the* Blutraben *conspiracy was the most powerful, as evidenced by our ability to bond with humans."*

My brow furrows. "*Blutraben*? And what kind of conspiracy?"

"*Blutraben are ravens in whom magic flows from vein to vane—enchantment woven in the very blood that sustains us. Blood ravens, for the less-perceptive ear. And 'conspiracy' not in plot, but in name—your kind's term for our gatherings,"* he clarifies.

"Blood ravens," I say, processing. "Do you mean like the *Enderaben*?" I ask, eyeing him skeptically.

"Absolutely not. There is little I have in common with those lifeless specters," he intones, bristling again.

Enderaben is a name pulled from the yellowed pages of children's storybooks and cautionary tales. Death ravens and the pets of Mortuua, the goddess of death, herself. Omen-bringers and watchers from the shadows. I remember the drawings in books—crude sketches of giant black birds with milky, vacant eyes and feathers that didn't gleam but instead consumed the light around them. Their shadows were always drawn oddly in pictures, jagged and twitching, living things trying to escape the bonds of their masters.

They weren't real, though. Just myths meant to scare you into cleaning your teeth at night and leaving offerings at temple. Fables invented by parents to keep their children well-behaved. What better way to do so than with creatures invented to give Mortuua eyes and ears in the human realm from where she sits, exiled in Nachternel.

This raven speaks in my mind, but not with death's cold breath. Something ancient and powerful, yes, but with warmth. Vitality. Sparks, not silence. And his eyes certainly aren't dead. The opposite, in fact. They are alive with knowing, with centuries somehow folded into a single glance. With blood.

A blood raven.

He was insulted by the comparison, like I'd just accused a king of groveling at the feet of a jester. Perhaps that's exactly what I had done. Because whatever this raven is, it's not from the bedtime stories. Not one of the silent sentinels of terrifying legend, made to observe and report and do so without emotion.

No, this raven definitely seems to feel. And *judge*.

I eye him warily. But I'm still not sure what to make of this. I've never heard of *Blutraben*. Or why he's here. And what having a "bond" even means, and what I'm to do with it. I'm not sure I can handle many more surprises about my heritage, my life, *myself*.

The raven simply watches me, and I get the feeling he can hear and see and feel everything I'm thinking right now, so I don't bother explaining it all to him.

Instead, I ask him the question now burning in the back of my skull. "Did my grandmother know this about me? That this…bond…exists?"

Did my grandmother, in fact, *know* this was inside me? That something ancient and magical had spilled itself into my blood, a secret waiting to wake? And if she did, *why didn't she tell me?*

We had spoken of countless topics in the time I had been with her. She had taught me a thousand things—about tea and history and dancing and lesson after lesson about manners, menus, and mundanity. But not this. Not the truth of what I have. What's inside of me. Not even a whisper of it.

Not even when her life seeped into my hands, and she had a final opportunity to give me knowledge that might have helped me, guided me, protected me. Instead, she gave me a coded, highly sensitive message I had no hope of deciphering on my own. And empty apologies followed by even emptier platitudes. Like I was ready to figure it all out with next-to-no information, ready to blithely take on the world with Agnethe, to live out gilded fantasies in a distant world with no heartache.

My chest aches with something tight and cold. And hollow.

Why didn't she trust me? And if she had been a seer, hadn't she known all of this would happen? Did she? And did she simply take the coward's way out by not telling me, letting me discover it on my own, in the worst possible way?

Why did she die with this still unknown to me, when it could have changed so much? If I'd known, perhaps I would've been more cautious. Maybe I could have protected Agnethe better—protected *myself* better.

Worse, this isn't a truth just about me. The raven said it was my blood. So it's a truth about our family. And she buried it, as though it were something shameful.

Perhaps it is. I've yet to find that out.

The raven's voice interrupts my musings. *"I suspect human influence might be the reason that I was only recently able to sense the bond. It was never apparent to me before, and it usually shows itself immediately after the passing of the current* Rabensblut.*"*

"Rabensblut," I repeat. "Is that what I have?"

"It's not what you have, *it's what you* are. *And you should be grateful for it, too. It's helped you to survive in these human games you seem so eager to play."*

My head snaps up in shock. "What? How did it help me?"

"The Rabensblut *often have increased agility, speed, and visual acuity, which should come in handy in your little competition."*

I retort, "It's not a 'little competition.' It's the only way to get back to my sister. Does Agnethe have it, too? *Rabensblut?"*

"Only fools mistake the first door for the only door," he says, *"and, no, there is only ever one Rabensblut at a given time."*

Now *I'm* bristling, though I'm certain it looks less impressive minus the feathers. "Are you calling me a fool?"

His head cocks. *"All humans are fools. But, in time, you will become…less foolish."*

"Does that mean I'll see you again?" I ask.

He dips his beak in agreement, then looks skyward. *"I will never be far. As your power continues to expand, you will need the wisdom of my years."*

"How many years? How old are you?" I ask, curiously.

"Not that old. Only four hundred fifty-three of your human years."

I nearly fall over. I try to process that information without insulting him again, and I notice him moving as though making to fly off.

"Where are you going?" I ask him, feeling suddenly worried. "How will I find you?"

"Use the bond. And, it's time I left you. You need to rest for your silly competition. Especially with all the romantic drama you've now added for yourself."

My mouth falls open at his saucy judgment. He lifts his wings and begins slicing upward into the sky, sable pinions silently carving the air. As he continues to rise, the prickling inside my head changes to a tightening. A pulling. A tether I didn't know existed that tugs at something just beyond my comprehension. As if part of me rises with him.

I want to be insulted by his quip about my love life, but I'm too distracted by the pull, and then worried when I realize I missed an important detail.

I rush forward, as if I can somehow catch up to him by running on the ground. "Wait! I don't even know what to call you!" I tell him.

A blur of shadow slashes through the sky, and in an instant, he's upon me, wind surging from beneath sable wings as he sweeps past so close to me the ends of my hair flutter in response. My scalp prickles once more.

"For the moment, King of the Blutraben; tomorrow, your mentor; and for such occasion as exists to address me by name rather than title…you may call me Roan."

The impact of my wooden krahbek against Dagmar's sends shuddering vibrations up my arms as I try to keep her from besting me in this skill. Naturally, I'm not succeeding in that regard whatsoever. I'm thankful for the distance the polearm provides me, because I hope it will help me avoid any injuries before the next trial tomorrow.

Dagmar presses her advantage, moving her arms up higher on the polearm, closer to the blades, to give her better control, and uses her superior strength to press me backward. I fight with all the might I have left, my arms and shoulders burning, teeth clenched in concentration, but my feet move backward, and I bump into something hard.

A deep voice skates along the side of my neck and the shell of my ear, caressing it as gently as a lover's. "Your downfall will be your kindness, *künnle*; you could easily hook your opponent's calf with your beak."

I startle, looking over my shoulder at Rafe Kriegeur's very smug, very close face. A stinging thwack to my thigh brings me back to reality, and I howl in pain and protest, hopping on one leg, away from Kriegeur and Dagmar. Dagmar, for her part, is grinning at me triumphantly. Either our blossoming mutual respect has once again died, or she has an odd way of showing her affection for her friends.

Incensed, I turn to Kriegeur. "I was *working* on it, but you distracted me!"

Kriegeur smacks himself on the forehead. "Oh, my apologies. I forgot that all battlefields are peaceful and quiet, which allows soldiers maximum concentration to strike down their enemies."

I huff in frustration and open my mouth to counter, but he cuts me off.

"You look like you're struggling more than improving, and that won't do you well on the front. Which, it looks like you'll be visiting since your luck in the Freiheit is bound to run out," he adds, smugly twirling that stupid dagger of his.

I wasn't going to allow some drug-addicted, privileged man to speak to me this way, even if he is enormous and deadly.

I snarl. "Luck is no match for wits, but I wouldn't expect *you* to understand that."

A flash of copper catches my eye, and I see Aric enter the training yard where my unit is practicing.

It's been almost a week.

Six whole days since his hands traced fire across my skin, since I lay against him, replete with satisfaction in the aftermath of our coupling. Since I traced the worry in his brow with my fingers. Since he told me to go back to my room.

We hadn't argued. There were no harsh words or slammed doors or me rushing off. No declarations of regret or shame. Just that fleeting interlude and then…distance. Like nothing had ever happened.

I've seen him since, here and there. In the training yard. Across the dining hall. Once, walking across the inner bailey from the infirmary, shoulders set and gaze fixed somewhere in the distance. Each time I've been near him, he's looked away or through me, not at me. Not a hint of acknowledgment.

And maybe my mistake was letting him have something we weren't ready to give each other: a promise. Of my affection and fidelity, of hope, of wishful thinking. Just because I am scared and lonely and desperate and want to be wanted. Just because, for that time, I wanted to be seen. Not as a helping hand, a burden, a cadet, a conscript, a challenger, or a means to an end. But as something worth cherishing, worth finding again. And maybe I also made the mistake of believing that, in sharing myself with him, he'd do the same with me, and that it would mean something for him in the same way.

He spoke as though he had more feelings than he could share. But wouldn't he have been unable to resist seeking me out if he did? Said something to me by now?

Instead, I'm left wondering if I had misinterpreted it all and it was only ever physical for him. Maybe the quietly deliberate captain, who touched me like I was something special, had only wanted comfort that I had assumed would lead to connection. Worse, maybe I somehow knew that and offered myself as that comfort, because some idiot, foolish, aching part of me thought that if I were enough for him to touch, maybe I'd be enough for him to want. Truly want.

And that makes me feel pathetic…and furious.

I'm tired. So tired. Of measuring my worth by how much space I take up in someone's life. Of giving without ever knowing if I'll be kept. I've done it as long as I can remember, and not just with Aric. With my parents, my grandmother, Valda, my uncles, Erwin, Agnethe.

If Stachtenbaste has done nothing else, it's helping me to learn that my value shouldn't come from breaking myself to lift up someone else. From knowing when to step in, yes. Supporting your fellow soldiers. But also when to stand your ground and guard yourself from the blows. I'm not less good for wanting to survive. Not less noble for protecting myself.

I know these things, and I am facing them. I wish I could say that I feel their conviction all the time. But the truth is…some nights this week, I've lain awake and wondered if I've expected too much. If I should've kept my mouth shut.

I hate Kriegeur's arrogance. Perhaps I share that quality with him. For isn't hope, in a way, a kind of arrogance? The feeling that somehow, you might get what you want just because you wish it? Maybe I'd be more content if I just made myself smaller. That's the part that makes me feel pathetic, but it's still there.

All of these feelings are tumbling through me. Wreaking havoc in my mind, causing nausea to stir in my belly as I watch Aric cross the training yard toward the equipment sheds. There must be something of that yearning in my eyes, because I can feel Kriegeur's gaze move from my face, following the direction of my stare as I watch Aric.

I look back at him and see the easygoing smile drop from his lips. He stalks close enough to me that I must tilt my head to look him in the eyes. I stubbornly do this even though all pretense of good humor has left him, and all that remains is the glint of cruelty in the obsidian depths of his eyes.

His voice is deep and low enough for only my ears. "You seem to mistake me for one of your teammates, Cadet, to insult me so freely. I'll have you remember, though, that my patience only matches the distance of a krahbek handle, and my mercy is as thin as its blade."

I feel fear—genuine fear—skitter down my spine at the look on his face. I was playing with fire by taunting Kriegeur. He is the son of the commander of the Aurengarte, a trained killer, and too stupid and emotionally fragile to take any threats from someone far weaker than he is so lightly forever. Not to mention if he is on any kind of drugs, it might affect his temper. I am about to step back from him when I hear the crunch of grass behind me.

"Is there a problem?" Aric's voice asks behind me.

Kriegeur smiles at his cousin, but it doesn't set his eyes sparkling like usual. "Not at all. Only that if you were a better captain, you wouldn't have such a lackluster unit with cadets that have bigger mouths than muscles."

The entire group of people around us goes silent.

"What did you just say?" Aric asks, his voice just as tight as Kriegeur's.

Kriegeur replies, "Oh, I'm certain you heard me just fine, even with your head shoved up your arse as it is."

There are a few short gasps. I'm sure if I could see myself, I would laugh at the comical way my head is whipping back and forth between the two taller men braced on either side of me.

Without breaking his cousin's gaze, Aric addresses us, "You're in luck, Gold Unit. You're about to get a demonstration on facing a krahbek with another weapon." He steps back and draws his sword, gesturing to an open grass space with his head. "Unless you'd prefer not to take on the challenge?"

Kriegeur follows him to the open space, cadets parting to make more room for them, even drawing the attention of units practicing nearby, who slow their own sparring to watch curiously.

Lotti and Otto find me at the edges of the crowd encircling the space where the two soldiers are poised to spar.

"What's going on?" Lotti whispers loudly.

I shake my head, unable to voice what happened.

"Did you insult Kriegeur's prick again?" Jarl asks from behind me.

"Darling, this is *too* thrilling!" Cyneric whisper-gushes as he wedges between me and Otto, grasping my hand.

I smile tightly. "Yes, thrilling." Which earns my hand a squeeze of encouragement from him.

Aric watches Kriegeur from several feet away, sword pointed at the ground. Kriegeur, for his part, looks completely unconcerned, twirling his krahbek in one huge hand until he's got a middling grip on it, the curved beak on the back side of it poised like a hawk mid-dive. He doesn't raise it, though, seeming content to simply wait.

Aric strikes first and fast. His blade, held between both hands, flashes in a diagonal arc meant to push Kriegeur off balance, to break through the reach of the polearm and finish the fight before it even really begins. But Kriegeur easily shifts, letting the blow glance off the haft of his weapon with a ringing thud. He pivots, using the shaft like a second spine, bending at the knees and letting the tip of the krahbek circle behind him in a lazy sweep that could have taken Aric's leg if he had been but a breath slower than he was.

They continue—strike, block, advance, deflect. Aric's movements are aggressive and calculated, his footwork tight, shoulder low, his blade always pressing forward like he's trying to thrust a needle into a storm. But the krahbek's reach keeps him at bay. Kriegeur yields ground with every step, but it doesn't feel like a retreat. It feels like he's toying with Aric, like a dancer conceding space to lure his partner closer.

My scalp tingles. *"While I'm enthralled by your messy romantic entanglements, nestling, I fail to see how this helps improve your fighting skills."*

I look over to see a dark shape at a respectable distance on the stone wall of the training yard. Roan is here, observing.

I think back in his direction, not exactly sure how to mind-speak to him yet. *"I am not romantically entangled with both of them, and it doesn't help improve my fighting skills."*

In that moment, Kriegeur's eyes cut toward me. Sharp, sudden, uncanny. Almost like he heard me. I freeze. Had I spoken aloud? No, no one on either side of me reacts. But something about his expression shifts, revealing a glimmer of surprise.

That instant of distraction allows Aric to lunge forward, sword angled low. He grabs the haft of the krahbek, moving to immobilize it or rip it from Kriegeur's grasp. I draw in a breath. He's actually going to beat him.

But then Kriegeur grins. I step forward to shout a warning, realizing what's about to happen, but I'm too late. Faster than lightning, Kriegeur plants his back foot, pivots hard, and uses the leverage Aric has given him. He yanks the krahbek's pole toward him, pulling Aric with it, and in the same motion his other hand flies to the small of his back. Less than a second later, the blade of his precious dagger glints at Aric's throat while Aric's sword dangles uselessly at his side.

Whispers and gasps ripple through the training yard.

"A cadet's folly," Kriegeur says icily to his cousin, "to believe your opponent is disarmed simply because you can't see a weapon."

He shoves Aric back sharply and pulls his krahbek from his hand, which falls away in acquiescence. Kriegeur then looks at me, his gaze still flinty, as he sheaths his dagger back at his waist.

He turns back to his cousin and barks, "Control your unit," before stalking off across the training yard toward the citadel.

My scalp tingles. *"I'd stay away from the big, brutish one, nestling. Some monsters wear smiles, and some hardly bother with disguises at all."*

CHAPTER TWENTY-NINE
A Dream Deferred, a Heart Denied

I'm running. No. Leaping. My feet don't touch the ground for long. Each bound carries me over water that gleams like molten silver, moonlight streaked across its surface like so much spilled paint. I don't question how I'm able to move this way; I simply continue. My limbs feel as light as breath, the air against my cheeks is cold and thin.

Suddenly, the sky shifts and I'm high. So high that the water is merely a shimmering thread beneath me, distant and trembling. When I look down—really look—the world dips. My stomach drops. I'm not falling, but it feels as though I should be. The wind howls in my ears.

No, not the wind. A person, screaming.

In a blink, I'm low, pressed against the earth, the scent of damp soil and moss filling my nostrils. It's black all around me, but the kind of dark that feels alive. I can't see my own hands; I can only feel the grit beneath my fingers. Something brushes the back of one—a slick, hundred-legged thing that skitters away before I can even muster a scream. My voice sticks in my throat. I imagine I can hear the sounds of millions of tiny legs moving around on the ground, creeping ever nearer.

Then…a growl.

Low. Wet. Close.

A sound so deep I don't so much as hear it, as I do feel it. It vibrates through the ground beneath my hands, through my very bones.

I jerk awake with a gasp, heart slamming against my ribs. My hand presses to my chest, palm spread wide as if to cage it there, to keep it from escaping. The night-dark dormitory seems too quiet now, too still. Through the peaceful rhythm of the deep and even breathing of my sleeping teammates, I imagine I can hear those legs again, crawling in the stillness.

I shake my hands, trying to dispel the repulsive feeling from them. I have been hopeful that the dreams would stop since Roan made himself known, but maybe they're something I will always live with. Perhaps the better focus would be living in a less horrifying place than this and under less dire circumstances.

"I'll get right on that," I whisper.

Sighing, knowing that sleep will be a long time coming for me now, I tentatively reach out my mind to Roan, hoping he's awake to talk.

"Are you asleep?" I ask him mentally.

After several seconds, I've almost given up hope, when my scalp tingles and a grumpy voice fills my head. *"Only fools waste the night's peace on fear when they could rest."*

I frown. *"Will you ever stop calling me a fool?"*

"I'll cease calling you one when you've earned the distinction," he quips, reminding me of a similar conversation I'd had with Kriegeur. Even the thought of Kriegeur, irritating as he is, is not enough to banish the lingering disquiet I feel, though.

"Can you meet me somewhere? I can't sleep."

A sigh sounds. *"I'm near the old chapel, and more fool me for sharing that."*

I grab my boots, sliding them on, not bothering to change from my night clothes into my uniform. In my work duties this week, cleaning the visitors' hall, I discovered an old passage leading from it directly to the portion of the outcropping where the ruins of the old chapel sit. Which means I don't have to circle the perimeter of the citadel's walls or go through the gaol to reach it.

According to Otto, who seems to know more about Stachtenbaste than anyone here, the island hadn't always been Stachtenbaste. At one time, long ago, it was the seat of the Bellatorian representative in the Gold Council, before Fracidaem claimed that distinction for being more central to the region and more connected to Embrathal. Before Stachtenbaste became something sharp and brutal and sequestered, it was someone's home.

Eventually, the land was donated to the crown. Maybe out of loyalty, or guilt, or both. After that, they built the first citadel, but it was simply a prison. Then, some enterprising Aurelian had the brilliant idea of killing two birds with a single stone: making the convicts into soldiers. So, the first citadel was torn down. Then built again and again until it became what it is today. A mausoleum of stone and iron, a monument to the sorrow and suffering on which it was founded.

The chapel, though, the one crumbling near the citadel's outer wall, choked with ivy and neglect, was older. Older than the citadel. Otto said it had once been dedicated to Proelian, the god of war. One of the gods the people of Bellatorius worshiped before Aurelia folded them into the faith that holds the sister goddesses above the others.

"Why didn't they just tear it down when they built all the new citadels? And the new chapel inside the inner bailey?" I had asked him.

Otto had shrugged. "Superstition, maybe, given what the legends say about Proelian and what he did to his father."

I had been surprised at that. Proelian is said to have been the son of Feuerignis, the god of fire. There isn't much in the ancient tomes about their relationship, but it seems Otto was able to find more than I had. I guess there is someone in the world who has had even more time to read old books than I have.

"What did he do to him?" I had asked, engrossed in the story.

"You've heard the legend of Feueroise's Flame, yes?" Otto had asked me.

I nodded my assent. Everyone had heard of Feuerignis's legendary sword, that long ago, when gods still walked the land and their shadows scorched the earth, Feuerignis forged a weapon unlike any other. In the molten heart of the world, he folded a blade in the ashes of his immortal phoenix companion, Feueroise, who gave its eternal fire willingly. The sword pulsed with power: heat enough to melt steel, light to blind armies, and flame that never died. It was meant to be kept, never wielded, as a divine warning—a balance to be preserved.

But, according to Otto, Proelian watched from the edges of the earth's forge. Born of fire and sun, he was a god of ambition and battle, aching to prove himself, so he stole the sword from his father.

The mountains trembled. The sky bled smoke. From that day forward, wars flared brighter, and Proelian's name was shouted with every victory. Feuerignis never told anyone that his son stole the sword, but he was never seen with it again, and so, too, were father and son gods never seen together again.

So, Otto reckons they built around the chapel and left it alone. Let it rot. Because even though the rulers of Aurelia would have us believe we've smoothed over old faiths and made all divine and orderly, many still fear the bones hiding beneath our feet in the soil. Still fear desecrating the wrong altar. Old suspicions die hard, especially when they involve thieving, vengeful gods.

Now, as I dash through the old, narrow passage wedged between one of the stairwells in the visitors' hall and a guest chamber, and break out into the midnight air, I can only think the ruins look small. Sad. Like something time has outgrown but couldn't quite bring itself to bury fully.

The bones of the building jut from the ground. Moss-covered stone walls rise unevenly, the upper portions long since collapsed or overtaken by weeds, leaving only a partial roof that allows moonlight to pour through in cold, silvery shafts. What remains of the ceiling arches like a ribcage overhead. Cracked, bowed timber and shattered tiles framing the night sky. I don't see Roan sitting on any of the rocks on the outer portion of the building, so I creep into what remains of the structure.

Inside, the air is thick with the scent of mildew and dust, age clinging to every surface like a shroud. The altar still stands, remarkably intact, though time has weathered its edges, blurred by cobwebs and the dry offerings of worshipers past, long since turned to ash and dust. Around the altar lay the abandoned carcasses of pews and prayer benches, their legs splintered and riddled with the gnaw marks of unknown vermin, stuffing torn out and scattered like innards. Moth-eaten tapestries still hang in tatters from rusted hooks on the walls, their once-vivid colors now faded into ghostly smudges.

A relic statue of a warped sword lies on its side by the altar, its decorative blade snapped and pitted with rust, the Bellatorian crest engraved in the blackened hilt barely visible beneath the grime. A dedication to Proelian, perhaps? Or Feuerignis. Discarded here, having outlived its use and its story.

The heavy silence presses in around me, like the chapel is holding its breath. Even the dust seems suspended, unmoved by time, clinging to every stone. Waiting for worshipers to return.

A flutter sounds from above me, and I see Roan dive in from one of the holes in the ceiling. He lands upon the altar, right where a shaft of moonlight falls, bathing his wings in its ethereal glow. They ripple with indigo and violet, and the eldritch shine from above glitters in his unearthly, crimson eyes. I'd be afraid if I didn't feel like I know him well enough to know that he means me no harm.

Even if he is kind of critical.

"It's sad, isn't it?" I ask him, gesturing to the detritus surrounding us. "How it's simply been left to ruin."

"I don't suppose many here have cause to pay tribute to and thank the gods. Let alone one who inspires the very conquest for which you now all suffer."

Roan preens fussily, picking at his talons with his beak, as if he doesn't enjoy the sensation of dust on them, which I find amusing considering he's a *bird* and has probably stepped in far worse. At this thought, his crimson eyes find mine, and I can swear they almost narrow in disdain, but he doesn't call me out on it, which I would guess is his idea of being magnanimous.

"What roused you from sleep, nestling?" Roan asks me as he returns to fussing with his appearance.

I frown. "Didn't you see?"

Roan stops preening and stares at me. *"Powerful as I may be, I cannot see your thoughts while sleeping."*

"It was a dream," I say. I explain my nightmare to him, recounting the feeling of flying, of crawling bugs, of the growling, and the screams. "They seem to occur more frequently when I'm under high stress. The third trial is tomorrow, which I would say certainly qualifies as stressful."

Roan huffs, both internally and externally. *"Joceran was similar."*

"Who is Joceran?" I ask. I grab a dusty tapestry and try to use it to wipe off a dusty bench. I frown when it doesn't seem to have done anything but smear more dust around. Shrugging, I sit down in it, deciding I'd rather sit and be dusty than stand and merely be less dusty.

"Joceran de Veend, my last bond. He was especially plagued by nightmares, fits of melancholia, and paranoia after inventing the Stahlvend."

Stahlvend. I've heard that before, but I can't remember exactly where. I don't want to interrupt Roan when he's speaking, though.

"I often wonder if the very invention through which he elevated his family hastened his demise. He became increasingly concerned that the knowledge of its rendering would be stolen from him."

"What happened to him?" I ask. I don't know when Joceran de Veend lived, but I clearly hadn't made it back that far in my family history research. Given Roan's age, it could be quite some time ago.

"He perished. At the age of six and thirty." Though he doesn't say so, I can tell that this pains Roan immensely.

"I'm sorry for your loss," I tell him, hoping it's the right thing to say.

His eyes meet mine. *"The memory comes less often, but when it does, it still cuts just as deep. When you are deeply connected with someone, you cannot help but feel inextricably linked to their mortality, even when you outlive them."*

I nod. "It feels somehow…wrong…to outlive someone you care about, does it not?"

Roan's head tilts. *"Not merely because of caring. Because you begin to wonder if, when they die, you also lose yourself. Your purpose. I did not hear the call again for these four hundred years."*

I am silent for a while, grappling with what Roan has told me about his own experience, and surprised by how much his feelings mirror mine, in a way.

"Sometimes I fear that…well, I worry that without Agnethe, my life doesn't amount to much." I twirl my fingertips through the dust on the bench beside me. "Inventory at the forge, translations at night, singing for those I'm not afraid to do it in front of. I hope that someone will see me as useful once Agnethe moves on. Now that Grandmother is gone."

I chance a look at Roan, but he merely watches me calmly and says nothing, like he's listening. Truly listening. At the thought of my grandmother, I feel the anger I had before surge within me.

"I'm so angry with her, Roan! Why didn't she tell me about all of this sooner? Prepare me? So that I could have a life after all of this?" I stand, pacing back and forth across the floor in front of the altar where he sits.

"*The* Rabensblut *don't share their gifts with others. This has only been done historically out of absolute necessity,*" he informs me.

I stop and stare at him, and my shoulders sag. "That sounds awfully isolating."

His gaze doesn't stray from mine as he nods. "*Responsibility often is.*"

I begin pacing again. "Perhaps Uncle Engilram will take me on fully at the forge. That is, assuming I make it out of the Freiheit, Stachtenbaste, and the military alive."

"*Do not borrow tomorrow's fear for today. Your purpose will yet become clear with time,*" he tells me.

I cease my pacing and sit on the bench again, hard, a cloud of dust puffing up around me. If a bird is capable of recoiling, I think Roan does in that moment.

"How can you be certain of that?" I ask him in a whisper.

"*The soul is not made up of only what you can give to others but also what you can give yourself.*"

I feel tears spring to my eyes, both at his quiet assurance and the realization, which I speak aloud, "I'm not sure I know what that is."

A twig snaps outside, and my head with it. Roan bleeds into the shadows behind the altar. Frantically, I race down the aisle of the chapel and out of the doorway opening, trying to be as silent as possible. When I see Aric staring among the choked weeds before me, I stop in my tracks.

"What are you doing here?" I ask him quietly, suddenly aware that dust covers me completely.

He looks nervous as he says, "I couldn't sleep. I saw you leave the building. I wanted to make sure you were all right with the trial happening tomorrow. But I thought I heard your voice. Were you talking to someone?"

I initially freeze, but force myself to look as relaxed as I can in that moment, which probably isn't very, and tell him, "Only to myself."

He rubs the back of his neck. "I see. Well, I uh, I've been meaning to speak with you. To apologize."

Hope blooms in my stomach, curls upward, spreading its fingers throughout my chest. Had he simply been too nervous after what had happened to speak to me sooner? Maybe he's not used to being in this position, one of vulnerability.

"Why do you want to apologize?" I ask, trying to sound nonchalant, but instead I sound breathless and silly.

Thankfully, he doesn't seem to notice.

"I took advantage of you by making things physical. You were emotional and stressed after the trial, and I shouldn't have pushed you into that." His dark eyes are earnest in the moonlight.

The idiot truly thinks he's apologizing by telling me how I felt.

Dejected, I start to walk around him. "It doesn't even matter at this point, Aric."

He grabs my wrist. "It does, Greta. It does because it's not what I want, but I'm worried the lines are too blurred for me. That I won't be able to function if I allow my fear for you to seep into every moment of my life. Maintaining distance is better for focus."

"Better for who?" I ask quietly, looking into his eyes.

He rears back, as if I slapped him, and drops my hand. I push fully past him then, heading back inside, and make my way up to my sleeping quarters. I'm not certain if I will be able to sleep more, but I drop into my bed once I'm in the dormitory, dust and all. While dawn is still several hours away, I know it will approach faster than I'm ready, and then it'll be time for the next trial.

I lie in bed for a while, wanting to cry, but my eyes remain uncommonly dry. I stare at the timbers on the ceiling, watch the moon arc over the sky through one of the small windows high on the wall as the night hours pass, sing songs to myself in my head. And between it all, I replay my conversation with Aric over and over, then the time in the bathing chamber, then every interaction I've ever had with him leading up until this very moment. I wonder if I can pinpoint the exact second when I might have saved my miserable heart from this repeated trampling with his self-pitying martyrdom.

After a time, my scalp tingles, and I hear Roan tell me, *"Gather dreams while the night still grants them, for tomorrow will take all it can."*

CHAPTER THIRTY
Miedrym's Melody

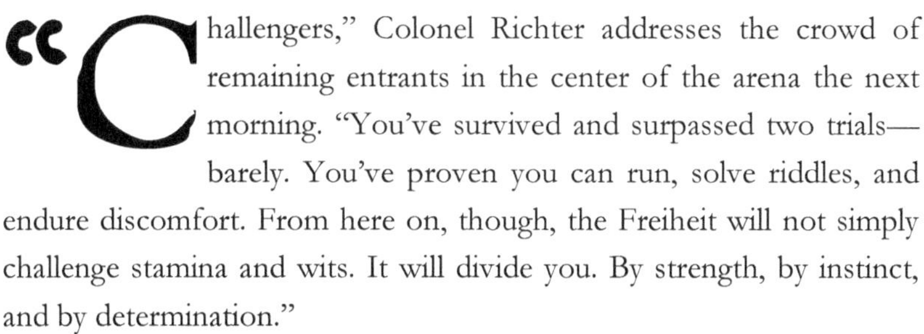

"**C**hallengers," Colonel Richter addresses the crowd of remaining entrants in the center of the arena the next morning. "You've survived and surpassed two trials—barely. You've proven you can run, solve riddles, and endure discomfort. From here on, though, the Freiheit will not simply challenge stamina and wits. It will divide you. By strength, by instinct, and by determination."

I'm dead on my feet. I barely slept. Not that my sleep brings much relief anymore, given my dreams. I finally drifted off at some point in the early morning hours, but the few stolen hours weren't enough to dull the ache in my chest or banish the fatigue from my steps. Both are still with me now, exhaustion making my limbs heavy, and hurt sitting behind my ribs like a stone.

I know I have to set it aside, at least for now. Whatever fractured between me and Aric, whether it's done or not, can't matter today. Not here, where the cost of distraction is my blood. Or worse.

Still, I feel it with each movement, as though part of me is slightly off balance. I hate how much space it takes up in my mind. I take a shuddering breath and try to focus on what Colonel Richter is saying, on the ground beneath my feet, the morning air in my lungs, the tense anticipation coiled in my limbs. Anything but the memory of what was said—and all that went unsaid—last night.

"These trials show you who you are when stripped of certainty, comfort, illusion. Some of you won't like what you see. Some of you won't survive it."

Her eyes sweep the arena. Forty-five pairs of eyes watch her. Forty-five sets of lungs draw anxious breath.

I've been avoiding looking at the platform with the officers on it. I haven't wanted to see him. For once, not to deny myself the possible rejection, but just to avoid the hurt it causes. He's in his usual seat next to Lieutenant Broadbente, but his eyes fix upon me. His face is a study in misery and tension. He looks upset, and I hate that it makes me feel bad for him. I hate that I want him to fix things when I know some problems have no compromise, no remedy, when one person wants to work through them and the other avoids the risk of heartbreak.

Colonel Richter is still speaking.

"The Blessed Sisters teach us that life is made of choices. That in each moment lies a balance between light and shadow, mercy and force, thought and action. The Freiheit is no different. Every moment is a decision, and every decision carries weight."

My eyes drift and find Kriegeur in his usual spot in the front row, but his posture is stiff, and his usual smug air is absent. His father speaks to him with quiet, clipped words that don't carry, but the effect on him is clear. Kriegeur's jaw tics. His shoulders tense like a beast bracing for the lash. Whatever is being said is not praise. The sight makes me altogether too curious and too sympathetic about, and toward, the lieutenant colonel, which are sentiments I most definitely should *not* be having.

I tear my eyes away before he catches me staring.

Later, I tell myself. There will be time to disappear into my head later.

Assuming I still have my head later.

"From this point forward, challengers, the trials will not grant you time to ponder. They will demand that you act. Commit. And when that balance breaks—because for some it will—pray it does not break you."

She steps back from her speaking position, ceding the platform to Major Berger. Her meaning and message must have conveyed, for the crowd is unaccountably somber, giving her only polite applause with none of the raucous cheering from the previous trials. Or maybe it's just that everyone realizes it will keep getting worse.

"Challengers," Major Berger booms, white teeth flashing. "Today's trial has four movements. Consider it a symphony of pain. Try not to hit a sour note. Welcome to Miedrym's Melody!"

The crowd begins to perk up, Major Berger's infectious smile and ridiculous puns apparently enough to invigorate even the most subdued onlookers.

"You will traverse a course with four obstacles in this trial dedicated to the god of music and dance," Major Berger begins, holding up four fingers as she paces along the platform.

I groan inwardly. I had seen the structures when we entered the arena, of course, but I had hoped it would somehow not translate to something that physical. I still haven't emotionally recovered from the first obstacle course. It nearly did me in.

"You must be one of the thirty fastest to complete it in order to advance," she adds, stopping mid-platform so the gravity of her words sinks in.

A ripple of shock cascades through the challengers and onlookers. That's as many people as were eliminated in the last trial, but this time, it's a quarter of the remaining challengers. It seems they're really trying to whittle the numbers down. I swallow nervously, shifting my weight from foot to foot in an effort to dispel the anxiety building within me.

"Patience. Calm. Quiet. Those traits will be your allies throughout this challenge and will help you avoid extending your time within the course. If you make a mistake but can decipher the riddle I'll give you before you begin, you will have the opportunity for the last step to be easier and faster.

"While the winners of the previous challenge will have five minutes deducted from their total time, challengers who crack and employ the riddle will receive a three-minute deduction to their overall time."

Every challenger stiffens with excitement at the prospect of reduced time. But *how* are we supposed to remain *quiet*? And *why*? Something about that particular warning sticks out to me and makes me very wary.

Major Berger points to the first obstacle. "For the balancing discs, you must cross a shallow pool with a series of platforms that require balance as you leap from disc to disc. Be careful, not only do they get farther apart as you go, they're as unstable as your last three ex-lovers. There's no time penalty for this challenge, but if you fall into the water, you must return to the beginning and restart the section."

My stomach sinks to the ground. Balance. Coordination. Speed. Not anything I'm particularly good at.

"The swinging bars you see are not merely swinging bars, no! You must swing across them, of course, but you may notice the boxes beneath them. They are pressure sensitive. Putting too much weight on one or more of them could have dire consequences. Not only that, but every time your feet touch a box, you will add fifteen seconds to your overall time."

I gasp along with the crowd. Every obstacle here is not merely physical in the basic sense, as the first trial was. They truly have increased in difficulty. On the surface, fifteen seconds doesn't seem like much time, but it could be the difference between surviving, advancing, and adding years to your sentence.

"After the swinging bars, you will crawl through a tunnel. Not an ordinary tunnel, of course, but one teeming with life of the many-legged and no-legged kind. There are no time implications for this portion, either, unless one of you has a phobia and it slows you down from progressing, that is. It's during this obstacle that your calm and quiet become even more imperative."

I look around the group of challengers, searching for my teammates. I see Berte, bold and brassy, standing by the front, unafraid to put herself immediately in the sight of the officers and leaders. Her determined gaze travels the obstacles as if calculating each step, but I catch the tiniest tremor in her throat. Not quite fear, but maybe the expectation and adrenaline coursing through her.

Then there's Stigander, tall, with his usual grim expression that belies any fear he might be feeling. The only sign he might feel trepidation is the slight twitching of his fingers at his sides.

And then…Dagmar. She could be carved from granite, she's so still. No twitch, no tremble, no tell. As unreadable as ever. Does the woman feel any emotion beyond rage?

I take in a deep breath. These are the people I have to run beside. Fight against. Maybe die with. If I'm honest with myself, I wasn't only looking to see if they're ready, but also looking to see if I am.

"The fourth obstacle is a real killer." Major Berger grins. "Quite literally, in fact. But it's related to the riddle, so you'll just have to wait and see what's in store."

She gestures for us to move toward the starting line, and we shuffle forward to the streak of red paint slashed across the dirt ahead of the first obstacle. It feels less like a starting line and more like a warning, an omen of the bloodbath this trial is bound to become. And from the sounds of it, that's meant both figuratively and literally.

"Challengers, your riddle! Learn it, repeat it, *use it*," Major Berger instructs, her voice rising like a drumbeat before battle. The rhyme that follows is fraught with double meanings, layered and shifting in its message.

Her words, amplified by the wind wielder, ripple through the air. Carried on the breeze, threading through our hair, clinging to our skin, and sinking into the marrow of our bones.

"In shadows, in light, in meadow or hall,
With cresting wave, but never stood tall.
From lowliest pauper to loftiest king,
Carried through air tho' not upon wing.
By many or few in joy's sweet refrain,
Or woven in echoes of sorrow and pain.
From tales built and broken, hearts mend or clave,
With rise and fall on line and on stave."

I am trying to remember all the exact words to decipher their meanings, but the starting horn sounds, and I guess that the speed with which that happened after the riddle was read is purposeful, so that challengers have little time to consider the rhyme. So only the truly "worthy" can hope to use it to their advantage.

At this point, the trials have conditioned me to move when the horn sounds and think as I go, so I rush to the balancing discs only to realize when I reach the bank of the pond that there aren't enough discs for all of us to jump them individually. We have to share the discs with other challengers.

A snide voice reaches my ears, "Hope they reinforced these discs, looks like they've got a lot of work to do to balance the weight of that arse of yours."

I turn to see a cruel-faced man about my age sneering at me. He obviously wants to embarrass me or keep me from getting on the discs, and I'm blocking his way. I have no patience left. My good humor is depleted.

"I confess I'm jealous of how easily balance must come for you, since you've clearly got nothing swinging between your legs," I snap.

I almost feel bad that I just insulted the man's prick when his face starts turning an ugly shade of purple. But it also feels remarkably good to have pushed back.

I immediately regret it when he starts to charge me.

A large, brown hand reaches out and chops the man right in the Adam's apple. He chokes and stumbles, falling into the water. I look in surprise at Stigander and Dagmar, both standing near me.

"Come on, de Veend, we'll get you across," Stigander says.

He steps onto the first disc, his legs long enough to simply walk onto it, and holds his hand toward me. I grab it gratefully and make the small leap onto it.

The ground beneath me lurches, not violently, but with an unsettling wobble that ripples through my legs and up to my back. Each muscle in my body tenses against the instinct to recoil, to jump off. The disc rocks with the slightest shift of weight. Not side to side, but in an unpredictable sway that makes it feel as though the world is rolling beneath us.

I brace my feet apart, shoving my arms out instinctively, fingers splayed to maximize my balance, like I can grab onto the air itself for purchase. The obstacle narrows to the disc I'm on, and I can only focus on remaining upright.

Dagmar and Stigander help me move from disc to disc, trying to figure out the riddle as we go. "Is it a sonnet or ode?" He asks.

"Certainly sounds as frivolous as poetry," Dagmar snorts as she waits for the disc we're on to settle from her leap to it. "I'm not sure I follow all the meanings. A 'sweet refrain'?" She shakes her head.

"A refrain is a chorus in a song. Usually, the part you repeat after each verse," I explain breathlessly.

The discs are too far apart for us to share them now, and we have to take them one at a time. I keep hoping Roan will show up anytime and help me a little with the physical parts. I didn't think to reach for him while listening to Colonel Richter drone and Major Berger put on her show. My brain hadn't been fully awake. Too much is happening now for me to try to reach for him while also doing something so physical, which means I have to figure out this obstacle alone.

I have one jump to make to the finish platform, but it's the farthest. I back up as far as I dare on the balancing disc and take a running leap, legs sawing through the air, arms propelling. My stomach slams into the side of the platform painfully, the wind knocked out of me, forced from my diaphragm like I've been struck. I start to slide off, my boots dangerously close to touching the water, when two arms reach out and grab onto both of mine, hauling me up onto the platform. Unprepared for how *still* the platform is compared to the balancing discs, I crash into Dagmar and Stigander, who pulled me to the platform.

Shocked, I say, "I can't believe you waited for me." I mostly direct this at Dagmar, because I get the feeling that Stigander would've waited regardless.

"Don't look into it too much, I need you to solve that riddle," she says, racing toward the swinging bars.

Stigander rolls his eyes. "Would it *kill you* just to be polite?"

Dagmar replies, "I'm not sure, but with other things trying to kill me right now, I'm not about to try to find out."

We reach a set of swinging bars, and Stigander, with his height and significant upper body strength, makes it across in record time without ever touching the boxes. So far, I have yet to see the consequences of doing so, as many challengers are still struggling on the discs, and several have made it past the bars ahead of us.

Before I begin, I reach out to Roan. *"A little help, maybe?"*

He doesn't immediately answer, but I've done what I can to reach him without having had much training with the bond yet. I reach my hands out, noting with dismay that Dagmar is already halfway across the set beside mine.

Stigander is yelling from the opposite platform, encouraging us to make it. "Stop being a fool and go!" Dagmar yells at him.

He cups his hands around his mouth and says, "You're not the only one who wants that riddle!"

On the second bar, my arms begin screaming. The pull in my shoulders feels like a rope fraying from both ends. I would do anything to be anywhere but here, my muscles feeling like they're unraveling at the seams. I don't have the strength for this; I wasn't built for it. I wasn't made to swing like some nimble thief across death traps and pits of terror. Sweat slicks my palms like oil, and every time my grip shifts, I feel a little closer to slipping—and falling.

I try to consider the riddle to distract myself from the pain in my shoulders. The first line about in shadows, light, meadow, or hall, means it can occur anywhere, at any time.

One more bar down.

The second line about a cresting wave that doesn't stand tall means it grows bigger, but metaphorically, not physically.

And the next bar.

The third and fourth lines tell me that anyone can participate, and it's something transmitted through the air, by a single person or many, whether happy or sad.

I make it past the next bar.

Whatever it is comes from stories, and they can break hearts or make them whole.

Only three bars left.

It rises and falls on a stave. Like a music staff. I look up and see Stigander and Dagmar waiting, close enough that they'll be able to hear me.

"It's a song!" I tell them excitedly. "Music!" But in my excitement, my feet touch one of the boxes beneath me.

I hear a voice scream my name as the earth falls from beneath my feet.

I scream as the box drops from beneath me. No, not a single box. Stepping on one seems to have started a chain reaction, and when the first falls, they all do, revealing a dizzyingly high drop from the ground. There's no way I can safely fall from this height without breaking things.

Like my neck.

Unprepared for the shift in the ground as I touch it, I hang fully suspended from the swinging bars. My arms are rigid and straight, and I haven't any clue how to swing to the next one without plummeting into the pit. Especially with my increasingly sweaty palms, which make my grip unpredictable and unreliable.

I feel my scalp tingle, and I know Roan is nearby. The relief I feel almost makes me start sobbing, but that can wait until I'm no longer hanging by my arms.

"I could've used your help a few minutes ago," I tell him.

"Challenge builds character," he replies.

"Well, my character must be extremely well built at this point," I think wryly.

I feel the energy surge through my limbs. A tingling that once unsettled me, crawled cold and strange beneath my skin. But now I know it means Roan is near. That the *Rabensblut* magic floods my veins, and instead of discomfort, it feels like coming home. Like stepping into the arms of a friend who's been waiting patiently in the shadows for me to arrive.

I swing my legs beneath me with far more agility than I know I truly possess and use the momentum to hurl myself into motion, grabbing onto the next bar. I swing through the remaining two and hit the platform, my arms and legs trembling. When Dagmar and Stigander see my feet hit the platform, they take off running, and I can't blame them.

They were more than generous in waiting for me as they did.

On legs like those of a newborn foal, I head toward the next step, which is the tunnels. I see other challengers diving into them, holding swords and other weapons.

"*Where did they get those?*" I ask Roan and look around me for any clues.

"*It was at the end of the platform near the bars. You ran past it.*"

I look behind me and squint at the platforms near the swinging bars. Sure enough, swords are leaning against it.

"*I don't think I have time to go back.*"

In fact, I don't see anyone else behind me, which means I'm last.

"*Others must complete the challenge, and you have no idea what will delay them in the tunnel. If it is your wish to continue, there is still time.*"

Without thinking, I dive in.

The tunnel swallows me whole, its throat narrow and damp, with the kind of darkness you can feel pressing close to you, like a second skin. My palms hit mud as I begin to crawl, and the air becomes thick, musty, warm. Rank with the scent of soil and something else. Something alive. I pause, just for a breath, and in the silence, I can hear the soft, skittering sound of tiny feet. A brush of legs against my own. Something cold and damp dragging over the back of my hand.

I clench my teeth and push on. Every sound is louder in here. My breath, the scrape of my boots. The nearly imperceptible hiss of something slithering past my knee. I remind myself to stay quiet, the Major's warning still reverberating in my skull, but the silence only serves to heighten the fear. Sharpen it. To stretch my courage thin.

Then I hear it. Screaming. Muffled through the tunnel's walls, but their undercurrent is unmistakable: pain. Panic. My heart begins slamming in my chest.

What horrors are waiting for me out there?

"*Are Stigander and Dagmar all right?*" I ask Roan.

"*Perhaps you should worry less for your comrades,*" he says dryly, "*And more about how you're going to employ the riddle you were given.*"

His voice doesn't echo through the tunnel because he's not physically with me inside of it, but it's inside of me. Despite my current surroundings, I feel a rush of gratitude weaving through the fear. I'm not alone. Not entirely. Even if the air is dank and the walls feel alive, I have Roan's voice to tether me to something beyond the mud squishing beneath my hands and knees.

"I thought we just had to figure out the riddle," I mentally sputter. *"Not actually use it."*

"The instruction was to decipher and *employ it."*

"And I thought telling them the answer *would be employing it. How exactly would I 'employ' music in the arena, anyway? By singing? You would expect me to sing in front of all those people?"* The very thought of it sends a fresh wave of fear skating down my spine, and this fear has nothing to do with being inside the tunnel.

I *hate* being the center of attention. I always have. Having eyes on me, judging and waiting. A wrong word, a wrong note, a stumble, and suddenly you're the story whispered behind hands between mean-spirited snickering.

Praise never felt fully safe. It could turn on you, grow teeth. Laughter always had sharp edges. Even silence could hum with expectation, with pressure to perform, to be perfect. I learned very young that it's easier to be useful than seen. Easier to disappear than disappoint.

And now, perhaps my only hope of progressing to the next trial is to put my greatest vulnerability on humiliating public display.

"I would think survival was more important than humiliation," Roan drawls.

"I might not survive the humiliation," I retort.

I'm nearing the end of the tunnel, as evidenced by the slivers of light I see piercing the gloom through gaps in the wooden door that covers the opening. There are more screams; they are louder. I guess the warning about noise is hard to ignore when faced with whatever horror is on the other side.

I press my palm to the rough wooden surface, finding the latch hooking it closed, and am about to slide it to the side and push the door open when I hear it.

A low, rumbling growl. So deep it vibrates through my hands and knees.

I freeze, my fingers curled around the latch, and try to stare through the cracks to see what might be waiting. I can't see anything through them, can't glean any information. It's clear, though, that whatever it is isn't human. And unlike the tunnel, it isn't quiet.

And it knows I've arrived.

CHAPTER THIRTY-ONE
Born to Be a Löwenard Breaker

"**R**oan," I begin in my head, "*what kind of creature waits for me on the other side of this door?*"

There is a pregnant pause. "*The beast is unusual. Not one I'm familiar with, but it is formidable in size. Possibly some abomination of human invention.*"

"*I get it, I get it, humans are terrible and we're singlehandedly ruining existence for everyone and everything else.*" I roll my eyes in the darkness of the tunnel.

"*I'm pleased to find you are so quickly enlightened, nestling.*" I'm not sure if Roan is that literal or if he's saying this sarcastically.

"*You may assume that I am both literal and sarcastic at all times in order to save your mind the trouble of determination,*" he says in response to my thoughts.

"But aren't you an unusual creature, Roan?"

A prissy sniff sounds in my brain. "*Yes, but you'll find the creatures of gods are far superior to those of man.*"

"The creatures of *WHAT?*" I say aloud, shrieking into the tunnel.

At the sound of my shriek, another growl sounds from beyond the door, closer than it previously was. The noise conjures up the worst sort of images in my head. Of massive shoulders covered in fur, matted from blood and battle. Of claws the length of my fingers and teeth jagged and sharp as broken glass, yellowed and slimy with saliva and worse. Of the smell of its breath, rank with the putrid stench of its kills left to rot between said teeth.

Even from within the door, I can sense its restlessness, picture muscles primed beneath a hide of midnight fur as it paces.

"*Its hide is golden,*" Roan corrects me.

"*Regardless, I'm sure it's a thing of nightmares, cobbled together from the worst parts of a wolf or bear or something. One wrong move and I'll feel it pinning me down, breathing in my face, right before it goes for my throat!*" I return with a panicky squeak.

"*I cannot imagine what has predisposed you to such vivid flights of overactive fancy,*" Roan says.

"Oh, I don't know," I begin, "*maybe it's the magical raven that speaks in my head that may have been created by a* god?"

"*I can assure you there is no 'may' about it.*"

I tell him, "*We'll have to discuss* that *point later, assuming I survive this. I have a lot of questions.*"

"*Humans always have many questions and offer little in the way of answers.*"

I suppose I should be more insulted at his continued derogatory remarks regarding my species, but I can't really argue with what he's saying.

I ask, "*How do I get out of here without getting eaten?*"

"*I cannot determine your exit from my vantage point.*"

Great. Just great.

"*I'm coming out,*" I tell him, "*but may need your help immediately.*"

"*I remain at the ready,*" he confirms.

I slide the metal latch along the door and press my palms flat to the wooden surface. Taking a deep breath, I push it aside, and it swings away from me, letting a solid shaft of light into the tunnel. The crowd is roaring. In the distance, I can hear the sound of metal against metal, of screams, and can smell the iron tang of blood in the air.

The door has opened into an antechamber of some kind. Metal gates surround me on all sides. In front of me is a doorway that leads into a larger section, which houses a second doorway at the rear. Presumably, the second doorway leads to my exit from the trial.

I haven't seen the creature; perhaps there's merely one, and it's distracted by other challengers. I stretch my fingers out, moving to lean against the gate to take a better look inside the larger chamber, when I hear the low growl to my left.

Turning abruptly, the sight of the beast takes me aback. It's as tall and wide as what I imagine a lion to be, its body a sleek coil of poised muscles and menace. Gleaming fur of neither gold nor gray but some smoldering, molten combination of both shimmers like hammered bronze in the afternoon sunlight.

Its head is leonine in structure, broad and imposing, but the muzzle is slightly narrower, more angular, and the ears point upward sharply, twitching at every sound like a wolf catching wind of its nearby prey. Its eyes, a cold, unrelenting black, lack any warmth, only calculation and hunger, and it blinks slowly, deliberately, like it's already decided the outcome of our encounter and is simply waiting for me to catch up. It reminds me of Lord Corvilian's black eyes, dangerous and glittering with malice.

Its tail is bushier than a lion's, long and plume-like. Its movements are unnervingly silent as it prowls, its massive paws cushioned by thick pads but tipped with claws curved like scythes. If I hadn't heard tell of the *Enderaben*, I'd wonder if this were another one of Mortuua's fabled creations. I recognize it, though, from drawings and descriptions of the palace and hearing stories from Eoforwine.

A löwenard. A massive beast that is a cross between lion and wolf. They're a symbol of the royal family and a favorite pet of Queen Beatrix. She's said to have several at Aurumstein, the palace in Embrathal, and more at the royal family's country estate in Verdantia.

It's both beautiful and terrifying, a portrait of lethal grace. And it looks as though it wouldn't oppose eating me.

That's when I hear the sound of gears creaking. I look around for the source of the noise, and notice the gate immediately in front of me has begun to lift from the ground, a very small gap starting at the bottom where its spikes meet the dirt beneath it. I squeeze my eyes shut, as if trying to block out the inevitability of my own gruesome death.

"I believe there is still opportunity to employ the riddle, thus avoiding prematurely burying oneself," Roan's voice interjects, betraying no apprehension about my current state.

I picture myself plucking out each of Roan's feathers individually. *"And how exactly would I employ the riddle? I—"*

Wait. Löwenards are said to respond to music, if I recall. Could it be that the music calms them?

I swear I can *hear* Roan's smug expression in my head, which shouldn't be possible, but here we are.

The gate is about a foot off the ground and moving steadily upward. The löwenard is pacing several feet back from it, as if it knows what to expect and is anticipating mauling me with great relish. I look outward to the stands, at the people cheering, I register the sounds of other challengers screaming, of metal, of the roars of other löwenards, and I feel my throat start to close up.

I try to quietly hum under my breath, a nameless, practically musicless tune. The löwenard registers the sound and pauses in its pacing. It lowers its head.

It's working!

Then it growls, its throat vibrating with the noise.

Okay, never mind.

"Your fear is loud. Louder than your voice. I suggest remedying that," Roan scolds.

"Of course, I'm afraid, there's a deadly animal in front of me and an entire crowd of people watching." The gate is halfway open. The löwenard could easily swipe at me, but it hangs back, like it's toying with me, waiting for the opportune moment to strike.

"You fear the silence after your voice, not the animal in front of you. Cowardice wrapped in modesty. A common human affliction." His voice drips disdain.

"I am not a coward. I'm here, aren't I? I'm here for Agnethe?"

"You wear her name like armor, nestling, but cower behind its protection. Were your places reversed, would you want your sister to hide behind her fear or use it to soar?"

Shame fills me at his words. But so does pride. So does determination. I know what Agnethe would want me to do. She'd tell me to sing even if my voice shakes, even if my notes fall flat. Even if no one claps.

I swallow hard. The gate is three-quarters of the way open. The crowd suddenly feels impossibly far away. My blood rushes in my ears to the point where I'm not even certain I'll be able to hear myself, which might be a blessing.

So I close my eyes and open my mouth. And I sing. The first song that comes to my mind. The last one I sang with Agnethe before everything happened. A song about someone who pledges to wait for the person they love for however long it takes. And in her honor, I don't think there's a better song I could sing for my sister.

O dearest love, I bid thee come,
Where flow'rs grow 'neath skies of brightest spring blue.
When stars have alighted and day's at last done,
In yon golden meadow, where I await you.

O dearest love, I bid thee come,
Where winter snow tempers the summer's dew.
When stars have departed and day's just begun,
In yon golden meadow, where I await you.

O dearest love, I bid thee come,
Where eternal sleep has now taken me to.
When you have joined me, our two souls as one,
In yon golden meadow, where I await you.

By the time I reach the lyrics of the third verse, where the song's writer has pledged to wait for the person they love even in death, the tears are streaming freely down my face. I don't know if I'll ever see Agnethe again. If the next place we meet will be Nachternel, when we've both passed on to the afterlife.

The anguish clogs my throat so thickly that I have to pause and take a shaky breath before quietly singing the last line in repeat.

In yon golden meadow, where I await you.

There is silence. Complete, total silence. I open my eyes, fat tears escaping my lashes to trail down my cheeks. The löwenard sits several feet from the door, peacefully watching me, tongue lolling as if it hasn't a care in the world. Utterly relaxed. I look up into the stands. Every pair of eyes I can see is on me for a moment of continued, deafening silence.

Then, the arena erupts in equally deafening applause.

I'm worried the löwenard will get startled by the sound of the crowd, so I don't waste any time hurrying to the door. I take one last look over my shoulder to confirm it's still where I left it. It's still sitting in the same spot, blinking lazily at me. Shaking my head in shock, I yank open the exit door and dash through.

Stigander, Dagmar, Berte, and several other challengers are on the other side of the door. Stigander's eyes look suspiciously watery.

"Gods, de Veend, where did you learn to do that?" He rasps.

I shake my head. "I didn't think I did anything that unusual—"

The starting horn sounds, and all the challengers startle. Major Berger steps toward the group of us outside the trial area.

"Challengers," she says, sweeping her arm toward the leaders' platform. "Please join me to receive judgment."

As I follow behind the others toward the platform, I swipe at my still-damp cheeks quickly, hoping no one saw the tracks of tears limning the dust there. A dark flutter in the corner of my eye alerts me to Roan's presence in the stands nearby.

"*You did well,*" he tells me.

"*I feel foolish for being afraid,*" I admit to him.

"*Bravery is easy when roaring into battle with an army at your back. Facing what you fear, with just one voice, and making yourself heard, still, is true courage.*" Warmth touches my heart at his words.

"*I'd not have made it through without you,*" I reply, "*you must have experience with facing your fears.*"

His voice filters through with a haughty edge, "*Fear visits me as does the breeze—briefly, and never twice from the same direction.*"

I roll my eyes. I'd say more except we've gathered in front of the platform. I'm struck by how few of us there are as I look around. My teammates are all still standing, which I'd noted with relief when I first left the löwenard, but could it be that those remaining have all passed to the next trial?

No, Major Berger said we were to receive judgment.

As if my thought of her manifested her presence, Major Berger steps to the center of the platform. "Challengers," she begins, "thirteen of your fellow challengers perished in this trial."

My breath seizes. Thirteen people *died*.

"That leaves us with thirty-two challengers remaining, and only thirty spaces. Would challengers Blumg, Damd, and de Veend please step forward?"

I swallow hard, looking at my teammates before stepping forward. I glance at the platform in Aric's direction and see him watching me with a pained expression, like he knows I've lost and pities me. It makes me want to crawl into a hole in the ground.

Major Berger addresses me and the other two challengers. "You are the challengers with the slowest times, with de Veend coming in last place."

Humiliation blazes bright and hot within me, as does hopelessness, because not only have I lost, but I am even further from being able to see Agnethe than I was before. Aric was right. This was a fool's hope. I clamp my lips together to keep them from quivering, lest they betray my desire to start sobbing then and there.

"However," Major Berger begins.

However? The crowd collectively leans forward.

"Challenger de Veend was the *only* challenger to decipher *and employ* the riddle. Thus, she receives a three-minute deduction from her overall time, placing her in the thirtieth spot and advancing her to the next trial. Blumg, Damd, you are dismissed from the Freiheit Tournament."

Shock floods my body. The crowd is cheering, but I can barely hear it, barely feel Stigander's large hand clap my shoulder, barely feel Berte excitedly hug me.

"You fucking *bitch*," I hear to my right before something heavy crashes into me.

My head hits the ground, and I'm stunned for several seconds. I register the woman challenger, Damd, who I just knocked out of the tournament. She kneels over me, and her hands wrap around my throat and squeeze. I begin frantically clawing at her fingers, which have an inhumanly strong grip on my neck, to try to dislodge them. I hear the sounds of feet rushing toward me as some come to my defense and others, I'm sure, have come to watch my demise with glee.

I try to swing my legs around to dislodge her when the pressure on my neck suddenly stops, and her hands drop away. Confused, I look at her face to see her eyes, wide with surprise, right before she keels over onto the ground, a dagger protruding from the side of her neck. I look at the dagger, then around me for my savior, only to spot Kriegeur standing on the platform, the fingers of his right hand twitching slightly, as if he'd released it only seconds before. When I look down at the blade in Damd's neck, it's then that I recognize it as the one he brandishes so frequently.

He leaps down from the platform and stalks toward us, the crowd parting to give him a wide berth. When he reaches Damd's body, he pulls the blade from her neck without ceremony, bright blood flooding the ground from the now-open wound. He wipes the blade on the fabric of her trousers and, without once looking at me, saunters back toward the platform and returns to his seat. Lord Corvilian looks at his son for several seconds after Kriegeur returns to his seat before turning his predator's gaze on me, eyes sharp with curiosity and something I'm afraid to identify and name.

I scramble backward from Damd's lifeless body and stand on shaky legs, letting Berte and Stigander flank me protectively.

Major Berger is frowning. "Well, I don't think any of us expected *that* to happen."

Colonel Richter stands and joins Major Berger. "Challengers, as unusual as the last few minutes' events have been, I must remind you that you are bound by the rules of the Freiheit Tournament, including those which may eliminate you. I ask the remaining challengers to please step forward."

Confused, we turn toward the platform, gathering closer. Colonel Richter nods at the usual wind wielder who projects her voice.

She says, "Victory does not always reward those with sword in hand or seal on parchment. Sometimes, she favors those who walk softly, listen longer, and strike only once—but well. A true warrior does not charge headlong into the fray without thought. They adapt. They learn. They calculate. In previous trials, you've tested your brawn and your brains. The next trial is a test of your nerve. Of your cunning. Challengers, your fourth trial begins now."

What? *What?*

Fuck.

No rest from the last trial. No chance to breathe after my throat was nearly crushed. No time for the tremor to even leave my limbs before they toss another blade at us. My heart rate hasn't even decreased from facing the löwenard, and now we're starting all over again?

Did they decide we weren't dying fast enough or something? I've fought with muscle, with my brain, through pain and fear. And now it seems they're demanding something more. Something calculating and cold.

"Challengers," Major Berger booms, "you've run, swung, crawled, and even sung your way through the past few obstacles." All eyes turn toward me, including hers, and she grins.

I shift nervously under the collective perusal.

"Now, though," she says and spins on her heel, facing the crowd in a semi-crouch, "we sharpen the game. Welcome to Proelian's Hunt—a trial of silence, shadows, and subterfuge."

She resumes her pacing up and down the platform. "Each of you will receive a name—a target. Your task is simple: retrieve something of value from that person without them knowing they were a target…and without revealing yourself as its thief. If they find out, you're out. If you're caught in the act, consider your journey in the Freiheit concluded.

"But should you succeed, you will prove what every seasoned commander knows—that the best warriors fight with more than just weapons."

She stops in the front center of the platform and holds up her hand, fingers splayed. "Over the next five days, you will observe your target without interference. No contact. Learn them. Watch them. Stalk them as the fox does the hare. Decide on the object you wish to acquire. And when the time comes, you strike!" Several challengers jump at the intensity and volume of her voice.

"You will have only the last two days to obtain your item. Strike before then, and you will be eliminated. In one week's time, you will present your chosen item to the Trial Panel of Lord Corvilian, Colonel Richter, and me. You will be judged on your ability to remove the item from your target and the difficulty it takes to do so undetected."

I look at Lord Corvilian, where he sits on the platform. The knowledge that he will, once more, be involved in deciding my fate at the end of a trial settles in my gut like a stone. It shouldn't rattle me. *He* shouldn't rattle me. But my hands are already cold, my throat already dry, and my mouth tastes like old fear and new outrage.

A man like him shouldn't affect my confidence, but he is both perceptive and cruel, which I've been able to judge from even our limited interaction. The first to look me in the eye and decide I'm guilty of all charges levied against me without any justification beyond my background and his own prejudice. Now, once again, he'll decide if I can proceed. If I move to another trial.

It's almost laughable how much power a single man wields with only a thought, a judgment. I told him not to underestimate me, and now I must prove myself to him. If he expects me to cower, not to try, he will be sorely disappointed. Then again, he'd probably enjoy watching me break beneath the booted foot he places on my neck.

Major Berger continues, "Only fifteen of you will progress to the fifth trial." My head whips back in her direction then. They're cutting the numbers in *half* after this trial.

"Only eight of you, however, will earn the guidance of one of our mentors. That's right, the best of the best will be watching and observing your performance in this trial and can choose to guide you through the remainder of the tournament following the outcome of this challenge. They will only offer their wisdom to those who prove themselves worthy of it." She turns toward the officers. "Will our potential mentors please stand?"

Lieutenant Broadbente, Major Berger herself, Aric, and five others I don't know are standing. My heart leaps when Aric stands. Is it possible he will offer to mentor me? Despite what's transpired between us and my disappointment, I still want to hope for a different outcome, even when I tell myself I shouldn't.

My scalp tingles, and Roan says, *"The dichotomous desires of humans never cease to baffle me."*

I almost snort aloud. *"You've never wanted two things that directly oppose one another?"*

"Never with such alarming inconsistency," he quips.

"Due to the unknown variables between targets and items, there will be no advantage given for this challenge. But there are also no rules beyond timing and identification. Sabotage is permitted. Do not share your target, or you may lose the game before it begins. So keep your secrets. Guard your prize. And may the stealthiest challenger succeed."

I line up with the others, the ache and fatigue from today's exertions beginning to catch up to me, my throat chafed and raw from Damd's wringing. I can still feel her fingers wrapping around my throat, fury and failure burning in her eyes. I hadn't even seen her coming until it was too late. No warning, no time to cry out for help. Which only reaffirms my belief that I make a terrible soldier. How will I do at subterfuge?

I glance over my shoulder at the platform, looking at Kriegeur, still surprised he saved me. He's in conversation with Colonel Richter, his face in its normal jovial-but-stupid-and-arrogant state. I frown. He hadn't said a word. He hadn't even looked at me. Just cleaned his blade, turned away, and walked off like he'd swatted a fly instead of ending a life. I should be horrified. *Am* horrified. Ending a life shouldn't be that easy, should it?

Although I suppose I could judge myself similarly, considering how quickly I killed that soldier at Lord Rocheburn's estate.

"Would you rather the large one let you die for the sake of clean hands?" Roan asks.

I reply, *"I'd rather no one die on my behalf."*

"Humans seldom learn from the lessons they wish for, only those sharp enough to leave scars," Roan intones. I send a mental eye roll down the bond.

My fingers tremble slightly as I accept my sealed parchment square from one of the officers distributing them. It feels weightier than it should in my hand. It's just a small scrap of paper. Insignificant and yet meaningful. Innocuous and yet heavy with premonition.

"Challengers," Major Berger yells after we are each holding a piece of parchment. "Memorize the names and ranks of your targets before destroying your parchment. Remember, guard your secret well, for it could mean the difference between advancement and elimination. At your marks, challengers! Let the hunt begin!"

I look around me at my fellow challengers as most of them tear into their parchment, eager to discover the identity of whom they'll be spying on and stealing from in a week. I find myself hesitating, imagining the worst possible outcome.

Please not one of the Schulz brothers, I think, since the others saw fit to warn me of their lecherous manners. I've endured much in the past few months, but nothing could be worse than having to hunt someone who would just as soon hunt me back. The idea makes my skin crawl.

Deciding to expose the wound and get the discovery over, I slide my finger beneath the sealing wax and pry open my parchment. I stare at the rank and name listed for several seconds without breathing. It seems I was thinking too small with the Schulz brothers. For it can be, and is, much worse.

"Why do I sense apprehension, nestling?" Roan asks.

My target is Rafe Kriegeur.

CHAPTER THIRTY-TWO
Proelian's Hvnt(er Gatherer)

Two days later, my team and I are toiling away at our laundry work duty, which was our misfortune to draw for this week.

The laundry house here at Stachtenbaste is more furnace than workspace—a cavernous building with a single hall choked with heat and steam and the sharp, acrid tang of soap. Along the far wall, multiple hearths roar with relentless fire, their confines kept full by sweating cadets hauling logs and stoking the blazes. A series of massive copper tubs dominates the center of the room, their surfaces perpetually rippling from the simmering water within. The tubs must be drained and refilled constantly, fresh water brought over by the bucketfuls from the cadets tending the fires.

Thick, wooden paddles lean against every wall, their long handles slick with water and soap. With these, cadets stir the sodden mass of linens and uniforms, lifting and plunging and wringing the fabric until our arms shake and our backs scream. Lye soap sits in fat cakes near each tub, crumbling at the edges from use.

Every surface in here is dewy with moisture—the stone walls weep with condensation, the wooden beams overhead are dark with damp, the floor is a swamp of scalding puddles and ash, the cadets themselves with rivulets of sweat pouring down their flushed faces.

Once the scouring is done, then comes the rinsing. Again and again, in troughs of frigid runoff water fed from the citadel's unique piping system, colder than ice and even less forgiving. Knelt on the wet flagstone floors, garments pressed between numb fingers raw and burned from the caustic lye soap, cadets scrub until their bones vibrate.

Even after the linens are washed and you receive respite in hanging them to dry, the steam clings to you. It soaks your tunic, mats your hair, fills your lungs until you feel like you're drowning in it.

There is no dignity in laundry duty. There are only aching joints, blistered hands, and the unspoken agreement that you'd rather peel ten thousand potatoes than rake your fingers across the ridges of a washboard even one more time.

It is back-breaking, thankless work, and I'm not sure how the washer women employed here do this day in and out without break or broken spirit.

The only advantage to having laundry duty is that the laundry house itself provides near-perfect scheming grounds, its massive size meaning that most cadets on work duty are far enough from each other where your conversation can't easily be overheard, especially over the noise. Though Major Berger advised us not to tell anyone, I immediately shared my target with Lotti and Otto in the hope that we could, together, figure out how to steal something from Kriegeur.

Otto pours another bucket of boiling water into the copper tub that he, Lotti, and I are slaving over. Lotti and I rotate our wooden paddles, stirring the bed linens in circles. The lye-laden steam curling from the surface of the water causes our eyes to stream with tears.

"Perhaps you could steal a lock of hair from his latest conquest," Otto suggests, his nose running, as he sets down the bucket and picks up a paddle. He is considerably better at paddling the laundry than Lotti and I are.

Lotti quips, "Who can even keep track of who it is?"

I frown. "I've never even actually seen him with a woman."

"Maybe he prefers men," Otto shrugs.

"Maybe he prefers goats," I shoot back, and we all laugh.

Lotti's eyes twinkle, although it could just be the soap. "You could always try seducing him yourself."

If I weren't already flushed from the heat of the room, my embarrassment at imagining this would be extremely evident. "I don't think I'm Kriegeur's type."

Lotti stops paddling, incensed by my own self-doubt. "You don't think beautiful is his type? You don't think breasts and arse are his type? Otto, tell her I'm right."

Otto's face *does* get redder. "Erm, well…that is, you're—well, you're pretty, Greta." He trips over the bucket he sat beside the tub. "Oh, Sisters!"

Lotti grins. "Oh, come on, Otto. You can think your friend is beautiful and still not want to bed her."

Otto shoots up, mumbles something about needing more hot water, and stumbles back toward the nearest hearth.

"You shouldn't torture him like that," I say, smiling. I have no illusions that Otto is interested in me romantically. But the poor man is shy about women and easily flustered when put on the spot.

"Where's the fun in that?" Lotti asks, groaning as she paddles the linens again.

When Otto returns with more water, I say, "Kriegeur's so full of himself, maybe I should just carry a mirror with me in case I meet him. He'll be so seduced by his own reflection that he won't notice me stealing something."

I use my paddle to gather wet linens from the copper tub, dumping them into a small bucket, then carry it over to the nearby stone basin along the wall where freezing water pours from the piping. Wincing when my hands touch the lye-soaked fabric, I begin rinsing the linens beneath the steady stream of icy liquid. The only blessing in the water's temperature is that my fingers quickly grow numb, and I can no longer feel the sting of the soap. As I rinse, I run the fabric across the ridges of a metal washboard propped against the basin.

When we've all rinsed our linens, we carry the sodden fabric to the drying yard behind the building, where ropes have been strung tightly in a grid across multiple wooden posts. Several cadets from our team are already outside, hanging the dripping linens from the ropes with wooden pins, leaving them to dry in the bright, midday sun, and retrieving those that are dry for folding.

Cyneric and Jarl, hanging their own batches, smile and wave at us when they spot us walking toward them.

"There's our songbird," Cyneric grins at me, delighting in his newfound nickname for me.

After the last trial, I expected mockery, backhanded compliments, even jests at my expense. I did catch Belinda and her toads sneering at me once or twice. But, to my surprise, my teammates seem to genuinely delight in my voice. To my even greater surprise, I don't mind that they do.

That night in our dormitory, they had asked me to sing, with playful elbows and grins—something before bed. So, I did. Quietly, tentatively. A lullaby that first night, a love ballad the next. They listen with rapt attention, the room going completely silent and still as I sing into the darkness of the space. It reminds me of singing with Agnethe as she played her rotte, like we often did in the evenings. I find the act brings me a sense of longing, but also peace. Something familiar.

In the laundry yard, where the air can sting your eyes and your back burns from bending, the songs have started to rise more freely. Once or twice, Lillen has picked up the refrain, off key but earnest. Jarl has joined us, as he displays his impressive catalogue of bawdy tunes. Stigander hasn't sung but has requested several familiar songs. Even Dagmar doesn't stray far when the team is singing.

Perhaps the rhythm and familiar tunes help to pass the time and soothe the aches in our bodies. Or possibly there is something in joining together in listening to and enjoying the music that reminds us we are more than what we're experiencing and makes it all just a little more bearable.

I'm not ready for the center of a stage or the attention of a crowd anytime soon. But, for now, I enjoy sharing music with my teammates, even if Cyneric insists on his silly nickname.

I roll my eyes at him, smiling, and begin pinning the edges of the linens to the rope lines. We all work in companionable silence for several minutes until Jarl's warbling voice sounds from the other side of the fabric I'm hanging.

"There once was a maid from Vallaurium fair,
With curls like sun on her head and down there,
With a smile and wink, she led me on a merry chase,
Then I stormed her keep at fevered pace!"

Several snickers break out from behind the linens. My scalp tingles a moment before I hear Roan's voice in my head.

"The boy's memory might be admirable, were it not entirely given over to songs of fornication."

Grinning, I turn toward the rows of sun-dried linens waving in the breeze. *"Some humans prefer humor and are not as devoted to intellectual pursuits as you are, Roan."*

"And, thus, humanity is ever amused and never wise."

"Humor can be a good coping tool, you know," I tell him.

"So can silence. I suggest he try it."

Lotti and Otto find me and join me in folding linens after they've finished hanging their freshly washed ones. Lotti says in a hushed tone, for only me and Otto, "I was thinking, perhaps there's some sort of poison in the apothecary you can give Kriegeur to sedate him and allow you to take something."

"And how would I get a poison? Then I'd have to steal from the infirmary *and* Kriegeur," I point out, shaking my head. "No, I hope to sneak into his chamber, take an item, and leave without him ever knowing it."

Otto frowns. "It's supposed to be something important to him, so it can't be just anything."

Lotti adds, "How are you even going to get into his chamber by yourself anyway?"

I hold up my folded bed linens. "With these."

After our afternoon work duties end and my team heads off to the dining hall for the midday meal, I sneak up the stairs to the third level of the main citadel building, the floor where most of the officers have their personal chambers. The last time I was on this floor, I came undone beneath Aric's hands. Now I find I can barely look at him. We haven't spoken since that night. I've not even set eyes on him except for the day he sparred with Kriegeur and then at the last trial.

He tried to find me then, eyes scanning the crowd like he hoped I'd be looking back. I had been, but I didn't want him to know it. So I turned and fled. Cowardly, perhaps. But certainly self-preservationist. I'm not ready to face him yet, to have the hard conversation I know is likely coming. Or even worse, to not speak of it at all. Not with everything still raw and loud in my chest.

It was easy to believe there was something real between us that night—when the fear was high and the silence was heavy and our bodies fit together like they already knew each other. But fear isn't love. Closeness isn't connection. I wanted to believe that he felt such a connection, that it meant something more. But now, with the distance of time settling in like so much dust, I'm beginning to wonder if it was just a fleeting moment wrapped in lust and adrenaline.

I don't know him, not really. Not in the ways that matter. And I'm not sure he wants me to. He's certainly made no move to let me find out. Has been content to let me go quietly for the sake of my safety or his mental well-being—or whatever bullshit reason he's given himself. And if he won't meet me halfway, I don't think I have the strength to keep walking toward him alone. I can't make someone choose emotion if all they want is escape.

My scalp tingles. *"You think only of him hiding, nestling. Were you searching for him, though, or for a moment in which to forget yourself?"*

Roan's question burns through my skull. Was I really looking for Aric to show me who he is? Or was I only looking for what I so readily accuse him of seeking?

I admit, *"It's a hard question. I'm not yet sure I even know the answer."*

There is a long pause before he says, *"Sometimes we hope touch will ease that which time cannot. You're not the first to conflate physical intimacy with emotional attachment."*

"Is this where you tell me I'm a fool?" I ask dryly.

"It's not foolish to desire. Or to feel. Only to dress one as the other and consider it a truth worth clinging to."

"How will I know when it's true?" I ask him, expecting some poetic raven explanation.

"When it refuses to flinch in the face of adversity," he says plainly.

I don't reply, considering his words as I creep down the hallway, past the bathing chamber where I met Aric, searching for some clue as to which one could belong to Kriegeur. Given the time, I know that almost everyone will be at the midday meal or on work duties, so I'm safe to snoop. I start opening doors, guessing that any that I'm able to open are not barred and, therefore, more likely to be empty. Most of the rooms are the same size as the dormitories the cadets sleep in, but house only two or three beds, a testament to the smaller number of officers and the greater comfort they're afforded due to their rank.

I pass a set of double doors on my right that open to another bathing chamber, this one even larger and more opulent than the one I had been in before on this level. At the end of the hall is a spiral staircase as part of the tower propping up this corner of the building. To my left is another long stretch of hallway, and to my right is a single door across from the stairs. I reach for the doorway, pushing it open gently, entering a short hallway dimly lit by daylight streaming in from windows with partially drawn drapes.

On hooks of iron embedded in the wall immediately behind the door hangs a beautifully ornate krahbek. I'm suddenly certain that I've found Kriegeur's room, given that the krahbek is his blade of choice and one at which he is expertly skilled. I quickly close the door behind me and then turn back toward the krahbek, staring at it through the gloom.

It looms on the wall like a silent sentinel. The ebony shaft upon which the blades are fixed gleams even in the room's low lighting, polished to the point of being reflective. The blades atop—axe, hook, spear—forged into a formidable bloom. Brutal but elegant. Beautiful but deadly.

When I lean in, I notice the faint pattern etched along the blades. It's so subtle I might have missed it had I not been staring, had the light not been angled just right. Not engraving, really. Almost like…veins…coursing beneath the surface of the metal. They ripple like the tracery of a feather. I run my fingers along the edge of the axe blade.

Whispers slam into my skull, flooding my brain all at once. Indiscernible but insistent. Heat pulses at my fingertips where they touch the metal. I snatch my hand back, gasping, and press myself against the opposite wall, eyes wide in shock and fear as I stare at the blade, half expecting something to leap at me from within its rippling depths. It almost felt like…like a call. A chill snakes down my spine.

My scalp tingles, but this sensation is comfortingly familiar. *"It is not the cold bite of metal that calls to you, but the echo of something older. Stahlvend stirs where* Rabensblut *runs, and the blood within you listens even if you do not."*

A memory stirs at his words. *"Stahlvend. You've mentioned it before. What is it?"*

Roan answers, *"Not steel alone, but grief. Grief and blood folded fifteen times beneath flame and hammer. Bled first without knowing. The metal drank as if it had been dying of thirst for eons before. A legacy of the* Blutraben *and the* Rabensblut *from which it was born."*

And it seems we're back to poetry.

I shake my head. *"I don't understand. It's in the metal? But how could that— no!"* Realization dawns. *"Roan, is this—is this made of the metal the de Veends developed? That my family forged?"*

"Indeed," he confirms.

I stare at the weapon in awe. *"How did Kriegeur get this?"*

He explains, *"There was a time when Stahlvend weapons were made in great quantities by enterprising* Rabensblut. *I'm certain there are many still in existence."*

Something in his words gives me pause. *"Stahlvend is made by* Rabensblut?*"*

"Stahlvend would not exist without Rabensblut,*"* Roan clarifies, although so much of this is still unclear.

I consider what he's told me, and I gasp, darting forward to touch the blade, feeling the whispers coil into my head. *"Is there* Rabensblut *in the steel?"*

"Stahlvend is not merely a substance," Roan confirms. *"It is a tether. A connection between the Rabensblut and blade. Between Blutraben and Rabensblut. Between gods and humans."*

The threads of my past begin to unravel. Grandmother's reticence, Engilram's deflection, even Walter's quiet declaration—"the world doesn't need more blades." My family had once armed the Aurengarte with superior steel. Now I know why they never spoke of it.

The ledgers I studied weren't just innocuous family history. They concealed truths purposefully hidden. Secrets taken to their graves I was never meant to exhume.

I shiver, pulling my hand back once more.

"And the whispers?" I ask him.

He replies, *"They are not whispers. They are echoes. Echoes of what already stirs within you. The whispers are not* to *you; they are* of *you. Reflecting your ability. Amplifying it. Answering it."*

"Because I'm a Rabensblut," I say.

"Blood sings to blood. The song ever remembers the singer. It will find you because it is from you. It speaks because you can listen. Now, unless you wish to whisper to the murder implements of your ancestors, I suggest you return to your search. Or have you forgotten your location and mission?" He asks sardonically. I swear, I can hear him side-eyeing me in my head.

"Shit!" I say aloud, realizing he's right. I've wasted so much time with my family history lesson that I've forgotten I'm in Kriegeur's bedchamber and supposed to be looking for something to steal.

The krahbek is certainly a good contender, although I'm not sure how I'd conceal something that large before the judgment, so I need to keep looking. I creep along the little alcove until I reach the main part of Kriegeur's chamber and stop short. If I needed evidence that officers are treated better than cadets, and that Kriegeur is treated better than the other officers, I need look no further.

The chamber is part of the round tower, its stone walls rising high into a ceiling inlaid with wood beams joined like the ribs of a ship.

Multiple windows punctuate the curved walls, each draped in heavy emerald fabric that pools elegantly on the floor, the jewel hue softened by the bright midday light streaming in through the glass.

Beneath my feet, a plush wool rug muffles my footfalls and guards against any chill that might be eager to seep through the ancient flagstones. In the center of the room sits a massive four-poster bed, stained a rich, deep chestnut, its posts simple in their carvings but no less beautiful for it. The bed curtains, which match the window drapes in material and color, are drawn back to reveal a mattress piled with furs, coverlets, and several plump pillows.

To one side of the bed stands a wide wardrobe with iron fittings, flanked by a stout, serviceable wooden desk covered in a few neat stacks of parchment, a sealed inkwell, and a quill. Most surprising of all, however, is the farthest wall: an entire arc of bookshelves, overflowing. Books in bindings of every color, size, material, and age—some in pristine condition, others so well-worn their bindings are cracked on the spines—are packed tight, sometimes stacked on top of one another.

I stare, stunned. Of all the things I'd expected of Kriegeur, his being a bookworm was not even on my list of considerations.

I circle the perimeter of the room, looking at all surfaces, stopping in front of a dry sink with an ewer and pitcher, along with various grooming tools, including a mirror.

"Well, there goes my mirror idea. He already has one," I laugh.

I wander to his nightstand, where three books lie stacked, each with dog-eared pages. These must be ones he's currently reading or has recently read. Or maybe they're important to him? Perhaps the places he's earmarked will provide insight into his psyche—something I can use to get my object. I pick up the slim volume on top. It's a book of poetry by the famous bard, Badurad Clineg, particularly well known for his romantic poems. The spine has creases in several places, and when I open the cover, it falls to a verse somewhere in the middle.

"I beheld thee conjure flame from frost,
Each mirror-glance a spell I dared not quench.
The spark thou wrought in me lies 'neath snow,

Cold-born, yet still it burns."

My eyebrows raise, not only because it's a poem about unrequited love, but because it's in old Aurelian. I suppose I shouldn't be surprised that Kriegeur is familiar with the language, given his nickname for me, and that he grew up in a privileged and wealthy household. My teammates had never learned it because of their station. That would definitely not be true of Kriegeur.

The book beneath it is even more curious. A volume of the legistadt, the Aurengarte code of laws. *Perhaps he's reading it so he can conjure even more ways to torture those less fortunate,* I think to myself sarcastically. But when I open it to an earmarked page, the passage I see is as shocking as everything else I've found so far.

"No freeborn man, woman, or child shall be stripped of land, home, or trade by decree of noble blood alone. No healer, herdsman, nor craftsman shall be pressed into servitude without just cause and fair trial in the eyes of the gods."

It's an old piece of legislation, based on the archaic language, probably from hundreds of years ago. It's obviously no longer in use since the farce of a fair trial doesn't seem to occur often, based on my own experience and that of my teammates.

I close the book and set it down, picking up the last book from the stack, one on the history of magic in Aurelia that looks particularly old. When I pry it open, the binding feels loose and fragile, like the pages could separate from it with even the littlest encouragement. The first earmarked page reads:

"In the elder days, the gods granted their favor freely, and magic dwelled among commonfolk and kings alike: the herdsman who called rain, the seamstress who wove dreams into cloth, the healer who soothed broken flesh with a whispered word.

But in the age of crowns, the great Houses decreed that no bearer of the gift might wed one without it lest the blood be thinned. So were commonfolk cast from the wellsprings of power and magic made the treasure of lineage, hoarded as jealously as gold."

I read the passage again. And then a third time. I can't believe what I'm reading. I mentally reach for Roan, who's been alive long enough to have possibly seen a different side of history.

"Is this true? Did commonfolk once have magic?" I ask him.

He answers, *"Some songs are not lost, only sung in places no ear dares linger. Some fires are not quenched, only banked low against the wind. What was given once is not so easily taken."*

Unnerved and unsettled, I restack the books on his nightstand and move to the desk. There has to be something I can steal from his chamber as my item. I pick up a book on the desk that looks nearly brand new. It's a book of folk songs, with musical notations. I flip through the pages, recognizing some of the tunes I've sung with Agnethe or my teammates. When I reach the last page, the corner has an earmark.

It's the song I sang to the löwenard.

I drop the song book like it's on fire and step back.

"Do you think he's watching me?" I ask Roan.

"It is possible that the large human simply enjoys the song," Roan says.

Shaken, I drop the subject and look around the room. So far, I haven't figured out what I will take from Kriegeur, and I only have three more days to observe him. It's both too little time and too much opportunity for him to figure me out. Biting my lip, I reach for the drawer on his desk when I hear it.

The bar on the door is beginning to lift. Someone is entering the room.

Blood rushes in my ears as I look around frantically. Under the bed? I bend over and see that it's too low to the ground. When I stand, I'm facing the wardrobe on the other wall. Frantically, I run to the wooden doors and yank them open, climbing into the shadowy wooden depths draped in uniforms and other clothing that smells surprisingly good. Clean, with a hint of peppermint and sandalwood. With me and the uniforms stuffed in, I cannot close the doors completely, but I pull them shut as far as possible, leaving a small gap.

Kriegeur enters my field of vision, stopping in front of his bed and stripping off his scabbard, followed by his uniform. With horror, I realize he's fully undressing. I'm stuck in my position holding the doors, but I know I should shut my eyes or turn my head to give the man privacy since he's unaware I'm here. But something in me can't resist the opportunity. I catch glimpses of his massive frame. The broad chest rippling with muscle and covered in a dusting of dark hair. Shoulders that curve not with softness, but with imposing strength. When he turns away from the wardrobe and removes his trousers, I see thickly muscled and powerful thighs and tight, well-defined buttocks. I swallow hard when I catch sight of the indentations in his backside, the muscles moving sinuously beneath his skin, which is a deep bronze even where the sun's rays have not caressed it.

Unless he trains in the nude.

I wouldn't put it past him.

Then he turns around, fully naked, and I almost let go of the doors.

Turns out that Kriegeur is not, in fact, hung like a flea.

He moves purposefully toward the wardrobe, and the blood pounds in my body so hard I swear the cabinet must vibrate in time with my heartbeat. My face is hot. My lips and fingertips feel icy cold. He'll open the doors, and I'll be exposed. He will figure out he's my target, and I'll be out of the Freiheit.

But instead of opening the wardrobe, he pulls a linen towel from where it drapes on the handle and wraps it around his waist. He turns toward the bed where he's discarded his clothes and weapons and picks up his dagger before he exits the room, presumably to the bathing chamber.

I can't believe he's taking that stupid dagger with him to bathe—

Oh, no.

It's the dagger.

I have to steal his dagger.

When the door shuts behind him, I tumble out of the wardrobe and race toward the door myself. Prying it open gingerly, I peer out to ensure the hall is empty before I dart out of the room. I mentally shake myself off and begin walking down the hall in the direction I originally came, trying to think how I might obtain Kriegeur's dagger without him knowing or getting caught.

Just then, a voice sounds, "What are you doing in the officer's hall?"

I turn slowly on my heel to see Aric standing in the doorway of a chamber across the hall and a few doors down from Kriegeur's.

My face turns red when I think of Kriegeur standing a few feet from me in all his naked glory. "I'm, uh, delivering bed linens."

He frowns. "That's not typical. We have to pick them up from the storeroom just like everyone else."

I shrug, trying to act bewildered but nonchalant. "I was just following orders."

"I saw you come out of Rafe's room," he says bluntly.

Blood drains from my face. "Y-you did?"

"Are you fucking him?" He asks, stepping toward me.

I rear back as if he punched me in the face. "*What?*"

Aric crosses his arms and stares at me. "Rafe. Are you fucking him?"

Suddenly, I'm angry. Irate, even. My face flushes as I say to him, "It isn't any of your business if I am, but *no.*"

Aric stares at me for several seconds before something shifts in his eyes. Understanding. And relief. "He's your target, isn't he? For the trial?"

I look around the hall before hissing, "Shut up! You don't know who's listening, and I'm not supposed to tell anyone."

He steps even closer to me, until he's near enough that I could touch him if I reached out my hand. "You need to be careful. Rafe is the worst combination of stupid and deadly."

I almost open my mouth to tell him I'm not so convinced of his stupidity anymore, based on his reading material, but something keeps me from telling Aric this. He does not seem to know this about his cousin. Which means that Rafe—I mean, Kriegeur—likely doesn't want him to know. I understand something of secrets.

The sound of a door opening and firmly shutting penetrates my brain. The reality of my situation hits. I am in a hallway of officers' bedrooms near Kriegeur's chamber, and anyone could see me. I have no reason to be here that anyone would believe. Without thinking, I reach for Aric's tunic, pull him toward me, and kiss him.

He goes rigid at first, but then relaxes, a hand finding my waist, the other gripping my shoulder. His lips tease mine gently, and I acquiesce, opening my mouth to allow him entry, his tongue slipping softly against mine. I lean into him, running my hands up his chest, my fingers curling around the fabric of his tunic.

Someone scoffs. We jump apart guiltily, faces flushed, lips swollen, and face our observer.

Of course, it's Kriegeur. He's standing there, toweling slung low on his hips, his hair damp against his shoulders, his eyes first taking in his cousin, and then moving from my toes all the way to the top of my head. Slowly. Torturously.

He smirks. "I'm surprised to find you breaking a rule, cousin, fraternizing with someone in your unit. Tsk, tsk."

Aric's mouth opens and closes like a fish, and he seems unable to reply. Rafe turns and stalks toward me. He leans against the wall when he reaches me, bracing his enormous arm on the stones above us. He's so close to me, his bare chest is almost touching my tunic. So close I can smell sandalwood and peppermint.

His voice is seductive, soft, but still loud enough to reach Aric's ears as he says, "When Saint Aric starts putting you to sleep with all his virtue, *kiinnle*, come find me. I promise I'm twice the trouble and ten times the fun."

My scalp tingles, and I hear an amused chuckle in my head. Rafe's eyes haven't left mine, and they suddenly narrow. He scans my face, like he's looking for something, anything. Gone is the carefree, arrogant son of a Gold Council member. The man looking at me now is calculating. Deadly. And, I fear, too perceptive.

My head whips toward Aric, who practically shudders with frustration and looks like he wants to punch his cousin. Then I look back at the hulking man standing in front of me. I do the only thing I can think of.

I turn on my heel and run.

As I dash down the closest spiral stairs, Roan's laughter still reverberates in my head. Irritated, I tell him, *"Need I remind you that you told me he was dangerous? Why do you now find him amusing?"*

"A blade may gleam with mischief as well as menace, fledgling. At least this one knows how to laugh before he cuts," Roan quips.

"*Oh, hush,*" I tell him, but his laughter follows close behind all the way back to the laundry house.

CHAPTER THIRTY-THREE
Stealth Bomber

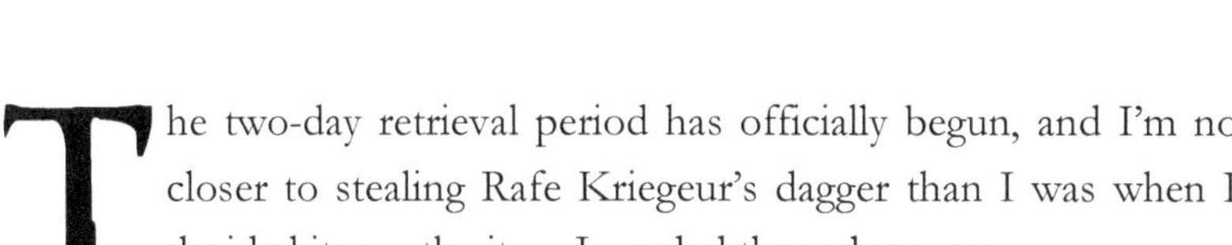

The two-day retrieval period has officially begun, and I'm no closer to stealing Rafe Kriegeur's dagger than I was when I decided it was the item I needed three days ago.

I've trailed him through the training yard, hoping he might set it down while sparring. No luck. He stretches with it. Runs with it. Does push-ups with it.

I lurked by him in the dining hall, thinking he might set it down while eating, and I could prepare to strike, but he doesn't. He wears it while eating, even twirling it maddeningly with one hand while spooning his food with the other.

I followed him through the visitors' hall to the war rooms, on the chance that I'd discover some step in his routine that I could use to my advantage, but he turned around and asked me if I was lost. I had to mumble something about work duties and then fled.

It turns out subtlety is not my strong suit—and Kriegeur never parts from that dagger. Not for a moment. I wouldn't be surprised if he sleeps with it tucked beneath his pillow. It's like he knows I'm watching or suspects someone is. When I think I'm being quiet, when I think I've finally outmaneuvered him, he knows I'm there.

In addition to my increasingly pathetic attempts at stealth-stalking Kriegeur, my movements have become a careful dance of avoidance—designed entirely around avoiding Aric. I've memorized his routine as much as Kriegeur's, but instead of doing so to follow him, I've done it in hopes that I won't have to speak to him or see him.

I know when he exercises, the halls he favors within the citadel, the corner of the dining hall where he sits, and at what times. I take the long way around, duck into nooks and alcoves, feign sudden, all-encompassing interest in the ceiling beams or cracked flagstones—anything to spare us more awkward conversation where I have to face the fact that I almost succumbed to him again.

The memory of his mouth against mine, my body softening against his, makes my skin prickle with humiliation. I was ready to fall right back into his bed and into that ache, mistaking comfort for connection, desire for meaning. And Kriegeur was there, watching and judging. Strangely, though, it didn't feel like an indictment of me.

When I repeated the interaction in my head for the hundredth time that night as I tried to sleep, and each night since, when I relived Kriegeur calling Aric boring and virtuous and saintly with mocking, and he put himself beside me, flirted with me…oddly, it felt like a warning. Or support. Like he was defending me.

As if I'd asked for his commentary or his strange kind of sympathy—or whatever smug, infuriating thing it was supposed to be. Still, it struck me that despite his absolutely irritating personality, his intentions didn't seem entirely dishonorable at that moment. Of course, I could be just as bad at reading him as I am at reading Aric. And if he *was* being supportive, that's even worse. Because I don't want or need his pity, or his attention, or whatever any of it means.

What I need is focus.

I didn't enter the Freiheit for them. Not for Aric's gentle touch or Kriegeur's teasing flirtation. Not for glory or fame or fortune.

I did it for Agnethe. And I can't let anything or anyone—not even myself—pull my focus from that.

With that in mind, I head up the southeast tower's stairs to the third floor. The one that will put me directly by Kriegeur's chamber door. I saw him heading toward the upper levels, presumably to his room, and I want to see if there is an opportunity for me to swipe that damned dagger. Perhaps he'll go into the bathing chamber again, and I'll be able to seize it then. At least this time I won't have to cower in his wardrobe.

Well, hopefully not.

Because if I can't nab the dagger, I'll have to resort to more extreme tactics. And I don't want to do it. I really don't. If Kriegeur never parts with it voluntarily—and after days of trailing him like a ghost, I'm all but certain he won't, I may have no choice but to try the one route Lotti suggested that I've been avoiding: seduction. Just the thought makes my stomach churn. Not out of fear, or even disgust, but dread at how obvious I'd have to be. How transparent. Putting myself on such a blatant display is neither typical nor comfortable.

Kriegeur flirts reflexively. He's been doing it with me almost the entire time I've been here. I'm not blind to how attractive he is. Most women wouldn't consider it such a great sacrifice. And if the rumors of his prowess are true, there could be far worse fates.

Blessed Sisters, if I have to sell a sliver of my soul for a knife, I'd at least like to enjoy it.

Though the idea of it only adds to my feelings of humiliation, I'm resigned to it. If I have to lie, steal, flirt, or fuck to make it through this— so be it.

Agnethe is worth it.

When I reach the third floor and exit the stairwell, I duck into the small, shadowy nook behind it with a direct view of Kriegeur's chamber door. Curiously, it's slightly ajar, and the sound of conversation reaches my ears. Despite his ostentatious nature, Kriegeur seems to limit access to his chamber. I've never seen his door partially open in the considerable time I've spent following him over the past several days. I tiptoe forward, flattening myself to the wall his door is flush with, and stop when I can peer through the hinge side into the chamber.

Kriegeur stands in the center, speaking to a man nearly as physically imposing, though striking in a different way. Where Kriegeur's skin glows a deep bronze hue, the other man's is polished ebony. Kriegeur's dark brown hair falls in effortless waves past his shoulders, while this man's black hair—liberally interspersed with gray—is threaded into tight braids that hang to the middle of his back. Time has etched its signature into his features. Lines frame his mouth, crease his brow, and have settled at the corners of his eyes. A man well into his fifth decade, and by the looks of it, he's earned every year the hard way. His expression is solemn, touched faintly with something like sorrow, though irritation tightens his gaze as it rests on Kriegeur.

A feeling I know all too well, where the lieutenant colonel is concerned.

"How many?" The unknown man asks, a voice as rich as the chocolate of his skin flows past my ears, warm and soothing in its decadence.

"Maybe half a dozen," Kriegeur answers, his voice clipped.

"Not possible," the man says tersely in return.

"That sounds more like you don't want to than you can't," Kriegeur counters.

The man's jaw tightens. "The Freiheit is going on as we speak. The grounds are teeming with Aurenclaste visitors and Aurengarte reinforcements. Not to mention your father's presence."

Rafe scoffs. "My father won't even notice with his precious tournament going on. With all the traffic coming and going, it's the perfect opportunity."

The man's mouth pinches. "How do you plan to explain away that number of deaths?"

My blood turns cold in my body. That number of *what?* My pulse starts pounding in my ears, but I force myself to remain still, unseen, straining to catch every word.

"When someone notices they're missing?" The man presses. "What story are you planning to spin then?"

"It's not difficult to claim there was an escape plot. Execution is completely justifiable and legal for that," Kriegeur says, shrugging, as if he didn't just casually mention murdering half a dozen people. "It's all very tragic, the necessary force. Clean and official. My father can even make a public example if he so desires.”

“And the *annullerian*?” The man asks.

At this question, Rafe looks more tense, his jaw tightening before responding. “That’s been a bit more…difficult. Hildegarde has spared what she can. It’ll have to be enough to get through.”

“A half dozen bodies, in two days’ time, with a lesser amount of *annullerian*?” The man questions, sounding incredulous and frustrated. “This is a fool’s plan.”

Bodies. He definitely said bodies. What in the name of the Sisters is Kriegeur involved in? And what’s *annullerian*? Is that the drug I saw Hildegarde give him before? As much as I’m loath to admit, senseless murder doesn’t make sense for Kriegeur to be involved in when he could easily punish people publicly with little recrimination given his position, rank, and status. This sounds like some other kind of plan.

“You’ve never minded my ‘foolish’ plans before,” Rafe counters, grinning at the man rakishly, which is more like what I’m used to, but it also strikes me as…off, somehow. Something about it seems strange. Different. It pulls at my memory, but I can’t examine it without risking missing what they say.

His companion rolls his eyes, and I like him for it. “Is that all?”

Kriegeur pauses, his demeanor shifting, almost like he’s nervous. Another oddity, and one which I would never believe if I weren’t watching it with my own eyes. “There might be another…but I haven’t figured it out yet.”

The other man frowns. “What do you mean you ‘haven’t figured it out yet’?”

Rafe responds, “I mean, she’s nothing like I’ve experienced before.”

She? Has he found some vapid cadet to moon after? I would think in following him around, I’d have seen her by now.

The older man snorts. “Let me guess, you’ve gone soft for some doe-eyed damsel in distress?”

“I’m not in a position to become attached to anyone, Conrad. Let alone some mouthy cadet who’s doing her damnedest to get killed in the Freiheit while making calf’s eyes at my prig of a cousin,” Kriegeur retorts.

I stare into the chamber, stunned.

He's talking about me. And I am not "making calf's eyes" or trying to get myself killed.

And what about me, specifically, is so different to him? I get the feeling it's more than my eye color or the sound of my voice. With the break in their conversation, it's then that it truly registers what has seemed so off about Kriegeur.

There's no performance in his voice. No bravado. Just calculation. Logic. Similar to how he acted when I overheard him with Hildegarde. This is not the brash, loudmouthed, smirking brute. No, whatever *this* Kriegeur has his hands in is likely bigger and far more dangerous than I can deduce from this single moment of eavesdropping. And is this Kriegeur the real picture of the man or a mask, like I'm beginning to suspect of his "normal" behavior?

And what does he want with me that he'd tell this Conrad man about me?

Like he has plans for me.

A door slams somewhere down the hall, and I jump. Rafe bites out a low curse, and the other man moves quickly toward the door. Panicking, I dash into the stairwell. I know I'll never make it down all the way before he sees me, especially because he's far more athletic and has urgency at his heels. So I enter the stairwell alcove and spin in a circle, walking into the hallway just as the large man—Conrad—exits Kriegeur's room, as if I had just climbed the stairs and am only now entering this level. I nod at him politely, and he returns it placidly before strolling into the stairwell, the picture of unhurried calm. *This* is a man accomplished at subtlety and subterfuge.

I look over my shoulder, watching as he leaves, and then turn back toward Kriegeur's room just as he, too, appears and looks like he's about to exit. He pauses when he sees me, his furrowed brow smoothing as he leans against the door frame, crossing his massive arms in front of his chest and assuming his usual dumb-but-cocky expression.

His eyes trace my body from head to toe before he says, "You know, *künnle,* I confess I didn't think you'd tire of Saint Aric quite so soon." One of his dark eyebrows raises, like he's waiting for me to refute him.

He's going to figure it out if I don't do something. Something drastic and different. With Agnethe in mind, I steel myself for what I'm about to do.

I start walking toward him, hoping I've injected enough sway into my hips, and force a breathy sort of laugh past my lips. I look into his eyes, then trail my gaze down his face, letting it linger just a bit too long on the strong line of his jaw, the column of his throat, the set of his shoulders and arms.

"Aric is more enamored of his duty than anything else," I say, wincing inwardly at both the ease with which I say this and the sad truth behind it. I drop my voice to a lower, husky pitch. "And I…well, I couldn't stop thinking about your offer."

I manage to move closer to him and now stand directly before him. I'm so close that if I inhale, my breasts will brush his chest. His black eyes glitter in the hallway's torchlight, and I have to force myself not to look away because I feel utterly ridiculous. A caricature of seduction. An awkward attempt that I know he's going to see through immediately.

He leans his head down toward me until our faces are a hair's breadth apart. His voice is intimate, amused. "If you're trying to make him jealous, *künnle*, wouldn't it be more effective if he were here to witness it?"

My lips part as I try to think of a retort, but my brain has gone to mush. My pulse kicks up at the invasion of my space and his nearness to me. "I, uh, well…" I stutter and lick my lips nervously.

His eyes flick down to my mouth, and my breath catches. Is he toying with me or testing me? And does he suspect I'm here for a reason beyond what I've told him? He can't find out he's my target, or I'm out of the tournament.

Before I can respond, he frowns slightly. "This is the second time I've seen you in this hallway in a week. What exactly are you up to?"

My mind desperately searches for a response, but my body answers first. Without further deliberation, I surge to my toes, wrap my arms around his neck, and press my lips to his.

He doesn't move for a moment, his body stiff with shock. But then, like a spark igniting dry kindling, he responds. His mouth claims mine with a hunger that pushes the breath from my lungs. One of his hands finds its way to the back of my head, threading roughly in my hair as the other splays against my back, pulling me into the bulk of his body. There is nothing gentle or measured about how his mouth eagerly slants over mine, almost desperate. His tongue traces along the seam of my lips, and I yield, parting them beneath his, the taste of peppermint flooding my mouth as he enters it.

He turns us, pressing me against the rough, wooden surface of his chamber door, his hands leaving my hair and back to slide down the curve of my arse, his fingers digging into my hips, pulling them against his own. He reaches behind me and fumbles with the door, pushing it open. I barely have time to register the shift before I'm propelled backward into the hallway of his chamber. He kicks the door shut behind him and stalks toward me, pressing me hard against the stone wall with his body before cupping my face in his hands and kissing me anew.

His mouth is fervent, devouring, like something inside him has snapped loose. I try to focus on my mission, sliding my hands down his back. It's becoming harder to think with his insistent mouth upon mine, the roughness of his beard against my cheek, that peppermint taste on my tongue, the scent of sandalwood flooding my nostrils, and the heat of his body warming mine. My fingers delicately explore the column of his spine, sliding down to the indentation at the base.

It's there that I feel it. The hilt of the dagger in a sheath at the small of his back, nestled beneath his tunic. Always close. Always guarded.

But thought of stealing it vanishes the moment his lips break from mine and slide, hot and urgent, along my jaw, the side of my neck, the sensitive hollow just beneath my ear. My body arches into his instinctively, curving toward the pleasure, a breathy moan catching in my throat. An accompanying noise leaves his own, but whether it's more curse or benediction, I'm not sure.

He grips the backs of my thighs and lifts me, as if I weigh nothing, wrapping my legs around his waist. Strong hands cup my arse, fingers digging into the flesh as he presses his hips against mine, pinning me even tighter to the wall. His cock, hard and demanding, is lodged against me just where I want it. He rocks his hips rhythmically into mine, setting every nerve ending between my legs on high alert. A feral sound escapes me at the unfaltering friction, and my fingers find their way into his hair, looking for something to anchor me while I feel completely adrift in sensation.

With his hips pinning me to the wall, I'm effectively trapped and at his mercy as he lowers his mouth to mine again, his hands sliding from my arse to the hem of my tunic. A low groan vibrates through his chest as his fingers slip beneath my tunic, his knuckles brushing the feverishly hot span of my stomach. I answer with a tortured mewl of my own at the brush of his callused hands against my bare skin.

"You're so soft. Like silk," he breathes against my mouth, kissing along my jaw, capturing my earlobe in his teeth.

His hands trail upward under my tunic, leaving a trail of fire in their wake. He's nearly to my breasts, his fingers reaching the edge of the fabric of my banding, and my nipples are drawn tight and aching, practically begging for him to touch them.

A sharp knock cuts through the fog of desire like a slap to the face.

My legs drop from Rafe's waist to the floor with a *thunk*.

A moment later, Lord Corvilian opens the door and strolls in.

If there were a hole in the middle of the room that I could crawl into and die of mortification, I would do it right now without question.

For his part, Rafe steps in front of me and speaks curtly to his father, "I don't believe I gave you leave to enter. We need a moment of privacy."

Lord Corvilian looks at his son, then at me, gaze calculating. I shrink back under the penetrating stare, hovering more behind Rafe's arm.

Like a coward.

So much for telling Lord Corvilian not to underestimate my strength. I would be more than happy for him to underestimate me. To not estimate me at all, in fact. Forget my name, too.

He turns to Rafe and says, "Privacy is not a right you possess, boy. It is a courtesy extended to those whose talents or blood might one day repay the kingdom's indulgence. You, I fear, have neither."

I wince at the man's harsh words to his son and feel sympathetic embarrassment that I witnessed the setdown. Since I'm close behind him, pressed against his arm and back, I can feel the slight stiffening in Rafe's spine at the words. The subtle evidence that he isn't completely unaffected by them is *almost* enough to make me want to speak up to Lord Corvilian. That is, until I look into his predator's eyes and feel all my bravado abandon me.

His black eyes bore into mine. "Get out," he says.

I don't need further encouragement to escape the tension or the humiliation. I scurry around Rafe's large frame, past that of his father, and quit the room.

Getting his dagger means I'll have to return. Apparently, seduction is a multi-step process, and it seems I'm destined for more of the cat-and-mouse game.

Except, in this case, I'm fairly certain I'm playing both parts.

It's the night before the trial presentation. Tomorrow, I'm expected to present my stolen item. I've spent the last day and a half trying to work up the courage to approach Rafe again. To finish what I started—or, rather, to do what I actually had intended to start, which is to steal the damned dagger. But I've barely seen him. Just glimpses from across the training yard or in the dining hall from afar. He sits there with Major Berger and Colonel Richter like nothing happened. Like I didn't press my mouth to his and nearly lose myself in the process.

It's ridiculous how often my thoughts have returned to it since it happened. The thrill of the moment, how good—Blessed Sisters, *dangerously* good—it felt to be consumed that way. Desired that way. And I hate that part of me wants more. That my skin still tingles when I remember his lips on my neck, the weight of his body pressing me into the stone wall.

It's purely physical, and I don't want to be ruled by that. I don't want to entangle myself with Kriegeur when he's playing some dangerous game, the plans he's weaving with his associate, Conrad, under his father's very nose. He is dangerous in more ways than one, and I'm trying to escape, not anchor myself to this place.

But desire is traitorous.

It slips past reason, snaking into my chest, alighting my nerves, whispering in my ear that perhaps the risk isn't so great, that the danger makes it exciting. The fact that I want it is even more terrifying than Lord Corvilian's notice or the thought of Aric finding out.

Sisters, what would he say if he knew? And how would I explain it all if he did?

I creep down the stairwell from my dormitory to the third floor. It's far past lights out, I'm only wearing my nightshift, and I shouldn't be anywhere near here. But I have a mission and must try to complete it.

My scalp tingles, and I hear Roan's grumpy voice, *"This hardly seems wise. These humans seem very particular about their curfews."*

"I don't have much choice," I tell him, exasperated. *"It's not as if I get much time to myself. The trial ends tomorrow, and if I don't have a good item to present, I won't make it to the next one, and then I'll have no way to get to Agnethe."*

He responds, *"No river runs straight to the sea, fledgling. Nor does victory come by only one path."*

"Perhaps not, but having a boat—or even an oar—makes the river far easier to navigate," I retort. *"This is the most straightforward path to Agnethe that doesn't begin with me getting sent to the front."*

"No," he replies dryly. *"It just might send you to the grave instead."*

"You can sit there judging me, or you can help me out a little," I say tartly.

I hear a long-suffering sigh in my head. My eyes go slightly blurry for a few seconds before clearing; all the darkened shapes and corners in the stairwell are suddenly more visible and crisp. Roan and I have recently discovered that he's able to share his keen night vision with me through the bond, which provides me with a better view as I skulk through the dimly lit corridors.

I tiptoe out of the stairwell on the third floor and into the hallway near Rafe's bedchamber, making sure the coast is clear before I dart over to his door. The flagstones beneath my feet are freezing, but I didn't want to risk the noise of shoes when sneaking around.

I gingerly lift the door handle, praying it's not barred, and breathe a sigh of relief when it unlatches with a soft *snick*. I make the narrowest opening I can still fit through and slip into the room, shutting the door silently behind me. I see the familiar dark shapes of the mounted krahbek, the pieces of furniture standing against the walls, and feel the soft carpet beneath my toes as I enter the central part of the chamber.

A shaft of moonlight spills from between the parted drapes, illuminating the bed directly in its path. The bed curtains are open, and I can see Kriegeur's sleeping form sprawled across the large mattress, the glow of the moon bouncing off his bare chest, arms, and shoulders, the coverlet having slid dangerously low on his waist, just draped over his hips. I stare for a few seconds, watching his chest rise and fall, mesmerized by the sight of the light dancing across the powerful muscles of his body, before I shake my head to clear my thoughts.

Focus, I tell myself. *Find the dagger.*

Spotting clothing discarded on the floor, I creep forward, bending down to rifle through the fabric, looking for the dagger and where he might have tossed it. After several minutes of crawling along the floor, I must face that it's not here. I look toward his bed with apprehension. What if he *does* keep it with him, even in sleep? Perhaps even as cliché as under his pillow, as I once jokingly thought, or clutched in his hand.

I pad over to the bed, my heart pounding. One of his hands drapes across his abdomen, and the other is stretched out across the mattress, like he's reaching for someone in his dreams. Since both hands are visible and the dagger is clearly not within them, under his pillow seems the next logical place to look.

My scalp tingles. *"Nothing like a blade beneath the pillow to cradle you to sleep,"* Roan drawls.

Just then, Rafe turns his head toward me and mutters something unintelligible. I freeze, knowing if he opens his eyes, he'll see me, and I'll be forced to continue my farce of seduction to allay any suspicions, as much as I'd hoped that wouldn't be necessary.

"It's *remarkable that you're not better at subterfuge, fledgling, considering how adept you are at lying to yourself,*" Roan says sarcastically.

I bristle at the tone and accuracy of his words. *"Hush, I'm trying to focus."*

I lean over to see if I can reach the pillow without getting too close to Rafe, my hand slowly edging toward his head.

A deep voice breaks the silence of the room. "Careful, *künnle*. Wake a man the wrong way, and he might decide to finish what he was dreaming about."

CHAPTER THIRTY-FOUR
Stolen Kisses and Stolen Thunder

I laugh nervously as I look at Rafe's eyes through the darkness. "I was just, um, trying to finish what we started earlier before your father interrupted us."

Bent over him as I am, my hand extended slightly beyond his shoulder, my face is unnervingly close to his. My braid slides over my shoulder and falls across his arm, but he doesn't give any indication that he notices. His gaze locks onto mine with complete focus. I wonder how much he can see of me, given that he doesn't have magical raven vision like I do.

He remains silent. My heart is pounding against my rib cage, and I sincerely hope that my voice lies better than my face is capable of doing.

I lick my lips and nervously try to fill the void his silence leaves. "How did you know it was me in the dark?"

For five, ten seconds, he still says nothing. Until finally, "I could be blind and half dead, and I'd know your scent anywhere. Ginger. Clean linen. And hope, as sharp as a dagger. Gods help anyone who breathes it in; they'd surely be undone."

Then he threads his hands into my hair and kisses me.

All thought of my mission abandons me in the wake of the fire blazing through my body as soon as his lips touch mine again. Delicious tingles ripple across my scalp that have nothing to do with ravens and everything to do with the strong fingers twined in the strands of hair at the base of my braid. I brace my hand on the mattress beside his shoulder, leaning fully over him as he ravages my mouth with his tongue, locking my elbow so I don't collapse on top of him in a boneless puddle of want. He seems to want me closer, though, and he tugs gently on my opposite arm, pulling until I lie against him, my palm splaying on the bare skin of his chest.

"Don't be shy, *künnle*," he says, skimming his lips along my jaw. "Climb on."

I sigh at the rasp of his beard on my skin, the warmth of his breath brushing my neck. I'm so pleasantly distracted that I blurt out, "I don't want to crush you."

His mouth freezes in its path.

Mortification courses through me, and I wish I could take the words back. I don't dwell on it often, this sometimes insecure feeling, and it's certainly never stopped me from pursuing physical pleasure. But pressed against someone whose body has been carved by war and discipline makes the thought flicker, quick and unbidden. A flash of self-consciousness that manages to worm its way through.

He moves his lips to my ear. "I've spent weeks," he says, voice rough, "imagining you naked and riding me, those glorious tits bouncing, head thrown back. That smart mouth of yours moaning my name until I'm half mad with want and fisting myself like some green schoolboy just so I can function. You couldn't crush me if you tried, *künnle*, but if you could? I'd welcome it."

I'm so shocked by his words that I let him pull me down fully on top of him, positioning my thighs on either side of his hips. With my legs stretched over the width of his body, my nightshift rides up over my hips, leaving the thin layers of my smallclothes and his coverlet the only barrier between our bodies. I moan shakily against his mouth as the thick ridge of his cock rubs at my sensitive flesh through the scant fabric, the coarse material providing additional friction exactly where my body wants it.

His hands slide up my thighs and underneath the back of my tunic, splaying across my back, fingers kneading my arse, tracing the bumps of my spine, sending goosebumps rippling across my skin. Emboldened, I push myself to a sitting position on his lap, placing myself directly in the moonlight pouring in from the window. I grasp the hem of my nightshift, pulling it over my head. My breasts spill from the confines of the fabric, nipples tightening from both the cool air of the chamber and the intensity of his gaze as he stares at me. One of his palms slides up the side of my ribcage until it's sitting beneath the swell of my breast, and his callused thumb darts out, rubbing across the hardened peak of my nipple. My head falls back in pleasure, forcing my breast more into his palm, which he rewards with repetitive circular motions that scrape the nerve endings enough to make me want more, but not enough to satisfy.

"Please, Rafe," I whisper desperately. "More."

Suddenly, I'm falling back against the plushness of the mattress, Rafe having grabbed my waist and rolled us until I'm lying on my back and he's settled above me. The coverlet has fully slid off him. The heat of his body burns into mine, where my inner thighs caress the bare skin of his lean hips. The rough hair on his chest teases my nipples as he takes in deep gulps of air, and his lips are poised millimeters from mine.

"Say it again," he commands, his voice low and rough with barely leashed desire.

"Please?" I squeak, squirming beneath him, arching my breasts into his chest to try and replicate the rubbing sensation, widening my thighs to welcome him where I need him most.

"Say my name when you beg me so sweetly," he purrs against my mouth, keeping his lips just out of my reach.

I lift my eyes to his. They're so close to mine I can see them glitter in the darkness. I watch his face as I murmur against his lips, "Please, Rafe. More."

He crushes his mouth to mine again and presses his cock against my core, rotating his hips in lazy circles that rub the blunt tip against my engorged clitoris through my smallclothes. He moves his lips to my neck, trailing kisses down to my collarbone, over the swells of my breasts, until his mouth hovers over my left nipple, his breath hot and insistent.

"Don't stop begging me, *künnle*," he instructs.

Despite the haze of desire, irritation flares, and I want him to be just as overcome as I am, just as out of control with lust. I dig my fingers into the back of his neck, grab onto his hair, and pull, arching my breast into his face.

"Fuck," he swears and closes his mouth around my nipple.

When the wet heat of his tongue hits my skin and his lips begin pulling, my eyes roll back into my head, and my neck arches, because nothing has *ever* felt this good. The persistent tug on my nipple, the roughness of his beard against the sensitive skin of my chest and abdomen, the surprising silkiness of his hair between my fingers, all compounded by the continued pressure of his cock rocking against me.

I trace my hands down his torso, wanting to feel how hard he is, how desperate. The coarse hair on his stomach tickles my fingers as I slide them down, down, the muscles jumping in response to my touch. I run a fingernail along the line of hair trailing from his belly button, feeling my stomach tighten at his sharp intake of breath. Without giving him time to brace himself, I wrap my hand firmly around the thick shaft and squeeze.

He releases my nipple from his mouth. "Fuck, Greta," he hisses through his teeth as my hand moves up and down. Hearing my name on his lips said with such intensity is more intoxicating than any wine, more inebriating than any drug. I respond with firmer strokes, running my thumb over the head, dragging the moisture beaded there across the tip. He surges upward and captures my lips with his, groaning into my mouth as my hand continues dancing across his flesh.

Suddenly, he reaches between us for my wrist, stilling my hand. Puzzled, I meet his eyes in the dark, and he grins against my mouth. "If torture is the game you aim to play, *künnle*, I'm not one to lose gracefully."

One of his hands pins my wrists above my head, though in truth, I don't fight him as he moves his mouth down my neck, dots kisses along the swells of my breasts, teases each of my nipples, and begins pressing his lips down the span of my stomach, his tongue periodically darting out to taste my skin. By the time he's reached my navel, my wrists are free from his grasp. All I can do is hold onto his shoulders as he hooks his fingers behind the fabric of my smallclothes, tugs them down over my hips, and tosses them to the floor. He uses his palms to press my thighs open and flat as far as they'll go, exposing my wet center to the cool night air of the room and the light of the moon.

He stares openly at me, and I would feel self-conscious if the look on his face weren't one of such indecent worship that I have no cause to doubt he's enjoying the view. He leans down and drags his tongue up the inside of my left thigh, and the sound that escapes my mouth is not one that I've ever made before. When his mouth hovers over me, I press his shoulders, suddenly concerned.

"Wh-what are you doing?" I ask, fairly certain I know the answer, but unprepared for it, nonetheless.

His teeth flash white in the dim light as he says, "Winning."

Then he slides his tongue up over my opening and swirls it around my clit, my hips jerking with each revolution.

Oh, my gods. Oh, my *gods*. How had I never heard of this? Experienced it? I'd rant against the injustice of the world on behalf of women who haven't yet either, but I can barely form coherent thought. I've devolved into a blubbering mass of sensation, my entire existence narrowed to the heat of Rafe's mouth on my body.

I cover my mouth with the back of my hand to keep from filling the room with too much noise, but he knocks it away. "Don't hide. Sing for me, *künnle*," he demands before drawing my clit between his lips. I'm a rotte string drawn tight, and Rafe is plucking me in just the precise way that makes music spill forth from my throat.

My head thrashes across the pillows, and I reach my hand up above me to brace it on the headboard. When I do, my palm brushes something cool and rigid beneath the fabric. Instinctively, my hand closes around the object.

Whispers slam into my brain. Overwhelming and lurid, they layer on top of one another, some seductive, others with urgency. They come from different directions, accompanied by the sound of screeching steel, of a rapid heartbeat, the gutter of a dying breath.

Just below the ribs. Left side. His heart.

Push. Twist. Watch him fall.

A kiss to the throat, and he sings no more.

Strike first. Strike now.

Horrified, filled with terror, my body stiffens.

Rafe must sense something in my body language, because he lifts his head and smiles at me. "You know, I don't usually have this effect on women—" his eyes look up to where my hand is beneath his pillow. Before I can even react, he's thrown the pillow aside and pinned my wrist, pressing against the side beneath my thumb painfully.

I cry out, and my hand opens reflexively, releasing the dagger from my grip, and the whispers leave me. I want to sob with relief, but the look on his face—tight with anger and, even worse, betrayal—keeps me from reacting further.

"Fuck," he bites out, and I flinch. "I'm your target, aren't I? For the trial?"

I swallow hard and say nothing.

He presses, "That's why you're here, isn't it? To steal from me, not 'to finish what we started earlier.'"

My mouth opens and closes like a beached fish as I try to formulate a response. "I—well—"

He makes a sound of disgust and releases my hands, balling his fists on either side of my head. "Or did my father send you to do what he's too cowardly to do himself?"

The shock of his question momentarily sucks the air from my lungs. When I'm able to breathe, to speak, I sputter. "No, I-I'm here for you, because I wanted to see you and—"

"If you ever want to pursue the stage, you'd better vastly improve your acting skills, because you're fucking lousy at it." He climbs off of me, taking the dagger with him and reaches for his discarded trousers on the floor, turning his back to me and pulling them on with angry, staccato motions. When he's covered, he faces me again and says, "Get out of my sight."

I scramble out of the bed, awkwardly sliding off the mattress to the floor. It takes me several moments to locate my nightshift, untangle it, and put it on. Several seconds more, still, to find my smallclothes and yank them on, shimmying them quickly over my hips. Once I do, I glance at Rafe's face. I'm surprised by the tightness of his jaw, the rigid line of his shoulders. He's angry, to be sure, but if I didn't know better, I'd almost say he looks…hurt.

I know I did what I had to by coming here, and that Agnethe is more important than anything, but I can't help but feel shame at the thought that I've hurt someone in the process. At least, in this case, Rafe was an unknowing bystander to my life, and were I in his shoes, I would be feeling upset and betrayed.

I step forward. "Rafe, I'm sorry, it's just that—"

He holds up a hand, and I stop, my teeth clicking shut.

"If I see you in here again, even the gods won't judge what I'll do to you," he says, curtly. "Get. Out."

Knowing his weapons expertise and the sheer size advantage he has, I don't wait for him to tell me again.

The next afternoon, an hour before the trial presentation begins, I'm moping toward Freiheit Field. Lotti, Otto, Cyneric, and Jarl all seemed to feel sorry for me and the fact that I'll be eliminated, and they took over my laundry duties. So I decided to take the opportunity to think and leisurely make the trek to the arena—and try to convince myself to accept that I'm stuck here for far longer than I had hoped.

Maybe it's for the best.

If I'm out, I'm out. No final trial. No last dance with death where I must kill someone or end up dying myself. No more crawling through tunnels or singing to beasts or stalking dangerous men that are dangerously attractive for bits of metal.

Maybe I can find another way. Maybe, once they send me to the front, I can desert. Slip away in the chaos. My uncles might find a way to free me. Or I could vanish. It's not such a terrible fate. Not compared to dying.

Except there are many ways of dying.

Not all of them leave behind a body.

As I try to reconcile myself to this fate, a cold chill spreads through me—the kind that makes me feel hollow. The kind that steals the memory of hope, that makes me forget what it feels like to fight for something. Fight for someone. Fight for *myself*, as I have been these past weeks.

I hate all of this.

Hate this place.

Against all odds, though, I had begun to feel like I was becoming someone. Not just the admittedly huge discovery of Roan and the Rabensblut. But someone more than just Agnethe's sister. Someone more than my grandmother's companion. Someone more than my uncle's assistant.

I have learned things. Ugly things. I can manipulate. I can use someone if it means getting what I need.

I've also learned that I'm strong. Not just the strength of enduring life's lot, but fighting strong. I'm clever and strategic and funny. I can lead.

I feel like I was starting to become myself. Not what I am for others. What I can offer, or fix, or be for someone else. That I'm…more.

Exactly what Agnethe asked me if I wanted.

And I want to get back to my sister above anything else. As it turns out, though, I also want the "more."

A winged shadow appears along the ground in front of me, a moment before my scalp tingles, and Roan's voice interjects itself into my thoughts, *"The journey to self-discovery is not undone by delay. The seed still holds the flower, even in the frost."*

I feel emotion clog my throat at his words, and I hurriedly dash the rapidly welling tears from my eyes, praying no one I know comes along to witness my self-pity.

"Greta," I hear Aric say behind me.

Of course. Of course it's him. The last person I want to see, except for maybe Rafe.

I take a deep, calming breath and slowly turn to face him, pasting on a falsely bright smile. "Yes?"

He looks at me strangely, as if he knows I'm faking it. "Are you all right? You looked upset."

"I'm fine," I lie. "Just tired."

He nods, looking unconvinced. "Did you get your item? For the tournament?"

"Why do you even care?" I ask him, bitterly. "We've not spoken in days."

"You've been avoiding me," he points out. "I've looked for you."

"You have?" I raise my eyebrows.

He steps toward me. "Of course I have. I haven't stopped thinking about you, about what happened between us, and wondering if—" he cuts off and looks away, appearing embarrassed.

"Wondering if what?" I whisper.

"Wondering if I made a mistake," he admits, his eyes meeting mine, "in how I handled things. In…in pushing you away."

I swallow. Oh, gods. Why is this happening now? When I have no idea what to do with this information?

When I don't answer, he looks awkward momentarily, like he regrets exposing his feelings. "So did you get your item?" He asks again.

I consider lying to him for a moment. To get rid of him so I can continue to wallow in misery. Because the burden of someone else's feelings when I'm still raw from everything that happened last night between me and Rafe feels like too much to bear; but as soon as we go to the presentation, he'll know I was lying, and I honestly don't see the point of trying to pretend any more.

"No," I admit. "He figured it out. So that means I'm out this round." I raise my chin, daring him to pity me. If he shows me even an ounce of it, I'll cry or scream or hit him or some combination of all three.

He steps toward me. "I'm sorry. I know you were counting on staying in."

I wrap my arms around my middle and nod, looking at the ground. "Yes, I want to get out of here. That is, I *need* to get out of here, to get to my—" I almost tell him, but stop myself again.

Then I wonder why I've hidden it from anyone. He tried to share with me. I will do the same.

I look him in the eye and say, "I need to get back to my sister. She's in trouble, and I—I don't know how I'll do it now," my breath hitches, and I can't continue. Can't explain more.

He steps even closer to me and cups my cheek in his hand. "We will figure it out. It will all work out in the end as it ought." He leans forward and brushes his lips against mine.

I'm so surprised by it that I freeze, unsure how to proceed.

"Hmm, maybe if you string enough empty platitudes together, you'll start to believe them, too, cousin," Rafe's voice seeps in between our bodies and douses my body in icy cold shock.

I jump away from Aric guiltily and stare at his larger cousin, who is watching us with glittering black eyes from a few feet away. I don't know how I expected to feel, seeing Rafe for the first time since last night, but a braid of tangled emotions tightens inside me, tugging at both ends.

Shame hits first. Not just because I deceived him, but because I let myself *enjoy* him. Even now, remembering the way his hands felt on my thighs, his mouth on my skin, makes my breath catch in my throat. A secret I don't want to admit, but that burns inside of me, nonetheless.

It started as strategy and ended up somewhere far past attraction. Desire.

And then there's Aric.

One steady; one wild. One who offers me protection and comfort, but at an arm's length and only on his terms. The other, who offers me nothing at all except the thrill of existing in a single moment and the intoxication of letting it consume you. I'm stuck somewhere between shame and longing, between desperation and determination, between survival and discovery, and not at all certain how to choose.

What kind of person does it make me to struggle with this so much? To be unable to sort through the mess of my own emotions and the bigger emotional mess I've created.

My scalp tingles. *"I fear the messiness is simply proof that you are human, fledgling. It is a hallmark of your species."*

Rafe's eyes narrow on me as Roan's voice sounds in my head, and I have to stop myself from looking around to see if Roan has somehow appeared and spoken aloud. I wonder what it is about me that gives away that I'm not entirely "present" when he's speaking to me? And why Rafe, of all people, is perceptive enough to notice when no one else has.

I don't know what to say. I haven't figured out how to tell Rafe to fuck off and mind his own business, while also acknowledging he has a right to be angry with me, without tipping off Aric to what happened between us. Before I can act, though, Aric steps in between us, like he's protecting me from the force of Rafe's scorn and says, "What's your problem? We were having a private conversation. And at any rate, it's not like she asked for this to happen."

"Actually, she did," Rafe says curtly. "Wasn't that the whole point of her signing up for this shit show?" The cousins stare at each other for a moment before Rafe turns and stalks toward Freiheit Field.

Aric starts forward. "I'll talk to him, he's just like this sometimes, but maybe he'll help if I—"

I step in front of him, holding my palms up. "Don't. It's not worth it. Short of threat to life and limb, there's nothing that can be said to convince him to help me. And we both know that any threat I make in that regard would be empty." Aric wraps his arm around my shoulders, and we stand there together, silently. I don't have the heart or energy to think about the implications or to deny him.

"*Would it?*" Roan asks me simply.

"*What do you mean?*" I ask him.

"*Would it be empty? A whispered word can cut a man faster than any blade,*" Roan intones.

I frown, considering his words, and I can't hold back a gasp when the realization hits me. Tearing away from Aric, I take off in a run toward Freiheit Field.

"What's going on? What are you doing?" He asks.

I call over my shoulder, "Finding a different path."

I can feel Roan's energy buzzing through my limbs, my *Rabensblut* surging through my veins, as I fly across the training yard toward Freiheit Field. When I spot Rafe, he's just crossed through the gate and passed the stone walls.

"Rafe, wait!" I cry out to him, and he turns abruptly toward me, eyebrows shooting up in surprise.

I'm moving so fast that I can't properly stop. I crash into him at full speed, and he instinctively reaches out to keep us from toppling over. His large hands wrap around my upper arms, steadying me. He scowls at his own hands, as if realizing what he's done, and snatches them back before crossing them over his chest.

"Gods, it's like hitting a wall," I say breathlessly. If only my *Rabensblut* allowed me to avoid getting winded after running. I put my hands on my knees and take several deep breaths, then look up at him and say, "I need—"

"I didn't think you'd come begging for it," he interrupts.

My face flames, and I stand up straight as an arrow and step back from him. "I'm not here for seduction, so don't bother trying to insult me by insinuating that I am."

He stares at me in silent challenge, his mouth compressed in an irritated line.

I attempt to appeal to his humanity. "Look, I *need* to make it to the next trial. So, I'm asking you—please—if you'll lend me the dagger so I can advance."

He laughs, but it's not the jovial sound he usually makes. This is mocking, derisive. Dismissive.

"Why would I do that? From what I can tell, you've got no money to bribe me with, and unless your cunt is magical, you've got nothing to persuade me with. So best be on your way." He flicks his fingers toward the challengers' entrance to the arena and turns, heading toward a different doorway.

My pride stings. Fury rears its head. How *dare* he presume to judge me when he doesn't know me, has no idea what I've gone through, how I've gotten here, and why I'm doing this? And since he's *certainly* got secrets and goals of his own he likely wants to protect, wouldn't he go to extreme lengths to do just that? The gloves are off. He's too angry with me to be reasoned with. Blowing out a shaky breath, I brace myself for what I'm about to do.

"I know about Conrad," I tell him, just loud enough for him to hear, but not so loud that it carries.

He freezes mid-stride. He turns around slowly and stalks back toward me until he's only a foot in front of me. I have to resist the urge to back up when I catch sight of the virulent gleam in his eyes.

"You'll have to restate that," he murmurs. It's not a request. It's a distinct threat. It dares me to repeat it, to make it known.

Well, apparently, I'm a complete fucking idiot, so I lift my chin as I say, "I know about Conrad. About the half dozen during today's trial."

He's so still he could be carved from granite but then something changes. His forehead smooths, his brows lower, his posture softens, and he smiles lazily at me. "I have no idea what you're talking about. Half a dozen what? Lovers? Apples? You'll have to be more specific."

The difference between what I knew to be true just a few days ago and what I know now is astonishing, and I am one-hundred-percent certain that his easy, dim-witted arrogance is an act. He is hiding something he doesn't want found, and I intend to use that to my advantage. Emboldened by my irritation, I lean forward and look up at him through the curtain of my lashes flirtatiously.

"I think you do," I counter. "More importantly, I think I'm about to go speak to Lord Corvilian and Colonel Richter in front of thousands of onlookers, and to keep me from telling them exactly what I saw, you'll give me your dagger."

His expression is thunderous. If he could strangle me then and there in front of the arena without arousing suspicion, I'm positive he would. I lean into him further and wrap my arms around his waist. He stiffens in surprise until I step back from him, his dagger clutched in my right hand, and he stares at it, slack-jawed, but doesn't move to take it from me.

"As a sign of good faith," I say, tucking the dagger into my boot to stop the whispers that have already begun, "I'll be sure to return this to you after it serves my purpose."

His jaw tightens and his fists clench at his sides, but he says nothing. With a nod and a smile, I head toward the challengers' entrance to the arena.

The adrenaline coursing through me is exhilarating, but the whispers still linger despite tucking the dagger into my boot.

"How will I focus with this blade talking to me?" I reach out to Roan.

"The echo is of your blood. Like any echo, it fades when you stop calling," Roan says loftily.

I almost groan aloud. *"But I'm* not *calling it."*

"You call it with your very being. It is you who stirs it. It is your guidance that will quiet its voice."

"Are you telling me I just need to ask it *to stop?"* I ask skeptically. The whispers have grown in number and volume, and I'm beginning to feel surrounded in my own head.

Feeling foolish, I consider my request before I think the words, trying to mentally aim them at the dagger in my boot. *"Um, hello…I appreciate the help, but you're sort of loud right now, and I need to focus. Would you mind just…not talking?"*

The whispers stop.

"Un-fucking-believable," I mutter under my breath.

"What's that?" Stigander asks as he comes up behind me.

"Oh, nothing, just slowly losing my grip on reality," I say, staring at my boot.

He nods. "So a normal day then?"

"Precisely." I nod back.

It's not long before the arena fills with onlookers, the officers and leaders have assembled on the platform, and Colonel Richter is stepping forward to address the challengers and the crowd. I fidget nervously, avoiding looking in Rafe's direction lest I do something stupid, like give his dagger back or vomit all over my boots.

"Challengers, the day has come. The trial you were given was one of silence and strategy. You were asked not to outfight your opponent, but to outwit them. To observe. To deceive. To take.

"Today, you will reveal your target and present the item you have acquired to the Trial Panel—composed of Lord Corvilian, Major Berger, and me. You will be judged not only on what you acquired but the difficulty required to obtain it."

She pauses, scanning the crowd of challengers before her.

"Only fifteen of you will advance to the next trial. Fewer still will earn the distinction of a mentor. These officers—seasoned warriors accomplished in battle and command—will only offer guidance to those who have proven worth the investment." She gestures to Lord Corvilian and Major Berger. "Impress us. Not with your strength or speed or charm. But with your cleverness. Your control.

"Present your item, and remember—failure in this challenge is akin to exposure. And in war, exposure is deadly."

My stomach tightens with anxiety. What in the name of the Blessed Sisters had I been thinking? Blackmailing Rafe Kriegeur was foolish enough. Doing it for the trials? Madness. I don't know what scares me more: that he didn't simply take the dagger back or that he could still expose my failure.

And now I have to stand before the judges, in front of everyone. Speak. Explain myself. Be watched, listened to, scrutinized. It's almost as bad as having to sing.

Where's a löwenard ready to maul you when you need it?

I steal a glance at the platform, looking at the judges, and can feel the weight of Lord Corvilian's stare already, as sharp as the dagger in my boot. Just waiting for me to stumble so he can twist it.

I watch as challenger after challenger presents their items. Many are impressive. Stigander has stolen one of Major Berger's prized dueling gloves. Dagmar managed to swipe Colonel Richter's personal journal. Other cadets nicked Lieutenant Becker's signet ring, Captain Algere's watch, and even Captain Schuster's dress sword. How they handled hiding the sword, I'll never guess.

Conversely, many cadets have failed to bring an impressive item or simply failed to bring one at all. A patch of uniform cloth. An empty wine bottle. A spare boot. A spoon.

Lord Corvilian couldn't hide his disdain at that one. "Tell me, challenger," he had said, "do you mean to feed your pride with this? It will need it after such a disappointment." I spared a wince in sympathy.

Berte is among the several who were unable to acquire an item, and she's dismissed when she presents herself empty-handed, eliminated from the tournament.

I'm last. And it's finally my turn.

Swallowing hard, I climb the platform and stand before the panel.

"Lord Corvilian, Colonel Richter, Major Berger," I bow to each one, taking care to really lay it on thick for Lord Corvilian.

"Challenger de Veend, who was your target?" Major Berger asks.

The wind wielder waits for me to begin speaking so she can amplify my voice for the crowd. My eyes flit briefly to Rafe, who stares at me in silent recrimination. I hear my own voice reverberate through the arena as I say, "My target was Lieutenant Colonel Ranulf Kriegeur."

The crowd begins buzzing like a stirred beehive. Whether with admiration or anticipation of a spectacular failure, I'm not yet certain. Perhaps they're looking to be impressed by my acquired item. Or perhaps they're hoping to witness the lion of Fracidaem maul the woman who dared steal from his son, even if it was my mission.

Colonel Richter says, "Present your item."

I hesitate, my eyes darting to Rafe once more before I say, "I stole a kiss."

The entire arena erupts in cheers, jeers, raucous whoops, and suggestive whistles. My face turns bright red. Dread fills me as I look to where Aric is sitting, and his stony gaze alternates between me and his cousin. I hadn't even considered *those* repercussions when I decided to put my conquests on such public display. I thought if I gave Rafe this— open myself up to the ridicule of the judges and the crowd, maybe he won't expose that I failed.

Lord Corvilian lets out a short bark of laughter. "I'd hardly consider that an accomplishment, knowing my son's reputation, Cadet."

Still with the "cadet" instead of "challenger." The prick.

I smile tightly, wanting to make the man eat his words. I flash what I hope is an apologetic glance at Rafe before I bend down, pulling the dagger from my boot in a single, smooth motion. I hold it up for the judges and crowd to see. "Then how about this? 'Rosamunde,' I believe he calls her."

If I could capture the expression on Lord Corvilian's face for posterity, I would. The shock is so exaggerated it's comical. Major Berger and Colonel Richter look equally surprised, their eyes meeting in some sort of silent communication. Major Berger then turns a sly eye toward Rafe, but he's assumed his typical oafish expression.

"What can I say?" Rafe says to the panel, his voice amplified by the nearby wind wielder. "If a pretty woman wants to get her hands in my trousers, who am I to stop her?"

He turns toward me and smirks as the crowd roars with laughter. I feel my free hand fist into the fabric of my trousers, and I look down at the wooden platform beneath my boots. While I might deserve his scorn, I'm unsure if public humiliation is proportional to my offense. Although I suppose he's also humiliated—a warrior of supposed unparalleled skill, having his prized item stolen and bandied about.

"Thank you, Challenger," Major Berger nods to me. She then turns to the group of challengers waiting below the platform. "We will deliberate and speak with the mentors and make our announcements shortly."

I scurry off the platform, eager to melt into the crowd and attempt a little anonymity. The way the other challengers part to make way for me disabuses me of any hope that I might blend in, though. I wait beside Stigander and Dagmar as the judges confer on the platform.

"That was a bitch of a steal, de Veend," Stigander grins.

He smiles so rarely that I find myself returning it. "You're telling me. But how did you get Major Berger's glove?"

We trade stories about stalking our targets, laughing at how ridiculous we felt. Dagmar declines to share her own secrets regarding her search, remaining quiet. When Major Berger steps up to the front of the platform, we fall silent with unease and anticipation.

She says, "The judges have deliberated. The following challengers will progress to the next trial: Brevic, Spengler, Schmidt, Peterssohn, Waldner, Schwarz, Frölich, Feltdgg, Langer, Wizer, Rötlin, Seiler, Wilhelms, Marcher, and de Veend. Please move to the front of the arena floor for mentor selection. The remaining challengers are eliminated and should exit to the stands."

She called my name.

She called my name!

Stigander, who also made it through, claps a large hand on my back in excitement, nearly knocking me over, and manages to do the same for Dagmar, who stands to the side looking bored. Of course, she was going to make it through after managing to steal something from Colonel Richter.

When the fifteen challengers remain in the arena's center, Colonel Richter steps forward to address us.

"Challengers, the mentors have watched your performance in the trials, have seen your capabilities. Now it's time for those abilities to be recognized. Mentors are authorized to oversee specialized training—including weapons, combat techniques, tactical exercises, and other disciplines intended to prepare their charges for the remaining trials.

"Mentors may requisition their challengers for individual training up to three times per week, not to exceed four hours per session. A mentor may pull a challenger from regular work or training, which must be justified and recorded.

"Mentors are not permitted to interfere or provide direct assistance during the official trials. Any attempt to manipulate the outcome of a trial will result in, at minimum, immediate elimination from the Freiheit."

She turns to the group of officers ready to select their charges. "Remember, mentors. Should your challenger win, you will receive a posting of your choice—subject to approval. So, choose wisely, train well, and remember that your challenger's failure is yours."

The officers come forward one by one and name their chosen challengers. Major Berger selects Stigander, impressed with his ability to steal from her. The other officers name their selections until only Aric is left to name his choice. My heart pounds so hard it feels like my entire body is vibrating. I don't have any reason to believe that Aric will choose me. I'm certainly not the most physically accomplished challenger. And I'm unsure what I am to him—a fling, a moment of weakness he regrets? He was tender with me earlier, more than I would have expected, but now he's heard what I did in the trial to advance.

For a moment, though, I allow myself to hope. Because if he were to choose me as his challenger, and he has permission to train me, it could be the additional advantage I need to advance through the competition. I might even have a fighting chance at—

"I choose Challenger Brevic," he says firmly.

The pounding of my heart doesn't stop. No, it just becomes jagged and sharp instead, slicing through me like so many blades. Heat pricks the back of my eyes, but I blink it away. Stupid. I was stupid to hope. Of course, he wouldn't choose me—not after our arguments or what he found out I did with Rafe. Clearly, he's not immune to more base human emotions. Like envy. And bruised pride. Otherwise, he'd not punish me like this—by choosing silence over guidance. Maybe it's not fair to hope for such ready acceptance, but it stings.

It's official. I don't have a mentor.

I catch the pitying glances exchanged between Stigander and Major Berger, standing near one another, but I force a smile in return, hoping it's enough to disguise my humiliation. That what I've done and endured still hasn't been enough to compel someone to help me.

I'm trying to quell the rising tide of hopelessness that threatens to pull me under when Lord Corvilian rises from his seat and addresses the crowd.

"After due consideration," he says, his gravelly voice unhurried but calculating, "I've elected to appoint one additional mentor."

A ripple of surprise cascades across the crowd of challengers and onlookers.

He continues. "This particular challenger demonstrated a level of cunning I found…impressive. And I am compelled to provide them with the opportunity to continue to impress me. Therefore, Lieutenant Colonel Kriegeur will mentor Challenger de Veend."

CHAPTER THIRTY-FIVE
Mentor? Hardly Know Her

The excited chatter filling the arena is deafening. After Lord Corvilian's announcement that the handsome, deadly Lieutenant Colonel Kriegeur will mentor me, the challenger who stole a kiss and his dagger, the onlookers are all champing at the bit. I, for one, haven't moved from my spot on the arena floor. I'm frozen in place, like I'm rooted to the dirt.

Of course. Of fucking course he's my mentor now.

Nothing screams "ideal mentor-mentee relationship" like having your tits in a man's mouth and then blackmailing him.

My stomach flips violently, as if it can't decide whether to churn from embarrassment or something far more dangerous. I can't even look at Aric, though I swear I can feel his stare boring into the side of my face like a hot poker.

I look to the platform and catch Lord Corvilian watching me. There's glittering, venomous triumph in his eyes, a satisfaction he doesn't even bother to conceal. Victory. Damnation.

He did this on purpose. Not because he believes I'm cunning. Not because he thinks Rafe would be a good mentor. No, he wanted to watch me squirm. To see if the gutter trash girl would grovel when the noble lord tightens the noose.

And maybe…maybe to punish Rafe, too, which lands in my gut with a sick twist. Lord Corvilian doesn't look upon his son with approval. It's the same cold contempt I've seen him wear when looking upon me. As if his son's very existence is offensive.

Because he resents him for what he isn't. For not having magic. As if it were a choice to make.

I consider the way Rafe jokes and smirks, the way he is always full of bravado, of arrogance. Is it a front for his secrets or armor against the father who despises him?

A flicker of sympathy rises in me, uninvited and unwelcome. With it, too, memories of belonging. The warmth of my mother's soft palm brushing my hair back from my face. The sound of my father's voice as he sang. The feeling of arms wrapped tight around me. I have few precious memories of my parents, but that they loved me, I am completely certain.

And because of that, I look to where Rafe sits and feel pity. I wonder if he's ever known what that feels like.

I hurry to the platform steps and take them two at a time to reach him. I'm a few feet away when Lord Corvilian steps into my path.

"Cadet de Veend," he says pompously, "I hope you recognize the advantage I've given you."

I look into his glittering dark eyes and wonder if there's a way I could fake falling and "accidentally" knee him in the groin, just to see the look on his face.

Instead, I bow and say, "My thanks, my lord, for the opportunity."

He looks down his nose at me. "I look forward to seeing what you can learn from my son. Do try not to fall on his lap in the meantime."

I feel my face heat at his words, a physical manifestation of the shame flooding my being.

My scalp tingles. *"Shame is not something given—it is something claimed, and only when you believe it to be true. You've no reason to claim what isn't yours,"* Roan tells me.

His voice sounds irritable, but I know he isn't upset with me. I'm fairly certain there might be visions of a great eye pecking floating through his mind.

"*No…not of the eyes,*" Roan says wickedly, and I have to keep myself from grinning lest Lord Corvilian think I've gone insane.

A large hand clamps around my upper arm and pulls. I barely have time to squeak a protest as Rafe drags me across the platform, as far from his father as physically possible without falling off the side.

"What did he say to you? And you to him?" He demands without preamble.

"Not much, just that he hopes I don't waste the advantage he gave me. He's forcing you to do this, isn't he?" I try to change the subject so I don't have to tell him what else his father said.

Rafe stares at me for several moments, as if gauging whether or not I'm telling him the truth, but then he bends down, takes his dagger from inside my boot, and stalks off.

"Wait, when are we training?" I call to him.

"Greta," I turn to face Aric, who has come up behind me on the platform.

The crowd has thinned out considerably, most onlookers returning to their duties, and the officers and leaders are already parading toward the citadel.

Aric asks, "What did he say to you?"

I'm beginning to feel like I'm in some kind of repetitive nightmare.

I sigh. "Who? Lord Corvilian or Rafe?"

"Either. Both. I asked to be your mentor," he tells me.

My head snaps up. "You did?"

"I want to protect you. Lord Corvilian denied my request. Probably because of this harebrained scheme he cooked up with Rafe," he says tightly.

I frown. "I'm not defending his regular behavior, but I don't think Rafe had anything to do with this particular scheme. And I appreciate the gesture, but it doesn't really help me understand how my mentor can help me, except maybe with training."

"We're supposed to work with you to train your strengths and bolster your weaknesses, physically and mentally. Mentors have a vested interest in their challenger winning because they get a different post if they do, so they choose the ones with the best chance of succeeding. So usually they want to work with you. To help you improve," he explains.

Something warm tingles in my chest. "Do you really believe I can win? That's why you wanted to choose me?"

Aric smiles at me and takes my hand. "I believe you *want* to win. And I want to keep you alive. Isn't that the same thing?"

Stung, I pull my hand from his. "No, it's not."

"You're angry," He sounds surprised.

"I am," I confirm, crossing my arms across my chest.

He runs a hand through his hair. "Look, I…I also wanted to make amends. I feel like I've bungled this entire thing."

"What 'thing'?" I ask.

"Us," he replies.

I stare at him blankly. "There is no 'us.'"

He looks uncomfortable. "I know. And I suppose I can't expect anything when you've moved on."

I know he's referring to what he heard about me and Rafe. "Aric, that was the trial. I did what I had to do. He was my target."

He nods, looking unconvinced. "I can imagine the kiss was necessary, given what I know of Rafe."

I almost laugh maniacally at the mention of "the kiss." Thank the Sisters he doesn't know of anything else.

He forges ahead, "I realized, though, that I was hiding behind duty for my own emotional safety."

"I don't know what to say," I admit, shaking my head.

He adds, "Say you'll give it a chance. I can picture it, Greta. A life where you're safe, honored, where no one can hurt you again. Where you can be with your sister. I can give you that if you're willing to try. To come to know each other. If you can trust me."

As I consider his words, how it would even be possible, my scalp tingles. I hear an inelegant snort in my mind.

"*What do you find so objectionable?*" I ask Roan.

"*He would guard you fiercely, fledgling, but only to bind your wings to the ground where he feels safe. It is a tragedy to see something made for the sky offered only a gilded cage. And sadder still when the one offering believes it a kingdom."*

Unsettled, I ask, *"What do you mean 'meant for the sky'?"*

He responds cryptically, *"Even fledglings must stay the branch awhile, gathering their strength. The sky will not be lost to you. Only when you go, make certain it is by your own wings and no tether leashed to your foot."*

"I don't understand. And I don't know what to do," I tell him.

"Choice is one of the greatest gifts bestowed upon man," he says, *"A bloom that unfurls in its own season. It is no gift to tear it open before its time, nor any kindness to force it to flower for another's comfort. You need not decide anything presently."*

"Where did you go just now?" Aric asks, breaking through my conversation with Roan and bringing me back.

"Just thinking," I answer. "And, Aric…I need more time for that. For thinking. To focus on the Freiheit, on my sister. On staying alive. I'm not sure the best way to do it all, but… I'll figure it out. When I'm ready."

It's the first time I've said such words aloud—to him or anyone— and as I do, I realize they're actually true. I do need time. To breathe, to think, to fight for myself and for Agnethe without the weight of someone else's heart in my hands. I don't know if I have space for the ache of another person's disappointment when I'm still clawing my way toward my own survival. The Freiheit isn't over.

Aric steps back, nodding solemnly. "I understand. Just…let me know if you need help. Or need me to talk to Rafe. You know he's required to spend a certain amount of time with you as a mentor."

I nod. "Thank you."

He turns and walks away, disappointment evident in the stiffness of his shoulders, the way the corners of his mouth turn downward, the way his eyes are cast toward the ground.

I hate seeing it—like I've just taken something delicate he trusted me to hold and smashed it into a million pieces. But I placed it down gently, knowing I can't carry his hopes and mine right now. It isn't cruel. It's honest.

The burn of guilt is real, but so is the flicker of relief. Maybe choosing yourself always stings. I wouldn't know, because it's the first time I ever have. Something about that, though, feels good despite the ache. Feels right.

A pleasant warmth flows across my scalp, down my neck, along my arms, and I know that Roan is sharing his pride in me. His support. It's one of the best feelings I've had in a long time.

"You carry the storm well, fledgling. It does not break you—it crowns you."

I'm on work duty in the forge that afternoon, finishing my shift. It's the most content I've felt during work duties at Stachtenbaste, probably because it's the most familiar. The heat wraps around me like a thick, occlusive blanket. The air is heavy with the scent of scorched metal and smoke and the comforting tang of sweat and soot and singed wool that reminds me of the forge at home. Sparks leap from the anvil with every hammer strike, bright against the dim glow of the hearth. It's a sight I've witnessed many times since I was small, tucked in the corner of my uncle's forge, listening to the sound of him shaping the world.

There's a steadiness here that none of the other work duties at Stachtenbaste offer. There are no screaming officers, no bruises from surprise blows, no blood, no tears, no slimy potato skins. Just heat and focus and the endless breath of the bellows and the churn of muscle. I know the sounds—the hiss of quenched steel, the satisfying ring of struck metal.

The bladesmith, Werner, was very excited to learn I had experience in a forge, but disappointed when I told him I did mostly administrative things. I told him I was willing to try more, though, so I tend the fires, manage the wood supply, work the bellows, take inventory of the metal stock, lay out tools, and sort repairs for sharpening.

My tunic sticks to my back, sweat drips into my eyes, but I have purpose. Heating billets, watching the metal glow the right shade of orange before pulling it free and bracing it for the strike. It's hard labor, and I know my body will pay for it later, but I feel useful here. Like I belong. The metal doesn't care who your parents were or whether you sang your way past a beast or kissed a man for a knife. All you have to do is withstand the heat, try not to disintegrate, and make something of what's left.

The forge can't protect me from what's coming. But while I'm here, sweating and blinking away smoke, I can almost believe I'm still at home. I'm still Greta de Veend. Not a prisoner, a cadet, a challenger. Still my grandmother's companion, my sister's guiding force.

I run a broom across the flagstones, gathering as much of the coal dust, metal shavings, ash, soot, and gods know what else from the floor as I can. Werner runs a neat forge, but smithing is dirty work. I can feel the grit beneath my boots as I move along the stones. A fine black haze lifts with every stroke, clinging to my clothes and hair.

Werner bustles into the main room of the forge from one of the back workrooms, carrying a bundle of metal in his wiry arms. You'd never know he's a smith from looking at him, as slight as he is, but the thinness of his frame belies a strength borne of years of working with his hands and arms.

"Sort the lot," he grunts, dropping the bunch with a clatter onto a workbench. "Remelt to the left. Shite to the right for discard or barter. Separate anything cracked, rusted, or too thin. Not worth the fire; we'll trade it."

I nod, setting the broom aside, and begin sorting through the pile of metal, trying to avoid getting cut on any sharp edges. Most of the metal seems salvageable, but near the bottom of the pile, I stumble across a broken blade that looks odd. It has the same unusual veining as Rafe's krahbek blade, the kind that looks like feathers. But unlike his blade, it's flat, darker, almost like it's dead. I don't hear any of the whispers when I run my finger along it.

Frowning, I turn to Werner. "What kind of metal is this?"

He shuffles over toward me and peers over his grimy spectacles. "Oh! Now that's a find! Stahlvend by the look of the veining."

"I'd not heard of Stahlvend until recently," I tell him.

"It's rare now," he says, "but once, the Aurengarte wouldn't carry anything else. Until the formula vanished."

"Vanished?" I ask innocently. This was more than Roan had told me.

He nods. "Died with the last in a family line. A descendant of the original inventor."

I'm suddenly very glad I didn't tell Werner my surname, or this conversation would be much more awkward. But a memory stirs at his last words.

"The inventor? Who was it?"

"Joceran de Veend. Name ring a bell?" He asks, watching me over his spectacles.

"No," I lie quickly.

He grunts. "Didn't figure. Old name. Lützenclaste. Shame about the formula."

"It looks different from the Stahlvend I've seen before." I frown, running my finger along the veining.

"Because it's broken, girl. Didn't you say you worked in a forge?" Werner asks tartly.

"Yes, but why does it matter that it's broken? What should I do with it?" I ask him.

"Salvage it, for tools, hinges, maybe armor fittings. Things you can fashion from the metal as it is. But not weapons," he clarifies, gathering the sorted metal from the workbench.

"Why not weapons?"

He says, "Stahlvend can't be remelted, reforged. Once the veining breaks, it loses its integrity. Won't be as it was before."

I suppose he's decided he's done teaching me about Stahlvend, because he hurries off to the back rooms again, leaving me to puzzle the broken blade in front of me.

I reach for Roan. *"I want to talk about all of this. This Stahlvend stuff. What it means for me. If Joceran invented Stahlvend, didn't you know about it? Weren't you there?"*

"Endure a little longer, fledgling, and the winds will carry more than riddles. Survive this trial, and I will open the oldest pages of your story—those writ in raven's blood and bound in shadow."

Sighing, I sort the rest of the metal and then take my leave to find Rafe for whatever in the name of the Sisters he's decided to do for my training. The only blessing about this training is the abbreviated work duties for several hours, multiple times a week.

I trek across the inner bailey, down the stairs from the outcropping to the training yards, and decide to try the officers' training yard first. Something tells me that Rafe won't want his forced mentoring to be as public as it would be in the cadet training yards.

The sun has begun its afternoon descent from its highest point, and though it still rests above the fortress walls, the angle casts long shadows over certain parts of the training yards. Units of cadets are sparring in the upper training yard, and the rhythmic thud of practice weapons hitting dummies reaches my ears, as familiar now as any melody.

When I reach the gate to the officers' training yard and peer inside, I find my instinct was correct. Rafe leans against the wall like he's posing for a portrait, one ankle crossed lazily over the other, a tankard of what looks like ale in one hand—the gentle afternoon breeze tugs at the dark waves of his hair.

I shouldn't find it appealing, but I'm also not blind.

I open the gate and enter the training yard, relieved to see it's empty of all but us. I send a prayer of thanks to the gods that there won't be anyone here to witness what will surely be my humiliation.

I stop in front of Rafe, and he peruses my form indolently from head to toe. "What, did you fall into a fireplace?"

Flushing, I reach up and wipe my cheeks, wincing when they come away with soot. I run my hands down my uniform, hoping to clear some of the dust from it, but the grime just smears instead of brushing off.

I shake my head and shrug my shoulders, feigning a casualness I don't feel. "I was working in the forge. I didn't have time to change."

He doesn't answer, just takes a sip from his tankard, closing his eyes when the breeze brushes his face once more.

I shift impatiently. "So, you're my mentor."

He opens one eye and stares at me, but doesn't respond.

"Aren't you going to mentor?" I ask him.

He raises his tankard in a mock toast. "Are you sure you want it? Seems you prefer other physical pursuits, if I recall correctly. I'm certain my stick-in-the-mud cousin would be all too happy to assist you in that."

I gnash my teeth together in frustration. "I need to be ready for the trials."

"Then get ready," he shrugs. "No one's stopping you."

"What am I supposed to do first?" I huff.

"I don't give a fuck," he says. He slides down the wall until he sits on the ground and leans his head back against the stone wall. "I'm required to be here, but what I do while here is none of your concern, and what *you* do here is none of mine."

I turn without another word, pulse pounding in my throat, and head for the equipment shed. If he's trying to punish me, to make me angry, it's working. The worst part is, he's not wrong to be angry with me. I did use him. Blackmail him. But I'd hoped for icy resignation, not this infuriating insouciance.

I yank open the equipment shed, still surprised when I see real weapons instead of the wooden practice ones I'm used to. Weapons with actual blades, sharpened to deadly precision, gleaming in the shafts of sunlight that pour in through the open door. I reach for a krahbek—nothing fancy, just standard issue steel and wood—but I immediately register the difference. The balance is nothing like the wooden stand-ins I've practiced with before. This has weight and consequence, and the head of the weapon pulls forward with every shift of my wrist. I choke up on the pole arm to gain better control, shut the equipment shed door behind me, and stalk toward one of the practice dummies in the yard.

My first strike is an overhead chop meant to split the dummy's chest, but the momentum carries faster than I expect, and the blade buries deep into the straw with a jolt that vibrates up my arms and into my shoulders. I have to yank it free, and even that's awkward. The angle is all wrong. I return to position, plant my feet shoulder-width apart, and then attempt a thrust with the spear tip, lunging forward. But it veers wide as I overcompensate this time for the weight. The haft dips too soon, and I nearly stumble forward, teeth clicking together, heart thudding in frustration.

I try to hook the neck—an impressive move when it's done right, but my arc is clumsy, my movements jerky. The metal scrapes across the shoulder but doesn't catch. My fingers are slippery with sweat, my head is beginning to pound, but I adjust my stance and clench my jaw, determined to land some kind of blow that looks remotely like I know what I'm doing. I spin and bring the axe blade around in a broad, sideways cleave, but the flat of the blade connects with the dummy, shaking the frame and knocking me askew in the process.

"Pathetic form. Are you trying to wound it or make love to it?" Rafe calls from his lounge spot on the ground.

Exasperated, I throw my free hand up in the air. "Then come help me! Tell me what I'm doing wrong."

He stands slowly, brushing the grass from his trousers and drains the rest of his tankard. For a moment, I think he will actually oblige and come help.

After a good three minutes of him preening, he looks at me with a falsely apologetic expression. "I don't hand out favors to those who threaten me. And you don't seem half eager enough to deserve it anyway."

My muscles ache, my temper is fraying, and the weight of everything—my guilt, my pride—clings to me as determinedly as the forge's soot. I stare at him incredulously until the rage floods through my system so rapidly, I swear I can almost see red.

"Not eager?" I ask, moving in his direction. "*Not eager?*" I repeat, my voice rising as I approach him.

I'm not sure what he sees in my face, but the huge man steps back from me as I stalk forward, and I follow, until his back presses to the stone wall. I'm so close to him we're nearly touching, the krahbek in my hand a threatening promise.

"You think I don't want it enough? I didn't crawl into this fucking *bloodbath* for the thrill of it. I entered this cursed tournament for one reason—the sliver of a chance to save my sister from a monster.

"I don't have the luxury of pride or indulgence or wondering whether I seem eager enough to satisfy some invisible standard I can never hope to meet.

"Only those privileged with choice dare question the desperation of those who have none.

"It's my ability you should be sneering at, not my motivation—and even that won't stop me."

I hoist the krahbek into both hands and turn, marching back to the practice dummy. With a frustrated scream, I spin, arc the blade, and slice the head off the dummy in one motion.

The only sound in the training yard is the dull thud as the dummy's head hits the ground. I turn to look at Rafe, my chest heaving with unspent anger, and find him watching me with an unreadable expression.

"Better," he says. "Do it again."

CHAPTER THIRTY-SIX
Bridges Burned and Lessons Learned

I enter the room alone.

No, not a room. A hall. It seems to stretch forever, lit by chandeliers so intricate, they resemble falling sunbeams—gold filigree draped with twinkling crystal. Each candle flame flickering from it is just slightly…off. The light is too yellow, too sharp. The glow makes my eyes ache.

I take one cautious step, then another, my boots sounding hollow against the marble floor, their soles slipping on alabaster veined with gold—lightning caught mid-strike. I try to avoid the golden wax dripping to the floor from the chandeliers above.

A hot splash strikes my shoulder. I startle, reaching up to brush the thick substance away. My fingers pull back, smeared with red.

Another drop hits my cheek.

Another in my hair.

A slow, rhythmic shower, as if the chandeliers themselves bleed.

I look up. The candlelight is gone. In its place: red seeping from within the gold filigree, trickling from hidden seams, from tapers that no longer burn. Far above, beyond the glittering gilt, something watches. Listens. Coiled just beyond knowing.

It is not behind me nor before me, but everywhere—in the corners of my mind, in the cracks in my consciousness. It finds me in the hush between breaths, the pause between footsteps. It presses against my skin. Suffocating.

The shadows begin to drift into the room. From the edges of the hall, they stir—curling across the marble like inky water, swallowing gold, dimming light. No sound. Only the oppressive darkness, spreading too steadily to escape.

Ahead, on a raised dais, lies a figure.

A woman, her back to me. A gown of molten gold pools beneath her like blood. The golden waves of her hair tumble to the marble floor. One pale hand stretches forward, as if reaching for escape that never came.

But she's still.

The shadows billow, teeming with menace, chilling me to my core. I reach the dais, stumbling up the steps, hands outstretched toward the fallen woman. The cold bites my skin, crawls up my wrists.

Seeking.

I touch her shoulder. I turn her, dreading what I'll find—that it's Agnethe. That I'm too late to save her.

But it isn't Agnethe. At least, I can't be certain it's her.

For there is no face at all. Only bone stares back at me. And on its brow, a crown, its metal warped and melting. From its sagging points—blending with melted gold, blood drips steadily, running along the curve of the skull, staining the fissures in the bone. Staining my fingers.

A gruesome portrait of finery and ferment, met in ruin.

Panicked, I try to wipe the blood from my hands, but the skin flakes away, exposing veins pulsing with red, with gold, with black beneath.

I stumble back from the figure, tripping over my skirts and something else in the process. I reach into the shadows and draw forth a golden scepter.

Even as I hold it, the gold begins to melt. It drips down my wrists, my feet—but there is no pain. Only a cold so chilling it numbs my very thoughts. The gilded pommel becomes obsidian snath, and the jeweled crown becomes curved heel arcing into gleaming blade, the surface rippling with feather-like veins.

A scythe.

The whispers crash into me—nothing and everything at once, heavy with treachery and promise. Pressure builds in my skull. Ice races across my skin.

I plunge the blade into my own throat.

And all goes silent.

I wake from my dream slowly, this time. Not with a sudden jolt of alertness but a gradual awareness that spreads across my mind, then my limbs, until my eyes are wide open in the early morning light filtering through the dormitory windows.

I could try to steal another hour of sleep, to see if the exhaustion can chase away the memory of the haunting dream. But the crawling sensation beneath my skin, the agitation I feel down to my bones, tells me that any additional rest would be a long time coming.

Sighing quietly, I tiptoe out of bed and the dormitory and start my morning routine of bathing and dressing. As autumn makes its presence known with each passing day, the water continues to decrease in temperature, and my baths have gotten progressively shorter. Lotti is right that the chill does help clear the last cobwebs of sleep from your brain, but I'm not sure it's worth the teeth-chattering cold that remains long after I've exited the water.

I dress quickly with numb fingers, fumbling as I shove my feet into my boots and yank my too-tight tunic over my head. I wince at the pull across my breasts, but as my other uniforms are being laundered since the forge leaves me covered in soot at the end of each day, it can't be helped. I traipse down the stairs and out of the citadel, heading toward the training yard, hoping one of the officers has already entered their training yard so I can slip in. The Freiheit challengers with mentors have been granted permission to use the superior, cordoned training yard for trial preparation. A fact for which I'm grateful since it allows me to practice in front of fewer people and with actual weapons.

I haven't tried to return since training with Rafe four days ago. I haven't seen him since then either. Not that I'm counting or anything. But I've been looking out of the corner of my eye for his hulking form, listening for that teasing voice, half expecting, half hoping to see him appear in the training yard to pull me away, as other mentors have done with their challengers. But the dismissal, silent as it is, is deafening.

He was still cutting that day, even after he told me to keep going. Still sarcastic. Still barely seemed to care. And even though I know I did what I felt I had to, I also can't blame him. I handed him a reason to hate me but still flinched when he took it.

Still, he helped me. Barely. Gave me pointers on my stance, my balance. Advised me on how to hold the real krahbek to keep it in line. He didn't have to do any of that; he could've stayed by the wall and done nothing. He certainly didn't do it with kindness. But it was something at least.

Now however, I'm not sure what to do, because I haven't seen him, and he hasn't sought me out. And I don't know if I'm more afraid to face him or never to see him again at all.

Because what horrifies me isn't his anger. It's this aching, humiliating truth sitting in my gut: that despite what I told Aric—about not being ready, about wanting to focus on the tournament, about needing space— my body is telling a different story. My thoughts are screaming discipline and strategy, but my mouth, my skin, the rest of me…well, it isn't listening.

Every time I think of what happened between me and Rafe—the heat of his hands on me, the look in his eyes as he stared at me, the sound of his voice as he pleasured me, I feel it. That sharp, unbearable, unmistakable desire. Curling low and hot but uninvited.

I'm not supposed to be thinking about sleeping with the man I blackmailed. I'm not supposed to want anything but survival. But it's there. Raw and persistent and humiliating in its truth.

To my relief, when I approach the gate to the officers' training yard, it's slightly ajar, which means at least one person is using it, but I push through the opening, resigned to the fact that someone will witness my ineptitude.

When I see Rafe standing with his back to me, I back into the shadows cast by the walls, sorely tempted to turn and flee.

He hasn't spotted me yet and doesn't know I'm watching. In truth, I'm not sure if he'd care even if he did, but I don't want to risk alerting him since I can't look away.

He moves through positions with his krahbek like it's an extension of his body. Fluid. Controlled. Merciless. His hands shift between grip positions effortlessly, blade slicing through the chilly air, each strike punctuated by a thud on the dummy absorbing the blow. It's not just that he uses the krahbek. He commands it.

The rising sun catches the glisten of sweat on his back, the sharp lines of his broad shoulders, the curve of his spine as he pivots.

My throat goes dry.

His raw athleticism impresses me—the discipline, the power, the instinctive coil and snap of his body. There is a break in his rhythm periodically, though. A moment where he shifts his weight and a limp reveals itself. Subtle, but there. An occasional hitch in his gait that's quickly buried by the next turn, the next blow. I can't say that I've noticed the evidence of his supposedly permanent injury often, but it must not bother him much.

Or he's good at hiding it. Like so many other things, apparently.

I can't imagine what it must have been like, fighting through chaos and agony, only to wind up here. Exiled to an island full of inexperienced cadets. Relegated to being a glorified babysitter while the rest of the world forgets that once you were brave. Once, you were important. And then there's his father, who sneers in his direction, who looks at him like he's not worth the dirt beneath his boots. Who clearly thinks very little of his non-magical son.

Maybe I understand his irreverence, after all.

He spins in another strike, slicing through the entire torso of the dummy, cleaving it in two. I can't imagine he'll linger much longer with how thoroughly he's destroyed it. I should leave before he sees me.

"Enjoying the show, *künnle*?" He asks, reaching for a waterskin on the ground near the dummy. He turns to face me, the muscles of his sides heaving from exertion.

My face flames red. "My apologies, I couldn't sleep and thought I'd try to practice. I didn't mean to intrude."

"The yard is yours," he says as he gathers his things.

"You're not staying?" I ask him, frowning.

"No," he replies, curtly.

"If it's because of me, I'll leave—"

"It's not," he interrupts. "I'm simply done."

I watch as he approaches the gate directly by where I'm standing, his limp more evident now that he's finished training.

"When are we training next?" I blurt out.

He stops and stares at me. "I think you can manage on your own."

I sputter. "But—I thought you were required to do it?"

He snorts. "Sure. But I don't exactly see anyone following me around to check, do you?" He moves to the gate again, brushing against my arm as he reaches for it.

Doesn't he want to get a different post? To get out of here? Maybe he's content with his lot in life, but I'm certainly not.

Frustrated, I begin, "But what about—"

He bites out, "Don't. Push it. Greta."

I'm so surprised to hear him call me by my name—only the second time he's done so, the other under *very* different circumstances, that my mouth shuts abruptly. I watch him turn away again and wince.

"Wait," I tell him, reaching for his wrist.

His reaction is instantaneous. In a blur of motion, he twists, slamming me into the wall. I cry out in surprise and with the discomfort of my back hitting stone. He presses his entire body against mine, pinning my wrist above my head, caging me by bracing his other palm against the wall. His dark eyes glitter with cold warning.

"Ready to slip a knife between my ribs, *künnle?*" He asks, voice low, borderline seductive.

With my free hand, I push against his shoulder, but it's like trying to shove a house.

"No, you arse, I saw you limping. I wanted to help," I tell him, though my tone is decidedly unhelpful right now. It would be easier to still feel charitable if my backside weren't smarting from the impact against the wall.

He frowns and lets go of my wrist, but doesn't step back. "What?"

Suddenly nervous, I look away and start babbling. "My grandmother's hands often troubled her. She had arthritis, you see. I used to have the steward make her a poultice with comfrey; it would sometimes help her…" I trail off when my gaze drifts back to his.

There's something in his eyes as he watches me. Confusion, curiosity, wariness. I can't identify which. But it's almost like he doesn't believe I'd offer help without any other motive. I lick my lips anxiously, unsure how to react to his continued assessment. His eyes drift slowly to my mouth.

My heart starts pounding, and I feel short of breath. I try to take in several gulps of air as surreptitiously as possible, but he's so close that my breasts brush his chest, the heat of his body seeping in through my tunic. This time, his eyes flick to my breasts, and almost like he's just noticed how tight the fabric is pulled across them, his own breathing hitches. My nipples harden, and my stomach tightens in response.

His pupils are dilated when he meets my gaze again, and even without his body against mine, the stare alone would pin me in place.

"What's going on here?"

Mortification, oily and unpleasant, slides into my stomach when I hear Aric's voice. I jump in response and try to pull away from Rafe, but he doesn't budge.

"I fail to see how what my challenger and I do in our training sessions is any business of yours," Rafe says, giving me a last, long look before he turns away from me and faces his cousin, the picture of smug charm.

I step out from behind him to see Aric and Dagmar standing at the open gate. Aric's face is tight with reproach and displeasure. Dagmar's icy gaze flits curiously between Rafe and me and what looks like amusement threatens to crack her normally impassive expression.

"Training," Aric crosses his arms over his chest and raises an auburn brow. He looks between me and Rafe. I want to squirm, but manage to stay still under the weight of his stare.

Rafe smirks. "Oh, you know me, cousin. I believe in *hands-on* instruction."

My eyes go wide. I know he's trying to goad Aric, and from the looks of his furious expression, it appears to be working. I glance toward Dagmar, hoping for solidarity, but her lips press in a firm line and her eyes dance, her amusement barely containing itself. I'm not sure if her laughter is at my expense, Aric's, or both. The sight fills me with more embarrassment but also irritation.

"Now, *künnle*," Rafe turns to me, as if imparting some great wisdom. He holds up his krahbek. "Next time, don't be shy—get your hands all the way around the shaft. It responds best to certainty, so apply confidence and pressure in the right places."

I want to hit him. Can I hit him? As much as I know he's baiting Aric, he's also castigating me. I wonder exactly how much trouble I'd be in if I struck him.

Instead, I go for a verbal blow, turning toward him and smiling earnestly, like I'm eager to please. "I'll try, it's just so much smaller than I expected."

A snort sounds from Dagmar, but my eyes don't leave Rafe's face. I'm destined for disappointment if I thought he'd be angry at me for my remark. Because, instead, his smirk spreads and he almost looks…pleased?

I chance a glimpse at Aric, and he looks…less pleased, but also more confused about exactly what's going on, like he can't decide if Rafe and I are feuding or fucking.

Rafe says to me, "Until next time, *künnle*, keep practicing your grip." He turns to Aric. "Always a pleasure, cousin. Do let me know if you'd like to observe up close next time."

With that, he shoulders his krahbek and saunters off with a wink, only the slightest limp affecting his movements, unfazed by every stare watching him leave.

CHAPTER THIRTY-SEVEN
Stellan's Slumber

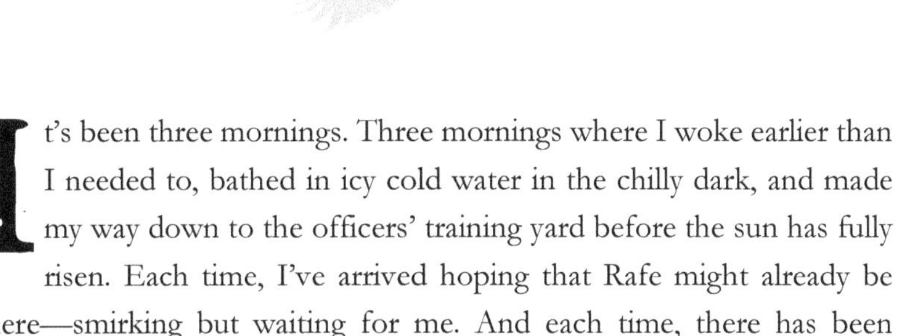

It's been three mornings. Three mornings where I woke earlier than I needed to, bathed in icy cold water in the chilly dark, and made my way down to the officers' training yard before the sun has fully risen. Each time, I've arrived hoping that Rafe might already be there—smirking but waiting for me. And each time, there has been nothing to greet me there except the practice dummies and the ache of ruined expectations.

Disappointment has settled into my lungs like a winter cough but matched—complicated—by a sliver of relief. If every encounter between us were going to feel like my entire body had been alit with flame and left to burn, then perhaps it would be better if I didn't see him. My nervous system isn't built for this kind of regular abuse. Now, one well-placed smirk or innuendo-infused comment and I'm just as liable to kiss him as I am to strike him.

I've only seen him twice since that morning when I'd last spoken with him. Once in the dining hall, from across the room, but only the back of his broad shoulders as they disappeared through the exit, while

I was frozen to the spot in the middle of the floor. The second was only yesterday, on the far side of the training yard, where he drilled a different unit in krahbek techniques. I caught just a glimpse of him turning, demonstrating some intricate strike, his voice jovial, face alit with humor. He didn't see me. Or at least, he didn't let on if he had.

To my everlasting surprise, I find I miss him. Not in the dramatic, longing sort of way of poetic love captured in novels. I missed the teasing, the way he gets under my skin without even trying. Lieutenant Broadbente is perfectly competent—good, thorough, direct—but he isn't even half as entertaining. Longbow drills blur together, my thoughts slipping at inopportune times when I should focus on footwork and bow height, on angle, and grip.

Given that I might need those techniques very soon so as not to die, this is less than ideal.

My only bright spot in the darkness of my own inner turmoil is Roan. I haven't found my human mentor, but I can always find my raven one. Or rather, we find each other. During those lonely mornings in the empty training yard, perched in the old chapel after lights out, or even just his voice finding me as I crawl into bed. We train when we can, through the bond and movement.

It's still new, our connection. Still unpredictable and unfamiliar, especially to me, but it improves each day. I am learning how to use the magic through instinct rather than dictation, how to react to the new abilities flowing through my limbs without panicking. Roan is patient, in his own, acerbic way, and he's proud when I get it right. There are moments now where I feel less like a drunkard fumbling through the dark and more like someone who is becoming what they were meant to be.

As I enter the Freiheit arena, though, all thought of that "becoming" leaves me in the face of fear. I don't know what this next trial will hold. None of the challengers or onlookers do, of course. The air in the arena is smaller, tighter. The stands are a fraction of their usual fullness, and only a handful of onlookers watch along with the officers, leaders, and mentors. The absence of spectators, alone, is enough to send a frisson of unease shivering down my spine. Whatever is about to happen, it doesn't need or want an audience.

I shift nervously on the dirt of the arena floor, rolling my shoulders to try to shake out the tension gathering there. My hands open and close, searching for an anchor to ground me, but finding none, so I begin digging my fingernails into the palms of my hands, letting the sting keep me focused on the here and now. I hate the anticipation before the knowing, like a pause before what I know will be a painful impact. There is too much time to wonder what will happen, whether I'm ready.

Stigander and Dagmar find me, standing beside me in silent solidarity. Neither is much of a talker, unlike Lotti and Otto, but their presence is a welcome comfort even so.

Colonel Richter steps forward on the platform, her gaze sweeping over the assembled challengers—only fifteen of us now—and the minimal onlookers. Her voice is calm, measured.

"Challengers, as you well know, any brute can swing a blade. But true soldiers are forged here," she taps her temple with two fingers. "In the mind. In the will. In the discipline to master not only your enemies, but yourselves. Today's trial is not of brawn, but burden. Not one of meaningless hurdles. But of fear. Longing. The blemishes you attempt to hide from the world and from yourselves.

"Today you will face what lies beneath. Not all of you will pass through unscathed. The challengers who overcome their obstacles with speed, clarity, and control will advance to the next trial. The rest will not.

"You might feel alone in what comes next. You are not, but this *is* a trial you endure alone. Only *you* will impact your advancement today. You and your strength of will."

She returns to her seat.

Major Berger steps forward with her usual flair. "Challengers, your trial today will be like a dream come true."

The crowd murmurs. The challengers look at one another in confusion.

She grins. "No, really. The fifth trial is dedicated to our god of dreams. Welcome to Stellan's Slumber! Challengers before me, you're still standing, still breathing. Well done! Just in time for a trip through the corridors of your own psyche. Today, you will not scale mountains, or leap across fire, or swim oceans—well, unless that's where your dreams take you.

"You will enter a potion-induced sleep designed to leave your body behind, but your mind…your mind will be thrust into the delightful theater of everything you fear, crave, and hate about yourself."

I don't need a trial to conjure nightmares. They come on their own, unbidden and merciless, piercing my consciousness when sleep dares take me. The idea of being forced back into my dreams, where my mind already turns against me, makes my stomach churn. For the past several nights, the same dream has tormented me: Agnethe, wasted away to bone on that dais, her empty eye sockets fixed on me with accusation. I've woken each time, nearly choking on the smoke and the awful fear that I'm already too late.

I don't know if I'm ready to see what else my mind hides. I don't want to know what this will dredge up and hold before me—like a mirror, but one I can't look away from. But there is no escape unless I forfeit. Forfeit Agnethe. My freedom. So I stand still, heart racing, dreading the coming dreams and the monsters they will unearth.

Major Berger says, "For your first obstacle in your dreams, you will face your fears, tossed headlong into three scenarios crafted from your deepest, most agonizing terrors. Real, imagined, remembered—the key is to endure, to overcome, and not be consumed by them."

I sense the challengers around me shifting nervously. It's one thing to be pitted against difficult obstacles, but the fears you've only *imagined* to be true? That is something truly terrifying.

I look to the officers' platform, unable to keep myself from looking for Rafe any longer, to see if he's at all affected by what I'm about to go through. To my disappointment, he's not in his seat. He didn't even show. For some reason, this is the thing that threatens to send my frayed emotions into tortured overdrive.

"In your second, dreamy obstacle," Major Berger continues, "it might get truly personal. You will be offered the object or objects of your strongest desire—power, love, freedom. And you must walk away. Refuse it. To crave is to be controlled."

I nearly grunt my agreement.

I look to where Aric sits on the platform, hair gleaming copper in the afternoon sun. He's leaned forward, elbows on his knees, his eyes on where I stand with Dagmar. Whether he's watching me or his charge, though, I'm not certain. I glance at Dagmar out of the corner of my eye. For once, she is not unaffected by Major Berger's description of the trials. Though subtle, the tightness around her mouth and eyes tells me she dreads the inner workings of her own mind just as much as I do.

"In your final obstacle in your dreamscape, you will face your worst enemy: yourself. You will be confronted with your greatest insecurities and weaknesses and be forced to destroy them to move forward, or they will destroy you."

Destroying my insecurities and weaknesses? Gods, I'll be here all day.

"Ten of you may advance. The ten who wake first will earn the right to face the next trial. The rest of you best pray you wake eventually with your minds intact," she says ominously.

They escort us to a part of the arena floor cordoned off by wooden fencing. Inside the fencing sit fifteen wooden platforms, and an attendant stands beside each one, holding a single glass vial of clear liquid. My palms start sweating as I near my platform and my blank-faced attendant. I'm almost tempted to flee, but the flap of dark wings near the top of the stands catches my eye, and I let the sight of Roan's form descending onto one of the upper benches steady me. I take several deep, shuddering breaths and climb onto the platform. The attendant hands me my vial, and I await Major Berger's signal.

"Challengers," she calls, "sweet dreams."

Before I can talk myself out of it, I down the potion, gagging when the bitterness hits the back of my tongue. I lie down on my platform, unsure how woozy it'll make me, how fast it'll take to work. When I'm on my back, I look into the stands, keeping Roan in my sights so he's the last thing I see before I fall asleep.

As my eyes grow heavy, movement catches my eye not far from where he perches. Seated alone on a bench all the way at the back is Rafe. I frown, wondering why he's not on the officers' platform, but then my eyes become so heavy I can't keep them open. My brain becomes so fuzzy I can't form regular thoughts.

I know no more.

I'm walking across the grounds of Stachtenbaste in the early morning. Mist as thick as wool clings to my legs as I trudge forward; the grass beneath my boots is slick. It feels like a normal morning at first, but something is off about the light. It glows without direction, pale and colorless. Like moonlight, but brighter. The air has a metallic tang, like I've bitten my tongue and can smell and taste the blood.

I crest a slope on the grounds and realize I'm in the livestock pasture. Below me, a cluster of goats graze in a lazy circle, but the longer I watch them, the more wrong they look. Their eyes glow faintly, a sickly yellow, and slitted vertically. Almost reptilian.

One raises its head and bares a mouth full of teeth no goat should have: jagged and serrated, like those in the maw of a wolf. Another stands with its front hooves turned backward, bent at grotesque angles as it chews, unconcerned. A third's limbs branch into twisted, antlered bone where hooves should be, clicking softly as it walks.

As if summoned by my gaze, *they all turn to look at me.* The air turns razor sharp as their heads lift in unison. For a breathless moment, they only stare. There are maybe a dozen in total, misshapen and glowy eyed, their bodies a parody of nature.

Then they move.

Without warning, they scatter and charge—not away, but toward me, hooves thundering across the sodden ground. The sound is wrong. It is not the rhythmic clatter of animals but a stuttering, jarring clack, like bone scraping across rock or teeth on iron. One bellows, a low shriek that tears through the mist. Another's jaw hangs open too wide, unhinged like a serpent's, rows of teeth gleaming, froth flying from its mouth.

I scream, stumbling back. I need to run; to run and flee back down the hill, away from the approaching stampede. My knees bend, ready to pivot in the opposite direction.

"*They are only memories,*" Roan's voice cuts through the fear, a tether in this twisted nightmare.

"They don't look like memories," I yell at him, too afraid to try to mind-speak to him.

"*Most fears do not. But they are phantoms of your mind. And the only way out is to go through.*"

Horrified, I gasp. "What?"

"*The only way forward is through the fear. Through them. When they charge you,* you charge back." His voice cuts through my panic like a knife.

I swallow hard, heart hammering. My instincts are telling me to turn and run. To wake up, to banish this place into nonbeing. The goats are coming fast—too fast. The slope is narrowing, boxing me in. Behind me is mist and ruin. In front of me, a storm of beasts straight from my nightmares. My legs quiver, and I can feel the memory of the beast that clamped down on my arm as a child. The goat in the pasture during the second trial that had lunged, its teeth grabbing my sleeve, tugging hard enough to rend the fabric, to wrench me off balance. I'd screamed in full-throated panic, and the moment I had, it had screamed back, gone rigid, legs locked straight. Then, it had toppled over in a dead faint, collapsing into the grass like a tipped-over statue.

Now, with these *things* bearing down on me like death with hooves, that same panic bubbles up my throat. I don't let it run away with me this time, though, barely holding on. I dig my mental hands into it, shape it. I grit my teeth, bend my knees, and run.

Not away. Toward.

The ground surges beneath me as I pick up speed, boots hammering against the grass, heart climbing into my throat, mist parting as my body cuts through it. The nearest goat rears up to meet me. I swerve toward it, face it directly, and scream. Raw. Guttural. Terrified. Angry.

Its front limbs stiffen, its back legs lock, and it topples, but barrels toward my legs, threatening to knock me down. When it reaches my legs, however, it dissolves against them into mist, disappearing.

Feeling ridiculous—ridiculously afraid and ridiculously angry—I charge into the fray, screaming like a madwoman, legs pumping, my breath burning in my throat. The next shrieks and explodes into mist as I tumble forward. Two more veer to flank me, but they, too, falter as I charge forward, dissolving as I press through.

I don't stop until, quite suddenly, the pasture is behind me. The goats are gone.

My gait slows, I suck in greedy lungfuls of air, and I stop for a moment, a laugh escaping me, breathless and a little wild. "A fainting fear. Who knew?"

Roan replies, "*Sometimes, fear is more fragile than it seems.*"

I nod and continue along the path, climbing yet another slope, not at all certain what to expect on the other side since my mind decided to treat me to monstrous farm animals. It's almost insulting, in a way. Has my life been so boring up until now that the greatest thing my fear-addled brain can conjure is animals that don't even have their upper front teeth?

When I crest the hill, the grass beneath my feet gives way, and before I can react, the world drops from my feet.

I fall hard and fast, tumbling through the evaporating mist and into shadow until I slam into something damp and unyielding. My breath leaves me in a ragged gasp, knocked from my lungs. The air here is stagnant and heavy. Quiet.

Then comes the skittering.

I sit up, dazed, only to feel a crawling sensation up my spine. Something cold and jointed moves across the back of my neck. Then another. And another. A low hiss enters the space, and the flicker of movement—everywhere—catches my eye, as light suddenly fills the cavern I've fallen into.

Spiders cling to jagged walls in trembling nests, black and glistening, their bodies swollen, twitching. Long-legged beetles swarm over my boots, climbing my calves. Ants bigger than my fingernails pour from cracks in the stone, flowing like water, rippling toward my hands. A centipede slithers across my knuckles, its needle-like legs brushing my skin in a hundred tiny pinpricks.

I can't breathe. Can't scream. My hands shake as I try to stand, finding my sleeves and hair matted with insects. A spider drops onto my shoulder, another onto my cheek. I reach up my hand to slap at it instinctively, but find my hand has frozen. Unable to defend myself, I must stand in place while the bugs teem over my body.

"Do not fight this with panic. If you hurt them or yourself, you remain. You must conquer your fear," Roan tells me.

"I-I can't!" I choke out, barely able to speak past the revulsion clogging my throat, not wanting to open my mouth lest they find their way in. My fingers itch to claw at my clothes, to rip them away, along with my hair and skin. "They're *everywhere!* How am I supposed to conquer this?"

"Fear need not vanish to be conquered. It need only obey. Let it walk beside you, not ahead of you."

"What do I do?" I ask him, my body trembling so violently, I'm sure I've shaken some of the bugs temporarily loose.

"Be still. Let them calm. Then move through anyway."

I close my eyes, shuddering. The feel of their legs—so many legs—crawling over me is enough to make me sob. Scream. But Roan is right. The more I move, the more they cling. I'm already covered in them. There is no version of this where I can emerge untouched.

There is only moving through.

I open my eyes. The light filling the cavern is coming from above. There is a ledge—a way out.

Taking a deep breath, I move forward slowly, consciously trying not to hurt any bugs. I raise my hands to grip the stone in front of me, teeth clenching as more pour down my back beneath my tunic. I fight the urge to brush them away, to slap, to stomp.

The climb is slow. Centipedes curl around my wrists. Spiderwebs catch my face like gauze. I'm shaking, but I don't stop. Don't scream. One handhold at a time. Then another.

"You are not your fear," Roan encourages. *"You own it; it doesn't own you."*

I reach the ledge at last, pulling myself to the surface above the cavern with strangled breath. As soon as my knees hit the ground above, the insects vanish. No scuttling, no crawling, no clicking.

Gone.

I collapse onto my hands and knees, waiting for my skin to no longer feel like it's moving. While convincing myself that I'm whole. Every brush of hair against my neck, my cheek, in the light breeze brings a new wave of fear, of disgust.

"*There is only through,*" Roan repeats. "*One remains.*"

I don't move from my position on all fours, but lift my head to see what I must face last. Churned earth and ash. The air is thick with smoke and the copper tang of blood. In the distance, thunder rumbles, but it's not the weather.

It's war.

I stagger to my feet, stumbling across a battlefield strewn with discarded weapons, fallen bodies, and banners burned to tattered pieces.

Then I hear it.

"Greta!" Cutting through the chaos like a blade, I would know that voice anywhere.

Agnethe.

She's collapsed among the detritus of battle, her gown stained with crimson, a jagged wound blooming across her chest. Her golden hair is matted with blood and dirt, her lips cracked as she gasps my name again.

My heart tears through my chest, and I scream, "Agnethe!"

Mud clings to my boots, weighing down my feet. The ground seems to stretch with each step, growing the space between us, no matter how fast I run. Screams rise from the field. Hands reach for me as I pass. Still I run toward my sister, breath burning in my chest, my hands outstretched.

Roan's voice cuts through my panic, "*You cannot reach her this way.*"

"She *needs* me, I have to—"

"*No, fledgling.*" His voice sounds as grief-stricken as I feel. "*You must confront the reality that you cannot save her with pure force of will. You must endure the grief, not surrender to it, to progress.*"

His words strike harder than any blade could. I falter and fall to my knees. The ground beneath me is wet and warm—too warm. Blood pools beneath my knees.

My sister still calls my name.

A sob catches in my throat. I crawl on my hands and knees in the direction of her voice. Not because I believe it will change anything, but because it is the last gift I can give her. And because I cannot bear not to.

She trembles in the mud, her eyes unfocused, her body already twitching with the last signs of life. I gather her in my arms, pressing my face to the top of her head, hot tears coursing down my cheeks, falling into the gold of her hair.

"I'm sorry," I whisper, "I'm so sorry. Sorry I wasn't faster. Sorry I couldn't save you."

I hear her breath rattle in her chest, and I look into her blue eyes, so like mine. Eyes from which the light is rapidly fading.

"I love you," I tell her, my voice cracking, "to whatever end, Agnethe, I love you."

"Greta," she whispers back, eyes fluttering closed, "don't fret so. With every end, there is a beginning."

My sister's weight in my arms sags, and she's still. Peaceful. Grief cracks open my chest, and the sorrow pours forth from me unchecked. Her last words pierce my heart, and it's a wonder I'm still able to draw in breath, though every inhalation feels like a dagger slicing through me.

Her form fades from my arms, the battlefield from my vision, but I remain where I am. Kneeling in the stillness.

Broken.

CHAPTER THIRTY-EIGHT
Waking Up is Hard to Do

The landscape of my fears dissolves in front of me, smoke unraveling like thread, blood sinking into the earth, and I now kneel on the plush carpet of a well-appointed dining room.

Sunlight filters through leaded-glass windows, casting gold-dappled light across a table set for two. The scents of rosemary and woodsmoke find my nose, mingled with a faint, sweet tang coming from the hearth.

I'm in a home. A simple one, by the looks of it. Simple but clean. Quiet. The kind of place where nothing ever goes wrong, where monstrous goats and crawling insects and bloody battlefields never dare darken the dreams of its inhabitants. Carved beams arch overhead, their joints dark with oil and age. A kettle sings softly over the fire. Fresh bread steams in a basket on the table.

I can see through the window that a garden blooms with lavender, thyme, and climbing roses brushing sun-bleached stone walls outside.

"Greta," a voice calls to me, and my head jerks up to see Aric sitting in one of the chairs at the table.

He looks younger. Softer. Dressed in a plain linen tunic with the sleeves rolled to his forearms, the picture of a relaxed country gentleman. He smiles at me pleasantly, blandly, as if none of the world's horrors have ever touched us. No trials. No blood. No Stachtenbaste. Just peace.

"Sit," he says, gesturing to the chair opposite his, "sit and relax."

"I don't understand," I tell him, but rise from the floor and sit cautiously on the edge of the seat.

He looks confused but still smiles as he asks, "What do you mean?"

"I mean what happened with the trials and Stachtenbaste? Where are we? Did we escape?" I ask him urgently, wanting to know what my dream is dangling in front of me as my greatest desire.

His brow furrows, and he does frown then. "Of course they're over. It's over."

Gods help me, for a moment I want to believe it. My body aches to simply sit, to breathe, to stay. Beneath the warmth, though, something inside me clamors in protest. The quiet is too clean. The light is too golden.

"And Agnethe?" I ask him hesitantly.

"Ah, yes, well…unfortunate, but it couldn't be helped. But you're safe now," he says, covering his hand with mine. "That's all you need."

A chill runs through me. This isn't safety. This is surrender. And would I trade the allure of safety for the reality of that surrender? My life is messy and terrifying and…well, awful. Is this version of peace, where I would be in a cage, as Roan said, better than the alternative?

It's tempting, which I suppose is the point of this whole exercise. To show me my most fervent desire. And part of me does long for the banality of the peace I knew before.

I look at my hands resting against the white linen of the tablecloth. Dirt cakes beneath my fingernails. Scratches and scars are covering the skin on their backs. Evidence of my struggle, yes. But also evidence I have fought. Fought and am still fighting.

I stand abruptly, dream-Aric looking at me with a frown as I do so.

"No," I tell him simply.

"No?" He asks, looking shocked.

"That isn't all I need," I tell him.

I turn and make for the door of the home, tear it open, and run through it.

The door behind me shuts with a gentle click, but when I turn, I'm not on the exterior of the country home where dream-Aric lives. In its place is a chamber of startling opulence. Firelight flickers across silk-draped walls and thick carpets shot through with colorful thread. An enormous, four-poster bed dominates the center of the room, canopied in gauze that stirs with an unseen breeze. Logs crackle in the hearth, and everything smells faintly of sandalwood and peppermint—familiar, masculine.

My breath catches, and I whirl to see Rafe standing a few feet behind me.

He doesn't speak. He doesn't have to. His presence fills the room as wholly as if he'd uttered words to me. He wears no uniform, just a loose linen tunic and dark trousers. His hair is tousled, and his dark eyes dance with promise. There is no smirk now, no cutting remark, and when he moves toward me, I don't retreat.

He crosses the room in three strides, eyes burning like the fire in the hearth. There are no flowery promises of safety. Just his hand as it cups the side of my face, fingers brushing the tangled curls back from my brow. Then, the press of his mouth to mine, fierce and possessive, his hands at my waist pulling me flush against his body.

The kiss begins slowly, warm and sweet, but it quickly deepens. His arms tighten around me, one hand reaching down from my waist to cup my arse. I gasp into his mouth, my pulse rioting through my body as his hips press into mine with unmistakable urgency.

I feel something tugging at the edges of my mind, but I ignore it. I know I should push him away. I should resist. But my body betrays me. I tilt my chin, lean into the heat, and curl my fingers into the folds of his tunic. The kiss is dizzying. The kind that makes thoughts scatter like dust in the wind, and all I can think is that I want this to happen. Want it with all of my being.

He reaches up to the neckline of my tunic, hooking his fingers under it, and pulls, rending the fabric in two in a single motion, exposing my breasts to his heated gaze. He leans down, his mouth trailing heat across them, tugging on one of my nipples with long, demanding pulls that rob me of my last coherent thoughts. I'm like a metal billet, molten and yielding beneath the force of his ardor as he worships my body.

"Greta," Roan's voice is a shard of ice in my mind, cutting through the fevered haze of desire. *"This is* not *real. Deny it—or be lost to it."*

My eyes fly open, lips parted, breathing still ragged. Rafe's head still leans over my chest, and his face—so close to mine—is so perfect it hurts. His eyes glitter up at me with want. The illusion is flawless. I hate myself for how much I want to stay. How much my body *aches* to remain in this room, with this version of reality. A version where I haven't betrayed him, where he looks at me as he did that night—like I'm something magnificent to behold. Not like something he regrets.

Realizing that this is what my body and mind want more than Aric's promises of protection and safety cuts deep, burning sharper than any physical wound. It hadn't been this hard to leave that desire, that illusion, behind. Maybe because, in reality, I've already left it behind. Because the quiet peace and safety I knew at Noetheim, knew before, has only ever been that—an illusion. And while part of me wishes to have it back, for things to be the same again, the larger part knows that will never happen.

I will never go back to doing the account ledgers, never go back to working in the forge, never go back to overseeing Agnethe's lessons, never go back to suffering through the fumbling embraces of men too quick to take without giving. I will never go back to singing in empty rooms, to holding my tongue, to wanting more but never taking it.

No, things won't be the same again because I am not the same. I am not that "me" anymore.

But the me that wants Rafe? That finds him maddening and intriguing and irritating and curious and suspicious and secretive and surprising, and—gods help me—desirable. That is who I am.

That is the "me" now. It's terrifying. And thrilling. And hard to reconcile with the fact that this dreamscape with him might be as close as I ever come to it again.

I'll never know, though, if I don't get out of here.

With distinct effort, like trying to drag myself through mud, I pull away from dream-Rafe. Step by step, I back toward the door, even as he calls my name, reaches for me. I don't speak, don't explain. I turn, open the door, and flee into whatever waits beyond.

When the door closes behind me, I'm once again on a battlefield, but it's bathed in moonlight, and the only occupants are four versions of myself.

The closest version of me sneers in my direction and says, "Welcome to your truth. Let's see which of us breaks you first."

This battlefield has no blood, no corpses, no debris, only silvery grass swaying gently in the breeze. Like the night itself holds its breath.

I stagger forward across the field, toward the four versions of myself, still reeling from the previous obstacle. These versions of me don't shimmer or blur; they are not ghosts or phantoms. They look real. Each one distinct, cast from the same mold I was, but forged by the corners of my mind. Their eyes gleam with disdain. Their posture smacks of judgment.

Though one has already spoken to me, already welcomed me to this final step, I do not yet know which one will start the obstacle in earnest.

I don't have to wait long.

One to my right curls her lip. Her arms are crossed tight beneath her breasts, her gaze raking me from head to toe. Her jaw is sharp, her eyes are narrow, and her face is tight with contempt. Her clothing is tight, emphasizing every curve. Her mouth curls as she circles me like a predator would its prey.

"Look at you," she hisses, "heavy where you should be light, clumsy where you should be quick. Do you think anyone sees a warrior? No— they see dead weight. A burden they'll have to carry when you fall."

I flinch. The words hit home, harder than I'd like to admit. They aren't words I've said before, not aloud. But they're ones I've heard. Whispered words by cruel girls, by exasperated training masters, by other cadets. And, in the back of my mind, at my own reflection, wishing I had Agnethe's slender grace, my grandmother's smooth elegance.

Sensing blood, this version of me presses, "Why are you even here? People here were born to be warriors. You? You were born for the settee in the drawing room, for eating cakes and drinking tea."

My fists clench, my nails biting into my palms. Shame pools in my gut.

Before I can respond, the second version of me steps forward. This one is velvet and sorrow. She wears my oldest dress. The one I would often wear for chores at the forge. Her eyes are wide and hollow.

"Without them," she murmurs, her voice a reedy whisper, "you're nothing."

My chest constricts.

"No one remembers the shield, only the life it saved. Without Agnethe to protect, without Grandmother to support, uncles to assist, you're nothing."

I stare at her, wanting to scream, but no words rise from where the humiliation tightens my throat.

The battlefield dims, shadows lengthening along it. When the third version of me steps into the light, she's wearing a training uniform, sweat stained and worn at the knees. Her voice is bright, brittle, laced with mockery. Her hair is tied back in a sharp braid. Her face splits with a grin that's far too wide and unnatural for her face.

"Look around you. Look at them. Your competitors. Faster. Stronger. Better. They make the trials look like an art form. You," she gestures to my form, laughing, "look like someone playacting soldier. In a uniform that's too small."

My shoulders stiffen.

"You were never meant to win," she continues, stepping closer, "you were meant to survive just long enough to lose. You know it. You doubt it. Deep down, you already believe it's over."

My breath hitches and my legs tremble. I lock my knees to try and keep myself steady.

"They will carve additional time next to your name if they don't carve your name into a headstone."

The wind stills.

The last version of me approaches.

She's different. Her hair is wild. Her eyes are rimmed red. Her fists shake at her sides. Her voice is not mocking, but furious.

"You don't want to save anyone," she tells me, "you want to *run*. You want to leave them bleeding behind you and choose yourself for once. And, gods help you, you *hate* yourself for it."

I recoil from her, bile rising in my throat at her words, but she presses on, heedless of my reaction. Or, perhaps, because of it.

"You're tired. Tired of being the older sister. The one to always give, to always sacrifice. Tired of never getting to want anything without guilt gnawing at you. You want to take. You want to walk away. You want to be selfish. You *are* selfish."

The words are fire in my gut. Burning too close and too real. I guess it's fitting that the person with the best ability to hurt me is me. The battlefield sways. The sky spins. The weight of them—of my own feelings—presses down on me like a stone, each word a wound carved deep into my skin.

I fall to my knees, breathing heavily. My fingers dig into the grass, trying to find purchase, to reclaim my grip on what's real and deny what's imagined, exaggerated, and exploited for the benefit of the tournament and this trial.

I'm not strong enough for this. Not steady enough. I am cracked glass, held together by desperation— brittle, ready to shatter at the slightest pressure. I raise my shaking hands from the grass and drag my fingers through my hair, digging my fingernails into my scalp, trying to summon some semblance of pain, a physical manifestation of the torment clawing at my insides. But nothing comes. No sting. No release.

Even in this, the tournament has denied me. Has stripped away everything from me until I'm nothing but an open wound—raw, exposed, untended. And no bandage, no tincture, no healer can reach what's been broken.

Roan's voice threads through the air. Pointed with command, but soft in its delivery.

"You are not broken, fledgling. You are many. And you are still yours. Embrace what shaped you. It is not meant to be your enemy."

My eyes sting. My mind recoils at his words. Not because they're wrong, but because they feel too gentle for someone who's failed herself so easily and thoroughly. Only moments ago, I had dared to think I was someone new, someone stronger, forged for the better by my experiences at Stachtenbaste and all I've endured. But a whisper, a jeer from my own voice, and I have curled in on myself.

If I'm so different, why do I bleed in all the same places?

"I feel like so many pieces, but not ones that make up a whole. Just…fragile. Weak. I'm Stahlvend—I cannot be mended once I've been shattered." I hang my head in defeat.

"Wholeness isn't strength—it is fortune. And fortune teaches nothing. You are not Stahlvend. You are its maker. *Steel may be reforged. But you, fledgling, are* forging yourself—*into what no blade could ever become."*

Roan's words are a balm to my battered soul. I have been broken, but I can choose what I do with the shards of my being—to remake them, to start anew. Even to give up and leave myself fractured.

As terrified as I am, though, I'm not yet ready to give up.

I stand on unsteady legs. I step toward the first copy of myself. I do not raise my fists, I do not scream. Instead, I wrap my arms around her. The figure stiffens. Shudders.

"I am strong enough exactly as I am." The figure gasps—and crumbles into a thousand flecks of moonlight, dissipating into the air like snow.

I turn toward the version of me who fears she is only a shield. Who whispers to herself in my old dress. Who looks lost.

I take her hand. "I am my own person," I tell her, "even though I love them."

The figure begins to weep—a soft, shivering sound that rends the air—before she fades into mist, leaving nothing behind.

I turn toward the cruelest version of myself, who waits to gloat over my failures.

I stare into her eyes, smile faintly, and nod. "I may fall. I may fail.

But it will never be because I didn't try."

The figure tries to scream, but the sound cuts short as she bursts into a spray of dust and is gone.

Only one remains. The angry one. The selfish one. The part of me that I fear the most and have tried hardest to bury.

Unflinching and without argument, I walk forward. I step into the shadow of her rage and pull this version of me close. My arms wrap tight around the shaking figure, as if holding onto something wild and wounded.

I whisper, "Sometimes I will be selfish, and sometimes I will be selfless. But wanting a life of my own *isn't* selfish. It is human."

Her shuddering increases until she trembles so violently I am shaking with her. Then she exhales a breath like wind passing through leaves. Her limbs loosen. Her head sinks into my shoulder. Then—gently, wordlessly—she folds inward, into me, and disappears.

The battlefield is quiet. The moon hangs overhead, brighter now. I close my eyes and take a deep breath, trying to quell the tremors still coursing through me. I feel bruised inside, like I've been hollowed and refilled. Remade.

When the light shifts, and the ground gives way, I wake.

I gasp as breath returns, sharp and painful. My palms press flat to the wooden platform beneath me, my back arching as I take in gulp after gulp of air, lungs drinking in my rebirth.

There are voices around me. Shouting. Footsteps rushing past. I sit up, dazed, as the sound of gasping and groaning fills the air around me. Some platforms are empty—their occupants already awake and gone. Others remain locked in sleep, limbs thrashing, lips parted in silent screams.

I scan the stands, searching for the one I want to share this moment with. When I find him, we lock eyes. Sapphire meets crimson across the distance. I pour my gratitude, my awe, my affection into the bond we share.

Roan. My mentor. My *friend*.

And though we've never spoken aloud, though we are nothing alike in form or flesh, I know he feels it, too.

I am forging myself day by day. I am clumsy. Heavy. But I am strong. I love deeply. And I'm learning how to stand alone. I am imperfect. But I do not stop. I want. I rage. I fear.

I am human.

And I am becoming.

I am becoming me.

CHAPTER THIRTY-NINE
Avrelian Lore or Story?

That night, after lights out, I sneak into the old chapel, the creak of the warped door announcing my arrival at the hush within. Moonlight filters through the holes in the ceiling and the remaining panes of glass in the windows. The air still holds the faint scent of damp stone and long-extinguished prayer incense, but no longer reeks of rot and mildew. With each visit, I've tried to salvage some of it.

The moldy tapestries have been pulled down and tucked into a chest behind the crumbling altar. Cobwebs have been brushed from the ceiling beams and furniture, and the dust—once thick enough to coat me like fur—has been relegated to the corners of the room. I've swept the aisle, cleared the altar of decades-old debris. I've even tried to rearrange the broken benches in orderly rows, leaving an open space where Roan and I can train.

At the center, perched with the solemn dignity only a monarch can possess, is Roan. He stands atop the stone altar, his inky wings folded, ruby eyes glowing faintly in the low light. Behind him, the old relic statue of Feueroise's Flame now stands upright.

I cross the room without speaking, footsteps echoing across the flagstones, and sit across from him on the altar's edge. The stone is cold, like always, but at least it doesn't cover my arse in dust and grime. I cross my legs on the floor before me, tucking my trousers beneath me so my skin isn't touching the cold stone, and fold my hands in my lap.

Raising my gaze to Roan's, I say through our bond, *"You said once I completed the last trial, you'd tell me more."*

"Indeed," he bobs his feathered head.

My conversation with Werner resurfaces. *"Can you tell me more about Stahlvend?"*

"To speak of Stahlvend, we must return to the beginning," he intones, talons clicking softly upon the stone as he settles more fully.

"Four hundred years ago, Aurelia was quieter, smaller. But even then, the roots of her current turmoil had already begun to climb beneath the surface. There was a young bladesmith called Joceran de Veend. Not yet legend. Not even yet a name in passing. He labored in the royal forge, one of many under the Vergildetbach family— skilled, to be sure, but unremarkable by standards of court and crown.

"Not long before, his father had died—a quiet death, not a dramatic one. But loss forges its own blades, and Joceran was vulnerable when struck. Newly wed. A new father. And the grief…it hollowed him. He stopped sleeping. His dreams turned to visions and whispers. He thought he was going mad.

"What he did not know—and what I would come to learn—is that when his father passed, his blood called to me. When a Rabensblut *falls, the conspiracy stirs in search of the next. His father had been bound to another. And when he crossed into death, so too did his bonded, at rest at last.*

"I heard the call. Followed it. And I found Joceran—young, raw, burning with sorrow. I observed him at first, as I did with you, before making myself known. Before sharing the truth of his lineage."

He tilts his head again, though this time he merely looks thoughtful, staring behind me, as if looking into the past.

"We were clumsy in the beginning. He spoke too much. I, too little. He mistook questions for conversation. I mistook silence for wisdom. Both of us were wrong. We quarreled. He said I spoke in riddles. I called him foolish."

My lips twitch. Not much has changed. His feathers ruffle slightly in irritation at my train of thought, but he doesn't acknowledge it.

"But the longer his grief continued, the more it took its toll. He returned to the forge night after night. When others had long gone home, he stayed. Out of desperation. Out of pain. He worked until his knuckles cracked, hammering and folding as if he could banish the sorrow with his hands.

"As he toiled away one evening, he failed to notice it. A small slice. Not deep, but enough. When his blood dripped onto the steel, it didn't burn away. It drank it. Absorbed it. We were then unaware of the significance. When he quenched the blade, though, everything changed. Veining like the barbs of a feather rippled across the steel. He thought it a trick of the light. An imperfection."

"But it wasn't," I whisper into the quiet, more statement than question.

Roan's voice is more thoughtful now. *"It barely took a drop. A single drop, folded just right, and the steel remembered. It held the melody of his blood like notes upon a stave. And when wielded…it sang."*

The moonlight ripples along his feathers as he shifts, turning them indigo, then violet, then turquoise.

"Did he know then what it was?" I asked.

"Once the blade was finished and married to its hilt," Roan explains, *"it was gifted to one of the Vergildetbach princes. A man of noble birth but little skill. But with that blade in hand, he parried what he could not see. Answered what had not yet struck. None called it magic, of course. Humans rarely do when the magic flatters their ego. The prince sang praises of Joceran's craftsmanship. Lauded the balance, the sharpness, as if it were skill wrought by hand alone. Joceran and I knew better.*

"Though the prince was not wrong. Craft and blood must go hand in hand to create something worthy. But the steel did more than cut. It knew. *So taken was the prince that he commissioned more blades. And soon, Joceran forged legends as much as blades. Nobles came with coin and favor in hand, hoping for might despite their mediocrity. And so ordinary men became extraordinary in battle. They moved with grace they had never earned, dodged strikes they should never have survived."*

"How have we not dominated Sarenaveld with such weapons at our disposal?" I ask him, bewildered.

"Like all magic, Stahlvend demands balance. It awakens only in the moment of need—at the edge of battle, not before or after. It cannot draft war maps or untangle the knots of political machinations. It cannot chart what has not yet been drawn. It

grants instinct, not foresight. Reflex, not reason. A wielder might move like a phantom in combat. But they will not spot the ambush in the hills. They will not see betrayal brewing in closed chambers. When the blood dries, when the quiet returns, so, too, does the silence in the steel. And the bearer, flush with victory, believes the brilliance was always theirs. Humans do love to take credit they aren't due."

"And does *Rabensblut* demand balance?"

"All *magic demands balance, fledgling. You are not exempt from that,*" he replies sagely.

"How have I not yet felt any kind of toll?"

He replies, "*The full strength of your magic has not been realized. Neither has your control. You are not yet all that you will come to be.*"

"Why did he keep it a secret?" I ask.

"*Many reasons. The duty of the Rabensblut is first and foremost to their guardianship,*" Roan says.

I frown. "What, exactly, are we guarding?"

"*The gods did not forge the world from a single breath. Why should understanding come any quicker?*"

It seems I'm destined for more explanatory conversations. Resigned to waiting for some of my answers, I lean back on my hands. "And the other reasons for concealing the truth of Stahlvend?"

Roan answers, "*A magic that requires no consequence of breeding or birth. No incantation or rite of passage. Merely contact. Such a magic is a dangerous thing to those who hoard privilege. They'd just as soon burn the truth as share it.*"

All of these answers seem to spur even more questions. One, especially, burns at the back of my mind.

"Why does Stahlvend react to me as it does?"

Roan tilts his head, feathers ruffling. He hops along the edge of the altar toward me, wings half extended for balance. "*That is a different matter entirely. To the ordinary hand, Stahlvend offers only instinct—subtle nudges, borrowed reflexes. To the* Rabensblut, *it speaks.*"

"You said it calls to me, to who I am," I remind him.

Roan replies. "*The same blood that shapes the steel flows through you. It is no mere tool. Not just a guide but a companion. An extension of your being. A partner forged in your likeness. To wield Stahlvend as a* Rabensblut *is to carry a living echo of your legacy.*"

So that's why I can hear the whispers, why they spoke to me from the blade in the armory. From Rafe's krahbek and dagger.

I glance sidelong at Roan, a smirk tugging at the corner of my mouth. "So does this mean that Rafe isn't as skilled with the krahbek as he thinks?"

Roan's voice sounds amused in my head, *"Tempting though your spite may find it, no. The blade has remained purely ornamental since the large one arrived. It has not seen action since Vitaheim."*

My eyebrows raise in surprise. "How do you know that?"

"Stahlvend may speak to the Rabensblut, *but we* Blutraben *sense it. Its presence, even dormant, its memories of when blood has kissed its edge. A privilege of being gods blessed,"* he says haughtily.

I open my mouth to ask him what exactly he means when he mentions the gods blessing the *Blutraben*, but another fills the air before the question leaves my lips.

"Hatching battle plans with a bird now, *künnle?* Or is it just gossip today?"

I turn abruptly at Rafe's voice, gasping, toppling over sideways onto the floor. Roan is equally ruffled. He spreads his wings, fluffing his feathers, hopping from foot to foot. He extends his head, opening his beak, and from the depths of his chest comes the eerie sound of words aloud, harsh and croaking. Nothing like the ancient, sardonic voice I heard in my head.

"Go away!" He caws at Rafe.

Rafe stops advancing down the center aisle and looks to where I push myself upright. "Well," he drawls, "it's definitely *your* bird."

Huffing, I push the hair falling over my face away from my eyes. "He's not *my* bird. And he's a raven, and far more interesting than you'll ever be. For one thing, he knows—"

An excruciating pain lances through my skull. I cry out, and my hands reach up to clutch my head.

Suddenly, Rafe is kneeling beside me, warm hands wrapping around my shoulders, steadying me. "Are you all right?"

I'm still reeling from the pain and trying not to vomit all over his tunic. I look up at his face silently, swallowing in an effort to keep my dinner in my stomach.

"*He cannot know. He cannot be trusted,*" Roan's voice says in my head, and I realize *he* was the source of my pain and also how close I came to revealing too much.

I can't focus enough to speak back to him through the bond, so I say, "I'm sorry," aloud to him, my eyes still on Rafe's face.

Misunderstanding, Rafe cups my cheeks and looks into my eyes. "Don't go soft on me now, *künnle*. Call me something awful so I know you're feeling better."

Irritated, I push his hands away from my face. "Ugh! You're the reason the gods invented plagues. Or perhaps you are one, sent to torment me."

Roan croaks his agreement.

Rafe sits back on his heels and says, "That's more like it."

I'm rubbing my temples with my fingertips, but something in his tone makes me look up in surprise. "You were worried."

He looks away, his voice gruff as he says, "You cried out. I'm not heartless."

My fingers still, and I watch his face closely. "I thought you were angry with me."

His eyes return to mine. "I am."

I frown. "Then why—"

"Because two things can be true at once, Greta," he says, his expression unreadable, "I can be furious with you and still not wish you harm."

My hands drop into my lap. "That's confusing."

"Tell me about it," he murmurs, eyes still on mine.

He says it like a joke. But his voice is too low, too rough around the edges. It doesn't seem like there's anything funny in it at all.

I stare at him for longer than I should. Trying to read the twist in his mouth, the strain at the corners of his eyes. He looks tired. Is it lack of sleep or something else? Did whatever he was planning with Conrad happen? Did it end as anticipated, or did something go awry?

The silence stretches between us, but it's not empty. It vibrates, heavy with everything unsaid. I'm suddenly aware of how close we are, with him crouching at my outstretched feet. If I reach a hand out, I'd be able to touch him, a fact which sets my nerves buzzing with awareness and makes me nervous. His eyes still haven't left mine. And it's dangerous because I both want him to keep looking at me and don't want him to see me. Not all the pieces that, even with the progress I feel I made, are still raw after the trial. A wound I just barely stitched closed that still needs time to mend fully.

I could try to say something clever. A barb about how he's terrible at reassuring people. But I don't. I just want to understand why he's here.

"What are you doing here?" I ask, rubbing at my temples again.

He eases onto the ground across from me. "I could ask you the same thing, since it's past lights out."

My fingers stop again, and I look at him incredulously. "Since when do you care about the rules?"

He snorts. "I don't give a fuck, but I thought *you* did."

My hands fall into my lap, fingers tracing imaginary shapes on my trousers, and my eyes follow, so I have reason to stop looking at him. "I'd wager there's much about me you don't know or realize."

Like that I speak seven languages but still fumble for the right words when I need them. That I hate being the center of attention, but keep ending up at the heart of every storm. That I used to bite my nails to the quick until my grandmother coated them in bitter salve.

He doesn't know that my grandmother was stabbed while I hid behind a wall and listened. That her death was sharp and senseless and soaked in blood, and I still dream about it. Still wonder if I could have stopped it. That my sister is trapped, and the only thing keeping me from breaking completely is the desperate hope that I can still save her. That I have magic in my veins now—or maybe always did, and that it speaks to me in feathers and riddles and eyes too ancient to fathom.

He doesn't know how much I've changed. How I'm not sure I want the illusion of protection and contentment anymore. That comfort and peace used to sound like everything I ever wanted, but now I'm not sure I'd recognize peace if it smacked me in the face.

And, Sisters help me, he doesn't know how much I want him to kiss me again. Because I still remember the heat of it, like falling into fire and wanting to get burned.

"Speaking of which," he says, "what was with your act during the trial today?"

My fingers freeze in their tracing. "What do you mean?"

"You had an unusual recovery," he says, and I chance a glance at him through the veil of my lashes.

"How so?" I ask, frowning.

He folds his arms and leans against one of the cracked benches. "Most challengers came to like they'd been tortured—stumbling, sobbing, screaming. A few tried to strike the attendants. I think one might've pissed himself."

He pauses and watches me, gaze discerning, as if he's trying to look beneath my surface to see what I'm concealing.

"But you…no thrashing. No crying. Just…still. Silent. Calm. Like you'd made peace with your inner demons instead of battling your worst nightmares. You were even still during the trial."

I shrug, fingers tapping along my thigh. "Is it hard to believe I might've had an easier time at it than others?"

His eyes narrow. "I've never had potion-induced nightmares. But I've sat by enough soldiers post battle to know what terror looks like when it lingers. What it costs to quiet it. I can't think that would be easy to shake. So imagine my surprise when you calmly leave the citadel tonight and have the wherewithal to hold secret council with your birdy overlord."

Roan grumbles in my head. I blink as I try to soothe him through the bond, only to find Rafe watching me intently, suspicion narrowing his gaze.

I'm trying to think of an appropriately deflecting reply when the door suddenly crashes open.

I let out a yelp at the noise. Rafe is already on his feet, dagger drawn, body taut with alarm, shielding me before he even registers who's arrived.

I stand, peering nervously around his considerable bulk, but feel my jaw go slack when I see Aric standing in the aisle. I emerge from behind Rafe's arm to stand beside him.

Aric's gaze flicks from me to Rafe and back again, like he's trying to assess the danger and the drama of what he's interrupted.

"What's going on?" He demands.

My scalp prickles. "*The entanglements of human affections are rarely improved by my presence. I shall take my leave before declarations are made or any garments are removed.*"

"*Coward,*" I say affectionately.

"*Is self-preservation cowardice or strategy? I choose to think of it as retreating with grace.*"

I don't know how he does it, but moments later, despite having never seen him quit the chapel, the flutter of wings through one of the holes in the roof appears as he ascends into the night sky.

"Fucking *of course* you're here," Rafe scoffs, throwing up his hands, "like a bad rash or a venereal disease."

"You would know," Aric retorts. "What are *you* doing here?"

Rafe crosses his arms and says, "Giving my challenger a pep talk."

Aric laughs, but it's hollow, like he doesn't believe anything his cousin says.

There's no love lost between them; that much has always been clear. Rafe jabs, Aric seethes, and if I'm there, I get caught in the crossfire of a battle I never asked to fight. I want to tell Aric that this is the exact opposite of giving me space. Interjecting himself into the conversation like this is not letting me decide or figure things out alone. But the words stick somewhere between my throat and my pounding temples, and I'm suddenly so tired my shoulders sag.

"It's fine, Aric," I say wearily, "we were just talking strategy where it's quiet and no one would overhear. No need to be concerned."

Rafe's head whips toward me, glittering eyes meeting mine in the moonlight.

He turns to Aric and needles me with perfect precision. "Yes, cousin. No need to *fly* off the handle. I just don't want de Veend *winging* her way through the rest of the tournament."

My fingernails dig into the palms of my hands as I draw them into fists. Did he expect me to tell Aric off? Maybe he did. But I don't want to defend myself any more than I've already had to. I don't want to explain, don't want to argue. I don't even want to make things worse between them. But gods forbid anyone ask what I want.

"Why do you even care?" Aric demands, turning toward Rafe, "it's not like you get to switch posts if she wins, like the other mentors."

I freeze. For a heartbeat, I can't breathe. The words sit in the air like so much rot, festering in the quiet that follows.

Is that true—Rafe stays even if I win? And is that by choice or by his father's design? The way Aric said it makes it seem like the latter. But worse—so much worse—is what Aric's question implies. That any investment in me, any care, any concern, must be transactional. Conditional. Measured by what someone stands to gain. My stomach heaves, sharp and sick.

I should say something. But nothing comes. All my cutting quips, my pointed arguments, sit in my chest like stone, too heavy to lift. I left the trial today certain that I am changing. That I'm beginning to believe I'm more than the sum of what others gain from me. But here I am again—silent, small, shrinking under the weight of someone else's expectations. Have I learned nothing, or does learning mean being torn open again and again?

Rafe's voice is deadly calm as he asks, "Why do you even care? She's not your challenger."

Aric steps forward, jabbing his finger into Rafe's arm. "I'm just trying to protect her."

Rafe smiles, but it lacks warmth. "Well, cousin, protection isn't ownership, so perhaps you should let *künnle* decide."

They both turn to me.

Suddenly I'm furious with both of them.

I don't want their expectation that I'll choose a side. I don't want to be the thing they volley between them just to prove a point. Neither of them asked me what I want. Neither seems to realize that I'm not some *thing* to claim or a problem to solve.

Their eyes are on me now—waiting, weighing—and something in

me rebels. I'm not a coin to toss, not a secret to hoard, not a taunt to dangle. And with both of them, I'm tired of being spoken of instead of spoken to. Of being the very thin excuse they need to wound each other.

I straighten, jaw tight. If they want to fight, they can do it. But they can do it without me.

I respond, "*Künnle* is deciding to go to bed so as not to be forced to bear witness to this cock-measuring contest any longer."

"Well, *künnle*," he drawls, his jaw tight. "Since you've encountered both, you'll have to let us know who the winner is."

My lips part in shock. That wasn't just crude—it was cruel. Wounded and lashing out, Rafe went for blood, and he didn't miss.

Aric turns sharply toward me, fury rolling off of him in waves, eyes bright with disbelief and betrayal—like I'd just plunged a dagger into his side and smiled while doing it.

My mouth opens and shuts several times, trying to form words in my defense but unable to make a single syllable. I look at Rafe, then Aric, then back at Rafe again.

He raises a single, dark brow.

My heart lurches in my chest. I want to slap him. I want to scream, I want the ground to swallow me whole. My humiliation is hot, jagged, loud. It burns in my chest, pricks behind my eyes. But I don't want to give leave to the burning that threatens to overtake me. Not in front of them.

So I turn and run.

CHAPTER FORTY
Practice Makes Perfect

The skeleton is no longer draped in golden splendor, collapsed before the gleaming throne.

No, the throne is overturned, its legs splintered, the golden scrolls upon it scorched black. Ash clings to every crevice, as if the entire thing had been burned from within.

The woman's gown has fared the same—torn, pockmarked with holes, scorched. The golden waves upon her head are singed, smoke still coiling faintly in the air, like it had only just now met its end.

Her hand is still outstretched, reaching for rescue, for deliverance that never came. But her fingers.

Each of her fingers is dripping gold.

Not jewels or finery. Immersion. As if her hands were plunged into molten ore and left to harden in death.

I back away, nearly tripping over myself to flee.

It's then I see it.

A figure on the opposite end of the vast, ruined hall.

Draped in a cloak so dark it consumes the light, the hood shadowing their face *entirely. In one hand is a scythe. The haft is carved obsidian, the surface dotted with moonstones, pale as milk. The blade glimmers in the little remaining light, the sharpened edge's reflective flash momentarily blinding me.*

A voice trembles from within the depths of the hood. Ancient. Knowing. Terrible.

"The words of the past are carved in bone, and the hands of the departed hold the key. Seek the sign where shadow and feather meet and let the keeper's legacy guide your way."

I open my mouth, but no sound emerges.

The figure raises a single hand.

And the cloak explodes into a hundred wings, their feathers flat and trailing smoke. The smell of ash, of burning, fills the air.

A conspiracy of ravens fills the room, circling above me, a cloud of feathers and beaks and talons. They are eerily silent as they move, not even a single caw marring the quiet of the room.

One dives for me, and I do run this time, sobbing frantically as I try to reach the door that moves farther and farther away the faster I move toward it. I trip, fall onto my knees, and look back to see what caught my feet.

The scythe.

Abandoned by its bearer, blade still shining, moonstones still glowing despite the dim. Sharp pain pierces my shoulder, and I scream, eyes meeting those of the raven now perched there.

It's no ordinary raven, though.

Up close, its feathers don't gleam with the iridescence of indigo and violet, but remain dull. The smell of ash from their barbs is so strong it threatens to choke me.

And its eyes.

Its eyes are milky white.

Dead.

These are no ordinary ravens, no.

They are Enderaben.

The winged beasts of the goddess of death herself. It opens its beak, and from it that same, ancient voice stirs.

"Even in death, the watch remains unbroken."

They swarm me then. Pulling at my hair. Raking at the skin of my arms, my legs. Tearing at the flesh on my face. I thrash, screaming, but they are everywhere. Relentless.

I find the scythe in my hand.

This time, I hear no whispers, no more voice. But I do not resist the urge to raise the blade to my neck.

To end it.

I would rather carve myself to nothing than let these monsters have more of me.

It's with relief that I plunge the blade into my own throat.

I wake with a start in the early morning light, reaching a hand up to my neck, searching for the place where the scythe punctured it. Finding nothing and feeling foolish, I sigh heavily. I stretch my limbs, toes, and fingers, encouraging my body to begin fully waking.

Others have begun to bustle within the room, milling around in various states of undress, flitting in and out of the bathing chamber. When Lotti had told me months before that I would become accustomed to the sights and sounds of my fellow cadets as they accomplish their morning routines, I hadn't believed it would ever seem normal, but now I don't bat an eye as I sit up and reach for my boots.

When I bend forward, I feel a trickle of wetness slip down my face and stare in confusion at the bed linens where the drop of blood has landed.

"Greta." Lotti waves at me, walking toward my bed, but then gasps, "You're bleeding!" Her face turns green.

I reach up a hand to my face, feeling the evidence dripping from one nostril. I reach for the corner of my bed sheet and wipe my face hastily, then tilt my head back to encourage the blood to flow back into it and not continue leaking.

"Uh…perhaps I'll come back later," Lotti says, clearly wishing to escape any potential sight of more blood.

I wordlessly wave her on with my head still tilted. I've only had a nosebleed once or twice in my entire life, and I'm not sure what prompted this one considering I was asleep.

My scalp tingles. *"Your blood answers—even in slumber—whether you intended to call it or not,"* Roan tells me.

Shocked, I reply, *"Do you mean I'm the one who caused this? I called my Rabensblut? But how?"*

"Your power continues to grow. One day, you will need not reach for it—it will

already be there."

"If it's something that I'm meant to be able to do, why am I bleeding?" I ask him, tilting my head back to its normal, upright position, waiting to see if the blood returns.

Roan answers, *"As I've said, balance must exist in all things. Magic is no exception. Force invites consequence—expend too greatly, and it will take in kind."*

"But how did a dream expend force?" I ask him.

"Some dreams are memories. Others, mirrors. And some, fledgling, are maps."

Maps?

"Like...a vision? Of the future?" I swallow nervously.

He answers, *"What is imagined and what is foreseen wear cloaks of the same cloth. Only the unraveling of time reveals what's underneath."*

Perhaps I am more like my grandmother than I thought. She bled for the truth. Perhaps I do also.

I replay the moment in the old chapel for the hundredth time, needle clutched tight in my hand as I stab it into the thick weave of the uniform I'm meant to be mending. The thread catches, tangles—just like everything else in my life. I tighten my jaw as I pull it through. Again. And again. Each puncture feels like it should let out pent-up frustration, but it doesn't. I'm still boiling.

Still stinging.

"'Since you've encountered both, you'll have to let us know who the winner is,'" I mutter in a mocking interpretation of Rafe's voice.

What a prick.

He'd said it with that perfect, affected joking way of his. It just wasn't funny. It was a dagger. Deliberate and sharp. He knew exactly where to aim to inflict maximum damage, just like with actual weapons.

I haven't seen him since that night. Not him, not Aric. Almost six days now. The next trial is nearly upon us, and I've neither so much as caught a glimpse of nor heard a peep from either one.

You'd think time would dull the edges. It hasn't.

I know he was angry with me. Maybe even hurt. But he put me on the spot in front of Aric. In front of someone who is in charge of my well-being here. I hadn't expected kindness from him, although the evening hadn't started so badly. I thought—I'd hoped—he'd understand. That he'd at least be fair. That he'd realize why I came to his room that night. Why I'd crept in, heart in my throat, to take the dagger.

But no.

Each time my needle stabs through the stiff fabric of the uniform, I imagine it's Rafe's smug face I'm jabbing. Work duties are in the weavers' building this week, and while I'm grateful I don't have to peel potatoes, stir laundry, or—horror of horrors—feed goats, I also wish the quiet atmosphere didn't afford me so much time alone with my thoughts.

Worse, my teammates are scattered this week. The weavers' building has many stations and rooms, and most of the team is not skilled enough with a needle to work on the finer-detailed tasks. So, I'm alone with the pile of officers' uniforms, stitching torn seams and reaffixing trim. My only hope is that I'll encounter Rafe's or Aric's uniforms and I can exact petty revenge by sewing their pant legs together.

I let the fabric slip from my fingers into my lap, pressing the heels of my palms to my burning eyes. My head aches faintly from the echo of my dreams. I lied when Lotti asked me if I was all right this morning, because I can't talk about it. Gods, there's so much I can't talk about.

And even without speaking of it, I'm obviously not good at hiding it. Rafe is far too perceptive. He has seen and picked up on things no one else has. Plucking at loose threads in an attempt to unravel it all. And I'm terrified he'll succeed when it comes to Roan. With what I am. He doesn't know only because no one knows what *Rabensblut* is. At least, anyone who did is long gone.

Despite it all, I want to speak with him. To storm up to him and shove him and scream in his face. But also, to explain. But I won't. Won't seek him out. Won't find him. Because I'm afraid of what I'll say or do. Or what he won't.

And I'm so godsdamned tired. Not just in my body, but in my mind, and the cryptic—possibly prophetic—dreams aren't helping my mental state. They twist through my sleep, laced with symbols and meanings I can't decipher.

And Aric—gods, that's fucked up, too. He said he wants to protect me, that he cares. But the second things weren't convenient or clear, the moment he lacked control over the situation, he lashed out. He said he'd give me space to decide on things, but then crashed into it with the subtlety of a battering ram.

""Why do you even care? It's not like you get to switch posts if she wins, like the other mentors.""

Like I'm just a ladder for someone else to climb. A means to an end—that what they stand to gain is the only reason someone would help me. And as someone still learning their value beyond what they can do for others, that hit me in a still unbelievably raw place.

He made me feel small.

They both did.

And I just stood there. Let them argue over my head like some weak-willed coward. Let them reduce me to something standing between them instead of someone standing beside them.

I should've told Rafe more about my choices. The desperation. The fear. And that not everything between us had been manipulation or strategy.

But now? Now I'm furious at him, at Aric, at myself, for even considering that either one of them deserves an explanation.

I pick up the fabric again, sighing, and shove the needle through. It punches through with a satisfying pop.

Did either one of them feel bad when I fled? Or did they feel smug? Or nothing at all?

I know Rafe pretends to be careless, thoughtless, like he doesn't give a fuck about anything except the very superficial, but I also know that's a lie. I know because I've caught glimpses of him that tell me otherwise.

I wish he were as stupid as he pretends to be. It would make this so much easier if he were thoughtless and simple. But he isn't. He's sharp. And I'm afraid he's eventually going to cut past seams I've stitched closed and expose the truths I'm not yet ready to speak aloud—and the ones I can't speak of at all because they aren't solely mine to tell.

The bells chime, informing me it's time for the midday meal, so I stand from my chair, stretching my arms above my head, rolling my shoulders, rotating my head, trying to work the stiffness out of my body that comes from being hunched over for hours on end. I shuffle into the main workroom and find my team, who chatter enthusiastically.

Jarl says, "All I'm saying is a trial by embroidery would be torturous. I might withdraw then."

Otto leans over to me. "They're theorizing what the next trial will entail."

Lotti rolls her eyes. "Except now it's only gotten ridiculous."

"Well, we all know I'd fail anything with reading comprehension," Stigander says wryly.

"You'd be excellent at a trial of silence, though," Jarl points out.

"Whereas you would be abysmal at it," Berte mutters irritably.

Cyneric raises his elegant eyebrows. "I'd *adore* a dancing trial."

"No one wants to see that lot hoof it across the arena," Jarl snorts, earning himself a wallop from Berte. "Ow, fuck!" She points in my and Stigander's direction.

I hold up my hands. "No need to feel bad on my account. I agree. No one wants to see us dance."

"Speak for yourself," Stigander sounds offended, "I am incredibly light on my feet."

Their ideas become more outlandish as we walk to the dining hall, from staring contests to pie eating.

"But what's the one trial you'd absolutely hate or that would make you withdraw?" Jarl asks me curiously.

"I keep thinking each time that the current one is the one that will do me in, so I can't really say," I shrug.

"What an evasive answer," he grumbles.

As we pass through the dining hall doors, Aric walks in our direction, as if he's on his way out. My shoulders tense slightly as his footsteps slow upon seeing us.

"Go on without me," I say to the team, who all watch me curiously but don't argue. Cyneric gives my hand an encouraging squeeze as they move away.

Aric nods at me and says, "De Veend," and keeps walking to the entryway.

"Aric, wait," I plead, following him.

He stops. Looks at me, his expression unreadable. "What?"

"I, uh, wanted to say I'm sorry. For what happened with Rafe," I know it isn't really my apology to make, but I didn't mean to embarrass him either.

"Why him?" He asks. The words seem sharper than is warranted.

I frown. "What?"

"Why him? Why Rafe? And I asked you if something was going on before, and you denied it. You could've chosen anyone else. You let me think it was because he was your target," he says, his voice low and tight.

I frown. "That's not—I wasn't apologizing for that. He *was* my target."

"Weren't you?" He asks.

Well, not *now*, I'm not.

I stiffen. "That's not fair."

He replies, "Isn't it?"

Now I'm angry, and I repeat what I told him before, "I did what I had to do."

He looks away from my face, and several moments pass. He exhales through his nose and turns his eyes back to mine.

"Fine. You don't owe me anything, Greta. But don't act like I imagined the choice you've made."

Frustrated, I throw up my hands. "It isn't a matter of choosing between you and him. Gods, Aric, it isn't a matter of choice at all—not about that. Instead, every day is a choice where I have to decide which part of my soul I have to sacrifice next just to stay alive. And I'm not even sure I will."

He doesn't answer, but a muscle in his jaw tics.

I scoff. "And even now, I'm the one explaining myself. But you— you don't. You just want me to hand over pieces of myself, to want to build something with you, when you've not given me anything in return. You want trust without having to give it."

Aric snaps, "I asked you to try. To come to know me, to *try* to trust me. To let me take care of you, protect you. I didn't demand anything of you.”

"And yet you judge me for not giving it to you," I snap back.

Silence. Thick and tense.

I sigh. "I'm sorry if I hurt you. I am. But you can't act like I've betrayed your trust when we haven't built it. When you haven't given me reason to return it."

"You're right," he says firmly. "Maybe I was looking for something that isn't there."

I feel frustrated and angry. He's still not getting it.

"Good luck tomorrow, Greta."

Then he walks away, leaving my unspoken words and frustrations burning on my tongue.

I don't even understand why he's angry. Nor why he believes he has the right to it. I never promised him anything. We never spoke of words like trust or loyalty until he brought them up to me—gods, was that only a week ago? We came together in a spark between desperation and attraction and comfort. It was heat and need and loneliness with no vows, no fidelity to uphold it. But now, he's acting like I've broken something sacred. Like I've betrayed him. As if what we had had been solid enough to fracture.

It feels like he's trying to pin something tender over something base and physical and pretend it was always there. It could have been. Maybe. In another place. Without Stachtenbaste. Without the trials. Without the blood on my hands, the ache in my bones, the whispers of steel and ravens in my mind.

He's jealous and frustrated, maybe, that I haven't jumped to give him an opportunity. I haven't even yet denied him, though. I've been avoiding it, but haven't said "no" definitively. His leaps are frustrating in their assumptions, exhausting in their certainty.

My scalp tingles slightly. "*Wanting without asking—your species' favorite form of sport.*"

I ask Roan, "*Then why do I feel guilty?*"

I did what I had to do. What happened with Rafe had been strategy, necessity, a move in a game I never wanted to play but have no choice but to win. My choices are not luxuries; they're survival. But telling myself that doesn't make it entirely truthful.

I could've walked away. I didn't have to want it. And I did. I *do*. Maybe that's where the guilt comes from—not in what I did or didn't do, but in how I felt while it was happening. The want that's still there. That had certainly never been part of my plan.

Maybe Rafe hasn't given me more than Aric has. In fact, he really hasn't. He's riddles and barbs and secrets. But what I have seen, I understand. The silence between words. The act that masks the hurt. The weight he seems to carry.

"Humans are often torn between the truth and the falsehoods they think seem nobler," he intones.

"I haven't lied to him," I protest.

"Only to yourself, fledgling," Roan quips.

"So, what should I do, then?" I ask, feeling weary.

He says, *"You cannot rush the root to take hold nor the bloom to lift its face to the sun. Hearts, too, follow their own season. Time will yield its knowing."*

I sigh. *"I was afraid you'd say something like that."*

"Do not seek wisdom if you wish to flatter your impatience."

I send a mental eye roll down the bond and head into the dining hall to join my team.

The bowstring pulls at my fingers as I nock another arrow. We're lined up in the upper training yard, humid afternoon air chasing the back of my neck underneath my braid's heavy weight, leaving a fine film of moisture across my skin. Autumn rears its head in the early mornings and evenings, but the afternoons still belong to summer.

On command, Lotti looses her arrow and it lands in the outermost portion of the target with a satisfying *thwack*. Mine veers off course and lands harmlessly in the grass beside my target.

Dagmar squints as she looses an arrow at her own target. "I'm not sure what happened to your skill since the first trial, de Veend. Trauma, perhaps?" Her words are casual, her tone anything but.

Why is everyone suddenly so interested in what I'm doing in the trials?

I try to force a casual shrug that matches her energy as I reply, "Fatigue, I suppose. Not exactly sleeping well these days."

She doesn't press me further, but the look in her icy blue eyes is sharper than an arrow's point.

I inhale slowly and try to reach out in my mind. Not to Roan, but to the *Rabensblut*. In truth, I'm not certain how I'm meant to accomplish it, but I imagine it's much like speaking to the Stahlvend whispers, like speaking to Roan.

If you don't mind helping me out here, I could use a little assistance so my teammate doesn't become too suspicious.

I feel a stirring. It's not the tingling, like when Roan reaches out. It's not like when he pushes energy down the bond and I feel a sudden burst of it coursing through my veins. This feels more like I've dipped my brain into a pool of power that coats every square inch of it. A thin film that flexes with thought, with intention, with action.

A hum buzzes through my mind, a rotte bow drawn across the strings, vibrating through my skull. My vision sharpens, and I can see my target as clearly as if it were a foot in front of me.

When Lieutenant Broadbente calls out our next fire sequence, I'm ready.

"Draw and anchor!" He commands.

I pull back the string tightly, bringing it to a point on my cheek. I feel the power flow down my arms and into my hands, creating a steadiness and rigidity I previously lacked.

He adds, "Steady…loose!"

Thwack. My arrow hits just left of center.

I grin at Dagmar, who only stares at me like I'm a puzzle she's trying to figure out. My head hums uncomfortably, and there's a slight whine behind my eyes, but it was worth the pain not to look quite as pathetic.

"Impressive. If you attended training lessons with half as much commitment, *künnle*, you might even hit something on purpose."

I whirl, my bow hitting me in the face when I clumsily stumble. Rafe is standing behind me, his customary smirk on his face.

"Unless you're so eager to avoid me that you'd rather publicly humiliate yourself," he adds, tilting his head.

Surprise and embarrassment flood me so thoroughly that I lose my grip on the *Rabensblut*. My limbs feel looser, my vision returns to normal, and the ache in my head blessedly dulls.

My cheeks burn hotter than flame. "I haven't been avoiding you, and I'm not humiliating myself!"

He raises a dark brow. "Oh? So, this is just a warm-up, then?" He asks, gesturing to the single arrow in my target…and the many in the ground around it.

"Maybe it's part of my strategy so my competitors underestimate me," I counter.

"Hmm, I fear you don't need to shoot arrows like a blind drunk for your competitors to underestimate you," he says, his expression thoughtful. He then smiles excitedly, as if he's had the best idea. "I know! How about we try *improving* your skill, just on a lark?"

Dagmar coughs, and I look over at her sharply. Her lips are twitching as she watches us.

"Do you mind?" I ask, huffily, hoping to shame her into ceasing her laughter.

"Not at all," she grins and stays exactly where she is.

"Come, *künnle*, time to fulfill my obligation," he says, gesturing toward the officers' training yard.

"I thought you had to get permission to pull me from training," I protest, wanting to avoid any private interaction with him lest I humiliate myself in ways far worse than with archery.

"Oi, Broadbente!" Rafe calls between cupped palms. The lieutenant looks up from the cadet he's guiding. Rafe points to the top of my head. "Taking this one for instruction."

The lieutenant simply nods and returns to speaking with the cadet. *The traitor.*

Dagmar holds out her hand. "I'll put your bow away."

Sighing, I reluctantly hand it to her. "My thanks."

"Enjoy your *hands-on* instruction," she grins and returns to her target, waiting for the lieutenant's next fire sequence command.

I stiffen but don't want to give her the satisfaction of letting her know she's bothered me, so I send her the most syrupy sweet smile I can summon before I turn to follow Rafe's retreating, broad back.

I walk several feet behind him, not wanting to speak to him, and he doesn't bother waiting. By the time we reach the officers' training yard, I'm so angry that he hasn't addressed anything, I'm practically vibrating. He holds the gate open for me wordlessly, and I walk through to find the yard completely empty. When the gate clangs shut, I turn on him and stomp forward, poking a finger directly in the center of his chest.

"How dare you accuse me of avoiding training. Especially in front of someone I'm competing against. And why are you even bothering with training me now? The trial is tomorrow."

He arches a brow again. "Which part offended you more—the accusation or the witness?" He ignores my question.

"You were cruel," I say, "and you know it."

He lifts a hand in mock defense. "Is it cruel to point out a lack of skill? Because I thought, as your mentor, that was my duty."

"I'm not talking about today," I snap, exasperated. "I'm talking about what you said in the old chapel. In front of Aric."

His expression loses its smug humor. I wait for him to say something, but he doesn't.

Filling the silence, I say, "You knew what you were doing. You humiliated me. You meant to."

He laughs bitterly. "And you didn't? Let's talk about your stunning performance in my chamber. Those breathy moans. The caresses. Then threatening me when I didn't help you and, let's not forget, telling the entire arena what happened."

I stiffen but don't have an immediate rejoinder.

His voice is tight as he presses, "Don't look so wounded. You used me. And when my knightly cousin rode in with his judgments, you didn't say a damned thing, even as I defended you."

"You didn't defend me! If you wanted to defend me, you would've said I was worth helping, even without the promise of a better post. That I mattered beyond being someone's stepping stone," my voice cracks on the last word, and I look away from his face, embarrassed I've revealed how much that part hurt.

Silence. When he doesn't respond, I tentatively look back at his face.

He's watching me, his expression unreadable, before he says, softly, "Why would I give you the courtesy you didn't afford me? Didn't you use me as a stepping stone to get to the next trial?"

I shake my head. "It's not the same."

He scoffs. "Isn't it?"

"This fighting is getting us nowhere," I fold my arms across my chest.

"On the contrary, fighting is how soldiers solve their differences." He beckons me with his fingers. "So show me what fight you have, *künnle*."

"What?" I ask him. He's lost his mind.

"Best put that fury to good use," he encourages.

I hesitate for a breath.

Then I charge, rage propelling me forward. I swing my arm, hand balled into a fist. He knocks my hand away. I strike with my other hand, and he blocks it with his forearm. I raise my foot to stomp his instep so I can hit him, and he steps back out of reach. He barely moves. Calm, precise, maddeningly in control. My outrage grows with every missed strike, every failed attempt.

I lunge, attempting to spin around and catch him on the back, but he twists, and I slide on the damp grass, losing my balance. I reach out to him to steady myself, and in the next breath, we're tumbling onto the ground of the training yard. He grabs me mid-fall and cushions me with his body, rolling us until we come to a gradual stop in the middle of the yard.

We've landed in a tangle of limbs, with me on my back and him braced above me, holding the bulk of his weight on his forearms. I take deep gulps of air, my chest brushing his, and his breath fans my cheek as he looks down upon me. We stare at each other silently for several moments.

"I'm sorry," he finally says, "for what I said. Then. And now."

My heart constricts.

I take a shuddering breath, "I'm sorry for what I did."

He says, "You did what you had to do. Were I in your shoes, I likely would've done the same."

There is a too-measured pace to his words, almost like there's something he's not telling me.

"If you understand, why were you angry?" I murmur.

He hesitates. Swallows hard enough that his throat bobs. His voice drops, "Because I wanted it to be real."

The blood rushes in my ears. My heart starts thudding against my rib cage in a way that has nothing to do with the exertion of fighting.

I swallow, too. Exhale shakily. Close my eyes, then open them slowly and look into his.

"It was," I whisper.

He swallows again. His eyes flick down to my lips, and mine part on a sharp intake of breath. His slight hesitation is the only betrayal of his uncertainty; he slowly dips his head toward mine, peppermint-scented breath filling my nostrils as his lips move closer.

Then—

The heavy creak of the training gate opening fills the yard.

Face tightening, Rafe pulls back quickly, just as Aric steps through the opening, halting mid-stride.

I scramble to a sitting position, scooting back on my hands in the grass, my heart in my throat.

Aric stares at both of us, eyes flicking back and forth.

Rafe, ever quick with his reactions, stands and brushes his trousers. "Cousin, we didn't know to expect your sparkling company."

I climb to my feet shakily.

Aric's jaw tics. "Clearly."

The tension is so thick, the blade of a krahbek could slice right through it.

"Lieutenant Broadbente didn't tell me you had training this afternoon," Aric says to me.

Rafe touches his chest. "Checking up on me? I'm flattered."

Aric ignores him and continues to look at me.

I shift uncomfortably. "Uh, well, I needed more training before the trial tomorrow. So, he pulled me from the unit session."

I don't want to make this any worse than it already feels, but Aric obviously doesn't like whatever it is he managed to see, nor my explanation.

He turns to Rafe. "Did you get permission to pull her out?"

Rafe lies blithely, "I didn't know I needed your permission to pull my challenger for training."

"Not mine," Aric bites, "Richter's. Or your father's."

At the mention of his father, Rafe's face tightens. "Are you really going to stand there and read the fucking rule book to me?"

Aric's eyebrows lower into a scowl. "Rafe—"

"I asked him," I lie, not wanting Rafe to get in trouble with his father. "As I said, I needed more instruction. But I'll go back to archery now."

Rafe frowns. "Greta—"

I cut him off with a small shake of my head, quiet but deliberate.

"It's fine. I'll go back and do some more terrible shooting." I glance at him to let him know I'm teasing. That it's all right. At least, I hope it is.

He holds my gaze, then nods once, face softening imperceptibly.

I scurry out of the training yard, eager to escape the awkward standoff, scalp tingling softly as I exit.

"Human romantic entanglements are tedious. Still, fledgling, you acquitted yourself well. Though your bow work remains an affront to both logic and divine will."

CHAPTER FORTY-ONE
Gehrvania's Cipher

The midday sun is high and heavy, thickening the air like breath caught in the throat of summer. The heat sinks into the back of my tunic, refusing to let go, as I walk alone to Freiheit Field for the next trial. The only respite is the hint of breeze creeping in from the trees across the river.

My boots make a soft squishing sound as they move across the damp earth. The ground hasn't dried from the morning dew, so they slap against it with every step, like the earth hasn't decided what it wants. Mud or dirt. Summer or fall.

I am well acquainted with the feelings of indecision.

The walk feels longer than usual, the weariness of my mind filling my limbs with lead, making me move sluggishly, like I'm trying to run through water. The arena rises ahead in the distance, waiting to see if I pass muster in today's challenge. The conversations, the echoes of the last week, feel like the harshest judgment, though.

Despite speaking with both Aric and Rafe yesterday and forming a tentative truce with the latter, I feel no closer to knowing what to do than before. They both hurt me. Different wounds, but deep, nonetheless.

Aric asked me for trust, like it's a promise I owe him. Like I am meant to strip myself bare, to open myself to him and wait, patiently, for him to do the same someday. He says he wants to protect me. Though what kind of protection requires my surrender? He didn't ask me to understand him; he didn't explain. He just wants me to believe in him without offering the same in return.

And Rafe…he hasn't asked for trust at all. He accused me of using him, and he wasn't wrong. He said he'd understood. He hadn't hidden it behind impassivity or measured words. He'd laid that hurt bare. He'd told me he wanted it to be real.

What scares me most is that it had been.

But it had been with *both* of them when things had happened. At least for me.

Am I developing some kind of pattern? Giving my time, thoughts, and feelings to men who can't—or won't—do the same? Aric, who thinks protection and trust are the same thing. Rafe, who hasn't made promises but is still capable of flaying me raw with the lash of his own pain.

Is it better to risk myself for someone who doesn't hide the fact that he has secrets, that he's dangerous, or for someone who doesn't recognize that he does?

I hear the thump of footsteps approaching behind me and turn to see Otto jogging up to me, breath ragged. His kind face is open and friendly as he slows upon approaching me.

"Are you ready for the trial?" He asks, falling into step beside me.

I snort. "Of course, I'm not ready. How can I be ready for something completely unknown?" I frown, looking behind us. "Where's Lotti?"

Otto shakes his head. "I'm not sure. She must've gone straight from her shift in the weavers' to the arena. I'll meet her in the stands."

I nod, and we walk in companionable silence for a few moments.

"Otto, do you think someone wanting to protect you is the same as caring for you?" I ask him, keen for an outside opinion on this emotional turmoil I'm experiencing.

He looks thoughtful. "I think…wanting to protect someone is a kind of caring. It means you don't want them hurt. But *truly* caring for someone means you trust they can get back up even if they do. One holds on too tight. The other stays close, in case you need them, but believes you don't."

I consider this and feel a sudden stab of regret in my chest.

Is that what I've done to Agnethe?

Held on too tight out of worry?

I thought I was shielding my sister, keeping her safe. Carrying the weight of burdens because I could, because I had to. But maybe it wasn't protection at all. Perhaps it was control. Fear masking itself as love.

And do I trust Agnethe will be all right without me? I worry she won't. But maybe—even worse—I don't trust that *I* will be all right without *her*. And Agnethe is the one who suffers for that fear.

I needed to be needed. In doing so, had I stopped seeing my sister as someone who might stand on her own? Someone who might not need catching. Or saving.

Roan's voice hums along our bond, *"Let those you love rise—or fall—by their own wings. Not yours."*

It hurts. Sisters, does it pain me. The idea of watching someone you love stumble, even fall, and not intervening. Not running to break that fall with your own body. Maybe, though, that's not really love. That's anxiety, doubt, dressed in falsehoods and calling itself loyalty.

Maybe real caring, as Otto described it, stands close but not over. Is there if you fall, but doesn't keep you from flying.

The realization that I hadn't really trusted Agnethe to stand on her own pulls at me. Not because she couldn't, but because I hadn't known who I was without her. And love without trust isn't love. It's fear.

And isn't that what Aric is trying to do?

Protect me. Asking me to trust him while keeping every part of himself sealed away. He doesn't want me to get hurt, that part I believe. But he also doesn't believe I can get back up if I am.

Rafe hasn't protected me. He hasn't tried to cushion the emotional blows I've received and has even dealt me some. He's called me out. He's accused me. He hasn't tried to shield me from the consequences of my own choices and actions. And he's been cruel, yes. He hasn't gone out of his way to make me feel safe.

But he doesn't make me feel incapable either.

When we reach the arena, I still don't feel like I know what I'm doing with this new perspective, but I feel closer than before.

Otto wishes me good luck, and I fling my arms around him, hugging him tight. He doesn't hesitate to hug me back. Grateful tears prick at the backs of my eyes as we part ways—he to the onlooker stands, me to the center of the arena floor where the other challengers wait.

It's time to face what's next and fall—and rise—on my own.

I take my place in the group of ten, the hems of my sleeves and the back of my tunic sticking to my skin as the humidity rises from the dampened earth of the arena floor. Beside me, boots shuffle, shoulders square, throats clear. Fidgeting from the other challengers, each trying to disguise the fact that they're nervous.

Behind us are ten stations stretched across the arena pit, evenly spaced in a long row. Each bears four identical podiums arranged in a staggered line, leading to a sturdy wooden crate, weathered and reinforced with iron bands. Behind each of those, taller than any challenger, stand enormous cylinders, fully shrouded in linen. The cloth is tightly drawn, pinned at each corner, concealing whatever lies beneath from all angles.

I narrow my eyes, rocking onto the balls of my feet, and crane my neck, trying to see what the cloth could be hiding. Is it my imagination, or was there a flicker beneath the fabric? Maybe it's another beast. Or perhaps it's a figment of my own fantasy, primed by too many nights of restless sleep and haunting dreams. Still, something about the cylinders unsettles me. Not just their size, which is massive. The way they're isolated and still. Like they're waiting for us. Looming ghouls poised to rob us of another piece of our souls.

I glance down the line of challengers again, catching bits of tension on the faces beside me. A clenched jaw here, a tapping finger there, a whispered prayer to the Blessed Sisters. The podiums, crates, and stations are arranged so that every line of sight leads to the mystery at each end. My heart races faster now, for I can't shake the sense that whatever hides behind that linen isn't just part of the trial.

It *is* the trial.

Colonel Richter steps forward to the front of the platform, and I brace my shoulders and lock my knees, apprehension coiling in my gut like a snake waiting to strike. The wind wielder moves her hands, projecting the colonel's voice as she commences her address.

"Challengers," she begins, "brute strength and raw instinct will only carry you so far in the field. I've seen soldiers rush in, with bared weapons and bravado, only to fall before they could ever reach the fight they were anticipating with so much relish. Why? Because they didn't think. They let fear, or pride, or haste dictate their choices. That will get you killed."

She clasps her hands behind her back, gaze sharp, and eyes each of us one by one.

"Today's trial is not only a test of knowledge, though you will need it. Nor is it merely about physical endurance, though it will demand that of you as well. No—today is about how you think. How you plan. How you pause, even under pressure, and make the right choice rather than the first one available.

"On the battlefield, in the chaos of war, you won't always have much time. But the time you do have must be used wisely. You'll be expected to recall information, assess risk, and anticipate outcomes. To adapt. The soldiers who survive are the ones who keep their heads when others lose theirs.

"This trial will put that to the test. I suggest you treat it with the solemnity it deserves. You have tools. You have training. You have minds. Use them. Instinct may win battles, but reason will win the war."

Stigander steps up beside me. "How many things, exactly, will win wars? I'm losing count from all her speeches."

The colonel returns to her seat, and Major Berger sweeps forward with her usual verve, boots striking the wood with crisp, deliberate purpose. She bends down toward us as if about to share a great secret— even though everyone in the arena can hear her perfectly.

"Challengers," she calls, white teeth flashing, "welcome to Gehrvania's Cipher! Today, you are invited to a trial devoted to our goddess of knowledge. A little exercise in logic and language. And if the old tongue isn't your strong suit, now is a great time to regret such a failing and hope your ignorance isn't fatal."

Languages. A flicker of hope stirs in my chest. I am *very* good with languages.

"Now before we get too comfortable," she drawls, pacing the length of the platform, "I should mention that today's trial isn't *only* about puzzles. It's also a rescue mission. And more importantly, a lesson in not getting in over your head."

She pauses, smile growing.

"Really. I mean that quite literally."

With dramatic flourish, she lifts one hand, and on cue, the linen shrouds drop.

A row of tall glass tanks stands revealed.

Inside each one: a person. Trapped.

And in one of them is Lotti.

I almost jolt forward, but a heavy hand grabs my arm and stills me. Stigander grips my bicep, staring grimly at his own tank where Jarl is trapped. When I look farther down the line, I spot Berte inside another. Perhaps she's Dagmar's rescue?

Major Berger's eyes turn back to the challengers. "Each tank is eight feet tall, three feet wide and deep, and holds precisely five hundred gallons of water. Water will begin filling them at a rate of ten gallons per minute, which gives you approximately fifty minutes before the tanks are full depending on your rescue's weight and height. When only ten inches of air remain, your rescue has roughly five minutes before things become…dramatic."

Her eyes coast over the group of challengers.

"That is," she says ominously, "assuming they can stay afloat that long under duress."

She turns, boots clicking sharply as she resumes pacing the platform.

"Now the winner of the previous challenge," she gestures to the challenger as she explains, "will enjoy a five-minute reprieve before their tank begins to fill. A modest, but distinct advantage. Don't waste it," she instructs him.

"At each podium, you'll find a sealed box containing a clue and a set of tiles—letters, colors, symbols. Solve the clue. Select your tiles. Take them to the next podium and fit them into the compartments on the outside of the next box. Do it correctly, and the box will unlock, revealing your next clue and tiles.

"There are four puzzles. Complete all four, and you'll earn the key to your companion's tank. Open it in time, and you both walk away. Fail…well, I don't think I need to explain what happens should you fail.

"Your first clue and tiles already await you in an unlocked starter box. Think carefully; move deliberately. Panic is a poor translator, challengers."

She claps her hands once and gestures for us to step up to our stations. She spreads her arms wide once we all stand before our first podium.

"Challengers, at your marks…decipher!"

The starting horn sounds.

I lift the latch on my first box, its lid releasing with a faint squeak of the hinges. I reach in, hands damp from nerves and the thick heat. The humidity makes the world feel smaller, like it's closing in on me and breathing down my neck, as if even the skies are leaning in to watch us.

Inside the box are dozens of square blocks, each marked with a single carved letter. They're arranged in no order, just scattered in the shallow, velvet-lined compartment like discarded teeth. Beneath them sits a scroll sealed with wax and stamped with Gehrvania's sigil—an unblinking eye.

I break the wax seal and unroll the parchment with trembling fingers, quickly scanning the text. As Major Berger said, the script is in old Aurelian, looping across the page as if someone had hastily scrawled the message.

My eyes flit nervously to the end of my station and Lotti's tank. Seeing the water pour in steadily sends fear and panic roiling through my veins. How quickly will it fill? How long do I have before it becomes critical?

A gentle hum spreads over my skull, *"Fly the sky you're in, not the storm you fear might be coming,"* Roan tells me.

I take a deep breath and lower my head to the parchment. I read the clue several times over to make sure I understand it correctly, wasting precious minutes since much is often lost in translation.

I am not alive, yet I can grow.
I cannot breathe but still need air.
I cannot drink but water kills me.
What am I?

I blink several times, the lines already blurring before me. My eyes flick up to the tanks once more. Lotti's pale hands press against the glass already, and her mouth forms words I cannot hear. The water has begun to rise rapidly; it's already hitting mid-calf on her. She's petite and doesn't have as much vertical space to go before the water reaches her head. Can Lotti swim?

I look back down at the parchment. I understand the literal meaning of the words, but the riddle is another thing entirely. It's not nearly as complex or layered as the scavenger hunt clues, but it's hard to think clearly when my heart is pounding with fear, when I feel pressure to work quickly.

Not alive but can grow. Needs air but not to breathe. I know this. I'd heard this before, hadn't I?

Something not alive but grows.

My eyes skim the letter blocks, fingers hovering over them. Too many options. No way to narrow it. My mind keeps leaping ahead. What if I fail? What if I pick the wrong word and waste time, or worse, it sets off some other horrible trigger?

Roan sighs, *"Give it breath, and it lives, but water and it dies."*

My head snaps up.

Fire. The answer is fire.

Heart hammering, I snatch up the letters that correspond to those in the common tongue. I look at the locked box in front of me. There are empty compartments inset into its front, each the size of a single tile.

I slot them in, one by one, pressing until each clicks into place. When the last letter slides in, a louder click sounds from within the box, and the lid lifts upward, opening.

I don't smile.

I barely breathe.

I just reach for the next scroll, already unrolling it with unsteady hands. I review the clue, read the words carefully, and think through my translation.

I am seen in rain but never in snow,
Bright and vibrant as the spectrum's glow.
What am I?

This one is simpler. The wording at least. And even the meaning.

A rainbow.

Yes. But to unlock the box demands more than just knowing the answer.

I peer into the open clue box and see a different set of tiles resting in its belly. There are seven, each one with a different color word on it.

The colors of the rainbow. Scooping up the tiles, I run to the next podium, to the next box I need to unlock, and stare at the compartment. There is a single, long channel inset within the top. The tiles are different sizes. Unlike the first clue, this isn't a spelling challenge, and I'm unsure how to order them in the space. Alphabetically? Or something more complex?

"*The sky writes its secrets in color,*" Roan says to me, and I startle at his voice, so focused on my task.

He continues, "*First a sparking flame, its edges blurred by dusk. Then comes the gold coin of a day's decline, then still and breathing as a forest. Memory sinks into sea, then twilight bruised and in-between. And last, shadow, the hush that ends it all.*"

I scowl, "*Are you giving me another riddle to solve right now?*"

"*Align them the same, and the lock will yield,*" he offers as his only explanation.

"*How can you be sure?*" I ask him, skeptical.

"*When you've been alive for over four and a half centuries, fledgling,*" he says dryly, "*you see many things. Among them, more clumsy riddles disguised as poetry than I care to number."*

I snort and look again at the words on each tile, then align them in the order of Roan's verse in the box's compartments.

Red for flame; orange for dusk; yellow for gold; green for forest; blue for sea; indigo for twilight; and, finally, violet for shadow. The hush that ends it all.

A faint click reverberates through the wood.

The box opens.

I look up to the other stations. Most of the other challengers are still at their first podium, brows furrowed in concentration, their heads occasionally looking up to observe the progress and paths of the others around them. Only one other person has made it to their second podium, and they look to be still translating.

I tear my eyes away and look instead toward the tanks.

My breath seizes in my throat.

The water in Lotti's tank has nearly reached her waist. Her mouth moves in silent words again when she sees me looking. Her face is pale. Not frightened, just yet, maybe encouraging? But the trepidation has tightened the skin around her mouth, and her eyes worriedly dart back and forth as if searching for escape.

By my estimation, roughly fifteen minutes have passed. That leaves thirty-five minutes before the tanks fill completely.

Thirty-five minutes until Lotti is dead.

CHAPTER FORTY-TWO
Promises and Other Drugs

I have thirty-five minutes left.

Thirty-five.

That thought alone is as sharp as a dagger. Thin and pressing to the side of my neck. Thirty-five minutes until the tank is full. Until the water swallows Lotti whole. Until her lungs give out. Until my hope will.

It takes longer to fall asleep most nights.

It takes longer to mend a seam on a uniform.

It takes longer to bathe, get dressed, and braid my hair.

It seems it takes no time at all to send someone to their watery grave.

My fingers shake as I reach into the box for the next scroll, struggling to slide my finger under the wax seal. It breaks unevenly, paper catching on an edge made tacky once more from the sun's heat blazing down upon us. I nearly tear it in half trying to open it quickly. My breath is too loud in my ears. My blood is pounding too hard in my veins.

The scroll won't lie flat. My hands are trembling so violently that the parchment repeatedly curls in protest. My vision blurs not from unshed tears, but from the sheer force of the panic clawing at me.

Focus. Translate. Read. You can do it.

But the letters won't stay still on the page. My eyes snag on the looping script, and for a moment, it feels like the words might lift off the parchment and scatter like leaves. I swallow hard and look up to anchor myself for a moment.

The officers on the leaders' platform at the end of the arena floor sit like a living gallery of judgment and boredom.

Colonel Richter is expressionless. Unmoving, as if carved from stone.

Major Berger is seated on the armrest of her chair, her usually merry eyes flitting from challenger to challenger with a grim countenance.

Rafe lounges in his seat with his usual insufferable ease—one elbow on an armrest, head tilted, smirk curling the edge of his mouth like he's watching a particularly bad play acting out in front of him.

His eyes don't match his body posture, though.

They're hard. Tense. Tight around the edges. Like something under pressure barely contained. Like someone trying not to reveal how closely they're watching and how much they care about the outcome.

Then there's Aric, sitting straight, arms crossed, jaw locked. His expression is a study in unaffected indifference, but, unlike Rafe, he doesn't wear it convincingly. His gaze fixes on my current podium, but it is cold. Like he's already calculating the precise moment I'll lose.

Maybe that's unfair. Maybe that isn't what he's thinking at all.

But it feels like it.

And ever since he planted the seed in my mind—that he didn't believe I could do this, only that I want to, I have been unable to shake it.

I'm terrified for Lotti but also afraid of proving him right.

"You're not the first to doubt yourself, fledgling. Don't let it waste time you cannot spare," Roan tells me.

"I'm so afraid I'll make a mistake. That I'll fail her," I tell him.

He says, *"You've survived worse with less. Do not dishonor my judgment by faltering now."*

I frown. *"Your judgment?"*

"A tale for another hour. Preferably one not colored by impending doom."

My throat tightens, and my spine straightens.

You've come this far, I tell myself. *You will* not *be the cause of Lotti's demise.*

My hands are still shaking, but now not only from fear. Anger. Determination. Defiance. I drop my eyes back to the scroll.

Focus. Translate. Read the clue.

I begin the painstaking business of translating the words before me, a process made all the longer by the ever-dwindling time limitation. When I feel confident I've gotten the words right, I read:

The wise one speaks in the night.
The fierce one roars with might.
The sly one slithers with grace.
The faithful one counts loyalty as one of its traits.

I peer into the shallow clue box.

Inside, about a dozen tiles lay scattered across the velvet lining, each etched with a single word in old Aurelian. Similar to the previous clue with the colors, these tiles bear whole words—names, perhaps? Titles. Nouns. Something that matches the clues.

I reach out, arranging them in rows to see them all clearly. My fingers brush the etched markings. Not all of the words are immediately familiar, but a few jump out at me.

Wolf.

I blink. That one doesn't even need translating. It's the same in old Aurelian as in the common tongue—the same shape, the same pronunciation.

I let out a slow breath. At least it's something to begin with—a foothold.

I scan the other tiles again, looking for a pattern, my brain trying to translate rapidly as I go. I see *hund* for dog.

The riddle parchment has curled up again, so the script is hidden, but I can feel the answers forming in my head: animals, traits, symbolism.

I run my fingers along the tiles again, cataloging them silently, making a mental list—*lewe* for lion, *katze* for cat, *slange* for snake. I repeat them in my head, pairing words with meanings, lodging them for Roan's benefit as much as my own.

I unroll the scroll and scan the riddle once more.

I murmur aloud. "The wise one speaks in the night."

I look at the tiles again. *Iule.* The owl. That has to be it.

"*I've known a fair number of owls,*" Roan muses. "*They speak in riddles, hoot at their own prose, and preen at their own supposed wisdom. I'd judge them marginally insightful on a generous night, and then only if the moon were feeling charitable. You have outwitted them twice already this day, and you're only human.*"

A laugh almost escapes my lips. "*They're not the only ones who speak in riddles.*"

I feel the feathers bristling in my head. "*I do not speak riddles, I am one.*"

"*Oh, unquestionably,*" I agree, setting the *iule* tile aside. "*An enigma wrapped in feathers and unsolicited advice.*"

I swear I feel a mind-speak "*harumph*" roll through my brain.

Next is the "fierce one." That has to be a lion. *Lewe.*

I add the tile beside the one I've reserved for "owl."

Then, "the sly one slithers." That one seems relatively straightforward. I set aside *slange* for "snake" with the other two.

The faithful one counts loyalty as a trait.

My eyes flick to *hund* for dog. That has to be the one. I palm the tile along with the other three and race to the next podium, heart thudding against my ribs. The compartments are equally sized and spaced apart, like the tiles, but I err on the side of caution and order them from left to right in the order of the clue.

Iule.

Lewe.

Slange.

Hund.

I step back, holding my breath.

Nothing.

No click. No unlocking. No motion.

The box remains locked.

"No, no, no," I whisper. "Come on—"

I look up at Lotti's tank.

It's more than halfway full. Water has reached her chin, and she's standing on tiptoe. Any moment, she'll have to begin swimming. Her lips are moving more rapidly now, as if panic has set in.

A hard knot tightens in my chest.

"*Roan,*" I think frantically, "*what did I do wrong?*"

"*There were two canines in your list,*" he replies. "*Perhaps the slot is meant for the other.*"

My eyes fly to the box—*hund* for dog.

I pivot, running back to the previous station, knees nearly buckling as I fumble through the remaining tiles. There—*wolf.*

I snatch it up, nearly dropping it in my hurry, and sprint to the following podium again. One breath. Two.

I yank out *hund* and slam *wolf* into its place.

Click.

The box opens with a hiss and a sudden shift of air, almost like the container itself has been holding its breath. I nearly let out a sob of relief.

Fingers shaking once more from adrenaline and nerves, I pull the scroll free, unraveling it.

My last clue.

I glance into the box. Letters again.

Another riddle, another lock. Twenty-five minutes, at best.

I don't look at the tank. I can't. Not just yet.

I translate quickly. The words are coming to me faster the more I've translated. The clue is simple, which only makes it more maddening to decipher.

> *I can be broken without touch.*
> *I can be made but am without form.*
> *What am I?*

I mutter the lines aloud to myself, brow furrowed. "Broken without touch...Silence?"

Roan's voice is soft in my mind, almost speculative. "*That would fit with the first part of the verse, for it can be broken without touch. It can be made by stillness, but it is not always created intentionally, which is implied.*"

I nod. "*You don't make silence. It happens.*"

I brush aside the tendrils of hair that have escaped my braid and are now stirring in the breeze kicked up from the river beyond the walls. I fight the urge to look at the tank again and stare resolutely at the scroll.

"*Trust?*" I think.

"*It can be broken,*" Roan says. "*It has no form. But it's a consequence, not a construct. Not made.*"

I scowl, scanning the letters again. "*Emotion? The heart?*"

"*Both break,*" Roan agrees. "*One has form, however, and the other is not made.*"

"*Spirit?*" I suggest.

"*Strengthened but not forged in the way this riddle demands.*"

Each seems possible in the moment, but they crumble like ash beneath scrutiny. Nothing fits both lines perfectly—something broken without touch, something made but formless.

"*Help me out, then!*" I say to him, exasperated. "*Since you've been able to tear apart my theories so easily.*"

"*You've made one, have you not? Something you live by now. Not with earth, or metal, or stone, but soul. And if you forget it now, it will be broken—not by force, but by failure,*" he tells me.

My mouth goes dry.

A promise. I'm living by my promise to Agnethe now. The promise I made to return to her. To take her home.

I remove the letter tiles from the box. Not just a vow. A binding. Something that doesn't exist in the world but exists within you. And once made, it can shape every action or unravel with no more than a stumble.

My heart beats faster now but with purpose. I gather the tiles and run to the end of my station, where the larger chest sits. I slot them into the channel one by one, spelling out the word. *Geheizen.*

A loud clunk sounds from within the chest. I reach out, pushing the lid up, and then peer inside. Lying on the plain bottom of the chest is a hammer, not unlike the large ones I've seen my uncle and Werner use in their respective forges.

I lean forward and grab the wooden handle. It's heavy—Sisters, it's heavy—enough that it requires both arms to lift it and that's still difficult.

The shaft is rough and thick, made for hands with a stronger grip than mine. I drag it from the chest, turn, and run for Lotti's tank.

The glass has warped her face, her pale skin, and the sluggish movements of her limbs. The water is only two feet or so from the top. She's swimming to keep afloat, but she's tiring. Her eyes are open but dazed, like she's sunk into some detached state of waiting.

"Lotti," I cry to her through the glass, "I'm here! You're almost out; just hang on a bit longer!"

Lotti stirs, her head moving forward, eyes meeting mine, but she doesn't respond. Her soaked uniform pulls on her like an anchor, and I can see how hard she's working just to keep her face pointed toward the air.

I grit my teeth and raise the hammer.

It slips, my fingers numb from fear and damp from sweat. The head falls to the ground, the impact shaking my arms. I try to heft it, my shoulders screaming in protest.

I glance toward the leaders' platform, not because I want to, but because I have to know.

Rafe is watching me.

He's not smirking anymore, not laughing. He's sitting utterly still, and his eyes burn into mine. I glance at Aric. His arms fold across his chest, his face drawn, and he looks tense. He seems concerned for me, which immediately makes me angry. The concern—the *doubt*—lights something deep and furious in my chest.

Roan's voice pierces through the haze, "*Let your fury be the weight behind the blow,*" he says, "*and I your wings in the wind, guiding the landing. Rage will give it force. I will give it flight.*"

I take a deep breath and nod, bracing my legs, tightening my grip.

"One," I say aloud.

I raise the hammer slightly off the ground.

"Two."

I feel the prickling—no, not just a prickle, it's a punch—of power start in my scalp, sliding down my arms, like lightning sizzling through my veins, across my muscles.

Roan says the last count with me, "*Three.*"

I swing.

The hammer arcs through the air, powered by fury and steadied by Roan. It strikes the glass with a thunderous crack, and the tank's wall explodes outward. Water surges forth, blasting shards and fragments over me and across the arena's dirt floor. I stagger back, drenched and coughing.

Lotti tumbles forward, gasping as the wave sweeps her free. I rush to her, pulling her from the wreckage. She clings to me, arms shaking, chest heaving with choked sobs.

"You're all right," I tell her, over and over, hugging her close.

Lotti nods. "No one else—" she cuts off in sputtering, water-soaked coughs.

"Don't try to speak just yet," I tell her.

"No one else," she continues stubbornly, "is even at the fourth podium."

I freeze.

I turn, scanning the other stations.

The tanks.

One—nearly full.

Another—mere inches left.

My stomach drops.

Only a few minutes are left, and some tanks are nearly overflowing. Not everyone floats the same, and their tanks fill at different rates with their weight displacement.

I look at Lotti one last time to assure myself she's all right.

"Go," she whispers.

I don't speak.

I don't think.

I run straight for the leaders' platform.

My water-soaked boots squelch with every step as I sprint across the arena floor, ignoring the shouts I hear from soldiers manning the tanks, the pounding of hands on glass, the roar of the crowd. My abdominal muscles burn from hoisting and swinging the hammer, my arms still tremble from the force of the impact, but I don't stop. Not until I reach the platform, hair plastered to my face, muscles quivering urgently.

I lock eyes with Rafe first and ask him, "Am I allowed to help the others?"

For a moment, he looks stunned—truly stunned. A heartbeat passes, and he doesn't speak; he stares at me like I've grown a second head.

Then he turns on that *fucking* smirk.

"Look at you, *künnle*," he says, spreading his arms, "bleeding heart and all. Should I start a choir while you play martyr, or do we skip straight to sainthood?"

A few of the nearby officers chuckle. One snorts. I don't flinch.

"It's not about that," I tell him evenly, eyes still locked on his.

Major Berger cuts in, her voice unusually somber, "There's nothing in the rules that prevents a challenger from assisting others."

Rafe drawls, "If this is a strategy we didn't discuss, it's a piss-poor one. You're helping the very people who'll gut you next trial. Or are you hoping kindness gets you a tie-breaker?"

Fuck the sisters sideways. I know he's putting on an act, but can't he rest from it for just a minute?

I barely have time to breathe before another voice enters—low, certain, and sharp.

"Do you think any of them would do the same for you?" Aric asks me.

The question hits harder than I expected. Not because it was cruel, but because it was sincere in its challenge. I hesitate for just a beat.

In that beat, the memory of Stigander striking the other challenger in the throat before he could hurt me, and him congratulating me on my steal of Rafe's dagger in the fourth trial. Dagmar's trust in me during the team trial and her quiet defense of me against Belinda.

Stigander, who cannot read.

Dagmar, who doesn't know old Aurelian.

And the other challengers, who I don't know, but whose rescues don't deserve to die for their friendship.

I know without a doubt that Stigander and Dagmar would help me if they could, if the positions were reversed.

I look at Aric and think about what he said in the old chapel, about how he implied that Rafe shouldn't help me because he wouldn't get anything in return. I think of Stigander telling me he wants to leave the Freiheit with his soul intact.

I shake my head. "It's not about what I get for helping or whether they'd do the same. It's about the fact that I couldn't live with myself if I didn't."

I turn without a backward glance and run for the stations.

On the dirt in the middle of the stations, I cup my hands around my mouth and shout the answers to the first clue as loudly as I can. Spelling out "fire," describing the shape of the letters unique to the language.

Heads jerk up down the line. Stigander looks at me, wiping sweat and maybe tears from his eyes. Dagmar drops her scroll and scrambles to arrange her tiles. Others hesitate only seconds before springing into action. I watch, heartened, as some rush to help those who cannot read and need help with even deciphering letters.

"The colors of the rainbow are next," I exclaim, explaining how the words look on the tiles and the order in which someone must insert them in the compartment.

"The animal order is owl, lion, snake, wolf," I yell when they're at the third podium.

I run in front of the stations, back and forth, shouting the order again and again, describing the letters, explaining the placement.

"The answer is promise," I tell them when they're at the last podium. My voice is raw, but I keep shouting until every box has clicked open.

I haven't even looked at the leaders' platform. I don't need to see if they approve or not. I chose what matters, what's important.

Stigander is the first to break through the tank. I turn just in time to see him slam his hammer into the glass of Jarl's tank. The force shatters it with a roaring crash, water gushing out in a torrent. Jarl collapses into Stigander's arms, coughing, alive.

Dagmar is close behind. She moves like a soldier trained for battle, for killing blows. Her strike to Berte's tank is clean and brutal. The glass gives way, and Berte falls out, gasping gratefully.

The others move, Stigander and Dagmar run down the line of tanks, helping the other challengers to break through their glass. I stand frozen as the tanks open in a symphony of crashing glass and rushing water, the sounds of rescue the sweetest melody imaginable. My heart pounds and my breath gasps from my body as surely as if I had been trapped in one myself.

We did it.

We saved them all.

I don't know if everyone made it within the time limit. I don't think the rules will flex even for that, but everyone is alive.

Matrons have escorted the rescues off the field to examine their breathing and check for any cuts from the glass. I catch Lotti's gaze as she leaves, her head turning to find me over her shoulder. She smiles at me, and she looks so damned proud it makes me want to break down crying.

The challengers shuffle toward the leadership platform, all of us heavy with water and weariness. The adrenaline has left our bodies and, with it, the fight. Stigander and Dagmar flank me, and he—surly, silent Stigander—wraps a burly arm around my shoulders and kisses the top of my head. He's trembling like a leaf. Dagmar doesn't touch me, which I suspect isn't so much to do with her aversion to physical affection, but more with her need to keep a tight rein on her emotions. Her icy eyes look suspiciously glassy as she nods at me in thanks.

Colonel Richter steps forward, her voice carrying across the arena.

"The winner of Gehrvania's Cipher is Challenger de Veend, who not only embodied the spirit of this trial—remaining focused under pressure and applying knowledge with precision—but, like a true soldier, she didn't consider her task complete until the entire unit was safe. She will receive a crucial advantage in the next trial." She dips her chin in my direction—acknowledgment of her approval.

The crowd erupts, louder than it has all day, louder than for any trial before. I hadn't thought about how many people were watching, how many might have been waiting with bated breath to see who lived or perished. I simply acted.

Not because I thought I'd receive praise for it, but because it was the right thing to do.

"*You gave what wasn't owed,*" Roan says, his voice cutting through the noise with unmistakable pride. "*That's how history recalls the names it should never forget.*"

My heart swells as I grin at the colonel, at Major Berger, who is grinning back, at each of my fellow challengers. I turn back to the platform and scan it, finding Rafe's eyes first.

He's standing beside his chair with arms crossed and one corner of his mouth turned up. It's not a scornful smirk. Not sarcastic. Just the smallest hint of a real smile. I know that I've surprised him, and while I didn't do it for him, I like that I have.

My gaze drifts to Aric.

He's neither smiling nor smirking. His arms are at his sides, his lips pressed together, watching me with a serious expression. Not just me— his eyes flick sideways to Rafe—a glance, quiet but charged.

When his eyes return to me, he smiles.

It's gentle, true. He even nods. It doesn't give me a thrill like it used to, though. Doesn't fill me with warmth or fire or hope. This time, it's only the sinking weight of unfinished business.

Because I know that we'll have to speak. Truly speak. And sooner rather than later.

While I'm still alive to do it.

CHAPTER FORTY-THREE
Pride and Nemesis

I'm in the hall again, kneeling on the ground.

I raise the scythe. The weight of it is staggering. It tries to resist. I don't feel fear anymore, only the desire for stillness. For peace. The Enderaben circle above me like spirals of smoke.

I lift the scythe's point toward my throat but do not yet stab the flesh there. The blade hovers over my neck. My hands tremble, but not from pain or anxiety. Something worse…the specter of my own mortality.

A beating akin to a heart fills the air. I press my hand to my chest to assure myself that my heart is still very much in my body.

Suddenly, the hall shatters like the water tanks. I clap my hands over my eyes to protect them, as so many shards of glass and fragments spill over me.

I'm in a completely different location when I remove my hands from my face.

A temple. A temple atop a mountain. The Enderaben are gone. So is the crowned corpse.

The air is cool, biting, thin enough that each breath feels labored, borrowed. Wind threads through the broken columns of the main chamber, hissing like a voice through cracked teeth. The temple is roofless and open to the vast blue sky above, where the pale sun hangs high and shimmering. No shadows shift to the side of its beams. No birds stir in its path. Marble stretches out in a great, circular expanse, its veined surface etched with ancient prayers, offerings, and symbols unlike any alphabet I know. Time has nearly worn the carvings into something that only exists in memory.

At the center of the open-air chamber stand two towering statues in contrast to one another. One cloaked in brilliant sunlight, golden and radiant, even in her deteriorated state; the other is veiled in shadow, her form hazy and dark, as though the light arcs away from her.

Levitia and Mortuua. Life and death. Birth and burial. The twin sister goddesses of Aurelia. Once painstakingly chiseled, their robes are chipped and pitted, their faces weathered by wind and rain. The hollows of their eyes are gouged with deep scratches—by animals, perhaps, or time itself. Together, they sit in silence.

I slowly stand and turn in place, the sound of my shoes upon the stone deafening in the quiet of the chamber. On either side of me, more statues rise from the temple's foundation, half lost to the weather and the passage of years. Aquaemus, bathed in sea foam, clutching a trident. Feuerignis, engulfed in flame, holding his sword. Gehrvania, arms outstretched, palms turned upward, her all-knowing gaze fixed on the skies above. Each one is ancient, still.

Waiting.

Beyond the pillars, the temple grounds fade into a neglected cemetery. Graves, clustered too close together, overseen by headstones split and chipped, their names faded to illegibility. Weeds claim the spaces between them, climbing into the cracks, nature's rebellion against the invading stone. Some of the headstones have toppled completely, half swallowed by dirt. Even the dead wish to leave this place behind.

The wind stirs, sending dry leaves gathered in the corners of the temple into whirling cyclones, then scattering them to the headstones.

A whisper rides the wind, not so much words as sensation. A voice I cannot place. A memory yet to occur. I step forward, and the marble beneath my feet trembles, causing me to stumble, to fall to the floor. When the trembling ceases, I raise my eyes to find I'm no longer alone. Between the sister statues stands a man.

A man with hair as black as pitch, skin as pale as the moon, and dark, fathomless eyes.

His mouth opens, and an ancient and powerful voice echoes from it, its resonance rippling over my skin, raising the flesh in its path.

"The conspiracy has stirred, risen," he intones.

"I don't understand," I tell him.

"All will be revealed in time, when the earth is stained red and the air falls silent," he replies, and his words send a chill down my spine.

"Why me? Why am I here?" I whisper.

"When the blood of ravens runs deep, power will rise, both terrible and great. Seek the sign where shadow and feather meet."

"I keep hearing that," I yell, "But I don't even know what I'm looking for!"

"The words of the past are carved in bone, and the hands of the departed hold the key. In the silence of stone and shadow, where the lost keep their vigil, truth waits in patience."

I shiver, "I don't know what that means."

He changes in front of my eyes, his nose growing, elongating; his figure hunching; his arms stretching out on either side of him. Skin, clothing, and hair are replaced by feathers as dark as night, iridescent with indigo and violet.

A raven.

A raven with crimson eyes.

The raven's gaze locks with mine. Its beak opens, "Follow the path where night lingers longest. For even in death, the watch remains unbroken."

The morning sun's golden beams are bleeding into orange across the training yard as it rises to midday's peak, the warmth already permeating my tunic a harbinger of the day's weather to come. I grit my teeth and raise my practice greatsword again, the hilt already slick with my sweat. Though the steel of a real sword is almost certainly heavier than a practice one, this feels like I'm swinging a tree trunk at Dagmar, given my speed and the accuracy of my strikes.

I meet her next hit with a two-handed block. The shock jolts up my arms, rattling my elbows.

She rolls her eyes, "Again," she says, stepping back into guard.

I exhale sharply and reset my stance. My muscles ache from the repetitive drills. My back burns from the effort of lifting the practice weapon. My legs feel weak and unsteady. The greatsword demands aggression and proximity to my opponent. It forces me to lean into blows when all I want to do is stay back, to have a moment to think, to breathe.

It doesn't help that I'm still physically and mentally recovering from the trial yesterday, and my brain is foggy from lack of sleep after being jarred awake by another strange and unsettling dream.

The memory of it scratches across my mind like the edge of the scythe I keep envisioning. I can't recall all the details by the time I'm fully awake, but I can still feel its weight in my hands, the press of marble beneath my feet, the eerie, unseeing eyes of the statues in the temple. Eyes carved with such precision and detail make it easy to imagine they can see.

Even now, beneath the weight of my fatigue, something keeps me on edge. A feeling that someone is watching me. Like the gods themselves have seen me. Judged me. Condemned me. I shake the thought away, trying to ground myself in the sting of sweat and the clatter of practice weapons. *Dreams are just dreams,* I tell myself; *they don't have eyes, they don't follow you into the day.* I repeat that mantra, pointedly ignoring Roan's previous, ominous words about their being "maps."

Another strike sends me hurtling backward.

I miss the krahbek.

I miss the distance it provides, the axe's slicing arc, and the spear's reach. It feels like a weapon made for people like me, who know their own weakness enough to know that we shouldn't get too close to our opponents or risk losing our heads.

"This thing is brutal," I groan, taking a break to lean my sword against my leg and shake out my hands. "Feels like I'm swinging a log."

"I don't think that has much to do with the weapon," Dagmar drawls.

I huff, "I like the krahbek better. It seems more my speed."

Stigander snorts from the side where he and Cyneric are practicing combinations.

"That's because the krahbek offers options. This," Cyneric says, stopping to heft his weapon, "this is just rude."

I laugh, "Exactly."

We continue to spar, striking and retreating. I frequently adjust my grip to learn the sword's weight and attempt to follow Lieutenant Broadbente's advice to let its weight work *with* me rather than against me. What a load of horse shit. I manage a diagonal cut against Dagmar's guard, but my foot slips on the damp grass in the follow-through, and Dagmar takes the opportunity to slam the flat of her blade against my ribs.

I stagger back, wincing.

I gesture to Stigander and Dagmar. "Why don't you spar and Cyneric and I…we'll supervise," I suggest, holding my ribs and hobbling a few feet away.

Cyneric grabs my practice sword from me and sets it gently on the ground at our feet. I suspect he mostly agreed with my assessment of the greatsword versus the krahbek to be supportive, since he doesn't seem to struggle with the weight of it whatsoever despite his lean frame.

"You know, darling, everyone is talking about you," he tells me, his eyes following Stigander and Dagmar.

"Are they?" I ask him, trying not to breathe too deeply. "What about now?"

He grins. "Oh, just about how you saved all the rescues in the trial yesterday and didn't have to help the others with the clues. That you could have let them try to figure it out."

A quiet falls over those nearby; Dagmar and Stigander slow their motions.

I look at Cyneric and say, "Someone wise once said, 'I'd rather lose with my soul intact than win with blood on my hands,' and I hope I'm never too far gone to feel the same."

I look back at Dagmar and Stigander, my eyes catching on the latter. He doesn't smile, as he does so rarely, but he nods at me. A silent thanks. I feel it land in my chest like the string of a rotte plucked on just the right note, filling me with warmth.

Berte interjects, "It's lucky for us someone around here knows how to translate old Aurelian. Would have been a pretty depressing trial, else."

"Lucky for Jarl, someone knows how to read," Stigander grunts.

Dagmar lifts her eyebrows. "Speak for yourself."

"Oh, were you in such a great position to help then?" Stigander asks, eyebrows raising right back.

"It isn't exactly common knowledge among the commonfolk. Where did you say you grew up again?" Berte presses me.

"Well, uh, here and there in Vallaurium," I offer.

It's a threadbare explanation, and one that won't hold up under any kind of examination. But not only do I not want to open myself up to the potential ridicule of admitting I'm from the Lützenclaste class, but it means talking about my grandmother. About listening to her voice recite syllable after syllable, repeating conjugations of verbs by candlelight. The scent of her perfume as she leaned in to point to the letters in her old texts. A soft cheek on the top of my head. A kind hand cupping my shoulder. My throat is suddenly thick with unshed tears.

Dagmar's voice cuts through the heavy silence, "You're all being gossipy busybodies," she says sternly, one hand resting casually on the hilt of her practice sword. "Back to training, if you don't mind. My partner needs a lot of work on the greatsword."

I laugh awkwardly, caught between embarrassment and gratitude. I know it was Dagmar's way of stepping in, cutting off Berte's question without making it a scene—her version of kindness.

I shift awkwardly and worry the toe of my shoe in the grass, "Um, thanks. I didn't want to set myself apart so much there, and I didn't know how to mention it without talking about everything, and it's just…not something I really feel like explaining right now."

She shrugs. "No need for thanks. But you can also tell people to just fuck off if you don't want to talk to them."

I laugh again, and this time it's genuine. "Maybe *you* can."

The words had barely left my mouth when I feel my scalp tingle faintly. *"Silence is not weakness. Your past is a door you choose to open—or keep shut. You owe no one the key."*

I blink several times, having lost my train of thought. I smile sheepishly at Dagmar again.

She is watching me. Not necessarily with suspicion but with consideration. Like she can't decide if there's something else going on or if I'm just strange.

She shakes her head. "I do wonder about you sometimes."

I frown. "What do you mean?"

She crosses her arms. "Well, you haven't really mentioned much about your background, whereas I can't get the others to shut up about theirs. And sometimes you get this look on your face—like you're listening to a conversation only you can hear. You were doing it during the trial yesterday. Makes me wonder if you're crazy—or hiding some crazy mind magic."

My insides go cold.

Roan's voice, darker now, slides into my thoughts, *"Be wary of the foe posing as friend. Not every outstretched wing offers shelter. Some only reach wide enough to encircle you."*

I make a mental "shush" at him. I'm certainly not going to make the painful mistake of almost revealing too much about him again. It took days to get over that headache.

I cock my head. "Hey, Dagmar…fuck off."

I hear a chuckle in my mind.

She raises her brows and grins before declaring, "On your guard!"

The shift into sparring happens fast, blades clashing like a storm. I barely have time to reposition my grip before Dagmar lunges. We fall into a rhythm, the clatter of weapons loud even with the background noise of others training. I block the first few strikes decently—I'm getting better, even with knowing Lieutenant Broadbente and Aric are observing from across the training yard.

Until my back foot slides on a patch of mud and I stumble forward with a grunt. Thanks to Dagmar's arcing blow, my sword flies from my hand, landing with a shameful thunk several feet away.

Dagmar lowers her sword and steps back, grabbing a waterskin. "You're still shit at this."

I groan, "You'd think by now I would have managed to develop *some* athletic ability."

Dagmar snorts, turning her head at the sound of approaching footsteps.

Belinda and her toads are flouncing by, bolstered by the weight of their own entitlement. Mette whispers something to Hartwin, who chuckles under his breath. Belinda's lip curls as she looks at me, my empty hands, and my sword on the ground.

"You tripped over your own feet out there, *grumple*," she says with mock concern, "I thought peasant girls were supposed to know how to work with their hands."

Mette and Hartwin snicker.

"Maybe her hands are too full of potatoes to grip anything useful," Mette smirks.

Hartwin, who wanders too close to me, says in a low voice, "Or maybe her hands are too full of something else, like one of the officers—"

The implication slides under my skin like a splinter, jagged and sharp. My eyes narrow, and I open my mouth to respond, ready to deal a verbal blow—

Otto steps in first, face flushed, putting himself between Hartwin and me. "Hey. Back off."

His voice is louder than it needs to be, and he's vibrating with anger, drawing himself up to his full height, which is equal to Hartwin's, but he's considerably heavier than Hartwin's reedy thinness.

Lotti joins in, her eyes gleaming with fury. "Greta's earned her place of respect here. Can't say the same for anyone who gets by on last names."

Belinda turns slowly to Lotti, lips pursed, her eyes narrowing, "You'll regret that, sunshine."

Dagmar drops her waterskin to the ground with a dull thud and steps forward, folding her arms across her chest. Several other team members—Stigander, Jarl, Cyneric, Berte—also advance.

"Are you planning to hit her with your wit or your fists?" Dagmar asks. "Either way, you'll miss."

A few scattered laughs flare from those around her.

I glance at Dagmar gratefully. Her tone is as dry as dust, but her message, like Otto's, is clear: back the fuck off. Hartwin, unable to handle being shown up, starts to move toward me, chest puffed up, jaw clenched.

That's when Aric appears on the edge of the training yard, pacing the perimeter of our training area. He doesn't approach, doesn't speak, just looks at Hartwin. It's quiet. Controlled. A silent warning.

Hartwin falters. The change in him is instant. His bravado wilts under Aric's stare, his step stuttering mid-stride. He shifts his weight like he means to speak, then thinks better of it. I watch Aric, wondering if he's going to step in, to say something, wishing he would.

Then with theatrical flair and perfect timing, Rafe saunters over to their side of the training yard, tossing an apple up and down in one hand, grinning lazily. His stupid act is back on in full force.

"Oh, good, a standoff!" He says excitedly. "I was growing tired of watching people wave swords like they're swatting flies."

A few nervous chuckles ripple through the team. I stiffen, but my eyes don't leave Belinda and her toads. I watch Hartwin shift his weight, no longer squared off but reluctant, uncertain. Belinda's attention swivels to Rafe with undisguised malicious glee.

She lifts her nose as she says to him, "It's good to see a person with breeding intervene. I was beginning to think these miscreants would get through their training without learning their place."

She looks smugly at the team, who all scowl back at her.

Rafe nods agreeably, "Indeed, it is. But until someone with breeding arrives, I suppose I'll take a...stab at it." He glances around. "Stab—because swords—no? Gods, tough crowd," he scoffs when the team remains quiet.

He takes a bite from his apple and turns back to Belinda with a dazzling smile. "Benedikta, darling, you simply don't have the presence to pull off menace, just volume. Perhaps try lowering your voice so you sound less like a congested poodle."

A few people snort. Otto tries—and fails—to hide his laughter behind his hand. My shoulders drop, loosening slightly, just enough to realize how tense I had been.

Belinda scowls and says, "This isn't your concern. And it's Belinda. You should know after all. You know my sister, Lodema."

Rafe puts his hand on her shoulder and nods sagely, "Right, right, Betina. See, everything becomes my concern when it threatens to bore me. And your speeches, Bernadette, rival the legistadt for dryness."

He steps between me and Hartwin, smiling, but his voice drops low, quiet enough that only we can hear him say, "Touch her, and I'll turn your bones into wind chimes."

Hartwin blanches. His puffed chest fully deflates. Whatever bravado had lingered from before withers beneath the menace in Rafe's tone, his voice having lost all of its cheerful oafishness. He steps back without another word.

I stare at the space Rafe now occupies, my thoughts racing to catch up. He had just pulled himself into my path like a shield. In front of everyone.

Then Aric's voice cuts through the silence, "This isn't break time."

He strides across the yard with purposeful steps, eyes sweeping across the group. His gaze snags on Hartwin, then flicks to Mette and Belinda, all three of whom freeze like children getting caught raiding sweets in the larder.

"You three," he gestures sharply to them. "You're not in my unit. Go find yours."

They scurry off without protest, Mette grabbing Belinda's sleeve to pull her away from Rafe. Hartwin doesn't look back.

Rafe smiles brightly, "Quite right, cousin! All these dramatics are positively invigorating. Does anyone fancy a verbal sparring match? Perhaps a dramatic swoon? *Künnle,* you look flushed. It's becoming."

My eyes widen in surprise, face reddening more as I look from my teammates to Aric to Rafe and back. I glare at him but have to compress my lips to keep from laughing.

Rafe, unfazed, continues, "Though, as Captain Everbrandt pointed out, perhaps we should return to our respective places. Maybe even review sword basics again. Now, this," he says, lifting my practice sword from the ground with reverence, "is a *sword.* The pointy end," he taps it gently for emphasis, "goes into the thing you want to die."

The team around me starts snickering. Otto chokes on his breath. Lotti snorts into her sleeve so hard she nearly drops her practice sword. Dagmar just grins. Aric looks on stonily but doesn't intervene.

I step back, resisting the urge to shake my head in bewilderment. That Rafe, who I humiliated in front of hundreds—maybe even thousands—of people, would publicly stand up for me. Our peace is cautious and newly made, not even something we've discussed since it happened. So I hadn't expected…this.

Roan's voice dips into my mind, *"You're surprised the blow to your opponents came from him? I suspect he is as well. But sometimes a thing meant to harm finds itself guarding instead. That's how change begins—sharp and unintended."*

I almost startle at the sound; I hadn't even felt the tingle then.

I look to Rafe, who saunters past me, leaning forward so only I can hear as he says, "You're welcome, *künnle*," and the low timbre of his voice sends shivers down my spine.

I swallow hard, hoping my face isn't betraying my feelings as much as I fear.

"Now," Rafe says, beckoning to the group with his fingers, "who wants to try me?"

Dagmar steps forward, stretching her shoulders and cracking her neck. They square off, the others spreading in a loose circle around them. The tension from before has evaporated, though anticipation has taken its place. I linger at the edge of the group, watching them circle each other, blades up, expressions playful but also coiled. Ready to strike.

"Think he's doing this for fun or to show off?" Lotti asks quietly from beside me.

"With him?" I ask. Shrugging, I say, "Probably both."

Otto leans in from my other side. "I think he's trying to distract us. Or himself, maybe."

"From what?" Lotti frowns.

Otto blinks. "From murder, probably. He looked like he *meant* the wind chime thing."

I guess Rafe hadn't spoken as quietly as I thought.

I dart a nervous glance toward Aric, wondering what he makes of all this. I still need to talk to him, to have the conversation I've been putting off from a combination of indecision and dread.

He's gone. The dread curdles in my gut.

Dagmar and Rafe meet in a clash of wooden swords. She puts up an admirable fight, but he is bigger and more experienced; and where she is fury and unchecked enthusiasm, he is precision and unrelenting force.

He knocks her sword from her hand, sending it flying across the yard, much as she did with mine.

After the morning training session ends, I'm halfway across the training yard to the citadel when I hear Rafe call my name.

I turn.

He ambles up to me, and the side of his mouth kicks up. "Didn't feel like sparring with me today?"

I raise a brow, "Well, I didn't want to embarrass you in front of everyone else by beating you. You've got a reputation to uphold."

He lets out a sharp, surprised laugh. Short but genuine. I smile and ask, "I'll see you later for training?"

His smile fades. His jaw tightens.

"I'll be gone for a few days. My father has decided I'm the best man to escort another batch of conscripts from Fracidaem. He didn't seem to think the mentee he forcibly assigned me was reason enough to stay."

My stomach drops. I try not to let my disappointment show, but I don't think I'm successful. I don't trust myself to speak, so I just nod.

"I spoke with Berger," he says. "You'll train with her and Stigander until I'm back. Look, Greta—"

"Lieutenant Colonel Kriegeur!" One of the Aurengarte soldiers is waving their arms in our direction. "Lord Corvilian has summoned you to his study."

Rafe's mouth flattens. He looks at me again and tells me, "You don't really need me, Greta. I can't teach you what you already have."

I blink. "But I'm an abysmal fighter."

He nods. "Agreed."

My eyes narrow. "Thanks for the encouragement."

He laughs softly and shakes his head. "I don't need to teach you determination—you've already got it. I don't need to teach you how to outwit someone—you're fully capable. I don't even need to teach you how to survive—you're already doing that." His voice dips lower, "And on top of that, you've got more compassion and heart than I could ever begin to understand. You might have to teach me a thing or two there."

I stare at him, dumbstruck and speechless.

He reaches out and brushes a wayward tendril of hair back from my face. It's an absent-minded gesture, one he doesn't seem to realize he was doing until it was already done. His fingers trail down the side of my cheek softly before he turns and walks away without another word.

And I…I stand rooted to the ground, watching him leave, heart racing.

"Sharp and unintended," Roan repeats in my mind. *"Like all good beginnings."*

CHAPTER FORTY-FOUR
Winging It

The moon sheds broken beams through the pocked roof of the old chapel, casting the splintered wood furniture and weather-worn stone in a silvery glow. The occasional breeze whispers through the fractured glass of the windows, tugging at strings dangling from threadbare upholstery and coaxing tendrils of hair from my braid. I stand in the open area in front of the altar, feet spread, wooden practice krahbek in hand, its blunted hook gleaming like polished bone.

I take a deep breath, slow and measured, before exhaling gradually. Then I move.

A forward thrust—a stab of my spear.

A tight slice from the side—a gouge with my hook.

Retreat, then pivot, then slash all over again.

Roan circles above me, dark shape skirting between rotting rafters, his wings arcing elegantly through the night air as sharply as steel. The bond between us pulses strongly and securely now, our connection growing smoother each day. I can feel when he swivels, returns, when he's watching, when he focuses his sight through mine. The presence of those sensations no longer startles me—it's a welcome companion now, like my veins thrum with a second pulse.

"*Left, hook high, direct downward,*" his voice threads through my skull like smoke, no longer jarring or tingling. It's just there—a part of me. I listen without question, adjusting the angle of the krahbek and slicing through the air, picturing my invisible target faltering beneath my blow.

Until recently, the power and connection were always accompanied by a tingle, a prickling sensation, like my body, my brain, my soul had been asleep before—and were finally waking up. Now, I barely feel the magic flood my body at all. It simply joins me, like breath filling my lungs, or adrenaline coursing through my blood. The tingling had already begun to fade, but Roan and I have met every night this week to train, and without the distraction and interruption of a certain pair of cousins, I've come a long way.

Occasionally, I'm able to pull it myself, as I had in archery training before. But still, it slips too quickly through my mind's grasp, like water through my fingers.

"*Loosen your grip, fledgling,*" Roan instructs from above. "*Let the motions ebb and flow as the tide.*"

"*I am letting it,*" I mutter, but adjust my grip. "*Maybe your tide is making too many waves.*"

"*And yet you are as a sailor regaining their balance on land.*"

I roll my eyes and smile, stepping into another spin, trying to channel all Rafe taught the cadets about using the krahbek—deliberate footwork, full-arm strikes that use your body's momentum, and fully completing motions.

Despite my improvement, I still have much to learn about working with my abilities—and Roan's. He can share not only the acuity of his vision, but also his *actual* vision with me, giving me valuable perspective from different angles. I am far from mastering watching the shared visions while I still need to see through my own eyes at the same time. When he does so next, the shift is disorienting, and the ground wobbles beneath my feet. I turn, overcompensating for the movement.

My boot catches on the edge of a chipped tile. I stumble sideways, slamming hip first into one of the benches with an ear-splitting crack.

With a groan, I slither to the ground gracelessly, krahbek clattering to the stones. My hip throbs as I lie still on the ground, catching my breath, watching through one of the roof holes as the clouds move silently overhead, filtering the moon through a milky haze.

"I'm not certain how you handle having such a clumsy bonded," I say aloud, not bothering with the silent mind link. "If your fellow *Blutraben* knew, you'd have to suffer the mortifying shame. King of the Ravens paired with the world's least coordinated cadet, barely capable of wielding a stick. I don't even know why you chose me."

"Kings do not embarrass so easily," he says simply.

I let out a watery laugh that gets caught halfway in my throat. My chest aches with the effort of holding the emotions in, holding myself together. The training, the fear, the pressure of the trials all weigh on me, digging into my skin like too-tight clothing.

I pull myself to a sitting position. "What…what will you do if I die?" I ask, barely a whisper. "Will you be all right?"

There is a long pause. When Roan finally answers, his voice feels sad, heavy, and older than the stones of the chapel around us.

"Blutraben are made to linger long after stone crumbles and names have been forgotten. I will remain. Not whole. Not unchanged. But here. You, however," he pauses, *"you are meant to fly farther than I ever could. I will see you reach the sky, even if I must fall to do so."*

The words pierce my heart like the spear end of a krahbek. I don't know what to do with this much faith in me, nor do I want to imagine a world where I can't speak with him like this or feel his presence.

I close my eyes. "What if I fail?" The words come out hoarse, "What if I don't win and I can't get out of here?"

He doesn't hesitate this time. *"I believe I've told you more than once, fledgling, that only fools think there is one path in anything."*

I swallow. "What if I'm a fool, then?"

The silence that follows is not one full of judgment, as it so often is when coming from Roan. Only the faint creak of tree limbs in the wind, the soft sweep of his wings as he descends, landing nearby with a gentle click of his talons on the floor.

"When Blutraben first hear the call of a bond," he tells me, *"they have the choice to accept it or to simply…move on."*

"You can choose that?" I blink.

He says wryly, *"Humans are not the only species to earn favor from the gods."* He hops closer. *"I chose you, not for peace, for I've known that in my solitude. Not for glory; fame means little to me. Not for duty, for others would answer that call had I refused. Not for joy, laughter, fulfillment. Those are your gifts to bestow, not mine to take. I did not choose you for what you could offer me."*

"Then…why?" I ask in a whisper.

He gazes at me, unwavering. *"I chose you for your sorrow. Because those who have fallen know how to rise. Should this path end, you will find another way. We* will find another way.*"*

The shell I have erected around my fears, my insecurities, my hopes, cracks at his words.

There is no one here but Roan, so I don't try to hold it in, to hold it back. There are no challengers, no cadets, no officers, no Aric, no Rafe, no Grandmother, no Agnethe, no uncles. No one whose expectations and desires weigh upon me so heavily that I forget my own.

The dam has broken, and rushing through it are tears. Heavy and relentless, burning hot pathways through the training dust gathered on my cheeks. I press my hands to my face, but it does nothing to stop the sobs that shudder loose from within.

All of it—the trials, the terror for Agnethe, for myself, the secrets I carry—pours out at once. And it *hurts.*

My shoulders curl inward, body hunching forward to cradle the pain, the grief threatening to crack my chest open. My breath comes in sharp gulps, stabbing between my ribs.

Roan doesn't speak. He hops closer, though, and settles beside me, tucking his head against my arm. His feathers are soft, his breath warm and even against my skin. He makes no grand declarations, no clever retorts. He simply sits patiently as the tears fall from my face and onto his inky wings, the feathers absorbing them like they're attempting to absorb my pain for me.

A large hand lands on my shoulder opposite Roan.

I gasp, my heart and stomach lurching. I instinctively twist away and nearly collide with Roan as he hops backward with a loud croak, wings flaring in alarm. My breath is sharp and stilted as I scramble backward, reaching for my discarded practice krahbek.

"Easy," Rafe says, "it's just me."

He's crouched nearby, one knee bent, the other foot braced lightly on the flagstones. His face is shadowed by the roof and the angle of the moonlight, but even in the dim, I can see the somber crease in his brow and the tightness around his mouth.

He looks exhausted. Not just in mind but in spirit.

I stare at him in dumbfounded shock. "You're back."

He nods. "About an hour ago. I thought you might be here."

Roan sidles up to me with an irritated croak, shaking his wings with deliberate irritation, muttering unintelligibly along the bond. I think I catch something about "sneaking, smirking brutes," but I don't respond. I keep my eyes on the man in front of me.

"When I came in," he begins, tapping his fingers absentmindedly along the side of his boot, "I heard you speaking. Then crying. I didn't know how to approach you without making you run."

I hastily wipe my hands across my face to banish the last of my tears. I'm certain that my eyes are red and swollen. The skin of my cheeks feels flushed and tight. I sigh heavily.

"Well, now that my humiliation is complete, there's certainly no point in running. You might as well stay," I tell him, settling back into my spot leaning against the bench.

He nods once and, without another word, lowers himself to the ground across from me. He leans back against the stone steps of the altar, long legs extended loosely in front of him, head resting against the worn platform as he closes his eyes.

I hesitate, then mirror his position—stretching my legs out, leaning my head back. Roan remains at my right, his talons clicking lightly against the flagstones as he shifts, silent but watchful.

We sit in the quiet for a while.

The chapel—and the world—seem to hold their breath. The breeze stills to nothing. Above us, the clouds clear from the face of the moon, pale light spilling through the broken ceiling. The stone beneath me grows cooler as night fully settles in, but my face still feels hot, tacky with the salt of dried tears.

After a long time, I tilt my head forward to look at him. I study him in silence.

He looks at ease, resting against the altar platform, legs crossed at the ankles. His head remains tilted to the ceiling, eyes closed. I'd suspect he's asleep, were it not for how his fingers trace small, distracted circles over the hilt of his dagger, now resting in his lap. The movement is too regular to be unconscious, too deliberate to be meaningless. It's not the motion of a self-soothing gesture made in dreaming.

His dark hair catches the faint moonlight, curling in soft, unruly waves past his shoulders, part of it pulled back from his face with a strip of leather. My gaze trails from the chiseled lines of his face, where his bronze skin glows softly, to the strong column of his throat beneath the dark edge of his closely cropped beard. Down to broad shoulders and a muscled chest that bunches beneath the dark linen of his tunic, narrowing to a lean waist. To thickly muscled legs stretched before him in easy confidence.

My mouth goes dry.

Sisters, he's handsome.

Beautiful, even—in a brutal, dangerous sort of way.

And even as exhaustion presses down upon me, a weight I couldn't lift if I tried—even now, hollowed out, emptied of everything but the fragile remains of grief, the sight of him still makes my stomach tighten. Makes my breath catch, shallow and quiet, like my body hasn't gotten the message that there's no room left for anything else.

I watch him for several moments before asking, "Are you going to say anything?"

He opens his eyes slowly, lifting his head to look at me. "Do you want me to?"

I shrug. "I'm not sure."

He looks at me for a moment longer. Then softly, he says, "I used to sit in the quiet with her often."

My brow furrows. "With who?"

"My mother," he answers. His voice is strong but hollow as he adds,

"After my father was done with her."

I blink, caught off guard by the information. "What do you mean 'done with her'?"

He looks away momentarily, then his dark gaze returns to mine. His voice is tight, brittle. "Beating her. Hurting her. Raping her in pursuit of more options to preserve his precious legacy."

A sudden gust of wind whips through the chapel, but I barely feel it. My mind is still processing what he's said—what he's given me. Rafe, who has never spoken of his past and keeps his innermost thoughts disguised beneath smirks and sarcasm, told me something raw. Something awful. Neither he, nor anyone, has ever mentioned his mother before. Now suddenly, I know of her suffering. The significance of it compresses my chest, and I'm caught between shock and sorrow. I don't know what to say, not really.

"So," he continues, saving me from having to come up with a reply, "I know that sometimes, more than anything, when someone is hurting, they just need another person to sit in the silence with them."

I swallow the tears threatening to surge anew. I want to say something right and useful, but everything I think of feels silly and insubstantial.

So I blurt out the first question that comes to mind.

"Your mother…is she better now?"

My mind flashes to the young woman I saw beside Lord Corvilian at the first trial. Too young to be Rafe's mother. Maybe she wasn't Lord Corvilian's wife, as I had assumed, but another relation or companion.

"She's dead," he says flatly. "So, yes."

My throat feels tight, but I have nothing sufficient to say to him. The words "I'm sorry" feel inadequate. Surely, he knows I am. Can tell by how the silence stretches to meet his pain. And he *is* in pain, whether he would admit it or not.

I think of what I'd want someone to say to me after being reminded of someone I've lost, what I would want someone to say if I had mentioned Grandmother or Agnethe. And rather than shallow platitudes meant to comfort the giver more than the receiver, I ask him a question.

"What was she like?"

He's quiet for a moment, black eyes glittering as they watch me, and I wonder if he'll answer. He finally answers, low and thoughtful, "She was smart. Gentle. Softer than anyone I've ever known." He shifts slightly against the altar steps, his thumb still tracing the hilt of his dagger, "But protective. She's the one who gave me Rosamunde. Named her. Before my father sent me to Magnivine, hoping to force magic out of me that I don't have."

Pity lances through me.

"How old were you when she died?" I ask softly.

He murmurs, "Twelve."

The answer is simple, but the ache behind it is weighty. Lingering.

This time, I do not refrain from the obvious. "I'm sorry," I tell him.

He nods, gaze fixed somewhere behind me, trapped in memory.

"My own parents—the ones I remember—died when I was not quite six," I tell him after a moment. "It was just me and Agnethe after that. And Grandmother."

"Agnethe is your sister?" He asks.

I nod. "Yes. She's just twenty."

He repeats my question back to me, "What's she like?"

My lips tug upward slightly, warmth spreading through my chest at his query. But I can feel the corners threatening to turn down, the shadow of fear and uncertainty threatening to overtake my happy memories.

"Smart. Sunny. Bursting with big plans, big ideas about what she will do, where she will go. She's bold in a way I've never been. Still am not," I confess.

He raises his brow. "Yes, entering a deadly tournament with fire, drowning, and literal nightmares is so timid."

I flush, plucking at a thread on my tunic. "I think I held her back more than I meant to. I tried to make her world smaller to keep her safe within it."

He seems to absorb what I say before responding. When he speaks, his voice is gentle.

"It's natural to want to hold on tight to the ones we love. Especially when we fear for them."

I tilt my head. "I worry she resents me." I look away from his face, unable to handle his study as I confess some of my deeper insecurities and share some of my past. "Some of the things she's said…I know she does, at least a bit. I don't completely blame her. I just—" my voice hitches slightly, "I just didn't want her to feel the way I did. When our parents died, the fear…the fear was like drowning. And I wanted to keep her away from the shore."

My eyes return to his. They're steady. Sympathetic but not pitying.

"She's lucky," he says, "to have someone who cares for her the way you do."

The words land harder than expected. Because of the weight they carry. The weight borne of memory. I realize that Rafe never had that care after his mother was gone. Maybe no one ever protected *him* the way I do Agnethe.

"One day she'll be grateful for it," he reassures me.

"I hope so," I reply quietly. "I just hope I can make it through. Get out. Go find her."

"Where is she?" He asks.

I hesitate. The truth rises in my throat, and the temptation to tell him is strong. But before I can decide what I want to do, he speaks again.

"You don't have to tell me if you don't wish to," he says, a half-smile tugging at the corner of his mouth. "But I'm rather good at keeping secrets."

I let out a small huff. "Yes, I've noticed." I shift on the ground, trying to bring feeling back to my legs and backside, which have gone numb from stillness and cold. "It's almost like you're two different people sometimes."

He smirks. "What about you with your strange bird cabals?"

Roan, who had been quietly observing, immediately croaks from beside me, "Go away!"

Rafe blinks. "Is that all he knows how to say?"

I purse my lips, mock thoughtfulness on my face. "I suspect you bring that out in Roan."

He raises his eyebrow again, eyes darting to Roan. "He has a name?"

I stiffen, realizing I've revealed more about him than I intended. I shrug with theatrical nonchalance. "I couldn't very well just call him 'bird.' He's very dignified. He'd object."

Rafe snorts. "*Künnle*, you were cuddling with the bird when I came in. I don't think he's as dignified as you believe."

Roan gives an offended flap of his wings, hops across my leg to the altar, and jabs Rafe's side with the sharp end of his beak.

"Ow!" He recoils, rubbing his ribs.

I burst out laughing. A real laugh with head thrown back and shoulders shaking.

Rafe looks at me strangely, brow knitting. His voice is softer as he tells me, "That sound might be even more beautiful than your singing."

I flush. The warmth rises fast beneath my skin, too quick to hide. I look away, studying a crack in the wall like it's the most interesting sight I've ever seen.

He says quietly, "I'll get her out."

My head snaps toward him. "*What?*"

Rafe swallows. "If you can't get out of Stachtenbaste. Or if…"

He doesn't finish the sentence, but the remaining words linger between us.

Or if you die.

Throat tight, I say, "You're stuck here, too, except for conscript trips. How are you going to get her all the way from Vallaurium?"

He closes his eyes briefly, taking a deep breath through his nose. "You'll have to trust me," he says at last, eyes reopening to meet mine. "Not only with her location, but with the fact that I can't explain how I'll do it."

I hesitate again, then I turn to Roan, who watches us with unblinking eyes.

"*What do you think?*" I ask him.

He sighs with the weight of centuries behind him. "*His gaze is veiled, and his path unclear—I will not lie. But some truths, fledgling, I've learned by feather and bone: there are those who guard what matters, even if they do not know why. On this, I believe you may trust him.*"

I turn back to Rafe and find him watching me warily.

"Where did you go just now, *künnle*?" He asks, voice guarded. "It's almost as if—no. Not possible." He shakes his head in denial.

I don't respond initially. I just look at him. *Really* look at him. Into his eyes, glittering jet above circles dark with fatigue. There's something vulnerable in him now. Something uncertain.

He clears his throat, clearly uncomfortable. "Well?"

I take a deep breath. "The last time I saw Agnethe, she was at Felsegeist Haus."

He stares at me blankly. "That doesn't mean much to me."

I say, "It's the house of Lord Rocheburn."

He pauses. This time, his face doesn't remain blank. Instead, it's a mask of incredulity.

"Lord Rocheburn," he starts, "as in the Duke of *fucking* Rocheburn? The lord chancellor of Aurelia?"

I gulp and nod wordlessly.

He presses a hand to his face, muttering something under his breath before saying, "Blessed Sisters, *künnle*. There are only so many powerful enemies I can make, especially since one is my father. You're sure it's not some minor country lord? Lützenclaste?"

I reply, "It's him. He's the one who has my sister."

For a heartbeat, Rafe just stares at me. Then his jaw tightens, his eyes harden.

"You have my word," he says.

He stands and walks toward me. When he's nearly at my side, he bends down, picks up my discarded practice krahbek, and then holds it in my direction.

"Now," he says, "show me what you were doing."

I stand stiffly before taking the weapon from him. My hand brushes his briefly, and something shimmers in the air between us—a fleeting tension, there for a breath, and then gone.

We move to the open space in the center of the chapel. I adjust my grip on the krahbek, shifting into the ready stance he drilled into us weeks ago. He crosses his arms and watches silently as I run through the basic cuts and defensive motions. Even without Roan, my movements are tighter and more practiced. Though still hesitant at times.

"Loosen your shoulders," he murmurs, stepping behind me, "and turn your hips when you pivot. You'll gain more power that way."

I do as he says, but my motions are jerky and awkward.

He moves closer. I freeze when his hands slide onto the curve of my hips—firm and deliberate. His fingers grip just enough to guide, adjust, and focus. The pads of his thumbs press against the crest of my pelvis, the edges of his palms tease the waistband of my trousers. For a brief second, one hand shifts beneath the hem of my tunic, brushing warm skin.

My breath catches, and my pulse races at the base of my throat.

He lingers, just a moment beyond "helpful."

I glance over my shoulder, primed to say something casual and unaffected, but the words never reach my lips. He's looking at me. Close. Closer than I expected.

And in that pause, he leans in.

His lips brush mine. Barely. Delicately. As if he's not sure I'll permit it. Then he pulls back. Not far. Just enough that coherent thought can reenter my brain. But the thoughts that do return are startled. Confused.

"I want you to focus on being ready for the trial," he explains, "not on anything else." His eyes hold mine. Serious. Determined. "On staying *alive*."

I nod, unable to speak. Instead, I pivot and spin into another slice, effectively cutting through the tension between us. We practice for a while longer. No words. Just motion and correction, drills and rhythm. Roan circles above, silent. He understands this is when I need to stand on my own two feet.

"Better," Rafe finally says into the quiet. He nods at me.

I lower the krahbek, arms aching, and return the nod.

Later—long after we parted in the old chapel, when he once again ran his fingers down the side of my cheek, sending shivers down my spine. When the night is bleeding into the dawn, I stare sleeplessly into the darkness of the dormitory, mind still reeling.

No matter what happens tomorrow in the trial, should I advance but not survive, Agnethe will be safe.

Rafe will get her out.

Something has shifted between us. Something in the shared grief we spoke into the cracks of the old chapel's stone walls. Something in the way he sat with me in the silence. An unlikely, blossoming trust. And maybe something more.

I don't know what to make of any of it, but one thing is certain.

For the first time in a long while, I have more hope than I ever dared feel. Hope can be a dangerous, empty promise. Foolish. Fragile. Even so, it's something to live for. And something I'd die for.

CHAPTER FORTY-FIVE
Lvnoch's Shadows

I step into the arena the next afternoon, heart hammering in my chest, mind racing. Six trials. Six weeks. Six brutal gauntlets requiring blood, cunning, and sacrifice.

My eyes sweep the arena's towering columns, the endless rows of benches teeming with onlookers, the center of the floor suspiciously absent of obstacles or indications of the coming challenge. My fingers tighten into fists, searching for a weapon I don't have, to provide the illusion of protection, of preparedness. I half expect traps to spring up from the ground or illusions to materialize from the walls.

The roar of the crowd feels distant, muted beneath the sound of my pulse pounding in my ears. I fall into formation beside the four other challengers, the familiar forms of Dagmar and Stigander flanking me on either side. We're not allies; we're all fighting to win. But having them nearby is still comforting.

Somehow, impossibly, I'm still here with them. Six trials, and the aches in my muscles have nearly taken up permanent residence. The feeling of helplessness, the scent of blood, and the sight of fallen competitors have etched themselves in my bones. And even though there's much I've endured, and I've done my best to build my strength and physical abilities, I know I would not have made it this far without Roan.

He responds at once, dry as ever, *"I'm honored."*

My lips twitch slightly despite the anxiety and tension coursing through me. Even now, his quips are grounding, anchoring. The bond we share, however, can't dispel the looming truth: only two will advance from this trial to the next. The field is shrinking fast, and every trial is a narrower path to traverse, with higher stakes.

My gaze flits to the other challengers: grim, wary, determined. Some have flirted with death more closely than I have. And now, the odds will demand more. Even with my gifts—my growing connection with Roan and my confidence in using the bond—there are no guarantees. Each breath could be my last. So as Colonel Richter steps forward to speak to us and the crowd, I inhale deeply, wanting to enjoy that breath as long as I can.

Colonel Richter's voice cuts through the noise of the arena like a blade, its bite commanding and merciless.

"Challengers," she begins, her boots thudding on the wood of the platform as she gazes upon us, "war rarely announces itself with clarity. In fact, it thrives on chaos. On uncertainty. It does not come with a list of obstacles or a well-marked path to survival. You will not always have the luxury of preparation. Of intelligence. Of knowing what's waiting behind the next door or around the bend.

"A good soldier learns to make decisions in the dark. To move forward with partial truths, with dulled instincts, and little time to think. You plan. You train. You try to stay a step ahead. Sometimes, though, all you get is a single step. A single moment. One chance. Sometimes, all you can do is play the hand you've been dealt.

"This trial will test your ability to do exactly that. You will receive little information. No map. You must trust your instincts, your training, your judgment—and hope they will serve you well. But remember: sometimes your best is not good enough. And 'good enough' can still get you killed."

A thrill of fear raises the hairs on my arms.

She returns to her chair, ceding the floor to Major Berger, who strides to the platform's edge with her usual dramatic flair, boots clicking with measured rhythm, arms spread wide, waiting for everyone's attention to shift to her.

"Challengers," she says, grinning, "I hope you're not afraid of the dark, because you're about to spend some quality time with each other. Your seventh trial is dedicated to our god of shadows, the moon, and the night. Welcome to Lunoch's Shadows!"

A wave of amusement and excitement washes over the crowd. Their reaction, however, is overshadowed by the strange ripple of awareness that runs through me, which I recognize as Roan. Something about Major Berger's words has unsettled or bothered him, but he doesn't explain, and Major Berger continues her speech, so I must listen to her rather than press him about it.

"Only two of you will leave this trial as challengers. The others…well, the shadows keep their secrets." There's a moment of silence as she pivots, gesturing grandly to the arena floor. "You stand on hallowed ground, where winners are made and failures are forsaken. Today, though, you will go beneath it. Into the dark belly of the island, where even Lunoch's gaze cannot reach, but his presence certainly can."

As her sentence disappears into memory, a sound splits the air—metal scraping on metal, harsh and jarring. The other challengers and I turn sharply to view the source: a section of the arena floor receding like a trap door, the earth falling in clumps, peeling back to reveal a door. It opens, deep and gaping, revealing only a darkened interior.

"This trial," Berger continues, calling our attention back to her, "is a test of faith in yourselves, in your instincts, and your resolve to claw your way through—even when you cannot see the path ahead."

Fear prickles along my skin. A trial in the dark, facing gods know what.

"You'll descend through four levels," she explains, "each darker than the last. Each with obstacles beyond mere darkness. The first level begins at seventy-five percent visibility and fades to fifty percent by the time you find the next door. The second level: fifty to twenty-five. Third: twenty-five to total blackout. And the final? Well, that's where you'll discover what you're truly made of.

"Look sharp, challengers, and be on your guard. As there are no rules beyond finishing first or second, anything on these levels can be used to your advantage. Conversely, anything on these levels can be used to your disadvantage by your competitors."

The tension around me spikes. My pulse races faster, heart thudding against my ribs. My gut twists itself in knots.

I look to Stigander, who meets my gaze and nods once, slow and steady. Then to Dagmar, who offers only the smallest jerk of her chin. Unspoken understanding passes between us that we will leave each other alone, no matter what happens.

The others, though…there's Athaulf, with a shock of hair so pale it flashes white in the sun, which reminds me of Brock. He stands on the other side of Dagmar, twitching with the unpredictability of desperate unease.

On Stigander's other side is a man of about thirty named Dirk who, belying his name, looks considerably less sharp than the other challengers, but the cruel smirk on his face makes me want to recoil in disgust. I recall Wazo's words during the second trial, about a dull blade still being able to cut, and I don't suppose he's ever been more right.

Berger claps her hands. "Finally, the challenger who won the previous trial will receive a ten-minute head start."

My heart jumps. *That's me.* Shock floods my body. Ten whole minutes could be the difference between survival and death. I've never been so grateful for a predilection for languages and deciphering as I am now.

I look past Berger to where Rafe sits on the platform. He's watching me. He nods in a quiet show of support. The corners of his mouth tip upward slightly, sweetly. A look of encouragement.

My eyes dart to Aric, seated behind him. He's composed, as always, but his expression is unreadable. There is a frigid stillness in his posture. I look away. I know I need to speak with him, but I'm not even sure I know how to anymore. Not with so much that needs to be said and so much hanging in the balance. Not when my life could end before I can even find the right words. It seems so pathetically small now to have worried about it before—what he thought of me, what he wants from me.

Major Berger's voice cuts in, "Challenger de Veend, at your mark!"

I nod, reach the starting line just before the door, and chance one last look at the stands where so many people cheer for me. I spot Lotti and Otto shouting and waving like mad. Berte and Cyneric are beside them, roaring my name. Jarl's arm is linked with Lillen's as they bounce up and down in place. Their faces are tight with worry but also full of faith. Faith in *me*.

I raise a hand and wave back, small but sincere, at my friends. It hits me then—I have *friends*. Friends, plural. Not just allies of circumstance or faces in passing. Real friends. It's more terrifying than comforting; their joy feels like both a lifeline and a weight. Because I just might lose them all. I might die and leave them waving at the space I've vacated, a ghost.

My throat tightens.

I seek the platform again, and Rafe catches my eye. He cups his hands around his mouth, and without the aid of the wind wielder, it cuts through the noise as he yells, "No mercy, *künnle*!"

A smile finally makes its presence known on my face. I tilt my head toward him in a nod of thanks.

The starting horn sounds.

And I dive into the dark.

As I step through, the door slams shut behind me, the metallic echo booming like a drum against the stone walls. I jump, heart leaping into my throat. The slam resonates long after it ends, leaving behind a high-pitched ringing in my ears. I exhale slowly, willing my heart rate to steady.

The door muffles the roar of the arena above, but I try to imagine the cheers, the hope, my name shouted by my friends in the crowd. I take another deep breath. This is the moment where the existence of the world above ends and the need for survival begins.

The air is cooler here, but thick, stale with dust and disuse. It clings to my lungs, forcing shallow breaths. The sound of my pulse pounds against my eardrums, and I wonder if I'm merely imagining that the walls themselves are pressing in, listening, too.

The floor beneath my boots is uneven, sloping gradually downward away from the door. The stones are slick in places where moss grows beneath their seams, encouraged by the underground damp. My nostrils sting with the acrid smell of burnt oil and smoke.

"Don't waste time being jittery," I mutter to myself, forcing my feet to take a step forward.

The room stretches before me, vast and mostly empty, though the edges are lost to the shadows. A pale, amber light glows from torches mounted along the walls. It's enough to navigate most of the chamber, though the far end fades to deeper gloom. I'm reminded of Major Berger's cautionary description: the deeper I travel, the darker it will become.

Roan says, "*Nine minutes remain of your advantage. Use it wisely.*"

I scan the walls and look for any signs of traps or hazards. The room is silent as a tomb—too quiet—and the stillness makes me feel edgy. My fingers twitch toward the nearest torch, then pause. What if it's a trap? Nothing here is ever that simple. I glance at the sconce again—just wood and oil-soaked cloth. No traps or enchantments that I can see. But the Freiheit has taught me that simplicity is a lie. Still, the darkness ahead is almost greedy. I weigh the risks. Roan says nothing. It's my choice.

"There are no rules, right? So, nothing prevents me from giving myself a light advantage to complement my time advantage," I say to myself as much as Roan.

I dart to the nearest torch, grabbing and easing the wooden handle from the sconce. Warmth brushes my face as the small flame flutters. Nothing happens. No traps. Just light. Holding it makes me feel steadier—less prey and more predator.

"*Well flown,*" Roan says, approval clear in his tone.

Encouraged, I hold the torch in front of me and begin a cautious advance.

"With this, I might not even need your help," I say to him aloud, testing the level of confidence in my voice. The torch crackles cheerfully in my hand, but the illusion of control only lasts a few seconds.

I stumble, and before I can even curse properly, something pricks my upper arm.

The pain is sudden and sharp, a biting sting that makes my breath catch. I don't realize I've dropped the torch until its light rolls away.

My hand shoots to my arm, my gaze following it, and my fingers brush metal. A dart is embedded there, thin and wicked, and what remains of the needle still protruding from my arm gleams faintly in the torchlight. I yank the dart free with a hiss, thankful for the rushing adrenaline that masks most of the discomfort. Whirling in place, I frantically scan the chamber for the source, but find no obvious mechanism, no visible archers.

Finally, I look to the floor and see that a thin network of crosshatched wires, each no wider than a strand of hair, covers the floor. This explains why I stumbled, rather than my own clumsiness, as I initially assumed.

"Tripwires," I breathe. "There are tripwires in here that must release the darts."

"*Are they ordinary darts or coated in pernicious substance?*" Roan asks calmly.

Panic floods me—was it poisoned? My vision swims for a second, but it might just be fear. I frown, rolling my arm. I flex my fingers, testing the range of motion. The sting remains, but nothing else has happened. No dizziness or numbness. No spreading heat. Nothing that would indicate any poison on the darts.

"Ordinary," I confirm.

"*Then gather your torch, but step lightly. No need to incur the talons of the trial unnecessarily.*"

I inch forward, carefully lifting my boots over the lines of wires. I bend forward when I reach my torch, relief surging through me as my hand wraps around the wooden handle. Thankfully, the oiled rag retaining the flame remains intact.

"I have it back," I tell Roan.

I sweep the torch low, watching how the light breaks. Some wires are so thin, they catch the flames like spider silk. Others don't show at all unless I shift the angle. My boot hovers midair, then plants down just beside one. I imagine dozens of darts pointed at me, ready to fly if I make a single mistake. My pulse thunders louder, and the shadows grow thicker with each step. The tension knots my back, and I slow the pace of my torch as the darkness increases to better see the ground, but don't cease moving. I can't afford to pause.

Suddenly, something thin and sharp tightens across my throat—not cutting, but catching just under my jaw.

A wire.

Reflexively, I jerk back, but it's too late.

The second dart hits harder, deeper, embedding itself in my right thigh. The pain is sharper this time, lancing up into my hip. My thigh spasms in protest, the muscle knotting up like it's trying to force out the metal.

Yelping and staggering backward, I groan, "Shit," and pull the dart free, gritting my teeth as I do.

I keep moving despite the pain.

"Three minutes remain on your advantage," Roan tells me when I'm about three-quarters of the way through the chamber.

"I'm making decent time," I pant. "Hopefully this will be quick with the torch—"

Another dart punches into my right leg—my calf this time, angled downward.

"Fuck the sisters sideways!" I snarl, yanking it out, fire burning in its path. I feel moisture where my fingers brush against my calf, and I'm not sure if it's poison or blood trailing down into my boot. I wait several breaths.

Nothing has happened yet, so I must be bleeding a little.

At least the darts aren't big enough to cause serious damage. The pain pulses in hot flashes. I limp forward, relying on the torchlight and sheer determination.

I'm so focused on my injuries, and the light is low enough, that I nearly collide with the far wall. I brace myself, scanning the stone, and spot a patch of shadow where the lines of the stone break.

As I sidestep toward it, I try not to think about what lies beyond this room. Who—or what—might be watching, waiting for me to walk through. When I reach what turns out to be a door, I'm ready to push it open, when, with the aid of my torch, I spot yet another tripwire stretched across the threshold. Careful to lift my foot high, and wincing at the pull in my leg as I do, I push the door open.

A gust of wind hits my face, unexpected and unnatural beneath the ground. I step through the opening, struggling to hold the heavy door while clutching my torch.

"*One minute remains on your advantage,*" Roan tells me, "*the other challengers are preparing to enter.*"

I let go of the door, which slams behind me, another gust tugging at my clothes. A faint scraping follows, a rhythmic squeal that sets my teeth on edge. Air shivers across my cheek. Something is moving, but what?

I frown, staring into the dim. "Could it be some kind of Luftella-related challenge?" I wonder. This was said to be dedicated to Lunoch, and we already had a Luftella obstacle in the first trial, but nothing else makes sense. The air shifts again, like something significant has exhaled across the chamber.

I clutch my torch tighter, my fingers aching around the wooden shaft. It's absurd how much comfort I've placed into something so small, especially as the increasing darkness means the meager light provides less assistance. I cling to it, though, like a shield.

I'm about to step forward when Roan's voice screams down the bond.

"*FLEDGLING, CEASE!*"

I freeze just as a massive blade swings past me, missing me by inches, stirring my hair in its wake.

My torch flickers wildly. In its wavering light, and with my eyes' adjustment to the darker room, I can see blades hung from above—slicing through the air in mechanical rhythm. They travel across the room, one after another, gleaming pendulums of death.

"*Look sharp,*" Roan says.

Is he taking pun lessons from Major Berger now?

"If that's a joke, you could have better timing," I tell him snappishly.

Roan replies, *"It was excellent timing. You dislike it because you're concerned."*

"Concerned doesn't even begin to describe it," I say, forcing a breath through my nose, "I need your help to see."

My vision momentarily blurs, but then returns sharper than before. The blades stand out more starkly, their motions clearer, the timing easier to track. I watch the nearest one sweep past me and bolt through the space just as it clears my frame.

"First one down," I murmur.

I count eleven more I need to go through. Each swings at a different speed. Each has its own rhythm, like the inner workings of some monstrous clock.

"Can you tell how close the other challengers are?" I ask as I duck past the third blade.

"I cannot say where they've flown—not without eyes on them or you sourcing their lichtfaden. *And that, fledgling, takes more than a glance. You must know the glimmer of their soul or stand near enough to feel it stir."*

I huff, "We'll unpack that whole statement later, if I get out of here. I feel like there's some stuff you've left out."

As I slip past the sixth blade, a strange sensation begins in my limbs. A faint tingling. They feel slightly numb. My calf aches with the heat.

My arm and leg feel heavy, like they're half stone. My hand doesn't want to close around the torch as well anymore, and I feel each pulse of my blood like it's vibrating through my veins. My vision, enhanced just moments ago, begins to soften at the edges, the torchlight smearing across the darkness.

"Roan," I whisper, "tell me you're doing this. Whatever this is with my arm and leg."

His silence answers me first, followed by his confirmation.

"No," Roan's tone is suddenly sharp, *"the darts which struck you were, perhaps, not so ordinary as they seemed."*

The floor tilts beneath me for a moment.

The door crashes open behind me. Not yet. Not now. *Please*, not now.

A scream echoes through the space. I nearly glance back but resist the urge. With my arm and leg as they are, I don't even think I can help the person anyway. And I won't survive hesitation.

The eighth blade misses me by a hair, and I lurch forward, my gait unsteady now. My legs feel heavier, the torch nearly slipping from my damp palm. My vision swims.

"*Poison,*" I agree, no longer speaking aloud.

I trudge on, awkwardly, and make it past the eleventh blade. The last swings in front of me, its speed terrifying. Only four seconds per sweep.

"*Shift to the far-right side. Let the blade pass, and only then move ahead. It is the longest span of time you'll have to cross.*"

Even though he can't see me, I nod and drag myself sideways.

The door crashes open again, just as I pull myself to the right side of the room, leg dragging behind me. I wait for several passes of the blade until I understand its rhythm.

One. Two. Three—*GO.*

I surge forward, running as fast as I can, nearly falling backward as I slam into a stone I hadn't seen coming. My torch has tumbled from my numb hand in my dash, bouncing across the floor, the motion of the blades and impact causing its light to snuff out completely. I hear screams again—closer this time. The others are gaining on me. I mourn the loss of light.

"*You must continue without it,*" Roan urges, "*I cannot mark the others, and the poison clings to you with each step. Every second costs, fledgling.*"

I nod again to no one and move toward the patch of blackness on the wall where the next doorway waits. I open it and slip through, the door slamming shut as soon as I step inward. After only a few paces, I'm nonplussed when I crash into another door.

I lean into the next one and push forward.

I immediately know why there were two doors when my eyes are flooded with searing, blinding light.

CHAPTER FORTY-SIX
Bright Ideas, Abysmal Results

Light explodes in my vision. Painful, glaring, complete. My vision blurs into a wall of white, the shapes dissolving into glowing apparitions and haloed hints. I stagger, disoriented, as my eyes struggle to adjust, utterly useless. I throw my hands over my face to block out the persistent beams, but even when I close my eyes and blink, shadows dance behind my eyelids, phantom images burned into my sight. There is no depth, no edges, and nowhere I can step safely; it is just an endless sunlight that leaves me blind and wincing.

Just when I fear I can no longer withstand the pain, the light cuts out. I gasp, falling backward against the door.

Near-total darkness. A thick, stifling black where shapes are vague impressions, and the perimeter of my own body feels far away. I run my hands down my sides, my hips, my legs, reassuring myself that I haven't been disembodied, am still present.

I blink rapidly, trying to force my eyes to adapt quickly, but they struggle to keep up. My breath rattles. The silence is total, stretching firmly across the chamber.

The light returns. Violently.

I jerk as it flares, just as overpowering as before. It's like staring directly into the sun during the peak of midday. The light punches into my eyes and leaves only sharp afterimages—forms and shadows I'm not sure are even really here, behind when it vanishes once more.

"Fuck," I bite out, stumbling once more.

The cycle continues. Bright. Dark. Bright. Dark. I'm not sure how long it's been going on. Thirty seconds? A minute? More?

When the darkness returns the next time, I grit my teeth and breathe through my nose, trying to calm myself. I tilt my head downward, bracketing my hands around my eyes. The next time the light flares, it still hurts, is still disorienting in its brilliance, but less. Enough that I can make out the floor that's beneath my feet. The lines between the pieces of stone. I watch the floor for several cycles, counting the seconds.

The light lasts five seconds.

Then darkness consumes the room.

I count patiently. One…two…three…my heart pounds in my chest…I reach fifteen.

Then, a blinding light again.

I wait for the cycle to repeat a few more times until I'm sure the pattern is the same: five seconds of light, followed by fifteen seconds of darkness. Just enough to disorient with both. Enough to rob someone of rhythm. Too little time for your eyes to adjust.

"Roan," I whisper, voice hoarse, "I need your vision help again. Please."

"It never left you."

"Then why can't I see?" I ask, fear growing.

"You've been poisoned, fledgling. Your eyes attempt to obey magic and instinct, and neither currently leads the charge."

I exhale through my nose. Of course. The darts again. My body is slowly failing me, one system at a time. And I have to keep going.

When the light flashes next, I carefully turn and sidle my way to the wall, blinking hard to hold onto the pattern of the stone surface. There are torches mounted here, also. I saw them flickering anemically when the light went out. Tiny beacons that—fleetingly—give me a sense of the direction I'm supposed to take.

I reach out and try to grab one from the wall.

It doesn't budge.

These, however, are fixed to the wall.

"Of course," I mutter, licking my drying lips. My throat tastes like dust and feels twice as dry. I let my hand fall from the torch as the light goes out again.

I can't stay here.

Not only will my competitors eventually join me, but whatever awaits me next won't wait for me to regain my composure.

My head is still tilted downward to reduce the impact of the light, and when it returns, I start inching my way forward across the floor. My steps are hesitant, more cautious shuffle than confident stride. My right leg, still numb and getting number, drags slightly, the offending muscles slow to obey my mind's directives. Even my other leg, which remains unharmed by darts, feels swollen and clumsy, like the poison has spread through my bloodstream and affected all motion.

One step. Another.

When the light comes again, I see it. A flash of metal on the floor. Spikes, dozens of them. My foot is inches from landing directly on one when I twist hard to the side. I stumble, pitching sideways with a yelp. My knee scrapes against something sharp, and the sound of fabric rending greets me. Pain burns through my trousers and stabs into my already injured leg. I brace my hands on my palms against the nearby wall, chest heaving from stress and pain.

The light vanishes again, and my body remains frozen in place. A trickle of sweat down my temple mirrors the trickle of liquid I feel on my calf.

"Let's hope that's not also poisoned," my voice is ragged, "and the only risk is lockjaw."

"*Don't be absurd,*" Roan replies, "*there are far more risks in being scratched by old metal than mere tetanus.*"

I groan, forcing myself to bend and press my hand against the cut. Blood beads there along the thin line. It stings and is sharp, but, thankfully, it's shallow.

"Thank you," I labor, "for being such a calming force in the face of turmoil."

Five seconds. Off.

Fifteen seconds. On again.

My existence has narrowed to the rhythm of my torment.

I wipe my sweaty, bloodied palms on my trousers, then press one flat to the wall, and continue sidling down the room. The stone is damp from condensation—hopefully nothing else. My head is pounding. My leg and arm are aching. My whole body throbs.

But I keep moving.

The torches have been left behind me as I cross the chamber. I can no longer fully lift my injured leg, which drags behind me like a stone, my muscles tightening with every forward shuffle.

My boot catches, and I barely have time to register the pull before my leg refuses to raise and momentum takes over. I pitch forward, unable to correct myself in time. My hands slam into the ground, stone scraping across my palms as they slide out from under me, my injured arm incapable of supporting my body weight.

They meet empty air.

Something is open beneath them.

Instincts screaming, I scramble upright with what little strength I have remaining, shoving myself backward just as a metallic hiss echoes from above. A breath later, the sound of rhythmic thuds echoes above my head. When the light returns, I can see blades—several of them— lodged into the wall.

Exactly where I would be standing had I not fallen.

I stare, wide eyed, at the daggers embedded above me. My body trembles, not only from exertion, but from the realization that my clumsiness and injury have saved me. If not for them, I'd be dead.

"Maybe a lack of coordination isn't such a failing after all," I mumble, voice shaking.

"*Victory and failure are matters of perspective,*" Roan intones.

"If you're making another joke right now, I swear…" I threaten him but don't complete it.

Light flares once more. The dagger handles aren't so far above me.

I reach up and dislodge one with each hand, wrenching them from the wall, and shove them into my boots. Then, grabbing more of the handles above me, I pull myself to standing, bracing my weight on the wall, forcing my legs to straighten. I shuffle forward quickly, hoping to escape the range of more shooting daggers.

Behind me, the door creaks open with a low metallic groan, followed by the sound of heavy boots and an unmistakable curse when the light flicks on again.

"Shit," someone howls. Dagmar.

I don't look back, I don't dare. One moment of distraction could mean another hidden pit, another volley of knives, another injury. Besides, the light is fading, growing dimmer with every step across the chamber, even the flashes that come are less bright, which means I have fewer moments of clarity.

I keep my eyes forward, head tilted low, and let the wall guide me.

The jab comes fast.

A burning spike of agony tears through my left calf. I scream, my body convulsing as a hidden spike slides cleanly into my muscle. The light comes on again, illuminating the metal shaft protruding from the wall that's buried inches deep in my leg.

Just as quickly as it came, the spike retracts with a sickening squelch, leaving behind a hot pulse of blood that pours relentlessly into my boot and onto the floor. I stumble, reaching down to clutch the injury, panting hard.

It would be just my luck to slip on a pool of my cascading blood and die that way rather than from an obstacle within the course, I think.

Light bursts again, fainter this time, and I can see how close I am to the opposite wall. The edge of the chamber. The next door.

Relief slams into my chest as hard as a flying dagger, and I limp forward, each step an exercise in determination.

The light dies and darkness returns.

Still, I press on.

I run as best as I can, my legs heavy, airways burning, needles of pain piercing my temples, and I crash into the wall. The light flares no longer happen directly overhead, but provide just enough illumination for me to see the door and sidle my way to it. I'm in near-total darkness when they go out in the space behind me.

The final chamber lurks behind this door. Despite the terror, the idea of pure darkness feels like a mercy compared to the blinding torment I'm leaving behind.

I wrap a blood-slicked hand around the door handle, clench my teeth, and pull.

Then I step into the void.

The heavy door slams behind me with a deep, metallic howl that echoes into the silence. Absolute, complete silence.

Darkness presses in on me like a shroud—not the kind that is merely an absence of light but one that feels thickened, heavy, almost alive. I blink, trying to adjust and see. Still, light spots dance behind my eyes, making a mockery of my efforts—a combination of lingering effects from the flashing light and increasing symptoms of the toxin spreading through my system.

At least this part is no longer blinding.

That doesn't mean it's safe either.

My vision, still blurry, maybe even a bit worse, offers little aid in the darkness. The boost from Roan gets me to "average" human night vision, which is nonexistent in total darkness.

"Roan," I murmur aloud, voice hushed, "any help would be appreciated."

"*Isn't being alive satisfaction enough?*"

"Roan," I push.

He sighs. "*Forcing too much of the* Rabensblut *into already overburdened senses—particularly those not accustomed to it—might cause undesired effects.*"

"Such as?" I pant, leaning against the wall.

"*Headache, nosebleed.*" I think those aren't so bad sounding, but he continues, "*Loss of consciousness, coma. Death.*"

Dread pools in my stomach. "And how much does it take to get to that point?" I ask him.

"*I've never tested it to its limits,*" he admits.

I exhale. "It can't be worse than what I'm experiencing now. If I don't get out of here, I will *definitely* die. I suppose I'll have to settle for the risk of a 'maybe.'"

Another sigh echoes in my head. Though it hasn't happened recently, with the influx of power, this time when Roan sends it flowing through the bond, I feel the familiar tingle—only, it's more of a pulsing sensation—surging through my skull. I gasp, doubling over as nausea spikes. My temples throb as if a vise tightens its grip around my head. But when I open my eyes again, the blackness is altered. Shadows and shapes have edges. The air ripples with texture, like the room before me is coated in ink, but the corners are still visible.

Hopeful, I take a ginger step forward.

My foot sinks.

Only an inch, maybe two, but enough to startle me. I rush forward on instinct, my injuries protesting loudly, and an ominous *thunk* sounds behind me. Something lies on the floor exactly where I had been standing. The head wound could've killed me.

Shaking it, the motion causing a surge of queasiness, I reach out with my toe to nudge the floor ahead. My foot finds several more spots that have slight give—pressure plates.

I continue on, feeling with my toe in front of me for give. My leg and foot can't feel much, but the change in how stable the surface feels beneath me is enough of an indication of which areas of the floor I should avoid.

Behind me, the door creaks open.

A dull thud, followed by a yelp, echoes into the darkness.

Someone else has entered.

I don't wait to see who it is. I lurch forward. As soon as I do, the sound of stone grinding against stone begins, and the floor beneath me rumbles.

I reach out instinctively, but my fingers meet a wall instead of open space. It's closer than I expected. Too close. I must've drifted farther to the edge than I realized while avoiding the floor plates.

I shuffle more toward the center. The wall follows me—a trap.

The walls are literally closing in.

I rush to escape the encroaching stone, only to feel a shove from my right as that wall moves inward. I take a step and spy faint movement in the dark. Portions of the wall are moving back and forth, impinging on the walkway.

I listen for the sound before choosing to go left, then quickly forward, weaving as the walls groan and reshape the space around me. I press myself flat against the stone several times as a segment juts across my path. Once, I have to backtrack, then turn sideways to sidle through before two segments slam shut behind me like jaws.

My feet step onto a different surface—smoother, level. I barely have time to breathe a sigh of relief when a rope net snaps up from beneath me, yanking me into the air.

My legs kick wildly, tangled in the rough grid. Panic surges.

"Use the tools available to you," Roan tells me.

The daggers.

My hands fly to my boots, and one is empty. I must've lost a blade somewhere along the way. I don't have time to mourn its loss as my right hand closes around the hilt of the other that juts from my boot. With shaking hands, I saw through the thick and resistant fibers of the rope. I drop to the ground in a heap just as I hear someone else get caught in one.

Hoping they don't *also* have a blade to aid them, I crawl forward, pulling myself to standing and collide with a wall. My hands find a seam, vertical, slightly recessed.

A door.

I must be done!

Using my good arm, I yank open the door and step through.

Something slams into my back.

I hit the floor hard, hands skidding across the stone, dagger clattering to the ground beside me.

It's still pitch black.

I begin to push to my hands and knees when a boot drives into my ribs, sending me sprawling with a choked cry of pain and surprise. My ribs throb. My head pounds. My legs scream in protest and pain. My right arm barely responds.

I roll to my side, groaning softly.

"*Silence is your shield,*" Roan warns, "*your opponent cannot see any better in the darkness than you can.*"

I swallow the pained whimper that was rising in my throat and struggle to my feet as quietly as possible. My legs quiver beneath my weight. Blood slicks my palm. I bend at the waist and find the source— the dagger I had dropped. I squint into the dark, letting the *Rabensblut* do what my eyes cannot.

A shape moves, vague and shifting. A man, I think, his arms outstretched and feeling the space in front of him for me.

He isn't holding a weapon. He must not have one, or he'd have used it.

Hand-to-hand combat. My worst skill.

Luckily, I brought a knife to a fistfight.

I don't want him to grab hold of it since he's uninjured and might use it against me. With effort, I take a lesson from Rafe and slip my dagger into my belt at the small of my back.

The man creeps closer. I move wide, circling. He must be more accustomed to the dark than I realized, because he turns toward the movement. Faster than I expected, he lashes out.

I duck and slam my shoulder into his gut. A masculine "oof" whooshes out of his mouth in a surprised grunt from the impact of the blow. I thank my stature for allowing me greater leverage.

I reach my hand around, slamming my left fist into his kidney, and drive my knee into his groin.

He cries out in pain and gags. Even wounded and in pain, though, he grabs my braid and yanks hard.

My head snaps back sharply, and his forehead collides with mine, head butting me with a crack. Stars explode behind my eyes.

Dizzy. Numb. Sweat and blood drench my skin and clothing.

"What's wrong, challenger?" He jibes. "Did you catch afoul of the darts back there? Must be affecting your arm."

He reaches up his hand and squeezes my right bicep, pressing painfully on the wound there.

"It's too bad you made it so close, only to remain so far," he sneers. "You fucking conscripts should know better than to dream of surpassing your betters."

I feel a surge of rage so hot it threatens to burn me from the inside out.

Not just at him.

At everything.

Lord Rocheburn, who presumes to take what he believes he has a right to because of his position as chancellor.

Lord Corvilian, who condescends to anyone without magic because he believes them to be inferior.

At the soldiers who'd held my sister back from me as she screamed for my release.

At every snide smirk. Every brush off. Every "less than" moment where I swallowed my pride.

What little vision I have remaining floods crimson. My lip pulls back in a snarl. Though I feel energy flooding my body, I force myself to go slack. Limp. Feigning a brokenness I refuse to give in to.

He steps closer, and his hands travel from my arm. They brush my hips. Linger on my breasts, squeezing painfully.

"It's a shame I don't have time to explore you. I believe I'd enjoy breaking you."

His words bring me back to a different time.

A different room.

With a different soldier.

Back to the *loubenstille*, that isolated, tiny cell at Lord Rocheburn's estate where the air was thick with mold and menace. The cold air that cut down to my bones. The small existence I had been given in that room, awaiting the lord's benevolent judgment.

That soldier had a casual cruelty, as though I were no more consequential than livestock—merely another toy for him to play with.

He'd told me what he'd do to me, what he'd do to my sister if I didn't comply, smiling as he threatened me.

I didn't scream then.

I didn't cry.

Now, in this new dark chamber, another creation of cruelty's design tears open that old wound. The words might differ slightly, the circumstances vastly dissimilar, but the threat behind them—the meaning—is the same. You are nothing. You are worth nothing. You are mine to use, to abuse, to do with what I want. Like my pain, my fear, my suffering, are things I owe them.

Only I am not who I was then.

And I am not alone.

I smile into the dark.

I wrap my weakened arm around his neck and pull him close, his surprise flavoring the air.

I murmur the exact words I spoke those months ago—only this time, with the anticipation of someone who knows their next act.

"You first," I tell him.

Then my left hand plunges my dagger into the side of his throat.

I shove away from him, pushing his sagging body away from me before it can take me down, but stagger back when his twitching, choking form drops and collides with my legs.

Breathing heavily, I lean in so I can see him closely. Watch as he chokes on his own blood, his eyes wide with pain and fear.

"A cadet's folly," I tell him, "to believe your opponent is disarmed simply because you can't see a weapon."

He goes still, unseeing eyes staring into the dark.

I'd once condemned Rafe for how easy it had seemed for him to kill Damd when she'd attacked me. But he'd done that to save me. This I had done with relish. The adrenaline has begun to fade, and I feel a rush of guilt. At my uncharitable thoughts. At my cold-blooded ability to kill.

Roan says, *"What needed ending has ended. Now go—the door awaits, and your story is not yet finished."*

With a trembling breath, my muscles protesting, I force my battered body forward through the dark, numb leg nearly immobile. I wrap my equally numb hand around my trouser leg, then use my good arm to pull it—and my leg—along with me.

I feel warmth bloom faintly in my limbs. It must be from Roan lending me a final push. It's not much—barely more than a whisper of energy—but it's enough to let me stagger over the still body of my nameless opponent, through the pool of his blood.

I don't spare him another glance. I don't know who he was. Only that he would've killed me, and I didn't let him. I defeated him.

My hand grazes the wall, searching, praying I haven't gotten myself turned around in the dark, and with all my injuries clouding my ability to reason. Every step is a betrayal of my body's desires, which all involve lying down. My left calf is still bleeding, and my ribs ache with every breath. My fingers finally meet the now-familiar feeling of the metal edge of a door.

I let out a sob of relief.

I lurch forward, hand twisting in the metal of the handle, and when the door gives, a sudden wash of light assaults my vision.

Sunlight. Actual, blinding daylight. It pierces my throbbing skull like another dagger, but I welcome the pain because it means it's over. It means I've made it out.

Sound follows closely behind the light as I ascend the slope from the exit door into the arena. The roar of the crowd hits my ears like thunder. Shouts. Cheers. Voices calling my name.

I hear my name closer than the crowd.

I blink rapidly. The world around me is awash in brilliance and staggering, saturated color that nearly brings tears to my eyes after what feels like an eternity in the shadows. I take one wobbling step, then another, and almost collapse. The ground tilts beneath me, and my legs barely support my weight. I'm vaguely aware of blood trickling from my nose—joining the steady ooze from the injuries on my legs—warm against my upper lip, the coppery taste hitting my tongue as it slips between my dry, parted lips. My whole body shakes, and I can't feel my fingers or toes.

Strong, sure arms wrap around me, catching me before I fall to the ground. The scent of crisp and biting peppermint hits my nose, and my body relaxes into the strength surrounding me even as I can't resist the urge to quip.

"You really are like a plague sent from the gods," I mumble into

Rafe's tunic as it rubs softly against my face.

His low laugh rumbles gently against my cheek, "More like a gift. You just haven't finished unwrapping me."

"In your dreams," I retort drunkenly, words slurring and voice cracking.

"Every night," he murmurs in agreement.

And then the abyss, darker than where I just came from, claims me.

CHAPTER FORTY-SEVEN
That's What Frenemies are For

I stare at the raven across the main chamber of the mountain temple. Its gaze locks with mine. Its beak opens. *"Follow the path where night lingers longest. For even in death, the watch remains unbroken."*

Its beak clicks shut, and all is still and silent for a moment.

Then light. A sudden, searing flare that blinds me.

Then darkness.

Then light again.

Darkness.

Each pulse of light seems brighter than the last, more severe. Brutal. One moment it's so bright I can't see, and the next it's so dark as to obscure everything around me.

I cup my hands around my eyes to block out the light's direction, which provides some relief. I look to the raven, poised between the statues of the sister goddesses. Levitia's statue holds a scepter that may have been made of gold in another time but now gleams with the subtle sheen of marble. In the statue Mortuua's hands is a scythe. Unlike her sister's object, this isn't part of the statue. It glitters silver in the light, a prismatic rainbow playing in the moonstones embedded in the heel and neck.

The light goes out.

Drip.

Drip.

The sound of water slowly falling fills the silent chamber.

The light returns.

It's not water.

Blood, black as pitch and slow as molasses, beads along the curve of the scythe's blade and trickles slowly from its point to a gathering puddle at the foot of the statue. It winds into the etchings on the marble floor, like it's returning to where it belongs.

A clap of thunder explodes across the sky. I jump, looking above me, but frown when the sky remains clear, and there is no sign of incoming rain in the clouds overhead.

I whip around, searching for the source of the noise. That's when I see it. Beyond the temple's marble columns, where the graves in the cemetery lie overgrown and abandoned, the earth has split—thin fissures, like cracks along a broken dish, snake between the headstones.

Hands burst from the soil—some with lingering flesh; with others, only the pale gleam of bone remains. Forearms, shoulders, and heads follow. Clods of dirt embed themselves in matted, brittle hair barely hanging on to decaying skulls. One by one, they pull themselves free of the earth.

They turn, as one, to look in my direction, and their eyes…their eyes are milky white, blind, and blank, identical to the haunting stare of the Enderaben.

I've lost count of their number. They slowly creep toward the temple, gaits jerky and uneven, as if they haven't figured out how to move and bend their limbs. Cloaks, gowns, and intact leather belts cling to the forms of the newly dead. Others are skeletons draped in tatters, stained copper from the soil. Sinew and skin barely cling to bone, indistinguishable from the fabric of their clothing.

Among them, one pulls ahead from the rest.

His skin hangs in strips, teeth exposed where his lips have rotted away. Lifeless eyes lock onto my face, and I know without question this is the soldier I killed in the bowels of the arena during the last trial. And he remembers. Wants his revenge.

He snarls, lurching into the temple chamber.

I scramble backward, foot slipping on the pooling blood gathered beneath the scythe. Without thinking, I wrap my fingers around the weapon's snath. Cold as chilling as ice penetrates my hands, but I pull despite the ache.

The statue's grip releases, the stone fingers breaking off and crumbling into dust.

The instant it's loose, whispers slam into my brain, telling me exactly where to slide the edge, where to jab the point.

The soldier charges. I raise the scythe.

I slash it across his neck.

There is no blood from one who is already dead. His head snaps back, barely connected to his deteriorating neck. Eventually, though, the weight of it is too much for the tissue to bear, and it falls from his body, which follows his head to the temple floor.

Unmoving.

I don't have time to breathe a sigh of relief.

The others are still advancing.

A dozen. Maybe two. Then more. Too many to count.

They surge over the headstones, crawl on all fours up the marble steps, flooding the chamber like water broken free of a swollen dam.

I swing the scythe wildly, catching one across the chest, another in the gut. Bones snap. Dust billows. I scream.

They do not fall.

Skeletal fingers claw at my clothing, pull at my hair.

I scream, and they consume me.

Then darkness. A darkness that no longer cedes to light.

The world knits itself back together slowly.

First comes the ache—deep, burning, and everywhere. Then the heaviness. My limbs feel like they're made of wet wool and stuffed with lead. A dull throb pulses on my right side through my calf, thigh, and shoulder. My mouth is as dry as ash. When I open my eyes, the ceiling above me is dim and unfamiliar—plastered stone with rough wooden beams. Dusk filters in through nearby narrow windows. Though I don't recognize the area I'm in, the smell of soap, of clean linen, of blood, of sick and suffering, tells me I'm in the infirmary.

I shift my legs and pain lances down my left calf, a pinpoint of fiery agony that spreads its fingers outward and digs its claws into the meat of my flesh. It feels wet, raw. The injuries to my right leg and arm are uncomfortable and sore, but not nearly as bad as this.

The memories trickle in, sluggish and hazy, dripping into the crevices of my mind, filling in the gaps.

The darts to my right biceps, thigh, and calf.

The spike to my left.

The trial. The light. The dark. The blood. The body.

Possibly bodies.

The blade in my hand.

A scythe? No, that was my dream.

A dagger. Pulled from the stone wall, tucked into my boot.

Then jabbed into the throat of my attacker.

A scrape of wood on the stone floor has me flinching in fear. Then a voice—gentle, awed.

"You're awake."

I turn my head toward the sound. The motion sends a bolt of pain through my aching muscles. Everything hurts, like I've had a fever. Aric sits slouched in a chair near the edge of my bed. His elbows are on his knees, and fatigue has etched itself into the handsome planes of his face. His uniform is wrinkled, hair mussed. Very un-Aric of him to look so disheveled. Almost like he has been here for some time and hasn't left my side.

For a moment, my heart surges, and I look to the other side of my bed. A dip follows it in my stomach. I'd hoped to see someone else here.

I turn back to Aric, and a voice—hoarse and creaky from disuse—slips from my lips. "Water…"

He's already on his feet, grabbing the cup on the nightstand beside my bed. "Hold on—I'll get it for you."

Drapes hang from the ceiling, obscuring my view of the rest of the room and protecting me from scrutiny in my enfeebled state. He disappears beyond the fabric wall, and the sound of liquid pouring reaches me.

"Here," he says when he returns to me from around the curtains, holding the cup gently to my lips.

I drink greedily, the cool water creating a fire of its own down my dry throat, both refreshing and overwhelming at once. I give a sputtering cough, lacking the energy to feel embarrassed when the water dribbles down my chin, which Aric wipes away for me.

"*Roan,*" I reach out to him, hoping he's listening.

"*Fledgling,*" his voice sounds relieved, though still tinged with concern.

"*How long have I been out?*"

He replies, "*You're nearing your fourth day. You've slept for over three. There are roughly four remaining until the final trial.*"

Three days. I've lost over three days to this.

Aric brings me another cup of water, and I drink more. I can't seem to get enough to banish the all-consuming thirst, the dryness of my throat, and the lingering foul taste on my tongue. I lie back on my pillows, exhausted by the effort of drinking.

"What are you doing here?" I ask Aric wearily.

He frowns, and he looks wounded, as if I had just jabbed the knife into *him* instead. "I'm not certain why you'd even ask that."

I stare at him, not providing further explanation.

He sighs. "I'm here because I care about you, Greta. Of course I want to be here."

"You have an odd way of showing it," I rasp. "One moment you're telling me you want there to be an 'us'; the next it's like I don't exist. One moment you care; the next you look at me like you disdain me."

He looks away, jaw tightening. "That's not really fair."

"Isn't it?" I press.

His face turns back to mine. "You said you needed time. You needed to think. I was trying to respect that. I didn't want to pressure you."

"But you still found time to seek me out when I was with Rafe. Like you were looking for a reason to be angry with me," I point out.

Aric says, "That was an unlucky coincidence. I…I couldn't always stay away."

"Was it a coincidence?" I ask, meeting his gaze. "You weren't giving me space, Aric. Not really. You just didn't want to talk. You kept appearing, like I still owed you something, even though you said I didn't. Without ever asking what I wanted."

His jaw clenches again, and I turn my head to look at the ceiling, swallowing several times. "Maybe it's not fair," I admit. "Maybe I made it harder than it had to be. But I can't help but think you didn't push because it was easier not to. And I didn't seek you out for the same reason."

He winces, just slightly, but remains quiet.

"You like order, Aric. Rules. Structure. Things tied up neatly and clear meanings and definitions and lines." I turn my head back to him. "But the longer I'm here, the more I endure…I realize how much I hate all of that."

I take a shuddering breath, the truth of the words bolstering my voice, adding strength. Certainty.

"I don't want everything spelled out and precise," I tell him. "I don't want guarantees. I like the not knowing. The adventure that comes with having to figure things out while I'm running at full speed. I want to feel things, to consider them, as they happen. Although I could maybe do without the ever-present threat of death following my every step," I say, smiling wryly.

He says quietly, "I'm not trying to cage you in."

"I know," I tell him. "But as much as I want to *be* safe, want Agnethe to *be* safe…you want something that *is* safe. And I don't think I'm safe any longer."

"I see," he says, clearly not.

I've long thought I needed answers to all of life's questions. A plan, a clear path from where I stood to where I had to go. That's what safety was to me. Certainty. Control. I still crave some of that. I need to know more about what's happening to me—more of what I am, what my grandmother hid from me, why these dreams won't leave me. I need to know if Agnethe is alive, well, and unharmed. I still want to survive— Sisters, do I want that. I want to find Agnethe, to find some peace among the ashes of this destruction. But, unlike before, I don't feel pressure to have every step laid out. I know I'm running toward her but don't know how I'll get there.

The Freiheit has been the worst, most terrifying thing I've ever done and will likely ever do. It's torn me down, physically and mentally, and forced me to rebuild myself from the ground up. And it's shown me what truly matters, and it's not the comfort of routine.

It's my sister. My friends. Roan.

They've taught me that my worth isn't found in what of myself I conceal, but in what I face. In the choices I make when everything has been stripped from me except the heat of the moment, the blood in my veins, the breath in my lungs. It's frightening not to know what's next. It's equally sad to realize that I never really did, and I spent far too much time being afraid anyway. I want the pain, the joy, the unknown. I don't want to fear all of life's endings but instead enjoy the in between.

I wince as I shift—maybe I can enjoy the in between with fewer injuries, though.

"Where's Rafe?" I ask Aric, who's still watching me.

He scowls. "Does it matter?"

"I'm just surprised he's not here. He's my mentor, Aric," I tell him.

"Who you apparently have been fucking," he says bluntly, hands closing into fists, "which I thought you were above."

I rear back like he's slapped me.

"*Envy is an ugly perch,*" Roan says, angrier than I've ever heard him. "*Especially when dressed as virtue.*"

I open my mouth, fury and humiliation rising in my throat, but before I can speak, a voice cuts in from just beyond my curtain.

"If you're jealous, just say so. But don't pretend it's about *her* morals when it's really about *your* pride."

The curtain snaps open in a single, sharp motion. Dagmar is standing there, her silhouette framed by the glow of burning candles. Her face is drawn and tired, and she's not without bandages herself, but her eyes burn with icy blue fire and it's all directed at Aric.

He stands stiffly, quickly. "We'll discuss this later, when we don't have an audience."

Dagmar crosses her arms across her chest. "Yeah? Maybe wait until she's not half dead before making her explain herself to you like she owes you something."

He hesitates, face taut, then spins on his heel and stalks out of the room without another word. My heart is hammering. I hate that even with all my newfound inner strength, part of me still wants to smooth things over. That I feel like I've failed someone. My stomach twists with the old desire to please, even though I don't want to.

Roan's voice is haughty with approval, *"This one has talons. I find myself quite fond."*

I ignore him, not wanting to draw any suspicions from Dagmar and look like I'm having one of those inner conversations she asked me about before. I push myself up to sitting on trembling arms and look into her eyes.

"Thank you," I tell her, "for speaking up for me. You said it better than I probably would have."

She nods but also rolls her eyes, letting her arms fall to her sides, which causes a slight wince.

"If you wait for permission to be angry at someone, de Veend, you'll wait a lifetime. Grow a spine, and use it."

I let out a tired laugh. "You know, I don't understand you. One minute you're kind to me, and the next you act like you can't stand me."

She doesn't flinch. "Because you started higher than most conscripts here ever dreamed—and you still act like you're asking the world's consent to exist. You want to fight? Then *fight*, Greta. Or don't. But stop wasting the ground you were given when the rest of us had to crawl."

I feel a flare of heat rise in my chest. "We are in the exact same place, fighting the exact same fight," I say sharply, "and I'll remind you that I got just as far as you did."

She nods. "And it's you and me in the final trial."

I freeze, my blood going cold.

She steps closer. "We were the first two out. We made it. Athaulf and Dirk are dead. Stigander…he lost his right hand. He'll live, but he'll never be able to work as a smith again; he'll have to train with his left now. Relearn everything with it."

"No," I whisper, feeling the blood drain from my face, "that's not possible."

"Of course it is," she snaps, though her voice sounds brittle, hollow with grief. "You and I barely made it out with whatever poison they put on those darts."

"Henbane," Roan informs me calmly and clearly.

My throat constricts. "But that means in the last trial, you and I, we have to—"

"Fight to the death, yes," Dagmar states bluntly, "and I won't go down without one. You shouldn't either."

Then, without ceremony, she turns and stalks out of the room, leaving my bed curtain wide open behind her. I lie there stunned. The light feels too bright; the air feels too thin. The room feels hot. Then cold. Everything assails me at once—pain of my body, torment of my mind, Aric's shocking words, Dagmar's blunt truths, and the awful, gut-wrenching knowledge that the final trial won't just be a test of my skill but a reckoning.

A reckoning only one of us will walk away from.

A rustle of skirts signals Hildegarde's arrival before I see her round my curtain.

"Well, look who's up when she should be resting," she scolds me, bustling forward while rolling up her sleeves.

"Just stretching a little," I tell her with a sheepish smile.

"Those wounds are barely stitched together," she snaps with gentle reproach, beginning to peel back the bandages on my legs. "Don't stretch them too far, or you'll stretch my patience to breaking."

I wince as she dabs at one of the wounds with some kind of tincture. "Your bedside manner is so comforting."

She grumbles, "I'm here to heal not coddle. Still clean. You're lucky, girl. No *wundsmeiten* this time."

I frown. "What's *wundsmeiten*?" I ask her.

"The salve we used on your burns before," she says matter of factly as she rewraps my legs.

"Oh," I reply with a blink. "I suppose Aric is punishing me."

Hildegarde looks up at me from her bandaging with a puzzled look.

"Captain Everbrandt," I explain.

"I know who he is, girl, but I don't know what he's got to do with *wundsmeiten*." She lifts my left calf, wrapping clean linen around it.

I frown. "He's the reason I got it last time. You said a 'certain handsome officer' had arranged it for me."

"Aye, I did. Lieutenant Colonel Kriegeur ordered it himself."

I sit up straighter, dislodging my bandages, which earns me a swat from Hildegarde.

"*Rafe* is the one who ordered the salve?"

Hildegarde hums, "Paid for it too, and it's not inexpensive."

I'm speechless. Even before I really knew Rafe, he was looking out for me. I need fresh air. I whip my legs over the side of my bed, tentatively planting my feet on the cool stone of the floor.

"Don't you dare," Hildegarde squawks at me, moving to block my path.

"I just need air," I assure her. "I'll be careful."

She stares at me for a long moment, searching my face. "Mind your stitches, then," she sighs and moves out of my path.

I start limping toward the rear door, the one that opens to the private herb garden attached to the infirmary. I just want to stand outside for a moment. Halfway down the rows of beds, I spot a familiar hulking frame.

"Stigander?" I call to him.

He's lying on his side, his back mostly turned to the room. I can see his right arm, though. Heavily wrapped and splinted. Shorter than it should be. I edge closer to his bedside.

"Beat it, de Veend," he tells me curtly. "Brevic already did the team's duty in checking up on me, so you're absolved of guilt in that regard. Besides, you look like shit."

I sit down on the edge of the empty bed beside his. "How did it happen?"

"Second room," he says in his typical brusque manner. "Caught afoul of one of those swinging blades. Used my belt as a tourniquet. They came in and found me after you and Brevic had made it out."

"I'm sorry," I whisper.

He rolls over and looks at me, green eyes flat with pain. "I wish I'd died."

My heart sinks. I touch the upper part of his arm, and he stares at my hand on his appendage, then grimaces at the stump, like it's the most offensive thing he's ever seen.

"I can't hold my children," he says, voice cracking gently. "I can't hold a hammer. My wife…she married a smith, a provider. Not…this mangled mess." His throat works visibly, and he swallows several times.

I sit quietly for several moments. The pain in his voice is so acute, so real. But I reach for comfort to give where I can.

"You won't always feel that way," I reassure him.

"How do you know?" He shoots back.

I shrug. "I guess I don't," I agree. I echo Roan's words. "You're not whole. Not unchanged…you might not yet even know all the ways in which that's true."

I touch the bandages on my legs and run my fingers along the linen edges. I think of my grandmother and her words to me when I was grieving.

"But one day you'll be less sad. I hope you'll hold on until then."

His eyes, glassy with torment and unshed tears, search mine, like he's looking for some sign of dishonesty, some indication that I don't understand or believe what I've told him. Eventually, though, he just closes them and nods once at me. He rolls back to his side.

Suddenly, it's all too much. The weight that's pressing down on my heart refuses to lift. The sharp words from Dagmar still echo in my ears, the despair in Stigander's voice lodges somewhere between my ribs, robbing me of breath. The tension with Aric is still thick and unresolved. I turn away from the infirmary garden door before I realize I've made a decision, my feet carrying me out the front and toward the main building. I had only wanted to escape the depressed stillness of the infirmary, but my path tilts upward, dragging me somewhere my heart recognizes it needs before my mind does. My thighs burn with every step, my calves protest, and my stitches pull too tight with every movement. But I can't stop. I need silence, but not that of miserable convalescence. I need the kind borne of understanding.

I want to sit in the silence with Rafe.

The upper levels of the citadel are mostly quiet at this hour, with shadows sitting in the corners and edges of the stairwell and halls. I limp up the spiral staircase, my breathing shallow, legs trembling from pain and too many days confined to a bed. Still, I push myself to the right level, bracing a hand against the wall to keep going. When I finally reach his door, I lift my fist to knock, but pause when I hear voices carrying from inside. Low, heated.

Heart racing, I hesitate only a moment before my fingers find the latch. Slowly, quietly, I ease the door open just enough to see Rafe speaking to the man I'd once seen him with—Conrad. Sending a quick prayer to the gods that they don't see or hear me, I listen with bated breath.

"We nearly got caught last time. Some of those conscripts were in rough shape, Rafe," Conrad admonishes him. "And now you want us to do it again this soon? How many this time? We might need to pause or even stop the missions until we're sure no one has figured it out."

I frown, trying to recall the previous conversation I'd overheard with Conrad. My still-sluggish brain struggles to remember, but then the memory catches up. The mention of bodies. A mission during the Freiheit trial. What kind of mission involves conscripts in rough shape? What were they doing to them?

Rafe replies, his voice sounding so weary it makes me ache for him. "Not as many…two, maybe three. I haven't been able to focus on abilities much with the Freiheit. But one…she's in the last trial, Conrad. I need to get her out. There's something different about her—"

Conrad scoffs. "This again? Rafe, I recognize you seem to care for this woman, but breaking someone out of Iron Gate when they're set to compete in the final Freiheit trial will invite more scrutiny than we can afford. It'll get us killed."

I almost fall over from shock.

Breaking people out.

The missions are *rescue missions*.

Rafe is breaking people out of Stachtenbaste.

But why? And to what end?

Rafe says, urgently, "Her magic, Conrad. And the raven with red eyes. Her magic is different; I can't even figure it out. It's like I feel something. Whispers sometimes, but I can't hold onto it yet. I don't even know what it is, and it's driving me mad." He pulls at his hair and sits down hard on the chair by his small desk.

My heart pounds even faster. He knows I have magic. He knows it has to do with Roan. The way he speaks makes it sound like he might eventually be able to figure it out. I'm not sure if I feel relieved or terrified at the prospect.

"Rafe, I know you want to save them all, but we can't," Conrad tells him. "We have others depending on us, hundreds at Hafenverre—"

"I KNOW!" Rafe explodes into standing.

I jump, hearing real frustration from him for the first time since I've known him. Real fear.

"I know," he says more calmly, "but her magic could be something helpful. Something we can use—"

"No," Conrad says bluntly, "we're not doing this. You can lie to yourself, but you won't lie to me. Figure out your fucking priorities and send word. We strike in four days' time."

During the final trial, I think. That's when they're breaking more people out.

Realizing Conrad means to leave Rafe's chamber, I run as fast as my wobbly legs can carry me, breaking into a room across the way, desperately thanking the gods that it's not occupied. I leave the door cracked to see when Rafe and Conrad leave the former's chamber.

I reach out to Roan and tell him, *"This changes everything."*

CHAPTER FORTY-EIGHT
You've Got Blackmail

The next morning arrives with a gray and feeble dawn, as if the sky itself is sapped of energy, of light. I wake with stiffness in every joint, my legs—especially my left calf—pulse with an intense, bone-deep ache. My body is a map of wounds and bruises, only now beginning to fade from purple to yellow. The dart wound in my arm itches beneath its bandage, and the muscle is sore and pinches with movement. Everything hurts, but I cannot lie still—not today.

I swing my legs over the edge of my infirmary bed, one hand bracing my side where bruises remain from my assailant's boot. My movements are slow and awkward, but I manage to dress myself, layering a tunic and trousers over the numerous injuries. I grit my teeth when I pull my trousers over my legs, the coarse fabric abrading my puncture wounds even through the bandages. I hobble toward the door, ignoring Hildegarde's noisy objections as she laments the state of my stitches.

I resolve not to return to the infirmary after today. I will no longer mark myself as an invalid. I will push through.

The air outside is thick and damp as I traipse across the training yard, dawn's mist clinging to my hair and uniform in a fine film. The gravel crunches beneath my boots, each uneven patch jolting my healing limbs as I fight to maintain my balance.

The training yard is still quiet, most of the cadets taking in their morning meals, so there's little to catch my eye as I cross. I see Aric and Dagmar sparring in the upper training yard instead of the officers' yard. They're locked in position—swords crossed in a clash of steel, bodies moving in rigid, deliberate rhythm. Even from a distance, the tension between them is palpable. Aric's expression is focused and hard, and his jaw clenches in concentration and irritation. Dagmar's eyes bore into his as she stares him down. Their sparring is impersonal. They are two soldiers fulfilling their duty, not bolstering their partnership.

My gut clenches. Their fracture is because of me. Because Dagmar stood up for me, and Aric hadn't protested. Aric is angry with me and hasn't sought me out, despite saying we'd "discuss things later." I'm not even sure I *want* to talk to him anymore. Not after what he said and the points Dagmar made. Is there anything worth resolving between us?

I can't help but feel the impact I've had on others. How I seem to leave destruction in my wake, whether I mean to or not.

Aric was a dedicated officer. Now he's distracted, compromised. Dagmar, who was once untouchable, independent, and a lone wolf, is now quarreling with Aric because of me.

And Rafe…he clearly has a carefully constructed façade that covers many secrets—is now exposed to me in a way he never intended. And by offering to help rescue Agnethe, he potentially further endangers himself and—according to Conrad—hundreds of others.

Because of me, they all bleed from wounds I hadn't meant to inflict.

"Do not carry the blame for steps not taken by your feet," Roan instructs. *"They made their choices; you must learn to accept that. To take responsibility for their actions is to unfairly castigate yourself and remove their autonomy."*

I stop briefly on the gravel path. Roan's words pierce me with their accuracy. I've carried guilt for Agnethe's pain, for Grandmother's death, for every loss that has scarred my life. Was blaming myself an attempt to control the chaos? By trying to give meaning to the senseless?

Pushing aside my self-pity, I exhale slowly and grimace at the pain in my ribs. I limp to the gate of the officers' training yard, anxiety clawing at my lungs. My heart starts to thud against my chest. Not just from the exertion or pain, but from my knowledge. What I overheard yesterday between Rafe and Conrad.

Rafe is smuggling people out of Stachtenbaste.

Somehow he can sense my magic—and possibly the magic of others.

Does that mean he has magic of his own?

I don't know if he'll pick up on the change in me. If he'll look upon me and immediately know that I know. That whatever feelings we've had are now shifted, altered by what I heard and what I must do.

I spot him standing near the equipment shed, hauling swords and krahbeks—two of each—from its depths, blades gleaming with deadly purpose. His dark hair is damp and pulled up with a strip of leather, and the back of his neck is slick with sweat. He has obviously been training himself before readying the yard for my arrival.

He looks up as I enter through the gate, and his dark eyes lock on mine. I stop and find myself frozen from the onslaught of emotions I'm feeling—panic, regret, hope, pain—everything and nothing all at once. Something hot and unsettled stirs low in my stomach.

He smiles at me—a genuine smile, not one of his smirks.

"*Künnle*, you're looking well," he says. "Far more upright than when I last saw you."

I smile stiffly and nod. The greeting is so very *Rafe*; it makes me want to hit him and cry from the familiarity of it.

His eyes scan me from head to toe, brow furrowing at the sight of my pinched face and the stiffness of my movements. I try to mask my limp as I shuffle into the yard, but my right leg refuses to bend properly, and the left flares with every step. My arms are leaden, like they're wrapped in chains. The resultant fatigue from an excess of bed rest is catching up with me, and my breathing is shallow by the time I stop in front of him.

He watches me hobble forward, his dark eyes softening, the corners of his mouth drooping slightly. "Is everything all right?"

I exhale a shaky breath. "No. Nothing is all right."

It only takes a moment for him to make it to my side. He grips my right arm gently, but it worries my dart wound and I can't help the wince.

"I'm sorry," he says sincerely, gently rubbing his thumb over the bandage. "What happened?"

"Oh," I begin breathlessly, "just this little thing called a deadly tournament and the fact that a bunch of people hate me," I explain with bitter and brittle sarcasm, arcing my arm in a sweeping gesture that only makes it throb more.

Rafe's mouth tightens, but he doesn't say anything immediately. So I tell him about waking up with Aric beside me, the way he accused me of sleeping with Rafe. About Dagmar coming to my defense, taking my side, and then departing with promises of death on her lips. Every word I utter feels like a shard of glass piercing my heart and burrowing deep. When I finish spilling it all, my throat is dry, and my lungs ache.

His expression darkens, gathering storm clouds preparing to unleash a torrent of punishment. He clenches his jaw and takes a step toward the training yard gate.

"That self-righteous, hypocritical little prick," he growls, "I'm going to—"

I grab his wrist, my fingers curling around warm skin exposed by his raised sleeve.

"Don't," I tell him, pleading, "it won't help."

He stops and stares at me, eyes staring into mine. His shoulders loosen slightly, and he exhales through his nose. He mutters something under his breath, but he doesn't leave.

"I don't want to think about Aric. Or what Dagmar said." I squeeze his wrist in a bid for him to listen. "I need to focus on the tournament. On things I can—somewhat—control."

He nods slowly and lets out a heavy breath. "All right."

We walk together toward the edge of the training yard, past the battered training dummies, to where he set down the weapons he'd removed from the equipment shed. The sun is rapidly gaining momentum, baking the dirt beneath us into dry clumps that disintegrate beneath our boots. I try not to limp, but every step causes more throbbing. I can still feel the tug of the stitches in my legs, the ache in my arm, the tight band around my bruised ribs. My muscles tremble from effort, and the exhaustion pulls at me like an anchor.

"For this final trial," Rafe begins, "they don't change it. The structure remains the same every year."

I nod, trying to focus on him, not my discomfort. "What is the structure?"

"Challengers are allowed two types of weapons," he explains. "They must select them by the end of today. Then once you're in the arena, you have to retrieve them first before fighting. The weapons are hidden inside a maze controlled by an earth wielder that can shift it as you progress."

"They use magic to change the course?" I ask him, horrified.

He nods. "The changes happen constantly. You have to find your way through it, dodging illusions and traps meant to slow you down or test you. Some cause injuries. You'll have thirty minutes to retrieve your weapons or enter the center ring empty handed."

My throat goes dry. "And once I'm inside the center ring?" I'm certain I already know the answer.

"You fight. One on one. Until one of you is dead. The one who survives becomes the champion…and is free."

I consider his words, the weight of them added to my exhaustion and injuries, until I feel like I'm pulling stones with me as I move.

"I want a krahbek," I tell him, "and a dagger."

He raises an eyebrow. "A dagger?"

I shrug. "In case I have the opportunity to take advantage of my opponent's folly, and she believes me unarmed."

He grins at my recollection of his words, and for a moment I allow myself to bask in that smile—genuine, warm, proud. I force myself to look away, shifting into a ready stance.

He does the same, and the sparring begins.

It's immediately apparent how far I've regressed in only a matter of days. Days of being bedridden and poison riddled have weakened me, dulled my already mediocre reflexes. My muscles protest every strike, and I can't get my legs to move fast enough. I'm clumsy—even more than usual—sluggish, and Rafe has disarmed me with almost no effort.

I don't want to ask Roan for help, though, and expend our energy.

This isn't a life-or-death situation. I'm not in a trial. So I grit my teeth and push through, forcing my body to respond to my commands and recall what it knows.

Rafe doesn't hold back. His movements are sharp, fluid, brutal, unforgiving. Maybe he's trying to provoke a reaction from me—determination, maybe, or rage.

"Push harder," he commands.

"I am," I insist, panting, "Sisters, do you think I'm not trying as hard as I can?"

We pause, circling each other, me with a distinct limp. Rafe has his own, but it doesn't keep him from dominating our match.

A scream splits the air.

We turn in unison toward the direction of the noise. At some point, Aric and Dagmar must have entered the training yard, because Dagmar is charging a practice dummy with a feral war cry.

In a single, elegant sweep of her sword, she severs the head of one of the practice dummies. It rolls to the ground with a gentle thud, and Dagmar straightens and turns toward us. Her eyes find mine. She doesn't say anything. She doesn't taunt me with words or expression. Just watches me.

I can almost hear her urging me to fight.

Rafe turns back to me, jaw tight. "You need to focus."

I huff in frustration. "Focus isn't the problem. It's skill."

"I thought that wouldn't stop you," he says sardonically, using my own brash words.

"I'll always keep trying," I reply, "but I have a limit. I'm not a soldier. I wasn't made for this."

"You're not trying," he argues.

"Yes, I am!" I shout, not caring who hears the words as they tear from my throat. "But I'm tired, I'm injured, I'm scared, and more than anything, I want to wake up and find out this was some fever dream and none of it has been real! But that seems less likely each day."

I drop my krahbek, dig my fingers into my hair, loosen my braid, and score my fingernails along my scalp.

Rafe steps toward me. "You need to—"

"No," I cut him off, voice vibrating with anger. "Whatever you're about to say, it's not going to change me into a killing expert like you in the next three days."

It was a low blow, and for a brief moment, he looked hurt, like I'd struck him with a real blade. But it's gone as quickly as it appeared. He smirks and moves closer to me, until his chest brushes my breasts, and he has to lean down to talk to me, his lips inches from mine.

He drawls, "Well, if you've resigned yourself to martyrdom, *künnle*, we may as well spend your last three days in far more…pleasurable…pursuits."

My face flushes. I feel stunned. Then my anger snaps the last thread of my control.

"You're a prick," I spit at him, throwing my dagger down to join my discarded krahbek.

I spin on my heel as best as I can and storm off. I ignore the burning in my legs, the stares of Aric and Dagmar as I pass them, and the curious onlookers as I exit the training yard. My boots crunch against the gravel as I limp toward the citadel.

My anger propels me toward the outcropping, and I climb the stairs with adrenaline fueling my limbs. Lotti is exiting the outcropping after her infirmary duties. She gives me a cheerful wave. I barely see it, only able to nod in her direction. I want to collapse into my bed, ignore training and work duties, disappear under the bed linens, and pretend none of this exists.

My feet have other plans, though.

I veer off to the side, around the edge of the citadel's walls, slipping through the overgrown foliage. I don't stop until I reach the old chapel.

As always, it stands quiet and still beneath the dappled light of midmorning. I push open the crooked door and slip inside.

I shuffle to the center of the room near the altar, take a shaky breath, and let the tears come. They course down my cheeks, barely a trickle at first, but then a deluge accompanied by body-wracking sobs that make my ribs ache.

I am exhausted in every sense of the word—physically, emotionally, spiritually.

More than anything, I feel hollow. Bereft of motivation and energy beyond fear. I kneel on the cool stone floor, hands braced against it to steady myself.

I hear Rafe's voice behind me, "Greta, wait!"

The echo of my name bounces off the worn stone and cracked windows. I turn just as he jogs into view, breath hitching faintly, one hand braced on one of the broken benches near the rear of the chamber.

"If I'd known you were that eager for an interlude, I would've suggested it sooner," he teases, his mouth twisted in a crooked smile—half amused, half mask.

My whole body stiffens. And not from pain. Fury simmers beneath my skin. My shoulders feel hot, a prelude to a surge of rage-induced magic, and before I can convince myself otherwise, I stand and charge toward him. My right arm hauls back, and I punch him hard across the jaw. The sound is wet and loud. His head snaps back with more force than I would've thought myself capable, a grunt of pain escaping him as he staggers back.

"Gods, *künnle*," he lets out a surprised laugh and rubs his jaw. "Where was that punch during the *Nachtrif?*"

My knuckles are still pulsing from the impact, but I glare at him. "How dare you?"

He sighs. "All right, I get it, the joke about the interlude was—"

"No," I bite out. "Not about that. How dare you treat me like I'm not trying? Like I'm not pushing myself. As if all I've done since I got here hasn't been a fight for survival. And now you feel entitled to criticize me? Need I remind you, *again*, that you're supposed to be helping me?"

He recoils slightly, his posture stiff. "I didn't ask to be your mentor. I've done what I could and what you've let me do. I worked with your ability, your willingness, and the limited time we had. You think this is easy for me? I have a lot more going on than you realize."

"I know," I say, my voice hard.

He blinks at me. "What?"

"I said I know," I repeat softly, but with a dangerous edge I didn't know I possessed.

He goes tense, his eyes narrow. "I don't know what you're talking about."

I step closer, until my body brushes his, and my voice drops to an almost whisper, "You can lie to yourself. But I won't let you lie to me," I say, mimicking Conrad's words. "I know. About Hafenverre. About breaking conscripts out. About how you can somehow sense my magic."

The dark bronze skin of his face drains of color and his mouth parts slightly, as if I've slapped him in addition to punching him.

"How?" He whispers. He looks like he's seen a ghost.

"Does it matter?" I ask wearily.

He leans into me angrily. "Yes, it fucking matters considering I could be executed if the wrong person finds out."

"I overheard you and Conrad yesterday. I came looking for you…to sit with you." I look away, embarrassed, swallowing the lump in my throat. My voice grows tight with anger, though. "I came looking for you and heard you talking. About me. About how I might be 'useful.'"

He scoffs bitterly, "Don't act like you have exclusive rights to being upset about dishonesty. I haven't told you anything because of the risk it poses to others. You haven't been forthcoming about your abilities either."

"That's not fair," I protest. "I have risks, too—Agnethe is trapped, I could go to war, the Freiheit."

"Isn't it?" He demands. "You have two people you're protecting: you and your sister. I have the weight of an entire village on my shoulders. Do you even understand the magnitude of that responsibility? We are not the same."

I stare at him, stung but unable to argue his point. No, I do not understand that kind of responsibility, and he knows it. Still, my anger spurs me on.

I say, "You have to get me out."

He stares at me in disbelief. "If you heard our entire conversation, then you know Conrad would never agree to break you out. You're too visible in the Freiheit. Too high profile. There's too much—"

"No," I repeat, "you will get me out. And Stigander. And Lotti and Otto and Berte and Cyneric and Jarl. And Dagmar, too."

He lets out a bark of laughter, dragging a hand down his face. "And what makes you think I'd do that?"

I dig my fingernails into my palms, steeling myself for what I say next. "Because otherwise, I will use the tournament to expose you. I'll tell them everything in front of the crowd. Just like before, except now I have more information. More details. The officers, the leaders, your father. It'll be over. For all of you."

I can feel Roan's presence in my head, like he's about to say something, but I keep my eyes and mind focused on Rafe.

He freezes. "You wouldn't."

I level my eyes on him. "I told you—only those privileged with choice question the desperation of those who have none. Dagmar promised she'll fight me with everything she has. I'm not strong enough to defeat her. I'm going to die. And then Agnethe will have no one, and Roan—"

My voice breaks, and I lose the ability to speak. The pressure in my throat swells, and I have to swallow to suppress the tears, the fear, the sorrow. Roan remains silent but steady in my mind.

Rafe is quiet for a while. He doesn't move. Barely blinks or breathes. Finally, he exhales like he's letting go of something within him.

"If I do this," he says quietly, "there's nothing more from me after this. We're done."

His black eyes meet mine, and the words hit me hard. Worse than the blows in the *Nachtrif*. Worse than the kick to my ribs, the puncture to my leg, the numbness of poison. Something inside my chest shrivels and dies. A blooming connection forever severed.

I swallow again and nod, the motion brittle and painful. "Fine."

"Fine," he echoes, then adds, "wait for my signal."

"What signal?" I ask him.

He turns to the doorway, and I think he will ignore my question as he moves to exit, but he stops right before it, keeping his back to me.

"When it happens, you'll know."

CHAPTER FORTY-NINE
Mortvva's End

The sun blazes mercilessly in the midday sky, a burning disc of white-edged fire that bleaches the stone walls of the arena and turns the air heavy with heat. The stands hum with noise—laughter, jeering calls, distant cheers that rise like trickles of steam from the tightly packed benches. People cram into every available space in the stands, along the walls, and leaning over the edges of the center floor. The scents of sweat, sun-warmed stone, and dirt fill my nostrils with each inhalation, and my skin itches beneath my uniform, already damp with perspiration.

The noise is overwhelming, louder than any crowd in previous trials. Combined. Everyone except the barest of skeleton staff is here. After all, this is their final chance to witness the glory—and violence—of the tournament. From the sounds of it, they've come expecting a show. Expecting blood.

My legs feel like I'm wading through syrup as I walk into the center of the arena floor, boots kicking up dust from the hard-packed earth. My stomach twists in knots, my heartbeat races so high in my throat I can't speak. Dagmar lines up beside me in front of the platform, silent. Her posture is rigid, severe. Her eyes face forward.

We don't speak. What more would we even say?

I shift on my feet, trying to dispel the pain that chases me. My injuries still throb beneath my clothing, and every step is a reminder of what I've already survived—and what my body still hasn't fully recovered from.

My ribs still feel battered, like I'm being kicked by another boot every time I breathe. The punctures in my right leg twinge every time I shift my weight, and the deeper wound in my left calf pulses with a persistent ache that makes my teeth clench even when standing still. The stitches feel less fragile than they did days ago and are less likely to rip open from the slightest movement, but I still don't trust them. Certainly not in the Freiheit, where every second demands total bodily commitment and exertion, and pain is almost a certainty. I don't know exactly what to expect in the first part of the trial, only that I'll have to push through it or risk facing Dagmar without a weapon.

Grimacing, I watch as the officers climb the stairs to the platform. Colonel Richter is in full officer regalia, ceremonial sword gleaming at her hip. Lord Corvilian sneers at me and Dagmar as he stands in front of his velvet chair. Major Berger, unaccountably solemn. Aric, straight backed and frosty. And then there's—

Rafe.

Everything inside me wants to buckle when I see him. Unlike the other officers, he's not wearing a dress uniform. He wears his regular tunic and trousers, irreverent as always. I haven't spoken to him— haven't seen him—in three days. Not since that moment in the old chapel where I forced his hand.

Cornered him. Blackmailed him—again.

He'd told me that if he did what I asked, got me out, that would be it. There was nothing more from him after that. That we were done.

I'd told him "fine" and pretended it didn't feel like a knife in my heart.

Because I didn't just sacrifice his trust and the growing friendship that had been forming between us. But also something fragile and genuine, blossoming beneath our quips and frustrations. Something that felt real.

The worst part of that sacrifice is that I don't even know if I can go through with it. If it came down to it, and my life were the price of silence, the price for keeping hundreds of people in his village safe, would I really expose him? I'm not sure.

"Truth unsheathed is a blade, fledgling—but only if you're willing to draw it. If you can't, don't pretend you would."

In other words, don't make threats if you don't intend to follow through.

I sigh inwardly. *"I thought you said he could be trusted?"*

"I believed so, but I am not infallible," Roan muses, though it sounds like acknowledging that is painful for him. *"There is still time for Sir Silent to make good on his promise, however."*

"Do you think I did the wrong thing?" I ask him.

There's a pause. *"I think you followed the only path you believe you had left."*

"You don't believe it was," I say the words I can sense hovering unspoken between us.

"To know all possible outcomes would require abilities beyond my reach. It is done now, and you must accept the disquiet that accompanies uncomfortable choice."

My gaze lingers on Rafe's face. His jaw is clenched. His arms drape with casual indifference on those of his chair, but his hands grip the edges. He doesn't look at me. Not a single flick of an eyelash in my direction.

I tell myself that he's avoiding me because he has to, because he's strategizing and trying to maintain his careless façade. In my heart, though, I fear it's because he's pulled away entirely. That he's severed whatever threads bound us together, including the threat of exposure.

Maybe he's decided to take the risk.

The crowd's cheers grow louder as Colonel Richter stands and makes her way to the platform's edge. The arena vibrates with the sound, and the air hums with anticipation and bloodlust.

My hands tremble at my sides, and I clench them into fists to steady them. I don't know how Dagmar remains so still beside me, but she possesses a control I can only ever dream of. My eyes dart toward the maze across the arena floor—the twisted mass of vines that conceal whatever horror waits for us beyond. In just minutes, we'll both run directly into its deadly channels to find weapons before time runs out.

Then we fight.

To the death.

I can't decide if I'm hot or freezing. My body feels suspended in an eerie, sickening in between.

I risk one more glance at Rafe. But he still doesn't acknowledge me. And my heart, already as bruised as my body, fractures in my chest.

Colonel Richter's polished boots catch the sunlight as she stops at the platform's edge, her graying-brown hair ruffles in the breeze, and she clasps her hands behind her back while waiting patiently for the crowd to quiet.

She begins her final speech almost precisely the same as she did the first. "Lord Corvilian, distinguished members of the Aurenclaste, officers and soldiers of the Aurengarte, and cadets of Stachtenbaste, welcome to the eighth and final trial of the Freiheit Tournament."

The crowd erupts, feet stomping on wooden risers, fists pounding against armored chests, cheers ringing out like the most ominous of songs.

"Today is the culmination of all that has been endured. Every blow, every cut, every break. And yet, it is not the heaviest strike or the deadliest blade that defines a soldier's true strength—it is their willingness to make the sacrifice others will not."

She pauses, and her eyes drop to me and Dagmar.

"Not all sacrifices are those you pay with your blood. Some you pay in what you give in order to take a life. That, too, is a death, albeit a quieter one. A piece of yourself you leave behind, buried the moment you make the choice. And yet, that choice is often what separates the protectors from the oppressors."

The crowd's full attention is entirely upon the colonel.

"Our soldiers must decide in a breath whether to hold, strike, seize, or spare. And so, too, will our challengers today. Because freedom does not come without cost."

Roan snorts in my mind, his voice dry as dust, *"Spoken like one of the oppressors."*

I shift my weight again and try not to wince as my fingers drift into my pocket, curling around the small glass vial Lotti had slipped into my hand this morning. Liquid that swirls behind the wax seal, barely enough to seem consequential. Not technically allowed but not technically forbidden either. I press my thumb against the glass warmed by the heat of my body.

I need all the help I can get.

Major Berger marches forward to address the crowd a final time. There is no dramatic flourish, grin, sweep of her arm, or clever turn of phrase. Instead, she stands tall in her pressed uniform, close-cropped black hair glimmering in the sun's rays. When she finally speaks, her voice is even and somber, echoing clearly from the platform across the entire arena.

"Today marks your final trial in the Freiheit Tournament," she begins. "What you witness now is not spectacle but a crucible of survival. Of choice."

The crowd remains quiet and respectful, sensing that this speech is not one for raucous cheering.

She turns to speak to me and Dagmar directly. "Your trial will consist of two parts—first, a maze grown and sustained in real time by earth wielders. You will have thirty minutes to locate and retrieve your two weapons. They may be concealed, guarded, or protected by traps or other mechanisms—some illusory, some real enough to maim or worse. Should you fail to retrieve your weapons during that time, or fail to reach the center in thirty minutes, you will enter the final battle without arms."

The air grows impossibly thicker as I listen, my heart beating sharply against my aching ribs. The tall hedgerows look even more ominous than before, their dark leaves glistening and sharp thorns protruding.

"Once within the center ring," Berger continues, her eyes only for us, "the challengers will fight. The final victor will be the one who is left standing. There can be no surrender or intervention. Only one may emerge from this battle."

A murmur ripples through the crowd, part sympathy and part excitement.

"As soldiers, to protect we must make impossible choices. Not just the saving of life, but the taking of it, too. Whoever emerges as the victor will carry the weight of that impossible choice with her every day following. As soldiers, we do so willingly because peace must be earned. Just as you must earn your freedom. Make no mistake, freedom will greet each of you in different forms when this day is done."

I swallow hard, my throat dry. It seems my life is a series of "uncomfortable" and "impossible" choices of late.

Dagmar shifts beside me. Is she nervous? Or just hurting as I am? Perhaps she's eager to get on with it. I don't look at her to find out; instead, I keep my eyes firmly on Major Berger and see her gaze shift. The sorrow. The respect.

"Challengers," she addresses us, "it has been our privilege to watch your progression through the trials, and whether you leave the arena whole or do not leave at all, you have earned your place in the Aurengarte. You are forged in valor and cast in strength."

She touches her fist to her opposite shoulder and bends at the waist, a sign of respect from one soldier to another.

I find myself returning the gesture, murmuring, "Forged in valor. Cast in strength." I can see from the corner of my eye that Dagmar does the same.

We have both uttered the final line of the Aurengarte oath. Though neither of us has taken it officially, the major has recognized our sacrifice and, without further trial, has told us that we have fought valiantly.

We have earned our place here.

We are both soldiers.

A moment passes as she stares at us, and I find myself blinking away the curious sting of tears. They are banished almost as quickly as they arrived when Berger steps back from the platform's edge.

"Challengers," she booms. "At your marks!"

My stomach gives a nauseating lurch as Dagmar and I step forward together, approaching the towering hedges. The entrance finally reveals itself, vines retracted by the skilled earth wielder that controls them, the archway dappled in shifting shadows from the angle of the sun above. The scent of crushed greenery and turned soil reaches my nose from its threshold.

The roar behind us grows louder; blood-hungry chorus reaching a fever pitch. That's what they've come to see. The final page of a conscript's story. One lives. The other dies.

Dagmar turns her head toward me slightly as we pause in front of the entrance to the maze.

"Whatever the outcome," she says to me, "fight for it. They want us broken. Make them regret it."

I turn to her. Her face is impassive and unyielding as if made of stone. But her words have feeling in them—she means them. She wants me to fight.

I nod once, firmly. "I will."

The starting horn sounds, vibrating along the soles of my boots, up through my limbs, and into my spine.

I step into the maze, heart thundering.

And the hedge closes behind me.

The sound of the crowd and the starting horn fade into silence behind me, and instantly, I'm alone. No crowd. No Dagmar. No Rafe.

No one.

I step forward into the halls of looming greenery. A strange hush settles over the path, leaving an almost reverent, peaceful quiet behind. The vines stretch to impossible heights above me, at least fifteen feet. The dense, green lace is so thick that it blocks out much of the light from overhead. It's darker here, like dusk has fallen over me—cooler, too. A faint, earthy scent fills the air—crushed leaves, clay, the heady nectar of blooming buds.

Even my footsteps are quieter on the uneven dirt path, as if the maze has smothered both light and sound. I turn slowly, taking in my surroundings. The hedges aren't ordinary. Beyond their height and their unlikely planting grounds, they have a *feeling*. Like they're alive.

"Unless you intend to plant yourself here, fledgling," Roan says, *"I suggest you move. Your time will deplete faster than you realize."*

I give myself a shake and loose a breath, Roan's words pulling me back into motion. I walk down the hedge corridor to my right, boots crunching softly on the ground. My injured legs ache with every step, and the stitches in my left calf pull uncomfortably, but I push on. I run my fingertips along the vines, partially for balance and reassurance that it's real and not an illusion. I snatch my hand back when a large thorn pierces my fingertip. I suck on my finger where the blood wells.

"Roan," I begin. "Can you see me?"

"Though the greenery does much to obscure you, your lichtfaden *glows brightly."*

"What is *lichtfaden*? You've mentioned it before, but not what it is."

"Life is a thread, spun through marrow and mind. It forms a path for those who know its pattern—one that can mend or unravel it entirely."

Often, I feel like Roan speaks in riddles. But unlike those in the challenges, only he can decipher them.

"As I once told you, I am a riddle. I do not speak in them."

"And yet, I find myself puzzling over your words as if they are," I argue.

"Life always seems a riddle until hindsight provides understanding."

I roll my eyes at his supercilious tone.

"Can you tell me what's ahead, or shall I continue wandering aimlessly?" I ask him, returning to my entire reason for wondering if he can see me.

"Ahead, you will reach a divide. When you do, choose the path to your right."

I round a curve of hedges. Just as Roan described, there is a fork in the path. One continues straight; the other curves sharply to the right. Without hesitating, I veer right. The vines rustle, like they're reacting to my movements, my decision.

The path feels endless. I jog along for minutes, guided by Roan's direction. Even though it's cooler within the maze, sweat beads along my brow and trickles down my back beneath my tunic. Even the vines cannot entirely dispel the heat pressing down from above. My wounds ache the longer I exert myself, especially my left calf. I wish I could claw at my other injuries, their surface itchy from heat and abrading fabric.

Without thinking, I reach for my *Rabensblut*, tug on the bond, and let a trickle of power suffuse my body. Enough to enable me to forge ahead without expending more physical energy.

"*Exercise caution, fledgling,*" Roan intones. "*Magic gives, yes…but it will take with both hands. It will burn through what you are to accommodate what you might become. Do not spend strength before you've measured the cost.*"

I scowl. "How can I know what I'll need before I've faced it?"

"*That is precisely my point,*" he drawls.

I protest, "I don't think your point has been made as strongly as you think—"

"*There is a clearing ahead,*" he interjects.

Suddenly, though, the corridor of the maze changes. Vines leap from the walls, weaving themselves across the path in seconds. The way forward is gone, sealed by an earth wielder creating a living barricade.

"Shit," I mutter to myself.

"*You'll have to retrace your steps,*" Roan tells me.

I spin around, frantically trying to recall my previous moves, heart pounding. My legs are cramping from the strain.

"*You've nearly arrived at the clearing,*" he tells me.

The hedge on my left shifts again, sprouting another wall where none existed.

A dead end.

"Fuck!" I hiss.

I turn again and return the way I came, Roan still navigating from above. Finally, a jagged curve reveals a vast clearing of packed dirt, misted by fog that rolls close to the ground. In its center stands a circular weapons rack holding a single krahbek. The curved axe blade gleams in the filtered light, whetted and waiting.

I push my aching legs to keep moving, slowing as I reach the weapons rack. I'm a few feet away when the fog picks up in speed, like the hedges are breathing and the mist is their exhalations. The clearing ripples—and then multiplies.

One clearing becomes five. Then ten. All identical. A hall of mirrors, but of magic and mist instead of angle and glass. In the center of each clearing is a weapons rack. And each rack holds a krahbek.

I spin, eyes darting across the clearings I can see. I know this has to be an illusion, so which one is real? Deciding I should try the original, I bolt to it and grab the pole. The moment my fingers close around the wood, white-hot pain surges from my hand and up my arm.

I scream and drop the blade. The wood hisses like an iron, and seeing the steam roll off it—knowing it's from where my flesh made contact with the hot object—makes me feel faintly nauseated. Blisters are already forming on my palm. I shake my hand, trying to banish the pain with movement, and turn toward one of the other clearings, when I'm thrown back through the air, tumbling toward the hedge wall, then through, and suddenly I'm in the middle of the maze once more.

Dread pools low and heavy in my gut. I have to start all over and find the clearing.

"Push on. You have fifteen minutes left. The clearing is to your left, then straight on." Roan's voice is tight.

I force myself upright, cradling my burned hand. The skin is angry and red, and I know I'll have to figure out how to fight while my dominant hand is searing painfully, but first things first.

"You wouldn't happen to have some secret magical raven healing ability you've been keeping from me, do you?" I ask pitifully.

"I do not keep secrets, fledgling. Secrets are nests of thorns. Eventually, one must sit upon the throne they have made—and then who is the one that bleeds?"

I grit my teeth and sprint in the direction Roan told me to go. This time, the maze lets me pass without incident.

"Yes, because you're so wonderfully forthcoming all the time," I retort.

"How pleasant for us both that you manage sarcasm even in your current predicament."

I smirk silently.

"I heard that," he huffs.

"I didn't say anything," I counter.

"And yet, it carried."

The fog parts, and the illusion has dissipated. The clearing seems smaller now, almost claustrophobic. This time, though, I do not immediately rush into it, but instead wait for the illusion to recur.

When the clearing multiplies, I wait for any telltale flickering from the scenes to indicate which are mirages. But nothing happens.

Roan says, "*The scent of iron is honest and not unlike blood. Search not with your eyes, but with your breath.*"

I run to the nearest weapons rack and approach, leaning in as far as I can without touching it. I take a deep breath. Smoke. Dried grass. Dust. My sweat. All the scents that fill my nose are distinct, and yet none smells of metal.

I run to the next and repeat, but meet with the same result.

When I reach the third, I take a deep breath once more. Smoke, moss, dust, sweat. Oil, like the kind used to polish blades. And something sharp with the faint tang of blood. Earthy.

My eyes fly open. The krahbek within it looks the same as all the others—curved, well forged, and balanced. I let out a shaky breath, reach my injured hand toward it—no sense burning my other one—and wrap my fingers around the wooden haft.

Cool.

Solid.

Real.

The weight is familiar in my hand and, even with my burns, comforting. Now I just have to make it to the center ring. Because if I'm late, I'll have to surrender it.

When I turn from the rack, the other clearings have disappeared. I run to the opposite end, to the hedges that grow there, and immediately plunge into their depths.

"*Your left, fledgling,*" Roan directs.

"Time!" I call to Roan as I run through the corridor of hedges. I have to see if I can find the dagger waiting for me and if I still have the minutes to spare.

"*Nine minutes,*" he replies.

This time, I see the next opening before the hedges can play any tricks on me and shift. Even as I near, they don't change. Before me is a pedestal of stone, moss covered and worn with age. On its upright end sits a single dagger. Waiting for me.

I approach, eyes narrow and posture wary. There are no illusions, though. No mirrored paths. No traps in sight. It almost seems too easy.

I lean forward, and my fingers just close around the hilt of the dagger when the ground drops from beneath me.

I scream as I fall, gravel scraping my back and thighs, the krahbek still clutched in one hand, dagger in the other. I slam into the bottom of a narrow pit, ankle rolling painfully upon impact. Pain lances through it, and I reach out to the dirt wall beside me to brace myself but catch my arm on a jagged root jutting from within it. It slices through my arm, blood immediately seeping from the cut, soaking into the frayed edges of my tunic sleeve.

"*Fledgling?*" Roan asks me, clearly concerned.

"I'm all right," I groan and push myself to standing. "At least, for the most part. I twisted my ankle. Cut my arm. Nothing life threatening."

The pit is at least a foot and a half taller than I am, and the walls are riddled with roots. The smell of rotting leaves and loam fills my nose. The edges of the vine walls I can see above me sway gently.

"The bigger issue is this giant pit I need to climb out of with an injured ankle. Oh, and then the death match I have to fight," I add.

I limp toward one side of the pit. I remove my belt and loop it around one shoulder across my chest. I slide my krahbek along my back, hooking it on the makeshift holster, then tuck my dagger into my boot. I reach forward, grab a thick root, and pull myself upward, grunting, pain blooming in my leg injuries. My ankle screams in protest. The burn blisters on my palm rip open.

"*Pity is a luxury reserved for the dead, fledgling. You're not far from the center ring. Seven minutes remain. Move.*"

I reach for another root when vines explode from the walls, their tendrils—like snakes—coil around my legs and waist.

I'm trapped.

CHAPTER FIFTY
Back to Black

I look down at my legs, tangled and immobilized by vines thicker than any rope I have ever seen. The green fibers coil around my ankles like a snare around prey. My breath hitches with panic, and my heart thuds painfully as I fumble to free my newly acquired dagger from my boot, then try to saw my way free, as I had with the rope net in the last trial. The vines tighten the more I struggle, clenching painfully around my leg injuries and twisted ankle. It's like they're sentient—aware of the discomfort they're causing and spurred on by it. Sweat pours down my brow, dirt clings to my skin, and everything below my waist throbs as I move.

The stink of the damp earth and crushed greenery increases as I pull against my bindings. Dust and fragments of torn leaves float in the air, kicked up by my fall and continued thrashing. The air has grown hotter, the vines have parted, and the sun beats down on me directly overhead, the heat magnified by the small space and my fear. Every movement I make is a punishment I put my body through.

"*Low and left,*" Roan instructs, "*the root bundle anchors the rest.*"

I don't question him. I twist my waist with a grunt, shifting to my side, and slice downward. My dagger jabs the base of the snarl, just where my left calf presses into the rocky dirt. The blade strikes something fibrous—tougher than the surrounding vines—and the moment I sever it, the coils enclosing my limbs slacken and release. I tear my legs free, scrambling out of the trap with a ragged gasp.

My ankle screams as I move. There is blood on my trousers' legs where my various wounds are, like my stitches have come open or are at least agitated. Still, I grit my teeth and push myself to standing, dagger still clutched tightly in my hand.

"*Five minutes,*" Roan says, "*the center ring is just beyond the nearest hedge.*"

As if on cue, I can hear the crowd's muffled commotion nearby.

I let out a breathless laugh. "Sure, climb out of a pit with a twisted ankle and wounded legs. Don't forget the bruised ribs. Simple."

Gravel shifts beneath my boots as I take a tentative step toward the sloped edge. My balance falters, my wounded ankle threatens to buckle, my sore legs tremble, my blistered palm burns. One false move as I climb, and I'll be back at the bottom. Or worse, crushed underneath collapsed earth.

"*Your blade is your anchor,*" Roan directs. "*Climb.*"

Checking to make sure my krahbek is still tied securely to my back, I stab the dagger into the dirt where it sinks in with satisfying resistance. I haul myself upward again, scrabbling with my free hand, until my boot finds a rock buried in the soil wall.

Roan pours power into my body through the bond.

"I thought we shouldn't spend strength…before we know the cost?" I pant from the effort and the sudden onslaught of magic.

Every muscle is on fire, and my brain hums inside my skull. Still, I climb—inch by torturous inch.

"*A warning for you, fledgling. But I am the one who keeps tally, and the gain merits the charge.*"

Roan guides me with directions from above.

"*To your right, firmer foothold. Rock just beneath the loam. Above you—angled root.*"

His voice is a tether in the chaos, a lifeline piercing panic and exhaustion. My limbs are shaking, my hands are scraped raw, and sweat drenches my face by the time I reach the edge. I pull my krahbek free first—terrified of losing it in the pit—and throw it to the ground. It clatters on the solid earth with a thud. I pull myself up after it, dagger clenched in my teeth. My elbows clear the lip, then my waist, and I finally roll, gasping, onto the grass just as the pit shudders and collapses further.

I scramble from its depths, stagger to my feet, and limp down the final stretch of the maze toward the center ring after retrieving my krahbek. My leg drags and my twisted ankle makes every step even more agonizing than they had been before. Blood leaks from my left calf into my boot. As I hobble forward, I plunge my hand into my pocket, surprised to find the glass vial still there and intact. I pull it out, uncorking it with trembling hands, and tip a few drops onto each blade of the krahbek, then my dagger, as I move.

Henbane.

Lotti had pilfered it for me just this morning and passed it with a damp palm as I left for the arena. I don't feel proud of this. I feel tired. Terrified. And certain I won't survive if I don't have every edge I can, which includes magic *and* poison.

Since Rafe has disregarded our agreement, I have little other choice.

I stumble forward as the last hedge wall parts and its vines slither away into the ground with a resounding hiss. The sunlight is blinding as I emerge in the center ring, my boots hitting hard-packed dirt just as the horn sounds across the field. My chest heaves, and I barely hear the crowd erupt around me in roars and cheers.

I have made it. Barely.

The hedges have vanished, drawn into the earth by the wielders stationed around the arena floor like they had never been there.

Across the ring, Dagmar is already there. She's bruised, scraped, her uniform scuffed and dirty. One of her sleeves is torn and streaked with blood. Sweat glistens on her face. She's breathing hard, but standing tall, with a gleaming sword in each of her hands.

My stomach flips. My heart races. My grip tightens on my blades.

I tuck my dagger into my boot and firm my stance on wobbling legs as best as possible. My time has run out. So has my ability to pretend this wouldn't happen. Unlike in the maze, there is no trickery here. No illusions. Just the ring.

Just me and Dagmar.

I tell Roan, *"I don't know how I'm going to do this."*

I can barely hear my thoughts over the noise. They're swallowed in the storm of cheers and stomping feet as soon as I think them. My hands tremble as I tighten them on my krahbek. My vision swims with exhaustion and pain. My ears ring, and my body protests every step. The sting of my wounds is sharp and constant. With all my injuries, my *Rabensblut* has allowed me to continue, but it hasn't given me any advantage.

My gaze lifts instinctively to the leaders' platform, searching for one person in the sea of onlookers. Rafe. I don't know what I'm even hoping for—a sign of encouragement, maybe, or some unspoken signal that he's still with me. I can't distinguish a single face through the shimmering haze of glaring sunlight and fear and panic. Everyone is a blur of color and noise.

"Is it cloudy?" I ask Roan. *"It seems like it just got dimmer, like it's not bright enough."*

Maybe I'm just on the verge of losing consciousness. It would be just my luck to faint before my big fight. To sleep through the ignominy of my violent death.

"Cloud cover does seem to approach," Roan answers, voice as steady as ever. *"Do not let it dull your focus, fledgling."*

My eyes flutter closed momentarily as I teeter on the edge of collapse and despair.

Roan's voice is gentle this time. *"Breathe through. Pain is not a wall—it is a wind. Let it pass through you, not stop you."*

I clench my jaw, inhale deeply, and open my eyes. I exhale slowly and feel the gust of pain as it breaks over me. Then, I steel my shoulders, plant my feet shoulder-width apart, and grip my krahbek with determination.

Across from me, Dagmar stands still, eyes bright and sharp with focus. She spins one sword in a lazy circle in her hand, but nothing is relaxed in her body or stance. She's ready as always.

Colonel Richter yells, "Challengers, at your guard!"

Time holds its breath.

Dagmar surges forward with a roar, blades flashing in the light, boots pounding the dirt. Energy from the *Rabensblut* fires through my limbs, but I barely have enough time to bring my krahbek up to block the strike. Steel crashes against steel with a whine that rattles my bones. The force drives me back several steps, and my ankle twists painfully as it bears the brunt of my weight.

Dagmar doesn't pause. She spins into another attack, this time slashing low with one sword while stabbing high with the other. I parry clumsily, the axe's heavy blade intercepting one blade as the other slices a shallow line across my ribs. It bites, but not deeply.

Not yet at least.

I stumble sideways to create distance. Despite the krahbek's reach, I've already allowed Dagmar to get too close to me; I've given her that advantage. I try to feint left and jab forward with the spear, but she's already there, already turning and blocking.

More blows. More crashes and clashes of blade against blade. My hands go numb from the constant impact. My arms ache. My legs burn. My breath comes too fast, reminding me of my bruised ribs, which now have a scratch on top of them.

Dagmar ducks low beneath the haft of my krahbek and rams her shoulder into my abdomen, knocking me off my feet. I hit the ground with a cry, falling, jarring my spine, and sending fresh waves of agony through my injuries. I roll and narrowly avoid a downward strike of her sword that lands where my chest had been.

"Get up!" Dagmar screams at me. "Keep fighting!"

I try. I push one foot flat to the ground and try to rise. The world spins. My ankle gives out. I fall again.

She doesn't attack. Not yet. She waits, her blades low, chest heaving as she watches me struggle to get to my feet.

"Don't you dare give up!" She bellows, voice cracking. "We didn't come this far for you to lie down and take it!"

"*Roan,*" I reach out, feeling my strength fade, "*I need more.*"

"*Fledgling, you will not survive the continued torrent of power.*"

I feel the wet trickle of blood from my nose.

"I won't survive anyway," I tell him.

I feel grief, thick and suffocating, coursing through the bond, accompanied by another surge of energy that gathers me to my feet. The crowd's roar dims to a faint buzz in my ears. Blood pounds in my skull. My vision begins to blur. Tall, broad, and furious, Dagmar filters through my gaze like I'm staring at her through water.

The sun dims further, or maybe it's me who is dimming.

I see Dagmar's swords glint as the blades point in my direction.

I feel my mother's hands in my hair as she runs a brush through it.

I hear my father's voice singing a lullaby while I drift off to sleep.

I remember my grandmother stirring tea in her drawing room, the spoon clinking gently against the porcelain.

I see Agnethe's small hand, plump with a toddler's youth, as it slips into mine.

The ache in my chest swells until it eclipses the suffering of my body.

A blade rises.

The crowd roars.

I blink rapidly as tears gather on my lashes. Once, twice—

The entire arena goes black.

The End

WHAT'S NEXT FOR GRETA?

If you've made it this far, thank you. Truly.

Greta's journey through shadows, steel, and secrets is far from over. The choices she's made—some brave, some brutal—will echo into the next chapter of her story. And yours.

If you're eager to know what happens next, don't miss a single step.

Visit www.hannahstandhaft.com to:

- Sign up for updates on the next book in the *Conspiracy of Shadows* series.
- Get exclusive behind-the-scenes lore and maps from the world of Aurelia.
- Receive alerts about special editions, bonus chapters, and early access opportunities.

Greta's world is steeped in shadow, but her story is just beginning.

Will you be there when the darkness lifts?

ACKNOWLEDGMENTS

I can't believe I can finally say this: I'm a published author.

This story has lived in my head for well over a decade, evolving and growing. There were many times when I wasn't sure if I'd ever actually get to this point.

But here we are! And I didn't get here alone.

First, to my daughter, Annie. You will forever be the reason I rise each morning, the reason I try harder, the reason I will continue to believe in the impossible. You are still the piece of my heart that lives outside my body, and the one who carries it with her wherever she goes. Every day, you teach me how to grow, care deeper than I ever thought possible, and love without end. Let this book stand as proof that it is never too late to follow your dreams and see them come true.

Next, to my mom, my fiercest supporter and unwavering cheerleader: thank you for urging me to keep going when I doubted, for listening (sometimes with horror—sorry, Mom) as I gleefully described the various tortures I was inflicting on my characters. You have given me so much more than life. You've shown me, by constant example, everything it means to be a good person. You've shared your strength, wisdom, and a love for which I will never stop being grateful. I will never be able to tell you enough how much you mean to me.

To my brother, Clif, who absolutely does not read romantic fantasy, but did anyway and encouraged me every step of the way. You're a stupid butthead (yes, I'm over 40), but I love you all the same.

To Lydia, who "locked in" with me so many nights through this, I don't think I would have accomplished this as quickly without someone to experience it with me. Thank you for being you, and for sharing in my joy when I finished. #madeitthroughsecurity

To Ashley, who let me lay out the entire plot of the series to her without a single complaint, only enthusiasm, and who has been one of my most loyal beta readers and loudest champions. I wouldn't have gotten through this without your encouragement and the endless memes and romantasy reels.

To Merissa, thank you for enduring all my theories, rants, late-night progress screen shots, and never-ending need to talk about this. I swear I'll write you a character who exceeds all expectations.

To my wonderful beta readers—Marina, Lotch, Acacia, Emma, and Liz—thank you for sharing in my excitement and enthusiasm, as I have built this story, and for the play-by-play, side-splitting commentary as you react to it. Your feedback has not only helped to shape this book, but it's also carried me through some of the hardest parts. Thank you for loving Greta as fiercely as I do.

To my ARC readers who have generously given their time, reviews, and your hearts: thank you for helping turn my dream into something real.

And finally, to you, wonderful reader. For picking up this book, journeying to this page, and (hopefully) looking forward to Greta's next adventure. From the bottom of my heart, thank you. You are the true magic in my story.

ABOUT THE AUTHOR

Hannah Standhaft is the author of the *Conspiracy of Shadows* romantic fantasy series. For nearly two decades, she has led high-stakes communication efforts in the corporate world while plotting magic, rebellion, and raven dialogue after hours.

A lifelong lover of stories, Hannah lives in North Carolina with her family and a rotating cast of rescue animals. When she's not writing or reading, you'll find her singing, meme sharing, doom scrolling, scheming new fantasy worlds, or updating her ever-growing TBR list.

Discover more at www.hannahstandhaft.com.

CHARACTER NAME PRONUNCIATION GUIDE

The de Veend Family and Noetheim

de Veend: dəh FAYNT
Vergildetbach: fair-GIL-det-bahkh
Margarethe (Greta): Mar-ga-REH-tə (GREH-tə)
Agnethe: ag-NEH-tə
Odina: oh-DEE-nah
Hrafn: RAH-fun
Engilram: EN-ghil-rahm
Walter: VALL-ter
Eoforwine: YOH-fohr-vee-nə
Burkhardt: BOORK-hahrt
Herman: HEHR-mahn
Valda: FALL-dah
Madam Boeschg: Madam BOHSHK
Sunna: ZOO-nnuh
Andebert: AHN-deh-bert
Merel: MEH-rel
Lorenz: LOH-rents
Tilo: TEE-loh

Vallaurium

Reinhardt Muller, Lord Rocheburn: RINE-hahrt MULL-uhr, Lord
ROHSH-burn
Captain Fiedlerg: Captain FEE-dlerk

Gold Council

Roderick Kriegeur, Lord Corvilian: ROH-deh-rik KREE-ger, Lord COR-
vih-lee-ahn
Fabian Weber, Lord Valenhof: FAH-bee-ahn VAY-ber, Lord VAH-len-
hohf

Stachtenbaste

Aric Everbrandt: AH-rik EH-fer-brannt
Belinda Bradleye: beh-LIN-dah BRAHT-lyeh
Berte Brauneg: BEHR-tuh BROW-nek
Brock Dürgg: BROHK DOORK
Cyneric Wyndhame: sin-EHR-ick VIN-dayme
Dagmar Brevic: DAHK-mar BREH-fik
Eduart Broadbente: EH-du-ahrt BROHT-bent-eh
Hartwin Faerberg: HART-vin FAIR-behrk
Heide Berger: HY-duh BEHR-ger

Jarl Braddocke: YAHRL BRAD-oh-kuh
Lillen Bloms: LEE-len BLOHMS
Lotti Grieves: LOH-tee GREEFS
Mette Bosques: MEHT-teh BOHSKS
Otto Weber: OHT-toh VAY-ber
Ranulf "Rafe" Kriegeur: RAH-noolf "RAYF" KREE-ger
Romilde Richter: roh-MIL-deh RIKH-ter
Stigander Feltdgg: STEE-gahn-der FELT-ook

GLOSSARY OF TERMINOLOGY

Animals

Blutrabe *(BLOOT-rah-buh)* — Extra-large raven with blood-red eyes capable of communicating with humans who have been god-blessed. *(Plural: Blutraben)*
Löwenard *(LUR-vehn-art)* — Lion-wolf hybrid that is calmed through music.

Deities

Aquaemus *(ahk-VAY-moos)* — God of the sea.
Efanwohl *(EH-fahn-vohl)* — God of wealth and prosperity.
Erdia *(EHR-dee-ah)* — Goddess of the earth and soil.
Feuerignis *(foyr-IK-nis)* — God of fire.
Gehrvania *(GAYR-vah-nyah)* — Goddess of knowledge.
Levitia *(leh-VIH-sha)* — Goddess of life (one of the Blessed Sisters / Twin Goddesses).
Luftella *(loof-TEL-ah)* — Goddess of the skies (weather).
Lunoch *(LOO-nokh)* — God of the night, moon, and shadows.
Miedrym *(MEE-druhm)* — God of music, song, and dance.
Mortuua *(MOHR-too-ah)* — Goddess of death (one of the Blessed Sisters / Twin Goddesses).
Proelian *(PRO-lee-ahn)* — God of war.
Stellan *(SHTEHL-lahn)* — God of slumber.

Geographical Features

Dorberge (Mountains) *(dor-BEHR-geh)* — "Gold mountains." Major mountain range that runs across Caelias, parts of Bellatorius, and parts of Vallaurium.
Flumevian (River) *(FLOO-meh-fee-ahn)* — West-east river from Navisia to the Stiriameer Sea.
Lusenbucht (Bay) *(LOO-zen-buht)* — Western bay off the coast of Navisia.
Oremer (Ocean) *(OH-reh-mehr)* — Western ocean off the coast of Navisia.
Salenorden (Ocean) *(ZAH-lehn-or-den)* — Northern ocean above Caelias.
Stiriameer (Sea) *(STEE-ree-ah-mayr)* — Eastern sea off the coast of Caelias, Bellatorius, and Sarenaveld.
Sundesol (Sea) *(ZUN-deh-zol)* — Southern sea off the coast of Navisia, Verdantia, and Sarenaveld.
Vereisten (Strait) *(FEHR-eye-sten)* — Strait connecting Stiriameer Sea and Salenorden Ocean.
Vichestrasse (River) *(FEE-keh-SHTRAHS-seh)* — North-south river that travels from the Eisianian Plain to the Sundesol Sea.

Holidays

Lunoktium *(loo-NOK-tee-um)* — Equinox (means equal night / moon), occurs twice a year when day and night are in ultimate balance, celebrates the blessed sisters.

Items

Krahbek *(KRAH-bek)* — Polearm weapon resembling a halberd, featuring a long shaft topped with a spear, an axe, and a curved, beak-like blade designed for hooking.
Rotte *(ROH-tuh)* — Musical instrument resembling a lyre.

Legal

Legistadt *(LAY-gi-shtaht)* — The Aurelian national legal code.

Magic

Lichtfaden *(LEEKHt-fah-den)* — Thread of living creature's life that winds throughout their being. For those who can identify it, they are able to track someone using its signature, as well as potentially control them or kill them.
Rabensblut *(RAH-bens-bloot)* — Capability to communicate with and through the Blutrabe.

Medicines / Illnesses

Wundsmeiten *(VOONTS-smite-en)* — Magic-infused salve that heals skin quickly, works well for burns, scrapes, shallow cuts, or for closing the surface of wounds without need for sutures or cauterization. Translates to "skin knit," pronounced "VOONTS-smite-en."
Fiebernacht *(FEE-bair-nakht)* — "Night fever" illness that has a high mortality rate when it strikes, similar to the "Black Death" in devastation.

Military / Police

Aurengarte *(OW-rehn-gahrt)* — Aurelian military force.
Palastgarte *(PAH-lahst-gahrt)* — Palace guard force.

People

Pfaetr *(PFAYT-r)* — Member of the clergy / Order of the Blessed Sisters.
Zan *(tsaːn)* — Magical healer / similar to "Doctor" title.

Places

Aurelia *(ow-REH-lee-ah)* — Monarchy with provincial magical council, similar to feudal monarchy with provincial governors. The crown holds sovereignty, but appointed representatives hold considerable power.

Bellatorius *(BEL-ah-TOH-ree-us)* — Easternmost province, typically the highest producer of Aurengarte (military) soldiers.
Caelias *(KAY-lee-us)* — Northernmost province, home to mountains, mines, and misery, as well as deadly work camps.
Embrathal *(EM-brah-tahl)* — Capital of Aurelia.
Felsegeist Haus *(FEL-zuh-gīst HOUSS)* — Residence of Lord Rocheburn.
Hafenverre *(HAH-fen-fehr-reh)* — "Safe harbor." Rafe's village.
Loubenstille *(LOW-ben-SHTIL-lə)* — "Quiet hallway." Holding cells in Lord Rocheburn's residence.
Navisia *(nah-VIH-zee-ah)* — Aurelia's westernmost province that is home to its primary port and maritime industries.
Noetheim *(NOH-tyme)* — Seat of the de Veend family.
Portaeli *(POR-tah-EH-lee)* — Capital city of Caelias.
Sarenaveld *(ZAH-reh-nah-felt)* — Neighboring nation and source of frequent skirmishes and conflict.
Stachtenbaste *(SHTAHKH-ten-bahst)* — Primary military / combat training center.
Sühneferme *(ZOO-nə-fehr-muh)* — Labor camp in Caelias.
Terraflore *(TEHR-rah-flo-reh)* — Capital city of Verdantia.
Vallaurium *(fah-LOW-ree-oom)* — Central and chief province of Aurelia, home to capital city and seat of the monarchy.
Verdantia *(fehr-DAHN-tsee-ah)* — Southernmost province and chief source of agricultural industry and output.

Religion

Heiligarte *(HĪ-lee-gahrt)* — "Sacred guard." Highest religious order in service to the Order of the Blessed Sisters.
Gleichvîger *(GLĪKH-fee-gher)* — "Agent of balance." Superior titled religious member of the Order of the Blessed Sisters. Reports to Hochvîger.
Hochvîger *(HOHKH-fee-gher)* — "High arbiter of balance." Holy leader of the Order of the Blessed Sisters.

Social Hierarchy

Aurenclaste *(OW-ren-klahst)* — "Gold class." Magical elite members of society.
Aurenkammer *(OW-ren-KAH-mur)* — "Gold Council." Appointed governing officials from each province.
Lützenclaste *(LYOO-tsen-klahst)* — Non-magical elite members of society, elevated due to societal benefit or provided service.
Arbenclaste *(AHR-ben-klahst)* — "Working class." Non-magical, commonfolk class of society.
Trübvolk *(TREWB-folk)* — "Lackluster." Derogatory nickname for non-magical commonfolk used by the Aurenclaste and occasionally the Lützenclaste to refer to commonfolk.

Words / Phrases

Alouisse *(AH-loo-EES-suh)* — "Little lark." Term of endearment.

Gesindel *(geh-ZIN-del)* — Lowborn scum / trash.

Grumple *(GROO-mpluh)* — Fat and clumsy person.

Herzeline *(HAIR-tsuh-leen-uh)* — "Little heart." Term of endearment.

Künnle *(KOOHN-luh)* — "Princess" diminutive nickname from küniginne *(KOOH-nuh-gih-nuh)*.

Liebelîn *(LEE-buh-leen)* — "Little love." Term of endearment.

Liebenette *(LEE-buh-net-tuh)* — "Little beloved." Term of endearment.

Müterine *(MYOO-tuh-ree-nuh)* — Endearment for a grandmother, similar to "grandmama" or "grandma."

Vögelein *(FEU-guh-line)* — "Little bird." Term of endearment.